Captain Hazard's Game

Captain Hazard's
GAME

*A Mystery
of Queen Anne's
London*

———✦———

David Fairer

Matador
Unit E2 Airfield Business Park,
Harrison Road, Market Harborough,
Leicestershire. LE16 7UL
Tel: 0116 2792299
Email: books@troubador.co.uk
Web: www.troubador.co.uk/matador
Twitter: @matadorbooks

ISBN 978 1803132 907

British Library Cataloguing in Publication Data.
A catalogue record for this book is available from the British Library.

Printed and bound by CPI Group (UK) Ltd, Croydon, CR0 4YY
Typeset in 11pt Adobe Jenson Pro by Troubador Publishing Ltd, Leicester, UK

Matador is an imprint of Troubador Publishing Ltd

For my readers

Characters

———∞———

Historical figures marked with *

COURT AND POLITICS

*Queen Anne, *the last Stuart monarch, niece of Charles the Second*
*Prince George of Denmark, *Prince Consort, Anne's ailing husband*
*Robert Harley (later Earl of Oxford), *wily politician with Tory sympathies, now out of office, Anne's confidant*
*John Churchill, *Duke of Marlborough, the great general, victor of Blenheim (1704) and Ramillies (1706). In October 1708 he is besieging Lille*
*Sarah Churchill, *Duchess of Marlborough, Queen Anne's friend and adviser, now out of her favour, supporter of the Whigs*
Arthur Maynwaring, *MP, the Duchess's secretary, wit and Whig pamphleteer*

RED LION COURT

Mary Trotter, *Chatelaine of the Bay-Tree Chocolate House*
Tom Bristowe, *budding poet working on his Virgilian georgic,* Covent Garden: A Poem in Two Books

Will Lundy, *Tom's best friend, mercurial law student of the Middle Temple, future Westminster Hall orator*

Mrs Dawes, *creative in the kitchen, inventor of the Covent Garden tapas*

Jenny Trip, *barista princess with a sharp eye and keen wit*

Peter Simco, *skilful coffee-boy with a bright future*

Jeremy Jopp (Jem), *does errands and hard lifting, training to be elegant*

Old Ralph, *sweeps and cleans*

Robert LeRoy, *Tallière of the Bay-Tree basset table, an adventurer*

Samuel Cust, *Whig with a Caribbean sugar plantation*

Barnabas Smith, *Whig cloth merchant*

Jack Tapsell, *Whig wine merchant*

Laurence Bagnall, *poet and critic with laureate ambitions, author of 'The Shoe-Buckle'*

Captain Roebuck, *old soldier of Marlborough's Flanders campaign*

Gavin Leslie, *down from the glens of Scotland*

David Macrae, *his friend and compatriot*

Charles Denniston, *runs a toyshop in Katherine Street, Mrs Ménage's landlord*

John Pomery, *his friend, private secretary to the Duke of Bedford*

Gabriel Winch, *cynical broker with business in Exchange Alley, suspicious of the Dutch*

Jacob Taylor, *another frequenter of 'Change Alley, not fond of the French*

Joe Garvey, *a third, a young man satirically inclined*

THE CITY AND EXCHANGE ALLEY

*Sir Charles Duncombe, *incoming Lord Mayor of London, 1708-9*

Sir Jasper Evington, *the Ancient Mariner of 'Change Alley*

*John Grigsby, *in 1708 'Mr Grigsby' was the cashier of the Sword Blade Bank, Birchin Lane*

Edward Barnes, *the Sword Blade notary*

Jack Grimes, *the first half of Grimes & Hitch*

Ned Hitch, *the second half of Grimes & Hitch*

*Sir Gilbert Heathcote, *richest commoner in England, a Director of the Bank of England, became its Chairman 1709*

*Peter Henriques, *commodity importer trading with the east*

Michael Henriques, *his progressive son, excited by science and experiment*

Willem Oosterhout, *Dutch entrepreneur running a Europe-wide system of intelligence*

Lambert Jansen, *Dutch dealer at Jonathan's*

Mr Rawls, *a Jonathan's share-hawker*

*Benjamin Levy, *Lombard Street banker of long experience*

George Rivers, *Alderman of the Mercers' Company, City Coroner and Common Councilman*

Samuel Rivers, *his son, a professional gamester taking on the 'system'*

Philip Roscoe, *a Director of the Bank of England, broker to the Duchess of Marlborough*

*Elkanah Settle, *the official City poet, responsible for the Lord Mayor's pageant*

ST JAMES'S

John Popham, *Second Viscount Melksham (Tom's Uncle Jack), Queen Anne's Deputy Treasurer, an unwilling courtier*

Sophia Popham (née Doggett), *Viscountess Melksham, a young banking heiress who has become a stepmother*

The Hon. Frank Popham, *newly-elected MP for Wootton Bassett, Wiltshire*

The Hon. Lavinia Popham, *independent and advanced for eighteen, recruited to Arachne's Web, a secret bluestocking circle*

Lord Tring, *heir to the Earldom of Welwyn, very fresh from the*

Grand Tour. *Lavinia's admirer*
Arthur, *the Pophams' tall footman*
Sidney, *their lad who fetches and carries for them*
Mrs Walker, *their dauntless cook*
Sir Charles Norreys, *Commissioner of Vandernan's gaming-house*
Julia, Lady Norreys, *his intelligent and bored wife, active in Arachne's Web*
Alexander, *their footman, her discreet ally*
Delarivier Manley, *controversial journalist and fiction-writer, chief weaver of the Web*
The Hon. George Sturgis, *well-connected rake and gamester*

THE LAW

Elias Cobb, *Covent Garden's resourceful constable, with semi-official interests*
Tobias Mudge, *his bold apprentice watchman, has ambitions to be an investigator of crimes*
Bob Turley, *watchman, strong-armed member of Elias's team*
Benjamin Hector, *Covent Garden magistrate zealous for the reformation of manners*
Sheriff Kirk, *knows the forms*
Richard Sumner, *Middle Temple barrister and Will's pupil-master, Lady Norreys's brother*
Mr Justice Oliver Lundy ('Hemp'), *Will's father, Old Bailey judge and strict upholder of the Law*
Mr Blackett, *an officious constable*

VANDERNAN'S GAMING HOUSE

Joseph, Lord Parham, *runs the Vandernan's system*
Joe Travis, *door-keeper of Vandernan's, close to Parham*
Joel Harkins, *Parham's enforcer, second member of the team*

Jack Beech, *daredevil highwayman who contributes to the Vandernan's economy*

Humfrey Corbet, *idle law student of Gray's Inn, frequenter of the gaming-house*

Isaac Ward, *another one, even more idle*

Ned Wilder, *and a third*

Mr Fleming, *a beau, flamboyant hazard-player*

Mr Nolley, *a reckless and unsophisticated player*

'No-Nicks' Nick, *a hapless player who doesn't give up*

Barbara, Lady Rastell, *female gamester of awesome reputation*

Sir John Simons, *the 'Hockley Hole gamester', part of the Vandernan's cabal*

Joshua Wakefield, *'Dr Convex', another member of the cabal*

'The Rector', *tenacious whist-player*

Mr Colleoni, *fop who loses with good grace*

'Dick', *former wig-dresser favoured by Dame Fortune*

ELSEWHERE

Adèle Ménage, *of Katherine Street, retired from the bagnio business, Widow Trotter's old friend*

Kate Primrose, *formerly 'Callisto' of Vinegar Yard, soon to be Mrs Joseph Quinlan of Soho Square*

Joan Cumberbatch, *hospitable keeper of the sponging-house*

Jack, *messenger from Custom House Quay*

*Abraham Darby, *beginning to exploit charked coal at Ironbridge, Shropshire*

Abel Broughton, *works for Darby, sees potential in the gas by-product*

Richard Morson, *proprietor of The Flagon*

Thursday

21 October 1708

Chapter One

⁓⁓⁓

IT HAD ALL begun innocently enough – with a casual remark after a hand at whist. But what a hand! Those cards alone would have made the event memorable, and Mary Trotter's thumb had tingled as she reviewed them: seven trumps in a tightly-formed phalanx ready for battle. Shoulder-to-shoulder they stood: the eight, nine and ten, the knave, queen and king, with almighty *Spadillo*, Ace of Spades, standing proudly alongside the rest of his family.

She couldn't avoid catching her breath, and her partner Mrs Ménage sensed electricity in the air. Adèle Ménage was an instinctive card-player who found calculation tiresome and liked to generate an element of surprise. This often disconcerted her partners, but Widow Trotter had learned to take it in good part and enjoy the ride. On this occasion the pair swept the board in triumph; and even their opponents, Mr Denniston and his friend Mr Pomery, accepted that it had been a privilege to be part of such a historic encounter – massacre though it was.

Over tea and cake, the four of them reflected on the game. That concluding hand had been mere chance of course – one in ten thousand. But the excitement had been intense, and they all felt exhilarated by the thought that their game of threepenny whist had attracted the attentions of *Fortuna*. It was as though for a brief moment the goddess had unveiled herself in their presence.

Mrs Ménage's words came out of nowhere:

'I am thinking Marie ... Could you not set up a basset table at the Bay-Tree?'

At first it seemed an absurd notion, and a dangerous one, and Mrs Trotter was not about to take it seriously; but as the urgings continued the idea took on a more certain form. She was forced to admit that her large upstairs chamber was little used. Once a fortnight the Mutton-Chops got very drunk around the punch-bowl, and the Good Fellowship Room (named after the Bay-Tree's previous incarnation) resounded to their high-flying Tory toasts and Jacobite songs. She had thoughts of making it a place for the ladies, above the coffee-room where a female presence was disallowed; but beyond the occasional afternoon tea or party at piquet it was hardly serving its purpose. Basset, it occurred to her, was a game favoured by the ladies; it would draw more custom into the house, and the additional income would be very welcome ... Gradually the idea gained on her.

Basset was the game of the moment, especially among the smart set. It was a kind of lottery played with cards – roly-poly without the wheel – and for the bank it was, almost without exception, highly profitable. It was this 'almost' which gave Mrs Trotter pause. The risk – though exceedingly small – had to be acknowledged. Gaming-house rumour told of one famous occasion when a stake of a thousand guineas had been brought to *soissant-et-le-va* ... a sixty-fold payout. No *tallière* could possibly honour it. No wonder King Louis had forbidden stakes at basset above a single franc! In France the thought that a footman or a valet might win himself a country estate was not to be tolerated. But any stout-hearted Briton had a God-given right to earn a coach and six by supper-time, and face utter ruin by breakfast.

And so, after much consultation and some heart-searching, Widow Trotter laid her plans, and the practicalities were all arranged. A license was obtained from the Groom Porter, a suitable table procured, and most importantly an experienced tallière engaged. Mr Robert LeRoy promised much and came with tales of White's and Vandernan's. He appeared to have been designed for the purpose, with a calm but alert manner, a twinkling eye to encourage boldness in his players, and enough of a French accent to lend an upstairs room in Covent Garden the air of a Parisian salon. The *ambiance* was completed by an elegant chandelier supplied with wax candles; there were green silk cushions for the armchairs, a new oval wall-mirror set with brass sconces, and a plush velvet curtain to conceal the chamber-pot in the corner. Everything was set.

As the inauguration of the basset table approached, Mrs Trotter's early enthusiasm became tempered by caution. The Bay-Tree's regular customers were apprehensive, and her friends urged her to tread carefully: set a limit to the stakes, establish fixed hours (perhaps two evenings a week?), confine the play to invited guests and select parties only … All of this was very wise, and the core of good sense in Mary Trotter saw the force of it. To begin in a modest way seemed best.

The result was that on a Thursday evening in October 1708 a private party of friends and well-wishers gathered in the Good Fellowship Room to put the basset table to the test. It would be a severe one, given that the cards had to compete with Mrs Dawes's pickled Newcastle salmon, which was sure to prove an attraction in itself.

A little before seven o'clock the chatelaine of the Bay-Tree was making a final survey of the room when the door opened and the familiar dark curls of her lodger peeped round it. Tom Bristowe occupied the chamber above and so had a close interest in the proceedings:

'Will and I have come to offer our services, Mrs T! You must give us instructions. No task too small!'

Widow Trotter suppressed a smile and shook her head:

'I fear you're a little late, Mr Bristowe – all the heavy lifting is done. We are well supplied with coals, and there's no fetching and carrying required. But I have a couple of aprons if you want to help out later.'

'Excellent!' declared a tall figure stepping up behind him. 'So, Tom was right – we have timed things perfectly. Always offer help when the job is done, he said.'

'But Will and I are ready for action, Mrs T … We thought we could become *puffs* for the evening. You know the arrangement: the house gives us some money to play with, and we encourage the other punters to push their chances just that little bit further.'

'We congratulate them on their boldness and whisper good fortune to them.'

'This is no gaming-house, Mr Lundy. If it were, then I would happily employ you as *orderly-men*: you could pace along Red Lion Court keeping watch for the justices.'

Tom Bristowe's eyebrows lifted:

'You know the jargon of the trade!'

'I've made it my business, Tom. But I must say I'm anxious about tonight. The Bay-Tree has a reputation …'

'But these are your friends,' said Will Lundy encouragingly. 'This is going to be a highly respectable table attracting only the most civilised *gamesters*.'

'Ah, that word! It keeps bad company does it not? Especially in sermons and pamphlets.'

'But yours is no hazard-table – there'll be no angry men cursing the dice, no outraged honour – no flashing swords! It may be warfare of a kind, but good order will be preserved. According to Tom here, basset is a reasonably chivalrous affair. It is French, after all.'

'Yes, and the field of battle is ready I see – and very handsome it looks …'

Tom was running his hand across the green baize, noticing how the nap ran away from the player and towards the bank.

'… I know Lady Norreys is looking forward to deploying her troops across it.'

Mrs Trotter brightened:

'I'm glad you encouraged her to come, Tom. You say she's a practised player?'

'Yes, very. But since there's no particular skill involved, she'll be in Fortune's lap like everyone else.'

'In that case,' said Will, 'I might take my chance once my friend here has explained the rules. I can be determined enough – provided I don't need to be skilful.'

Tom looked uneasy:

'No, but it helps to have a modicum of prudence and sobriety. If you can manage those, Will, then I'm sure I can explain the thing to you. We shall watch the game closely and you'll see how it works. I don't suppose card-play was ever encouraged in the Lundy household?'

'Utterly proscribed – just like the tavern and the playhouse! But I have to say there was a large supply of prudence and sobriety. On that score you need have no fear.'

'I'm not sure I want my guests to be prudent,' said Mrs Trotter. 'I confess I hope for a degree of reckless abandon …'

A hint of wicked anticipation played across her face.

'… I don't wish to break my players entirely – but some transfer of funds would be welcome. A basset table is no charity, gentlemen. There's business to be done! … The bank is ready, and I've secured a healthy sum. It won't all be on show tonight of course, but arrangements have been made. I'm told a substantial bank is absolutely necessary for the reputation of a table.'

'I hardly think it will be at risk tonight,' said Tom. 'But I'm sure the play will be lively enough.'

'Well, I trust my friends will enjoy themselves ...'

Widow Trotter paused for a moment and turned to look at the clock, before remembering that she'd had it removed. In contrast to the Mutton-chops, her basset-players were best left unaware of the passing of time. Instantly her purposeful countenance returned.

'... If you truly want to be helpful, gentlemen, then perhaps you could wait in the coffee-room and direct our guests up here? The Popham party will be arriving soon, and I wouldn't want Lady Melksham to feel awkward. Are you sure she'll be happy to be here, Tom?'

'My aunt will be conflicted as always, Mrs T – the social whirl and the social forms! But Uncle Jack will make her easy, and having Lady Norreys at her elbow should help.'

'And could you please remind Jeremy not to go anywhere near the salmon – not within six feet! Once the dish is prepared it is to be entrusted to Mrs Dawes alone. I don't want to be scraping fish off the stairs.'

'Understood, Mrs T. You can rely on us. Decorum – and the princely salmon – will be preserved!'

It was spoken with a flourish, and Widow Trotter took their salutes. She watched as the two young men, like a comic partnership on the stage, negotiated their exit in a series of mock bows – Will inclining his tall figure with elegant ease, his hair flopping over his temples, and the stockier Tom bobbing satirically. What a remarkable pair, she thought – so light of heart and yet robust and resourceful, and the surest allies in a crisis – something she knew well. The thought gave her a twinge of unease; but it soon passed and her confidence surged back. Tonight would be the start of a new adventure for the Bay-Tree, and she was intensely curious as to how it would all work out.

There was someone else witnessing the playful performance. At the other side of the doorway an open-mouthed Mr LeRoy had been attempting to make his entrance, and he hung back in some confusion. The *tallière* knew that Widow Trotter was determined to make her basset table polite but hadn't expected such delicacy, such *finesse*. The two young men in passing gave him a florid *au revoir*, and for a moment he imagined himself at a Court levee. He stepped into the room with trepidation. Mary Trotter was no Queen Anne, but at this moment the chocolate-house proprietor was almost refined away, and what faced him was a woman of presence, her auburn hair swept up under a tall tiara of lace. A lawn scarf played round her shoulders above a simple, close-fitting dress of dark green muslin. The room was not a large one, and she didn't want to take up too much of it. That must be left to the gamesters.

She stretched out a hand to the new arrival:

'Welcome, Monsieur LeRoy! At last you see the room in its fresh guise. I trust you approve of the table and furnishings. We are no White's, I confess, but I want the place to be intimate and comfortable.'

Robert LeRoy maintained a degree of *sang froid* at the information. Yes, it was certainly no White's … but he supposed it would do well enough for a private table – and one where he could rule. The thing would be orderly and select. Just a single table, but who knew what triumphs and disasters were in the offing? He smiled inwardly as he thought of the delicious uncertainties that lay ahead.

He was now in front of the mirror adjusting a small bob-wig that gave his face a boyish look. His eyes flickered in his hostess's direction:

'Who were those young blades, Mrs Trotter? I detected an element of the burlesque in their courtesies. Am I wrong?'

'You are not wrong, Mr LeRoy. Tom Bristowe and Will Lundy are fast friends of mine and enjoy their liberties. Mr Bristowe is poetical, and Mr Lundy a student of the Middle Temple ...'

'Ah!'

It was a mere monosyllable, but an eloquent one. It spoke of suspicions confirmed, of a certain wariness, the hint of a challenge to come.

'You should know that Mr Bristowe's uncle and his party will be at the table this evening – Viscount Melksham is Her Majesty's Deputy Treasurer – has oversight of the Privy Purse ...'

'Ah! ...'

This was a very different sound, and Mr LeRoy's eyes sparkled. It was clear that note had been taken. He awarded the titles a slight nod of the head.

'... Then I shall enjoy taking his guineas, Mrs Trotter – so long as they are his and not the Queen's! I trust he will leave that particular purse at home?'

Widow Trotter attempted an encouraging smile. Without question, her tallière was a difficult man to read. Some awkwardness was making itself felt, until it struck her that in the governor of a basset table a degree of enigma could be an asset ... Well, she was prepared to wait and see.

But her curiosity was aroused, and she couldn't resist a further gentle push. She looked him in the eyes:

'Will Lundy's father is a judge at the Old Bailey – 'Hemp' Lundy ... Perhaps you've encountered the name and know of his reputation?'

This time the 'Ah!' was forming but no sound came. Instead Mr LeRoy swallowed and attempted a smile:

'Indeed, Mrs Trotter, I should have made the connection. We can only hope that Mr Lundy *junior* will not report us to the authorities ...'

He sensed her uneasiness and gave a little laugh.

'... But have no fear – I am confident our game will not attract the attention of the magistrates. We shall maintain a table of repute, and I trust a highly profitable one!'

She heard the words 'our game' and knew there was a ticklish point still to be settled. It had been agreed that the bank's profits would be divided equally between them, and any loss also. But she had said nothing about limiting the stake. Tonight the players were her friends, and it had been settled in advance that a two-shilling stake would be the evening's maximum. This was well understood. She knew she must tell him, and so she broke the news, almost casually ...

Mr LeRoy was taken aback. The expression on his face was one of disappointment and annoyance, with a hint of derision about the mouth. No, this was certainly no White's! He had been looking forward to some 'deep' play as the night wore on. It was when the drink was flowing that a practised tallière would expect to harvest the fruits of his conjuring. He was having increasing doubts about Widow Trotter and her table. Worryingly, he recalled that some mention had been made of a *salmon* – the word being spoken in hushed tones that suggested its arrival would be a special event. Was the evening really to reach its climax with a pickled fish? ... He had taken this to be a light-hearted joke, but now he couldn't be certain. Robert LeRoy was a man who took his gaming seriously.

An hour later all the guests had assembled and the room was humming. The game had begun to find its rhythm, and the tallière's hands moved quietly and smoothly. The handsome kidney-shaped table was full, with Robert LeRoy in snug occupation at its centre and the players seated around him across the green baize, their chosen cards spread before them. Alongside the tallière's right hand every eye could see the glittering bank with its little towers of gold and silver – shillings, crowns and golden guineas – winking at them in the candlelight. It was a dragon's hoard in miniature within reach of their outstretched fingers – so very near and, with Fortune's help, waiting to become theirs.

Mr LeRoy was maintaining an even pace, allowing the communal ritual of basset to unfold with natural ease. Moments of drama and frustration must never disrupt the progress of the game. When things were going well he felt like the director of a musical ensemble with the instruments weaving their varied sounds together. It was a game of *pianos* and *fortes*, and the occasional resounding *tutti* as applause broke out. A single turn of a card might bring simultaneously a bitter oath, a sharp intake of breath, a laugh, and a little cry of triumph. The tone shifted from dark to light, and back to the deepest gloom. But always things were moving on: the next card was revealed, and everything became possible. Each punter was sure the tide would turn and sweep all before it. Just a few minutes more and things would be different.

Basset was also a spectacle. Each punter had a full suit of thirteen cards, and their selected ones with their coins formed changing patterns on the baize. The concentration was intense for both player and watcher. Eyes flicked across the table – none quicker than the *croupier*'s, whose role it was to note the losing cards and claim their coins for the bank. Widow Trotter was watching the play eagerly, delighted at how everyone was absorbed in the to and fro of the game. She was longing to play, but conscious that having a share in the bank would be awkward: she would be winning from herself and losing to herself …

Will was standing alongside Tom, fully absorbed in the action and trying to master its different stages. At regular intervals the tallière dealt the top two cards from his pack, one after the other, and his voice called success and failure: 'Queen wins! – Seven loses!' … 'Three wins! – Eight loses!' The calls were intoned like verse couplets declaring a win and a loss. 'Five wins! – Knave loses! …' On top of a punter's winning card a matching sum was added, but the coins on a losing card departed to the bank. It was absurdly simple, Will thought, and yet something else was going on: punters were turning down the corner of a card or adding another coin to it. With several cards before them, each punter managed her forces – keeping faith with their King, or removing a disappointing nine from the fray, only to find that the next card …

Will whispered:

'Why are they turning the corners, Tom?'

He whispered back:

'They are making *paroli!* – letting their bet ride further, hoping to reach *sept-et-le-va*.'

'What is that?'

'The bank then pays *sevenfold*, Will. And if you want to risk more, you then turn over a second corner and move to the possibility of *quinze-et-le-va*.'

'Ah! Fifteen times the stake!'

'You've mastered it already! But every time you do this, you're tempting Fate and risk losing all.'

'This looks an even chance to me. I was told basset worked in favour of the bank.'

'Indeed it does,' said Tom with a smile. 'The bank has certain favours awarded it: if the two turned cards are the same, the punters lose. Also, the first card of the hand gains the bank half the money staked – and he doesn't pay out on the final card.

'It begins to cast a spell, I admit. This Mr LeRoy has something of the priest about him. He's conducting it like a religious ceremony.'

'Three wins! – King loses!' came the call.

A cry of despair was heard from the Popham end of the table. The croupier magicked away four shillings from Lady

Melksham's King, uncovering the face of a scowling monarch. The piles of coin alongside Mr LeRoy were beginning to assume alpine proportions.

'Put not your trust in princes, my dear!' whispered her husband as he removed his humble Three from the baize, along with six shillings.

'Basset is a hateful game, John – so very subversive! There's no *precedence* – and the Court cards must fight it out with Twos and Threes …'

Lord Melksham placed a comforting hand on his wife's arm:

'Well, you'll have to give the little fellows a chance, Sophia – I've had great play with my Three, have I not? You should swallow your pride and risk a Two – we've not had one this hand – and let him restore what your King took from you.'

Around the table, the punters were in various ways attempting to guess and to calculate, pursuing a whim, a conviction, or a superstition – even forming a battle-plan … But each turn of a card treated all that with contempt. What seemed like choice and agency was in reality only guesswork. There was no pattern or purpose to the way the cards fell – no priorities, no consistency or consideration … It was not a game for the powerful or those who wished to be master of their Fate. The punter deserved nothing – and more often than not it was nothing he was left with.

Mrs Ménage's attitude, however, was one of glee at the vagaries of Fortune. Her threepences were as adventurous as others' shillings, and they came and went quite happily. She took delight in the game itself, in watching the other players and reading their thoughts. To lose a few shillings at the end of the evening was a fair price to pay for all the pleasure it gave her.

As the hour passed, the rhythm of the game was gripping Widow Trotter completely, making her heart surge and sink in response to the play. She couldn't take her eyes off the table, and the quiet clink of coin on coin was undeniably arousing. She had to stop herself from running a continuous calculation of the assets of her bank, feeling something akin to the excitement of Exchange Alley with its fluctuation in the price of stocks.

Over to the tallière's right, Mr Denniston and Mr Pomery were becoming increasingly grim-faced while each encouraged the other not to lose heart – surely a change in the wind would blow some success in their direction? Alongside them, Lady Norreys was being silently philosophical. She was used to deep play and took comfort from the thought that were this Lady Rastell's table in Arlington Street she would be severely mauled by now.

From the house's perspective all was going swimmingly, and Mrs Trotter's thoughts began to turn to the salmon, which would be ushered into the room at the appropriate moment. But at this point she was loth to disturb the rhythm of play – and especially the flow of coin across the baize in the direction of the bank. Her friends could surely remain peckish a little longer. Wine was being dispensed from the sideboard by the door and along with the warm fire was contributing to the genial mood in the room.

By now Will Lundy had joined the fray, confident of having mastered the elements of the game and eager to show his mettle. He had tied his hair in a knot behind his head and was ready for serious play. There was something about the nonchalance of Robert LeRoy that was provoking, and Will longed to be the bold adventurer. Someone had to turn the tables on the bank and discompose those serene features! But things had not begun well. He had been over-ambitious for his Knave and had paid the price. The answer, he decided, was to lie low and build up his resources more modestly – then he would strike …

After a short while the last cards of the hand were called, and Mr Denniston decided to withdraw from the battle and relieve himself behind the curtain. Tom was invited to take his place and slipped into the seat beside Will.

'Shoulder-to-shoulder, eh?' he said. 'Perhaps I'll bring you luck.'

'It's a pity we can't work together,' said Will. 'What a strange game this is – no competition and no collaboration – just the bank against the rest of us!'

'I never trust bankers, Will. And this Mr LeRoy makes me shiver. But I'm delighted for Mrs T. The bank must be some fifteen pounds up at least.'

Mr LeRoy was now shuffling the pack with an easy motion, his lace cuffs swaying gently. People were refilling their glasses and assessing their finances. Mr Denniston was re-adjusting his clothing and heading for the sideboard. Will was taking encouragement where he could:

'Your uncle is doing well, Tom! He has quite a little bank of his own!'

'But Aunt Sophia is in the dumps. I do hope this isn't going to prove a disaster for her – Uncle Jack will never hear the end of it. But I'm sure the Doggett fortune can stand the strain.'

'I can see her exchanging sympathy with Lady Norreys. The Fates have been cruel to her too. You must commiserate – I know she would welcome it.'

It was spoken lightly, but the tone was a sly one. Tom reddened:

'I may have to. She told me she was confident of doing especially well tonight and was sure the company would be congenial. She said the occasion was *propitious*.'

'Was that her word? …'

Tom nodded.

'… In which case, perhaps she has made a sacrifice to the Fates? We know her special rapport with those ladies, don't we!'

Tom looked over, and Lady Norreys's dark eyes caught his.

She shot him a rueful look, raised her hands and glanced down at the empty baize before her. In return Tom pointed encouragingly at the ceiling. She nodded and dived into a velvet pouch that was evidently well filled. Tom felt confident her evening was far from over and a resurgence was overdue.

Will watched the dumb-show with amusement. Basset was truly a riveting game – perhaps because there could be no concealment, and no appeal. The lawyer in him found this intriguing. The thing was so simple in principle. Where would your card appear? To the left, or to the right? With the elect, or the outcast? It was a sheep and goats matter, and there was nothing you could do about it. He watched Mr LeRoy shuffle the pack as fastidiously as any fine lady managing her fan – wrists and fingers working in harmony, keeping anticipation alive. The man was playing God, and clearly relishing the role.

Within a few minutes the next hand was under way and the pulse of the game had re-established itself, when a man's loud laugh was heard from beyond the door. The sound jarred with the mood in the room, and the players glanced apprehensively at each other. A moment later the door opened, and two figures appeared ...

Chapter Two

⸺⸙⸺

EVERYONE SAW THE bottle first. The thing was being held out toward the company, and the gentleman holding it was beaming with the confidence of a man who assumed that with his arrival the party could at last begin. He crossed the threshold boldly, his sword scraping against the door:

'Mrs Trotter! My dear lady! How splendid this is. Let me salute you!'

The greeting was spoken much more loudly than was warranted by the place and the occasion.

'Ten wins! – Knave loses!' came the response from the table. The tallière's voice chimed reassuringly. The game was going on, and the players were being called to attention.

Aware of the awkwardness, with a few sharp strides Widow Trotter placed herself in front of the new arrival and greeted him with a quiet 'Welcome, Sir,' trying not to let her embarrassment show.

When the man's fair-haired companion stepped into the room she at once became easier:

'Ah, Mr Popham! A warm welcome to you also. You were not expected, gentlemen – but I'm sure we can accommodate you.'

Lord Melksham stirred and lifted his head:

'Frank my boy? Are you here? Well well! ...'

'Two wins! – King loses!' came from the table in a tone of slight annoyance. At this, the croupier immediately swooped, causing Lady Melksham to scowl at her King – then at her husband – then at her newly-arrived stepson. The moment was a complicated one.

Tom Bristowe was turning round to greet his cousin, who had placed a restraining hand on his noisy friend's arm and was introducing him to their hostess:

'Mrs Trotter – this is Mr Sturgis. We have strolled over from Vandernan's ...'

'Damn'd dull there, eh Frank? We thought something might be stirring at the Bay-Tree! News is abroad of your table, Mrs Trotter, and I had to take a look ...'

Mr Sturgis surveyed the circle of basset-players, who to his mind were not far from dullness themselves. An uneasy silence had fallen. All attention was focused on the red-faced newcomer, and on the empty glass in his other hand.

'Cheers to you all!' he declared, and lifted it to his lips.

'Ace wins! – Five loses!' came the reply from Mr LeRoy's tightened throat.

By now it was the voice of the tallière that seemed the interruption. Will grinned at the goings-on and calmly placed two more shillings on his seven. He caught the eye of Tom's cousin and gave him an encouraging wink. Francis Popham, M.P. was clearly embarrassed by his companion's volubility. The Honourable Mr Sturgis, however, was eager to be sociable:

'Frank here said we shouldn't be welcome – ha! ... But this is a convivial party, Frank – and I see a well-stocked sideboard to boot! How very cosy ...'

He grinned warmly at everyone and shoved the bottle into Mrs Trotter's hands. Then he put a finger to his lips, swaying slightly.

'... But your father is scowling at us. Let us not interrupt the play! We shall take our station by the sideboard!'

His first step was erratic, but Frank Popham guided him by the arm, with Widow Trotter trailing anxiously in their wake. She was trying to maintain a smile and was wondering if it was time for the salmon.

'Seven wins! – King Loses!'

It was spoken sternly and with emphasis. Will's heart leapt. He was struggling to concentrate and wondered whether he should turn his card. There were two sevens remaining in the pack ...

'This is a bad night for the royals, Mr LeRoy!' said Lady Norreys, who had been watching the commotion with some amusement. 'I have to say your dealing is positively Cromwellian!'

Others laughed. Robert LeRoy's hitherto unruffled brow was showing signs of a frown. Mr Sturgis's entrance had succeeded in stirring up the players, who at this stage of the evening were beginning to feel that a degree of merriment wouldn't come amiss.

Mrs Trotter took the initiative. She leaned over Mr LeRoy's ear, and he heard the disturbing word 'salmon' whispered into it – this would be the final hand before the company took a break. The now thoroughly discomposed tallière managed to conduct the remainder of the hand briskly and with a degree of decorum, until he and everyone else sat back to witness the entrance of the long-expected fish.

The door opened and a white-aproned Mrs Dawes, culinary genius of the house, was revealed. Between her forearms she held a large dish on which a salmon of heroic scale was displayed. It was an entrance to match Cleopatra's before Antony, and the air in the room was suddenly lovesick with the delicious sharpness of the sweet pickle. The salmon glowed pink and enticing, surrounded by little red beets and sprigs of dill. With a combination of grace and superhuman strength Mrs Dawes laid the dish down in the centre of the sideboard. The creature was three feet long, and after four years roaming the Atlantic it had returned home to the Tyne in a consummate state. A ripple of applause was its fitting tribute.

Robert LeRoy admitted defeat, and looking at the tempting spread he was almost prompted to declare *droit de tallière*; but Viscountess Melksham was given precedence. In truth, they were all paying court to the fish, and it was some while before conversation moved onto other topics.

Eventually Tom walked over to join his uncle and cousin by the fireplace. Frank Popham had successfully detached himself from the Honourable Mr Sturgis, who was loudly monopolising Lady Norreys, smothering her in *dear Lady*'s and affixing his free hand to her arm. She in turn was practising statuesque indifference.

Lord Melksham looked across at them and shook his head:

'Dear me, Frank! What in God's name are you doing? Why bring that popinjay here?'

'In truth, he brought *me*, Sir – I had little say in the matter … George is a difficult man to shake off.'

They could hear his voice across the room.

'He's as pickled as the salmon,' said Tom brightly, 'but with none of that creature's quiet dignity. Not the politest entrance, was it!'

Frank was now looking at the floor. Lord Melksham sensed his son's uneasiness and was uneasy himself. He spoke quietly:

'I didn't know you frequented the tables? And in company with a man like that …'

There was a moment of awkward silence before Frank responded. He looked up cheerily:

'Have no fear, father. Once parliament begins I shall have other matters to occupy me. Time hangs heavy in the recess. I'm impatient to show my mettle! You know how much I – *we* – have prepared for this.'

'Good, good!' said his father. 'Indeed we have. I just wish Mr St John could be there to guide you ... But this Sturgis fellow ... he has something of a reputation. I need not tell you ...'

'George is a bit wayward, father – but he has a good heart. He can be generosity itself – I've certainly found it so. As a parliament man I shall need to mix with all types – some of them unappetising characters like the ones I encountered at Wootton ... It is damned hard not to be entangled in obligations – promises are extracted and uncomfortable alliances made. Independence is difficult. It is far easier for you – you can be your own man.'

It was a firmly-made point from the new politician of the family, elected that summer as one of the two members for the Borough of Wootton Bassett in the County of Wiltshire – in the interest of Henry St John, late Secretary at War. The new Parliament was prorogued until November, and so this hopeful sprig of the Pophams fresh from the Grand Tour had yet to make his mark on the nation's destiny.

Lord Melksham gave him a fatherly smile:

'I trust you'll look to me for advice when you need it, Frank. And to Tom too – I'm sure this wise young fellow won't be stinting! Politics is a dirty trade – but you'll have to learn from experience like we all do ...'

He was on the brink of offering some sage moral counsel, but broke off.

'... Ah! I see my wife's fan beckoning me – a summons not to be ignored! ... Good luck with the play, gentlemen – I hope Dame Fortune will favour you. This basset is a confounded bit of trickery, is it not? Have you watched the man's hands closely? All that lace!'

He left them looking at each other in puzzlement.

The table was filling again, but Tom didn't move. He leaned towards his cousin and half-whispered:

'What is it Frank? Something is troubling you ...'

There was no immediate reply, and Tom knew his intuition was right. He and Frank had been close all their lives, and since childhood Monkton Court, the Pophams' decaying country house, had been his second home. From the moment his cousin arrived he had sensed anxiety beneath the assurance.

Frank looked down at the carpet again:

'I'm in the mire, Tom ... indeed, if it wasn't for George ...'

'What do you mean? Has something happened?'

'At Vandernan's – I've had a run of foul luck at hazard.'

'*Hazard?* You've been dicing? But that's a place of deep play – nowhere deeper ... at Vandernan's men lose fortunes in an evening. It's no place for a novice ... How stand your affairs? – truthfully now!'

Frank looked into his cousin's eyes, then shied away – they were blazing.

'Little short of ... two thousand.'

'Two *thousand?* ...'

Tom was forced to whisper it, disbelieving.

'... Who knows of this?'

'Only the crowd at the gaming-house. To them it's a handy sum, but nothing memorable. I was assured I could recoup it in a single evening ...'

'But how did you settle? I've heard of men staking their clothes – stripping off their shirts and shoes for a final throw ...'

'I gave them a note, Tom.'

'A promissory note? For the *full sum?*'

Silence was the answer. Tom was trying not to tremble at the news.

'But George Sturgis settled on my behalf. He has an account

and bought up the note – he says he'll not press for the sum until things are easier. It was thoughtful of him …'

'*Thoughtful?* Did he not introduce you to Vandernan's in the first place? Tell me he did not!'

'He did – but it was half my suggestion. We had fallen in with a pair of parliament-men just arrived from the shires.'

Tom was shaking his head. He could picture the scene: a couple of country members with more money than sense determined to try the delights of the metropolis:

'So you were ready to make your mark, eh Frank? Show them how to win big – and win with style.'

A satirical note was creeping in.

'I didn't look for this, Tom. I can see you're angry. I'm angry with myself. I downed too much port – and somehow …'

'Somehow the power of the game claimed you. You were riding your charger into the thick of the fray, enjoying the thrill of it.'

'Everything happened so quickly – the stakes – the dice – yes, the thrill of it. It was over in a few minutes – or seemed so. I lost track of time … I can't tell my father, Tom. You mustn't ask me to!'

'So, the Honourable Mr Sturgis has your note, does he? Well, we must hope the gentleman has no need of a large sum himself. Your promissory note could end up touring all the gaming-houses in London. Anyone might knock on your door.'

Frank was pale and stunned:

'I'd not considered that …'

'Two thousand!' muttered Tom, half to himself. 'That's a terrific sum … What are we going to do?'

It became a rhetorical question. The game was about to resume, and Tom noticed with slight alarm that the newcomer Mr Sturgis had seated himself at the table alongside Lady Norreys. Her velvet pouch was open, and with intense concentration she was deciding which cards to place before her, studiously ignoring her neighbour's fascinated gaze. Mr Sturgis was watching her hand as it fingered one of the many pearls that adorned her silk turban. Lady Norreys, thought Tom, would always hold something in reserve. She had no need of promissory notes – there was a treasury on her head.

The Honourable Mr Sturgis looked down, and with a strange, self-directed grin he carefully placed a solitary penny on the single card in front of him. It was the Queen of Hearts. The extraordinary move drew all eyes toward him. Was the visitor making a point about the modest little game he had joined … or was it a tentative venture on another noble lady at his side?

Will may have lacked experience of cards, but he was beginning to understand how they could have their own silent language. Perhaps more was in play than coins? He glanced at Lady Norreys and saw her move an equally derisory penny onto the Knave of Clubs, and then turn her serious attention to the other three cards.

The hand was under way, and Mr LeRoy was re-establishing the dignity of the game as the pairs of cards were turned over with an elegant twist of his fingers, two by two, as if drawn out of the air.

'Three wins! – King loses!'

There was a ripple of amusement around the table, and Tom saw his aunt's face noticeably brighten. This time she had a two, three and four in front of her.

For several minutes the play continued, and Widow Trotter was once again held in thrall by the ritual. At this stage things were breaking even with the bank, and around the table smiles and frowns were finely balanced.

Mr Denniston and Mr Pomery were working in concert now, with the one going for odd numbers and the other for even – as if this would somehow offer more chances and insure against any severe loss. Mr Pomery's spectacles lent a studious aspect to this strategy. Further along the table Lord Melksham was radiating confidence. If his wife was at last deploying her infantry, he had decided the court cards were due for a good run. The Jack, Queen and King made a handsome group against the damasked silk of his waistcoat.

Will was beginning to find humour in all of this, admiring the ingenious means by which players were attempting to guide their fortunes. He could only think of basset as a form of religious rite with the congregation trusting to Providence. But the one deity Will saw before him was Robert LeRoy intoning the names of the cards as they showed themselves to left and right – fortunate and unfortunate, the elect and the reprobate.

The most assured person at the table was Mr Sturgis. Encouraged by the acceptable claret, he began to be impatient with the sedateness of the game. He had been having a good run at the gaming-house, and both dice and cards seemed eager to favour him. The new hand was about to begin when he decisively set down his glass and reached into his waistcoat pocket. With a determined look on his face he extracted two large coins and set them on top of the Queen of Hearts. Their gold was radiant in the flickering candlelight, and even at a distance the hooked nose of King William could be made out, his flowing locks and laurel crown. There was an audible intake of breath around the table … Two five-guinea pieces …

Widow Trotter went cold and looked in alarm at Mr LeRoy, as did the croupier. But the lace cuffs did not rest. The tallière's manner continued calm and dignified, and without any discernible hesitation he made the call: 'King wins! – Eight loses!' … What was going on? Will and Tom looked at each other. This should not be happening – but of course Mr Sturgis was not to know of the informal limit on the stake. The other players hesitated, yet continued to play as before, glancing at Mrs

Trotter who was rooted to the spot uncertain whether to speak. It was too late now in any case. She caught Adèle Ménage's eye and saw that it reflected her own fears. There was tension in the air as everyone waited, hardly breathing. Each call cut through the silence. And each time the expectation increased ...

And then the decisive words came:

'Queen wins! – Six loses!'

A sudden burst of sound filled the room. All eyes were fixed on Mr Sturgis's Queen. With awesome calm the tallière took five two-guinea coins from the bank and offered them to him; but the Honourable Mr Sturgis made no move to receive his winnings. Instead he turned over the corner of the card. With a ten-guinea stake he was set on a course for *sept-et-le-va*.

There was sudden silence. The other players – or rather, all but one – remained stock still, giving attention only to Mr Sturgis, while his eyes were fixed on his neighbour. By his side Lady Norreys calmly moved two shillings onto her nine of clubs as if unconcerned ... People held their breath.

'Four wins! – Ten loses!' ...

The game had suddenly changed its character. It was now a duel between Mr LeRoy and Mr Sturgis – two piles of gold, head to head.

'King wins! – Five loses!'

Everything was still. After a pause, the tallière's lace shivered again. The next card was a Queen ...

And the second ...

Another Queen!

Cries of amazement burst forth. Mr LeRoy looked around the table intending a frown of disapproval but was unable to suppress a sigh of relief.

'Banker wins!' he said calmly.

The second Queen had banished the first, and the punter was the loser. The twenty guineas were now the bank's. It was a delicate moment, and the croupier hung back for an instant before taking possession. Mr Sturgis, however, was well used to the rough and tumble of fortune, and while others exclaimed and fluttered around him, he maintained an expression of indifference, his mind working quickly. Without even looking up, he retired his Queen and pushed forward an Ace. Once more he reached into his pocket, and this time drew out four five-guinea pieces. With exquisite precision he formed them into a little column on the prostrate Ace and sat back in his chair to await the stroke of Fate.

No-one else was moving now. Even Lady Norreys appeared caught up in the drama of the moment. There was a faint smile in her eyes as she glanced down at her neighbour's card – and at her own Ace with its modest half crown. She paused only a moment before adding a second. Their destinies, large and small, were linked.

While these events unfolded before her, Widow Trotter was scarcely breathing. She was fascinated by the scene. Mr LeRoy, she acknowledged, was directing it in masterly fashion, allowing the tension to build and maintaining a total stillness while the players made their moves. He seemed conscious of the pulse of the game, and now he set it going again with another pair of cards.

'Four wins! – Nine loses!'

The pace was still a measured one as the play went on.

'Three wins! – Six loses!'

All harmless enough.

'Two wins! – Seven loses!'

Will gave a groan – but no-one seemed to notice as he bade farewell to his silver … The infantry were doing well again, but what about the powerful players in the pack? When would they appear?

'Ace wins! … . King loses!'

There it was. The Ace of Spades. The Honourable Mr Sturgis had fully recouped his loss. It had to be admitted the man was a bold player. He looked over almost politely at Widow Trotter, who returned him a nervous smile. This was her basset table, and the man was perforce her guest. She had set this up and would have to take the consequences, whatever they were.

Mr Sturgis's Ace was to receive its winnings of twenty guineas. His hand reached out. But it was not to take the coins. Instead he gripped the corner of the Ace between his fingers and turned it over, pressing it fastidiously down as if to leave no room for doubt. He was making *paroli!* – parlaying the bet – letting his twenty-guinea stake ride for *sept-et-le-va*. Two more calls, and each an even chance. Make, or break. He was now in play for one hundred and forty guineas …

Tom was watching all this in horror, sweating involuntarily – and not merely because of the fire. His anxiety for Mrs Trotter and her enterprise was clutching at him, and he felt his heart pounding. Cousin Frank's affairs were still in his mind, and now this was happening. Things were not about to end well.

The call came.

'Five wins! – Knave loses!'

Then, only a minute later, Tom saw his fears realised.

'Ace wins! – Four loses!' …

Everyone exclaimed at once. The table was now a theatre, and the atmosphere electric. Tom looked wonderingly at Mr Sturgis. The man who had half-stumbled into the room, flushed and unsteady on his feet, was now the coolest person in it. The game seemed to have transformed him. His movements were well under control. Tom had expected something heedless, not this steely calm. He had thought of serious gaming as a fever, not icy calculation. He and the others watched intently. Now the play was for *sept-et-le-va*.

Surely, this time, the Ace had to lose? Tom looked at the now-thinned pack of cards in the tallière's hand. Somewhere inside was the final Ace – where would it fall? One hundred and forty guineas rode on it.

Once again Mr LeRoy's timing was perfect. He allowed several seconds for the drama of the moment to establish itself – before continuing the deal:

'Nine wins! – Seven loses!'

And then:

'Six wins! – Two loses!'

Now there were only three cards remaining. Which of them was to be the Ace? The final card would not pay out, and so the odds were one-in-three.

With a coy hesitation, and a flourish of lace, the final pair of cards was produced …

'Ace wins! – Four loses!'

Mr LeRoy was superb. He showed not the slightest flicker of pain but seemed to revel in being the centre of attention. The man reminded Tom of a conjurer holding a fairground audience in thrall.

This time the whole room went quiet. All eyes were on a single player – the others were scarcely attending to their cards. Once more the tallière offered the money – and once again it was declined. The second corner of the Ace was turned over. Mr Sturgis was in play for *quinze-et-le-va* … Three hundred guineas.

The new hand began with hardly a pause. Mr LeRoy knew when to raise the pace of play, and no-one was thinking of adjusting their cards.

'Eight wins! – six loses!'

'Seven wins! – Ten loses!'

The calls were calm and clear, like the tolling of a bell, and Widow Trotter knew what kind of bell it was. Her throat was tight and she felt almost suffocated.

'Two wins! – Queen loses!'

Tom and Will glanced at each other. There was nothing they could do. There was something inexorable about it – like steps to the edge of a cliff ...

'King wins! – four loses!'

Closer and closer it came.

Mr LeRoy's hands remained relaxed and supple ... This had turned into a duel between two ice-cool players. Nothing could be done. Fate was in the cards, and had to be left to work itself out.

'Five wins! – King loses!'

'Ace wins! – six loses!'

The last words were scarcely heard in the commotion.

Lord Melksham looked anxiously at Tom and Will, and over at Widow Trotter. Their hostess was remarkably still. At this precise moment she was surveying her lovingly furnished room, her eyes coming to rest on the stripped carcase of the salmon which still had pride of place on the sideboard. The room was stifling, but she had to remain calm and not let her feelings show. She tried not to catch the eyes of those around her, and remained motionless.

There was to be no respite. Mr Sturgis waved away the proffered money yet again and turned over the third corner of his card. He waited for Mr LeRoy to continue the hand. He was now intent on *trente-et-le-va*, playing for the sum of six hundred guineas. The other players had been struck dumb. By this time the Ace of Spades, lying on the green baize with its four gold coins, seemed to have a talismanic power, as if it were drawing down the influence of the planets into that small room.

'Four wins! – Six loses!'

'King wins! – Eight loses!'

And then it came. The tallière's fingers turned over an Ace, followed by a seven ...

31

The seriousness of the moment was not in doubt, and there was silence. No-one in the room was unaware of the consequences of this run of cards. Now Mr LeRoy felt the embarrassment directly, and for the first time that evening the tallière seemed to hesitate. He looked down at the neat columns of gold and silver before him, unsure what he should do. The bank was about to be broken, and these piles of coin were in no way sufficient; but his hand once more made the offer. Mr Sturgis lifted his right arm to wave him away; but this time, as he did so, Lady Norreys gently set a finger on his wrist. It was the slightest touch but it had an immediate effect. Mr Sturgis froze, glanced sideways at her, and then spoke quietly to Mr LeRoy:

'I have had a good run, have I not, Sir? I shall take my winnings if I may.'

Late that night, in an unsalubrious alley at the western edge of Covent Garden, the Honourable Francis Popham M.P. walked disconsolately and with little sense of direction. The midnight gloom was failing to be a sympathetic companion; his head was throbbing and his steps unsteady. In the drama of Mrs Trotter's basset table he had been replaying the scene of his own disaster at the gaming-house. Every new thought, rather than let in a little light, seemed to add a layer of darkness, black on black. The weight of it was becoming too much to bear.

At the threshold of a new career, ready to fulfil his cherished ambitions and the glittering hopes of his family, he had allowed himself to play the fool. Puffed up with pride and wanting to impress his new friends, he had sunk himself in his own estimation. This was what the preachers called *debauchery*. The idea brought a bitter smile. He had allowed himself to play the part of a dupe in a satiric comedy. The very banality of it! He could hear the audience laughing.

The young man had finally parted company with an ebullient George Sturgis in Long Acre. Frank had refused the offer of a nocturnal jaunt in his chariot, not wishing to be jumbled elbow to elbow by Robert LeRoy. That insufferable prig had joined them and was surprisingly animated for someone who had just become several hundred pounds the poorer – in a queer way the man seemed to want to cling to his adversary. As for his own losses, they were easily spoken yet hard to grasp: *two thousand guineas* – the words reverberated in his mind like a spell. Indeed it was a kind of magic trick: he hadn't strictly lost them, because he had never really had them. Where had this lost wealth come from? Where were these riches he had thrown away? A half hour at the hazard table – it can hardly have been more – had passed like a ghostly interlude. He remembered the pats on the back, the friendly grip on his arm, the shouts of encouragement – all exciting an idea of brilliant success. For a glorious instant he had been Dame Fortune's seducer. But then suddenly everything had stopped. Gilded figures drifted away; bejewelled ladies turned their eyes elsewhere, and he began to feel nauseous – like a shipwrecked sailor choking on a beach.

Frank was jolted out of these thoughts by a sound behind him. It was his own name – *Mr Popham!* – not shouted, but spoken unthreateningly. And he caught footsteps getting closer. In response he turned around, ready for an affable greeting, and out of the night came a stick, swept hard against the side of his head. He staggered back and immediately felt a strong arm forcing itself against his chest, the elbow dug painfully into his ribs. He was pressed flat to the wall, the man's fist now crushing his throat. His name sounded again, only this time it was hissed between clenched teeth. He tried to note the face, but in the dark saw only a pair of eyes blinking beneath a hat. He struggled to catch his breath, but the fist held him tight, the fingers crushing his windpipe. Another sudden shock jarred him as the head of the man's cane was forced into his side. He found himself trembling in pain and bafflement.

'Mr Popham! – This is no place for a midnight stroll. Do you take the air after your unfortunate *adventures?*'

The word was spoken sarcastically. The cane was pushed further, searching out his left kidney.

'Who ... are you?'

This was whispered with the little breath he could muster. There was no answer – only his name again:

'The *honourable* Mister Popham ... I have a message for you ... a message for you to *deliver.*'

The brick wall was forcing the point of Frank's dress sword against his calf – another sharp pain. The stupid thing was adding to the panic he felt on every side. Now he could hardly breathe.

He managed to choke out '*What?*'

The other voice was composed and clear:

'You will tell your father not to *meddle* – do you hear? We wish you to be a good and dutiful son ... Warn him to mind his own affairs – not to poke around in places where he does not belong. *Do you follow?*'

The pressure on Frank's throat relented slightly and he was able to whisper out a response:

'This is madness – I know not what you mean.'

'Your father knows well enough. You are to be our messenger. Tell him, he were best leave stones unturned, do you hear?'

'What stones?'

'You are a fool, Sir! Our message is simple enough – even for you! ... Do you understand? Will you be our messenger?'

The crush on his body was suddenly more intense.

'Yes!'

This came out as a whimper, something like an injured dog. 'Off with you!'

It was spoken in contempt. With a quick turn the man pushed him away, and in a few strides he was gone. Instinctively Frank's hand clutched the hilt of his sword, but he held himself in check as the figure dissolved into the night – something told him a sword-fight would not end well – he was taking desperate breaths and his knees were shaking uncontrollably.

Here, added to the horrors of the day, was a fresh humiliation, and above all a fear – not physical, but a fear of the message and what it might mean. The man's threat was real enough – he felt it in his pulsing chest – but what lay behind it? Was his father caught up in some risky business that was leading him into danger? He knew he must carry the message, but what might he learn when he did so? He choked at the thought, sensing the arm still at his throat. There were no marks on him, but his whole body ached and he was close to sobbing.

And what of his own unwelcome message for his father? Nothing had been said at the Bay-Tree, but news of his loss at hazard must surely reach him soon. Was this the moment for a confession? It would be a mighty double blow. He couldn't bring himself to go home, and yet he would have to face the truth soon. Self-disgust rose up in him. The ruffian in the night had given him a role in another very different drama – and not a heroic one. This was surely cowardice without conscience?

Friday

22 October 1708

Chapter Three

───◦◦◦───

IN THE BAY Tree's coffee-room the following morning, the daily supply of news included gossip much nearer home. The drama of Mrs Trotter's basset was the hot topic around the tables, competing favourably with the siege of Lille, the illness of the Prince Consort, and the fragile state of the Ministry. Indeed, the sharp fall in Bank of England stock seemed as nothing to the near collapse of Widow Trotter's basset-bank. The room was busy, and as she looked around she caught her customers' furtive glances and began to wonder if she shouldn't post a bulletin on the front door giving everyone the full story.

It was a cold autumn morning, and today she badly needed the reassurance this room always gave her. She leaned on the bar and inhaled the heady fragrance of the place that told her she was at home. The crackling fire with its bubbling cauldron, the mingled aromas of bitter coffee and sweetened chocolate, with hints of fruit and spices – even the fug of tobacco that hung around – helped draw her mind from the chilling thoughts that were crowding in. Without doubt, the previous night had been a disaster. She couldn't banish the thought that in setting up the basset table she had taken a step too far. Was it *hubris*? Had she aspired too high? There was a possibility that the Bay-Tree would now carry the taint of a gaming-house, however unfairly

– and as for her own finances, well, things could hardly be more serious.

She knew she ought to have established the house rules firmly and ensured that her tallière enforced them. At first she had felt sorry for Mr LeRoy, who had borne the same heavy loss as herself; but after some thought, much of her concern was dispelled. On the matter of the stake, it was his wilfulness that had brought this on them both. Mrs Trotter's guests had been quick to commiserate, and even those who were nursing losses professed to have enjoyed the evening. Adèle Ménage's threepences had in the end become a full two pounds, and the finances of the aristocratic ladies were robust enough to take the blow. As she left for her coach, Lady Norreys had given her a friendly hug and asked to be kept informed about the next basset evening.

As for the Honourable Mr Sturgis, he had been seen carrying Robert LeRoy from the scene in his handsome chariot – a generous gesture that told her these two members of the gaming fraternity were well acquainted. Beyond that, she was trying not to let her suspicions loose. Mr LeRoy's parting words had assured her their losses would be repaired at the next table and the bank would be in a healthy state in no time – in the jargon of the trade, she would 'get home again.' Such things were easily spoken, and she began to see that her tallière had the practised ease of the gamester himself. But she would never 'get home' unless the stakes were raised. The man was ignorant of the full threatening picture – and 'home' was a word she didn't use lightly.

Widow Trotter's doubts about the enterprise were swelling up again when a familiar voice caught her attention:

'You must not be sad, my Lady! – Above all, you must *not* be *sad!* …'

Elias Cobb, the Covent Garden constable, leaned on the bar beside her. His face was doing its best to lighten her mood.

'… Where would this place be without your good cheer?'

He placed his penny on the bar and removed his hat.

'Oh Elias – I'm finding it very hard this morning … You've heard about the events of last night?'

'I've heard that your table was a vast success – that it had better food than the finest ordinary, and more drama than the Theatre Royal!'

'You give me too much credit. It was a small affair as these things go … but I've taken a great hit …'

The constable's substantial frame settled itself against the bar. He lowered his voice:

'Rumour says it was hundreds of pounds, Molly. Can that be right?'

'Yes, something over three hundred for me on the evening – more than my wage bill for a full year! … and Mr LeRoy too, of course – though I've come to suspect he has larger resources … Oh, Elias, how could I have been so foolish? I had planned an evening among friends, but by the end we were having deep and dangerous play – certainly too deep for me. I had not planned on this at all.'

Elias Cobb could see how sharply the blow had struck and he hesitated to inquire further; but they were old and trusted friends, and if there was anything he could do …

'The bank – are you able to carry the sum?'

'Not immediately. This is something I must arrange today. I need to venture into Birchin Lane. I had funds enough for the present and was thinking to build up the bank over time … but things slipped out of hand.'

'Ah, yes, your Mr LeRoy … I trust he has paid his share of the loss?'

Mrs Trotter tried to sound confident:

'I have a bundle of paper notes under various hands – to be negotiated.'

'*Paper credit!!* …'

Elias spat out the words in contempt and shook his head decisively.

'… Scraps of paper floating around – light as air! I'd never trust those flimsy things, nor the people who trade in them. Give me good solid *specie* – metal you can rub your fingers on and dig your teeth into!'

'You are behind the times, Elias. Business doesn't deal in bags of gold anymore – though I admit I'm always glad to count the coins at the end of a day.'

'You can melt down your coin, Molly, and still have the value – but try setting fire to that precious paper. Where's *value* then? Just a whiff of smoke! No, no – give me money to have and to hold. Like a good wife. Something of substance!'

Widow Trotter smiled benignly on her old friend:

'I love coin as much as you do, Elias – and nothing else is taken here. But we must *flirt* with paper occasionally. I'm sure there'll be no problem.'

<hr>

And so, holding her pocket-case close, Widow Trotter made the best of her way eastwards into the City. Bounded by its ancient walls and gates, this was the core of London, the great mart of the nation where opportunity ruled and wealth grew out of nothing. The scent of money was almost palpable, competing with smoky chimneys and sweating horseflesh. Here Dirt and Beauty went hand in hand, with Trade blessing their union. Along Fleet Street into Cheapside and on to Cornhill the thoroughfare was one long avenue of shops – no shortage of coin here! – and Mary Trotter found herself in a surging tide of commerce as relentless as the River Thames itself. To right and left, the window displays were little gilded theatres that allured the fancy and fed the eyes with colour. She paused in front of a miniature cottage moulded out of spun sugar and twisted ginger which had sweetmeats spilling from it like guineas; in another window, coloured silks were spread out in a rainbowed wheel of fortune; in a third, a group of china jars and ivory snuff boxes appeared to be in lively conversation as they flaunted among miniature posies. The shops offered a gift to the imagination: swags of delicate lace made patterns in the air; hats and scarves hung from invisible threads; silver chains coiled across black velvet. Everything was there to catch the eye – and open the purse.

Along the pavement the human displays were equally fine, with gentlemen in skirted coats and cocked hats pointing their canes, and ladies under extravagantly tall top knots being trailed by page-boys encumbered with parcels and hat-boxes. Widow Trotter's pocket-case was clutched even tighter as if in resistance to the temptation to spend and spend.

She rounded the slight bend into Cornhill, and the full magnificence of the street stretched out before her. There on the left the handsome Royal Exchange was presiding over the scene with its storied clock tower and elegant arches. If the City was the kingdom of international trade, then this was its regal palace. But Mrs Trotter's mission today was leading her in a different direction. At the entrance to the Exchange she turned her back on the Corinthian pillars and negotiated the crossing of the busy street, making her way beneath a narrow arch into a side alley.

At once the noisy bustle of Cornhill was left behind. Now she was even deeper in the land of commerce, but this was a different scene. In Exchange Alley little was on show – quite the opposite. It was a place of bowed heads and furtive glances, with groups of dark-suited men in consultation. Others stood watching from doorways, assessing the pedestrian traffic for likely clients. No two-shilling whores these, though in principle their trade was hardly different and their propositions equally seductive. Curiosity and opportunity were the stimulus. Brokers and dealers circled each other.

The alley twisted snake-like through a series of passageways, with offices and shops intermingled. There were no elegant displays here: the emphasis was on practical needs: stationers, scriveners, barbers and gentlemen's hatters. And of course there were coffee houses – not for leisure, but for work. In this closely packed enclave you were within hailing distance of every piece of hot news or chilling rumour as it arrived. Exchange Alley was the first port of call for any snippet of information – false as well as true – that might nudge the market, sway the public mood, create sudden alarm, or rouse a spirit of adventure. In particular, Jonathan's was the hub of the business, and as she walked past the place, the door to her left swung open and cries of 'Who deals?' and 'What price?' flew out. She turned her head and glimpsed a pair of men inside shouting to each other and gesticulating urgently. It seemed something was causing a flurry today, and she sensed an electric charge in the air. But perhaps it was merely excitement of the blood?

Nevertheless she was beginning to feel uneasy, and Garraway's Coffee House to her right was also noisy. Suddenly a man hurried out, beckoning to another stationed further up the alley. The two of them sprinted off together leaving Mrs Trotter in their wake. She looked round and hesitated. As she did so, a young man in a tightly-buttoned coat stepped forward. He had noticed her pocket-case. With a slight incline of the head, he doffed his hat and inquired in silken tones: 'Do you wish to make a purchase today, ma'am? – I have bank stock at a hundred and twelve – an excellent opportunity after the recent fall ...' He began walking beside her. '... or perhaps something more speculative? There are great possibilities for Mr Hancock's rape-oil soap – he's taking subscribers this very moment – over in the Three Tuns ...'

Widow Trotter's stomach shifted slightly at the thought. A thick brownish oil spread over the skin? ... whatever next!

'... Also, extracting inflammable air from coal ... There are great opportunities, ma'am! You would not believe ... We have a special purchase of stock ...'

She gave him the courtesy of a friendly look:

'Forgive me, Sir, but I am about other business today. You must excuse me!'

His eyes were dark and intense, and they remained fixed on her:

'Then please let me give you this.'

Seemingly from nowhere his thumb flicked out a small card. She took it and glanced down. *'Michael Henriques – Factor and Broker. Birchin Lane.'*

'Mr Henriques – thank you. As you say, there are so many opportunities ...'

The man bowed again, more deeply this time, and she was allowed to continue on her way.

At the end of the alley was a narrow passage that led into Birchin Lane itself, a thoroughfare packed with offices of notaries and brokers. Emerging into the street she saw a sign above her head: *Henriques. Commodity Importer*, and over on the other side were the offices of the Sword Blade Company, her bankers.

It was a reassuringly faceless exterior. What had once been a shop was now displaying in its window a printed list of stock prices above a cursory arrangement of dry autumnal blooms. It couldn't match the pretensions of the Bank of England, but it seemed trustworthy enough. Only fourteen years old, the Bank of England was proving to be the big bully of the market; but recently it was not having its own way, and a fall of over ten per cent had shaken confidence a little. During this time the Sword Blade, with its firm base in land and property, had held its own and was outfacing threats to limit its ambitions.

In truth, the Sword Blade office had little to show for itself, but its door was solid and freshly painted and the main room was busy and comfortable with a log fire giving out enough warmth to put clients at their ease. A rumble of voices from an interior office indicated that a lively meeting was in progress. Widow Trotter availed herself of one of the comfortable chairs and waited, amused by the two heavy oak desks across the room at which the company's public business was transacted. They formed a stark contrast: one was scattered with papers in untidy heaps, while the second was uncluttered, with a neat pile of files set to one side.

When the moment came, she made for the tidy one.

The face that welcomed her was familiar – a face that could tell a tale, as the saying went – and indeed it was a story she partly knew. But today there was serious business to be transacted and their polite exchanges were soon over:

'My dear Mrs Trotter. Welcome!'

The voice was reassuringly rich and dark, like malmsey. It was not unlike a dignified sermon-voice.

'Thank you, Mr Grigsby. I trust that you – and the company – are flourishing?'

There was a humour in the tone that dispelled any awkwardness in the question.

'Indeed we thrive, Mrs Trotter. We are both in robust health!'

The sentiments were more cheering than the face that uttered them. The man's neatly-tied linen cravat supported a countenance which seemed to have a natural inclination to droop. Every feature hung heavy. He smiled at her, but the manoeuvre was effortful and only emphasised the weight that had to be lifted. His movements, however, were precise, and the eyes were warm. Mr Grigsby she knew to be a sympathetic gentleman, and so she began her story of the previous night's events in an easy frame of mind.

As the tale of the basset table unfolded, the cashier shook his head. The heavy jowls swayed, the brow lowered further, and a look of kindly sorrow added to the gravity of the moment. A quiet 'tut tut' – not a censorious one – came from his lips; and as she drew out the bundle of Mr LeRoy's paper notes from her pocket-case he reached over and took them from her, spreading them out on the desk in front of him.

'Let us see what we have,' he said. 'Three hundred pounds you say?'

'I think you'll find these notes are for three hundred and twenty, Mr Grigsby. A deposit to offset what I owe. I gave Mr Sturgis two hundred in cash and a note for the rest of the sum – four hundred – to be drawn on my Sword Blade account.'

'I see,' he said, lowering his head further. She folded her hands in her lap and waited. There was silence as he ran through the documents. Once more the jowls began to swing – more quickly now. He cleared his throat:

'Hmmmm … "Three Sword Blade notes – number 41 for twelve pounds ten shillings; number 19 for twenty-three pounds; number 66 for thirty pounds … Six Bank of England notes – number 114 for fifteen pounds" … hmmmm …'

Again there was silence. He turned and extracted a file from low down in his pile. He leafed through it, then turned back to the papers on his desk.

'… "One note under the hand of Mr Richard Mason for twenty pounds, payable to William Scrimpshaw, dated the 24th instant; one note under the hand of Crofts for thirty pounds, payable to Mr John Mead; one note under the hand of Fisher for twenty-five pounds …"'

He glanced again at the paper in his file. Widow Trotter shifted in her seat. The atmosphere had suddenly grown chilly.

Mr Grigsby raised his head a little and looked at her. The weight of the world seemed to tell on his heavy cheeks as he spoke:

'I greatly fear, Mrs Trotter … I have to tell you that payment on these notes has been stopped – stopped earlier this year. They are no longer current.'

'*Not current?* What can you mean?'

'They cannot be honoured. What my files tell me is that the notes – all of them – were in a wallet that was lost on March 26th – dropped by one of our clients while on his way here from the Mine Adventure office on Snow Hill. He was very distraught – I remember the incident well. Of course, the notes were stopped at once, and advertisements printed in the newspapers. The gentleman offered a reward – as much as *twenty guineas* … but the time has elapsed on that … These pieces of paper are worthless, Mrs Trotter. I am so sorry. You will have to raise the matter with Mr LeRoy.'

'Do you mean that Mr LeRoy stole them?'

'No, not at all. These things circulate freely until redeemed – or until someone *tries* to redeem them …'

Widow Trotter was hardly breathing.

'… From what you say, your gentleman – your *tallière* – is not unacquainted with several gaming-houses of the capital? Such bank notes and promissory notes are kept for settling debts and are easily passed on. A wise gamester will take his winnings in coin and pay his losses with paper. It is a veritable whirligig, Mrs Trotter! The law is very lax about such things, and in a case like this it has much catching-up to do.'

Her face was reddening by the moment – words and images flashed through her mind. Embarrassment, fear, and anger were debating the matter inside her. How could she have let this happen? What should she do?

Her next words were hesitant ones:

'The note I gave to Mr Sturgis – for four hundred …'

'Dear lady, your account as it stands cannot cover it – not the *full* sum at least – only a half. From our records, a loan of two hundred pounds is needed to cover the deficit, if one could be arranged.'

The little word *if* slipped quickly by, but left its mark. She had always thought it a fearful syllable. How much hung on *if!* ... The tiny sound uttered in conversation could bring anything into doubt, undermine the boldest argument, challenge the firmest belief.

'But cannot my note also be stopped?'

Mr Grigsby's gaze continued intent and well-meaning, but his words were not cheering:

'The note has not got into the wrong hands, Mrs Trotter. It has not been lost or stolen. I fear there are no grounds for the bank to invalidate it ... but let us see what transpires. You will have to confront Mr LeRoy. Much also depends on Mr Sturgis. If he does not press the debt ...'

If again!

'... if he is content to allow you time – then I'm sure we can come to some arrangement. The Bay-Tree is your freehold property, is it not? You have excellent security for any loan that we – or another party – may advance.'

The dagger was pressed to her heart, and she fought to remain calm. Her mind was working hard. She was turning the situation round in her head – conscious of a mismatch between Mr LeRoy's debt to her, and her debt to Mr Sturgis ... How could she be trapped in the middle – unable to pursue the one, yet bound to settle the other?

Now anger was fighting it out with fear.

'Unfortunately, your promissory note to Mr Sturgis has your signature on it ... In return you are left with an assortment of notes, none of which has currency. It is an unfortunate state of affairs. I heartily condole with you, Mrs Trotter.'

She reeled out of the Sword Blade office and stood for a moment on the pavement to steady herself, her free hand gripping a post.

Birchin Lane was full of life, and all around her business was brisk. She wondered how many other people had hesitated outside one of these doors contemplating ruin and wondering where to turn. Her case was not wholly desperate – not yet – and she had committed herself to nothing with the bank. As the thoughtful Mr Grigsby had explained, this was something to be taken up urgently with Mr LeRoy. The tallière's image came to her mind and with it a tightness in the stomach. It was not a confrontation she relished, but it had to be faced. A voice was telling her that the man was slippery – someone well versed in the entanglements of profit and loss, in the making and breaking of fortunes. She suddenly thought of the Bay-Tree, and the pain was almost palpable. Not yet, she thought – surely not yet? There was no cause for panic. But she needed to consult her friends. This was a labyrinth through which she must step with extreme care.

She crossed the street again and headed back into the twisting alleys.

Chapter Four

B ACK ON HOME ground, Widow Trotter pushed open the door of the Bay-Tree to find the coffee-room at its liveliest. Ripples of conversation reached her through the warm, spicy air, and she could see a lot of animated nodding, smiling and frowning. The cauldron over the fire was humming to itself, and something else was bubbling up too. She at once became part of it.

There was a shout from one of the tables:

'What news from 'Change Alley, Mrs Trotter? The *Albemarle!* – what have you heard? …'

The booming voice was that of Jack Tapsell, a substantial wine merchant sitting with his cronies by the fire.

'… Barney here tells us the whole cargo is lost! Indigo and diamonds …'

'And one *hundred tons* of coffee!' said Barnabas Smith, cloth trader. 'Imagine it! Now that's a shocking waste!'

'I trust you've a good stock in the cellar, Mrs T – or it'll cost you. The price is bound to soar. A hundred tons of coffee! – imagine it!'

'And indigo too – in Looe Bay they'll be swimming in the stuff,' said Sam Cust, plantation owner. 'A shame they don't have tons of Jamaican sugar drowned as well!'

It was an odd idea, but for Widow Trotter a picture was beginning to form:

'I did sense some commotion in Jonathan's, gentlemen, but was about other business. This is the Indiaman, is it not? ... But surely, I read only yesterday that the ship had come safe?'

Jack Tapsell was shaking his head slowly in an impression of wisdom:

'A false report it seems, Mrs Trotter! You know how little these things are to be trusted.'

His companions drew on their pipes and contemplated the extent of human duplicity.

'Someone at the Exchange will be rejoicing – mark my words,' said Jack. 'Set up for life! By tomorrow he'll be hunting for a country estate. It's happened before, and will happen again. A private messenger sent post haste from the scene – and a dealer can make a fortune.'

'But how do we know *this* isn't false news now?' said Sam Cust somewhat philosophically. 'Who is to say the Albemarle isn't safe in the roads already?'

'The coffee is nothing. Think about those diamonds! The finest stones you can imagine. Report says there's a thousand guineas reward to be offered on their recovery. The wealth of India!'

'A *thousand?*'

'Aye – and the Queen's pardon! Now, if that's not something to set the smugglers at each other's throats ...'

It was an uncertain world, and Mrs Trotter left them to their speculations. Such fortunes to be played for! In her head she could still hear cries of '*Who buys?*' and see the wild eyes and waving hands.

In relief she turned to the bar, where Jenny Trip was entertaining a pair of smartly-attired gentlemen. The scarlet lappets on her head-dress swayed as she caught their eyes in turn, and her white hand was extended to one of them. The man

raised it elegantly, drew it towards him, and inclined his head –
a courtly gesture that reminded Mrs Trotter of an old print of
Queen Elizabeth. What she thought of as Jenny's 'snuff-taking
ceremony' was popular with the bolder clientele, and these two
newcomers were clearly being charmed.

But the expression on Jenny's face altered. She called
over:

'Mrs T! – Mr Bristowe wishes to talk with you – he has
some news to share.'

Widow Trotter nodded and was about to move on, when
one of the gentlemen swung round:

'Ah, our hostess! ...'

The face was florid and fleshy, and the greeting was
followed by an audible sniff and a twitch of the nose as the
man raised a finger and inserted some errant snuff into his
left nostril.

'We were about to enquire of this polite girl ... your basset
table, Mrs Trotter – is it ... does it *operate?*'

The man at his side turned round also, and from within a
flaxen periwig a pair of heavy-lidded eyes appraised her:

'Its fame has reached us, madam. We hear it is a select and
well-appointed table.'

She was already becoming uncomfortable:

'I fear play has been suspended, gentlemen – temporarily –
to permit one or two adjustments to be made ...'

Her voice dried. Embarrassment was creeping up on her,
heightened by a feeling that the men were suppressing smiles.
There was a hint of satirical curiosity in their looks which she
did not like.

'You are certainly fortunate in your *tallière*, Mrs Trotter
– Robert LeRoy is a man of consummate skill. We miss him
terribly at Vandernan's. There is none better in the management
of a pack of cards.'

'Yes, such calm and confidence! We are quite devoted to him.'

'You always feel he is doing his *best* for you.'

The words came almost as a sigh. The friends' eyes met, their two heads slightly tilted in duet. Widow Trotter expected them to burst into song at any moment.

'Does he no longer practise at Vandernan's?'

It was a direct question. They both breathed in sharply.

'Mr LeRoy became … dissatisfied. He felt he was not appreciated by those with authority in the place.'

'Oh, I understood he was still the banker there …'

'Alas no – and like many a successful bank, I think he has a mind to a life of greater leisure.'

'The fruits, Mrs Trotter, are to be savoured.'

'The rewards of *skill*.'

It occurred to Mrs Trotter that the *skills* of the basset table (to judge from her limited experience) were far to seek – unless they were those of neat-handedness and dexterity.

The two men were looking at each other again. Mary Trotter's mind was racing:

'You speak of Mr LeRoy, Sirs, as an artist who has *sharpened* those skills – something of a magician perhaps?' she added, with a dextrous emphasis of her own and a knowing look that kept the two of them in her sights.

'Yes indeed,' replied the flaxen wig, a little lamely.

'Exactly so,' echoed his friend, glancing over at the tables. 'You will find him most satisfactory, I'm sure … when do you expect him to return here? Where is he now?'

'I cannot answer either question, gentlemen. Mr LeRoy has no firm contract with me. Ours has been an informal arrangement.'

Widow Trotter decided the game should end there. She nodded a welcome, and the two of them turned away from the bar, leaving a grinning Jenny behind them.

'I heard a new word the other day, Mrs T,' she said. '... *Connosewer* ... Do you think our gentlemen are *connosewers* of the card-table?'

'Indeed I do, Jenny. As always you have hit the nail ... I think our Mr LeRoy has perfected his *craft!*'

She wondered to herself just how far that craft extended. How sharp was his practice?

Meanwhile, on the second floor of the Bay-Tree Tom Bristowe had been pacing his chamber like a prisoner measuring out his cell. He had deserted his writing-desk where the manuscript of *Covent Garden: A Poem in Two Books* (an optimistic title) lay scratched over with disordered jottings. His thoughts were in disarray, and the writing of verse had failed to settle them. Vegetables – especially root vegetables – were proving resistant to poetic treatment, and he had spent the previous half hour wrestling with a couplet on the radish. It was no use. His thoughts kept turning to the events of the previous evening, and he now found himself, pen suspended, gazing at the wall trying to make sense of the double disaster.

Cousin Frank and Widow Trotter were both in trouble ... no, in real danger. The more he thought about their plight the more anxious he became. At the basset table he had seen how easily substantial things could melt away. Now all was unsure, and his two friends couldn't trust to firm ground any more. In his georgic poem he had been writing about the returns of the earth, the rootedness of Nature, and how it nurtured life and strength – but in the world of gaming ... all was up in the air, blown hither and thither.

But before he did anything, he needed to open his heart to his wise friend Mrs Trotter – he knew she could keep the secret of Frank's calamity. Perhaps she too might wish to talk? She had gone to Exchange Alley to see her banker, and he was apprehensive of what she might have found there. After all, the place was a byword for risky dealing, peopled with stock-jobbers and sharpers …

There was a knock, and Tom turned to see his landlady standing in the doorway. For a moment each remained silent, breathing the troubled air between them, until, playing the host, he offered her the single armchair while he turned his desk chair round and sat down beside her:

'So, Mrs T, you have survived your venture into 'Change Alley?'

He was trying to sound genial, but the look on her face was not encouraging: the eyes were slightly puffy and her chin hung loose:

'I've certainly a tale to tell … but Jenny has told me you also have news, and she didn't speak it lightly – I trust it's nothing to give you concern?'

Her voice was strained. Behind the formality Tom sensed a struggle to hold her thoughts together. He suspected things had not gone well over in the City. But perhaps talking for a moment of his own worries might help lighten hers?

'It was a dark day for you yesterday, Mrs T – and also for the Pophams … I have told no-one – but there's something I have to share with you …'

'It will go no further, Tom,' she said, at once relieving him of the need to ask.'… Your family? Not a grave matter, I hope. You must tell me what is weighing on your mind.'

'Oh, Mrs T! So much is weighing – and so heavily. It's Frank – Cousin Frank – he is in deep trouble. A difficulty not unlike yours … and for him no less serious. A gaming debt – what they call a "debt of honour."'

'Ha! Yes, that foolish notion! There is much nonsense spoken of female honour, but *men's* honour can be truly absurd … You are not about to tell me of a duel?'

'No no – it is not something so easily settled … He has made a fearful loss at hazard. He was drawn into some deep play at Vandernan's gaming-house and found himself drowned. He has to find a vast sum – it's not a loss he can cover …'

This was coming too close.

'… He is not being pressed at this moment but might be at any time … George Sturgis has bought up the promissory note. It is a stay of execution – but I would never trust that man.'

Mrs Trotter felt a footstep on her grave, and gave an involuntary shudder:

'Oh – yes, a case very similar to my own … Hazard and basset! How easily we stoop to folly! … Can I ask the sum? Are you able to tell me?'

Tom's response was quiet:

'Two thousand pounds.'

She breathed out heavily, feeling the weight of it:

'Oh Tom – that's a vast sum indeed. And you say the *Honourable* Mr Sturgis – the man's title makes me wince! – has it in his power …'

She was reluctant to finish the thought.

'Yes, poor Frank is at his mercy. It's a frightening state of affairs. I have presentiments, Mrs T … There is something about that man which chills me – for all his *bonhomie*.'

'I think he rides easily over difficulties. I just hope he doesn't ride over people as readily.'

'If only Frank had not brought him to your table …'

'Yes – *if* … But it wasn't chance. I think Mr Sturgis sniffed an opportunity.'

'Frank says the man had insisted on trying his luck at a new table. He was full of confidence, was he not?'

'Confidence – and assurance …'

She hesitated to bring forward the thought that had been niggling her.

'... Perhaps he felt assured the play would favour him.'

'What do you mean?'

She told him about the two gentlemen she had encountered in the coffee-room – her suspicion that the newcomers were gloating at her discomfiture:

'They are both particular admirers of Robert LeRoy. They were paying tribute to our tallière's dexterity and were eager to call on his services again. It seems Mr LeRoy has left Vandernan's – and I suspect not willingly. They spoke of some difficulty there but tried to brush it away.'

'So, Mr Sturgis's triumph last night was managed, do you think?'

'Who can say? We cannot make that claim yet. But the thought has been tapping at me all day ...'

She hesitated.

'... There can be a fellowship among gamester's, Tom – especially winner and loser. Each knows how easily their places may be reversed. Heads and tails – odds and even – the game needs both ... You know that Mr Sturgis carried Mr LeRoy off in his chariot?'

'What!'

'After the game. They were seen in the Strand – Mr LeRoy looking every inch the gallant! Do you not think it strange? I'm beginning to wonder if there had been some arrangement between them – some manipulation.'

'Sleight of hand?'

'Yes.'

They fell silent for a moment, contemplating the possibility of collusion and what it implied.

Then Tom spoke, hesitantly:

'And you have Mr LeRoy's paper ...'

There was another pause. She averted her eyes, and in that instant – no words needed – his suspicions were confirmed.

'... Oh, dear Mrs T ... I hope what I'm thinking ...'

'Alas, Tom, you have run ahead of me. If I said that all his notes are worthless ...'

'*All?*'

His heart sank as she proceeded to tell him about her visit to Birchin Lane and what she had learned there – that the paper had possibly been circulating round the gaming-tables of London for months – like a stinking handkerchief no-one wanted to pocket.

'Mr Grigsby advised me to confront Mr LeRoy. The man surely cannot avoid making reparation? It's the one thing that comforts me – that he has paid me in what is not legal tender.'

Tom hesitated. It occurred to him that the notes were not forged but withdrawn – he would have to ask Will about the legal question. So much was uncertain. How firm was a promise on paper? What was to be taken on trust? How far did it extend? Was Mr LeRoy himself a fraud?

Widow Trotter's thoughts were running in parallel. She pictured the tallière in her mind's eye, enthroned at her basset table with a king's ransom of crowns and guineas – her coins! – before him. Yes, the bank of the Bay-Tree had been solid enough. But what of the bank of Mr LeRoy?

She saw that Tom was sunk in gloom and tried to brighten her countenance. Together they must think about what was to be done. Something practical was needed.

With a thrust of her arms, she left the chair:

'We have to do something, Tom! We must inquire into this *Honourable* Mr Sturgis – how secure his honour is and who his friends are. What is his credit? Does he have "bottom," as the traders say? We must certainly investigate Vandernan's and what goes on there. There may be someone who knows more about Mr Robert LeRoy and why he was sent packing – if that's what it was. And I have to confront the man himself, however painful it may be. Perhaps you should ask Mr Lundy? – this is the kind of inquiry that will appeal to him. And your uncle too – he's such an honest gentleman and will surely want to know more about Mr Sturgis and Mr LeRoy. New friends, or old friends? ...'

The words were unstoppable with hardly a pause for breath. Tom looked in admiration at his landlady, who was now turned toward the window, hands on hips, eyes directed through the casement glass to the big city beyond.

'... Out there, Tom – just think of it! – how many schemers and jugglers are busying themselves, every man seizing his chance, with nothing but self to guide him ... *Sordid self-interest!* – isn't that what the pamphleteers call it? Well, perhaps we shall have to do some scheming ourselves – learn the tricks of the trade and take our own chances? I wonder if there are any rules, or is this a game with none? I doubt the law is going to help us ... but we shall see.'

Tom saw to his relief that the Trotter sparkle had returned – although her determination was alarming. The lady had a mission, and nothing was going to stop her. With such enthusiasm lighting up the chamber he even began to detect in himself an appetite for the task ahead.

Chapter Five

WHILE WIDOW TROTTER made her way down the stairs to the coffee-room, Tom sensed a new energy in himself. His mind was limber and alert, as if he'd heard a bugle call. The desk beneath the window with its inkwell and scattered papers spoke of recent torpor and admonished him. With a surge of confidence, he turned back to his work determined to make some poetic progress before *Covent Garden* was consigned to the drawer. A new task was looming, and this old one would have to take second place.

But the creative spurt was brief. After a while he heard a sudden sharp crack – then silence. He looked up, distracted. At that moment he had been running the phrase *humble kale* across his tongue and found that it gave pleasure ... A second much louder crack brought him to his senses and made him jump to his feet. He reached up to the casement before a third stone could shatter the glass.

In the cobbled alley below he recognised the gentleman, pebble in hand, silently waving. But why this furtiveness?

He called out: 'I'll come down!'

A moment later at the side door he found a familiar figure, but one that had undergone a change – the eyes were stained with red, and the face had a haggard look.

'Frank! … What the deuce?'

His cousin said nothing, but Tom knew why he hadn't wished to make a formal entrance into the coffee-room: this young man had been through a hard time.

'I wasn't expecting this,' said Tom awkwardly as they made their way up the stairs. He was wondering what story Frank had to tell and knew it would not be a comfortable one: his cousin was still wearing last night's clothes.

'I've been up all night, Tom! … I've not been home.'

The implications were clear: poor Frank had not dared return to Pall Mall and his parents. Vivid images flashed across Tom's mind – of his cousin back in the gaming-house desperately trying to recoup his losses but sinking even deeper until hauled off by the beadles to the Fleet … It was something of a satiric sketch and he banished it – but the idea remained.

He seated Frank in the armchair and quickly thrust his poem in a drawer, embarrassed at how it had distracted him. He knew he should have been giving thought to his cousin's affairs. He leaned forward and spoke softly:

'So, your father still knows nothing of your escapade at Vandernan's …'

It wasn't posed as a question and there was no reply. Frank swallowed hard as if holding back tears, a look of abject despair on his face.

'… Where have you been?'

A pause, and another swallow.

'Walking the streets …' It was said in a whisper.

'*All night? …*'

Silence again. Another troubling image flashed into Tom's mind, even more vivid this time. He flinched from it.

'. . We ought to have had words last night, Frank! We should have talked things through – but you stuck so close to Mr Sturgis …'

'Ah, Tom! What have I done? I thought George was a friend – he was the one who was sticking close to *me*! But last night I saw something else … When I left here, Robert LeRoy was waiting for us in Long Acre …'

'Ah! That must have made for an awkward scene?'

'On the contrary, Tom. There was a lot of grinning and good cheer – you can imagine how I felt. It seems the plan was for the three of us to explore what the Strand had to offer. Can you believe it? The pair seemed to be fast friends … I left them to it, and they jaunted off in George's chariot.'

Tom's fears were confirmed.

'This is certain, then?'

'I saw it with my own eyes. It was blatant – the two of them in collusion. I thought of poor Mrs Trotter – there was surely some dirty dealing there? And as for Vandernan's, I have been re-living my adventure at the hazard-table – the few moments I can recall clearly – and I'm convinced advantage was taken – that there was some sharp practice. Mrs Trotter's case is different, I know – but when I think back, I see George at my elbow constantly pressing me, drawing his friends around us, full of encouraging words …'

Frank was painting a picture, and it was an all too familiar one.

'… The pair of them are *rooks* – *sharpers* … There is such confidence in them.'

'I think you must be right. But suspicion is not evidence. We must talk with Mrs Trotter. Not many minutes ago I entrusted your secret to her …'

'Tom!'

There was alarm in his cousin's eyes.

'It is for the best. We can trust her completely, and she deserves to have the full picture. We must hold our forces together on this. Word has already reached her of Mr Sturgis's chariot! I assure you she has been having her own suspicions of Mr LeRoy.'

Tom was expecting his cousin's countenance to lift a little – but if anything, his look grew darker. He was gazing distractedly into the far corner of the room, as if at a ghost.

Tom sensed something was wrong:

'Is there anything else you need to tell me? You must tell me all – or we shall make no progress with this.'

With great effort Frank dragged his eyes back to his cousin:

'There is more to my story, Tom, which you haven't heard … Something much more serious.'

Tom was apprehensive. Frank's countenance was eloquent. The young man was not just ashamed – he was afraid:

'Something else happened last night …'

Tom listened intently to the story of Frank's encounter with the ruffian. It was clearly no common assault, but a larger warning – a threat of violence against his father.

'What can it mean, Tom? Do you think my father is involved in some dubious business? I can scarce believe it – I hate to think he is in danger.'

'I suspect there's some connection with your debt, Frank.'

'But how could this be?'

'You say the man knew of it.'

'Yes, he spoke mockingly of my *adventures*. He knew about my humiliation.'

'And you must have been followed – the man surely didn't encounter you by accident. There's surely no coincidence here. There must be a common thread.'

Frank sighed at the thought. He saw there was nothing left but to grasp the nettle and talk with his father immediately – about everything.

Tom agreed, and told him so:

'I suspect your losses at the hazard-table will figure. From what you say, Uncle Jack may be about some difficult business – making unwelcome inquiries perhaps. Are you sure you took no hint from him about what they might be?'

'Nothing. He was his genial self yesterday, was he not?'

'Well, now you must be completely open with him. You have to return to Pall Mall and lay your cards on the table …'

Tom checked himself. The image was an uncomfortable one, but for the first time he glimpsed a lifting of his cousin's features.

'You could say the die is cast, Tom!' came the reply.

Tom understood what a doubly difficult interview it was likely to be – two alarming revelations, each leading to awkward questions:

'What if I came along with you, Frank? It might help to have another voice besides yours.'

His cousin's relief was palpable, and he was more than happy to agree.

But for Tom there was another more practical motive. It was important to know if his uncle was caught up in some clandestine business and had given some offence. What dangerous forces had he aroused? Frank had allowed himself to be drawn into a murky world, and if there was a connection to be made with the threat to his father, then they needed to know of it. At the back of Tom's mind was a remark Widow Trotter had made about a gamesters' fellowship. It was a chilling idea. He began to wonder if this might be more than comradeship – a fraternity perhaps? If there were 'gentlemen of the road' then why not 'gentlemen of the tables?'

Little did the two cousins know, but while they talked in Tom's chamber, down in the coffee-room a scene was playing that would change the picture dramatically for both of them. It began routinely enough when the face of Tobias Mudge appeared in the doorway. On his watchman's rounds he was rarely hesitant, but today he was seeking out Widow Trotter for a quiet word, and when he saw her by the fire in conversation with one of the Bay-Tree regulars he beckoned her over. The hostess had been doing her best to encourage a convivial atmosphere, and she greeted him warmly. But the usually chirpy young watchman was about more solemn business. Together they found a station by the corner of the bar.

'You have a dark face on you, Toby.'

'Yes – and for a reason, Mrs Trotter. I carry a message from Constable Cobb. He cannot come himself. It's something he says you ought to know about – before it's the talk of the streets … one of your card-playing people …'

'You mean one of my guests at the basset table?'

'Yes, that's it – a gentleman who was here upstairs last night.'

'You must tell me, Toby. Has something happened?'

'A body, Mrs Trotter – they've found a body. You must keep it to yourself until Mr Cobb can tell you the particulars. You see … the *circumstances*, well, they were *peculiar* … I can't tell you more. But he wants you to know that it's a Mr Sturgis – or was … Mr Cobb says he won a lot of money here last night.'

Widow Trotter drew in her breath and nodded. George Sturgis dead!

'Yes, a great deal, Toby. He swept the board … was this a robbery then? How terrible! The gentleman was well soused when he arrived, but composed enough in his play …'

'I can't say, ma'am – you must ask Mr Cobb about all this. He'll come round here when he can. He thinks the particular *circumstances* …' (that word again!) '… are sure to concern you.'

He paused. Widow Trotter began to feel uneasy – as though a finger were pointing at herself:

'Well of course, yes, I am *concerned* …'

But as she spoke she heard the ambiguity. Her hesitation underlined it. She was longing to bombard Toby with questions but knew she must wait for her old friend Elias. It seemed the full sum of the watchman's message had been delivered.

'... But Toby – why this visit, when you cannot tell me more?'

'Rumour, Mrs Trotter. The gossip will begin at any moment, and Mr Cobb wants to reassure you. He will tell you all. You must believe nothing unless you hear it from him.'

This was enigmatic, and her own curiosity was now at full stretch:

'And this is for my ears alone, Toby?'

'Oh yes, of course. You're to keep mum.'

'Then mum it is.'

As the watchman turned to leave, the hum of conversation in the room suddenly died, only to surge up again as the door closed behind him. Bewigged heads turned back to the tables and conjecture was renewed with some nodding and nudging. Widow Trotter stood frozen to the spot, not knowing where to turn. Her coffee-room was always expectant for news, and the arrival of the Watch had brought a swell of interest. She thought of the place as a character with moods and responses of its own, and at this moment they echoed hers. She longed to share her thoughts with someone. But the conjectures must remain her own. The death of George Sturgis was dramatic, and the implications could be momentous. As if things were not complicated enough already!

But the chatelaine of the Bay-Tree was made of resilient material. She turned to the room, offered her people a radiant smile, and spoke words that were designed both to placate and shamelessly to titillate:

'Yes, gentlemen. We are promised news! – But in the meantime it seems we must be patient. Despite the fate of the Albemarle, we do have a good supply of coffee!'

Chapter Six

MEANWHILE, TOM AND Cousin Frank had slipped out of the side door of the Bay-Tree and begun making their way westwards towards St James's. A quick wash had made the errant young man a little less like a vagrant, and they set off along Red Lion Court in determined spirits. The arcaded piazza of Covent Garden was its usual organised turmoil, and as they wove their way past the market stalls Tom began to think himself inside his own poem. He felt the liveliness, variety and clutter of the place. An exuberant miscellany it certainly was, but in his poem it needed to be more than that. The thing must be given a shape and a sense of direction. The thought made him glance at his cousin, who was walking a little ahead as if needing to take the lead. Frank was silent and apprehensive, and no wonder: it was an uncertain mission that didn't bode well. As they walked on, Feste's little song arrived in Tom's mind like a welcome friend: yes, 'what's to come is still unsure,' he thought to himself. 'In delay there lies no plenty ...'

Without warning, his cousin swung round:

'*Flowers*, Tom! Don't you think we should arrive laden with polite *bouquets* – as extravagant as possible! ...'

It was a wild gesture, and a welcome distraction perhaps.

But Tom had been thinking of a more subdued approach given the circumstances. His frown stopped Frank in his tracks.

'… You don't like the idea?'

'I was thinking some choice fruit would be more welcome. We don't want to be too celebratory, do we?'

His words were overheard by an old woman with a basket, who stepped forward:

'Ripe peaches, Sir?' she inquired courteously – it was no street cry. She held the basket out to him and drew back the coverlet. The fruit lay like birds' eggs in a nest. Tom beckoned to his cousin:

'Look at these Frank! They have a perfect bloom on them – I love the way they are defying the season.'

'Then peaches it is! I trust you have cash enough? You may need to take out a loan.'

The woman looked offended:

'The very last of the year, Sir – and fit for a royal table! They're from the greenhouse at Syon Park – my nephew is an under-gardener there.'

Well, it was a story, and Tom wanted to believe it. The woman had honest eyes and was not a familiar face in the market, so perhaps it was true? Certainly his aunt would appreciate their lordly breeding! He picked up one of the peaches and at once his churlish doubts cleared. He weighed it in his palm, felt the soft downiness that gave slightly to the touch, lifted the fruit to his nose and drew in the exquisite scent of summer.

The woman drove a hard bargain. Tom's half-crown secured him the prize, and the blushing fruits – four of them – were received into his silk kerchief. He cradled them with due tenderness.

The Pophams' townhouse in Pall Mall rose elegantly from the street but did not assert itself. Its neighbours along the terrace were equally dignified, each one proud of its station within sight of the royal palace. Arrived at the door, Frank pulled the bell, and half a minute later it opened to reveal the Pophams' footman, himself a lofty structure in braided scarlet. His eyes welcomed the young gentlemen, who marched in with a friendly nod.

'Is my father home, Arthur?'

Frank asked the question with a casualness he did not feel.

'Lord Melksham is expected shortly, Sir. But the ladies are here – Lady Melksham and Miss Lavinia. They are just back from the Exchange. It was a good catch today – Sidney was fully laden!'

A cry from the direction of the drawing-room confirmed there was excitement in the air, and when Frank and Tom entered they were met with a scattering of boxes and fabrics. Cousin Lavinia was lowering a saffron-tinted stole across her shoulders while her stepmother watched. Tom shielded the gorgeous sight with his arm:

'Sublime Aurora, goddess of the dawn!'

'Hello Tom,' said Lavinia soberly. 'That's a lofty strain – I thought you were writing about turnips?'

'*We've* been bargaining too, Sis,' said Frank. 'What do you say to these choice items?'

Tom stepped forward and displayed the peaches; but his aunt's attention was elsewhere. She was giving her stepson a look normally reserved for street-sweepers:

'Well, I have my answer Lavinia! – your brother has spent the night under a hedge.'

'It was a *wall*, mother – indeed quite a respectable one.'

There was laughter at Frank's reply, although on this occasion Wit and Truth were in accord.

Lavinia scrutinised him:

'We've been conjecturing about your fate, Frank. We left you in dubious company ...'

'Does that mean you both intend to stay for dinner?' Lady Melksham asked, examining the peaches. 'If so, we need to tell Mrs Walker. These are very fine.'

'From Syon House, aunt – the Duke's own greenhouse,' said Tom. 'The very last of the season.'

Lady Melksham's features lightened:

'Then we must do them justice ...'

'... Mr Sturgis has a *reputation*, brother,' persisted Lavinia, her eyes narrowing. 'I hope you didn't add to it last night. You were without the respectable Tom here to chaperon you ...'

While she spoke, Frank was lifting the lid of a hatbox from which an ostrich feather sprang out. He drew back in mock alarm:

'Well, Sis, Arthur told me you'd had rich pickings – from half the globe it would seem! ...'

Lady Melksham sighed:

'Had I been favoured last night with Mr Sturgis's good fortune we could have ransacked the Exchange! ... Poor Mrs Trotter – I felt sorry for her. With those winnings he could purchase her Bay-Tree twice over! ... It seems the man can do no wrong. And to think his stallion won a match at Newmarket last week – a stake of *two thousand guineas!*'

The words reverberated across the room. Frank stiffened and reddened simultaneously.

'Frank! Don't crush that feather! The hat cost me five pounds!'

He drew back his hand:

'I really must go and change my clothes, mother, if I am to grace your table. I don't want a further reprimand from His Lordship.'

'Indeed you should! Your cravat has half the dust of Charing Cross on it.'

Tom intervened:

'Frank and I need to have a word with Uncle Jack when he comes in. It's on a matter of business …'

He had aimed for nonchalance but didn't quite achieve it. Lavinia snorted:

'Ah, *men's* business, mamma! Do you hear that? Important affairs! But we all know it's just solemn gossip.'

'You're entirely right, cousin … But you must allow us men our own scandals. We promise not to encroach on yours!'

The exchanges continued for a while in this bantering vein; but eventually the two young gentlemen were able to extricate themselves from a conversation that was becoming difficult to manage. Curiosity and suspicion soon gave way to talk of shoes, and so they left Lavinia and her stepmother to conduct their equally pressing business.

When he arrived, Lord Melksham meant business too. He swept down the hall with determined speed, sword swaying beneath an ample dress-coat surmounted by a chestnut-coloured wig of splendid excess, an ebony cane gripped in one fist and a sheaf of papers in the other, buckled shoes clattering along the parquet. Without inquiry or greeting he at once disappeared into his closet, leaving Arthur the footman to summon his son and nephew to his presence.

This was not the easy-going gentleman of routine but a man who had returned fretful and impatient to settle things; and as Frank and Tom stepped into the room they knew that their news – or some version of it – had already arrived.

'Father …'

Frank stopped in his tracks, frozen by a piercing look from a face that was usually benign and comfortable. There was silence: his father was not proposing to help him.

'… Father … I owe you an explanation …'

Still no reply, but the angry look was beginning to register pain and disappointment too.

'… I have been very foolish – and I see news of my predicament has reached you. I had wanted you to hear the story from me directly.'

In response, Lord Melksham glanced at his nephew who was standing at Frank's shoulder like a fellow-conspirator:

'I see you have brought Tom along – do you expect him to plead for you? I'm surprised you didn't come flanked by Will Lundy also! This is no court of law … but I shall hear you out – before I throw you into the street …'

Frank went cold. He looked for a hint of a jest in his father's eyes but didn't detect any.

'… You call it a *predicament* – such an easy word! … But you must tell me everything. You mustn't spare me … How much is the debt? You know how these things can grow in the telling.'

'Two thousand guineas, Sir.'

Frank hung his head and there was a moment of uneasy calm.

'*Two thousand?* …'

Nothing followed, except a loud exhalation.

'… I heard *five* … No doubt tomorrow it will have risen to *ten* – and my friends will look at me with smiles of pity. Then you will be in the Fleet, and your mother will be selling the furniture …'

'Father, I can't say …'

'No more! I don't want any hand-wringing – I want a full account – how this came about, how the debt stands, and what determination you have come to … Then – and only then – I shall fling you through the window.'

Lord Melksham's face was still remarkably set. No seat had been indicated, and so the two young men remained standing side by side while Frank attempted to arrange the happenings at the gaming-house into a coherent story, although in his mind it was no such thing. Throughout the account Tom remained in sympathetic silence, thinking it best to wait.

As so often, an account became an explanation, which in turn began to sound like a string of excuses. After a couple of minutes, dry-throated, Frank halted.

His father's wig took on a judicial gravity:

'So ... you were the worse for drink, were you? – your friends urged you on – you suspect some underhand trick – it all happened so quickly – a sudden turn of fortune ... What am I hearing? Oh Frank, you of all people! I had thought better of you. How could a level-headed young fellow like you let himself be made such a fool? "Bamboozled" – isn't that the new *lingo?* You were thoroughly *bamboozled!*'

The vogue word was given added colour by a curl of the lip.

Frank shivered with embarrassment. Yes, his father was right. It was an age-old story, and he was no different from countless other fools gulled out of their senses. He was a pigeon well and truly plucked.

'You say George Sturgis has the promissory note?'

'Yes, father.'

'How long has he been your friend? The man is slippery as a fish – everything is in play with him, and I suspect he's been playing you too! If he took on the debt it must have been for a reason ... The fellow certainly does well out of it all. I hear he had a huge win at Newmarket a few days ago – and now it's poor Mrs Trotter ...'

Tom felt his uncle's anger was beginning to find another channel. He wondered if it was time to speak out. But he was pre-empted.

'... What did you make of the basset table, Tom? You've been keeping your counsel. I was watching you during the game, and you looked very thoughtful.'

Tom hesitated, conscious of having to tread carefully. He replied firmly and quietly:

'We think, Sir, that Mr Sturgis had another friend in the room.'

It was enigmatic, but it was enough. He paused to let the idea register.

'Oh? You interest me, Tom! I wonder who you can mean? ...'

The implication had struck home.

'... I saw you were giving the tallière close attention. What conclusion did you come to?'

'Somewhat akin to yours Uncle, I suspect ... I know you were watching him closely too. Mr LeRoy was very handy with the cards, was he not? – I've seen nothing so accomplished since Mr Fawkes's performance at the May Fair ...'

He could see from the half-smile on his uncle's face that he had touched the spot.

'Ah yes, Fawkes the conjurer!'

'Do you not find it an added curiosity, Sir, that Mr Sturgis and Mr LeRoy were observed later that evening charging up the Strand together in a chariot?'

Tom and Frank had agreed he should be the one to make the revelation. And it had the required effect:

'Truly? That's brazen indeed ... So you suspect Mrs Trotter was fleeced?'

'We do – but we cannot prove it,' said Frank.

Tom pressed on:

'Mrs Trotter has told us she had two cocksure gamesters in the Bay-Tree this morning who spoke warmly of Mr LeRoy's considerateness – is that not an odd way to speak of a tallière? It seems he has left Vandernan's – and we wonder why.'

Lord Melksham was sinking deeper into his chair, brow furrowed in thought:

'But does this have a bearing on Frank's misadventure?'

'Cards and dice, Sir – dealing and casting – both are tricksy things. And George Sturgis, as you say, is a slippery customer.'

Enough words had been spoken. There was a moment of calm while the two young men waited like soldiers expecting the judgment of a court martial.

'I shall remit the defenestration,' said Lord Melksham with proper solemnity. 'You raise a topic of significance. What you say of Vandernan's and Sturgis interests me in a particular way …'

Frank glanced at Tom. Another pause followed. His father rose from his seat.

'… I think this calls for a pipe … You can both sit down.'

He walked over to his desk and took hold of the tobacco-jar while the two of them drew up chairs. They knew something of import was imminent and were also conscious of their own revelation to come. They watched him filling his pipe while he gathered his thoughts together.

He reached down to the fire:

'Two days ago, I attended the Board of the Treasury – an august body that holds the nation's finances in its hands …'

Tom and Frank remained silent as he lifted the glowing spill and began setting it to his pipe. They were intrigued to know where this was leading. He appeared to be settling in for a long voyage.

'… I am not formally a member of the Treasury Board – neither is the Duchess of course. But as her deputy I have day-to-day oversight of Her Majesty's finances – a position of great trust, gentlemen, and an independent one. The 'Privy Purse' is precisely what its name implies – an income privy to the Queen, free of Treasury scrutiny. It is not a 'supply' matter. But as you can imagine, from time to time there needs to be some sharing of information. The Purse has disbursements which require negotiation, and out of mutual courtesy, at the invitation of the

Board, I consult with them about anything that might touch on Treasury business – it is all regular enough and serves us both well …'

He drew on his pipe, pleased with the successful negotiation of an awkward topic.

'… But all this is a preamble, gentlemen – I must remember I'm not in committee now! … You understand that what I tell you is *in confidence* …'

Lord Melksham's frown became more confiding – it was a mode he always seemed to relish.

'… At the Treasury Board I am of course excluded from reserved items; but on this occasion the contentious business reappeared, and my presence was forgotten. The pulse of the meeting was high, and I was able to gauge the cause …'

He leaned forward.

'… That upstart *Bank of England* is acting the bully again! The institution is assuming greater powers, and the government is ever more dependent on it. The Bank's Board is levelling with the Treasury itself! They are like two generals jockeying for command … I want to say Eugene and Marlborough, but *both* their armies are paid and clothed – and armed – by Bank of England debt! …'

These were high matters. Frank looked questioningly at his cousin, but neither spoke.

'… In relation to the Bank, gentlemen, no doubt the pamphlet war has escaped you. You are fortunate if it has. The cries of "monopoly!" and "financial tyranny!" on the one side, and "security!" and "public credit!" on the other – I shall spare you the arguments. But you need to know that a new settlement has placed even more power in the Bank's hands. Its charter is now to be extended for *twelve* more years, and its grip on the nation's finances is stronger than ever …'

Lord Melksham drew again on his pipe, and the smoke

swirled around like the mist of battle. Frank and Tom remained transfixed and not a little puzzled.

'... The Bank's *Directors* (what a pompous title!) are powerful men, and the government is thoroughly indebted to them. These gentlemen know what a hold they have. After all, it was they who financed the Union with Scotland, and now they fund the war. They have just compounded for *a million and a half* – think of that! The loan will keep Marlborough in the field, and the war will stagger on. The nation is deep in debt, and shall be for years to come ... Yes, we gain our national glory, and the tyrant Louis must be faced down ... and yet the thing drags on like a wounded snake. I see no end to it!'

'But what of Oudenarde, father? I have not heard you speak like this before – and in such bleak terms! – surely Oudenarde was a notable victory?'

'A mere ripple, Frank, you must agree – not the turning of the tide that was looked for ... All the hopes of the summer are fading ...'

A look of despair was beginning to show itself.

'... I can see no resolution ... And now the Duke besieges Lille! – but what will that achieve? A distraction merely – a sop to the Dutch! These are Autumn manoeuvres – little more.'

Frank was becoming uneasy. He had never considered his father a politician, and yet there was a fervour here – and a distinctly Tory one. As for the National Debt, he comforted himself that it made his own two thousand look pretty meagre.

Tom hazarded the important question:

'But what of Mr Sturgis, Sir? And Vandernan's? This is not a matter for the Treasury Board, surely?'

'Ah yes – you ask where all this is leading! You've been very patient. Well, I'll tell you ... I have wind of a *plot* ...'

The word was spoken with a conspiratorial glance toward the corner of the room.

'... Something that arose in Privy Purse business. I can't go into detail – but it concerns Sir Gilbert Heathcote ...'

It was a formidable name. The cousins looked at each other.

'... A man of vast wealth, gentlemen – and therefore vast influence. Yet he is restless to accumulate more and to crush all rivals. Heathcote is the great engine of the Bank – its most powerful voice – and he bids to be its next Governor ...'

Lord Melksham's voice softened.

'... I caught sight of a paper – a note rather than a formal letter. I knew immediately it was not for my eyes, but for the Keeper personally – the Duchess. The thing had found its way into the Privy Purse papers. It was a missive from Sir Gilbert to Her Grace. He was guarded in his words, but it alluded to a *negotiation* between the two of them – no mere exchange of pleasantries. Heathcote and the Duchess! ... You may wonder what they could find worthy of discussion ...'

He drew again on his pipe.

'... But it takes little imagination to see what might interest the Duchess ... The Bank pays for our Whig war – her husband's campaign! And she has a strong bond with Heathcote. She knows he is of her party – always has been. Sir Gilbert is an entrenched Whig, and the determined enemy of Mr Harley and everything he stands for. Above all, he is the implacable foe of the Sword Blade and its Tory supporters. You are not to know this, but over the past months the Bank and the Sword Blade have been at war – more covert than Marlborough's campaign but closely fought none the less. The Bank is determined to destroy its rival.'

'But where is George Sturgis in this picture, father?'

Frank was becoming impatient, but also anxious. Part of him was not eager for the answer.

'Ah well, from the note it would appear that in this business our Mr Sturgis acts as a go-between – feeding intelligence from the Bank to the Duchess, and in turn from her to Heathcote and the Bank. I need not say how valuable this traffic could be for both of them. It was only a brief reference, but the link is clear. The Honourable Mr Sturgis is part of the Duchess's card circle – White's and Vandernan's are not his only places of resort. He is a denizen of the Marlborough set – Whigs to a man – and woman! This is George Sturgis's natural element, and of course he can profit from the messages he carries. It is possibly little more than gossip; but in the world of high finance chatter is everything. A whisper behind the hand can make your fortune. A word in the ear can ruin a man.'

'But the Treasury Board, Uncle …'

'The Board knows nothing of this. As you would expect, Heathcote's name frequently arises. But about him they are – how can I put it? – *not of one mind*. That is the polite expression. But there was little politeness in the words I heard spoken. The Treasury is divided between those who regard Sir Gilbert as an overbearing dictator and others who see him as the bulwark of the nation's credit (that is how they talk of him!). Strong words flew around; and in the heat of the moment it was remarked that Heathcote was surely *in league with the Marlboroughs* – to the extent of by-passing the Queen and her ministers! There was anger on both sides.'

Lord Melksham's pipe gave its own emphasis to the point. A tense silence descended. Frank and Tom knew their moment was near.

'Did you say anything yourself, father?'

'No, no – I kept my counsel, as you might expect. It was not for me to play the informer! But I thought of the note and the evidence of Sturgis's part in this. I have little to go on, but I suspect there is more to be uncovered – something in train which may not be in Her Majesty's best interests.'

'The Queen and the Duchess are still at daggers-drawn?'

'They maintain a show of peace – but there is no trust anymore. On the contrary, all is poisoned with suspicion. The ground is fertile for plots of every kind, and you know how mistrust breeds conspiracy – they feed off each other. It is difficult terrain, gentlemen … I trod carefully, believe me!'

'Does this mean you have spoken to no-one about it?'

There was an urgency in Frank's voice as he posed the question. His father sensed it:

'What makes you ask? Have you had some intimation of this business from Sturgis himself – from your new *friend*? …'

The word fell awkwardly. It was a difficult moment, and all three men felt uneasy. The sudden flush on his son's face made Lord Melksham take a step back.

'… There is no imputation, my boy, believe me … But you must know how this connection of yours unsettles me. I don't doubt your innocence in all of this …'

There was a further pause while Tom and Frank hesitated.

'… You ask me a direct question, gentlemen. To give you an honest answer – I did voice my suspicions – in conversation when the meeting had closed. But it was in confidence …'

'Did you speak of George Sturgis?'

Frank's father began to feel uncomfortable. He was unsure where this was leading:

'His name did arise … Is there something you're not telling me, Frank? There is clearly some intent behind your questions. What else have you done?'

'You are right to be angry with me, father. I have behaved foolishly and deserve every reprimand for it … You know that I did not return home last night. In truth, I walked the streets accompanied with my own miserable thoughts. You can be sure I rebuked myself more violently than you have done … and as each hour passed I could not bring myself to enter your house – wretched though I was ...'

Lord Melksham was intent on every word.

'... I have to tell you that last night I had an encounter in the street – a violent one. But it was my mind that was the more troubled ...'

'My boy! ...'

Frank cut his father short:

'... It was a man bringing me a message – and one that was reinforced by a hand at my throat ... it was a message for you, Sir – and I swore to deliver it ...'

By now Lord Melksham was motionless and open-mouthed.

'... I was to advise you not to *meddle* in affairs that do not concern you. Those were the man's very words. Of course, I did not understand them – but from what you now tell us ...'

'The man threatened you? – Frank! What can I say? ... Who was it?'

'I could not make out his face in the dark. The ruffian had been following me. But the threat was not his – he was strong and could have run me through in an instant ... No, he was the bearer only – the message was from someone far more powerful. It is not to be taken lightly, father ... You ask me what else I have done ... Tom and I need to ask you the same question.'

Lord Melksham sat slack-jawed and silent, trying to take in what he had just heard. The pipe hung loose in his hand.

'The power-brokers at the Bank, uncle – do you think word has found its way to them? – that you have stumbled on something they do not want known?'

'Something they wish to keep secret at any cost?' added Frank.

'But I *know* nothing. It is only hint and supposition – a strong one certainly, but ... You are right – this must arise from my conversation after the Board ...'

Lord Melksham's eyes searched the room, as if looking for a sign. The pipe fell against his knee.

'... But ... Do you see what this means? My suspicions ... There must surely be a plot ... *Aaah!* ...'

He leapt to his feet.

The animation was startling. It was not the response they had looked for. But the hand flapping at his breeches gave the answer.

'... There is more to be found, gentlemen! There's some import to it. The Duchess? Her Majesty? Where might this reach? ...'

His mind was running fast.

'But father ... is this not a warning? You seem to be treating it as a challenge. Whoever these men are, they are *very* dangerous.'

'The threat was against *you*, uncle – do you not understand? These are people who won't hesitate to use violence.'

Lord Melksham seemed hardly to be listening. He continued to speak:

'Sir Gilbert Heathcote ... George Sturgis ... where might it reach, do you think?'

Tom and Frank looked at each other. There was no talking to him. They could only retrieve the pipe and settle him back in his chair. Then Tom found himself addressing both father and son:

'All this talk of plots can be distracting. If Frank has been the victim of a trap, then it is there we have to look first – to George Sturgis and his friends. But you must promise to do nothing precipitate, uncle. Allow matters to cool ... and I think the same holds for you, Frank. Both of you must keep your peace. There is a strong chance you may be watched!'

The gravity of events was unveiling itself. Lord Melksham began to think of his family, and how much he would hazard if he acted incautiously:

'But it is vital we get to the bottom of this affair, Tom. We may have only glimpsed a part of it. Who is to say? I do have a responsibility – nay, a *duty* – if it extends further and … involves Her Majesty.'

'I don't suggest you do nothing, Sir – but that you are circumspect. Do not draw attention to yourself. You must leave the *actions* to others.'

'To others?'

'Yes, both of you must take care. Frank's disaster at the gaming-house is part of the picture. The ruffian alluded to it. We have to ask ourselves why? … '

He turned to his cousin.

'… What might connect your loss at hazard with the activities of George Sturgis and the threat to your father? This is where we must begin.'

'We?'

'Mrs Trotter is involved too – thanks to Sturgis and LeRoy. Her loss is very great, and what threatens her is equally serious. I have to inform her about all we have discussed.'

Lord Melksham gave a slow nod:

'Yes, Tom. Mary Trotter is a resourceful lady. We need to act in concert with her.'

'Good … And I must also add my friend Will. You know that we keep nothing from each other – and with his knowledge of the law … He is sure to want to help.'

The tautness in his uncle's face lessened slightly:

'It is good to have such friends … I know you will keep us informed, Tom. Frank and I will pass on any news that comes our way …'

'But leave the initiative to us, uncle! A careless act could jeopardise all.'

Tom knew it was presumptuous of him – all these warnings! But he sensed a greater easiness in the air – a sign that consensus had been reached. He looked at father and son, and smiled to himself. There was something very attractive about the Popham confidence, but sometimes the family's briskness needed to be tempered.

Feeling the pressure of the moment, he couldn't resist summing up. When the words emerged, he was disconcerted to hear himself beginning to sound like his landlady:

'Yes,' he said. 'George Sturgis is surely the key. He is somehow deeply involved in all of this ... I think that is where our investigations must begin.'

Chapter Seven

⚬⚬⚬

'AH, THERE YOU are, Tom! – Come along – we can talk freely in the parlour. There is something I must tell you.'

With no more ado, Widow Trotter turned and led the way along the side of the bar while a silent Tom trailed after her. He had arrived back at the chocolate house ready to share his news from St James's, but a single glance told him he wasn't the only person with hot intelligence. Something was cooking. Within seconds he found himself in the Bay-Tree's holy of holies, full of anticipation.

Widow Trotter's parlour was her inner sanctum, a wainscoted room beyond the bustle of the kitchen where she could do the accounts, have a quiet supper, read a book, or enjoy a private chat away from the public conversation of the coffee-room. It was also a place for serious thought. Tom settled himself into a chair by the oak table and leaned on one elbow, contemplating his landlady as she stood at the sideboard and began silently to pour a couple of glasses of madeira. She was considering how to break the news of Sturgis's killing and needed to collect her thoughts. But an impatient Tom couldn't resist offering a tit-bit of his own:

'I think I can match you, Mrs T – news for news! I've just got back from Pall Mall …'

He watched as her back flinched slightly at the words and her pouring hand steadied itself.

'... Frank and I have had a memorable interview with my uncle. It touches more than a little on your own affairs.'

Tom felt hopeful and a little apprehensive, like a card-player who had just laid his ace.

The glint in Mrs Trotter's eyes as she turned round confirmed she had a strong hand of her own; but her curiosity was irresistibly aroused.

'Well then,' she said. 'Let us set things before us and see what the picture is ... I hope your news is more encouraging than mine. Perhaps I should be the listener first? Mine is unfinished business — at least until Elias arrives, when I hope to hear more.'

Now Tom's curiosity was aroused. But it was Widow Trotter who prevailed. She eased back in her chair, cradling her glass between her fingers while Tom told the story of Cousin Frank's nocturnal misadventures, of his encounter with the ruffian, and the man's warning for Lord Melksham.

'It was a chilling message, Mrs T! Frank was left in no doubt that the threat is a violent one. Uncle Jack is being warned to stay clear of something — and we suspect Frank's huge loss at hazard may be part of the picture. The ruffian made contemptuous reference to it.'

A thrilling scene was forming, and already Widow Trotter's mind was running on ahead:

'Poor Mr Popham — that must have been a shock to him ... And so you carried the message over to Pall Mall? ... and how did Lord Melksham receive it?'

'With some excitement. He said it confirmed something that had been troubling him — some affair to do with the Duchess of Marlborough.'

'Do you know what?'

Tom made the most of the moment. He looked her straight between the eyes:

'A *plot!* – being hatched within the Bank.'

The word was electric:

'Aha! ... Now, that I can easily believe. Some financial jobbery perhaps? Am I right?'

'You are unerring, Mrs T. But it is no more than a suspicion at present.'

'But what has this to do with your cousin? And with me? I have no connections with the Bank of England. My affairs are in the care of the Sword Blade ... Unless ...'

'No, no – this involves the Bank. In particular it touches on *Sir Gilbert Heathcote.*'

He paused. The very name carried weight, and it thudded down on the table between them.

'Heathcote? ... Is he not the richest man in England?'

'The richest *commoner*, Mrs T. That is what is said. He is himself a bank! He lends and deals like an institution!'

'He would make a formidable enemy ... You are making me uneasy, Tom. I'm not sure where all this is leading. You say it touches on my own affairs – I'm not clear how ...'

'If I was to mention the name of George Sturgis ...'

He paused. A change came over Mary Trotter's features. What had been a look of lively interest was now one of foreboding. This grew while Tom spoke about his uncle's discovery of the note among his papers: how it appeared to show that the Honourable Mr Sturgis was acting as a channel of communication between Heathcote and the Duchess – between the Bank and the Marlboroughs.

'... Do you see what this means, Mrs T? Uncle Jack believes he may have stumbled on a conspiracy – or why threaten him like that? What do they think he may uncover? George Sturgis looks to be caught up in something ... We are wondering if taking on Frank's debt may be some manoeuvre ... Of course, Frank wants to confront Sturgis directly – try to discover what he knows. But I spoke against it. I warned them both to lie low. I suggested that you and I – with Will's help – might see what we could uncover?'

This was a bold move. It had been a headlong speech, and Tom paused for breath. He took a sip of his madeira, awaiting her response. But his words were met with silence and a look that could only be described as solemn. Mrs Trotter set her glass down on the table:

'Oh Tom! ... Mr Sturgis ...'

'Yes, he could be the key, don't you think?'

'George Sturgis is dead.'

'Dead? ... But only last night ...'

He paused in shock, trying to get his brain to accept the idea.

'... Dead? ... Do you mean killed? Or has there been an accident?'

'No accident, Tom. A rapier through his heart – so the word is. You can imagine how the coffee-room has been humming with rumours. Toby Mudge broke the news to me before any of this was known – but he gave no particulars. He said I must wait for Elias – that there was something odd about the killing and I was not to listen to any gossip until Elias could tell me the facts ... I wonder why this secrecy?'

Tom drank off his glass of madeira and caught his breath:

'This confirms our worst fears, does it not?'

'I think your uncle may be in even greater danger – that the threat delivered to his son is no empty one.'

'You speak of rumours ...'

He gave her a questioning look.

'It is only coffee-room news, Tom, but one physical detail is so remarkable that I think it could possibly be true ...'

'What? … about the body?'

'Yes – it is being said that something was found in Mr Sturgis's mouth.'

'His mouth? – Do you mean something had been placed there … or …'

He paused. His imagination was beginning to play tricks.

'Yes, Tom. Someone – the killer it must be – had pressed a pair of dice into his mouth.'

It was grotesque – but the picture was an eloquent one.

'Dice? … That speaks of gaming does it not?'

'Yes, Tom. But not cards. It must be *hazard* … This is another message! And an even more cruel one.'

The same thought was in both their minds, but neither dared speak it. Tom hesitated:

'When was the body found?'

'Not until after nine this morning it seems. It was slumped by some bins – in an alley. But he had certainly been killed during the night.'

'A duel was it? If so, it was an underhand one – not a fight between gentlemen.'

Widow Trotter shot him a disapproving look; but she spoke in forgiving tones:

'A *gentleman* can be a cold-blooded murderer like anyone else, Tom. But this one showed no regard to the forms. From what I've heard, Mr Sturgis's sword was sheathed.'

'And where is this alley?'

'Angel's Yard – an insalubrious hole not far from the rear door of Vandernan's …'

The name made him start.

'… But these are just coffee-house rumours. I am trying not to credit any of them until our friend calls … One thing does unsettle me. From what Toby said, Elias wants me to hear the truth directly from him … it suggests the incident touches on me particularly – that he knows something beyond the stuff of gossip.'

Tom was deep in thought, and it was very like the one troubling Mary Trotter: the fact that besides George Sturgis there had been a second desperate young gentleman roaming the streets of Covent Garden during the night – one who was indebted to Sturgis for the vast sum of two thousand guineas, incurred at the hazard-table ...

Neither of them gave voice to this thought, but their eyes met. Both hesitated to carry conjecture too far – Constable Cobb might call at any moment. And yet they longed to thrash the matter out. Tom was frowning and trying to be patient. His eyes were exploring a Dutch landscape which held pride of place above the hearth. Mrs Trotter stirred herself and retrieved the decanter of madeira from the sideboard along with a saucer of sugared almonds. The few words between them were stumbling ones – hesitant comments and trivial observations – nothing to the purpose.

The painting was more eloquent. Tom gazed at the rural scene of meadow, stream and woodland, complete with its rustic cottage and straggling fence – a tranquil pastoral ... and yet, there in the foreground were figures hard at work: a peasant was mending the fence, and brawny-armed women were bent over the stream, washing lengths of linen cloth, with more of it spread out behind them across row upon row of tenter-hooks.

It seemed an emblem. Tom felt it almost physically.

He was stirred from his reverie by Widow Trotter, who finally spoke out:

'There is some mind behind this, Tom. I'm sure of it! I dread to hear more. What shall we discover next?'

As if in answer to her summons, a sudden commotion from the kitchen told them the long-expected messenger was about to appear. A moment later Elias Cobb's face showed itself round the parlour door. He had scavenged a small fruit tart and was biting into it as Mrs Trotter invited him inside.

It was not a dignified entrance, and the unshaven jaw was occupied with the pastry; but his expression was a serious one.

'You'll take a drink, Elias,' said Mrs Trotter, and reached for the decanter of claret behind her.

'Gladly Molly! What a day this has been. Such a commotion! Young Mudge brought you the first news, I know …'

'Yes, Elias – but it was a strange message. He said I had to await the full report from you.'

'Good! I've trained him well. There was reason, I assure you. Jenny tells me the Bay-Tree has been buzzing.'

The constable seated himself and spread his legs, looking at his two friends, both of them silently expectant. He nodded particularly at Tom:

'I'm glad to see you, Mr Bristowe. You will understand that the goings-on in Angel Yard touch on you and your cousin no less than Mrs Trotter here – indeed, perhaps more so … It is a terrible thing!'

'We have just been talking of it, Mr Cobb. Mrs Trotter has been trying not to believe all she has heard. I assure you she has been Good Sense personified.'

'But now you're here, Elias, we must know everything. We were promised more – but a part has already reached us … there has been a rumour about *dice* …'

She hesitated, and the word trailed off into silence.

The constable caught the apprehension in her voice:

'So much is true, Molly. A pair of dice were found in the poor gentleman's mouth. It was a message of course …'

Tom looked at Widow Trotter, and their faces fell.

'… I'll not beat about the bush, Mr Bristowe … It was intended to point the finger, and we may be pretty sure to whom it was directed.'

He turned his gaze full on Tom, whose mouth opened involuntarily. A tentative sound came forth:

'Frank – is it not?'

'Indeed, Mr Bristowe, your cousin. I fear that is the case.'

'But how can you be certain, Elias?' said Mrs Trotter. 'Mr Sturgis was a notorious gamester. White's and Vandernan's were his second homes. He surely had made enemies, perhaps important ones?'

'What you say is true, Molly. There is no denying Mr Sturgis's wild reputation … but I have to tell you – there was further evidence found at the scene.'

This was a revelation.

'We have heard of nothing more, Elias,' said Widow Trotter. 'The rumours seem to have proved true.'

'So they have. But, as I say – something more has been found.'

Tom and Mrs Trotter looked on in astonishment while Elias sat back and reached into the pocket of his greatcoat. What he drew out was a torn piece of paper. Without saying anything, he held it out for Tom to take:

'I found this in Mr Sturgis's coat. I think you will recognise it, Mr Bristowe.'

Tom went cold as his fingers turned the fragment over. There, without mistake, was his cousin's signature: 'Francis Popham'. It was written at the foot of a page, but most of the document had been ripped away.

Tom looked at the others. The same thought was in their minds:

'This is Frank's signature, without a doubt … but what was it attached to?'

He already suspected the answer but stopped himself.

Mrs Trotter spoke in hushed tones:

'The promissory note, Elias. Do you not think?'

'I do, Molly – and if you look along the edge you can make out part of the script.'

Tom was looking at the paper with growing bafflement:

'But I don't understand. If this is Frank's promissory note, then why rip it in two? It would invalidate the document.'

'Exactly,' said Elias. 'That must have been the intention.'

'And why preserve *half* of it? I take it the rest was missing?'

'Yes, Mr Bristowe. That is the curious thing – unless the purpose was to implicate Mr Popham further? I can think of no other reason.'

'It suggests there was a quarrel and the killer tore up the paper.'

'Neither makes entire sense,' said Widow Trotter, 'but we have to consider what this fragment is meant to show. If anything, it points to your cousin's innocence. The killer arranged the scene with too much deliberation.'

'Mrs Trotter is right,' said Elias, reclaiming the paper and gripping it tightly. 'It is my excuse for *removing* the evidence … I assure you, even Toby doesn't know of this! I decided it would serve only to confuse matters at tomorrow's inquest … I've done nothing of the kind before, Molly – but in these circumstances …'

'I'm very glad of it, Elias. If nothing else, it should avoid Mr Popham being brought before the Coroner's jury …'

The constable was looking somewhat shame-faced; but she detected a lifting of Tom's spirits.

'… As for the promissory note, Tom – we can but hope that your cousin's debt is now cancelled.'

'That would be a deliverance, Mrs T. I hardly dare think of it.'

Elias was reassuring:

'Well, I have made my report to the Magistrate, and nothing was raised about that particular debt. Some dispute over gaming was assumed – and the location of the corpse was noted. As you can imagine, the name of *Vandernan's* brought a shake of the head – such is its reputation among the Justices. The killing seemed to take on something of a sordid character.'

'But Mr Sturgis's winnings at the basset table were surely mentioned?'

'Yes, Molly. And a possible robbery was considered. No money was found on him ... The killer carried a sword, and the victim was dispatched with a single well-executed thrust, so this was not a street thief ... but we can only speculate. All that will be discussed at the inquest.'

Widow Trotter knew that for all the disturbing nature of his news, her old friend had secured them valuable time. She also knew that at some point Elias must be let into their secret. She couldn't help but think the idea of robbery was a distraction, as were the dice and the signature ... Taken all together, this was reinforcing her suspicions that behind the curtain another story was waiting to come into view. To remove George Sturgis from the scene had perhaps served a wider, possibly political, purpose?

Chapter Eight

—∞∞∞—

WILL LUNDY PRODDED the glowing coals with a poker and set his kettle on the grate. On the table beside him the dishes were set out and a tin of fine *bohea* was in readiness. After another relentless day in Westminster Hall this tea-making was a ritual he had come to value, not least for its simplicity and precision. It relaxed the body and allowed the mind to settle. The benches of the Chancery Court were numbingly uncomfortable at the best of times, and today they had been packed. Escape was impossible if you didn't want to lose your place. Now back in his attic chamber he could slide blissfully down in the armchair and turn his thoughts to other matters, allowing the legal cant to slip gently away: *mala fides … suggestio falsi … suppressio veri …* He smiled at the pompous names the Law bestowed on lies.

Now he could let sophistry go. The Law may be wedded to Truth, but the attachment was a difficult one. He was becoming exhausted by the endless wranglings and contradictions, the indignant confutations and ingenious evasions – all the mental and verbal clutter of legal dispute. How hard it was to hold onto facts and find what was just, especially when these were not the same thing. He found himself looking philosophically at the kettle. Could it be an emblem of the moment? The thing was beginning to steam, but soon its seething contents would be poured out and transformed to calm refreshment.

But peace was not yet. He began to hear tramping steps getting ever louder on the stair, and a few seconds later an almighty hammering on his door elicited a wider smile. He recognised the bailiff's summons and shrank from it instinctively. "A dun! A dun!" he cried out in fear. In response the door creaked slowly open, accompanied by a familiar voice:

A dun!
Horrible Monster! hated by Gods and Men,
To your aerial Citadel ascends;
With Vocal Heel thrice thund'ring at your Gates!

A grinning Tom stepped across the threshold:

'Hello Will! I've come to consult you on a point of law.'

Will frowned and rubbed his chin:

'Tea *and* a consultation? … That will certainly raise the fee, Mr Bristowe.'

'You lawyers are always lining your pockets!'

'We must have some recompense for the tedium.'

'The news I have for you is far from tedious! *I could a tale unfold* … and my only fee is your refreshing Chinese leaf.'

He stepped towards the fire, removing his hat and loosening his muffler. Will paused for thought:

'A fair bargain I suppose. After five hours in the Court of Chancery anything remotely human is welcome. And if it is news from the Bay-Tree, then I'm all ears.'

Tom drew up a second chair and settled himself while his friend played the host. Here underneath the eaves of the garret was a less than polite scene: the teapot was a brown homely thing, and placed between them was no lacquered tea-table but a stout bit of joinery that was usually piled high with books. The quality of the tea, however, was not in doubt, and the Stepney bun that accompanied it was reassuringly fruity.

There was indeed a tale to tell, and as Tom's story unfolded, Will saw that the drama of Widow Trotter's basset table had been only a prelude. Since the night before, it seemed events had moved swiftly and the picture that formed was more sensational than anything Westminster Hall could offer:

'I don't believe this, Tom! I was expecting some news, but what are you telling me? Murder – fraud – assault – conspiracy … and all in a few hours? I'm wasting my time here – I need to be in Covent Garden!'

'And we need your help, Will. Our friends are in trouble. Widow Trotter faces the loss of the Bay-Tree, Frank the ruin of his reputation, and Uncle Jack, I daren't say what … It doesn't bear thinking of. Nothing has taken shape yet, but it's an alarming state of affairs. I can't help but believe all is connected somehow.'

'And money is at the heart of it, Tom. You can be sure of that. Poor Mrs Trotter – I hate to picture her wandering back through Exchange Alley clutching her worthless paper. What she must have felt! … and poor innocent Frank – what a price to pay for an hour's foolishness! I know you couldn't tell me last night, but someone should have guided him home. He was not fit to be wandering the streets.'

'He left with George Sturgis …'

'Even worse! … and you say Sturgis and that *faux* Frenchman Monsieur LeRoy were in league together?'

'This is how it looks, Will.'

'Well, if that's so, it was a remarkable piece of acting on the tallière's part – but I suspect he's well used to playing the role.'

Will's lawyer's mind was working fast. There had been so many revelations that he hardly knew where to begin:

'You said you wanted to raise a point of law, Tom – was it something particular? There's so much chicanery here.'

'It concerns Mrs Trotter and her paper. I was thinking about promissory notes and everything connected to them. They are legal tender, are they not?'

'Certainly – but they have become so only recently – just three years ago, by statute. Until then they were not recognised as bills of exchange. There is an awkwardness with them, as you might expect – a *promise to pay* between A. and B. being used to settle a debt between C. and D. It can lead to problems!'

'This is what I told Frank last night. If George Sturgis had decided to use Frank's note to settle a debt of his own …'

'Then another could enforce it – any third or fourth party – a complete stranger – much like Mr LeRoy's bits of paper. These things are the stuff of crime, Tom – difficult to trace.'

'But an individual could stop payment?'

'A bank can – in case of a theft, let us say. But it can be highly convenient to keep the paper moving. They have *currency*.'

Tom was shaking his head:

'This is a labyrinth, Will.'

'Yes, and ordinarily a lawyer would revel in entanglements, but in cases like these … However, there is one legal fact that you need to know. I'm not saying it's the answer to Frank's case, or Mrs Trotter's … but any gaming debt *above ten pounds sterling* cannot be legally enforced.'

Tom's spirits rose:

'What! But surely, there are many debts of thousands of guineas – huge losses at the tables …'

'Hold, Tom – hear me out … Such debts are not enforceable by law. But another code has even greater force – and *severity* …'

Will's features hardened to a judicial scowl.

'… The code of honour.'

'But that is not law, Will.'

'No – but it can be more powerful than any law – and certainly more dangerous.'

'Do you think George Sturgis's killing … ?'

'It bears the marks of a gamester's quarrel, Tom. The rapier – the dice – the place also, within yards of Vandernan's. You know how dice and duelling are near allied … and yet …'

Will paused and set the teapot down, resting his arm on the table while he thought.

'… The business of Frank's signature puzzles me. You say the promissory note was torn in half?'

'Yes. Most of it was missing.'

'The intention is to point at Frank, of course. But in doing so it would seem to cancel the debt. We are meant to picture your cousin seizing the note and thrusting his sword through Sturgis's heart. But why should he leave his name behind in the pocket to advertise his handwork? We have an ingenious villain – or a stupid one.'

'But whoever ran him through may not have known the thing was there.'

'True – in which case the note had already been torn … if so, then why? It's a nice question.'

He reached for the remaining bun and, knife in hand, sliced it neatly in two. Tom admired the exactness:

'Performed like a good lawyer, Will.'

'That's what your fee is for!'

'And you must admit I've given you excellent value.'

'Agreed – we are quits. The debt is settled between us!'

It was a light-hearted moment; but the phrase brought the full seriousness of the situation back to them. Logic could take them only so far, and simply talking would resolve nothing.

They both chewed thoughtfully.

'What can we do, Will? Mrs Trotter is in desperate straits if she cannot extract the three hundred from Robert LeRoy. When we parted just now she was determined to confront him – but is unsure of his whereabouts. Her message had been brought back

… I wish I could believe he will settle matters with her. The man must have known his notes were worthless.'

'Well, that could be our first task – to track Mr LeRoy to his hiding-place. I doubt he'll be calling at the Bay-Tree again … But we also need to see the larger picture … It occurs to me – if he and George Sturgis were in league, then might our Mr LeRoy be in danger too?'

'I had not considered that.'

'And this supposed plot between the Duchess and the mighty Gilbert Heathcote – is your uncle being fanciful, or could there be something in it? Perhaps Sturgis trespassed where he shouldn't? Did he know something he shouldn't? … These are heavy matters, Tom!'

'Uncle Jack is already convinced of a conspiracy – and when word of the murder reaches him he'll be entirely off the bit – it will confirm his suspicions beyond question. We have to pursue this, Will. I'll send a note round to Frank – he needs to hear the news about Sturgis. I'll suggest he comes to the Bay-Tree tomorrow. I assured him and Uncle Jack that we would find a way to help them, and they agreed to leave matters to us. My uncle was all for charging in at full speed. And now with Sturgis killed …'

'Yes, friend Tom, before we do anything further, we must consult your esteemed landlady. I do believe a little of Widow Trotter's warming madeira will help us see our way! We cannot act without her knowledge, and she will have the latest news, don't you think?'

'An excellent plan for tomorrow, Will – if you are sure the Court of Chancery can spare you?'

'Well, I can certainly spare it!'

An hour later Tom made his way down the rickety stairs and stepped out into a noisy Pump Court, where a group of students were having an uproarious time putting the old pump to playful use. Water was spraying everywhere and he had to stick close to the wall. As their cries echoed from the brickwork it struck him what an incongruous place the Inns of Court were – such a mixture of solemnity and wildness. How many pompous gentlemen of the Law had left a careless youth behind! (He tried to picture Will's father, Judge Lundy, running around the yard with a bucket, but that was too much for his imagination.) Suddenly he felt older than his years, and his eye caught the elegant sundial which projected between the facing windows above. He had visited Will in the Temple many times, but its import had never struck him directly before. Beneath the dial's pointer a board offered a chilling announcement: *Shadows we are, and like shadows depart.* And as if to drive the message home, there above it on the face itself were painted three enigmatic letters: T. O. M.

Saturday

23 October 1708

Chapter Nine

⸺⸺

EARLY NEXT MORNING the Bay-Tree was humming. The brisk air and the first coffee of the day encouraged a feeling of anticipation. News was freshly brewed, and there was promise every time the coffee-room door swung open. People were readying themselves. Wigs were crisp, cravats white, cuffs pristine, shoes well shined, and in most cases eyes were bright – the dust and grime of the city had yet to settle over things. Even in the street outside where people were beginning the business of the day, sounds were just a little sharper, pavements cleaner, the kennels less choked with dung. As the day wore on, all this would change as human commerce asserted itself and the awkward confusions of life began to accumulate.

From her vantage-point behind the bar Widow Trotter was trying to absorb some of this lively spirit, but she could only anticipate more anxiety and frustration. She wasn't at all hopeful that the coming day would set matters right. Indeed, she was beginning to question whether rightness was the true state of the world at all. The liveliness of the coffee-room conversation could be deceptive. She knew that in these early hours of the day, rumour had the authority of news and news the thrill of rumour, and sometimes they embraced disconcertingly.

All the early talk around the tables was of the Siege of Lille. Indeed it was set to be the dish of the day, re-heated and re-dressed with each report. Impatient hands grasped the newspapers, and eyes scanned the columns for the latest intelligence from Brussels. The siege had been grinding on since August, the French reinforcements being held at bay while the Lille garrison resisted every attack the allies could mount (the town had the finest defences in Europe). But now in October the climax was approaching and snippets of news were eagerly consumed. Every boat that docked in the Thames might bring a story from across the channel; official packets were hurried to the War Office; scribbled letters from the scene were carried post-haste – and yet somehow word-of-mouth appeared to outrun any sweating horse. Conjecture took wing, and reported facts fought their own endless battle with hearsay.

Around the table by the fire, the Chocolate-house generals were offering their opinions freely, until the Bay-Tree itself seemed to be in the thick of the action. With a paper in his hand, any man could become a strategist, and it was Jack Tapsell who was holding the floor:

'I tell you! – the town cannot hold out above three or four days longer!'

'But the mines under the breaches – they are surely a difficulty?'

'No longer, Barney! It says we have fifty pieces of cannon on the batteries – on the very top of the counterscarp, and it is certain new breaches will be made before the garrison can prepare any further mines ...'

Jack's tobacco-pipe thrust itself forward as if assisting with the assault.

'... *The Post Man* is clear on the matter.'

His friend Barnabas was sceptical:

'But we have heard such boasts before, Jack. Why should this be different?'

In reply, the paper was waved in his face:

'This report is from General Wilks himself – who has come direct from the camp. It says he has returned here to be cured of his wounds.'

'Well that's very fortunate for him!' said an unconvinced Sam Cust with a shake of the head. But what about his men? These generals may whistle cheerily and think all is going to plan – but what of the men left behind? He may have carried all confidence away with him! All this talk of *breaches* – Mark my words, the poor infantry will be shitting theirs!'

At the corner of the table, Captain Roebuck stirred himself:

'You speak truer than you know, Mr Cust ... Namur in '95 – now *that* was a very devil of a siege! Bits of parapet were flying around everywhere. I'm not ashamed to say I soiled myself more than once ...'

His friends offered a respectful silence.

'... A siege never has the romance of battle. You spend most of your time *digging* – and at Namur the clay was as thick as a bull's hide. What I remember most was the digging – there was more work done with spade than with musket, I can tell you ... No, give me a clean battle any day!'

He clutched his old campaign wallet to him like a physical memory.

'You've seen a lot, Jonah!' said Barnabas Smith.

'Aye, too much. But we have much to be proud of, do we not, gentlemen? Thanks to the Duke – God bless him! – we English can hold our heads high again.'

'But if these Tory peace-makers have their way ...'

'Ha! Then all will unravel! Our Grand Alliance will be no more, and Louis will soon be back to his old imperial tricks.'

At this prompting, Jack Tapsell's solid frame shifted on the bench, and the table shuddered:

'There are some who will not rest till the Duke is brought down. All this bleating about the cost of the War! The glorious name of Marlborough is dragged in the dust. He is under siege himself, is he not? Even his victories are grudgingly spoken of.'

'Aye – our very own Mr Bagnall has not helped matters. His *Oudenarde* is a disgrace – hardly the rally we looked for!'

'Blood and bodies, Captain – that is his theme – all the cost of battle without the glory. And the ode is intended to celebrate! … I'm waiting for him to show his face in here. We all know Laurence Bagnall is in Harley's pocket. The verses are a parcel of wind!'

Sam Cust's eyes lit up in a mischievous grin:

''Tis said there's a riposte in the making, Jack – a parody. I suspect our laureate of the shoe-buckle will be roughly handled.'

'In that case, I promise to be the poem's first performer! I'm sure the Bay-Tree will provide an appreciative audience …'

His voice rose confidently, and he swung round to take in the whole room, embracing it with his arm.

'… This place has been Bagnall's own theatre on occasion, has it not Mrs Trotter?'

Widow Trotter, who had been catching the drift of their talk, smiled over at them in return. Yes, the poet of *The Shoe-Buckle* had not been seen in the place for at least a week – and she now understood why. She held onto her benign face:

'Mr Bagnall is a gentleman of fine feelings, Mr Tapsell. I trust you will not treat him cruelly. Good humour is our watchword here, as I'm sure you know. We like all voices to be heard.'

'Aye, this is a mixed house indeed – especially above stairs! Courtiers gaming, and papists hatching their plots. At least in this room you can hear sound common sense!'

'You give us nothing less, Mr Tapsell. We always look to you to provide *equilibrium*!'

She gave the word due emphasis and was pleased to see his friends beginning to laugh. The place was a little like a theatre, and occasionally the audience needed to be wooed.

It could also stage its own dramatic effects – and did so now.

As the laughter came, the coffee-room door opened sharply, and a wild face appeared. The visitor was breathing heavily.

'News, boys! News! … *Lille has fallen!*'

'Is it certain?'

The man raised his hat in salute to his listeners:

'Down at 'Change the talk is of nothing else. I've come from there directly.'

'And that is where we were heading, Sir!' said Barnabas Smith. 'Perhaps we should do so expeditiously!'

He looked at his friends. A triumphant expression now occupied Jack Tapsell's face, and Captain Roebuck's eyes lit up:

'History is at your bidding, Mr Tapsell!'

'What will this do for the stocks?' asked Sam Cust.

'We shall soon find out,' said Jack, pulling himself to his feet. 'It will certainly bring relief to the Duke – and discomfort to his enemies. The Bank stock is sure to go higher … Let us sniff the air down Cornhill way …'

He paused and acknowledged their landlady.

'… If there is any little errand we can do for you over there, Mrs Trotter … ?'

It was a sly thrust in the guise of politeness, and not one she appreciated.

'I wish you joy, gentlemen. My own affairs are unaffected by these sensational developments.'

And with that, the three merchants hurried out of the room, their thoughts turning to the day's trading in wine, cloth, and sugar.

The visitor, however, did not follow them but strode calmly towards the bar, unfolding the scarf that swathed his neck in cochineal-coloured velvet. There was an extravagance to the man's appearance that amused Mary Trotter – it was not a figure known to her. She was intrigued even more when he held out a hand to her across the bar:

'I take it you are Widow Trotter? It is an honour to meet you ma'am! Samuel Rivers at your service!'

She acknowledged the young man uneasily, wondering if there might be an irony in his elegant address. He was certainly presuming a great deal:

'Welcome to the Bay-Tree, Sir. You know how to make a memorable entrance.'

'Do I not? You must forgive me for that. These *men of business* are a constant amusement to me – I take delight in flushing them out. Did you see how their bodies came to life, and their eyes shone? ... The glint of profit, Mrs Trotter! The eagerness of bulls and bears!'

He placed his penny on the bar.

'Your news set them in a fever, Mr Rivers – but you seem untroubled yourself.'

'Your perceptiveness does you credit, ma'am. Indeed I am remarkably calm ... perhaps because the news I brought with me is an entire fiction of my own ...'

Widow Trotter was lost for words and could only stare.

'... It had a grand effect, did it not? Scurrying off like mice! ... But I must introduce myself. My friend Will Lundy should be here to do the honours but he's just taken a quick diversion into the market. We are fellow-templars, he and I, but my friend Will subjects the Law to serious study – unlike myself! He has spoken of you and the Bay-Tree in the warmest terms.'

Mrs Trotter was finding it hard to absorb all this, but things were beginning to make sense:

'I share your admiration for Mr Lundy, Sir. And any friend of his is always welcome here.'

'I'll let him explain, Mrs Trotter – but we are here to see your lodger Mr Bristowe – and *yourself* ...'

He cast an eye around the now quiet room, lowering his voice to something above a whisper:

'... Will thought my experience might be of some use to you ... I understand you have been dabbling in the black arts of basset? – forgive me if I put it harshly!'

'No, Mr Rivers, I have indeed been a *dabbler* – and have been soundly punished for it.'

'So I have heard ... and you are not the only one to have *hazarded* more than you should?'

Widow Trotter was unaccustomed to such directness; but there was an honesty in his boldness that was beginning to charm her:

'You seem to know something of our story, Mr Rivers ... Thanks to you the coffee-room has half-emptied, so I think we shall be able to adjourn to my parlour – though you may need to awaken Mr Bristowe. I have to say you are about your own business remarkably early.'

'On the contrary, Mrs Trotter, this is somewhat late for me – by rights I should have retired to bed two hours ago ... I like to catch the day once it has warmed through and all the busy people have settled matters. I love a substantial breakfast and find that dinner provides it. I assure you my affairs don't call me abroad till the candles are lit ... "Hide me from Day's garish eye!", as the poet says.'

Widow Trotter was scrutinising her visitor while he talked. He was thin and sinewy; a redness in the eyes was offset by the pallor of his skin; and a tautness in the cheeks gave his features a sharpness that hinted at an acute mind. These traces of dissipation seemed only to emphasise the animation. This was a restless young man, she concluded, who lived on his wits – perhaps literally so.

'You must tell me more when we are in conference, Mr Rivers. I have heard that name before – there is an Alderman Rivers – one of the City coroners – you're not by any chance … ?'

'Guilty as charged – you have found me out! … I am a great disappointment to my father, Mrs Trotter; but he has learned to tolerate my passion for gaming in the hope that my wild oats will be quickly sown. Of course, these Common-Council men know how to indulge themselves in their turn – but I cannot afford their vast complacency! Pater and I have settled on a division of labour: while he makes his money by the stocks, I make mine at the tables; he grows fat on his interest, and I grow exceedingly thin on mine. My task is the more consuming – but the rewards can be considerable if you know how the system works …'

A genuine enthusiasm was creeping into his voice.

'… Yes, I keep my head above the waters. Indeed, my father and I end up advising each other on our respective professions.'

Widow Trotter hadn't thought of gaming in quite these terms, but she could see that fortune and risk were at play in both. The turn of a card, the roll of the dice, a rise in the stocks – all were subject to Chance.

'You speak eloquently on this, Mr Rivers.'

'Only because I remind myself of it constantly. I won't say it amounts to a philosophy – but it sees me through life pretty well.'

'But is it an *honest* life?'

Mrs Trotter found herself speaking out in her turn. To give him credit, the young man didn't flinch but gave her question the consideration of a frown:

'That is a thought I address frequently. Possibly it is not – especially when I try to steer my Fate and bribe the goddess Fortune … But I assure you, there is as much cheating and intrigue in 'Change Alley as at White's. And there can be more honesty in gaming than in City *speculation*.'

'That is a fine word, Mr Rivers – you speak like a visionary. Does imagination play a part?'

'Yes indeed. The eye and the hand, Mrs Trotter – *speculation* and *manipulation* – the two are close cousins!'

Mrs Trotter was already learning something, and the jargon of the trade (or was it an art?) was striking. This was a young man with a profession, as he thought it, and she was curious to know more. Will Lundy had evidently invited his friend to bring his knowledge to the table, and she was beginning to see that if their investigations were to bear fruit, then they needed to understand better the worlds of Sam Rivers and his father – uncomfortable though that might be.

Chapter Ten

———

AT THAT OPPORTUNE moment a jaunty Will Lundy arrived at the Bay-Tree bearing a posy of pink roses. He doffed his hat to Widow Trotter and presented his gift with a polite bow. She in turn accepted the flowers gracefully but with a niggling thought that this wasn't an impetuous generosity. Her suspicions were confirmed when Will glanced at his grinning fellow-templar:

'I take it Samuel here has introduced himself, Mrs T?'

'He has, Mr Lundy. Indeed we are now thoroughly acquainted – so you do not need to do the honours ...'

He saw her eyes narrowing.

'... You will surely want to know that while you were *marketing*, Mr Rivers seized his opportunity. He made an entrance worthy of the Theatre Royal. No stage messenger ever delivered a summons better – he succeeded in half-emptying the place. Mr Tapsell and his friends galloped off to 'Change Alley like runners at Newmarket. You should have been here to see it.'

The look was unrelenting, and those final words were spoken with intent. Will knew the game was up:

'I'm glad the little scene was well played, Mrs T. Of course, I couldn't be present myself ...'

He paused uneasily.

'... I trust there will be no repercussions ...'

'I hope not, Mr Lundy. Our gentlemen-traders look upon the Bay-Tree as their second home, sometimes too loudly, it's true – but I would not have them mocked. They were my husband's dear friends and will always be welcome here.'

Samuel Rivers stepped forwards:

'The device was entirely mine, Mrs Trotter ... You must allow me to take the guilt on myself.'

As a sign of contrition, he pushed back his collar and lowered his head before her as if readying for the scaffold.

Widow Trotter hesitated just long enough to mark the seriousness of the charge:

'On this occasion, Mr Rivers, you are reprieved. But you must remember we are a Chocolate House, not a Club. The Bay-Tree is convivial, not unruly. In this place I hope it is possible to be easy without indulgence, to argue without quarrelling, to be jocular without offence. On those terms, you are warmly welcome here.'

'I subscribe to your formal articles ma'am, and shall commit them to memory!'

Will was watching the performance with amusement – Mary Trotter's raised hand was almost queenly. Gloriana! he thought.

She smiled by way of encouragement, and became easy herself:

'Of course, I shall have to placate Mr Tapsell and his friends ... but I'm sure they'll be none the worse for their excitement. The siege was the hot topic when they arrived, and they do love a savoury rumour with their early coffee ...'

In this way the awkwardness was smoothed over, and a quarter of an hour later Widow Trotter had settled the three young men around the table in her parlour. A newly-risen Tom was buttoning up his shirt while Will was arranging his roses in a glass bowl. Before them were a pot of coffee and a platter of crusty bread, cheese, several curls of butter, cold ham, and hard-boiled quail's eggs. What was breakfast for Tom and Will was Sam Rivers's late supper.

It soon became clear why Will had thought to bring him along. For all his lack of years Mr Rivers was a seasoned gamester, and his credentials were impeccable. As he explained to them, Vandernan's was one of his favoured playgrounds. He had first entered the place as something of a valuable commodity. With an indulgent father bankable for a six-figure sum, the novice was there to be initiated into the game's mysteries. By a Law of Nature, he would be relied on to supplement the income of his friends and be encouraged to bewail the unkindness of his mistress, Dame Fortune. This was the scripted scene. But for months now young Sam Rivers had declined to play his part. Somehow the cards seemed to be his cousins, the dice his benefactors, and his mistress a kind patroness caressing her favourite. There were certainly nights of losses, but these would be redeemed by radiant mornings when blessings descended in showers of gold. In no time at all this novice was a seasoned practitioner ready to commiserate with his less fortunate friends when Chance played them false.

'I am a kind of businessman, Mrs Trotter,' he said. 'I scorn Chance. I trust to my skills and am always ready to seize opportunities. The hazard-table is my 'Change Alley, and Vandernan's my Jonathan's ...'

There was no denying the confidence of this, though the others sensed the precariousness beneath it.

'... Gaming is not mere accident and confusion. The trick is to see it as an ordered *system* – one not divine in its operation, rather a human machine in which numbers of men are joined in one interest, one business … It is this system you need to understand … this is remarkably good cheese, Mrs Trotter.'

'It is good country cheese, Mr Rivers, from Chelsea cows – the butter also.'

By now she was becoming accustomed to the young man's frolics.

Tom intervened:

'So, you think there is hope for Mrs Trotter to recover her funds?'

Samuel Rivers raised his eyes:

'Ha! The old fallacy! … *Hope*, Mr Bristowe is a will o'the wisp. It were best not to let her lead you astray. No Sir, forget Hope – and don't trust her sister Chance either. They are Sirens, and the thoughts they bring are dangerous. Along with their other siblings, Nature and Fortune, they are best avoided! … No, it is a more decisive figure that you must welcome – Opportunity. You must take hold of her at once, and make sure your grasp is a firm one! …'

He turned his attention momentarily to the boiled eggs, while the others watched him in fascination.

'… This holds true for the stocks as it does for cards and dice. I keep reminding my father of this – usually to good effect. He is not unwilling to learn from his precocious offspring!'

'So, you play the market as well as the gaming-table?' said Will, genuinely curious.

'Yes, a little – though *play* is a slippery word. These are no frivolous exercises – you rather "play" as on an instrument, mastering its possibilities.'

Widow Trotter was beginning to find this amusing:

'But why are you telling us this, Mr Rivers? Are not these your *secrets*?'

'Is it your wish to help us?' said Tom.

'I would not be here otherwise, Mr Bristowe! Will's invitation appealed to me. You see, I take satisfaction in exploiting and defeating *system* – whether it be in the mechanisms of play or the ordering of the Universe. I know you are not part of the system – that on the contrary you have been injured by it and long to extricate yourselves from it – both your cousin Frank, Mr Bristowe, and yourself, Mrs Trotter. In this I am ready to be your ally, if you will have me ...'

It was a modest enough remark, but there was some boldness behind it.

'... Believe me, I don't preach ideals or claim any virtues – I am no priest of a higher power! ... No, the figure I respect most of all is Risk. She is someone I am prepared for – and I keep my tools – my weapons – to hand ...'

The speech was gaining momentum and drawing them in as they listened. Was this a Siren-voice? Or was there some practical sense to it? Almost to reassure themselves, Mrs Trotter and her friends began to consume their breakfast while he talked on.

'... Risk, Hazard, Fortune, Chance, Fate – all are different! Risk is calculated in a way that Hazard is not. Risk is something you bargain for and with, and it may be assessed. In comparison, Hazard is a field strewn with traps where your steps are uncertain. Risk knows the odds, Hazard is unclear about what lies in wait and the direction from which danger comes. Beyond these two, Fortune offers an over-arching pattern, while Chance is momentary, a thing of the instant. You *have* your Fortune, you *seize* your Chance – she is Opportunity's giddy sister! And Fortune bears a message where Chance does not ... But beyond them all, my friends, is *Fate*. About her I can say nothing. She is implacable – not to be won or wooed. Who can know that terrible lady? With her you can only shudder and move on!'

For all Mr Rivers's protestations, there was something of the sermon about this, and as with many a sermon it was hard to gainsay. It had a confident sweep that went beyond advice and deliberation. None of them knew what response was expected, and there appeared to be little room for questions.

The flow of words was over for the present, and Widow Trotter felt a vote of thanks was looked for. Instead, she swallowed most of her dish of coffee and blinked as if emerging into the light:

'So, you think this moment is our opportunity, Mr Rivers?'

'Every crisis is an opportunity, Mrs Trotter, and the killing of George Sturgis is undoubtedly that. It is a shocking thing. From what Will has said, both you and Frank Popham have found yourselves entangled with him. You have had your adventures! I would be glad to know more … You must tell me all!'

The words hovered between a request and a demand.

As he watched the nervous animation in the young man's face, Tom had become increasingly uneasy. He knew that the full story as it touched on his uncle's political suspicions would have to remain a secret. All the talk of risk and hazard painted a lively picture, but not one that could reassure him. This spirited fellow had the confidence of a practised gamester, but he wondered about the substance. Was there something to bear the weight of their trust? Was there honesty and integrity? In the figure of Samuel Rivers he was glimpsing the very character of gaming itself – its combination of assurance and recklessness, under the guise of calculation.

But at this point there was no turning back. With his experience of the gaming world Sam Rivers could be valuable to them, and if they used him carefully it must surely work to their advantage? … . . This thought gave Tom pause. Were they not being drawn into the hazardous game themselves? He watched Will and Widow Trotter giving Mr Rivers their full attention, and checked himself. He must be guarded and alert.

Samuel Rivers was certainly a good talker; but he could be a good listener too, and as the three friends began to piece together their story of the hazard table and the basset table, of the dice and the promissory notes, he was all ears, even though he'd heard the tale of the unfortunate gamester countless times. But given the murder of George Sturgis, this did have an intriguing mystery hovering over it.

'And so,' said Widow Trotter in conclusion, 'we are left with many uncertainties in a world of which we know little. We would value your guidance, Mr Rivers – but you must forgive us if we cannot share your confidence. You speak of *risk* in rousing tones, but I assure you the risk I face in losing the Bay-Tree is a grievous one – it is no mere monetary embarrassment. I lose my very livelihood and all that is precious to me ... and poor Mr Popham faces the loss of his reputation, and perhaps much, much more – I dare not think what.'

'I feel the weight of it, Mrs Trotter, believe me. But every first step has to be a confident one, otherwise you will never begin the journey.'

'And what do you think our first step should be?' asked Will.

'That you must decide. It is to be your inquiry ...'

He looked invitingly at Widow Trotter, who was not slow to respond:

'For me, the most urgent thing is to find Mr LeRoy. I had a Holborn address for him, but my message has been returned – it seems he has left London. With your familiarity with Vandernan's, Mr Rivers, can you tell us what you know of him, and where he might be? From the start I found him elusive – a man hard to read. If he has fled, then ...'

She was unwilling to complete the thought.

"Yes indeed, Mrs Trotter. Robert LeRoy is an enigma, and such things invariably excite my curiosity. As you will be aware, he has been the banker at Vandernan's basset table, and his reputation as tallière has been high in certain quarters – although far less in others. This was a phenomenon that interested me, and so I thought it worth my study. I regret I was never one of his *friends*, perhaps because Hazard remains my greatest love – or possibly for another reason ... I have to say my occasional flirtation with basset was instructive. As I told you, I like to know precisely what risk I am taking, and at basset it is Chance that rules – or ought to! Somehow, for certain friends of his, Chance was taking a holiday, and the sly goddess *Favour* slipped into her place – quite against the principles of the game which usually ensure that the bank will emerge with a comfortable profit.'

The look on Widow Trotter's face was eloquent:

'This confirms my suspicions, Mr Rivers. I sensed some collusion between Mr Sturgis and Mr LeRoy. How it was done I know not, but there was an intricacy – a trickery – about his dealing ...'

'The man is something of a magician – an admirable skill when properly directed! I am glad you noticed this yourself ... but there is much more about Mr LeRoy which I was able to discover – something that he had scrupulously concealed. I think you may find it the key to his secret chamber ...'

Sam Rivers couldn't suppress a slight smile at the appositeness of the phrase.

'... Our Mr Robert LeRoy, the elegant and precise tallière – a man of such Gallic manners and *étiquette* – is in reality ... Bob Leary.'

'Ha! ...'

The cry came from Will.

'... I suspected he was not a true *monsieur*.'

'My friend Adèle had sniffed him out,' added Widow Trotter. 'But *Bob Leary!* – that name is delightful – I can understand his wish for a *nom de tallière*. It has a touch of the Irish, if you ask me.'

'You are right, Mrs Trotter. Bob Leary of Dublin – no less!'

'Well, well – no doubt there's a story to tell – if I could only hear it from his own lips. I'm more than ever eager to find him. Do you have any idea where he might be?'

Sam Rivers half-turned toward Will as he replied:

'I shall make some enquiries at Vandernan's – discreet ones of course. My friend Mr Lundy here doesn't know this yet – but he and I shall be paying the place a visit tomorrow evening. I think it is high time this young man came to know something of the gaming-house and its ways. And I intend to teach him.'

It was said cheerily, but there was sudden apprehension in the air. Will was caught off his guard:

'But … I know nothing of gaming – I'm the rawest of beginners …'

'And that is perfect for my purposes, Will! Your face will not be known. Tomorrow at Vandernan's you will be an unfledged pigeon, the very meekest of lambs. Believe me, you will have the wolves licking their chops!'

This was not a comfortable prospect. The thought of being made a sacrifice to a set of predatory gamesters was a chilling one. He looked pleadingly at Sam whose features were suddenly animated – this was a man anticipating some excellent sport:

'But I have very little money to stake and cannot carry any great loss.'

'There is no difficulty, Will. In this venture you will be my plaything! You yourself will be my *stake*. I shall deliver you up to some cunning gamesters, believe me, and we shall see how things unfold. Any winnings will of course be shared! …'

By now, Samuel Rivers was positively glowing at the prospect.

'… If you are to achieve anything with your investigations, then all three of you must understand something of the arts of gaming – of odds and probabilities, casting and reckoning, the particular disciplines of uncertainty. As I said, in this trade we employ both speculation and manipulation. The rules are to be played by – but also *with*.'

A look of cunning gave them no doubt that his would be an unorthodox experiment.

'And what game do you intend to teach him?' asked Widow Trotter in a voice rather more unsteady than usual.

'Hazard!'

'But this is very dangerous!' said Tom at once. 'The throw of the dice is pure chance, surely? My Cousin Frank rapidly lost a fortune. The very name declares it – as you told us yourself.'

'Yes, Mr Bristowe – but the *art* of the game is to turn Hazard into Risk – to edge your play from possibility toward probability – to nudge the odds. Hazard is a time-spending, money-wasting game, I confess, but one that allows a degree of science to tip the scale ...'

Once again, the three friends reeled at the confidence – almost amounting to certainty – of the young man's pronouncements.

'... I admit that caution is necessary. Hazard is the most bewitching sport, and when a man begins to play he knows not when to leave off ... But calm your fears – I shall be there to watch over Mr Lundy. He is a man of sense and reason, not apt to act unadvisedly. And in this scene his very innocence will work in his favour. He will not be suspected or doubted.'

They began to wonder if there was some subtle plot hatching in Sam Rivers's mind. Widow Trotter was especially concerned. All this talk of odds and probability seemed dubious to her – just another way of admitting the uncertainty while thinking you could bring it under control. She knew all too well the dangers of self-deception, and at that moment it occurred to her that this cocksure young gamester must be reminded of the perils of dice-play. Had these not been laid open to them in the most terrible way? She swung round in her seat and got to her feet:

'Let me stop you for a moment, Mr Rivers. You are exciting us with your bold talk – and yes, you are almost giving us Hope (however much you decry it) ... But I need to recall you to the fate of poor Mr Sturgis. His body was dumped behind Vandernan's, his heart run through – and a frightful message thrust into his mouth ...'

She reached out to the top drawer of the sideboard and pulled it open.

'... The lure of the gaming-table is dangerous. It can bring you riches – or it can be your death warrant.'

To clinch her point she slid her hand into the drawer and took out a piece of cloth. Laying it carefully on the table before them, she unfolded it to reveal a pair of ivory dice.

There was a sudden intake of breath around her.

'Mrs T! Are these ... ?'

'Yes, Tom. Elias asked me to place them here for safe keeping. They are the dice taken from Mr Sturgis's mouth.'

Tom and Will hung back, but Sam Rivers leaned forwards:

'Let me take a look ...'

There was a pause while he took up the pair of dice and held them – almost caressed them – in his two hands.

'... These are indeed Vandernan's dice – and beautiful they are too. Unmistakeable!'

'So they are certainly from Vandernan's?'

'Oh yes. Do you see? The tiny pips are of lapis lazuli, each one carefully set into the ivory – blue on white. The box-keeper guards them carefully, as you can imagine. It means that any substitution of false dice – if such a thing were attempted – is impossible.'

His breathing was intense. The others watched him closely – none of them spoke. He was now holding two corners of each die very gently between forefinger and thumb – as if weighing gold leaf. He stopped breathing. His hands became motionless, so that the only movement was the slightest shudder of the dice themselves. He repeated the process a second time.

'Well, well! How very curious! … I ought to be surprised, but somehow am not … These are false dice, my friends!'

Chapter Eleven

—∞∞∞—

AFTER HIS EXTREMELY late supper, a yawning Samuel Rivers left the Bay-Tree and went off to his bed, leaving the others to finish their breakfast and reflect on the scene that had just played out. They could only look at each other in silence, until Widow Trotter spoke quietly:

'Your friend is a prodigy, Mr Lundy. I know not what to think. He certainly had an answer to everything.'

'I knew he was deep in the gaming world, Mrs T, but had not expected such philosophising! You were right to challenge him about his confidence. He wants to defy the universe – with cards and dice as his weapons.'

'I'm not sure,' said Tom. 'Are they not rather the tools of his trade – like a wood-turner's lathe, or an artist's pencil? There was a deep satisfaction in his words – a pride in his craft.'

'Yes, you're right … the moment he held those ivory dice in his hands …'.

'It was almost sacramental. He looked at them in wonder.'

'And when he told us of the skill in giving them their bias – how to drill through the pip and inject the tiny drop of mercury …'

'The idea excited him.'

Widow Trotter was listening:

'Yes, gentlemen – weapons and tools. How very subtle falseness can be – how intricate its ways! ...'

She was in danger of becoming philosophical herself.

'... Mr Rivers has plans for those dice, Will ... As I led him out, he asked if he could make use of them tomorrow night.'

There was a moment of shock. Will sighed audibly and ran a hand through his hair:

'Oh heavens, what am I being led into?'

'It seems you'll not be playing by the rules.'

'But is this for any purpose, Mrs T? I am happy to do all I can, but subjecting me to the perils of the Hazard-table ... I need to know why. False dice or true, where will this take us?'

It was a pertinent question. Tom was becoming anxious too:

'Surely he can't be expecting you to win back Frank's two thousand? That is surely fantasy.'

'I think he has his own rules,' said Will. 'It was all a strange mixture of calculation and playfulness.'

'Yes, he spoke of Opportunity as though it was an amusing flirtation!'

'He's certainly a mystery to me,' said Widow Trotter. 'I don't know what he has in mind. But remember, the stake tomorrow night will be his. It seems he is welcoming Risk – that other favourite lady! Perhaps he has plans for you, Will? You may be serving a purpose of his own?'

Tom picked up the thought:

'I wonder. I've been thinking about Uncle Jack's suspicions. Perhaps our Mr Rivers has sniffed out something himself – about Vandernan's and its *system*? There seemed to be some purpose behind his curiosity. Perhaps he too wants to discover more about Bob Leary and George Sturgis?'

'Well, I am content to be part of his game, whatever it is – so long as it will help our cause.'

If the early morning had witnessed some drama in the Bay-Tree, by late afternoon the place had settled into an easy quietness. The occasional rustling newspaper or clinking teacup could be heard above the hum of conversation. Even the squeak of a pen was audible from the far corner of the room, where Laurence Bagnall (author of *The Shoe-Buckle*) was composing some contemplative verses suited to the mood of the hour. It had occurred to him that between Milton's *L'Allegro* and *Il Penseroso* – the poet's celebrations of cheerfulness and melancholy – there was room for a delicate ode that explored the claims of the balanced life, and he was intending 'Il Moderato' to find its place alongside them in the classic pantheon.

Tom Bristowe had given him what encouragement he could and was now seated in silence nearby, reading some recently printed verses in praise of wine. He was beginning to think that this anonymous poet somehow managed to bestride all three moods, adding a generous pinch of wit too.

Everything in the Chocolate House, therefore, was as it should be at this time of day, with a calm thoughtfulness interposing between the activities of the day and the adventures of the night.

This meant that the interruption, when it came, was even more marked.

It began with a shout from outside in Red Lion Court. The cry echoed from the walls and was loud enough to be heard inside the coffee-room – it was a confused noise of protest mounting almost to a scream – a mixture of 'Let me be!' and 'Hands off, you villains!'

At once newspapers were lowered; Laurence Bagnall's pen lifted from his page leaving unfinished a couplet on the joys of equanimity; Tom Bristowe swung round at a voice he thought he recognised and jumped to his feet. Widow Trotter looked up anxiously and slipped out from behind the bar while Tom half-ran to the door.

Outside, a struggle was going on. A young man was being held by two burly-looking characters. His arms were pinioned and a cudgel was being held to his face.

'Frank!'

Tom strode towards them. His cousin was writhing in protest:

'Tom – thank God! We need to talk. Tell these rogues to unhand me!'

It was a theatrical phrase but seemed to do the trick. Tom reached out a pacifying arm and they loosened their grip a little.

'We must execute our commission. You'll come with us!'

'Calm yourselves, gentlemen,' said Tom. 'If you release your hold he will not flee. This gentleman is my cousin – I'll vouch for him.'

'So, you'll stand bail, will you?'

Tom understood what was happening. Now Frank Popham was drawing himself to his full height and dusting off his coat with his free hand. Mrs Trotter had stepped out of the Bay-Tree and was at Tom's shoulder:

'Where are you taking him?'

'Somewhere to cool his heels! It will be commodious accommodation, I assure you.'

'We are arresting him upon an execution for two thousand guineas.'

'At whose suit?' said Tom in alarm.

'Here is the writ. Read it for yourself!'

He took the paper from them and his eyes scanned it:

'But this makes no sense ...'

He handed it to Widow Trotter.

'... it cannot be! This debt is not enforceable − it is here in the name of Vandernan's. There has been a mistake.'

'No Sir, no mistake,' said the fellow with the cudgel. 'Just the old story! There's been some wild play here, has there not? Some heedless flirting with Dame Fortune?'

He smirked at his fellow bailiff.

'But I happen to know the debt was transferred,' persisted Tom. 'It was settled by another gentleman ...'

The two tipstaffs looked at each other:

'Well, you're mistaken, Sir. This paper says otherwise. You must take the matter up with the sheriff. We have a job to do.'

Frank Popham was losing his composure again:

'This is nonsense! Utter nonsense, I tell you! You cannot do this − I am a Member of Parliament!'

'There is no basis for this arrest, gentlemen,' said Tom more calmly. 'Can we not settle this over a dish of coffee − or a dram?'

His eyes were indicating the door of the Bay-Tree a few yards away.

'You can be my guests, Sirs!' added Mrs Trotter. 'We can sort the matter inside. It seems we are attracting an audience ...'

The bailiffs looked at each other. The whisky was tempting, but they were in no mood to accept any polite invitations:

'You can keep your fancy coffee, madam! This is not to be settled by witty talk. Come Sir! You must with us!'

They tightened their grip.

'We must send for Constable Cobb!' declared Mrs Trotter at once.

The bailiffs were annoyed:

'The constable has nothing to do with it! This is a civil matter.'

Tom sensed the situation was becoming more dangerous. He put out an arm and touched the head of the cudgel calmly:

'We shall not stand in your way gentlemen – but let us have a moment, I beg you.'

Frank looked despairing:

'I can't understand this, Tom! At Vandernan's my brain was a little fuddled, but what I do know is that George Sturgis settled this account himself. My own debt was to him. I signed the note!'

'But did you sign anything else?' asked Tom. 'How befuddled were you?'

Silence.

'We must go,' said the second bailiff. His companion swung his cudgel back and raised it threateningly. They both began to pull him away:

'Leave whining, Sir! Come with us!'

Tom suddenly remembered Will's advice:

'But no! Surely such a debt – a debt of this size – cannot be enforced by law? You have no authority in this.'

There was consternation:

'A debt is a debt!' shouted the second bailiff. 'We must about our work! You must take up the matter at the sheriff's office.'

Frank was deeply embarrassed. Red Lion Court had become a theatre, and all eyes were on him as the men began marching him off in the direction of the piazza.

'We shall do just that, gentlemen!' cried Mrs Trotter. 'Don't despair, Mr Popham! I'm sure this can be settled today.'

It was a hopeful thought, but an uncertain one. All they could do was watch as Frank was led away at a brisk pace, followed by a pair of impish boys acting as escort.

⌘

Half an hour later, the Honourable Francis Popham found himself in distinctly unfamiliar surroundings. The sponging-house was a three-storied building that jutted out into one of the insalubrious streets beyond the Covent Garden piazza. The past century had not been kind to it, and as he was ushered into the reception-room he felt the fustiness of a place that was an odd combination of home and prison. A small fire occupied the hearth and there were curtains hanging at the barred windows. It was a room where food had been eaten several hours earlier; but the aroma of rabbit stew was now combining uneasily with the mould along the outer wall.

He was not alone here. As a holding-house for debtors it had a mixed clientele. A grim-looking character was hunched over a table; further along, a dapper young gentleman was reading a paper, legs crossed to display his silver buckles; and a second older man in a brown worsted suit lounged comfortably beside the fireplace, drawing on his pipe. It was a strangely domestic scene. It aspired to be a coffee house, but the dirty tables and odd bits of debris on the floor suggested otherwise. Above the mantelpiece was displayed a reminder of the building's true purpose: a framed list of 'House Fees' gave extortionate prices for 'fire', 'candles', 'bedding', and other necessaries. This was no free market. In this place your debts were likely to mount rather than diminish.

It was a resigned Frank who found himself confronted by the proprietor of the house, a stout, big-boned woman with a delicate lace cap tied round her chin and a butcher's blue apron clinging to her hips. This lady, he decided, needed no cudgel to enforce her rule. The brawny politeness was evident in her speech of welcome, which set out firmly the regulations of the place and what was expected of him, but with a degree of deference that could easily be mistaken for sarcasm. There was a slight bow of the head as she spoke:

'It is exceptional, Sir, that we are able to entertain a Member of Her Majesty's *Parliament* …'

She gave the word its full four syllables.

'... and one whose indebtedness is of such magnificent proportions. No mere trade-bills either! but the most respectable – nay honourable *liability* – Two thousand guineas is a regal sum, Mr Popham! Mr Cumberbatch and I are pleased to welcome you. Fortunately we have a most decent double-windowed room available on the next floor ...'

'I don't intend to remain here, Mrs Cumberbatch,' said Frank as graciously as possible.

'Many of our guests have said the same, Mr Popham – but you may find that *eventualities* are a long time coming ...'

'This is absurd! ...'

Frank was becoming restive again.

'... It is a mere gaming debt – and one I am not liable for.'

'Be that as it may, Sir, it is clear you did not make the appropriate *arrangements* with Vandernan's.'

Mrs Cumberbatch had the knack of endowing abstractions with particular menace.

'What arrangements? I tell you, this debt is a false imposition. I can only think they wish to embarrass me to the utmost! I assure you, all I need is a little time ...'

'Ah yes, Sir, *Time* – a precious commodity. It comes upon us so quickly – or it takes an exceedingly slow course ... I hope for your sake, Sir, that it is the former. Meanwhile, you will settle yourself and take some tea?'

Frank seemed to have found himself in a grotesque parody of the Bay-Tree, which made the discomfort even greater. Was this real, or would he wake up at any moment? He decided to make the best of things:

'I would like first a sheet of paper and writing materials. There is an urgent note I must send.'

'Yes of course. As you'll have seen, Sir, the paper will be a shilling – but we supply pen and ink with it.'

'How much?'

'Rest easy, Mr Popham. We shall add it to your account. Have no fear.'

'My account? But …'

'Our terms are ten shillings a day.'

'What! But I could rent a mansion for less.'

'Indeed you could, Mr Popham, indeed you could. But at the present moment your *necessity* is pressing … I shall bring you the writing materials.'

With the tea delivered and the note dispatched, Frank tried to settle down at one of the tables. It was an unsociable place. None of the other inmates had anything to say, although the dapper gentleman raised an amused eyebrow in his direction and gave him an alarming wink before turning back to his newspaper. It struck him that the place was in reality a waiting-room where some could wait for days, perhaps weeks, and by the time they left it would be for the Fleet – whither the sponging-house debt would no doubt follow them.

His heart therefore leapt in relief when Mrs Cumberbatch reappeared and made an announcement:

'You have a visitor already, Mr Popham! He is waiting in the closet over the hall. Follow me.'

He did so eagerly. Help was at hand, and the misunderstanding would surely soon be resolved.

But instead of a familiar face from the Bay-Tree, the person who confronted him was a stranger, and one of foreboding aspect. He had the accoutrements of a gentleman – cravat, peeping linen cuffs, shiny buckles and silver-topped cane – but he was wigless, and the features were distinctly those of a bruiser, topped by hair of an aggressive spikiness. At Frank's entrance the figure was bending slightly toward him, holding a cocked hat in his other hand, a look of ill-disguised contempt on his face.

'Mr Popham! What a state of affairs this is. Most unfortunate!'

Frank hesitated in the doorway:

'To whom am I speaking, Sir?'

The man gave a dismissive sweep of the arm:

'My name is of no account … I am not here on my own behalf. I come from some gentlemen who have your welfare very much at heart. If you close the door behind you, then we can talk. What I have to say will surely concern you.'

This was an uneasy encounter; but Frank had little choice. There were two small chairs. The man indicated one, and when Frank had seated himself he sat down on the other. The corner of a table jutted between them.

Frank took the lead:

'Whatever your message, I hope it will be brief.'

The response was a cold smile and a shake of the head:

'I'm sure you will want to listen, Mr Popham. It is in your interest to do so. You are in extreme danger.'

An awkward silence followed as the stranger's eyes locked onto his. Frank's thoughts were racing ahead in fear and bafflement. He felt a blush forcing itself into his face. When the stranger spoke again, it was to the purpose:

'You were given a warning, Mr Popham – and a message to carry … I trust your father has received it?'

Frank was not expecting such a direct question. He was suddenly back in the dark alley:

'Yes … I told him … He was puzzled by it.'

'No, Mr Popham. I think your father understands very well … Of course, if he does not, then you yourself will suffer the severest penalty. Do you understand me? …'

The gaze was unrelenting.

'… You will wish to tell him that, and ensure he takes a step back. We ask nothing more.'

Frank was determined to be bold, but stuttered slightly as he swallowed:

'*We?* … Who is it has sent you? Why are you here? … Is all of this your doing?'

'Questions!'

The word was spoken in amusement. There was no immediate move to answer– just another pause. The man placed his hat on the table and reached for his snuff-box. Frank declined the offer and watched as the man carefully removed one of his gloves. There was an odd politeness about the stranger's behaviour that sat uneasily with his ruffian face. It was surely not the man in the alley? This voice was oily in tone, and sly in manner.

'I am here to help you, Mr Popham. You are in a perilous position. Two thousand guineas is a considerable sum! …'

Frank was becoming impatient:

'So, you are here about the debt! What is that to you, Sir? The debt is between me and George Sturgis … and my father is not involved in any way!'

'In a strange way he *is*, Mr Popham – and that is why I am here. You know, of course, that Mr Sturgis is now dead. This circumstance changes matters considerably …'

Frank was stunned:

'*Dead*, you say? No, no! … I don't believe you!'

'Oh yes, Mr Popham. There is no doubt of it. His body was found yesterday. Murdered – run through with a sword … Has the news not reached you?'

'No. I knew nothing of this.'

His mind was racing. So, Tom's note now made sense. The summons had spoken of 'serious developments.' A euphemism indeed – although the phrase had been underlined. It seems his cousin had intended to break the news to him in person. There could be no pretence of resistance now. He was in the stranger's hands and could only wait and see what unfolded.

'In that case,' the man continued, 'you will understand that the killing of George Sturgis puts you in acute danger. All eyes are beginning to turn to you ...'

It was a chilling image. Frank was about to protest but bit his tongue before the words came. He could feel a threat approaching.

'... You were wandering the streets throughout the night, angry and afraid – and what is more, Mr Sturgis had your promissory note in his pocket. Your losses at Vandernan's had been heavy indeed – far more than you could possibly cover. You had no account at the gaming-house, and no arrangements had been put in place. You faced utter ruin – not only to your purse but to your reputation ... and then your magnanimous friend Mr Sturgis came forward. He settled your debt himself, and you wrote a note to him for the sum of two thousand guineas. What a friend! It would give you time to organise your affairs – and being such a friend he would not press you for payment until the embarrassment had passed ...'

The stranger gave an eery smile and looked for a response, as if reading a story book to a child. Frank was desperate to break in, but knew he should hold his peace till the full picture had formed. He needed to know the worst of it.

'A charge of *murder*, Mr Popham – unthinkable, is it not? ... But I advise you to think about it now. It would be an ignominious end – and destroy the reputation of your family ...'

This was too much:

'Murder? How dare you! What are you suggesting?'

'No man had better motive – none an easier opportunity. The evidence points in your direction and you have no alibi that can save you.'

'What evidence?'

'Such is easily found, Mr Popham. There need be no difficulty in it.'

Frank was speechless. The man's assurance was extraordinary:

'But all this makes no sense. You admit that George Sturgis was my rescuer. Why should I kill the man who had saved me from ruin?'

'Because he now had power over you. Was that the reason for your confrontation?'

'What confrontation? This is a mere fancy of your own!'

'It is a scene easily imagined. A jury could learn of a quarrel between you – perhaps a careless threat? ... As I said, such things can be found.'

'This is entire fiction – there is no truth in it – as you well know!'

'What *I* know, Mr Popham is unimportant. It is what others can be made to know that is vital. Your life hangs on it. We are in a world of fictions, are we not? People can be made to know anything – so long as they believe they see it.'

There was a terrible logic to the stranger's threat. Frank was himself trying not to see George's body:

'If George Sturgis is dead, then what has happened to the promissory note?'

'An excellent question, Mr Popham. Well, let me tell you ... there is a story here, but not one for your hearing. Let us say it is a little secret which you may not yet share.'

This coyness was infuriating. Frank was by now struggling to hold back his anger – he needed to hear everything the man had to say. He was also genuinely curious.

'Why are you doing this? What is your own motive? ...'

Again, no reply.

'... Who are you?'

'A friend – if you will allow me to be. You must listen further. I have a proposal to put to you.'

'Why must I? All I have heard thus far is a tissue of threats and insinuations – nothing more.'

The stranger continued to tread his own path:

'Your father, Mr Popham … Do you love your father? Do you wish to save him from harm?'

'This is impertinent, Sir! …'

Frank stopped himself.

'… Of course, yes. You need not ask it.'

'Then you will want him to avoid danger?'

'Yes.'

He had to know where this road was leading.

'Your father's oversight of the Queen's finances is a heavy responsibility. Her Majesty needs to have complete trust in his discretion.'

'That is true – and she does … but the Duchess of Marlborough is Keeper of the Privy Purse. My father is merely her deputy.'

'Of course – but it is well known that Her Grace's position is more honorary than practical, and that a coolness in her relations with the Queen has made matters *problematical*. Viscount Melksham finds himself in an awkward position between the two of them.'

'That is not for me to say.'

The stranger's features set themselves into an angry frown:

'I have to tell you that the Duchess is outraged by your father's behaviour. She feels herself undermined at every turn. Lord Melksham has been spying on her and voicing suspicions. This is intolerable! Her Grace has made it clear to the Queen that he must be dismissed …'

This was news to Frank. Given its source, what credence could he give it? He let the remark pass by.

'… It is time that your father gave up such an onerous office. The Duchess can no longer work with him. You must persuade him to resign, Mr Popham. That is what we require of you. Otherwise he will be sent packing in ignominy and disgrace, his son branded a *murderer*. Of that I can assure you. Have I made myself clear?'

There was no polite indirectness now. This was an outright threat:

'As clear as crystal, Sir. I now see why I find myself in this sordid place – how my own threatened disgrace has been managed. It *has* been managed from the very beginning, has it not? You have attacked me because you have no grounds for attacking my father ...'

If he thought the man would demur at this, he was mistaken. The eyes continued to hold him in thrall.

'... Do you have the honour to admit as much? I want to hear it from you, Sir. As a man of honour you must give me that satisfaction.'

The stranger gave a short laugh:

'Ha! Do I hear you speak of *honour*? Forgive me for smiling! Must I remind you that your debt of two thousand guineas is a debt of *honour*? It is the gentleman's code. At the gaming table we expect men to pay their debts – and woe betide him who does not ...'

There was a devilish cleverness to this which was chilling. The man was right.

'... But you must not see matters in these terms, Mr Popham. As I said to you, we wish to be your friends. Let me put it simply and clearly ... If your father resigns his royal appointment, then your debt will at once be cancelled. All suspicion regarding Mr Sturgis's death will be lifted from you, and you will be free to serve your country honourably ... Now tell me, is that not a noble offer? And a generous one under the circumstances.'

The directness of this was shocking. Frank needed time to think; but it was clear the man was insisting on an immediate answer. There was only one move he could make:

'Will I be released from this place?'

'Instantly, Mr Popham. I have authority for it. Your singular gaoler will be more than happy. You may walk free now.'

'Then I accept your terms, Sir. I shall do everything I can.'

'Excellent. You have a week, Mr Popham. Seven days ... Do not disappoint us.'

Chapter Twelve

⸺◦◦◦⸺

THE FRANK POPHAM who returned to the Bay-Tree was almost a ghost-like figure. Stepping out from the sponging-house, he had instinctively turned in the direction of the chocolate house rather than towards Pall Mall, as if at this desperate moment his home was to be found there. The elements seemed to agree. A boisterous wind tugged at his coat and drew him forwards encouragingly, the swirling dust pricking his eyes. An empty wicker basket danced along the cobbles ahead of him.

He knew he couldn't confront his father until he had come to terms with himself. What had he just done? As he walked, he could hear his own voice: 'I accept your terms. I shall do all I can …' Did he really say those words?

He had to escape that place, of course, and the Devil's bargain had been extorted from him – but what was he to do now? To dissolve into air was hardly possible, but the alternatives were all painful and humiliating – except perhaps for one – to throw himself onto the ingenuity and determination of his friends at the Bay-Tree. The thought gave a momentary lift to his spirits. After all, he had a whole week …

George's murder had stunned him, and to be told of it and be implicated in the crime at the same time was a double shock. He tried to dispel his mental picture, but fancy insisted on painting the scene in vivid colours with the body slumped at his feet. Against this, his calmer judgment was struggling to offer reassurance: the man's threat was chilling – but it was a threat, not an accusation. It was clear these people knew he was innocent. Most likely, they also knew who the killer was.

But his thoughts didn't stop there, and they led him in an uncomfortable direction … Perhaps his father might be willing to retire from Court? After all, the alternative – his son executed, and the family plunged into scandal and disgrace – was surely unthinkable? … And the answer was simple – indeed it might be a choice his father would willingly make? His responsibilities as Deputy Treasurer were a constant source of unease, and Court life was soured by politics. The Duchess was a formidable enemy, and her Secretary Arthur Maynwaring was sure to be dripping poison into his patroness's ear. The man had borne his father a grudge ever since they had clashed some months earlier. Perhaps this business was Maynwaring's sweet revenge? …

With thoughts like these churning in his brain, Frank strode up Red Lion Court in troubled mood, longing for society and some sympathetic advice. His spirits began to lift when he saw the Bay-Tree sign ahead, waving as if to claim his notice. The building's upper stories leaned out slightly in a gesture of welcome, and through the window the evening candles were beginning to glow. He pushed open the coffee-room door, propelled by the wind that whistled around, and closed it carefully behind him.

Inside, the atmosphere was warm and aromatic. Ripples of amusement were bubbling up around the tables, and a general conversation appeared to be taking place. He walked quietly up to the bar and laid down his penny. Jenny Trip gave him a smile of welcome, then turned away. Her attention, like everyone else's, was directed to the table nearest the fire, where a corpulent gentleman in an unkempt wig was on his feet, holding up before his audience what appeared to be a printed handbill. It was Jack Tapsell. Frank had evidently chanced on a moment of raillery – whether good-humoured or not he was yet to discover. The room was full of grinning faces, except for a sober-suited figure seated at another table who was attempting a look of calm indifference, not altogether successfully.

By the fireplace, Mr Tapsell was favouring the room with his eloquence, and in full satirical mode was preparing to read from the paper waving in his hand – a welcome *corrective*, he told them, to Mr Bagnall's *Oudenarde*:

'No patriot he, gentlemen! No celebrator of our great general! No – our laureate of the Bay-Tree has favoured the nation with a Tory rant against the War! ...'

And there at the next table was Laurence Bagnall himself. His poetic reputation as author of *The Shoe-Buckle* commanded rather less awe than it once did – at least from the merchant-traders of the Bay-Tree.

'... These lines are hot off the presses, my friends – and piping hot they are too! They deserve to be delivered in this place. Their anonymous author is clearly a man of wit and sound principles! ...'

There was a sudden expectant silence. The moment of performance had arrived. Jack Tapsell raised a quizzical eyebrow and announced the title with due ceremony:

'Verses on Mr Bagnall's *Heroic Ode upon the Duke of Marlborough's Late Victory.*'

Then he cleared his throat and gave the lines the flourish they deserved:

"The Critics oooh'd – his baffled readers aaah'd –
Yet could make nothing of this Oudenarde ..."

An ironic cheer went up. Jack paused a few seconds to let the hilarity subside – and then caught the moment:

> *"… Like shiv'ring soldiery, they cringe with fear*
> *At tortur'd metaphors that blast the ear;*
> *Our poet takes us to the field of battle*
> *In words that groan, and bang, and scream, and rattle –*
> *With verses harsher than the noise of war*
> *He plucks Defeat where Victory was before.*
> *Great Marlborough to his Nemesis must yield:*
> *'Tis mad Pindarick slaughter wins the field!"*

The audience applauded enthusiastically. Mr Bagnall was on stage, though not in the way he would have chosen. He felt the summons. With as much dignity as possible he rose to his feet, brushing his wig aside so as to take a comprehensive view of the room.

'I am honoured, Mr Tapsell! It is given to few poets to win the tribute of verses like those. Although I heartily deplore their *Whiggish* sentiments, I can applaud their vigour as a tribute to my humble ode! But like many a satirical squib, the thing is unjust – monstrously so! The field of battle is harsh and cruel, and it demands a style that paints war's violence in its true colours. Cannons and muskets are not things of harmony. nor suited to mellifluous notes! If my language is tortured, Sir, it is merely to convey the horrors of human slaughter. I shall say no more … though in my defence permit me to quote Mr Shakespeare: *The words of Mercury are harsh after the songs of Apollo!'*

Mr Bagnall resumed his seat, and a hum of approval ran through the room – one appreciative soul even applauded lightly. But Jack Tapsell was not to be fobbed off with critical niceties:

'You betray a noble cause, Mr Bagnall! You injure our heroic troops!'

'It is War does that, Mr Tapsell! ... But you are right. It is not the politician's *noble cause* that I celebrate – but the infantry's *bloody sacrifice*.'

During these exchanges Frank Popham was leaning on the bar and caught Jenny's eye. There was a lively look there, and a slight smile appreciative of the repartee. It struck him how much wit and knowledge the girl would pick up in this place – it was indeed a 'penny university'. He pushed his coin towards her and was about to speak. But he was pre-empted:

'These are gentlemen of fine words, Sir, are they not? How they make them serve their turn!'

'They do indeed – though it is often in play of course.'

'But they send them into battle too, I think!'

'Jenny – you speak true! There may be no quarter given – especially in wit.'

'You are witty yourself, Sir. I can tell.'

'But sometimes that is not enough, Jenny ... Sometimes words will not serve ...'

The thought trailed off into a sigh.

'... I need to speak with Mrs Trotter – and Mr Bristowe too – if they are here?'

'If I may say so, Sir, I think they will be glad to see you. They have been in a flurry since you were taken off.'

Indeed, Frank Popham was welcomed into the parlour with surprise and relief. The rueful young man was soon ensconced well away from the skirmishes of the coffee-room and was recounting his adventure in the sponging-house. He had resolved to spare them none of its embarrassment. His mind would explode if he didn't share his troubles:

'I was determined to heed your warning, Tom – to hold my peace in all this and do nothing rash – I truly was! But events have overtaken me. George killed! I still cannot credit it.

I know you were about to tell me the news when I was hauled away ...'

'I couldn't risk a full message to Pall Mall, Frank.'

'No, of course. I understand ... And what of my own note? – I wrote it less than an hour ago – do I take it the thing hasn't arrived? ...'

Tom and Widow Trotter looked at each other. Their silence was answer enough.

'... Ha! Why am I not surprised? I suspect pleading letters from that house are encouraged to go astray. The Cumberbatches have a thriving business!'

'You have done well to escape so quickly, Frank ... but at what price?'

It was a sharp question, and his cousin felt it.

Grim-faced, he told them of his unsavoury visitor and the poisonous message he had delivered:

'... And so, I had to hear about George from that creature ... hear him gloat over my plight and threaten me with a charge of murder! I fear I took it badly, but what could I do? The man was a rough-looking fellow for all his polite airs, and he held me in the palm of his hand like a sparrow about to have its life squeezed out ... Newgate and Tyburn, Tom! The very thought is terrifying! I saw no other course but to agree his terms. What else could I do? They are ready to bring evidence against me – hired of course! Wandering the streets throughout the night I have no-one to vouch for me ... And what can I say in my defence? I have only the vaguest memory of it – I was so befuddled ... What a bloody fool I've been, Tom! How I've run heedlessly into this disaster!'

By now he was close to tears, head bowed, one hand clutching his hair as if about to pull it from its roots.

Widow Trotter had been listening intently but saying little. She recognised a young man drained of his youthful self-assurance. This was real fear, and it needed no extraordinary sympathy on her part to understand it. She leaned towards him:

'It is a glimpse of hell, Mr Popham. But I assure you, the threat of violence is often greater than the act. Our imagination sets to work, and we paint the picture in vivid colours … Believe me, I have a frightening picture of my own …'

The two young men could see it in her eyes.

'… You say they have given you seven days?'

'Yes, Saturday of next week. That is when the debt will be called in. My father must resign his post. These are ruthless people, and they are determined to remove him from the scene. His suspicions about the Bank and the Duchess are surely proved?'

'Yes, gentlemen, the whole affair smacks of conspiracy. But that is its weakness … A conspiracy depends on trust and secrecy. The plotters find they must trust each other, and the more intricate the plot, the more precarious it may prove – especially when politics shows its ugly face …'

She sat back in her chair and looked at the ceiling.

'… I have been comforting myself with this thought – believe me!'

Tom smiled at her:

'Yes, we seem to have two conspiracies here. George Sturgis and Robert LeRoy had their own little plot.'

'That is why we need to bring the two plots together. I can only think that in both cases our Mr LeRoy will have something useful to tell us – if we can track him down.'

'Ah, Robert LeRoy!' said Tom, looking at his cousin with a sharp eye. 'Or *Bob Leary*, as we now know him to be …'

Frank heard the words and almost choked. This was yet another revelation.

'What!'

'Yes, he's Irish Bob, it seems.'

'How did you discover this?'

The two of them glanced at each other:

'This is where *we* have a story to tell *you*, Frank.'

'You could think of it as our own plot,' said Mrs Trotter. 'The beginnings of one, at least.'

'And Will has brought in reinforcements …'

This was the language of field strategy. Frank was becoming alarmed:

'So, matters have moved on?'

'Indeed they have. Thanks to Mr Lundy we have gained admittance to Vandernan's.'

Frank's eyes widened:

'How was that managed? Have you found yourselves a spy?'

'An informer of sorts,' said Tom. 'The gentleman is a denizen of the gaming-house – and Will is to venture there with him tomorrow night.'

'He is Mr Lundy's friend – a fellow-templar.'

Tom and Widow Trotter were beginning to sound like a pair of conspirators themselves.

'Tell me more!' said Frank with enthusiasm.

And so they told him of Samuel Rivers. They gave a full account of the phenomenon – his gaming philosophy, his particular fondness for the hazard-table, his attachment to Risk, his confidence of success.

Frank was cheered; but his look was sober and thoughtful, and it was his misgivings that found a voice:

'You warned against *confidence*, Mrs Trotter – and yet here is a gentleman who is bursting with it. You spoke of the dangers of *trust* – but you are ready to trust this man with so much …'

'You're right to be cautious, Mr Popham – and we need to tread carefully. But Samuel Rivers knows Mr LeRoy – Leary! – and has encountered George Sturgis and his circle. Indeed, he has suspicions of them himself. This is something we have to pursue.'

'The game's afoot!' said Tom, half-muttering to himself. It was hardly the traditional rallying-cry – more a recognition that what lay ahead of them was a precarious combination of battle and play.

The three of them did not have long to wait before events moved on. An unnecessarily loud knock on the parlour door revealed the sturdy figure of Jeremy, his eyes bright beneath the thatch of hair. He needed no invitation to speak:

'A letter has come in for you, Mrs Trotter – good paper – and sealed! Your name is written with a flourish.'

She gave him a knowing look:

'Thankyou Jeremy – observant as always! Any reply?'

'None, Mrs Trotter. The boy said it was from the gaming-house! But it's certainly addressed to you …'

'That's quite enough, Jem … if I may be allowed to read it?'

Jeremy handed it over a little sheepishly.

'How goes it in the coffee-room?'

'Quieter, Mrs Trotter. Nothing has been thrown.'

'I should hope not! You must tell me if Jenny needs assistance.'

'Yes, Mrs Trotter.'

He nodded twice and backed slowly out of the room, leaving the three of them to contemplate the letter. The character of the hand was a confident one, which left little doubt as to its sender.

Mrs Trotter broke the seal and ran her eyes over it:

'Excellent! This is indeed from Mr Rivers. He has already been busy on our behalf.'

She read it aloud to them:

Esteemed Mrs Trotter!

I appear to have been fortunate with my first throw. I have a sniff of Mr Robert LeRoy! A discreet inquiry – made in an off-hand way with the assistance of Madam Geneva and her cousin Sir John Barley-corn – has elicited the hint that he has indeed left London secretly and sought the rural shade. There has been a sight of him at Islington – presiding over one of the tables there. A little out of season, but I would suppose usefully quiet for his purposes. For it seems he has fled. I do not know if his financial arrangement with you is connected to this – but an early visit there could be fruitful. A Sunday jaunt beyond the smoke and stir of the city may be a pleasant diversion for you?

I can report that arrangements have been made with our friend Mr Lundy. He is to place himself under my tutelage tomorrow, when I hope to initiate him into the mysteries (more truly the science) of dicing. I anticipate our nocturnal visit to Vandernan's with impatience.

If you are to pay a visit to Islington, may I respectfully suggest you take a male escort. An unaccompanied lady at the tables can convey a particular message you may want to avoid. I heartily wish you well with your enterprise!

You shall have our news from Vandernan's on Monday.

I am your respectful servant
Samuel Rivers

'Well! A resourceful fellow, our Mr Rivers!' said Tom, not a little impressed by the speed of the report and its good sense. Part of him had doubted whether the young man's professions would amount to anything; but this was helpful and practical.

Widow Trotter thought the same. Her determined look told the others a decision had already been made:

'Islington it is, then!' she said, with some eagerness. 'No time is to be lost!'

She turned toward Tom, but no words emerged. The inquiring look was enough, and the Trotter eyebrows were eloquent.

There was a moment's hesitation, but no more.

'I ... cannot let you venture there alone, Mrs T,' came the reply. 'Are you for a hackney?'

'I'm sure we can procure one for tomorrow, perhaps eleven o'clock? I don't see why an investigation should not also be a *Sunday jaunt?*'

Sunday

29 October 1708

Chapter Thirteen

It was an unseasonably warm day for their Islington jaunt – almost late summer rather than full Autumn – and being a Sunday, and such a fine one too, a hackney had been procured with difficulty. The driver played the traditional surly coachman to perfection, almost persuading Tom and Mrs Trotter that they were spoiling his holiday and he would rather be smoking his pipe at the rank in Long Acre than drag himself off to that ungodly resort. The two of them were trying to cultivate a cheerful humour and not brood on their difficult mission, but the man brushed away their pleasantries and seized his whip with a shrug of the shoulders. As they climbed aboard, they noticed the outline of a coat of arms on the door, its paint now faded and scratched. Evidently this coach had seen better days – and perhaps the coachman had too?

Once aboard the low-slung vehicle, however, they raised the tin sashes and determined to enjoy the air. Creaking in protest, the coach soon found a swaying rhythm as the pair of horses settled into an even trot, so that it was almost comfortable.

But their anxieties couldn't be suppressed for long.

'Are we on a wild goose chase, Tom?'

She was gazing out at Lincoln's Inn Fields which were moving at a stately pace outside their window.

'It has to be tried, Mrs T. We must confront the man. From what Samuel says, our Mr Leary is installed at one of the tables – doubtless as *Monsieur LeRoy*. Yours is the last face he will expect to see.'

'Yes – or *want* to see …'

The coach made a sudden turn. The sun caught her auburn hair, and a flicker of wicked anticipation showed itself.

'… It would be good to make the experience as uncomfortable as possible.'

'Are you hoping for contrition, Mrs T?'

'No, not from him – I don't look for that. I would expect to see some *shuffling*. The man is a master of it after all – as I know to my cost.'

Tom smiled at the neatness of the idea:

'Yes, a *deal* of shuffling. A nice thought!'

They had somehow found their way back to good humour.

'I suspect he will be effusive, Tom – apologetic to a degree – full of innocent surprise … and if that is so, then I intend to be ruthless …'

She swung round.

'…I shall not spare him, Tom!'

The gentle northward climb out of the metropolis finally brought them to Islington spa and the New River Head with its two large ponds stretching out to their left – reservoirs that helped supply London with fresh water. Children enjoying their holiday liberation were chasing over the grass, and other figures strolled at leisure or turned to take in the view. Behind them, the distant dome of St Paul's commanded the southerly prospect, encircled by a scatter of miniature spires which showed above the rooftops and marked the various City parishes. In front of a windmill by the outer pond, patient anglers with rod and line gazed at the water.

The coach rounded a lofty brick wall and came to a halt some distance from a narrow gate around which an assortment of traders had stationed themselves – pedlars, hawkers and flower sellers. Bare-footed boys were playing tag and screeching loudly while a pair of discharged soldiers looked on, propped on their crutches, caps in hand, easing their backs against the wall.

The coachman received his shilling and sixpence with no false show of gratitude. It was clear the place gave him no pleasure.

'The usual rabble!' he muttered with a contemptuous swing of the head. 'And 'tis little better inside, I assure you!'

There was a melancholy in the man's voice that told them he had known its better days.

'The place has sunk, then?' asked Widow Trotter. 'It's some years now since I came here.'

'Oh, you'll find it changed! Twenty years back – in Mr Langley's time – the place had some style. The season should have ended by rights, but 'tis a Sunday resort now. I don't bring the coach too near ...'

He nodded almost respectfully toward his vehicle.

'... This was Lord Bethel's coach. He used to set the tone of the place. "New Tunbridge Wells" it was indeed! Such parties of pleasure they had ... Not that the waters did him much good, poor gentleman.'

Widow Trotter and Tom looked at each other – they had not expected this garrulity – or these sentiments.

'And what of the gaming tables?' asked Tom hesitantly.

'Aye, the tables are busy enough – you can be sure of that. But 'tis only hardened gamesters now – a few card parties, but mainly dice – the Children of Fortune! Rooks and tricksters, all of 'em!'

A couple of threepences and a sprinkling of charitable halfpennies saw them through the gate into a topiary crescent which acted as a kind of entrance-hall to the gardens. On either side a pair of plaster busts offered welcome, looking disconsolately out from their niches of yew. Shakespeare's brow was furrowed, while the blind Milton gazed ahead in visionary rapture – unaware of the human faces that were peering at him through a grate in the wall, like prisoners behind their bars.

So far, the holiday spirit was proving elusive; but a fiddler was scraping out a jaunty tune somewhere in the distance, and after a few steps they turned a corner into the gardens. Ahead of them stretched a lime-tree alley, and they began walking along it in a more buoyant mood, a crisp carpet of fallen leaves under their feet and a continuous arch of pale gold hanging in swags above their heads. It was a glorious setting and in truth deserved a matching foreground of elegant couples in promenade. The reality fell short, but it was a lively scene nonetheless. They passed the fiddler who was sawing merrily with his bow while a boy and girl danced a jig, kicking up leaves with their feet. A dog was chasing a ball to shouts of encouragement from a pair of young apprentices in their Sunday clothes. Family groups ambled along, and City tradesmen released from their weekday labours strolled arm in arm with their wives. Young girls huddled together, all bonnets, ribbons and parasols.

The finery on display was bright rather than elegant. They passed some good muslins with edgings of lace, and a scattering of fringed petticoats – even a few muffs and ebony canes – but the walk was busy and there was too much running and chattering for any form to be observed. This was not a place for high heels and lofty peruques – and silks were the preserve of the *bona robas*. These expensively dressed ladies moved along the avenue like stately galleons, satin sleeves billowing, top-knots borne aloft, perfumed feathers swaying. Their sidelong glances disturbed the air around them: matrons as they passed stiffened and scowled, daughters blushed and looked away, husbands stole a glance. Piratical gallants in tightening breeches held them in conversation, while more business-like men drew briskly alongside and led them off to the shrubbery alcoves on either side of the walk.

'The œconomy of life, Tom!' said a thoughtful Mrs Trotter. 'I'm glad I left my feathers and silks at home!'

'And happily my Popham suit is still in its drawer!'

As he spoke, a figure in a heavily-powdered wig brushed past them, his dangling sword catching Tom's knee. The man spun round, and with a cry of 'A *thousand* pardons!' he met Tom's startled gaze, doffing his hat with a flick of the wrist. The face was a mask of white lead, save for a nicely-placed patch above the chin, a pair of rubious lips pouting like strawberries, and eyes that leapt from their sockets.

'What a throng, my dears!' he declared. 'The *canaille* so loves its Sundays – one might be at Hockley-Hole!'

A reply stuck in Tom's throat, and he could only smile awkwardly.

'You must enjoy the show, Sir!' said Widow Trotter. 'It is life's pageant – and you yourself are a part of it!'

The man gave a bell-like laugh:

'Ah, yes indeed Ma'am! One must play one's part! One must indeed …'

He gave a little bow and turned, scanning the walk ahead, and in a moment his strutting steps had taken him off.

Tom and Mrs Trotter continued to enjoy the passing show. There was something to catch the eye at every turn, and Tom decided he liked it better than the fashionable parading in St James's Park. Admittedly the elegance of the Mall was unmatched, and the intrigue and gossip there could be entertaining – especially when cousin Lavinia was of the party. But that was a pompous exhibition, whereas this was improvised theatre. In the further reaches of the gardens romantic scenes were being enacted, some of which were progressing beyond the rehearsal stage. The two of them had left the main walk and were following a gravel path that wound its way past a succession of secret arbours woven out of sycamore and hazel – rather less secret now: in the October sunlight these rustic bowers were rapidly shedding their summer clothing – much like the actors.

With averted eyes and quickened pace the pair pressed on. The same thought had struck them both, but it was Widow Trotter who spoke:

'This won't do, Tom. I think a dish of coffee is called for! I can't think myself into a holiday mood – not until our little matter is concluded. We need to steel ourselves for the gaming-room.'

'Yes, there's a job to be done, and 'twere well it were done quickly … Lead on, Mrs T!'

In this determined frame of mind they soon reached the hub of the gardens. The main building was a two-storied brick structure with a brewhouse alongside it, and several outbuildings, one of which housed a public latrine. Next to this, in uneasy proximity, was the spa itself. It was a modest affair – little more than a tap which dribbled into a broad marble bowl. Tom and Mrs Trotter looked inside, caught a whiff of sulphur, and turned away for more gratifying refreshment. What they sought was coffee, and this was being dispensed from an unpromising shed nearby. Inside, the place was all smoke, backgammon, and nodding heads. Outside a few benches and trestle tables offered a more congenial setting, and they were able to find a perch there. The hostess of the Bay-Tree gave a sniff, and Tom was amused to detect a flash of distaste:

'We are a long way from Red Lion Court, Mrs T!'

'I don't have hopes for their coffee, Tom – but as fuel, it will do the job. I think two dishes are going to be needed.'

Indeed, the infusion, when it came, was grainy and bitter; but the first mouthful promised to do its zestful business, and they began to feel restored.

In front of the main building the concourse was crowded with all sorts of people – some were awaiting the lottery or taking a break from gaming; others were browsing at the stalls which had been set up along the wall selling toys and knick-knacks of all kinds.

Tom was casting his eye along them when he saw a figure heading purposefully for the entrance. He had just enough time to nudge Widow Trotter:

'Look! See who it is!'

Her face lit up:

'We have him, Tom!'

It was Robert LeRoy. He was dressed in his basset-table uniform and looking every inch the tallière of the Bay-Tree from his powdered bob-wig down to the silk stockings and buckled shoes. But here among the holiday crowd the man was incongruous – more like a liveried footman hurrying on an errand.

'So far, so good,' said Tom. 'He's surely bound for the gaming-room.'

'And there we shall follow him – but not until I've taken a second dish of this deplorable concoction ...'

Tom's face registered surprise.

'... There is a certain satisfaction in sampling the bad – it sharpens one's appreciation of the good.'

This casuistical argument was clearly an excuse for delay – and he caught a look in her eyes that seemed to admit as much.

'Mrs T ... We must seize our opportunity. We have to face him before he's drawn into the game. It will not be easy – but of the two torments, the spa coffee is surely the worse?'

With that thought they pushed the two dishes aside, the dregs still lurking, and rose to their feet. The challenge ahead seemed suddenly easier.

There were two gaming-rooms on the first floor of the building, and as they reached the top of the stairs they met a contrast of scenes. In the room to the left card-games were in progress, with the tables occupied by the fair sex – though here the term was approximate. Wives had escaped their husbands, and the tense silence that brooded over the place spoke of serious whist.

Over on the other side, a sudden raucous outburst told a different story, as did the scent of beer and tobacco that wafted out when the door opened. This was the hazard-room. Play here was equally serious, but there was no requirement for a clear head. Instead, intermittent cries of anguish and triumph signalled that the fickle gods were playing their own game too.

Tom and Widow Trotter hesitated, conscious of their breathing. They knew where he would be! In apprehensive silence they approached the hazard-room. Suddenly the door swung open again, and a familiar face was in front of their eyes:

'Lord! – if it isn't my young friend! Come to take your chance? …'

A hand was on Tom's arm and the white mask bent close to his ear.

'… Fly this place, Sir! – it is the haunt of rogues and vagabonds! You will get no joy from these dice, I warrant you … Come and commiserate with me over a brandy … I swear it will cost you less! I have taken a severe beating …'

Tom flinched slightly, and the man lifted his head, only to notice Widow Trotter who was hanging back slightly. He looked at her, then back at Tom.

'… Ah! *Je compris*, my friend! …'

He gave an outrageous wink.

'… I wish you both joy!'

With a wave of his handkerchief he made a polite farewell and began to negotiate the stairs.

Widow Trotter remained stock-still:

'Well!'

The word hung in the air. Never had Tom seen her so out of countenance. But on this occasion he could only laugh:

'Fuel to the flames, Mrs T! Mr LeRoy will reap the whirlwind?'

'The wrong metaphors, Tom … I intend to *drown* him!'

And with that, in sudden determination, Widow Trotter stepped past him and thrust open the door, ready to encounter the foe. Now it was Tom who hung back.

Her entrance was so bold that heads turned. The room at that moment was silent and tense, and the interruption was resented. One of the gamesters hung over the table, the dice-box tight in his fist. He paused, arm in the air, and glared. Unabashed, Mrs Trotter scanned the room from left to right – and then from right to left. All sorts and conditions of men met her gaze – but there was no sign of Robert LeRoy.

She closed the door discreetly and they stepped back to the stair-head.

'Do you think … ?' she said.

Tom nodded:

'It must be … Whist!'

Mentally on tip-toe they moved over to the card-room, where the decorum of whist was being observed. No sound came from within, except for a little suppressed cough which only emphasised the quietness. Widow Trotter pushed at the half-open door, and instantly saw Mr LeRoy – or at least his back. He was at the far side of the room in whispered conference with another gentleman who was shaking his head disconsolately. The room was substantial, consisting of four tables with a line of chairs set against the left-hand wall where a couple were already waiting. Mrs Trotter beckoned to Tom, and they seated themselves on the two nearest the door.

There were more seconds of silence before a creak of chairs and ripple of conversation signalled that one of the tables had finished a rubber. Mr LeRoy turned to give the players his attention, and his eyes caught Mrs Trotter's. His gaze froze. His body froze also. What transfixed him was the look on Widow Trotter's face as she got to her feet. It wasn't murderous anger – she was no Medusa – but it was a look of sorrowful accusation, edged with contempt – like an arrow trained on his forehead.

He stood as a statue just a little too long, causing some of the whist-players to look round to see what had caught Monsieur LeRoy's attention and brought a pallor to his cheek. He recalled himself and leant over the table, and with unnecessary fussiness began performing some routine ceremony with the cards and tokens, aware that the hostess of the Bay-Tree was slowly approaching. His hands were shaking a little. The seconds ticked by, and he was relieved to draw himself up to his full height and step away to let the next rubber begin.

Now he felt Mrs Trotter's silence. This disturbed him even more. He looked at Tom, who was also on his feet:

'You must give me a moment …' he said. 'We must talk outside.'

'Perhaps we should talk *here* – Mr *LeRoy!*'

Widow Trotter spoke firmly and delivered the name with full French intonation, to satiric effect.

'No! … A moment – I insist! …'

He quickly stepped over to the first gentleman, and the two of them conferred briefly. By now, all four tables had paused from their play.

'… I shall leave you with Mr McKay, ladies …' he announced, trying to sound calm.

At that, he moved to escort his visitors from the room. But Widow Trotter stood her ground. Her voice remained loud.

'Mr *LeRoy* has some important business to transact – *have you not? ...*'

The company were all watching, curious to see how this hand would play out.

'... May I have your assurance the matter will be settled?'

Mr LeRoy's pallor had now turned to a deep blush:

'Yes indeed – of course! Let us confer outside ... I'm sure we can conclude things amicably ...'

He forced a smile and attempted a polite gesture with his arm – but it looked awkward, hinting at desperation.

'... Mrs Trotter – please!'

In the pressure of the moment the French accent had disappeared.

The hostess of the Bay-Tree relented, and with calm dignity she led the way out of the room. Nineteen pairs of eyes followed them to the door, and as it closed a burst of discussion began.

The lady had undoubtedly won the hand, they concluded.

Chapter Fourteen

*'I*KNOW WHY you have come.'
'Yes, and there is a great deal to be said – but not in this place! A staircase is for apologies and excuses – and I want neither. We have much to talk about, have we not … *Bob Leary?*'

Widow Trotter pronounced the fatal name with emphasis, and the effect was dramatic. He flinched and his eyes looked away:

'How did you discover … ?'

Somehow he couldn't complete the sentence – so she helped him:

'… your *deceit*, Mr Leary of Dublin? … Well, like most pretence, it can't outrun the truth for ever. The reckoning comes when the game is over. In your case, Mr Leary, there has been a great deal of sport. You have sported with people's lives, have you not?'

'But … I don't …'

Again he was lost for words.

'You will remember my friend Mr Bristowe …'

There was a wary exchange of nods between the two men.

'… We both wish to have a talk with you. There are things that have been hid for too long – and there are more than just money matters to settle. You need to understand that Mr

Bristowe and I know something of what has prompted your flight ... Indeed, we believe we may be able to help you ...'

Tom saw the implications but resolved not to show it. This was Mrs Trotter taking charge. There was a confident look as she began leading them down the stairs. At the same time a couple of young gamesters were leaping up two at a time, eager for the hazard-room. They squeezed by noisily.

'... Let us get out of this place, Mr Leary. We need to be where the air is clearer. It will encourage you to be open with us – and for us to set out our thoughts to you.'

The man found a voice at last – though a hesitant one:

'Then ... can I suggest a stroll by the river?'

'Capital! Shall we walk past the Wells?'

This was agreed, and a few minutes later the three of them had left behind the walled gardens of the spa and to all appearances were a group of Sunday strollers enjoying the pastoral scene. It was windless, and to their left the tranquil New River (really a narrow canal) flowed through a grassy meadow, setting a meditative mood. But there was no calm of mind in this little party, which remained tense and apprehensive. On both sides there were things waiting to be explained and discovered.

Tom knew he ought to speak, but he was unwilling to divert the conversation when Widow Trotter was steering it so expertly. He thought he could discern her strategy: – assume anxiety in your opponent and encourage it; speak with confidence; don't ask questions too early; pretend to know more than you do; offer to help him out of a difficulty; and keep the big threat in reserve. Tom couldn't help thinking the hostess of the Bay-Tree would make a fine gamester herself ...

The silence was becoming awkward. Bob Leary was walking between the two of them and felt at a disadvantage. He also was hesitating to speak, but knew he must say something about the bank notes and his sudden flight. He had expected Widow

Trotter to confront him, but it was clear she was biding her time and awaiting an explanation.

He finally spoke:

'You say you want no apology, Mrs Trotter ... but you are owed at least an explanation. Not an excuse, but an account of how all this happened ... I do you the credit of believing you understand how affairs have gone on.'

It was a tentative remark, but there was nothing tentative about her reply:

'You are right, Mr Leary. This is not just a debt to be settled between you and me. We both know that larger forces are at work. Mr Sturgis's death has been a shock to us all, and the prospect is a dark one. We must piece the story together and find the larger picture. Mr Bristowe and I need to hear more about the system of which you are a part. We know you have not acted entirely for yourself but are entangled in something beyond your control.'

This was a bold move – a suspicion delivered as knowledge. Bob Leary looked startled. Tom was also surprised but tried not to show it. He gave a supportive nod:

'You are not here in Islington for a change of air, Mr Leary, are you?'

His question was more than rhetorical, but there was no response.

Widow Trotter pressed on. The man had to know that she wasn't the only concerned party – that Tom would have his own questions to ask:

'You know that Mr Bristowe's uncle is Lord Melksham, Her Majesty's Deputy Treasurer, and that as Frank Popham's cousin he has an interest in this affair. Both he and I are curious about the late Mr George Sturgis and his activities – in which you have been involved. I'm sure you know that he bought up a huge debt of Mr Popham's ...'

She paused, but again there was no response.

'... And of course you know what a ruinous debt – a *shared* debt – our basset table incurred thanks to the unlimited stake ... In respect of that sum, Mr Bristowe and I have sought legal advice and the matter is going forward. I'll be open with you, Mr Leary: you will be required to settle the three hundred pounds in legal tender – not stolen paper. As for the larger business ... the stakes are high. Matters of State are involved. The whole affair cannot be more serious ... but from the look on your face I see you understand this all too well.'

It was as if the sky above them had darkened, and Bob Leary's look reflected it. Her own expression was uncharacteristically grim. Now Tom was prepared for anything – Did Mrs Trotter somehow know more than he had thought? Or was this last *ultimatum*, as he suspected, a daring cavalry charge to panic the enemy? She was taking a great risk – all guns firing! Tom looked over at Leary, who continued to maintain a slow, deliberate tread along the path. He couldn't be sure what the man's response would be.

'You don't ask much, Mrs Trotter ...'

It was spoken with undisguised irony. There was a pained hesitation before he continued:

'... Yes, I do know something of what you hint at ...'

But before he could say more, a sudden cry rang out, and an inflated pig's bladder bounced along the grass beside them, followed by two chasing boys. They ran past, kicking the ball while half-wrestling with each other. It was a disconcerting interruption. Any lingering pastoral decorum was gone, and a sudden urgency took its place. Mr Leary, as if shaken out of thought, was now resolved. His tone hardened:

'... As for the three hundred pounds – I cannot pay it, Mrs Trotter ... Not *will* not -- *cannot*. You must understand that.'

She was touched to the quick. Her response was immediate:

'Well then! The law must take its course – there's no more to be said!'

Tom looked anxiously at her. But Leary wasn't finished:

'No! There is a *great deal* to be said, Mrs Trotter! A story to be told – if you will consent to hear it. If all you require is your three hundred pounds, then this interview is at an end … but from what you have said, there is something else that alarms you?'

Tom felt he had to break in:

'Yes, Mr Leary, we have things to fear – and you are not without fear yourself, are you? If you truly have a story to tell – *your* story – then we are eager to hear it …'

Now it was Tom's turn to take a chance:

'… I would like to think that we are not opponents here – but caught up together in something dangerous. Am I right?'

Bob Leary looked across at the river, which continued to move placidly at its own determined pace:

'Let us find a place to sit.'

A little further on was an ironwork seat half-set into a tall hornbeam hedge. Here they settled themselves, with Mr Leary again feeling a little like a prisoner between his guards. He looked at them in turn, and in his mind's eye saw a pair of innocents who were pretending to more power and knowledge than they had – two good people being drawn into a world they had yet to understand. But it would be easy to underestimate their boldness and resolve. After all – somehow – they had discovered his secret …

He spoke softly:

'Yes, Mrs Trotter, I'm Bob Leary of Dublin – "Irish Bob!" – I confess it …'

A long-hidden Irish burr emerged as he spoke.

'… I have a history – and one that still pursues me, however hard I try to throw it off … But now I must leave all behind and win my fortune elsewhere! I lodge with my aunt not far from here – but by the week's end I shall be gone.'

Tom was surprised:

'It isn't we who have prompted this?'

'No, Mr Bristowe, I had chosen this course – I leave from Harwich on the Friday packet.'

'Holland? But this is desperate, Mr Leary!' said Widow Trotter, who saw her three hundred pounds scattered on the waves. 'Is it the Law you flee? Because if so, I swear …'

'No, no – I run from something more pressing, believe me! … But you must allow me to tell my tale from the beginning. You may think it a serpentine one, but it will bring us to the present moment, and to the difficulties you both face. If I cannot settle my debt in money, Mrs Trotter, I can perhaps give you something to help you through this and bring you restitution … You must trust me so far. Before you act any further, you need to know what it is you are engaging with. I know only a part – but that is enough!'

He settled himself on the seat, clasped one hand in the other, and with a solemn air began to give them his story.

Chapter Fifteen

'M Y TROUBLES BEGAN when I was apprenticed to a Dublin watchmaker. He was a violent man and gave me enough beatings to turn my arse to shoe-leather. He called me indolent and over-delicate – but the truth was, I could put my fingers to the finest work. He took no pride in me – rather, it vexed him to see a slip of a boy more dextrous than himself.

'Before my term was out, I could take no more – I fled him and his shop! You may imagine how he pursued me – with a vindictive determination. And he had the law on his side. He accused me of carrying away two gold watches, and I was hunted like a felon. Had they caught me it would have meant hanging … But I eluded my pursuers and by some miracle I found a saviour – a soft-hearted captain who let me board his vessel for Bristol.

'To shorten the tale – in Bristol I pursued my skill with playing-cards. I had always found they sat with my hands like silken gloves. I could work them deftly and knew I could make them do my bidding. In the taverns of the city I used my skill to amuse and entertain – yes, and to fleece too … But it was the fair I enjoyed the most. I began to have ambitions in that line and decided to try my luck in London – at Bartholomew Fair, no less! … And it was there I found a *patron* …'

He spoke the word with caution.

'… The Fair is a dangerous place for a youth, and I was glad to gain a friend. But I soon discovered I was expected to be in service again – that I was part of a gang and all I earned was for the common pool. In truth it was for our patron's coffers! All too soon I was made to set the cards aside and put my fingers to more profitable use.'

'You were picking pockets?'

It was a naïve question.

'Yes, Mr Bristowe. In the gang I became "Light-finger'd Bob" …'

He gave a rueful smile and unlocked his hands.

'… "He who fears the gallows shall ne'er be a good thief" – That's the saying! Well, I was in terror of hanging, and the scaffold was but a single mis-step away … I knew I had to leave.

'During this second "apprenticeship" I had put by a little money of my own, and so, before the law could take me, I took passage for France. I was determined to use my talents in a country that values *finesse* and *savoir faire!* I knew I was master of my profession, and to be handling cards again was a joy. After Smithfield – believe me! – Paris was a place of enchantment, and before long I had moved from the tavern to the *salon.*'

Widow Trotter was following all this with fascination:

'You have seen something of the world, Mr Leary …'

'*LeRoy*, Mrs Trotter! I was now a figure of enchantment myself. For three years I was in my glory – welcomed in the highest circles, dining at the finest tables. I had an apartment in the Marais – and kept a coach!

'When King Louis introduced a new game – Faro – I at once became its master. It is like basset, Mrs Trotter, but rewards *expertise* – and I had huge success at the Faro table, especially as the bank … Let me say, I could *feel* the cards …'

Widow Trotter and Tom exchanged glances.

'Cards of a particular manufacture, were they?' she asked.

'Let us say, they responded to the most sensitive fingers.'

Tom's question was brusquer:

'Then where did it all go wrong?'

There was a hint of satisfaction in Tom's tone, but Mr Leary met it with a half-smile:

'I was unfortunate in two things, Mr Bristowe ... I allowed a *Marquis* to become over-indebted to me, a man who had the ear of the greatest in the land – and I do mean the greatest ... The gentleman could not pay me and faced ruin ... And so I found myself threatened with a new lodging – in the Bastille.'

Widow Trotter couldn't suppress a gasp.

'And what was the second thing?' asked Tom.

'Oh, just a little matter of the *war*. It was the damn'dest coincidence, and out of my hands! Marlborough's rise was my fall. I had no choice but to flee the country and leave all behind.'

'And so, you returned to England?'

'Yes, Mrs Trotter. I was back in London – but I returned only half a Briton. My French ways did not count in my favour. Only among gamesters did I feel at home. I assure you Mr *LeRoy* was no disguise – it was the person I had become.

'For a while I led a roaming life, but I was always drawn back to the metropolis. And this was where I was to fall in with another gang – a very different set of men, and yet a gang it was.'

He paused and took a breath.

'Vandernan's?' asked Widow Trotter, eager to hear the continuation.

'Yes – I said my story would find its way home, and indeed the place did seem a home to me. I would eventually be back in the station where I was happiest – the bank. Only this was *basset*. In France the game has lost its passion and become a penny sport. But here in England it is still an *adventure!*'

He looked at Widow Trotter and hesitated, knowing he had stepped a word too far. Her gaming-room expression returned:

'Tell us about this gang, Mr Leary.'

'At first the cards were just an evening indulgence. By day I now had an honest trade at a Barber's shop in 'Change Alley. (Believe me, I'm as nimble with a razor as a deck!) My gentlemen were remarkably free, and in that nest of traders and stock-jobbers with every shave I picked up a daily bulletin of news – and helped circulate it too. I had as well been at Garraway's! Many things I heard and overheard – of bulls and bears – of trades and puts, with advice and opinion of all colours – and wagers galore! I soon saw that card-sharpers and stock-jobbers are close akin. Both are ruled by greed and fear – a greed for gain, and a fear not of loss but of missing a chance for gain … That paradox is the key to our hearts! …'

Bob Leary's tone had grown enthusiastic at the thought.

'…But I had a story too, and I shared it with those who would listen. Not the earliest scenes of course – that was a page not to be turned! But my Parisian adventures gave a burnish to my character, and tales of my success at the tables were well received. My gentlemen saw me as a kindred spirit. I told them of my tricks, and they told me theirs … This was how I formed a connection with a certain peer …'

'Ah!' said Widow Trotter, at last getting a scent of the prey.

'I thought I had found a true patron. He was generous to a fault, and his *gratuities* were more than monetary. I had encountered him at Vandernan's where I had begun to venture, and he showed an interest in me. I gave him a sample of my skills. We became close … and – fool that I was! – I entrusted my secret to him.'

'Your Dublin secret?'

'Yes. He swore to silence – it was a bond between us …'

Widow Trotter sighed.

'… The upshot was, I found myself in demand. My lord was influential in the place and installed me as the chief tallière at the basset table. This was coming home indeed! I slipped back easily into the role and wished for nothing finer …'

He broke off. The thought of what he had left behind gave him pause – as did a young couple ahead of them who were sauntering across the grass with arms interlocked, each lingering step in tune with their thoughts.

Widow Trotter glanced across at Tom. She was in two minds about Mr Leary. The villain had tricked her and brought her to the brink of ruin – and yet the man seemed to think there might be a way through and he could guide them to it. She was astute enough to see that she couldn't trust the Law to save her. Perhaps Robert LeRoy might indeed be of help to them?

The two lovers progressed out of earshot, allowing Bob Leary to continue. His voice was less soft now as he moved from memory towards the uncomfortable present.

'I should have understood that my role as a Vandernan's banker would not be an entirely innocent one. I was not looking to be a virgin in a nunnery! – after all, I knew the dealer's tricks and had exploited them myself. I could draw a lamb to me so it would lick my hand whilst I gathered its fleece … I was ready on occasion to assist or hamper a punter's chances – to nudge Dame Fortune's elbow. Such things are part of the game – an exhilarating part, I will admit!

'But then the interventions became … *systematique*, as they say in France – planned and methodical. I had no say in the matter. A word would be given, and I would be expected to align the fates accordingly …

'To be brief, I became aware that there were certain favoured people for whom the bank was a generous benefactor. This itself was curious; but stranger still was the reverse – occasions when large sums were in play, and the punter paid dearly.'

'But isn't that the old story – the bank cheating the players?'

'Yes, but such *organised* losses of hundreds were accepted with resignation – as if a transaction had taken place. On those occasions I was especially vigilant. I sniffed a settlement. At moments like these I suspected I was acting the bank in every sense – funds disbursed, and funds received.'

'That's very strange,' said Tom. 'You were given instructions?'

Mr Leary gave a silent nod.

'Is there a like arrangement for the hazard-table?' said Widow Trotter, her thoughts turning to Will's coming mission to Vandernan's.

'Yes, perhaps more so. In the general run of play all is as it should be, but on occasion the game takes a different turn. It is entirely surreptitious, but the box-keepers know what's what. They have a whispered watchword between them …'

He hesitated.

'And what is that?' said Widow Trotter, sensing discretion in the air and determined to dispel it.

Robert LeRoy paused only for a moment:

'It is Captain Hazard … They speak of "A subscription to Captain Hazard" or "a bequest from Captain Hazard" … it is said with a knowing smile. Contributions and gifts! – it's the language of the tables. But for them it has a particular meaning … I found myself using the term after a notable transaction had been concluded.'

It was directly the language of finance. By now, both Tom and Widow Trotter had turned their thoughts to Frank's experience at Vandernan's hazard-table. The question needed to be put, and it was Tom who did so:

'I am thinking, Mr Leary, of my Cousin's great loss – his two thousand … What do you know of that?'

They had reached a critical juncture. Bob Leary chose his words with care:

'It seems that on that occasion Mr Popham may have been playing Captain Hazard's game – unbeknown to himself of course. It is what George Sturgis suspected. The mechanism was there – and it is likely that the *word* had been given. George certainly thought so – and he was observing the play closely.'

Mrs Trotter's mind was busy:

'Ah yes! ... Mr Sturgis. We have come back to him. I am wondering how you regarded him? Mr Popham thought him an ally. He accepted the debt onto his own account so that Frank might have a period of grace ...'

'I have been pondering this, Mrs Trotter. George was a difficult character. He could be whimsical and act on impulse – often generously. A warm friend – but in liquor he was dangerously unpredictable ...'

He looked into Widow Trotter's eyes.

'... I fear you had experience of that on Thursday evening – poor George's last evening on earth ...'

Aware that their talk had brought them back to the Bay-Tree, he hesitated. Widow Trotter did not. Her tone hardened:

'That evening at the basset table, Mr Leary, the two of you appeared to be firm friends. And I believe that during the interval you decided between you that it would be amusing to play Captain Hazard's game?'

Shamefaced, he turned away. The accusing finger was pointing at him, and he couldn't evade it.

'Yes, I'm ashamed to say we did ... but I tried to discourage him. Those two Queens were a masterstroke I thought ...'

'But Sturgis persisted, did he not?'

'Yes, George was very bold, and determined to press on – so I gave him a run.'

Tom could take no more of this:

'A *run?* ... You are a cheat and a scoundrel, Leary! – and a flippant one too. How dare you sport with Mrs Trotter like that!

You have thrown her very livelihood into danger. Not only did you play your silly game, but you paid her back with worthless paper. You are a man without honour. You disgust me! …'

'Tom!'

Widow Trotter was alarmed – their careful drawing out of the man's story was at risk … But Tom was not to be diverted:

'If you have any decency in you, Mr Leary – and in God's name, I really believe you do … then you will make her reparation. You must live up to your professions! Before you flee the country, you have to give us something …'

Tom was poised on the brink, ready to threaten the man directly – with the Law and with his fists – but he saw anxiety in Mrs Trotter's face and drew back.

'… You promised us help. What can you give us?'

Robert LeRoy thought for a moment:

'I can encourage you to stay resolute and continue digging. There is something to be found. George Sturgis is the key to your predicament – for both of you – and if you wish to discover who killed him, then the answer is in Vandernan's. I was never one of the *cabal* – I simply observed and overheard – but I know certain things are being hatched by the great people there. The place is more than a gaming-house – not your customary den of thieves but the centre of some illicit business – a highly secretive one! Something is always going forward … Those stolen bank notes could be the clue. That paper I gave you was Vandernan's money! Notes and bills of all kinds circulate through there, and little care is taken about the soundness of them. The place is an exchange – and I suspect it reaches out east to the Royal Exchange itself and its dubious suburb, 'Change Alley …'

There was another cautious hesitation.

'… I have a friend over there – a trader – who can perhaps give you practical help. I know that he also has become caught in Vandernan's net. There is a chance you may be able to help each other. He is a factor in Birchin Lane – a good man who is close to breaking …'

Widow Trotter's nose tingled slightly.

'… His name is Michael Henriques …'

She said nothing, but saw again the dark-eyed young man in Exchange Alley. She still had the card that he'd pressed into her hand:

'I'm acquainted with Birchin Lane, Mr Leary, and will be sure to seek him out.'

At this moment Tom's thoughts were still on Cousin Frank and George Sturgis:

'Are you telling us Mr Sturgis acted in my cousin's interest? Can you be sure it was not to bring Frank into his power? The word is that Sturgis had some high connections. Could he not have been one of that *cabal* you speak of?'

'Your question is a reasonable one, Mr Bristowe. But that evening, when we left the Bay-Tree, I could see that George was in some kind of trouble. He was deep in his cups and determined on a whirl in his chariot. He wouldn't tell me of it, but I knew something was gnawing at him. When Mr Popham refused to join us and walked away, I heard him mutter "Poor Mr Popham! I have done my best for him!" I made little of it – he was speaking by fits and starts. All he could say was "I am marked out!" and "I know too much!" and "I have been very foolish!" It sounded like boasting, and I took it all lightly – as merely a drinker's dumps. When I left him, the last words I heard were "I have given displeasure, Robert, and must repair my fortunes!"'

Widow Trotter heard all this with concern:

'His *fortunes*? Do you think it possible he returned to Vandernan's that night?'

'The thought had occurred to me – but it is mere supposition. I understand his body was found in that vicinity?'

'*Displeasure* … Was there someone he had displeased? It is an odd word … you *displease* a patron for example.'

Mr Leary's eyes shifted slightly, but he gave no immediate response. Tom jumped in:

'You have said little about your own aristocratic patron there, Mr Leary. Might they have been one and the same person?'

Up to this point Bob Leary had appeared willing to talk. But these questions unsettled him. He was suddenly ill at ease, and their curiosity could no longer be contained.

Widow Trotter asked:

'Who was the generous patron you *thought* you had found – the man who was lavish with his *gratuities*? –You imply that he is your patron no longer.'

'Does His Lordship perhaps lead the cabal?' asked Tom.

'Why this sudden flight, Mr Leary? What threat has been made to you? Have you also displeased this man?'

The bombardment on both flanks was unrelenting, and the questions flew like cannonballs. As he sat between the pair of them, Mr Leary felt not unlike the city of Lille. The garden seat was beginning to take more of his weight. It gave a creak as he rearranged himself.

Tom's eyes narrowed:

'You are not … fleeing Justice, are you, Mr Leary?'

Now he knew he must speak, or sink entirely:

'Please – I surrender! … There is only so much I can tell you. You are right to ask these questions. I have been asking many of them myself! But there is one question I can answer without hesitation … No, Mr Bristowe, I did not kill George Sturgis – I am not *fleeing justice*, as you phrase it! If anything, I am fleeing *in*justice …'

They were silent now, and expectant.

'… As for George, all I can give you are my suspicions … He was well connected – as the brother of a Baron he moved in a circle far above mine. I only had glimpses. But I know he was taken up with important affairs, and important people. There were hints of high politics – matters of State. You are right about that, Mrs Trotter! But I cannot say more. I think George had made an enemy, or had angered some important people … I could not swear to it, but I have been asking myself if his friendship with Frank Popham might bear on this? I overheard someone make an angry remark against his father, Lord Melksham.'

The seat shuddered again.

'Can you say more?' asked Mrs Trotter.

'It was "A curse on him!" That was all I heard. It was a passing remark, but spoken in real anger. I thought it strange … That is all I can tell you.'

'But there is something else you have finally to tell us, Mr Leary … three questions which perhaps amount to a single one … … Who was your aristocratic patron? Why did he withdraw his favour from you? … And why are you fleeing the country?'

She stopped. It was a towering question. Her gimlet eyes bored into him.

'You are right to press me, Mrs Trotter. How can I give you an honest answer? … In recent days I have been troubled about Vandernan's and my role there. So much so, that on two occasions I dared to go against instructions. A huge loss became a great gain – and a great gain became a huge loss! … it was very foolish of me – but I was tiring of Captain Hazard's game. Basset, when played with good sense and good grace, is an exhilarating thing. You are poised between light and dark, between wonder and despair. If you let it take its course, it will excite every emotion … But whenever I played their game it lost its excitement for me. It was mine no longer. There were no delightful turns of Chance. I myself was Fate, and all was decreed in advance.

'Thursday evening at the Bay-Tree was the breaking-point. Before that remarkable salmon I was in Heaven and savouring every minute of the play. Every turn of a card made my fingers thrill with pleasure. But after the salmon – bound by George's instructions – all the magic ceased. I was no longer a part of the game ... And then George's killing was decisive. Believe me, Mrs Trotter, I now fear for my life. When I went against instructions the fury at Vandernan's surpassed anything I had expected – my patron too! My secret was no longer safe – a secret that could hang me! And with George's death I know these people will stop at nothing to protect their interests. I am resolved to have done with it.'

The pause was electric.

'Who was your patron, Mr Leary? Do you think he and his confederates killed George Sturgis – and are now threatening you?'

His voice in reply was quiet – an almost childlike murmur as if he didn't want to hear his own words. The Irish tones were clearer than ever:

'You must do what you can. You perhaps have the means to find the truth! I suspect large forces are involved ... As I said, you should find Mr Henriques ... and, as for Vandernan's, I can name two gentlemen to you. The first is my patron, and the other his *confrère* ... Together they are formidable. I'm sure they are the dark heart of this affair ... The one is Lord Parham ...'

Widow Trotter glanced over at Tom, but he looked blank. The sound of the second name, however, had a very different effect:

'... The other gentleman is Sir Charles Norreys.'

Chapter Sixteen

———∞∞∞———

WIDOW TROTTER TURNED to watch as Bob Leary's legs propelled him at a swift pace along the grassy path back to his duties in the card-room. The man looked almost carefree – but he left consternation behind him.

Tom stood transfixed:

'Sir Charles Norreys! ... I cannot believe it. What does this mean, Mrs T? ...'

His mind raced back to the basset table, thoughts leaping over each other.

'... On Thursday – lady Norreys and Sturgis – there was an intimacy between them that evening, was there not? ... Is it possible that Sir Charles ... do you think ... ?'

Mrs Trotter was also recollecting the scene:

'I see where your thoughts are leading. We need to sit down and talk – but not here. I suggest we look for some refreshment. The taste of that spa coffee still lingers!'

'Perhaps a little entertainment too? This is a Sunday jaunt, remember. There's sure to be something stirring at the music-house.'

'Good – my spirits need a lift. Our Mr Leary had plenty to say for himself. We have a lot to think about.'

They began walking back themselves, pondering. Tom's features were knitted into a frown:

'Everyone is playing a game, Mrs T, and there's nothing light-hearted about it – after all, a game is a serious thing, is it not? You must watch every move, work every advantage, outwit your adversary, steer between the cheats and rogues ... It's no easy pastime.'

'Not the way these people play it. A game is fought by rules – and the winners are those who exploit them best – or twist them most cleverly ...'

'Or defy them most brazenly.'

'Ha! – that is unfortunately true. As you say, it's a serious business ... but that doesn't mean we cannot be at ease while we consider our play.'

Having established the important principle that good humour keeps the mind alert and prompts serious thought, they crossed over the river.

Beyond a set of walled gardens laid out with flowers and shrubs – now well past their best – stood Sadler's music-house, a substantial building with a lofty pitched roof from which, thanks to an open window, the faint tones of an organ beckoned them. The sprightly sound grew louder as they approached, and minutes later they were inside, mounting the stairs to a long upper room where the instrument could be heard to full effect, accompanied by the percussive rattle of crockery and cutlery – entertainment and refreshment in one! This was no elegant tea-room, however, but something closer to a busy tavern with pot-boys scuttling amongst the tables, laden with jugs of beer and flasks of wine. They found a small table by the wall being vacated by a couple of citizens who had evidently consumed enough cakes and ale for a party of six. The place was hardly conducive to quiet deliberation, but the very busyness gave them privacy. Trays flew by their ears, and cries of 'Coming, Sir! Coming!' rang out.

Suddenly a fiddler struck up a tune at the far side of the room, adding to the cacophony. Whether this was accompaniment or competition for the organ was impossible to say.

'The music-room!' declared Widow Trotter with a laugh.

'We can speak freely here!' Tom almost shouted. 'No danger of being overheard!'

A flask of wine and two generous slices of cheesecake promised to do the trick, and Widow Trotter soon gave an impression of good cheer. But the taut lines around her eyes told Tom a different story, and when the inconsequential talk petered out, he broached what had been at the front of both their minds.

'We cannot let Bob Leary slip away scot-free. We must ask Will's advice this evening ...'

'Alas, Tom, I have few hopes there, and my own negligence is to blame. My agreement with Mr Leary was an informal one – there is nothing on paper. It is a matter of honour, not law. The only settlement either of us looked to make was how to divide the *profits*.'

The word died on her lips. The irony was too painful, and Tom felt it:

'To hell with these damned gamesters! ...' The curse shot from him with genuine bitterness. '... All this talk of *honour* is the merest hypocrisy. It's a kind of violence – only the powerful can invoke it, and only with swords can they satisfy it.'

'Yes, but we must be cautious, Tom. There must be no talk of satisfying honour or going to law. If we are to find a way through this, it will be by craft. I suspect they have not just gold coins in their pockets, but people too – men of authority and influence.'

'That's a dismal thought.'

'I cannot forgive Leary for what he's done – but he has told us much that we can use, and I truly believe the matter of my six hundred is tied up with your cousin's debt. Leary said that George Sturgis is the key – and now we know the man had offended his masters. What was the phrase ... ?'

'I have given displeasure.'

'Yes. A chilling phrase. I suspect that both Sturgis and Leary angered the *cabal* – and now Sturgis has been killed, and our Mr Leary is in fear of his life ... These people are dangerous, Tom.'

'And if we can believe what Leary says, my uncle has made enemies. He has stumbled on something incendiary ... All this fits with his suspicion of a plot, does it not? – the Bank of England, Sturgis, Sir Gilbert Heathcote, the Duchess ...'

At that instant the music-room organist ended his piece with a *fortissimo* flourish, and a spattering of applause broke out. It was as if those characters were taking a bow.

He flinched slightly and reached for his wine.

'And this Lord Parham, Tom – you've not encountered him?'

'The name means nothing, but Uncle Jack will surely know the gentleman – the *ermin'd tribe* and all that! He cannot always choose his acquaintances.'

Widow Trotter sensed more than a touch of despondency:

'I suspect this must be difficult for him? Lord Melksham has such zeal in a good cause – not always in his best interest, perhaps.'

'You've come to know him, Mrs T. I'm proud of Uncle Jack and couldn't bear to see him harmed in any way – but he can be so heedless! I only hope we can keep him out of danger. It's an odd thing to say, but he has been something of a second father to me.'

'Not an odd thing at all! I've never met your father, but I suspect Canon Bristowe was the one to keep you in order?'

'He and the Usher at school between them – they were an unholy alliance! In comparison, my time with the Pophams was always a vacation.'

'That certainly gave your uncle the advantage ... and I suspect if he were with us now he would urge you to be cheerful ... To that end, I suggest we do justice to these majestic cheesecakes, and then see what is happening over in the gallery. I recall a series of frescoes of the classical gods doing intemperate things in the brightest of colours. Very innocent Sunday fare!'

Eight o'clock was the time appointed for their evening rendezvous with Will Lundy. He duly arrived at the Bay-Tree after four hours under the tutelage of Sam Rivers, who had pursued his mission with a schoolmaster's rigour. Understanding the niceties of hazard was a challenge even to Will's legal brain, and he was sure the intricacies of chancery law were as nothing to the dicers' jargon which was ringing in his ears as he approached the chocolate house: *If either eight or six be the main, and the caster throws either 4, 5, 7, 9, or 10, this is his chance, which if he throws first he wins, or otherwise he loses; if he throws 12 to 8, or 6 to the same cast with the main he wins* … Numbers hadn't held such sway over him since his mathematical exertions at Oxford. He knocked on the side-door of the chocolate house to their insistent rhythm.

He was welcomed into the back parlour, happy to accept the offer of supper – or 'dinner' as he was now thinking of it. Having breakfasted with Sam Rivers at three in the afternoon Will's day was already becoming that of a dedicated gamester. He eyed the slices of crusty ham pie with anticipation.

Tom and Widow Trotter were eager to tell him about their Islington visit. It may have lacked something as a Sunday jaunt, but the excesses of Sadler's Wells had been some compensation.

Will listened intently, wearing his Westminster Hall face. To him, Bob Leary's story had all the ingredients of a rogue's tale – something that would do well as a sixpenny pamphlet – *The History of the Irish Sharper!* Part of him – the sceptical legal part – was suspicious of the man's story, but his friends had heard it from his own lips and felt its truthfulness.

Their account of the goings-on at Vandernan's was remarkable too. If Leary was right, then the gaming-house was a kind of criminal exchequer – a business that reached beyond the gaming tables to the City world of finance, to stock-jobbery and the criminal economy. He didn't like the smell of it.

'No fire without smoke,' he thought, and reached for a second slice of pie.

During this manoeuvre Tom turned the conversation to the challenge of the night to come, eager to hear what Will had learned about the notorious game of hazard. He longed to make a joke of it, but not on this occasion – his friend would be dicing with the Devil:

'Are you ready for the fray, Will?'

'As near as I'll ever be. Sam is a rigorous instructor, and he drilled me in the discipline of hazard. But he kept reminding me that I have to appear a novice – as if I could be anything else! I assured him the role would come naturally.'

'Perhaps you were becoming too skilful, Mr Lundy?' said Widow Trotter. 'Does it mean he wants you to *lose?*'

'No, simply to be *very lucky*. In the normal run there's little skill in the game – it's as hard to lose as to win. But Sam says the art lies in the fine calculation of the odds. He has studied the winning and losing chances between setter and caster and has drawn up tables ... Sam has made it into a science.'

This flew over their heads.

'More difficult still!' said Widow Trotter.

'I think Sam is laying a trap with me as the bait – a pigeon ready to be plucked! He says the seasoned players love a tyro in the art. They circle round, embrace him and encourage him. He'll be allowed to win a little at first to help build his confidence – they will declare him a genius! – then, once his courage is up and his ambitions roused, he will find the game slipping away. He will sink ever deeper – but always with the hope that he'll recapture that lucky spark … Sam suspects false dice will be used …'

'Ah yes, the dice! … '

Widow Trotter spoke the words with relish and glanced toward the sideboard drawer.

'… I have decided you can take the dice entrusted to my care – if it will help you both. After all, at Vandernan's they will be back home, will they not? … and in your hands they may do some good – I have wit enough to know how you might employ them!'

'So, you'll allow it!'

'Let us say I can see the appropriateness. Those false dice don't belong at the Bay-Tree, and I'll be glad to see the back of them. I'm sure Elias can have no objection … Besides, our Constable Cobb's understanding of material evidence seems to have undergone a recent change.'

Will was beaming with relief.

'They will be put to excellent use, Mrs T. I know Sam was looking to make them an essential part of our performance!'

It was a dangerous word – Vandernan's was not a theatre. Tom felt he had to say something:

'You must rein in your confidence a little, Will. Please be circumspect! Tonight, you'll be among treacherous men. You've said they will be puffing up your self-belief – the more reason to be cautious.'

'Dear Tom! You're right of course. It's the excitement in the nerves – the risk of the thing … Here with you and Mrs Trotter I can sound bold – the two of you give me courage. But trust me, when I'm in the gaming-house the fear is sure to return, and with it the caution. Will Lundy of the Middle Temple will not be forgotten!'

Tom began to think that Sam Rivers had transfused something of his buccaneering spirit into his friend:

'I do hope so, Will.'

Widow Trotter's concerns were also niggling her:

'The dice-play will be important, Mr Lundy. But while you are in Vandernan's there is more to be done – you must watch and listen and see what scraps you can collect. Remember, you are a spy as well as a player. You and Mr Rivers need to work together.'

'Have no fear, Mrs T! Samuel is more than ever curious to uncover the Vandernan's "system" – and now after your encounter with Bob Leary I shall have more to tell him. I know he'll be interested.'

'But Tom is right …'

There was a sudden intensity in her tone.

'…You are going into a dangerous place. You must be on your guard at all times. I need to remind you these gaming dens are illegal – as the preachers forever remind us! They survive by vice and bribery, protected by crooked magistrates and lax authorities – Vandernan's notoriously so! The place works by its own rules – so have a care. I've no doubt it will be gay and genial – but keep watchful. You'll not be in the Good Fellowship room.'

'Wise words, Mrs T,' said Tom. 'I think he is duly chastened … but for all this caution, I'm concerned about your name, Will …'

'My name?'

'Yes. You do know you'll be in a place where the name of *Lundy* will raise eyebrows? Your father is no friend to law-breakers! The mention of 'Hemp' Lundy will unsettle not a few and put them on their guard.'

Will checked himself:

'Ah – I'd not given thought to that … But I cannot go under another name – that would bring impossible difficulties.'

'Then best make a point of it!' said Widow Trotter. 'You are the son of a hanging judge who is rebelling against a tyrannical parent – a good story, don't you think? It's something anyone would understand.'

'Excellent, Mrs T! That's how I'll play it …'

He glanced uneasily at Tom.

'… if the question is put.'

There was a serious look on his friend's face:

'Will … Please remember, you are not just playing an innocent – you *are* an innocent – a pigeon! The gaming world is new to you. Remember how easily Frank slipped into disaster … Have a care what you drink!'

Will gave him a scorching look – Mrs Trotter was at that moment replenishing Tom's glass with a golden hock. Will reached for his lemon cordial and raised it to his two confederates:

'I shall be on my best behaviour I assure you. I shall carry your warnings with me … You have prepared me for the challenge ahead, not least thanks to Mrs Dawes's thoughtfulness. If I'm to be plucked and roasted I don't wish to be reminded of it … It was good of her to serve up ham pie, and not pigeon.'

Chapter Seventeen

⸺◦◦◦⸺

WILL HAD EXPECTED Vandernan's gaming-house to be secure – but not in quite this way. As he hovered behind Sam Rivers at the entrance, he felt like a knight before a Norman castle. There was no moat and drawbridge, but this urban equivalent was forbidding enough. Facing them was a door fashioned out of solid oak, hinged with massy iron, and set with ranks of steel spikes that would resist the stoutest shoulder (or even a battering ram, Will thought).

It was after eleven, a time when honest folk were a-bed – although around Covent Garden on this Sunday night there were enough of the dishonest wandering the streets to keep the Watch well occupied. The Theatre Royal might be shut, but in the theatre-passage off Drury Lane, play of a different kind never ceased.

In response to Sam's knock, a hatch to their right swung open and a pair of eyes appraised them:

'Mr Rivers – greeting!' came a voice. 'And a guest, is it, Sir?'

Sam smiled and nodded, and a moment later the slab of black oak swung open. Will was anticipating an unearthly creak, but the hinges had been well greased. They stepped into a narrow passage that served as an entrance hall.

'A Sunday precaution, Will!' said Sam, and handed sixpence to the doorkeeper, who nodded thanks.

'Yes indeed, Sir,' he said, 'our *reforming* friends are busy again – though at Vandernan's I like to think we strive to keep the sabbath holy. We keep vigil religiously!'

'Quite so, Mr Travis! We do not load our asses, do we? Neither do we tread our wine-presses. We bring not our burdens into Jerusalem!'

'All burdens are left at the door! ... Mr ...'

He was smiling at Will.

'Lundy,' said Sam, gesturing to his guest. Will gave a nod of acknowledgment.

'Welcome, Mr Lundy!' said the doorkeeper. 'No, indeed – nothing burdensome here! May you enjoy your evening, gentlemen – and take some profit from it.'

The doorkeeper turned back to Sam:

'Lady Rastell has a party in, Mr Rivers – though the Fates are not being kind. There has been sound of lamentation! Lady Rastell has a distinctive voice, Mr Lundy, and a fine store of curses.'

They laughed, and Sam led his guest along the hall. After a couple of steps something made Will look over his shoulder. He saw the burly Mr Travis with lowered head pencilling into a notebook.

The hall opened to a large wainscoted room bright with a hundred candles. Talk and laughter filled the place, which was surprisingly busy. Will stood for a moment and took in the animated scene: it was a Dutch painting come to life. There was elegance certainly, but formality had now relaxed into looseness – fine coats were unbuttoned; silk cravats dangled; lace was becoming limp in the humid air, and peruques were uncurling. He noticed a pair of them draped side-by-side over the back of an armchair like drowsy judges sleeping off their dinner.

There were two card-tables in the room, and at the far end was a fully-occupied basset table – what had been Robert LeRoy's domain.

Will looked around:

'But I see no sign of hazard, Sam! This is cards only ...'

He was instantly answered by a distant whooping, which seemed to echo from some subterranean world.

'The dicing is down in the cellars, Will. We shall resort there soon enough, I promise you. But first we would do well to settle ourselves. Let us have a drink and overlook the cards for a while.'

Will sensed he was to be initiated gradually.

It was clear that Samuel Rivers was a familiar face in these parts, and several introductions were made. Will smiled a lot. Eyes scrutinised him; words of greeting were edged with curiosity. He sensed that pulses quickened slightly when the words 'first visit' were uttered. One gentleman unashamedly shot a look that said, 'good catch, Mr Rivers!' He felt welcome but was made to feel a little like a yearling at Newmarket yet to show his paces.

'What do you make of the gamester, Will?' said Sam when they had a moment to themselves. 'You see the species itself before you!'

'A very sociable tribe – and a miscellaneous one.'

'A *mixed bunch*, as one would say in the market ...'

Sam drew closer to Will's ear and lowered his voice as if talking business.

'... The tall, stooping gentleman over there by the first table is – would you believe? – a man of the cloth, or *was*. He still wears black – though the garment of righteousness was stripped from him some years back! The difficulty was not his devotion to gaming, but to the worship of Belial ...'

'Yes, I suppose that's a disqualification.'

'To some degree – but Vandernan's does not hold with excommunication. They still accord him his title. The "Rector" is a tenacious player of whist and collects his tithes with some regularity.'

Will couldn't resist glancing at another figure lazing on

a couch over by the left-hand wall. The man was garbed in a brocaded nightgown of yellow satin embroidered with flowers:

'Who is the bird of paradise over there?'

'Yes, a fine plumage, is it not? That is Mr Colleoni. A man rightly proud of his noble name! – though *coglioni* would be more apposite … I have to say he always loses with careless grace. The man is negligent in many things – but meticulous about pronunciation.'

'And by the fireplace, Sam – the purple scarf …'

Will gestured toward a gentleman in a handsome skirted suit embroidered with silver, who was smiling broadly and raising a glass.

'Ah yes! A man worth your study, Will … A mere twelvemonth ago Dick was dressing wigs in Cheapside at threepence a time – and look at him now! – all spruced up in velvet and becuffed in lace! Vandernan's can transform your life, Will!'

'The place is certainly more genial than I expected – and with ladies too.'

'But of course! A few of them find their way here. I see Lady Rastell has brought a pair of country misses with her – one very much the blushing *ingénue*. She herself is a formidable player, especially at piquet. You must expect no mercy from a female gamester, Will!'

'Is that why the satirists castigate them – out of fear?'

'Exactly so. A woman's power at the tables unsettles them, and some men cannot endure losing to a lady … although I know of one who will happily sacrifice himself in that way as a prelude to another kind of sacrifice.'

Will began to think that, despite his distaste for the dark side of the place, Sam Rivers felt at home in Vandernan's and relished its lively character.

'More wine, Will!' he said, beckoning the waiter. 'You are

allowed a second glass. The claret here is very good. The French enemy is thoroughly despised, but exception is made for the Bordeaux trade …'

Will was about to demur – but too late:

'Sam, …'

'I know, Will – you are becoming a little anxious – it's only natural. But you must be patient. Things happen in their own good time! You will have seen that I put the word about – cast the bait into the current. Trust me, we shall have a fish or two showing interest shortly. Your presence has been noted.'

He was as good as his word, and as Will raised the second glass to his lips, Sam's eager face indicated something was about to happen:

'Don't look round, Will, but a pike is swimming lazily in our direction – the monarch of the stream himself!'

The hairs on the back of Will's neck bristled slightly, but he continued to appear calm and easy.

A moment later he became aware of a rubicund face hugged by a glistening black wig. The man stood next to them, saying nothing, but inviting attention. His nose flared.

Sam did the punctilious thing:

'Sir Charles – this is William Lundy of the Middle Temple …'

There was a barely detectable incline of the head and a flicker of recognition.

'… Sir Charles is the Commissioner of Vandernan's.'

'You have a flourishing place here, Sir,' said Will lamely. The remark was ignored.

'Ah yes – *Lundy* – a name of some notoriety in the law.'

Will bridled but forced his features into a slight smile:

'This place is not my father's world – but fortunately I can escape the old man's clutches!'

'You interest yourself in the practical side of the law, Mr

Lundy, do you not? I find you assist my brother-in-law, Richard Sumner?'

Will began to feel uneasy:

'Yes I do, Sir.'

'And I'm given to understand that earlier this year you gave my wife assistance – on a stupid matter of her pocket-book?'

The word "wife" was spoken a little raspingly, and "pocket-book" was weighted with contempt.

'Yes, Lady Norreys was in danger of being embarrassed – I was glad to help her.'

Will paused, not risking more.

'Hmmm … My wife is a headstrong woman, Mr Lundy – as you no doubt discovered – and she enjoys her cards – by God she does! She has been known to show herself in here … I see Lady Rastell is striving to ruin herself … I suppose we should be grateful.'

'Her Ladyship has not been favoured by Fortune tonight,' said Sam. 'But perhaps her luck will change?'

Sir Charles Norreys glanced round at her table, allowing Sam a surreptitious wink. When he turned back, the look of contempt had not dissipated but was if anything stronger:

'To think she was once a beauty! … I have to say, nothing wears out a fine face like the vigils of the card-table. I never knew a thoroughgoing female gamester hold her looks two winters together.'

A reply to this was difficult. Will hesitated, but Sam came in boldly:

'I have heard it said there is nothing so alluring as the face of a lady discomposed by the heat of play.'

'A nice thought … Yes, Mr Rivers, the card-table is a practised seducer: it encourages a woman to lose her fortune and her reputation simultaneously – and in the genteelest manner.'

Sir Charles was beginning to warm to the repartee. Will

plucked up courage and gave him a full-eyed look:

'Yours is no mercenary consideration, Sir. Lady Rastell's loss would surely be the house's gain?'

'Ha? Vandernan's can be generous, Mr Lundy! – though the bank's losses are merely loans, you understand. Our devotees return the principal with interest … Although in Mr Rivers' case the account is mightily overdrawn … Are you for cards tonight? Or the hazard-table?'

Will glanced cheerily in the direction of Sam, who had stepped away from the two of them:

'Oh, I thought I would take my chance with hazard, Sir. I may be a novice, but I have great hopes. I think the wine has given me heart! …'

Will's face was radiant, naïve. His unguarded expression was nicely achieved.

'… I was all for basset! – I knew your tallière to be a master of his craft … But I understand Mr LeRoy is here no longer? I confess I wished to see him in action again! I encountered him at the Bay-Tree chocolate house several days ago.'

The look that came over Sir Charles's face was hard to define. It was simultaneously curiosity and suspicion:

'The *Bay-Tree*? Well, well … I looked in there myself on Friday – a dull enough place! I had wind of a new basset table and wished to investigate. It is useful to know what rivals we may have. News reached my ears that our Mr LeRoy had decamped there, but the man seems to have vanished – I was not able to ascertain whereto …'

So, Sir Charles Norreys had called at the Bay-Tree … Now it was Will's turn to be surprised. He tried not to let it show and side-stepped the implied inquiry:

'I fear, Sir, that Mrs Trotter's scheme has been abandoned – your rival is no more! It was altogether a delightful evening – but, unlike Vandernan's, the bank was unable to withstand a substantial loss. I fear it won't re-open … the late Mr Sturgis swept all before him!'

Will threw out the name nonchalantly and took another sip of his wine.

Sir Charles's response was brusque:

'A sorry business! The man moved in murky waters.'

Will waited to hear more, but Sir Charles was suddenly reticent; he had left an opening that must not be declined. Will swayed very slightly and continued to beam:

'Mr Sturgis's body was found near this place, was it not? Did the poor man make an enemy here, perhaps? At the Bay-Tree he played boldly and won his triumph! Mr LeRoy took it in good heart and even seemed to be offering *encouragement!*'

This was said almost laughing. Sir Charles was looking distinctly uneasy. He was irked by Will's breezy conjectures – conversation had sunk to gossip – and yet something was holding him. Will was unsure where this would lead and knew he was taking a risk. But Sir Charles was willing enough to push things further:

'Did you exchange words with Sturgis and LeRoy? Tell me. What do you know of them?'

'There I must tread carefully, Sir … Some who were present thought they detected a co-operation – *collusion* – between them. LeRoy fled without settling his share of the debt, and now poor Mrs Trotter faces ruin. She is even more anxious than you to know his whereabouts. If you dig him out, I'm sure she would be glad to know … Did you detect any cheating here? I trust he did not defraud Vandernan's?'

Will was giving his naivety free rein.

At the word 'cheating' Sir Charles's nostrils flared again and there was a slight twitch of the cheek:

'He defrauded no-one Sir! – neither the house nor his players. Such a suggestion is without warrant. When we take your money, you'll have no cause to whine.'

At that moment, Sir Charles's attention was distracted. A gentleman in a blond periwig had sidled up and was turning his face toward his ear. Will hoped this wouldn't end their exchanges but thought it best to look politely away while they talked. The man's voice was a half-whisper, which made Will give his words particular attention. The first muttered sentence he couldn't make out; but then two words, spoken unguardedly, reached him. They were clear enough ... 'Captain Hazard.'

There was an expression of assent, and the man turned away in the direction of the cellars. Sir Charles closed down the conversation at once:

'I am needed elsewhere, Mr Lundy. I trust your first visit here will prove a memorable one.'

And with that curt remark, and a sniff, he was gone. It was an ambiguous wish, and Will felt the pepperiness of it, and of the look that accompanied it. Out of the corner of his eye he saw Sir Charles move towards the table where Lady Rastell was still fighting her losing battle. A few onlookers were gathered round, adding to the tension that seemed to emanate from that side of the room. Will shivered at the thought of being on display in a place like this.

Sam Rivers was back by his side.

'So, what did you learn, Will? I must say you played the innocent lamb to perfection. I was trying to keep a straight face.'

'Did you hear our conversation?'

'Only by snatches.'

Will sighed and shook his head inconsolably:

'Sir Charles is a difficult person to love ...'

He paused. Sam began laughing.

'... He is what we lawyers call "irritable" – both inattentive and easily excited. The physicians consider it a medical condition ...'

Now Will was trying not to laugh himself.

'… In the witness box he would be easily provoked. I have been taught that such a man can be played upon! Yes, I do think I conveyed a touching naïvety. Let me quote an old courtier at you … "Plain dealing and simplicity are the best game a man can play."'

'Not a bad motto for what you are about tonight, Will! … but what did you *learn?*'

'I learned, Samuel, that the mere mention of the name "Sturgis" disturbs him. I also learned that the hunt is on for poor Bob Leary – and that Sir Charles, would you believe, has visited the Bay-Tree in search of him … He was hoping I might know the man's whereabouts … How did you come to know what he and his friends do not? You must have your own office of intelligence?'

Sam tapped the side of his nose:

'That would be telling … but it says much for my sources, does it not, Will?'

'Undoubtedly. You can be sure I left Sir Charles in ignorance about Islington … But I learned something of more immediate import from the gentleman who interrupted us …'

'What, exactly?'

'I heard a phrase being secretly spoken – one that seemed to have the force of a watchword in this place …'

Will broke off with a provoking coyness and looked Sam Rivers straight in the eye.

'… Captain Hazard.'

'Ah! … I think you have trumped my Ace …'

'So, you have heard the phrase?'

Sam hesitated just long enough to be awkward:

'Yes … A verbal cipher. Did this come from Bob Leary?'

'Tom and Mrs Trotter say he was helpful to them. Is this the watchword for the cabal, Sam? … Why did you not tell us?'

'I pride myself on knowing more than others – on what you

call my "office of intelligence." It is how I survive in the system. It was not to keep you in ignorance, believe me – just something I held in my sleeve.'

'You sound like a true sharper.'

'I told you, I know the trade.'

'Do you help us, Sam? Or are we helping you?'

'They are not alternatives – we work together!'

It was a mercurial exchange. Neither man spoke it, but the matter of trust was suddenly there between them.

Will sighed:

'This is an uncomfortable world, Sam, is it not? I like to think we are friends who can rely on one another.'

'You touch me to the quick, Will … I confess, my worst transgressions are sins of omission, not commission. You need to understand that of me. I would never do anything to harm you or your friends. Indeed, I feel a special allegiance to Mrs Trotter above all. In that, my private ends are nothing – believe me!'

'On that basis, Sam, let us continue our work. I'm sorry – I should not have spoken like that – I should not have been suspicious.'

'On the contrary – if you are to succeed you will need that quality in good measure …'

He gave a knowing smile.

'… But there is something you need to know, right now … The gentleman in the flaxen wig who whispered with Sir Charles …'

Now it was Sam's turn to pause for effect:

'… That is Lord Parham.'

'Bob Leary's patron? Then we are in luck if both of them are here tonight … Is the game afoot, do you think?'

'I smell something in the air … We must be ready.'

Before Will could reply, there was a sudden intake of breath audible from around Lady Rastell's table, as if some precious vase had fallen. A cry of 'By all the Gods!' told them the Fates had struck her another blow. Curiosity drew the two of them in that direction, and they joined the ring of spectators who had gathered round. The scene that was being staged had the look of a final confrontation. All the other players had risen from the table, leaving Lady Rastell seated opposite a young man of striking appearance.

The contrast could not have been more complete. Her ladyship was visibly unsettled – she wore a confection of pale blue satin over which hung an esclavage of silver chains that rose and fell with each quickened breath; her dark hair was gathered under a precarious topknot of lace, and exquisite pendant earrings trembled on her neck.

Opposite her was a figure garbed informally. No silks and buckled shoes here. The young man was shod in dirty boots and leather breeches, like a postman after a hard ride. His coat was handsome enough but distinctly rumpled and discoloured by dust. He wore no wig and had his hair gathered in a queue. A scarlet kerchief hung carelessly across his chest.

The man was smiling confidently on his opponent – a gaze that was met with a look of wide-eyed alarm.

'It's Jack Beech!' said Sam in the lowest whisper.

'The highwayman?'

'None other.'

Will leaned forward to try and catch the conversation.

The man might as well have been holding a pistol to her head – though it remained tucked into his belt.

'... That is my offer, Lady – *odds and evens!* Is this not a gallant proposition? I tally you a single card – which if your Fortune decrees, the sum you owe me shall be quit and my hopes – which so mightily offend you – be set aside forever ...'

His words were interrupted by a busy murmur round the table.

'... And if the Fates choose otherwise, I assure you, Lady Rastell, your debt will still be cancelled ... but concerning the other matter between us – you will agree to settle it to my satisfaction.'

He caressed the word and leaned back in his chair, appraising her with a lazy confidence, eyes smiling. His right hand was resting on the deck of cards, one finger stroking the top card slowly. It took a moment before she could find her voice.

There was a muttered 'Shame!' from beyond the table.

'It is the Devil's bargain, Sir!' said Lady Rastell, looking at her antagonist with a mixture of contempt and pride, 'and you are a bold devil for proposing it ... *Fifteen hundred?* ... You value me highly – no slave in the market ever commanded so much.'

Hearing the sum, Will let out an involuntary whistle – it was as much as he might hope to earn from five years' work ... He could feel the danger in the air – the madness – as something physical.

'... Well, then ...'

Her neck was blushing. She was trying not to look at the faces that were pressing in around her.

'... I choose *even!* ... and may the card make all even between us!'

It was spoken like a challenge. She had come to a determination, and her face showed it. The slightly hooded eyes began to blaze.

Jack Beech roused himself and coolly took the deck in his hands. The shuffle was purposeful, precise. Each card might bring him what he wanted, and the moment was to be savoured.

His hands became still. The pack was tight, and his finger was sliding the top card out, when she stopped him:

'No! ... You will let me choose. I shall pick the card. If my Fate is to be declared, I would have the gods decide it – not you!'

He was caught off balance:

'Do you not trust me?'

'I have faith in the cards, Mr Beech. Perhaps in this final hand – at last – they will be my friends.'

He was nonplussed and a little annoyed. But the murmur around the table gave him no choice:

'Very well. Take your card.'

Without hesitating, she leaned forward and reached out to the pack, which was still being held tightly in his hand. He pushed it towards her so that she was touching the proffered card. She made a calculated pause and ran her fingers across the whole deck as if thought were guiding her. Then decisively she slid the jutting card aside and chose the one below it.

She calmly placed it, face-down, on the green baize between them.

'Turn the card, Mr Beech. See what the gods have given you.'

The play had been reversed. Lady Rastell was dictating terms.

Almost sheepishly he complied – and flipped the card over with deliberate casualness – and there for all to see was the two of diamonds.

The place was suddenly a miniature theatre. The audience exclaimed, and there was a scattering of applause. Lady Rastell showed no emotion and sat perfectly still:

'Such a little card, is it not, Mr Beech? A poor two – and yet how strong and wise its voice … It tells us that honour is preserved on both sides.'

Will and Sam stepped back from the table, slightly dizzy from the drama that had played out before them.

'Extraordinary!' said Sam in a tone of admiration. 'What a remarkable lady. Now there's a female gamester for you, Will!'

'Not one to tangle with, I think. I'm now beginning to understand the force of those small oblongs of pasteboard … how much they can betoken – and how our fate can depend on them.'

'That's the allure of the game, Will – how it can have such power over us. After all, does it not give us our very language of fate and chance?'

This was a philosophical proposition Will was not ready to explore just yet:

'I need another drink, Sam – before we move down to the cellars. I only hope the drama of the evening is over with, and in our game we shall not face such powerful forces.'

'That may be a vain hope, Will – if I know anything of hazard!'

Chapter Eighteen

※

Midnight, and in the card-room of Vandernan's the chandeliers were being lowered and candles re-set for the hours to come. From his seat, a solitary Will began to sense the shifting mood of the place. A few of the gamesters had slipped away, but others were continuing to play in the half-light with widened eyes, and ears alert to the lowest whisper. As ever, elation and despondency rang the changes. Around the tables there was plenty of confident talk – boasts and taunts recalling the evening's battles – but at the periphery was a more pensive taking-stock. For the quieter gamesters, thoughts of suicide alternated with dreams of a country estate. The world was turning. In the alcoves, shadows were at play as silhouetted figures gathered around small Venetian girandoles.

Some minutes earlier, Sam had gone down to the hazard-room and suggested his friend remain to await events. At this moment Will was feeling like a tethered goat sniffing the scent of lion in the darkness.

With the light now dimmer, he looked about him and drank in the sheer romance of the place. He could sense a power stirring – one that was unfamiliar and yet had an insidious appeal. Many long days in Westminster Hall had trained his mind to look for facts and find solutions in them – to know there was no short-cut to the truth. Through a process of structured thought and rigorous argument, the untidiness of life might be brought to order.

But in this room daylight resolutions melted away. For a few hours life offered something more immediate. Those forever-distant things, dreams and hopes, were here within reach ... He had not drunk much – but enough to settle into the Vandernan's mood. He could understand the character of the place and these people. For a moment he imagined himself in a gloomy side-chapel of a church with its dim religious light infusing itself into him. To what saint were these people making their devotions? He was seated in one of the alcoves and his wine-glass was almost empty.

A few feet away in the shadows he was aware of a pair of gentlemen talking in low voices between themselves. To this point he had not heeded them; but after pondering the nature of the mental world and the intricacies of human thought he began to register their half-muttered exchanges. Syllables, then words, then a phrase or two became audible. As if in court, he began to attune his hearing, and his chin settled on his chest so that to a bystander he appeared to have sunk into an alcoholic slumber. But this was Will's posture of deliberation. He was fully alert and realised that a conversation was taking place that would repay attention. He settled further into his semi-recumbent stillness and gave ear.

One phrase struck him at once, and the words were unmistakeable: 'The Honourable Adventure.' This was the pretentious title of a lottery scheme that had caught the imagination of the nation and had been attracting funds not merely from the wealthy but from men and women of all ranks in society. As their muttered talk went on it became clear this was no incidental reference: they were discussing the subscription, and in terms that suggested the assets were at their disposal.

They were speaking low, yet with obvious relish. He caught the words 'quarter of a million' and felt a sudden responsive thump in his chest. He fought to keep still. Fortunately, there was a burst of laughter from the room that disguised his twitch of astonishment. Where was this conversation leading?

As the men warmed to the topic, their speech grew a little less hushed, and Will found he could follow their words more closely. He was used to taking shorthand in Westminster Hall and longed for his pencil and notebook. They were soon discussing stocks – it was the language of 'Change Alley. East India stock, Hudson's Bay stock were briefly mentioned – but then something completely different – some ingenious project concerning "inflammable air," and how it could be drawn out of coal ...

Will was having to suppress a smile – it was a leap from the sublime to the ridiculous! But it was this latter topic that appeared to excite them. Will was unpractised in the language of the market, but as the talk continued, he picked up a curious line of thought – it seemed there was to be a covert scheme to purchase stock with the intention of raising its price. They referred to it as "the enterprise," and the phrase "to the skies" told Will it was an ambitious one, with others involved – a true conspiracy! He listened carefully. It would appear that a pamphlet extolling the project and its possibilities was imminent. There were some more words he didn't understand, but he picked up the idea that at the climax there was a plan to "make an *almighty put*" – this was twice spoken. Will was trying to picture what this action would involve – some great weight being thrust aside? Perhaps a shove from behind? What jargon! But with what warmth the two of them were playing with the idea. He would have to ask Sam about this.

Their talk returned to 'The Honourable Adventure,' and Will began to see how the full plot fitted together. Funds from the lottery would be used to invest in the inflammable air scheme ... Even Will, in his ignorance of the ways of the City, could see this was a wild and fraudulent proceeding, with more than enough hazard to delight any hardened gamester. He began to wonder what Samuel, with his fondness for the goddess of Risk, would say – perhaps the idea would delight him? It certainly came under the category of an *opportunity* ...

Will was pondering this when yet another shock made him start – this was truly the busiest slumber he had ever enjoyed! ... It was those words again – the watchword. He heard it distinctly. One of them was to 'go downstairs to meet my old friend Captain Hazard ...' Will could hear the smile in the voice as he spoke. Was this to collect, or deliver, he wondered?

And suddenly he was aware of movement as the two men rose to their feet. The main chandelier was being hoisted towards the ceiling, its fresh candles beaming out and bringing life and glitter to the room once again. Will opened his eyes and noted the two men who were showing their backs to him – stock traders, no doubt, who were laying their ingenious plan. Or was it a different relationship? One was clothed in a comfortable brown worsted, the other more finely clad in a skirted coat of dark crimson with embroidered cuffs. An oddly-matched couple, he thought – one a scrivener perhaps, or a denizen of Jonathan's? And the other his wealthy client? ... But then Will checked himself. Perhaps the figure in his finery was drowning in debt and the plain-John was a banker as rich as Croesus? Men did not always wear their wealth on their backs.

But then the finely-dressed gentleman turned and showed his face. In the new candlelight his flaxen wig was illuminated, and Will recognised the features ... It was Lord Parham.

As the light returned, Will had no time to digest the discovery. Sam Rivers was striding over towards him, flinging out a nervous arm in a gesture of admonition:

'Will! I thought to see you mingling – but what do I find? You are taking your ease and talking to no-one.'

'Ease? …'

Will responded with indignant confidence.

'… Sit yourself beside me, Sam, and you'll learn what my *ease* has accomplished. It has been the most profitable slumber any man ever enjoyed!'

Sam warmed to the exaggeration, and a sudden animation in his sharp features showed his curiosity was caught. He followed instructions and sat down.

Thanks to his regular devotions in Westminster Hall, Will was well-practised in the concise summary, so it didn't take long to relate what he had overheard. But he was aware of being a dramatist too – the identity of one of the men would be kept back to achieve its full effect. After all, Sam had taught him that it was wise to hold something in your sleeve …

Will didn't use the word 'conspiracy' but what he described was undoubtedly that, and as he told the tale Sam's response was something close to silent rapture.

'… Is it not the boldest of schemes, Sam – and the most dishonourable? The *Honourable Adventure* indeed! Even I can see the dangers … And they spoke of their plan with such glee – though some of their language was new to me. They said their venture is to culminate in *an almighty put*. They seemed very pleased at this idea – whatever it is. What is a *put*, Sam?'

His friend's light frame twisted round in excitement:

'Ah – so they are going to destroy their own scheme! This is bold indeed! The price will plummet, Will. They are creating a bubble – a *genuine* bubble in their case – one made not of air but of *gas*! …'

Sam smiled at his own wit.

'… and they will finally explode it – after having made a wager on the scheme's failure.'

'So, they will be rewarded if the price falls?'

'More than that, Will! Their gain will be commensurate with the loss. It is an *inversion*. They invest in a bad outcome – and the worse the outcome the greater their profit.'

'So, money can be made out of failure?'

'Oh yes indeed. The *put* is a devilish mechanism. It means you can have a stake in disaster – and welcome it!'

'This truly is a game, Sam.'

'Theirs is a double reward. They gain from the rise, and then gain even more with the fall ...'

'Not a happy outcome for those who hold the stock ...'

'It is the worst kind of theft, Will. The unfortunate purchasers are drawn in by the success and pay a premium – then they are forced to sell when the bubble has burst – if they are able to sell at all! The whole thing may go up in flames – like fire-damp in a coal-mine. And there will undoubtedly be casualties ... The thing is a terrible risk – and to venture lottery funds is foolhardy in the extreme. I can hardly credit it! ...'

Will could detect a degree of admiration in Sam's voice as the scale of the 'enterprise' became clear. He had to admit there was something neat, even satisfying, about it. The scheme was a kind of cheat, yes, but nothing that the game didn't allow. Prices in any market will always respond to demand – why should men not find a common interest and work together? *What's ought but as 'tis valued?* The only deception was in the secrecy of the collaboration. Will's lawyerly mind whispered that some use could be made of what he had just heard.

But Sam was right – it was time to see what was happening in the cellars. Raucous sounds told him there was some lively action going on. Will reached into his pocket and his fingers felt for the dice. The very touch of them made his mouth dry. What should have been reassuring was the opposite. Sam had identified them as 'high fulhams' – dice destined to favour high numbers: 4, 5, 6. But would he be able to use them at any point? What if the cheat were spotted? Perhaps he would escape with a beating, or was there something worse in store?

Suddenly the adventure was real, and the danger of the moment was palpable. Will remembered what Tom had urged on him (with that intense look he sometimes adopted!). Yes, my friend, he thought to himself, I shall try to be wary and remain in control – not be swept up in the excitement of the game … but such admonitions are easily made …

He looked at Sam, whose eyes had been inspecting him silently. Their question did not need to be spoken aloud:

'Yes, Sam, I'm ready.'

'Good. Remember all you've learned, Will, and keep a clear head …'

Sam leaned forward and spoke a low reminder:

'… Always make *seven* your main – have the odds in mind at every cast – picture my tables – never run ahead of the arithmetic – don't let yourself be hurried! – watch the faces – be cautious with your betting – don't be tricked into taking an "even" chance (nothing in this game is even)! You must mingle in the room at first, allowing the other gamesters to make much of you – let them be encouraging. But be wary of their advice. Follow your own judgment! In good humour you can let them guide you a little – this will please them – and if I'm right, they will allow you some small wins. But you must eventually strike out for yourself …

'Do *not* use the loaded dice on your first visit to the table – your precious fulhams must be left till later when the other gamesters think they have you at their mercy. Remember, you haven't the experience to be a setter, so you must *only cast*, do you hear? There is money to be made from setting, but not until you are master of the mechanisms of it. As caster, I suspect you will be given fair odds at the beginning, but don't let that make you

feel secure. Remember, over-confidence is your greatest enemy! …
Avoid side-bets until you are completely settled at the table …'

Will was beginning to smile, and feel a little easier:

'Sam! Sam! … I thank you. You have taught me exceptionally
well. If I keep all this in my head I shall deserve to win mightily! …'

Sam's tone changed:

'Don't use such language! You are not here to *win mightily*.
Merely to survive will be a triumph. Remember, we are in this
place for you to make friends, not enemies! … My account will
cover you for the *fifty pounds*. Do not – *do not even think* of
exceeding it!'

Will thought of Frank Popham's disastrous night at those
very tables, and shuddered. Yes. He was duly admonished.

But would all this work out as planned? Yesterday's Bay-
Tree conversation came to mind. What Sam had said to them
about risk, fortune and chance was very fine in theory – but in
practice? The only ground of truth was experiment, and events
could overturn all. But whatever the outcome, there was no
stepping back now. The game had already begun, and perhaps
Captain Hazard would have a say?

Chapter Nineteen

⸺◊⸺

THERE WAS LITTLE of the romantic about Vandernan's hazard-room. The stone steps led down into a substantial vaulted space reminiscent of a Gothic undercroft; but what might have been a subterranean temple for unholy rites was closer to a noisy schoolroom without the teacher. Will's first impression was of warmth and clubbability. Men in groups were drinking and smoking, some overlooking the two gaming-tables, and their glances noted him as he approached. Instantly he felt the compressed energy in the place. It was convivial certainly, but it was hard to dispel the thought of being trapped in a cellar with men whose passions could boil easily.

He looked around him. There they all were – the winners and the losers! The magnetic force of hazard was binding them in a close embrace. Which would be his fate? He remembered Sam's advice and knew he must think only of Opportunity, but there was no benign goddess to guide him – only Widow Trotter facing ruin for the want of three hundred pounds. She was a formidable lady, but what could her spirit do here?

The fifty pounds in gold and silver weighed heavy in his pocket – and even heavier in his mind when he thought that the sum could secure him a house in St James's for a full year. He pictured the Pophams' townhouse in Pall Mall and clasped the bag more closely.

He didn't stand alone for more than a few seconds before a bustle of new acquaintances was around him – a youthful trio who were bursting with swagger and joviality, all sword-knots, silver buttons, fob-watches and Mechlin cravats. Smiles beamed forth, and a glass was raised:

'Ha! A fresh face! You are welcome to the Academy!'

'Do you intend to *tempt the dice?*'

'Pour the young man a glass, Ned!'

Names were exchanged – Ned, Isaac and Humfrey – young sprigs, it turned out, from Gray's Inn – though he soon discovered these fellow students had no intention of devoting their lives to the Bar. But the name of 'Lundy' was known to them and provoked some hilarity. There was a mock shiver from Humfrey, a weasel-faced youth who was now holding the bottle:

'So, your father is Hemp Lundy? Well, well! Have a care, Sir! Don't let Hemp hear of your Sabbath escapade – or you'll be *beating hemp* in Bridewell!'

The others giggled. Isaac, a rather dreamy-eyed young man, gave him a serious stare:

'Are you acquainted with Westminster Hall, Mr Lundy? I have been told it is a very grand place – full of old gentlemen in gowns, all looking incredibly wise, and very, very *busy* …'

More laughter.

Will couldn't stop himself:

'You should look in there one day, Mr Ward! I understand some business called *The Law* is being carried on. You might find it amusing for an hour or two!'

Ned took a handkerchief from his nose and shook his dark locks with mock solemnity:

'Westminster Hall? I doubt he would, Mr Lundy. Humfrey and I paid a visit there some months ago and told Isaac about it.

But, as a matter of principle, our friend is determined to see out his days at Gray's Inn without having set foot in the place.'

Will felt old, and his stomach was tightening. He was about to respond when a sudden commotion broke out at the adjacent table. There was an explosive cry of 'Go *again*, *Trusty!!*'

A second of silence was followed by another loud cheer. One of the gamesters was on his feet. The three templars broke into laughter:

'That's our Hockley-Hole sportsman, letting his dog off the slip!'

'Sir John has a lucky devil at his elbow tonight! He flings his main religiously!'

'But *what* religion? He's made some hellish bargain!'

The gaming talk was bubbling around Will, and in a few moments he too was looking down at the hazard-table. There were five players seated at it, their coins scattered before them. Four had evidently seen a meagre harvest, but the fifth – a character of bright eye and ruddy cheek – was still on his feet, smiling radiantly. In front of him was a positively architectural mound of coin, gold amongst the silver:

'Forgive me, friends – I've not been so *warm* these past three months!'

Sir John's apology was taken for the boast it was.

'As for me, gentlemen ...' announced the setter, a melancholy figure with nothing but bare board before him, 'Caster and setter – I've had the worst of it both ways! I'm playing on trust now. All I can offer is my watch, though I'll be needing that for the pawnbroker tomorrow. I am a man of considerable *promise*, however!'

A wit was quick to respond:

'We all know your promises, Nick! ... And with a name like yours, you've been a serious disappointment to the fraternity – and so, I hereby christen you ...'

He looked around at his friends.

'... *No-Nicks* Nick!'

There was delight all around:

'No-Nicks!'

Glasses clinked, and the name was repeated loudly – to the embarrassment of the young man concerned who could look forward to a soubriquet for life.

"'Tis a *nick*name to be proud of!' remarked a wag, to more laughter.

Will sensed the abundant good humour, but he wasn't fooled. The air was volatile.

'What can you promise us, Nick?' asked the man seated to his right. 'Your clothes will hardly do the business – and you have no estate.'

'I have the promise of one!' was the over-eager reply.

'*Promise* again!' said another. 'You are certainly a young man of expectations. We are *promise-cramm'd!*'

More laughter.

There's wit in the room, thought Will. These are no simple gamesters – more a fraternity with its own *lingua franca* – the tongue of their trade! He felt the stimulus of it and the itch to belong. It was troubling.

He stepped aside from the group and walked over to the second table, where Sam Rivers was seated with half a dozen other gamesters. He knew he needed to accustom himself to the pace of the game, which was conducted in brisk fashion. Hazard allowed little time for careful thought. Sam caught Will's eye briefly, enough to wish him well and signal caution before turning his attention back to the table. Seated to Sam's left was the caster, a chubby character in a waistcoat that struggled to contain the flesh within. The gentleman was so well-rounded that his arms hardly reached the board. But he flicked the dice-box with practised ease and was occupying his seat contentedly, a handsome collection of golden guineas before him.

Will tried to work his mind to the procedures of hazard as Sam had taught him. The instruction had been intense, and the information had poured into his brain so quickly that he was concerned some of it had leaked away. Happily, the action was less noisy here, for the moment. The large man, with a certain dignity, declared his *main* as seven and promptly cast the pair of dice, which settled on two ones, or *ames-ace* as it was called – and with that he lost his guinea stake (a caster *threw out* with a two or a three). With a main of seven again, he cast for a second time, but now *nicked* with an eleven (always a win with a main of seven) and the coin made its way back to him.

Newly heartened, the gentleman cast for a third time, giving the box a good rattle. This time the dice showed a three and a two. Five therefore became his *chance*, and from this point he would continue to throw for as long as it took to win or lose: he would nick with his chance, but now throw out with his main … At this point there was a sudden flurry of interest with side-bets coming in – including Sam's. The setter offered 3 to 2 against a five being thrown, and Will's mind ran through the arithmetic – yes, it was fair odds – this bank was above board. He watched as Sam pushed a silver crown forward, and he wasn't alone: along the table to Sam's right was a glowing guinea, and opposite him a couple of half-crowns. The large gentleman confidently staked two five-guinea pieces. Will already felt his heart pulsing quicker.

After two more casts – a four and a six – nothing had been decided. No main, no chance. To Sam's right, a second guinea joined the first. Will had shown that of thirty-six possible casts, a seven was the likelier with its six chances against five's four – hence the odds. There was something satisfyingly precise about hazard's system which had an appeal for him – it gave the game a rigorous logic around which you could play with the permutations of probability. In this setting he at last saw how cheating – and favouring – could happen once the night and the drink and the manic energy of the play began to combine. The eyes would tire, the brain become less acute, the emotions grow giddy; it would be tempting to see pattern amid the randomness and feel you were riding the sportive animal brilliantly. What was an entirely mathematical procedure would slip easily into hoping – daring – willing – hazarding! Will began to understand how, as the hours rolled on and the excited energy mounted, a *false box*, a quick *peep* and *slur* in the casting might be perpetrated, or favourable or unfavourable odds sneaked in by the setter at an opportune moment when vigilance had slipped …

With a neat flick of his wrist, the man cast again – and the dice settled to show a one and a four. He had flung his chance, and the bank counted the cost – but with some small mitigation: one punter had taken the odds on the main. Sam gained another half crown. The large gentleman took his reward of five guineas. To an accompaniment of conflicting laughs and scowls, the play went on.

Will could feel how the momentum of the game would take hold, and the pulse of it pull you along. Each rattle of the dice was a kind of climax, an emotional instant – a thrilling 'now!' that could become a craving …

He felt a hand on his shoulder:

'You are deep in thought, Mr Lundy! …'

Will turned. It was Isaac.

'… You contemplate the folly of human life, perhaps?'

'Its follies and enchantments, Mr Ward! … In truth, I was trying to steady my head by meditating on the power of the moment.'

'Ah yes – how fleeting and decisive it is? I see you are already initiated into the mysteries of hazard! Our guiding spirit put it so well, did he not?

Whatever is to come, is not –
How can it then be mine?
The present moment's all my lot,
And that, as fast as it is got,
Hazard! is wholly thine!'

Will blinked innocently:

'So – hazard is your mistress? You subscribe to Lord Rochester's creed! Is he not a dangerous patron?'

'Dangerous certainly, Mr Lundy – that is why we cherish him! Is that not why you are here? ... Come and share a glass with your friends – and then we shall join the other table and see if we cannot charm our mistress into smiling on us? Dr Convex has settled himself too securely at this table – and I don't like the dice!'

Will heard this last remark with interest but tried not to show it:

'Dr *Convex?* Do you mean the large gentleman?'

'Yes, we have awarded him that name – it allows much ribaldry. The man has a magnificent curvature, does he not? We like to think that somewhere in the world there is a limber Miss *Concave*, who will fit him to a T!'

'Well, he seems to be in favour at this moment, does he not?'

'Yes, highly favoured by the right people. Come!'

Will allowed himself to be guided back towards the other two templars, who were seated round a bottle of port at a small table by the wall. They were looking at him welcomingly. A genial interlude was in prospect, but Will glanced at the bottle and stopped in his tracks:

'I think I'll take my chance at the table, Mr Ward. Let me see if I can pick up a lucky fifty!'

It was spoken with bravado – very much in the spirit of the place – but his words gave him pause. These young men were at home here, and it might be profitable to draw them out a little – but how to do that without allowing them to reverse the play?

In the event, the matter was decided for him:

'All in good time, Mr Lundy! First, there are things you need to know about Vandernan's …'

Isaac's hand clutched at Will's coat.

'… I can feel a bulge in your pocket – and a substantial one! Before you risk your own stake, you need to settle yourself into the ways of the house. It is good to have friends in this place, Will – believe me!'

So, this is how it happens at the beginning, he thought. Friendly encouragement – a genial drink or two …

What he 'needed to know,' it seemed, was nothing to the purpose – certainly nothing to match his instruction by Sam. As the four sat and talked – and drank – it was clear the intent was to ease him into a devil-may-care mood. Will was alert and kept his glass never less than half-full – though he allowed himself to show a degree of wide-eyed inebriation. As the talk became livelier and the anecdotes more extravagant he was able to slip in a few innocent questions:

'Up in the card-room just now, there was a memorable duel played out – a fine lady and a dusty vagabond – a *knight of the road*, so I was told. She all silk and jewels, and him in his working attire – with a pistol in his belt!'

Will's face was marvelling at the image he had conjured.

'Yes – we hear Jack Beech was at his tricks again!' said Humfrey.

'Jack has a steady hand – with cards or a pistol! And he wins mightily with both!'

'What do you mean?' asked Will.

'He plays with a "friendly deck" – one that responds to his hands.'

'As the women do also!' said Ned.

The three of them laughed. Will allowed dawn to break across his face:

'Ah I see! But, to win the lady – he sacrificed fifteen hundred … fifteen *hundred!*'

'Money means little to him, Will. He can take all he needs whenever he runs short – it's hard to refuse Jack! … But the challenge he truly enjoys is playing for a lady's favour. She turned the tables with him, did she not?'

'Yes,' said Will. 'As calm as you like.'

'Lady Rastell is a *heroic* gamester,' explained Isaac.

'Aye – and she sets a high price on herself!' said Ned. 'The story is, that was how she and George Sturgis came to terms – only on that occasion she lost!'

'Poor George! Given their history … she cannot be said to have mourned excessively.'

Isaac shook his head in mock disapproval. There was more laughing.

Will was struck dumb. So, Lady Rastell and George Sturgis had a 'history'? … He hesitated to say anything, his mind running swiftly. But he couldn't let the moment pass.

'*Sturgis* – is that the gentleman who was murdered in here?'

'Not in here, Will …'

'Though not far away!' put in Isaac, helpfully. 'Yes, the man was run through not a hundred yards hence.'

'A gamester's quarrel was it?' said Will eagerly as he lifted his glass.

The others suddenly looked uneasy.

'It is not decided,' said Humfrey. 'A street assassin, more like.'

Will sensed an awkwardness with the topic. But Isaac was happy to say more:

'They say he had a big win that night at basset. Not George's game as a rule – but he always took what came his way.'

'On this occasion it *came his way* thanks to Robert LeRoy, I hear,' said Ned.

'Now there's a name! Where has he vanished to?' said Humfrey, genuinely curious.

'Wouldn't Joe Parham like to know!'

The wine was loosening their tongues. What an irony! Will was longing to bombard them with questions but knew he must be cautious, so he held back to watch where the current would flow.

'George had a good heart,' continued Isaac, with a touch of sadness. 'I was here that day – Thursday. He rescued a lamb from the wolves – took a note for his friend's losses. A couple of thousand! The box had been playing its tricks, and the poor gentleman was befuddled ... It had been like snatching a rattle from a child ... Lord Parham was none too pleased at it – as it seemed to me.'

Will couldn't keep silent:

'Not pleased at what? Did he not wish the man to lose?'

He tried to make it sound a casual question.

'Oh no – the reverse! He was put out at seeing him let off the hook ... This friend of George's was a political gent – a Member of Parliament, no less! – Lord Parham interested himself ... I think he would fain have seen the gentleman *ruinated!*'

Isaac spoke the word with emphasis. The others smiled.

'A Tory then, was he?' said Humfrey.

'Still is, I suppose ... But the young squire will have run back to the country by now!'

More laughter. Isaac reached for his glass.

Will jumped in:

'Does the box play *tricks?* ... because if ...'

'Don't fret your mind with that, Will – I'm sure you'll ride your luck fairly, like everyone else. *Chance* is the biggest trickster here!'

'And Dame Fortune, of course,' added Ned with a sigh. 'We are Fortune's children, and she's a fickle mother!'

'No, Ned. She's a peevish mistress! She likes to be wooed …'

A far-off look came into Isaac's eyes.

'… She will give you the key to her chamber – but you must treat her gently.'

Will felt he had to get a grip on this maudlin gamester talk:

'Do women not come down here to the tables? Is hazard only a game for the gentlemen?'

'We are favoured with a lady on occasion – though seldom, I admit. It takes a bold woman to throw dice with the men! Lady Rastell likes to take her chance. Who knows but she may look in here – if she's recovered from her play with Jack Beech.'

'I'm surprised,' said Will innocently. 'Does he not take great risk to his life – a highwayman – playing here in public?'

'Ah well,' said Humfrey with a knowing look. 'He has some *protection* in this place. Jack is a valuable punter. He likes to borrow a little money on the Queen's highway to stake himself at the tables … Rumour is that tonight he brought in a few notes he'd been gifted by the Bristol mail!'

It was a seemingly confident and light-hearted Will Lundy who took his place at the table. Things had reorganised themselves in the interval. At the second table Dr Convex had gathered up his haul of gold and silver, with some paper which he folded carefully into a wallet – about eight hundred pounds in all. He tipped the box-keeper a guinea and departed well satisfied with his night's work. Others took the opportunity to settle their losses. This left Sam Rivers, who came over to his protégé and muttered encouragement. The words 'modest' and 'vigilant' were left humming in Will's ears as Sam mounted the stairs back to the card-room. He said he would return.

Now there was only the one table. Sir John Simons and 'No-Nicks' were in their seats ready for more – the latter still fully clothed. Thanks to his timepiece he had found enough credit to continue playing and had even begun to show some *promise*, to the consternation of his two friends. By his side, Sir John's countenance glowed as before, though his fortunes had cooled somewhat. Ned, Humfrey and Isaac sat down too, which meant that with Will they made a table of eight.

Ned was eager to be the setter, and the first main was called by Sir John, who had shifted his allegiance to five. He set things off with a guinea stake – and promptly doubled it by immediately throwing a two and a three. Ned took the blow stoically, and for a few minutes, play continued in a subdued tone with everyone watchful, as if taking the measure of the new table. Will noticed that Ned declared the odds without pause, and with a quiet briskness that made it seem an easy routine. After three losses a caster passed the box to his left, and so, when his neighbour failed for the third time, it was Will's turn to call his main.

'Seven!'

He spoke the word with uncertain bravado, which he thought hit the right ambiguous note. On Sam's advice he had as yet placed no side-bets, and so a full fifty pounds was his to play with. Aiming to be bold but not reckless, he staked a silver crown, took the box in his right hand, and flung out the dice, which nestled together in front of him showing five and two. A cheer went up – rather too loudly to be without irony – but he persuaded himself it was intended to encourage the newcomer. He had *flung his main*. He took a crown from the bank and left it in front of him, doubling the stake. He threw again.

Another cheer rang out. Six and one.

Feeling slightly embarrassed at his success, he drew the two crowns towards him, leaving the other two as the stake for his next throw. He risked a fleeting glance around the table but stopped himself. He must ignore the watching eyes, or it would unsettle his play.

This time he threw an eight. This was now his chance.

'Six to five,' declared Ned – the right odds. Eight had five possibilities as against seven's six.

A few side-bets came in. Will himself added a third crown; Isaac and Humfrey – perhaps in support – added crowns of their own; on the other side of the table, Sir John Simons, beaming widely, put down a handsome five-guinea piece. Ned, as the bank, breathed in sharply, but remained still.

With all the bets laid, Will shook the box hard. He couldn't avoid feeling the responsibility, and his fingers were now gripping it more tightly as if unwilling to release Fate. It proved to be an awkward throw. One die dropped before him showing a two, and all eyes followed the second while it rolled to the end of the table in front of Ned, as if carrying a message to the bank. It wasn't a welcome one – a six! Will had thrown his chance. All at the table – all except for Ned – gave a loud *hurrah!*

Things could not have begun better. Will was feeling flushed with his – and thanks to him the other players' – success. How easy it was to be popular! Sir John was casting a beatific smile on him like a saint from a church window.

The ritual continued. Will staked an ambitious two crowns, and again with seven as his main he cast afresh, this time with more assurance.

A five – his chance! Now seven would lose.

Once more, at odds of three to two, the side-bets came in, and with a sudden zest for the moment Will added a third crown. He cast again – and again.

An eight … an eleven … a four … another eleven … another eleven … and yet another eleven … Eyes began to be raised. His fellow-gamesters looked at each other … then back at the box as

Will shook it firmly, feeling slightly embarrassed and unwilling to release the dice. Finally, he began to throw again.

A ten ... a six (he breathed more easily).

By now there was a distinct tension in the air. Both his main and chance were proving elusive. Several more coins had been staked around him, and the silence was striking. He cast again.

Another six ... another six ... an eight ... a six ... and then a FIVE!

They were there for all to see: a four and a one. He felt a surge of delight. The tide was joyously sweeping him along.

The other punters were enjoying the ride too – though poor Ned as the setter was a caricature of ruefulness.

Again, with a main of seven, Will cast, this time staking a full guinea. It took only one throw.

A seven it was!

Will was scarcely breathing, and the other gamesters were beginning to eye him differently. Could this young man do no wrong?

Doubling his stake to two guineas, Will threw again.

A four fell, but the second die spun dizzyingly round on the board, on and on like a child's top. They watched fascinated until it came to rest on another four. This was his chance ... at the next throw an eight would nick it.

Confidence in the lucky gamester was mounting, and at odds of six to five some bold side-bets came in from all sides. He cast again. Seven or eight – which would it finally be?

The answer came at once – a seven – his main! The four and the three lined up, side by side, and all eyes flicked from the one to the other, as if disbelieving ...

The mood around him changed. Now the silence was different, and Will felt his face beginning to redden ... Nothing was said. There was no commiseration or complaint, just a sense of the fullness of the moment emptying out in disappointment.

Suddenly Will knew the force of hazard – felt its name branding his soul. He sensed how warmth could turn to chill, confidence to suspicion, friendship to enmity.

The game had begun, and a challenging night stretched ahead of him.

Chapter Twenty

'… Cupid and Bacchus are my saints –
May Drink and Love still reign!
With Wine I wash away my cares –
And then to Love again!'

T HE TWO GAMESTERS swayed as one, their arms round
each other's neck. Glasses and tankards were raised in
salute, and other voices joined the chorus. But there was little
harmony in the raucous performance, and the stone vaulting of
the hazard-room turned sound into noise. The sentiments were
jovial ones but edged with a note of melancholy that said life,
however bold and passionate, would never be enough.

An hour had passed, and the mood of the room had altered.
The peep o'day boys were settling in. The song came to an
end, and to the sound of the applause Will emerged from his
temporary refuge behind the curtains of the privy. His hazard
adventure was under way, and he had survived the experience so
far, at the cost of just seven pounds.

It was an uncomfortable ride at times, and at one point his
fifty pounds stake-money had shrunk to a handful of guineas.
But he knew the picture could have been much darker. His
'friends' had acted their part, and their encouragement made

his dice-play distinctly enjoyable. He was caught up in the rhythms of the game and the ebb and flow of its emotions. But he had resisted the demon's whisper and stayed low. Despite the impression he gave he had remained in control and kept the mechanisms of hazard in mind. However, as time slipped by and the wine flowed, he had begun to feel Bacchus tickling his cheeks. It was an amiable sensation, but this was one deity he wanted to keep at bay. He felt the need to break off for a while.

At the far side of the room the rakish chorus had settled down to laughter and conversation, and the place was once more a gaming-room rather than an alehouse. He was expecting to be beckoned back to the tables at any moment; but fortunately, everyone's attention was turned on the unlucky Ned Wilder whose state had sunk from precarious to dire. After a series of unfortunate casts the young man was being comforted by his fellows – a role that Will couldn't help thinking was intended to be his own. He must soon return to the fray; but before hazard reclaimed him there were things he wanted to tell Sam – and a few urgent questions he needed to ask.

Will didn't believe in guiding spirits, but just as he was wondering whether to mount the steps to the card-room he saw his friend descending them. At first glance those restless eyes and taut features suggested anxiety, but Will knew it was the engine of Sam's mind hard at work – here was someone who didn't come to Vandernan's for ease and affability!

They found a spot in one of the bays not in direct view of the tables. Sam listened eagerly as Will told him about his 'friends' and what he had learned from them about that fateful day in the hazard-room. When George Sturgis took Frank Popham's debt on himself it was to the annoyance of Lord Parham, who it seemed had some political motive for seeing the young MP ruined. Sam was intrigued:

'So, it could have been an act of generosity?'

'Yes – a rescue of sorts. And Parham was angry. This isn't how I was thinking of it – and they spoke warmly of Sturgis.'

'I only encountered him across the table,' said Sam. 'But I have to say I never regarded him as one of the *cabal*. An agreeable enough rake – but loud and cocksure, like all of them.'

'Perhaps something had happened to turn Sturgis from Parham's ally to an obstruction – like Bob Leary? He and Sturgis seem to have been frustrating His Lordship's plans – whatever they were. The boys confirmed that he is trying to track Leary down.'

'So, word of Islington hasn't reached them?'

Sam seemed surprised – and not a little pleased with himself.

'No ... and something more: they said that when Frank lost his money the dice-box had been *playing tricks*.'

'Well, that does not surprise me,' said Sam. 'It's all part of the game here! ... While you were at the table just now, did you notice anything suspicious about the dice or the box?'

'No, it was above board. I was watching everything carefully, just as you told me, and looking for patterns.'

'So far, so good. You've acquitted yourself well – seven pounds is less than I feared! Let us see what success you'll have with the two little fellows in your pocket – I expect them to add some bounce to your game.'

It was an uncomfortable idea. Will couldn't suppress a sigh:

'Nothing can be trusted in this place, can it, Sam? There's falseness and deception everywhere.'

'Life in miniature, Will, only here the deception is carried on with cards and dice, and men challenge each other across a little table. It's not unlike Parliament or the Courts. Much depends on how you play your hand. Politicians and *lawyers* make excellent gamesters.'

He looked at Will approvingly.

Will thought it best not to be dragged along the path of similitude. He made a side-step:

'There was something said about Jack Beech which I thought would amuse you – that he plays with a special pack of cards. He must have trusted them to deliver Lady Rastell to him.'

'I think Her Ladyship was a step ahead there. Barbara can outface any man – even a highwayman in arms! When I left her just now, she was dealing death-blows at Piquet.'

'*Barbara?* ... are you acquainted with her?'

'We have conversed ... I've had a few *jousts* with her in the past.'

'Across a *little table*, I trust?'

'Oh, indeed. We see *eye to eye* about certain things.'

The conversation was enigmatic.

'Sam ...' Will paused. 'Could you introduce us?'

Sam swallowed, taken aback by his briskness. The request merited a suitably brisk reply:

'Business or pleasure?'

'Very much to the business ... My new acquaintances let slip that she had been more than friendly with George Sturgis – that they were lovers. From what they said, he had once *won her* – had succeeded where Jack Beech failed.'

'What? ... Yes, it's an amusing idea – too good to be true, perhaps? It would be disappointing if it were false news – like the fall of Lille ...'

He thought for an instant:

'... Well, she has packed off her two nieces to Arlington Street – and, given what she said upstairs, she seems determined to make a night of it. I think she intends to come down here ...'

Will was about to exclaim, but Sam laid a finger on his lips:

'... Say nothing more! Let us see what transpires. One hazard at a time! There is more play to be had, and good money to be made. I saw Dr Wakefield emerge even heavier than he is already – weighed down by gold!'

'Ah, *Dr Convex!* …'

Sam looked puzzled.

'… That's how Ned and the others speak of him – not very kind, is it?'

'I think Joshua would wear it as a badge of honour! The man is a buoyant individual – he floats on a veritable lake of money.'

'Wealthy? Not a Doctor of Divinity, I hope?'

'No, medicine is his practice … He's a *pox-doctor.*'

Will looked puzzled:

'And does that bring him great wealth?'

'It most surely does – when you think how generous his clients can be … Believe me, Dr Wakefield knows more awkward secrets of the great and good of this metropolis than anyone … Let us say, he has a healthy income …'

'I suspect he has taken payment from Vandernan's tonight! – Isaac suspected that the dice at his table were co-operative.'

'Oh yes – if he knew which way the bias was, it could prove very profitable … and that, my dear Will – thanks to your little cubes of ivory – is how we ourselves are going to play. You recall your instruction in the business?'

'You say they are *high fulhams*, biased to 4, 5, and 6 – and thus favouring casts of eight to twelve. It couldn't be simpler!'

This was met with a sigh and a shake of the head:

'Those are not the words I want to hear, Will. *Nothing* is simple! Things can go awry – and you can be sure at some point they will. But the mathematics will prevail in the end … Remember! Patience, observation, and calculation are the watchwords.'

'And our agreed signals?'

'Yes. We may not need all of them – but you must stay sharp. And be careful with your stakes – not to draw any sudden attention. Over-confidence can look suspicious. Steady and quiet – at least for a while.'

'And if I look confused and unsteady, it is for a reason.'

'Of course – but in moderation. No falling over or spewing up! Avoid the theatrical at any cost.'

'Have no fear, Sam – I've just left some of my guts in the chamber-pot. I was hoping to clear my head.'

There was a sudden shout from one of the tables. Oaths inappropriate for the sabbath were being delivered. Will and Sam stepped out of the bay in time to see an agitated gamester on his feet fling the box across the table. Attempts were being made to pacify him and prevent his hands from doing any further damage. It was clear that drink had been taken.

That was when Will noticed a familiar figure descending the steps from the card-room. He nudged Sam's elbow:

'Look! – Do you know that man? He was the one I heard talking with Lord Parham about *The Honourable Adventure* and the inflammable air subscription.'

'Now that is curious!' said Sam. 'I wonder what his part is to be? The gentleman in question has considerable resources – no mere dabbler in stocks! That is Philip Roscoe – one of the Directors of the Bank.'

'The Bank of England?'

'The same, yes … It makes me ask if he is interested in the scheme in a private capacity, or …'

'Or is involving the Bank in the business? Surely not?'

'I wouldn't be so sure. If any man is part of the *system*, it is he!'

'But he looks so commonplace – I took him for a stock-jobber.'

'No, Will. Such a man does not need to wear plumage.'

Will gave an intake of breath. He had just recalled something else:

'And it was he who spoke to Parham of his friend "Captain Hazard" – how he was looking forward to encountering him ...'

'Well, I think we both know what that means?'

'... That Mr Roscoe expects to receive a generous premium tonight – and that the dice will favour him ...'

Sam nodded. Will at once saw the complication:

'... So – is this to be a battle between us? A duel of the dice?'

'It will certainly add to the entertainment! We must be more than ever vigilant ...'

Sam's face lit up at the thought.

'... I think it is time we re-joined the tables, Will. Let us see if we cannot give Mr Roscoe a bumpy ride!'

The first thing Will noticed was Sir Charles Norreys standing by the far wall. The Commissioner was well positioned to overlook the activity in the room, and his arrival suggested he had an interest in the goings-on.

The session began with tips to the box-keeper (always recommended), who handed the box to the first caster – a Mr Fleming. This gentleman with shining face and pinprick eyes was one of the songsters who had entertained the room a few minutes earlier. Now he clearly meant business. He removed his coat to reveal a richly embroidered waistcoat that might have done service at a birthnight ball. The cream silk woven with flowers and butterflies took every eye, and the distraction was increased by the lace cuffs that hung down from his wrists. The contrast with the no-nonsense worsted of Mr Roscoe who sat to his left was striking. Will looked further round the table. The impoverished Ned Wilder had retired from the scene, leaving Humfrey Corbet and Isaac Ward to continue with play. Humfrey was to be the setter. Another of the songsters – a Mr Nolley – was peering into a mirrored snuffbox not much larger than the ruby ring adorning his finger. The ring alone would cover a substantial debt! Will knew he was surrounded by money. Suddenly his forty-three pounds – more than an attorney's clerk might earn in a year – seemed a paltry sum. But who knew what might grow from it? He gave a shiver of anticipation.

Mr Fleming called a main of seven and staked a golden guinea.

Play began with a ritual first shake of the box. On this occasion it had an ominous sound, and for the first time Will was put in mind of bones rattling in a coffin. Not a portent, he hoped.

The dice settled to show a three and a two – a five was therefore Mr Fleming's chance. Will remained still and observant, but Sam immediately staked a modest half crown, almost surreptitiously as if dipping a toe in the water. Without hesitation Mr Roscoe extended his brown woollen arm and left a five-guinea piece. The odds were three to two, but Mr Fleming didn't add to his stake, and his face was expressionless as he shook the box again …

A four and a one – the chance! At the very first cast Mr Roscoe's side-bet had been rewarded. Will looked for a glimmer of pleasure, but the man's features were impassive; he did, however, glimpse a flicker in Sam's eyes – should it tell him something? Fleming looked a little disappointed as if he had missed an opportunity. Humfrey, the setter, muttered to himself, wishing he hadn't assumed the bank so eagerly.

For his next cast Fleming found more confidence, and with the main still seven, he staked a two-guinea piece. His lace cuffs swayed, and the dice rolled …

A pair of ones – ames-ace!

Humfrey appropriated the two guineas a little too eagerly as Fleming gave a dignified sniff. Will looked across the table at Sam and sensed his mind working.

The next cast brought Fleming another chance of five. At once, Roscoe pushed five guineas forward; Sam, with a nicely calculated pause as if he were debating the matter, followed with a hesitant two guineas. Seeing this, Will staked a guinea of his own.

The next two casts were indeterminate, but at the third cast the dice showed a three and a two. The chance. Will had won again.

He sensed that something was happening and wondered whether to sit quietly and observe or continue with the side-bets. He was uneasy about following Sam's lead too often. In the end he chose his moments carefully, and after a further ten minutes he found himself only two pounds sterling in deficit from his original fifty.

At each call of a main Will had been glancing at Sam. Given what he knew of Mr Roscoe's expectations he had been observing the dice closely, looking for a pattern. It wasn't dramatic or obvious, but it was becoming clear that the lower numbers were being favoured. And at that moment, out of the corner of his eye, he saw Sam raise a finger to his left temple and give it a little rub.

A sign. Yes, Sam evidently thought the same. It signalled that the dice were *low* fulhams. A moment later Sam placed his hand on one of the golden guineas in front of him, tapping it with his finger. *Take care*, it said – *keep it steady*.

As the minutes passed, their suspicions were confirmed. Sam had been right. The tendency would be scarcely noticeable in normal play; but they were alert to the possibility of loaded dice, and Mr Roscoe's actions left little doubt: he was more confident in betting on fours, fives and sixes rather than higher numbers.

The test came when Roscoe became the caster. He promptly declared five as his main, and within only a few casts he had flung it three times. Poor Humfrey was badly holed and taking water fast. In the battle between the bankers, the might of the Bank of England was supreme.

Mr Roscoe's stakes rose as his winnings mounted, and Will began to detect a hint of smug satisfaction in the man's movements – the easy loll back in his chair as he surveyed the action; his unhurried breathing; above all, the way he caressed the box as if it were a soft willing hand.

Both Sam and Will were able to benefit from their knowledge – but discreetly. Sam would make a fortunate gain, then Will would strike a lucky chance. Sometimes both of them won together. When his time to cast came, Will stuck with his main of seven and flung it twice; but chances of five and six were profitable too. Sam was bolder and followed Roscoe with a main of five. He flung it three times. Suspicions might have been raised, but Sam's expressions of surprise were entirely convincing, and Will's slightly bleary devotion to the glass of wine at his elbow didn't suggest a mind making careful calculations – the young man was simply riding a lucky streak.

Mr Roscoe's stakes became even bolder as his assurance grew, and after half an hour of play he was in profit by some five hundred pounds. As the banker, Humfrey was managing to hold on by his fingertips, and had not Mr Nolley been playing with such all-or-nothing recklessness he would have sunk entirely. Sam was showing a gain of a hundred and ten; and Will – who was by now struggling to remain composed – was up by no less than eighty-five.

The arrival of Lord Parham on the scene added to Will's apprehensions; but His Lordship's half-smile as he watched the game suggested he was more than happy with the conduct of things. His glances toward Sir Charles Norreys were eloquent. Will longed to wipe the look of satisfaction from their faces, and spontaneously his left hand reached down into his coat pocket. The twins were there! – the two little ivory dice with their pips of lapis lazuli – the *high* fulhams! The game had been going well enough without them, but what might he achieve *with* them?

He felt a surge of contempt for Vandernan's, with its sham conviviality, its false friendships, the tricks and cheats that were ingrained in it. He took a good sip of his wine and felt ready for the challenge – not pausing to question his own duplicity.

Will was the next to cast. He was now determined to give the loaded dice a run – if only he could make the substitution. But he must be patient, and the game had to continue. His first cast lost him a guinea; but he won it back with his second. He took note that once again Mr Roscoe was the greater beneficiary, and he began to resent how the man, with his judicious side-bets, was leeching on others' success. The thought of frustrating him was too good to resist.

It seemed unlikely that Will would be able to exchange dice during play – the table was full of watchful people. He knew, however, that to do so in mid-session would have the greatest effect and allay suspicions; but how might it be done? Anything *theatrical* (dread word) had been prohibited by Sam, and he did not have the conjuring skills of a Robert LeRoy. Should he spill his drink? Have a fit of coughing and drop them? … The idea was ludicrous – fairground stuff! – and he would doubtless end up scrabbling on the floor on his hands and knees.

But Will was forgetting that human life is not always directed by choice and will. His namesake did not have everything its own way. At this critical moment in the game, he was unaware of another resource to hand. He had not allowed for the intervention in human affairs of *Opportunity*.

Chapter Twenty-One

⊸⊷⊶⊷⊷

THE GODDESS TOOK the form of Lady Rastell, who chose that moment to appear in full panoply at the head of the stairs. Her resonant voice hailed Lord Parham, who at once stepped forward to acknowledge her. Around the table all eyes lifted and heads turned, except for Will's, and in an instant the dice in his pocket found themselves in the casting-box. Those two little dice which had been on a dark journey in recent days were now back where they belonged, keeping their secret to themselves.

The eighth place at the table was Lady Rastell's, and she eagerly settled herself by Sam's side. The two of them nodded acquaintance, and Will was poised to continue. She glanced round the table at the circle of men and bestowed a condescending smile on them all:

'I trust the dice are fair and generous tonight, gentlemen?' she said, smoothing over the contradiction and placing a silk bag in front of her. There was unanimity of silence, which seemed to reassure her.

Will scratched his right temple for a moment while he thought, then pushed a golden guinea uneasily forward. A rattling sound filled the air.

'Seven!' he declared, and immediately flung the dice. The game was under way again.

A three and a six gave him a chance of nine.

'Three to two!' came the voice of Humfrey.

Will staked a second guinea, and this was matched by Lady Rastell's five guineas. She shot him an enquiring glance.

The others were still, except for Mr Nolley, who unhesitatingly staked a five guinea-piece himself, and Isaac Ward who risked a couple of crowns. Mr Roscoe, statue-like, held his peace.

Will flung the dice again.

A five and a four showed. The chance. Short and sweet. And profitable!

Will's slight giggle of surprise was accompanied by a low murmur of pleasure from Lady Rastell. He took his four pounds gratefully, leaving a guinea behind as the next stake. Mr Roscoe was imperturbable.

Continuing with a main of seven, Will threw once more. This time the dice settled to a four. A low chance this time.

'Two to one!' declared Humfrey.

Will paused as the bets came in. Sam staked only a crown, Mr Nolley another five-guinea piece. Mr Roscoe hazarded a full ten guineas and settled back in his chair. Will made a quick decision: he didn't want to arouse suspicion, and so staked a further two crowns. Lady Rastell didn't stir.

Will shook the box hard, and cast an eight.

Muttering to himself, he gathered up the dice and threw again, this time untidily. One of the dice was a three, and the second – once Mr Fleming had lifted his lace cuff – showed a four. The main of seven! Will had lost. But so too had Mr Roscoe, who shifted in his chair and eyed his neighbour's flamboyant arm with annoyance. Humfrey accepted his winnings with a barely muffled whoop of delight.

Mr Roscoe didn't know it yet, but this throw set a different pattern for the game. He was prepared for setbacks, and there was the usual alternation of ups and downs – but now slightly more of the latter, especially when he staked boldly. As the minutes rolled by, Mr Roscoe's substantial profits diminished, and he began to question his strategy. His body stiffened. He became more attentive. Slowly and surreptitiously, however, Will's high fulhams were asserting themselves. The easy flow of the game found a different channel, and mathematical probabilities began to have their inexorable effect. The box moved from one caster to the next, but the expected pattern failed to form.

At one moment, Will caught Mr Roscoe directing an inquiring look at Sir Charles Norreys, who had walked up to the table to see how all was progressing.

If the banker was finding his funds melting away, the credit of both Sam and Will – evidently much to their surprise – was moving in the opposite direction. Lady Rastell, by her judicious side-betting, was also showing a good profit. Mr Roscoe's frustrations grew, and the mood of the table began to change.

The crisis came when Roscoe was the caster once again. Persisting with the lowest main of five, he continued to have no luck with the initial cast and became convinced that the higher mains were being favoured. It made no sense, but it was the only rational explanation. All was not as it should be, and the banker took it as a personal affront. A face hitherto serene was growing creased and thunderous. No-one else appeared to be troubled by this, but the grunts and growls from Mr Roscoe were beginning to be noticed.

In some desperation he felt that decisive action was needed, and so he reverted to the more conventional main of seven and staked a defiant ten guineas – only to find, with his very first cast, that a three and a two were looking up at him. The dice were mocking him! An expletive flew from his lips, tight though they were, and there was a ripple of laughter round the table. One of the joys of hazard was the fickleness of Providence, and this cast seemed to carry a message for the hitherto favoured banker. The gods had turned on their chosen.

But perhaps not? A chance of five offered itself – the lowest possible. Determined to take advantage, Mr Roscoe pushed forward a veritable hoard of fifty guineas. His colour was rising. Everyone else at the table swallowed hard, their minds working – except for Mr Nolley, who broke off from taking a pinch of snuff to stake five guineas. Eyes turned toward Lady Rastell, who was toying with a five-guinea piece herself. But after a couple of seconds, with a shake of her head, she withdrew her hand. Will – as a gesture of wicked sympathy – laid down a crown.

The table was silent as Mr Roscoe began to cast. He shook the dice firmly and seemed to be muttering some sort of incantation.

Eight – then a ten – and then … a seven. The main! A six and a one. There they were! He had indisputably lost.

His response was a far from gracious one. He threw down the cup.

'Enough of this! I demand the dice be changed! Norreys? We must have new dice!'

Sir Charles stood there, highly embarrassed and a little baffled at what was happening. He too had noticed the slight shift in the play but could find no explanation, except that Chance had momentarily gone against them. But Mr Roscoe's demand was powerfully made.

'Of course, Mr Roscoe! Vandernan's is entitled to substitute the dice at any time. I can assure you these are our own dice – no imposition! But Mr Jennings will happily change them for you.'

There was some fuss being made as the box-keeper took up his wallet and searched for a fresh pair of dice. He looked at Sir Charles, who stopped him:

'I shall take those!' he said, indicating Will's high fulhams. 'You may use these in their place, gentlemen! …'

The Commissioner's hand went to the pocket of his waistcoat, and he drew out new dice.

'... On my honour, Mr Roscoe – I think you will find these entirely satisfactory.'

There was no gainsaying that. He accepted them gratefully.

During all this commotion, Lady Rastell had risen to her feet:

'I think I shall retire, Sir Charles – Lord Parham – I have had a memorable visit tonight, have I not, gentlemen? As always, Vandernan's entertainment has been unmatched!'

She took up her bag, which was now heavier by forty pounds sterling. Seizing the moment, Will stood up also:

'I think time calls for me too. Thank you, friends!'

He moved unsteadily away from the table, leaving Sam to continue playing with the others. He had taken only a couple of strides when he heard a warm female voice:

'Thank you, Mr Lundy!'

He turned. Lady Rastell was smiling on him. She knew his name.

'Your Ladyship!' said Will, 'I cannot think you have anything to thank me for. You owe it all to yourself. Your play was most judicious.'

'But that is thanks to you, Mr Lundy ... Let us sit for a moment – in the card-room I suggest. We cannot talk here.'

Upstairs had become a little quieter during Lady Rastell's absence. The drama of basset was over, though a lively game of ombre was in progress at one of the tables, and four gentlemen were deep in whist at the other. They seated themselves on what Will now thought of as Mr Colleoni's couch, and he watched as she settled herself, adjusting the interlinked silver chains around her neck. Her opal earrings swayed and glimmered in the candlelight. Will began to think he had moved from one hazard to another.

But Her Ladyship was entirely calm:

'When I first join a gaming-table, Mr Lundy, I find it wise to begin by following in the steps of the caster. It is possible he knows something I do not …'

There was a glint in her eye.

'… Before I descended the stairs tonight, I had a vantage-point over the room. And while everybody – save one – was looking at me … I, Mr Lundy, was looking at you …'

Will went cold.

'… I have to say you were admirably *deft* – most quick-fingered! – and so I decided to take your lead and trust my fortunes to you …'

In her face were the stirrings of an ironic smile – but also something more. She looked down at her lap on which the bag of coin heavily rested.

'… As you can see, you have not done badly by me.'

Will was hesitant:

'I have done exceedingly well by myself, Lady Rastell – one hundred and ninety pounds. Unimagined wealth! … But in my case it is ill-gotten – as it seems you know. I cannot ascribe it to skill or chance – not even to a novice's luck! It is a cheat.'

'That is no cause for shame in this place! …'

She waved a jewelled hand toward the room.

'… In Vandernan's you leave scruples at the door … But you have been well instructed, have you not? Mr Rivers hinted to me that you are here not to try your fortune – but that something more has prompted you.'

By this stage of the night, Will was longing to be open and honest. He was finding the endless deception exhausting. But he couldn't dispel the thought that within these walls, and among these people, the truth could be dangerous:

'You are right, Lady Rastell – I am not here for myself, but to help a friend. It is not a story I can tell – but it involves someone

I think you know – *knew* ...'

He corrected himself, embarrassed. His voice had sunk almost to a whisper.

'... George Sturgis.'

'Ah! ...'

The syllable was spoken with a mixture of sadness and acceptance. There was no surprise in her voice, but it was accompanied by a look of curiosity.

'... I shan't ask how you know this, Mr Lundy – we both have our discretions! Safe to say, George's death shocked me ... but it did not surprise me. Do you understand? I cannot say more than that.'

The distinction was revealing – this was no hostile witness, and she spoke low. Her private voice was a quiet one.

Will didn't choose his next words – they just slipped out. But they emerged kindly:

'Who killed him, Lady Rastell?'

There was a slight pause. The question did not unsettle her. She was thinking:

'It wasn't a gamester's quarrel, Mr Lundy, I am sure of that – whatever the appearance. No, it was somebody powerful – somebody *with* power. George seldom spoke of it, but he had a larger life. He mingled with the Great in a secretive way – City people, money-men! I know something of them, and they are never to be trusted. He could be a foolish boaster, but about such things he said little. The last time I saw him, there was an air of desperation about him.'

'When was that?'

'Just two days before he died. He had been down in 'Change Alley – for what purpose I know not. George was always free with his money – perhaps he was indebted to someone? But I would think it unlikely. His credit was good. But there was something preying on his mind.'

'And what about Vandernan's? This place was his haunt, was it not? Did anyone here wish him ill?'

Lady Rastell was looking a little uneasy at the questioning, which was becoming persistent:

'I couldn't say, Mr Lundy. Is that why you have come here? You think the answer is in this place? I told you, I cannot believe it was a gamester's quarrel ...'

She broke off.

'... Ah, I see! You understand more than I allow ... Yes of course, Vandernan's is more than a gaming-house – I think we both know that. It is a place of business too. You were witness to my encounter with Jack Beech tonight, were you not? ... *His* business is a thriving one ...'

Will could think of nothing to say. Her Ladyship, however, was becoming fluent.

'... This is something of a thieves' den, and Sunday night is its trading hour. There was a committee met here this evening. You must ask me nothing about it – but you may wonder why the bankers and the money-men are in tonight. Are accounts being settled, perhaps? I merely conjecture! ... But if you wish to explain George's death – if that is your intention – then Vandernan's has been a good place to start ...'

Lady Rastell stopped in her tracks, surprised by her own volubility. She stirred herself.

'... You intend to wait for your friend Mr Rivers, do you not? ... I quite understand! ... But I'm sure we shall meet again under other circumstances.'

Will felt a warm pressure on his hand. He choked slightly, baffled by his hesitancy, which he hoped wasn't being read as sullenness. Away from the table, he was fighting off the effects of the wine:

'I'm sorry, Lady Rastell – you must think me ungrateful. But there is more to do tonight.'

'Then you must do it!' she said with a knowing smile. 'I wish you and your friend success – I do, heartily ...'

She rose quickly and turned to go. But then stopped.

'... I am sure money is at the heart of this, Mr Lundy. In these times it speaks more eloquently than religion does. The Bible can be so naïve:

Wealth gotten by vanity shall diminish – but he that gathereth by labour shall increase ...

Pah! What innocence! We know better, do we not?'

She lifted her bag and shook it, then briskly walked away, leaving him standing by the couch feeling awkward and impolite. A very assured woman, he thought – and an encouraging one! – though his own courage at that moment was faltering. Will didn't quite know where he was. He felt the weight of coin pulling him to earth, and yet his head was light – his heart too when he thought of the riches he was now master of ... As for Lady Rastell's revelations, he needed to consider what she had told him – and perhaps hadn't told him.

Lingering in the card-room, he took another glass of wine and overlooked the ombre for a while, pondering the tangles of human life.

Finally, he stirred himself and decided to face the hazard-room again. Sam hadn't appeared. He told himself he would not rejoin the table – but he was curious to see the state of play.

Down in the hazard-room things had come to a pause, and Sam was chatting to Isaac Ward. On the near side of the table, a few feet away, Philip Roscoe was gathering up his winnings. Not surprisingly, the banker's fortunes had markedly improved since the replacement of the dice, and it was the confident and assured Director of the Bank of England who was settling his account with Humfrey Corbet, who as setter had borne the brunt of

Mr Roscoe's success. Sounds of agitation were coming from the young man, who was pleading with his implacable creditor. Humfrey was finding it hard to cover his losses, and Mr Roscoe was standing over him in some impatience. Will watched the scene play out, feeling a little sorry for the templar.

Humfrey reached into a side pocket of his waistcoat:

'But I have a note here – for four hundred …'

Mr Roscoe brightened a little as Humfrey handed it over, expecting a Bank of England note. Even a Sword Blade note would in the circumstances be acceptable. But this! His eyes ran over the paper. It was a promissory note for four hundred pounds – yes indeed – but the beneficiary's name made him shiver … George Sturgis! He looked for the signatory …

'Mary Trotter? …'

The words were spoken with disdain. He glowered at Humfrey.

'… No, no! This thing will not do at all – I cannot make use of it. You will have to make arrangements with Vandernan's – or your own bank.'

'But the note is legal tender …'

'That may be so, given the new Act – but I am quite at liberty to refuse it. I think you will find that others will also. I would not accept this, even for a hundred!'

Will gazed in amazement. To hear the name 'Mary Trotter' coming from the lips of Mr Roscoe was startling enough – but to see the promissory note itself, there in Humfrey's hands, made him shudder. Widow Trotter's debt – and the fate of the Bay-Tree – was within reach. Will's mind worked quickly. How had Humfrey procured the note – and from whom? And what should he do? This was Opportunity indeed – and one he couldn't allow to slip by.

Chapter Twenty-Two

A DISCONSOLATE HUMFREY Corbet was folding his note away when Will put an arm round his shoulder.

'Counting your losses, Humfrey, poor fellow?'

'It's been a punishing night, Will. The setter had a bad time of it, did he not? I was looking to make a tidy sum ... You were in high favour!'

'Sheer luck, Humfrey. Dame Fortune was indulging me! My turn for the lash will come ... Our Mr Roscoe thinks winning is his privilege.'

Humfrey looked toward the banker:

'Yes, a gentleman who could buy this place and half the people in it – and yet he cannot negotiate a promissory note. The man questions my credit!'

It was said with ill-disguised anger. In response Will swayed slightly, and grinned:

'Tut, Humfrey! Credit isn't everything. A man is ... worth what he's worth ...'

Will's words didn't make sense, but they were offered as a deep truth.

'... That note of yours – I think I heard a familiar name ...'

Humfrey looked puzzled.

'... On your note – *Mary Trotter* – is that right?'

'Yes – Do you know her? Who is she? And why is she indebted to George Sturgis? I know the man is dead, but the note has currency still ... but Roscoe thinks it beneath him.'

'Perhaps he's afraid to put himself in a dead man's shoes?'

He gave an accompanying shiver. Humfrey persisted:

'Who is this Trotter?'

'The hostess of the Bay-Tree – not far from here.'

'The chocolate house? Pah!! ... What is *her* credit I wonder? Roscoe seems to think it's naught – and the *Sword Blade* too! ... Not the sweetest words to a Bank of England man.'

'How much is the note for? Let me look at it.'

'Four hundred.'

Humfrey unfolded it and handed it to Will.

'Yes, it's her signature ... She's a worthy lady – but not I think worth this amount. But who knows? I'd be willing to take the risk.'

'What do you mean?'

'I have one hundred and ninety in coin ... What do you say?'

Will's grin had widened.

'No, Mr Lundy.'

'Gold and sterling silver, Humfrey! Real money in your pocket – not flimsy paper!'

'But the note is for four hundred.'

'You heard what Mr Roscoe said. A note is worth only what can be negotiated ... How did the thing come into your hands?'

It was an important question and Will tried to sound casual. But Humfrey bridled at the directness of it:

'Legitimately, I assure you! My Vandernan's account was settled earlier this evening, and this was owed me.'

Will looked down at the paper:

'A handsome settlement – but not in coin.'

Humfrey looked slightly awkward:

'It has currency, Mr Lundy. You can be assured of that. I shall not let it go for less than four hundred.'

He looked closely at Will and saw a young man who was the worse for drink and seemed remarkably free with his winnings. It gave him an idea …

Will in turn caught the slight sparkle of interest in Humfrey's eyes, and it was he who spoke first:

'Well then, Humfrey, let's cast for it. *A full four hundred!* If that is what you reckon the note is worth, then you'll accept the challenge. I'll match the sum! An even chance – your note against my coin. Ha?'

'An even bet, you say?'

'Assuredly! … What about *odd or even?*'

Humfrey tried to work his mind into position. He felt there was something very wrong. Why would anyone stake coin against paper – at even money?

'But surely, *even* would be favoured by the higher numbers, Mr Lundy, would it not? Four and six? *Odd* by the lower – one and three. How can I be sure the dice are sound?'

'I must defer to you on that, Humfrey – I have no idea about such things …'

Will hesitated – then resolved himself. He gave a little laugh.

'… What do you say we cast for *one* and *six* – the highest number and the lowest?'

Humfrey was looking doubtful:

'But how would that work? What about the other numbers? The objection is the same.'

'No – I mean, if I cast for *one* and *six* – highest and lowest, and you cast for …'

Will paused. He swayed slightly and his eyes nearly closed.

'… I'm sorry – I'm confused now.'

Humfrey looked at the sleepy and muddled young man and thought it would be foolish not to seize what was on offer:

'Yes, Will – you cast for one or six, and I'll cast for the other numbers. You win when one or six are shown – and I the rest.'

Will lifted his head and displayed a damp furrowed brow to his adversary. There was an uncomfortable pause.

'Very well, Humfrey ... But how do we decide?'

'Fifty casts, shall we say? My note for four hundred against your coin.'

Will gave a heavy nod:

'But someone must adjudicate ... Mr Rivers!'

He shouted over to Sam, who was hovering nearby. Sam walked over, looking curious about what Will was up to. Humfrey happily explained their idea, but was distinctly annoyed when a glowering Sam at once took issue with the plan and attempted to explain the odds:

'Do you not see, Will?' said Sam. 'You have only six and one – but Mr Corbet has two, three, four, and five. That cannot be right! That is no even chance.'

But Will was insistent, and there was an angry edge to his voice:

'You must let me play my own game, Mr Rivers! Do you not see? I feel lucky tonight. I know Fortune is with me!'

Sam was looking furious and shaking his head. 'Then you're a fool! But so be it. Throw away all you have won – and more – for a mere piece of paper!'

'I think Mr Lundy has decided,' said Humfrey firmly.

And so, the challenge was accepted. The dice were procured from the box-keeper, and the three of them sat down at a small side-table away from the others. None of them wanted to be in a circle of curious onlookers. As for the game, nothing could be simpler. Fifty casts. No choice, no strategy, no decisions. They were entirely in the hands of the dice and whatever force they imagined might be directing them –Chance, Fate, Fortune,

Providence – they could take their pick. Probability might be a reassuring guide through life, but Accident always had a say too.

Humfrey was trying not to feel sorry for Will. He knew he was about to take advantage of the fellow's inexperience and his tipsy state – but if the young man had set his mind on that document, then the more fool him. Why should he quarrel? …

As for Will, he couldn't take his eyes off the note. It was there on the table before him, with Mrs Trotter's signature at the bottom. An inoffensive bit of paper, fragile and yet so very powerful. Her fate, and the fate of her beloved Bay-Tree, were determined in those few scratched words – a promise which, not unlike a death warrant, had a terrible closure. He imagined seizing hold of the thing, ripping it to shreds, and flinging it in the flames – but that could not be. Opportunity had once again given him an invitation, and he knew he had to take it. There was also something wonderfully exhilarating in placing yourself in the hands of Chance.

Nothing Will could do would alter the outcome, and so he invited a slightly surprised Humfrey to do the casting himself, declaring that he would simply watch. Alongside them, Sam kept the score, glowering with obvious disapproval. There would be fifty casts. Will would win the throw when one of the dice showed a six or a one …

Five and two was the first throw; and the second was three and four. Then six and one. That seemed to be the message, Humfrey thought: all six numbers, and Will was already behind, two to one! Those seemed to be the right odds. He cast again with a light heart: two and two. Even better! Will shivered slightly but tried not to show his discomfort. Sam's teeth clenched and he marked his paper three to one in favour of Humfrey.

The fifth cast was two and one, and the next five and one. They were now even. Humfrey took up the dice with a little less confidence and gave the box a thorough shake. Two and two again. Then five and four. He became easier – probability appeared to be reasserting itself. Ahead five to three … But then he threw one and one, followed by six and three … They were even again, five casts each!

Sam himself was becoming gripped by the game. An audience would have been buzzing.

Humfrey continued to throw. Three and five – three and three – four and four … He was breathing easier now, although he felt perspiration tickling his neck. He was well ahead, eight casts to five. The way was becoming clearer.

Will's thoughts, however, were on the ending of his dreams of wealth and the loss of the Bay-Tree – a double blow but felt as one … and what would happen when word of his recklessness reached his father? … Doubts were rising above him like a thundercloud. He reminded himself to breathe.

But the little ivory dice continued to play their own game, oblivious of any human consideration.

Two and one – three and one – four and one – two and one – four and one … It was a pattern, a rhythm. However hard Humfrey shook the box, the pips of lapis lazuli seemed to be mocking him. He paused and looked at Will with a mixture of disbelief and fear in his eyes. This was not happening. He was two throws down.

Will said nothing in response. For all three of them it seemed unwise to interrupt the silent dance of the dice.

They continued. Two and three – five and four – five and four again – three and three – three and two. It was an intricate minuet. When would the turn come – if at all? Sam marked the score: thirteen to ten in Humfrey's favour.

Two more casts, and it was fourteen to eleven – the mid-way point. Will was having to face the possibility of disaster.

Five and one – three and one – five and six – six and five … if the Fates were indeed dictating this, then they were amusing themselves. Will was puzzled why his mind was reading the random numbers as a pattern, as if a silent message were being conveyed. Fifteen to fourteen in his favour.

Then, four and five showed.

So, twenty casts remained, and the gods had made all even again. Will was shocked he could even think in those terms …

Sam whispered that the accounts were balanced, causing Humfrey to pause in his casting. The young man was about to speak, but checked himself, not daring to break the spell. He too felt there were presences not to be offended.

Four more throws, and the totals were still level. Sixteen throws were left. By this time Humfrey was having to acknowledge that something was not right. The castings were not going as they should. But where did the blame lie? In the dice? His arm? His calculations? Probability itself? Perhaps he had been mistaken and it was indeed an even chance? He stopped himself from pursuing the thought. He must press on to the end.

Three and one – four and one – five and four – six and six – four and three … Eleven casts remained, and it all was in the balance, twenty to nineteen in Will's favour. Both young men were aware how much hung on this, but each was trying not to think the thought, lest it should realise their fear. Will needed six more casts to favour him.

One and five – one and five again! – six and two – one and six – five and four – three and two – one and six … … … . six and three.

Will had to stop himself from shouting out. Sam looked up from his notes and couldn't suppress a smile:

'You have done it, Mr Lundy! As it stands, twenty-six casts are in your favour.'

Humfrey said nothing, but slumped in his chair, disbelieving. Then, as if protesting at the gods, he hunched forward and with rapid motion continued to cast ... but the same unrelenting pattern was confirmed. One throw was his, the other two Will's. Twenty-two lost to twenty-eight.

At that moment Will longed to run over to the fire and make his final cast of the night. It would be thrilling to see Mrs Trotter's promissory note consumed in the flames. But he knew he should present it to her so they could watch her immolate the thing herself, with her own hands, in the grate of the Bay-Tree. The chocolate house was saved! Will's chest was swelling in victory, but he checked himself and took Humfrey's hand. He knew the young man's devastation.

'It was not meant to be, Will!' said Humfrey. 'I have been the biggest fool. I should have taken your offer, should I not?'

He slipped away, the commiserations simply confirming his humiliation.

A few seconds later, with the coast now clear, Will and Sam burst into radiant smiles and seized each other's hand:

'Will! What can I say? A triumph! Thank God for mathematics, eh?

'Thank God for Mr Huygens.'

'Ah yes, you remembered. The perfect pupil!'

'It struck me forcibly at the time, and I still cannot credit it. After all, there are but two aces and two sixes, yet the caster has two fives, two fours, two threes, and two deuces – how can that work out?'

'Well it does, Will – as you have shown. The odds in your favour were five to four. That is what Huygens says. And what was your score? Twenty-eight to twenty-two! You have been an illustration of a profound mathematical truth!'

'No, a mystery, Sam. My brain will never work it out.'

'*The Laws of Chance*. Don't you feel it strange that something so random as casting dice can be subject to law. We live in a world of numbers, Will. Your hopes and prayers were answered by Mr Huygens – not by God.'

'So, no Providence – just mathematics?'

'In sum, yes.'

The two of them laughed and went off to find some wine. Will's mind was still wondering at what had just happened. But the computing of numbers faded away, to be replaced by the picture of the joy on Widow Trotter's face when he returned to the chocolate house carrying the note. The nightmare was over for her! And in addition, unbelievably, a small fortune was weighing down his own pockets. He would have danced for joy had he been light enough. He smiled to himself. His mission was accomplished. All had worked out for the best.

Chapter Twenty-Three

A DISTANT THUD and a sudden cry told them something was wrong. The gamesters in the hazard-room looked up in alarm. The dice-box was set down on the table and questioning eyes met other eyes. What was happening? … Another thud, a brittle crash, and frantic shouts emanating from the card-room confirmed their fears. At once chairs scraped on the stone floor as men jumped to their feet, hurriedly stuffing coins and papers into their pockets. One or two of them ran up the steps to join what was sounding like a riot. Raucous threats and screams of defiance filled the air. A gang of men wielding staves and clubs were pouring into Vandernan's, urged on by a figure in a cocked hat who barked orders and waved a quarter-staff toward the gaming tables like an angry prophet:

'There's your man! Take him!'

The man in question was a startled Jack Beech, who kicked back his chair and swung round to face them. He drew his pistol, but they were on him before he could cock it, pinioning his arms by his side. Blows rained down as he tried to fling them off. Not content to be observers, other gamesters were pitching in, and within moments there was a general mêlée with fists flying and heads cracking.

Then, from a far doorway a ghost-like figure appeared. It

was Sir Charles Norreys, his face chalk-white, his mouth open in bafflement and outrage:

'Stop this!' he cried from a tight throat. 'Stop this at once!'

But his words were lost in the hubbub. One of the card-tables was flung onto its side as men wrestled each other, their feet sliding on a carpet of playing-cards. Chairs were kicked over. A stick caught one of the chandeliers, and as it swung, lighted candles were flung to the ground.

Sir Charles was furious:

'Who is in charge? Control your men!'

But the invading force was itself under attack as bottles became weapons and glasses were flung at faces. Swords were out and oaken staff met steel blade.

During the commotion Will and Sam cowered in one of the alcoves, paralysed, not knowing whether to run or stay. But there was no avenue of escape. Occupying the hall entrance, with a grim-looking guard at his shoulder, stood a tall figure who watched the proceedings with icy satisfaction. His lips were moving, but the words he murmured were audible only to himself:

'And the people of the land went into the house of Baal, and brake it down; his altars and his images brake they in pieces!'

With so much movement everywhere, this man's stillness was striking. His eyes scanned the room like a lighthouse commanding a stormy sea, until they came to rest on the alcove where Will and Sam were sitting. Only moments earlier the pair had been re-living their triumph, recalling what they had learned about Vandernan's and its 'system,' and delighting in their dicing success. Now they were caught in this accusing eye-beam and felt dangerously exposed.

'Who is that man looking at you, Will?'

Will knew only too well:

'It's Benjamin Hector, the Magistrate. The man is a hot reformer – the Society for the Reformation of Manners. He knows my father!'

Sam felt the shiver in Will's voice:

'So, this is no mere raiding-party – it is the vengeance of the Lord on the abominations of the heathen! ... '*I will draw out a sword after you: and your land shall be desolate!*'

'Sam! You know your scripture!'

'Ah, Will – I was a believer before I became a sneerer.'

'In my experience it's no great leap ... This means trouble for me, Sam!'

The magisterial stare was interrupted when reinforcements arrived. A constable with a pair of watchmen flexing their staves pushed through towards the fighting. At once Will's eyes brightened:

'It's Constable Cobb! – and Toby Mudge!'

There was a glimmer of hope. Elias was directing his young watchman to the hazard-room. But around him the action was chaotic. The man in the cocked hat had lost his headgear and much of his authority as he scrapped along with the rest. Alongside him, the doorkeeper's fists were flying in all directions. Only Mr Hector and his henchman appeared to command the room. By now Will and Sam were standing in the alcove, backs to the wall. It was clear that the invaders were gaining the upper hand. But a last resistance was continuing. One of the Vandernan's waiters seized the bottle from their table and launched himself at the enemy with a loud battle cry.

Will's mind was busy elsewhere. Thinking of the likely aftermath, he had allowed the low fulhams to fall on the floor behind him. Now he was fingering the promissory note in his pocket – he couldn't risk the thing being found. If only he had burned it when he'd had the chance! Here in the card-room the fireplace was well out of reach or he would have made a run for it. He looked around in desperation, sensing disaster.

In the room all dignity was lost. At that moment a snatched peruque of ample proportions soared through the air and caught itself on one of the chandeliers before coming to land on the floor nearby, followed by a guttering candle. Like a benign planetary conjunction, the two objects came into temporary alignment. A tiny flame began to frizzle the generous curls of human hair.

Without a second thought Will bounded over the table with the note in his hand.

Oblivious to all else, he crouched down and held the corner of the document to the smouldering wig. The flame was precarious, but after a frustrating eternity the paper began to darken and smoke. He tried to keep his hand steady. Never in his life had Time moved so slowly and with such indifference. The violent swirling around him made the unhurried flame seem more leisurely still. His hopes were screaming out with each laborious second.

The large boot which stamped down upon the paper crushed Will's hand too. He gave a cry of pain and despair as he saw the flickering flame die. Towering over him was the Magistrate's burly lieutenant. The man seized Will's collar and jerked him away like a rag doll, while the other hand picked up the still largely intact promissory note:

'Eager to destroy this, were you? ...'

His eyes scanned the document.

'... Mr Hector, Sir – look at this! Here's a name will interest you!'

Will was horror-struck and tried to rise, but the man's tight fist swung him to the side, causing him to turn over on his right ankle. He yelped with pain a second time ... The *name!* He knew what name that must be ... but what of the signature? Did it remain? He went cold and tried to get a glimpse but could see nothing. Part of the paper was burnt away, but very little.

Curiosity made the Covent Garden magistrate bestir himself, and he walked over while his henchman dragged Will to the wall. Now Mr Benjamin Hector was examining the promissory note, his face betraying a look of surprise and satisfaction.

'Well, well … George Sturgis! Now why would you wish to destroy this – Mr *Lundy?* …'

He gave Will an unsettling smile.

'… after all, this is a valuable piece of paper, is it not? Four hundred pounds!'

The word *hundred* was spoken with undisguised relish.

Will could say nothing – his tongue seemed to be filling his mouth. He was still half-lying on the floor, hurt and humiliated. He was about to call on Sam, who was watching from the alcove; but he resolved not to draw his friend to the Magistrate's attention. His glance told him that if the worst happened Sam would be able to report back to the Bay-Tree.

Will was allowed to struggle to his feet, and he found a voice, though not a confident one. He half-muttered:

'The thing is mine to do what I wish with it …'

'Oh! Is that so? … It seems you have been lucky tonight! The *gods* have smiled on you, have they? You have been favoured by that whore, *Fortune?* …'

The sarcasm was mounting.

'… What foul deities have you been worshipping here, Mr Lundy? And on the Sabbath! – a double outrage! What will your father say when he discovers he has spawned a child of Belial? … Not only that, but his son is possessed of a paper picked from a dead man's pocket. That is the case, is it not?'

'I know nothing of that. I won the note.'

'You *won* it? Good fortune indeed! … Then why should you now wish to destroy the paper? – four hundred pounds, no less!'

Will was desperately trying to think like a lawyer, not like a suspected criminal:

'It is a gaming debt, Mr Hector – not mine. I want nothing to do with it! Such things are worthless – a scrap of paper written after a night's debauch. No bank would honour it. This place is full of such stuff. They circulate here like leaves in Autumn.'

Will was attuning his words to Mr Hector's own. The Magistrate lifted the paper close to his face. There was an uncomfortable silence while his eyes moved back and forth across the charred paper like a caterpillar on a leaf. He touched it with his hands, narrowed his eyes further and tilted his neck. His lips began to form silent syllables:

'Hmmmm … A curious document which would seem to tell a story of its own. It needs to be investigated further.'

Mr Hector folded the paper.

'I know nothing of its history, Sir – no doubt the thing has been in many pockets before mine.'

Will knew he was flirting with risk here. The Magistrate opened the paper again and glanced at the contents:

'As notes go, it is a poor thing indeed! I see it is to be drawn on the Sword Blade Company?'

'Yes.'

Mr Hector grunted and gave him an intense stare:

'And from what poor fool did you win this?'

'The gentleman has left – I did not ask his name … but the note may have come into his possession a few hours ago. Such flimsy currency leaves no track behind it.'

The Magistrate's narrowed eyes spoke of his suspicions. Will had often seen that look from the bench – it was a speciality of his father's! But he knew it could betray a hint of admiration for a resourceful witness. He hoped to God that was the case now. He could almost believe he was in court.

The next question was direct and inevitable:

'Then – I ask again – *why* did you attempt to destroy it?'

Will had been preparing for this:

'For a reason you will understand only too well, Mr Hector. I did not wish to be suspected. I thought – rightly it seems – that its possession would raise awkward questions. I discovered this Mr Sturgis was killed in a quarrel just three days ago – and yards only from this place. I had been hoping to pass the thing on as quickly as possible. It is poisonous!'

The Magistrate was gazing into his soul. Will returned the look unblinkingly, refusing to lower his eyes. He was resolved to brazen it out.

'But how … ?'

Before Mr Hector could say more, at that moment a fortunate interruption deflected his attention:

'We have some order now, Sir …'

It was the first constable, standing feet together as if on parade. His hat – badly torn and no longer cocked – was clutched in one hand, and he was pointing across the room with the other.

'… All is ready for you.'

Indeed, behind him the physical violence appeared to have come to an end. A couple of gentlemen were sitting on the floor nursing their wounds, a few sported handcuffs, while others were huddled together beyond the basset table. They had been joined by half a dozen stragglers herded in by Toby Mudge from the cellars. Some were shocked and silent, others were murmuring resentfully. Sam Rivers was now part of the melancholy band, his eyes darting around the room as if searching for an escape route. Will watched them all and thought of Milton's rebel angels.

The Magistrate looked satisfied:

'Do you have your man, Mr Blackett?'

'We do, Mr Hector, Sir – Mr Beech is well secured! … As

for the other gamesters – what do you wish to happen? We have some blood – but no bodies.'

'I would have them searched, and their pockets emptied. Every last coin. Every shred of paper. They will take away no *filthy lucre* from this place! … And, Mr Blackett, …'

The Magistrate's face darkened.

'… An inventory must be kept. Names taken. And tell your men, if I find *any* discrepancy it will be regarded as theft, do you understand? …'

The constable nodded to show he did indeed understand. His look suggested that the very thought appalled him.

'… You may begin with this gentleman, who appears to be weighed down with his sordid gains. It seems he can scarcely stand. I'm sure he'll be glad to be relieved of such a dead weight …'

Will searched for the hint of a smile, but the Magistrate was intent on his business. He turned to walk away, still holding the note. Then he looked back.

'… Your father shall hear of this, Mr Lundy. I advise you to decide what you'll tell him … Speaking for myself, I am disappointed in you …'

He observed the first coins emerging from Will's coat pockets.

'… *Thou shalt not desire the silver or gold that is on them, nor take it unto thee, lest thou be snared therein.*'

It was the voice of the preacher, and it chilled the air.

Mr Hector had taken only a few steps more when his path was blocked by an indignant Sir Charles Norreys demanding to know what was happening. The anger was all the stronger for being suppressed in a half-whisper. Will was eager to hear what was being said, but his attention was distracted by the sight of his recently acquired fortune piling up on the table beside him. Sam's winnings had been even greater, and so he was happy for Will to keep his share. And a fortune it certainly was – a hoard of extremely filthy lucre such as he had never known – or might know again. One hundred and ninety pounds, building up into turrets of gold and silver – his own miniature Byzantium. There was a hollow tugging where his stomach should be.

He tried to listen to the conversation behind his back and caught enough to learn that the incursion was bigger than planned. The constables and their men were to arrest Jack Beech only; but Mr Hector had determined on a more lavish production. Such a blatant polluting of the Sabbath must be punished, and he would seize the opportunity. A posse had been raised from the Society for the Reformation of Manners, who were more than eager to descend on the ungodly.

Sir Charles was protesting – but also issuing threats of his own. Will was astonished to hear him deliver a warning:

'You know the arrangement we have here, Mr Hector. You have exceeded your authority and need to know with whom you are dealing. I assure you it is not just myself!'

Benjamin Hector stood his ground:

'You may have other Justices in your pocket, Sir Charles, but not me.'

There was an electric pause, and then the tone darkened and the volume grew louder. Will knew Sir Charles was forgetting where he was:

'I don't think you understand! If you persist in this, you will open Pandora's box. Believe me, Mr Hector, there are people who will be very unhappy. We have *protection*. I warn you now. You were best take off Jack Beech and leave us be. Do not persist with this!'

'You know I cannot do that, Sir Charles. These men demand the law be upheld. This is no church matter – the law of the land has been breached.'

Will was hoping to hear more, but Constable Blackett was demanding his name and signature. As he signed, he glanced at his pile of treasure – so tall and handsome, but as fleeting as the promissory note in the Magistrate's pocket. He bade his wealth a silent farewell and moved to join the gang of reprobates beginning to empty their own pockets.

Constable Cobb, who had been attending to a waiter with a broken head, stood up and looked around. He was wiping blood off his hands when he saw Will making his way towards him. The usually bright-eyed and confident young man was thoroughly crestfallen, and Elias grasped the awkwardness of the moment. Looks were exchanged but there could be no friendly greeting. There was merely a brief whispered exchange between them.

For his part, Will had judged this wasn't Elias's enterprise, and Elias at once suspected an adventure originating from the Bay-Tree. Their mutual looks seemed to confirm these thoughts:

'I cannot explain, Elias – but I've learnt much in this place.'

'Say nothing – I understand. This is Constable Blackett's business – I insisted on being present. You'll be lucky to escape Bridewell. I'll do what I can.'

And that was all they could manage, but it was enough. Elias had a job to do. Around them, one or two coats were being removed, but other gamesters were beginning to protest loudly. The resentment in the room was mounting.

Will was comforting himself with the thought that in his interrogation the name of 'Mary Trotter' had not been mentioned. Had her signature been obliterated? Was the damaged document now invalid? He could not be certain, but it was the hope he must cling to. He sought out Sam and shared the thought with him. As for their own predicament, they could only commiserate with each other and await the outcome.

As with many negotiations, an agreement was reached that was no more than satisfactory for both parties. Constable Blackett, however, had his villainous highwayman; the reforming

Magistrate gained a few customers for Bridewell, where, while beating hemp with heavy mallets, they would be able to contemplate the evils of gaming and learn to respect the Sabbath; and Sir Charles Norreys secured the immediate release of the more influential of Vandernan's customers. Sam Rivers was not among them.

For some reason – perhaps because of his father – a now penniless Will Lundy was spared correction and allowed to slip away into the night, where he stood, dizzied by the whirl of emotions. The past few hours had been an extraordinary adventure, a test such as he had never known. He tried to begin drawing together some of what he had learned, but it was impossible. It would all have to wait till the morrow. At that moment he was thoroughly exhausted in mind and body. He could only picture his own chamber and bed. He just wanted some peace. Above all, he longed for a place where he might be himself again – if he ever could be.

Monday

25 October 1708

Chapter Twenty-Four

‒‒‒‒

NEWS OF THE overnight events at Vandernan's reached the Bay-Tree early. The intelligence was delivered with the morning milk – and, ten minutes later, with the morning bread. It meant that the place was altogether well provisioned; and in the coffee-room as customers began arriving, the words 'Jack Beech' were breathed in with the aroma of freshly ground beans. His name gave the first coffee of the day an extra smack: 'Jack Beech' raised eyebrows, shook heads, and brought a mixture of smiles and scowls. 'That villain Beech!' could be distinctly heard, but there was also the occasional 'poor Jack!' spoken more quietly.

Soon more news was coming in through the door, and the picture gained some lively details. The raid on the gaming-house began to grow into a full-scale battle between the gamesters and the mob. The place had been wrecked – pistols fired – throats cut – furniture thrown from windows. Those with confident voices were relishing the drama, while others shivered and looked toward the fire.

Widow Trotter's mind, however, was not dwelling on the unfortunate highwayman. The reports of riot and mayhem were deeply troubling – Vandernan's raided on the very night Will was there! Her imagination was rioting too, and she was finding it hard not to think the worst. Part of her wanted to circulate amongst the tables and pick up every snippet, and yet she feared the jumble of fact and fiction that often went for early news. Better to wait until she could trust the messenger! And so, she kept to her station behind the bar and pondered, trying to shut out the snatches of loose talk that reached her ear.

'At least two dead, I assure you!' said a heavily breathing gentleman who had just settled himself at a table, '... a bad business altogether!'

He shook his head and pressed his hat to his chest.

'And one of them the Watch!' said another. 'Is that not so?'

'Aye, like as not. It was a furious fight. They say Jack Beech is sure to follow – his life hangs by a thread!'

'Well, thread or rope – 'tis much the same in the end!'

A flurry of laughter reminded everyone that life would go on.

Widow Trotter heard herself sigh, and the sound disconcerted her. She allowed her eyes to survey the room, if only to reassure herself that the familiar world was still in place. To her left, the fire crackled merrily enough, and hanging above it the old black cauldron was simmering quietly; across the hearth the platoon of silver pots and pewter jugs stood in line ready to serve, watched over by the nearby clock with its solemn ticking that refused to be hurried by anyone or anything; a little further along the wall, Anne Bracegirdle as the Indian Queen continued to look out from her frame with a confident smile, her crown a headdress of swaying feathers; and alongside her the Dutch landscape reposed in its eternal late summer; even the messages pinned to the notice board were awaiting their moment patiently, and by the far window the wooden pegs held a sociable arrangement of hats and scarves happy in each other's company.

By the outer door, the tall looking-glass reflected back the busy human scene. Peter Simco in his green livery and neatly-tied apron was performing graceful motions with his coffee-pot; Jenny Trip was taking orders for early morning snacks; and a humming Jeremy was popping in and out of the kitchen with a tray, trying to look elegant. There was nothing here to alarm, and so much to cheer her. But the more the old familiar pleasure swelled up in her, the more she felt a coldness in the chest, a tightness in the throat. All this ... the place, the people ... what was to become of it?

It had been arranged that Will would call to make his report at ten o'clock – a sensible time, they had thought, which would allow Will a modicum of sleep. How unsuspecting they were! Now, every minute till then would be painful ... and if he did not come? She tried not to think of it, half hoping he might appear sooner to quieten their fears. She wondered whether to wake Tom with the news of the raid; but there was nothing either could do until a more certain report came in. Best let him lie, she thought.

But Tom hadn't been able to lie. Once the smell of coffee had worked its way up the stairs to his room, he had felt the call and found himself whistling while he shaved. A few minutes later, full of anticipation, he sprang through the door by the bar, eager for the news of the day.

He encountered not an animated Widow Trotter relishing the buzz and bustle of a Monday morning, but a woman who was doing her best to smile, despite eyes that said all was not well. Tom stopped in his tracks, sensing something was wrong. It took only the raising of his eyebrows to draw the unsettling news from her, and he leaned across the bar to pick up the half-whispered sentences. They could do little but exchange anxious words, both aware of trying not to speculate on how big a disaster the raid on Vandernan's might prove to be. Neither wanted to alarm the other. They knew how imagination fuelled itself.

This was borne out by the small talk around the tables, which was becoming ever more fanciful:

'You can be sure Bridewell will be humming!'

'What a treat for the whores this is like to be!'

'A bit of company for them.'

'It will raise the tone of the institution.'

'The hemp is sure to have a delicate beating!'

'Who knows but they'll be beating out Jack Beech's rope?'

'Now there's a dark thought for a bright morning! ...'

Dark and light were being woven together with little distinction – just idle talk to ease down their shot of coffee. At the nearest table, three friends set aside their newspapers. They were tired of hearing about the latest breaches in the walls of Lille and were glad to find a lively topic on their doorstep:

'Is Vandernan's not one of your haunts, Gabriel?'

'No, no. Too costly for me! – No, I lose my half-crowns to Mother Strickland.'

'Down Codpiece Alley? That's a low place.'

'Low but honest – there's none of your silver-spoon sharpers there – and they let you keep your shirt – It's a principle with them!'

'Aye, they'll spare your shirt, but take your house. That's generous indeed!'

The remark brought spirited laughter. At the bar, Tom couldn't avoid catching Widow Trotter's eye. He reddened, but no words came. Their silence was eloquent.

The men continued their banter:

'I wish I had fortune enough to lose *honourably*! I would be like old King Charles, who would sit down with friends of an evening to lose a hundred with good grace. He gained much honour by it!'

'Aye. Charles had a delicacy of taste altogether – in his dicing and his whoring.'

'How a man loses tells you much about him – more than how he wins.'

'That's true. It's the same with liabilities. A man's debts *are* his credit. I know one who parades them at the Exchange – swears he can raise a quick five hundred in a single tour of the walks – and with no surety. On his credit alone!'

'That makes sense to me, Jacob. Money is an upside-down world. What people think you have weighs more than what you truly have. What men will give you counts for more than what you give them.'

'Spoken like a philosopher, Gabriel!'

Widow Trotter, who admired the wisdom of wit, found herself nodding in assent. Tom turned around to look. She gave him an encouraging tap on the arm:

'Go and sit down, Tom, and I'll have Jenny bring you some toast. See what you can pick up from our friends over there. Perhaps there'll be some grains of wheat amongst the chaff?'

Tom was happy to be instructed and was soon settled at the table with the others, a dish of coffee before him and a heap of quince preserve nestling alongside his toast. By now the three men had reverted to bigger business. An ebullient Jacob Taylor was regaling them with his thoughts on the Public Credit – a topic on which he had decided views, particularly on the machinations of the hated French. He was a big-boned man and his wig shook while he talked:

'The ruin of our credit is what the French want, gentlemen! – it's their reason for fighting this war. The Spanish throne is a pretext only. Believe me, it's *London* they fear – the wealth and might of the City. Without that, our trade and our navy would be – – – nothing!'

His hand sliced through the air. His slightly sour neighbour, Gabriel Winch, nodded sagely:

'It's true what you say, Jacob – Exactly so! But remember, the French are merely our enemy ...'

It was an enigmatic remark delivered in a dry voice, and he emphasised it by lifting his dish of coffee slowly to his lips. He savoured the taste while his two friends looked at each other.

'... Our enemy is in the field and can be faced. But our *rival* – well! – that's a more dangerous thing. Our rival lurks behind our back.'

'You mean the Dutch, do you not?'

'Aye, Joe, the Dutch! ... We may think they are our allies, but we are protecting them and letting them dictate. For all the Duke's brilliance in the field, the true war is between London and Amsterdam.'

Tom chewed as he listened. By his side, Jacob Taylor looked doubtful:

'By that rule, Gabriel, you think we should go hard with 'em?'

'*Harder*, at least. This endless pother about the barrier! – It's all that concerns the Dutch. It seems we have to defend Amsterdam at all costs. There's quite a tale I could tell you about that ... Now ...'

Alongside him, Joe Garvey, a young man who had spent part of the discussion scribbling in a small notebook, looked up:

'Are you for 'Change Alley this morning, Gabriel? It's become your haunt.'

It was a neat side-thrust. Gabriel Winch was left out of his guard, but accepted the check with good humour:

'Yes, Joe ... Garraway's has a good class of client. But I thought I should look in at Jonathan's in spite of the bustle – it's usually worth the sixpence on a Monday – gives you a sniff of what the week has in store. And of course, it's good to smell all that ink and paper. The place is full of the stuff! – everyone waving their paper around or scratching away with their pens

– it's hardly a coffee house any more – rather a grand attorney's office! … But they do serve a decent drop of the dark liquor.'

'Everything is paper now,' said Joe. 'Perhaps one day soon the esteemed Widow Trotter will be refusing our coins. We shall all of us be signing notes!'

Gabriel leant forward and lowered his voice to a whisper:

'Let us hope there will be a Bay-Tree to welcome us. They do say our good lady has taken a bad hit with her basset table … Can you enlighten us, Mr Bristowe?'

The invitation emerged from the corner of his mouth – Gabriel Winch had an ironic countenance.

This thrust Tom to the front of the stage, and he needed to swallow before he could offer a coherent response. He tried to seem easy about the topic:

'Mrs Trotter regards her basset evening as a failed experiment, Mr Winch – and not one she is anxious to repeat! Gaming-tables belong in gaming-houses, don't you think? This morning's news about Vandernan's is sobering.'

'And surprising too,' said Joe Garvey. 'I had thought the place was under protection – like White's. After all, there have to be places where the clergy and the Justices can play without fear of disturbance!'

'And the City men and parliament men …'

'And the lawyers and physicians …'

'And the lords …'

'And the ladies – let us not forget the female gamesters. They love nothing better than to ruin their husbands.'

A rueful look gave an emphasis to the thought.

'Yes Joe, a sad fact. I know one who says his wife's card-play costs him more than his coach and six.'

Gabriel smiled judiciously:

'Fair's fair, Jacob! A gentleman should be able to maintain both.'

Tom had set a hare running and was finding it hard to keep up. He knew he must join in the chase:

'But why is the Law so hard on gamesters? Surely, stock-jobbing has more than its share of rogues and cheats. What is 'Change alley but a mighty gaming-house? – and one under less regulation.'

Gabriel Winch adjusted a cuff:

'You say true, young man. Fortunes are won and lost almost playfully – and with very little thought for the life to come.'

'If your clients were to hear that, Gabriel …'

'Ah, but they would be the first to agree, Jacob! Subscriptions, lotteries and wagers – I find people are eager for anything that might bring a profit.'

Joe Garvey shook his head:

'You are a broker to men's greed, Gabriel!'

'No – to their aspirations. Everyone has the right to be adventurous – to make what they can of life's chances …'

He looked at the others.

'… I suspect all of you have your share in the lottery …'

Tom was amused to see the other two respond with an awkward silence.

'… Yes, *The Honourable Adventure* – what a noble name for a sordid enterprise!'

'Sordid? Do you know something we don't?' asked Jacob Taylor.

'I do know one thing – those bankers will not lose by it! The people run the risk and the bankers make the gain. The adventure is ours, but the honour is theirs. And what an *honourable* cause the war is, gentlemen! Bribes and subsidies, guns and uniforms! It will certainly keep thousands of mercenaries in our pay.'

'That's your cynic humour, Gabriel.'

'No, no – I am ready to wave our Union Jack along with you

all … but it's a strange world we now live in. I have three clients who are wagering on the Duke's death.'

Tom was startled:

'Marlborough's? Is that possible? Is it allowed?'

'Any wager is possible, Mr Bristowe. Anything at all. I have others staking large sums that Prince George will die before the month is out … and as for the siege of Lille …'

A sudden chill had descended. Gabriel Winch thought it wise to step back.

'… But *projects* are the thing in fashion, and the more fanciful the better. The big call today is for a *gas*, would you believe? An inflammable air drawn out of coal! It seems our snug fire over there holds more secrets than we know of. We are all to be transformed! … It is a marvel, gentlemen – oh the genius of our age!'

The others looked at the hearth, wondering to themselves. Jacob Taylor stirred and reached down into his pocket:

'Well, look at this, Gabriel. Here's a new project to set your pulse racing. One even more ethereal.'

He took out a paper and unfolded it for the others to see. It was Joe Garvey who read the title aloud:

'*For carrying on an undertaking of great advantage, but nobody to know what it is.*'

A glow suffused Gabriel the broker's face:

'But that is the perfect project, Jacob! What can possibly go wrong – when there is nothing there *to* go wrong? I predict it will have great success!'

'What an ingenious nation we are, Mr Winch!' said Tom, 'chasing bubbles! – or do you think the coal-gas scheme has more solid prospects?'

'Airy prospects undoubtedly – it is sure to *soar*. I am recommending the subscription to my clients. I would certainly buy stock myself – if only the Law allowed …'

The qualification was made with a slight twitch of the cheek that could almost be mistaken for a wink.

'Who is the projector?'

'That's not a word I like, Mr Bristowe. It has a hint of trickery. I prefer *proposer* ... The proposer in question has credentials. He works for a Mr Darby over in Shropshire. They are beginning to produce charred coal ...'

'I always prefer a log fire myself,' said Joe Garvey wickedly. 'Considerably less oppressive to the lungs! ... I would suggest a project for growing more trees, especially in London ... Now that is something I would certainly subscribe for!'

Tom grinned but felt frustrated. He wanted to hear more from Gabriel Winch, but things were moving on. The gentlemen's talk would never settle on a topic for long.

It was at this moment that he heard the door open behind him and noticed Widow Trotter's face light up. He looked over his shoulder to see Will Lundy approaching the bar. He felt a sudden surge of relief and his heart thanked God for it. But there was an unaccustomed slouch to his friend's gait which didn't bode well, and Widow Trotter's concerned look reflected it. Tom was eager to be up and join them. The talk at his table had been instructive, but his attention was now elsewhere. Besides, Jacob Taylor was beginning to offer his considered thoughts on the Baltic timber trade, and so it was assuredly time to leave. Tom drank off his last mouthful of coffee and made his apologies. There was another conversation beckoning.

Chapter Twenty-Five

'I HAVE BEEN in a strange world, Mrs Trotter.'

Will Lundy leaned back in his chair as the pot of coffee was set down on the parlour table alongside a plate of lavishly buttered cinnamon buns. The look on his face was evidence enough. His eyes were bloodshot and there was a pallor to his skin. Lack of sleep was partly to blame, though there was a haunted aspect too which suggested a troubled vigil. But Will's manner was as ever genial, and he was anxious to share everything with his two friends. He had called round early, knowing they would be longing to hear the story of his night in Vandernan's, and he hoped he could do the events justice. It had been a turbulent episode with all the elements of a successful stage drama: alternating hopes and fears, sudden gains and losses, intrigues and revelations, suspicions and confrontations; a set of remarkable characters, even a moral fable of sorts – and certainly a memorable battle in the final act.

Neither Tom nor Mrs Trotter wanted to press him too urgently, but he was eager to talk, and with the added encouragement of a chicken leg from the kitchen he found his voice. He began with the invasion of the gaming-house and the fate of Sam Rivers hauled off to Bridewell with a dozen other malefactors. His own escape had been fortunate, perhaps due to the intervention of Constable Cobb.

'So, Elias was a part of it, was he?' said Mrs Trotter who was taken aback by the news.

'Only to assist – the raid was none of his doing. I saw him tending the wounded.'

'I feel badly for poor Mr Rivers. You did well to escape ... You say the Reformation of Manners people had a hand in it?'

'It was chiefly their enterprise – and can you guess who was leading them? A certain magistrate we have encountered before ...'

Tom's memory was working fast:

'Not ... Hector? – the new-broom Justice?'

'The very same – and he was in fine ranting mood. He even quoted scripture! It was he who took the promissory note ...'

The fateful words had tumbled out, and the shock was instantaneous:

'The *promissory note?* ... what note was that? Was this your winnings?'

The look on Widow Trotter's face told him she had another note in mind. Will hesitated, not knowing whether the revelation would count as good news or bad.

'It was your note, Mrs Trotter ...'

The words made her snatch her breath:

'*Mine?* ... But how did you come by it?'

'I had won it – cast for it!'

'What! How?'

'It was through a calculated risk, Mrs T – I had been tutored by Sam Rivers, remember.'

For the next few minutes Widow Trotter was held spellbound while Will told them the full story – from the ingenious dice-game with Humfrey Corbet to his frustrated attempt to immolate the note. He ended with the slight hope that its signature might no longer be legible.

Widow Trotter lived every second of his account and could only wonder aloud:

'If the paper could speak, gentlemen – what a tale it could tell us!'

Tom, however, was beginning to feel uneasy:

'So, the thing is now in the hands of the zealous Benjamin Hector?'

He was trying to sound matter of fact, but his voice was unsteady.

'Alas, yes,' said Will, 'and my fortune along with it. I was about to become a rich man!'

Widow Trotter tried to be encouraging:

'You were thoughtful and heroic, Mr Lundy – and resourceful too!'

'I was so very near! – so close to destroying the thing … Now I'm fearful and hopeful together. Hector didn't mention your name, so there may be cause to hope … *Out of the frying pan into the fire* – or perhaps the reverse?'

The grim humour reflected their mixed feelings. Tom at this moment was thinking of George Sturgis:

'You say this Humfrey fellow had received the promissory note from Vandernan's?'

'Yes, in settlement of his account.'

'Then the question is, how did it find its way there?'

'It surely came from the body?' said Widow Trotter darkly. 'It confirms the link to Vandernan's – if the killer took it.'

'Was there talk of Sturgis last night, Will? Did you pick up any hints about his doings?'

'Ah, Tom! *Hints* there certainly were – but far from being *picked up*, they were offered me on a silver platter! … For this, I need to tell you about my couch-conversation with Lady Rastell …'

The name had its due effect:

'The famed Lady Rastell? You must allow me to tell Cousin Lavinia – but perhaps it's not for a maiden's ears?'

'No maid need blush at my little scene, Tom … But what she told me brought a glow to my own cheek, I confess … it appears that she and George Sturgis had been lovers.'

Mary Trotter's eyes widened:

'Lady Rastell told you that?'

'Not in those words – but she spoke of him fondly. She was quite frank and was holding little back. She said his death was not a surprise to her – that something had been preying on him. He mixed with powerful people – *money-men*, she called them. Sturgis had a *secret life*, she thought. I remember she used those very words.'

Tom looked at Widow Trotter:

'Secret life? – money-men? – as if we needed more evidence! … This surely touches on Uncle Jack's conspiracy?'

'Lady Rastell was confident his death was not a mere gamester's quarrel.'

'Well then, this points us in the direction of the City, does it not? …'

Mrs Trotter spoke the words with more than a little apprehension. But she also sniffed a new adventure coming her way.

'… Perhaps it's 'Change Alley that holds the key, gentlemen? All those hugger-mugger people shaking hands and taking notes! It's clear my return should not be delayed. I need to call at the Sword Blade office, and I'm determined to have my interview with Michael Henriques. Bob Leary thought he might be of help to us.'

'This is your factor in Birchin Lane?'

'Yes, the mysterious young gentleman who tried to interest me in some dubious projects – dirty manufactures, both of them! Soap made from rape-oil, would you believe! – and combustible air extracted from coal. I thought myself in the world of satire, Tom!'

Her face mimicked the idea.

Tom responded with a grin:

'Yes, my friends in the coffee-room were full of it just now – the gas, that is! – Gabriel Winch thinks highly of its prospects.'

Will was not sharing in the humour:

'Mrs Trotter! You must certainly seek out Mr Henriques. Your gas was being discussed in Vandernan's last night, and in terms that suggest it is no trivial thing. Quite the contrary – substantial money is involved. If we are seeking a conspiracy, then this coal-gas scheme is undoubtedly part of it.'

Will told them of the conversation he had overheard in the card-room – about the plot to make a fortune dealing in the stock, and how it appeared that lottery funds were being misappropriated.

When he had finished, Tom let out a long, low whistle – like wind through cloister ruins:

'And this was Lord Parham, you say?'

'Yes. And the person who was sharing his secret was a certain Philip Roscoe ...'

Will saw no recognition in their faces.

'... A gentleman who happens to be a Director of the Bank of England.'

Tom had used up his whistle and could only stare in amazement.

'The Bank? ...' said Widow Trotter. 'But this is a labyrinth, Will! How far does it extend?'

'Who knows? Parham and Roscoe referred to the scheme as "the enterprise" – as if it were a great play for them.'

'It's a cold world out there,' said Widow Trotter, glancing toward her newly-laid fire spitting in the parlour grate. 'So much deception and trickery!'

'But here's something else to chill you,' continued Will. 'I need to tell you more about Vandernan's – how on a Sunday evening it transforms itself into a bank of sorts ... a criminal exchequer.'

'That's a good name for it,' said Tom.

'But that is exactly what it appears to be. Lady Rastell told me there had been a meeting at the gaming-house earlier in the evening. Her money-men were congregating, and some of them were there to receive funds from Captain Hazard.'

'Aha! So you've witnessed Bob Leary's cabal in action, Will?'

'And were they playing Captain Hazard's *game?*' asked Widow Trotter.

'Indeed they were – and with relish ... Your dice were put to excellent use.'

'You were able to employ the dice?'

'With practised skill, Mrs T! Believe me, I was able to *have some fun*, as the canting crew say. I caused great consternation to Mr Roscoe, who was quickly transformed into the angry banker!'

Will's account of his adventures at the hazard-table provided a light-hearted interlude. But they knew there was a shadow behind it all, and one they couldn't ignore.

'There is one name I haven't spoken yet,' said Will. 'A gentleman who, it turns out, is no mere social butterfly but the very Commissioner of Vandernan's – a man who has authority in the place ... Sir Charles Norreys.'

'So, Bob Leary was right,' said Tom. 'He and Lord Parham together! ... Was Sir Charles there last night?'

'He was, and I had the distinct honour of exchanging words with the Baronet himself – and what a delight that was! ...'

Will didn't disguise the irony in his voice.

'... He's a sneering sort, Tom, happy to look with contempt on all around him – especially gamesters of the female sex. He's proud of his wit, but it's the shallow and rakish kind. He talked dismissively of his wife. There's no marital love there, I fear.'

Tom frowned:

'Poor Lady Norreys. No wonder she needs her own friends. My uncle has no high opinion of Sir Charles – he thinks him a dolt. But he doesn't yet know of the connection with Vandernan's.'

'The man is not to be dismissed, Tom. I've no doubt he is at the heart of things. Last night he was giving directions, and he protested vehemently at the raid. It seems the place has had a convenient *arrangement* with the Law – one that had been violated. Our Sir Charles was enraged and ended up threatening the magistrate with a higher authority.'

'A settling of political accounts perhaps? That warfare will never end!'

It was a heart-sinking thought, and the three of them relapsed into silence. This was a moment to take stock, and as Widow Trotter rose to her feet to pour out some more coffee, she voiced the question that was on all their minds:

'Well, gentlemen, *what are we going to do?* We cannot simply sit back and wait on events.'

'You're right,' said Tom. 'We have come a fair way already, and now that Will has unlocked the secrets of Vandernan's, we have a picture of what could be facing us ...'

He lifted his dish of coffee to Will.

'... You've visited the Underworld, my friend! Thank God you've come back to us!'

'I second that,' said Mrs Trotter, pledging in similar fashion. 'The hero has returned!'

Will looked uncertain:

'But it's also a magical world, Tom. That is what disturbs me most. It's a battlefield *and* a theatre – a world of challenges and possibilities. It sets the pulse racing, believe me! I was beginning to think myself invincible.'

Tom looked at his friend and saw someone who would soon be returning to the grind of Westminster Hall. Poor Will! he thought. After the exhilaration of Vandernan's, how tiring the struggle with laborious truth must seem; how heavily those hours of legal argument would hang on him! Tom knew his friend had glimpsed another kind of life and was feeling unsettled by it.

'You've heard the siren-song, Will. It's good you understand that.'

'You mustn't let me return there, Tom!'

His look was intense. It was no casual remark.

'On that, Will, you have my solemn promise. Besides, we now have other things to occupy us. We must look beyond Vandernan's! The cabal are pursuing their dark deeds in the City. The gaming-house is just their Sunday playground.'

'You are right,' said Widow Trotter. 'The City calls ... So, let me return to my question, gentlemen ... What do we need to do?'

'Well, you've told us your next mission,' said Tom. 'Exchange Alley! I suspect your Mr Henriques will have something to say.'

'I dearly hope so. Bob Leary said the young man was close to breaking. If his business is in trouble and Parham and the others have a hand in it, then he may be only too willing to talk.'

'I think your curiosity is going to have a feast.'

'I would ask you to come with me, Tom, but I plan to approach him as a likely client – a woman of business who has some hard-earned guineas ready to be put to work.'

'Irresistible, Mrs T!'

'As for you ...'

She turned on Tom what he thought of as her brigade-commander look.

'... Do you think another visit to St James's is called for? It would be good to know that Lord Melksham and your cousin are both safe and not about to do anything rash. I'm wondering if Mr Popham has confronted your uncle about the Treasurership?'

'I've been wondering that myself – not an easy interview! You're right, I must go over there. Poor Frank is going to need my encouragement.'

'And see if you can discover more about Sturgis and the Duchess – your uncle's conspiracy. My nose tells me more is bubbling up ... And what does he know of Lord Parham and his cronies? Perhaps there are others in our picture?'

It was quite a bulletin. Tom felt like saluting her:

'Agreed then! I shall invite myself to Pall Mall this afternoon and take pot-luck with a Popham dinner.'

'Excellent! – and make sure you present my compliments to your Cousin Lavinia. I would be surprised if her sharp wits haven't told her something untoward is going on.'

During these arrangements Will had been regaining a zest for their investigations. Simply being in their company was enough. He took a mouthful of the dark coffee and his neck shivered:

'Can I consult your nose too, Mrs Trotter? You mustn't think my contribution is over. Remember, I have a ticklish parental meeting of my own to negotiate ...'

He turned to Tom.

'... if you hear thunder from an easterly direction, it will be coming from my father's chambers in the Temple.'

'Ah yes, Will. I'll keep my ears pricked. You would be wise to go and confess your transgression before Mr Hector delivers his charge-sheet.'

'Poor Mr Lundy,' said Widow Trotter with a sigh. 'Yet another test – as if you had not been challenged enough these past hours! ... But rather than confess, should you not present your Vandernan's experience as a charitable errand on behalf of Mr Popham and myself? You have nothing to apologise for – quite the contrary.'

Tom nodded:

'And you could try to enlist your father's advice – without revealing too much, of course. Does he not have his own City connections? You told me he dined in Mercers' Hall only a few weeks ago. Is that not Alderman Rivers's company? ...'

'Yes, Tom, it is! That's a fine idea. Father does indeed know people in the City – Common-Council Men a speciality!'

'Then that is our triple plan, gentlemen!' said Widow Trotter. 'I'm for 'Change Alley – Tom for Pall Mall – and you for the Temple. The Bay-Tree militia will sally forth! Mr Lundy has shown us what boldness and ingenuity can do. Let us see if we cannot find a few villains and smoke them out.'

Chapter Twenty-Six

———∞———

Widow Trotter felt doubly uneasy returning to Exchange Alley. The scene was much as before: the narrow lane twisted between shops and offices with dark figures scurrying past or gathered in doorways, but now the muttering and glances somehow felt more threatening. Nor had she noticed the smell before. It was not the customary alley-stink of sweat, smoke and urine – quite the contrary; nor was it especially strong. No, it was a faint, lingering caustic scent – limewash perhaps, or even quicklime? She noticed that the paving stones did look clean, so this was possibly a Monday morning wash? In a mistrustful mood she read it as an emblem of the place: the new week was setting out to expunge all the dirty dealings of the previous one ...

Her own dealings began in the Sword Blade office, where on this occasion she was offered a dish of coffee. The astringent potion set her up for what was to follow – an awkward interview with John Grigsby. His voice was benign as before, but his pendant features were if anything more weighed down by the gravity of what he had to say. All he needed was a black cap to pronounce sentence. His opening 'Dear Mrs Trotter' was sympathetic as usual, but what followed was stringent as bitter grapes. He knew his message would be uncomfortable for her.

Her breathing stopped when the crucial words came:

'Your promissory note for four hundred pounds was presented here this morning, Mrs Trotter.'

'But I thought ...'

She hesitated. She had come to negotiate, but this revelation pre-empted her. There was only one immediate question she could ask:

'... Was the note physically whole?'

Mr Grigsby's eyes narrowed slightly. His jowl shuddered, but his voice was calm and clear:

'Ah ... then I need not inform you of the poor condition of the note. It appeared to us that an attempt had been made to destroy it. The bulk of the paper was, however, intact, and your signature legible beneath the charring ...'

Her heart plummeted. As Will had said – so very very near!

'... This is a difficult state of affairs, Mrs Trotter, and not one we regularly encounter. But I must tell you that we had little choice other than to decline payment.'

For a moment there was hope:

'Is it not legal tender then, Mr Grigsby?'

'It is a valid document, in that it is a signed promise to pay a certain sum ... In spite of the damage, the intent remains clear. However, as you know, in your case the bank is unable to honour it, given that your account here falls substantially short of the sum required.'

Widow Trotter's head was beginning to ache. The language of logic and calculation cut through the tangle of hopes she was clinging to:

'What does that mean, Mr Grigsby?'

It was a naïve question, but she was foundering and could think of nothing else.

'It means, Mrs Trotter, that if payment is to be made, the bank needs to assure itself that the amount can be covered. In your case, we shall be happy to advance the sum – provided security is given.'

'Security?'

'The money required will need to be underwritten by you on sufficient surety – on your assets.'

'By that you mean ... my property ... ?'

Mr Grigsby's head gave a slow, sustained, sympathetic nod. Words would be too cruel. It was left to Widow Trotter to spell them out.

'... You wish me to mortgage the Bay-Tree.'

'To transfer your interest in the chocolate house to the bank ... Yes.'

The word *interest* was a chilling one. It meant everything. Her business. Her home. Her security for the future.

A sudden indignation swelled up in her – the nonsense of it all!

'But Mr Sturgis is dead!'

'Alas, Mrs Trotter. That no longer signifies. A promissory note is now quite the equivalent of a bank note – a promise to pay. A bank's reputation rests on its preparedness to honour that promise. It is not one of our own notes, but the fact is the same – the gentleman in possession has the right to expect payment.'

The word *gentleman* was a harsh reminder that within the last couple of hours someone had entered that office carrying the note and had demanded settlement. Her next question was spoken tentatively:

'This gentleman ... Do you know his name?'

'He did not give it ... I have to say the man had something of an ambiguous character – not a sort we generally encounter here ... if I may speak candidly, he bore the impress of a fashionable costermonger ...'

This was spoken with a delicacy of enunciation that made its own point. Mr Grigsby saw Widow Trotter's sudden discomfort.

'... I said what I could to him, but he was a man of few words and revealed nothing of himself. Needless to say, he left no address. I spoke of delay and of the necessity of making arrangements for payment – but this failed to reassure him. He did not depart a happy man.'

'I am grateful to you. Mr Grigsby.'

'It is not for me to advise you on what course you should take, Mrs Trotter – but might I suggest a degree of caution. As the bearer of the note, the man will surely press you for the debt.'

A chill struck her. First Frank Popham, and now herself!

'I am well and truly trapped, Mr Grigsby, am I not?'

'Alas, Mrs Trotter, it will comfort you little to know that the Sword Blade detests such pieces of paper. You can well imagine how they unsettle and complicate financial transaction. By making them legal tender the Law has sanctioned dubious dealings and precarious debts. Bank notes have at least a guarantee behind them, but such scraps of paper, often written under pressing circumstances – forgive me! – belong in gaming-houses! ...'

He leaned forward and softened his voice:

'... For your own peace of mind, I recommend that you make arrangements within the next day or two. Our notary, Mr Barnes, will be able to draw up the document quickly.'

It was all so polite, so considerate and sensible. But there looked to be no escape. She badly needed to think and take advice. Necessity – itself an implacable creditor – was closing in on her.

The speed of all this had been a surprise. In a few hours only, the note had flown from the magistrate's possession into the hands of a mysterious figure eager to realise the sum before questions would be asked. For the first time she was beginning to understand how money worked, and how it moved: hand to hand, pen to paper, materialised and dissolved, channelled through good and bad, from victim to fraudster, rewarding and corrupting; poured out lavishly, hoarded avariciously, building power and buying influence; a medium of desire which could also drain resolve and destroy peace of mind. The more she contemplated money, the more it became the driving element of life itself.

But this would never do! Her immediate thought had been to hurry home to the Bay-Tree and leave the tangled maze behind; but as she stood outside the Sword Blade office and watched the mid-day bustle of Birchin Lane, she knew she had a job to do. Her instinctive determination returned. She steadied herself and resolved to banish airy speculations and set about her business. She needed to cut through the complication and find the truth, for herself and for her friends.

And there, facing her, was the next challenge. The sign read *Henriques. Commodity Importer*, and she strode resolutely towards it.

Widow Trotter stepped inside, and as the door slowly closed behind her she was intrigued by the scene. It was hard to know what kind of room this was – part office, part emporium. At the far end beyond a partition she saw a clerk, clearly an apprentice, who stood pen-in-hand before a high desk absorbed in his ledger-work. But immediately before her was a very different space. A large round table was spread with swatches of coloured silk and some intriguing objects in ivory and bronze that spoke of long journeys from the east. Above her head, a lantern in finely-chased silver hung on chains from a roof-beam, and alongside it dangled what appeared to be a golden incense-burner – a lingering sweetness in the air confirmed it. On the walls around were finely woven hangings, and shelves displaying vases, clocks, and carved figures. She felt she had stepped into an eastern bazaar. Nothing could be further from coal and rape-oil! ... She was puzzled, and hesitated, Michael Henriques's card pressed between her fingers.

Only then did she notice the two figures seated together in the corner of the room over to her right. They were sharing a pot of tea, and neither of them was Michael Henriques. For a moment she thought she must have mistaken the door, and she paused a little awkwardly. But the taller gentleman had risen to his feet and greeted her with a gesture indicating a third empty chair. He was plainly dressed, with a natural elegance of bearing heightened by the finely shaped head and eloquent eyes. Nothing was spoken, but the invitation was a welcome one, and when he pointed to the china teapot she smiled and nodded. A solemn ritual! But there was nothing cringing or effusive about it – this man was no shopkeeper. Widow Trotter sensed that when he finally spoke it would be to the purpose.

But she couldn't stay silent any longer:

'Mary Trotter ... I am here to find Michael Henriques – he gave me his card.'

Her host exchanged glances with the other man and smiled:

'Michael is over at the Exchange, Mrs Trotter. I am his father, Peter Henriques.'

A slim hand reached out. As she shook it her eyes were drawn to an exquisite emerald intaglio ring set in gold:

'That's a fine ring, Mr Henriques. Who is that lady?'

'You have a sharp eye, Mrs Trotter. She is the Empress Agrippina, mother of the deplorable Nero! I'm happy to say my wife and I are more blessed in our own offspring! Michael is a busy young man. I am sorry he is not here. High 'Change finishes at two, and so I don't expect him before then. I promise not to enquire about your business unless you wish to tell me – but do stay a moment and drink tea with us. This is my friend Mr Levy.'

Widow Trotter had not expected all this politeness, and another handshake followed.

'Benjamin Levy ...' the man said, and fixed her with a warm, deep gaze. Above the grey beard was a soft parchment face etched with good humour.

'... You catch us in a peaceful interlude. We are comparing our troubles!'

'I am sorry to hear you have any, Mr Levy. But a moment of calm is precious in Exchange Alley, I'm sure. What is your line of business?'

'Financial instruments, Mrs Trotter – loans, contracts, insurance, securities ...'

'As a notary?'

'Ah no! I am an underwriter. I arrange guarantees.'

Peter Henriques smiled on his friend:

'When so many are floating and bobbing on a sea of speculation, Mr Levy is the anchor!'

Widow Trotter blanched at the image. It was too close to home, and she could see only shipwreck:

'You are a reassuring figure, Mr Levy. Does that mean you allow others to take risks but remain secure yourself? I admire the wisdom of it.'

'Ah, dear lady – if only that were true it would all work beautifully. But the world is full of villains. Honourable dealing has always been my custom, but in these times, trust is a rare commodity!'

'My friend is very sore today, Mrs Trotter. A client has reneged on a debt. The man is broken, so there is no recourse to law.'

'So, you are ... a guarantee of value, Mr Levy? You stand behind all the paper that whirls around 'Change Alley?'

'I, amongst others ... The nation's bullion, Mrs Trotter! The vaults of Lombard Street! How easily that store of value is forgotten, and yet without it the nation is nothing. All else is air!'

'But there is good profit for you, is there not?'

'A very uncertain one – and in 'Change Alley wealth breeds itself with ease. Their paper goes off adventuring whilst my gold stays at home. But too often their loss becomes mine, and my substantial loss is their paper gain. I sometimes think I am like a wife who keeps house prudently while her husband flirts with every harlot in the city.'

'So much is changing,' said Mr Henriques. 'The old pride in trade is disappearing. The merchants remain over in the Exchange, and the stock-jobbers have fled here to the Alley.'

'They were *thrown* out, Peter – remember that. And with good reason! But from here they pour scorn on the true traders across the road. "Hang trade!" they say, "Trade is an ass to stock! There's more to be got by stock in a day than through a year's merchanting!" And while the honest merchants risk their ships across dangerous seas, the adventurers of Jonathan's and Garraway's play with their paper to their heart's content.'

Mrs Trotter had found herself caught up in what was clearly a regular grievance. She watched intently as a rather theatrical Benjamin Levy drew a coin from his pocket and held it out to her:

'An English *crown*, dear lady. Exactly *one ounce* of sterling silver! Here is true value! …'

Widow Trotter thought of Elias – this was a man after his own heart!

Mr Henriques poured her some more tea:

'You must forgive Mr Levy's *anathema*, Mrs Trotter – though I wouldn't wish to contradict a word. 'Change Alley has indeed become a gaming-table … With my son away, my friend and I can rail without fear of contradiction. Michael is far more amenable to modern speculation and is happy to deal in the stocks. It is a cause of contention between us … But I must say nothing more. That may be your business with him!'

'I see your business here, Mr Henriques, is of a special kind – there's so much to take the eye. Is this your merchandise?'

'Yes, these are samples of our wares – I like to display them. Our prime connections are with Syria, Turkey, and Morocco, but we have sources in India and China too. It is an exotic trade … but we face many frustrations at present. The war makes all uncertain. The merchants' difficulties are ours too. The Danube trade is sunk, the routes through Holland and Flanders are often impossible, and with French privateers and Barbary pirates, the seas are perilous … but you must not let me deliver my speech on the subject!'

Benjamin Levy twinkled and lifted his hands:

'You see, Mrs Trotter – troubles on every side! … And yet somehow we survive!'

'My son has little time for my *extravagances*, as he calls them. Michael has faced severe difficulties himself and has encountered real villainy, but the young man looks to the future – to the wonders of science and experiment. He delights in all things new and speaks of *material improvements* and *national advancement*. Patents excite him beyond measure! And how do you think he is going to repair the fortunes of the business? … by coal and soap! A very different world, is it not? I have no thought to display either here!'

The genial conversation continued, and Widow Trotter felt surprisingly comfortable in this old-style company. Part of her longed to speak about her own troubles, which were not far from theirs. But she knew it was wiser to keep her concerns private, at least for the moment. She had already resolved to make her way across to the Royal Exchange and thrust herself into the busy throng. There was a good chance she would encounter the junior Henriques – a young man she was more than ever eager to meet. And there might be an opportunity to explore the shops too?

She thanked the pair warmly for their company and left the place with a tug of unease. Their world was torn between old and new, and things they had put their trust in were becoming uncertain. She was heartened by their resilience, but behind the good humour she knew the company's troubles were genuine ones. It concerned her to think that they might only be beginning.

Chapter Twenty-Seven

—∞∞∞—

WIDOW TROTTER EMERGED from the labyrinth of Exchange Alley and looked across the street at the magnificent façade of the Royal Exchange which towered above Cornhill like a profane cathedral. Indeed, it struck her that its only rival for grandeur in the City was the new St Paul's – two edifices that marked out the kingdoms of God and Mammon. It was with some relief that she was leaving behind the secretive windings of the alley; but facing her was the equally daunting prospect of universal commerce.

The broad entrance arch, a full two storeys in height, was far larger than it needed to be and seemed to extend an invitation to the whole world. She tried to catch some of that confidence and raised her head expectantly; but once under the portico all pretence to classical grandeur slipped away. She became caught up in a busy crush of porters and messenger-boys, with hawkers shouting their wares on every side – everything from spices and fruit to second-hand shoes and spectacles. This was the place for corn-cures, glass eyes and ivory teeth, and for all manner of allurement. Along the wall, tightly-packed stalls offered their displays: here were ranks of apples, chestnuts, lemons, oranges and pomegranates, all in their polished uniforms; and there an enticing assortment of powders, tinctures and elixirs. She wove

her way circumspectly through it all, past men eager to catch her
attention and nimble children with eyes at pocket-level. Notices
and advertisements flapped on every pillar.

Inside the colonnaded quadrangle of the Exchange the
contrast could hardly have been greater. The crush was much
the same, and yet the immediate impression was of order and
solemnity. This lay congregation had its own rituals, here in
the service of trade. During the two hours of High 'Change,
negotiations were conducted in low voices like a humming of
bees. There was urgency and haggling a-plenty, but nothing was
shouted or broadcast. Looks and gestures were more eloquent
than speech. This lent an element of secrecy to the proceedings
and an almost grotesque politeness, all the more remarkable for
the multitude of figures that were huddling together, drawn
from the four corners of the earth.

The court was surrounded by elegant arches that gave it the
appearance of a Florentine piazza. But its single statue was a
remarkably solid rendition of King Charles the Second, plumb
centre, presiding over the scene with a jowly patience – other
kings and queens of England were confined to niches along the
enclosed upper gallery, their stone effigies gazing on the scene
below. In truth, there was little history in this place – all the
commerce was between present and future, the perfect alignment
of demand and supply.

Widow Trotter paused under the colonnade and wondered
whether to launch herself through the crowd of men. She
suddenly felt utterly out of place. After all, she was no merchant
and had nothing to negotiate – no wines, sugar, timber, rum or
jewels. There was no Trotter cargo of tea and spices waiting to
unload at one of the Thames wharves. Her own little paper-
problem shrank to nothing amidst all this material plenitude,
and around her the music of different languages reminded her
that much of what she took for granted was supplied from this

market of nations. The produce of every climate was gathered here, and her own Bay-Tree bore witness to it. In the chocolate house the harvests of India, Mexico and the orient were combined. The food of one continent was dressed with a sauce from another. A leaf from China was sweetened with the pith of a Jamaican cane.

If Michael Henriques was somewhere in this crowd, she decided, then it would be best to mount the stairs to the gallery from where she could survey the whole courtyard. And so, after a few minutes she found herself on the Exchange's upper floor among a row of small shops on either side of a walk. These were partitioned pinfolds from which beckoning calls of 'Fine linen, sir!' and 'Gloves and ribbons, ma'am!' answered each other. Ignoring the solicitations, she was making her way towards a window when she caught sight of two familiar figures browsing at a haberdasher's close by. The elder woman was holding up a silk handkerchief, while the younger ran her fingers over some lace trimmings.

It was a pleasurable surprise, and Mrs Trotter was not one to forego anything that might prove a fortunate meeting. It didn't take many strides to bring her by their side. Her old friend Adèle Ménage was in company with Kate Primrose, the former 'Clarissa' – more recently 'Callisto.' The girl was looking remarkably fresh in a pink gown with embroidered sleeves. Her hair was ringleted, and a hat box lay at her feet. A slightly startled Mrs Trotter gave her a broad smile, which she returned.

'I'm delighted to see you Kate – and looking so radiant! Life must have treated you well these past months. Do I take it Callisto is thriving?'

It was meant light-heartedly, but the question died on her lips when Kate gave a detectable shiver. It was Mrs Ménage who replied:

'Ah Marie! The "Callisto" is no more ... our friend has been telling me her excellent news. We must share it with you if you will join us. Let us find a quiet corner and unfold the tale ... This is truly a fortunate meeting! – You see, I myself have a *bonne bouche* for you! News barely one hour old ...'

This was impossible to withstand, and Mrs Trotter seized the chance to satisfy her curiosity. Only when the three of them were gathered in front of an empty shop at the far end of the promenade could the serious talk begin.

It transpired that life for Kate Primrose had taken an upward turn. The world of Vinegar Yard was behind her, and she was quite the lady.

'I am to be *Katharine Quinlan*,' she declared, pronouncing the name clearly and looking at Adèle with evident pride.

'*Mrs Joseph Quinlan*, Marie! – does that not have a fine ring to it?'

'Your friend, the clerk in the Excise Office?'

Mrs Trotter recalled her encounter with the man on the dark stairs of Kate's tenement when she had mistaken him for a thief.

'Yes – you have met him, of course. It is Joe who has *thrived*, Mrs Trotter. He has such a wonderful clear head for figures – and the Excise Office is a place of many opportunities.'

Again, Adèle Ménage couldn't resist offering a gloss:

'Mr Quinlan has knowledge of the warehouses, Marie! Do you see? He knows what is in store and what cargoes are expected ...'

'It is very useful knowledge, Mrs Trotter. Joe is able to learn things that the gentlemen at the Exchange are eager to hear – men who will pay well for advance intelligence ...'

There was a natural confidence in her words, and a look which said this was a time when a lowly clerk with a turn for business deserved success. He was someone who could make the system work for him.

'... We are to be married in three weeks' time, Mrs Trotter – and are to rent a house near Soho Square!'

This was a lot to take in at one breath. Widow Trotter's heart warmed to her, though there was a chill undertow of resentment she was fighting to suppress.

'You must give Mr Quinlan my good wishes, Kate. He has done well to take his chances.'

Mrs Ménage intervened again, her face rippling with joy:

'Pepper, Marie! ... Mr Quinlan has made a fortune from *pepper!*'

'Hardly a fortune, Adèle,' corrected Kate. 'But he made use of what he knew.'

Widow Trotter was granted the full story, which featured a huge consignment of black pepper shipped from Malabar, held secretly on a Thames lighter and waiting to unload.

'... Joe knew the price of pepper would soon fall, and he found a way to gain from it. The fall was greater than his highest hopes ... He understands these things – though it baffles me.'

Widow Trotter's generosity of spirit began to flow back. Dear Kate, she thought, what a headlong journey you've had – from Vinegar Yard to Soho Square!

Their conversation wound its way for a good five minutes more until the subject of Joseph Quinlan's resourcefulness had been exhausted. Then Mrs Ménage leant forward in a slightly conspiratorial way:

'But it is time for my revelation, Marie! Something to amuse you, I think – it concerns your tallière, the remarkable Mr *LeRoy* ...'

She gave his name a flourish.

'... The gentleman is not all that he appears! ...'

Widow Trotter was a little disappointed. This was not something new, and it made her own news redundant. But she smiled at her friend encouragingly.

'... I heard it from Monsieur Basire yesterday at our Huguenot church. I told him of my basset victory, and of our *pretending* Frenchman ... and would you believe, he had encountered the gentleman at Paris ...'

Suddenly the prospect brightened.

'... Robert LeRoy had a reputation *dans les salons* ... a man of dangerous skill at the card-table. He played at Court and impoverished not a few ... But, Marie, his fate was an ignominious one – he was driven out! Fortunate to escape with his life! ...'

This was a little dramatic, but Widow Trotter was reassured that Bob Leary's tale had evidently been no exaggeration.

'... And what had been his crime, do you think? ...'

There was a shameless pause, and an intake of breath.

'... He was a *spy*. Can you believe, Marie? It was found that he was supplying more than gossip to his masters – secrets, political and financial – cryptic information!'

This certainly counted as a revelation – if it could be trusted. Widow Trotter knew what a skilled embroiderer gossip was. It was not easy to think of Bob Leary as a daring patriot:

'A bold man indeed, Adèle! But it would seem he got little reward from us!'

'No, no ... not from us, Marie. He was a spy for the *Dutch*. His masters were in Amsterdam!'

Widow Trotter froze, and her thoughts suddenly found a different channel. It was a startling idea, but it did make some sense. In taking ship for Amsterdam Mr Leary would not be an exile!

More was said, but nothing that added to the already vivid picture – until Adèle's voice suddenly took on a tone of triumph.

'And now for the peak of my news – the culmination!'

Widow Trotter swallowed – there was to be more!

'Who do you think I saw here, but twenty minutes ago?'

'Here – in the Exchange?'

'Yes, in the court below! ... Our Mr LeRoy – seated on

the benches in the colonnade. He was watchful – I think he expected someone!'

Widow Trotter was conscious of her friend eyeing her closely and awaiting a reaction, but she needed to be careful. This was not the moment to untie her own parcel of news, satisfying though that would be. There was much to be pondered and she needed to be alone with her thoughts. She allowed their talk to reach its *culmination*, then made her departure. Full of anticipation, she hurried round to the north side of the gallery and found a convenient window. There were now two figures to interest her, but one question loomed large: what was Bob Leary – a man sheltering in fear of his life – doing in this populous place?

She looked out. Beneath her, the floor of the Exchange was seething, and an incessant hum arose like an ocean murmur. Hundreds of merchants, tradesmen, and dealers in all kinds of commodities were gathered into their national 'walks.' It truly was the globe in miniature, and as Widow Trotter cast her eyes from group to group she felt she was journeying across the earth itself. Down on the left, a pair of bewhiskered figures in furs and shaggy thrum-caps looked as if they had just landed from the Baltic; another group in Spanish flat-crowned hats and short cloaks were more poised, took snuff and shrugged their shoulders gracefully. A patriarchal figure in a cinnamon-coloured surtout was shaking his head at a pair of petitioners who appeared to be seeking his custom. All around, heads and hands were talking. She noticed some men had gloves tucked under their arms as they gesticulated closely, palms opening, fists closing, fingers wagging. Business of all kinds was being done – and not only in commodities. On the far side of the court under one of the arches, a group of young men with roving eyes were lounging, hands in pockets, whispering among themselves.

At last, half-hidden by the splayed calves of King Charles,

there was Michael Henriques – she was sure it was him – dark-clothed, in deep conversation with a no-nonsense looking gentleman in a plain russet suit. So, he was indeed here! She noted his location. But there seemed to be no sight of Bob Leary, who had probably slipped back to his refuge in Islington. Such a throng of people! Her eyes began to range again, this time more randomly.

And then she saw him. Leary was making his way slowly along the far colonnade, his attention fixed on one walk in particular. He hesitated and then stood, glancing anxiously around. She could think only that he had come to meet someone and was waiting to make an approach. She looked over in the direction of his gaze and saw a striking figure in a long black coat and scarlet breeches, a knitted woollen cap pulled over his ears. In front of him another man was holding out a paper and the two of them were scrutinising it together. Widow Trotter cast her eye on that part of the court and saw alongside them a man in white Puritan bands and a tall hat. Widow Trotter had a good eye for such things. Yes, she thought, this was certainly the Dutch Walk.

Moments later the gentleman and his paper had moved off, and she watched as Leary made a tentative approach – this was not Robert LeRoy the confident tallière but a sneaking Bob Leary wary of all around him. Above the crowded court she had an excellent vantage from which to read the dumb-show that began to play out below her.

The man showed no surprise at Leary's approach. There was no greeting or shake of the hands – the encounter lacked the formalities. Both had solemn expressions. Leary's opening words were delivered closely to the man's left ear while the gentleman's eyes darted from side to side as if searching out danger. There was an immediate frown and a shake of the head. In response, Leary's hand reached out for his elbow. A half-turn away brought further speech from Leary, now delivered more rapidly as he shifted to his right to continue confronting the man. There was little room for manoeuvre, and so the two of them remained in an awkward dance together. At last something seemed to be resolved, and the man's hand delved into his pocket. It remained there while he spoke further, bringing the full weight of his body close to Leary's chest. His face was stern and set in a determined expression, and his words – she could almost hear them in her imagination – were delivered slowly and directly. Then, with a discreet lack of fuss the hand emerged and a tiny parcel was pressed into Leary's palm. In an instant it was in his pocket. Widow Trotter was transfixed. In the Theatre Royal the scene would have compelled attention, and no less here.

But there was no applause at Bob Leary's exit, which was observed keenly before the man turned back. She felt the scene hardly needed words: something had been asked and refused, something determined, and something – what could it be? – handed over. The scene opened up further dramatic possibilities. What exactly these might be, she was yet to find out.

Chapter Twenty-Eight

———

THE EXCHANGE CLOCK chimed two, and instantly the character of the place was transformed. All argument and negotiation ceased. Like elves at dawn, the miscellaneous congregation of furs, silks, feathers and woollens slipped away as if a wand had been waved over their heads. But these men were not about to melt into air. They had substantial things on their minds and were heading for their dinners or towards an alehouse for some communal reflection on the trading of the day.

Widow Trotter had resolved to await the close of business and catch Michael Henriques as he left the court. It seemed to her that for the previous two hours the young man had been in a different mode of trading – the representative of his father's affairs rather than his own – and she decided that her finely-tuned purpose wouldn't be well served in the midst of a haggling throng. Fortunately, he was leaving the place in solitary thoughtfulness, and when she stepped out before him he took a moment to collect himself:

'Ah yes, I gave you my card, did I not? …'

The dark eyes recognised her, and the tone was welcoming.

'… You must forgive me – being away from my office I have no documents to hand – and I'm unable to offer you a seat.'

He removed his hat and gave a slight nod.

'Perhaps the bench here will suit us, Mr Henriques – if you have a few moments to spare? I called at Birchin Lane a short while ago, and your father directed me here.'

The suggestion was accepted, and they settled themselves at the back of the colonnade where a convenient bench ran the length of the court. She was carrying her pocket-case (emptied of its worthless paper), which gave her the appearance of a woman who meant business.

But from the beginning she knew there could be no pretence. Her idea of being a woman with a deal of money to invest would not be appropriate. This was no occasion for role-playing. She was reminded of Bob Leary's words – that Michael Henriques was close to bankruptcy – something his father also hinted at – that his son had met with villainy. Perhaps that would be a bond between them?

It took little prompting to encourage him, and his eyes brightened as he expatiated on his favourite topic – the inventiveness of the present age and the wonderful opportunities for harnessing new discoveries:

'Our knowledge grows, Mrs Trotter, and our ingenuity with it. The natural world hides many treasures, and the human mind will surely reveal them. There are secrets within Nature that might be unlocked and worked for our use. There is a wondrous power in every plant and mineral! ... But sadly, inventions require money, which today must be sought in the market – noble patrons are rare as unicorns ...'

The enthusiastic flow continued. His voice was warm, and his language became transformative. He magicked the world with every word he spoke. In his imagination, soap became silky to the touch, and a dirty lump of coal seemed capable of breath itself. There was an innocence in his manner that told her he was not privy to the coal-gas *enterprise* – the chilling term Will had heard used in the gaming-house. She could only think that unless something was done, Henriques was destined to become a victim once more and his beloved projects nothing but torn-up paper. The Vandernan's plot was already moving towards its consummation.

Widow Trotter felt a sharp tug on the reins was necessary:

'Mr Henriques – What you say excites so many ideas – but I must confess to you … I am not here as any kind of trader or purchaser, but as someone who needs your help – and perhaps can help you in turn.'

Michael Henriques shot her a half-amused look. He had his father's face, but more mobile:

'You would flourish as a trader, Mrs Trotter! You speak our language of commodity – of one that looks to gain while bestowing favour. Are you saying you have a proposal that will work to our benefit?'

His mind was agile, and Widow Trotter knew she mustn't be won over too easily by his quick understanding. She composed herself:

'There is a name I must speak to you, Mr Henriques – but I'm unsure how you will respond.'

'There is a way to find out.'

The card was on the table. It was an invitation.

'The Honourable Mr George Sturgis.'

The effect was immediate – a sudden frown and a tilting of the head:

'A name indeed – now *only* a name, of course …'

His grip on his hat tightened.

'… I was sorry to hear of Sturgis's death – but alas, I cannot mourn the gentleman … I am interested that you mention his name to me. Do you know of a connection between us?'

'It was a throw of the dice, I confess … but, coupled with the name of *Vandernan's*, I have been led to expect you might be able to help me and my friends …'

His young eyes narrowed. Widow Trotter softened her tone. She didn't want to sound riddling.

'... We are in deep trouble, Mr Henriques. I was told to seek you out – that you have had experience of Vandernan's and its ways.'

'You were told ... may I ask by whom?'

'By Robert LeRoy.'

'Ah – another name! The picture is beginning to form ... But you are being enigmatic, Mrs Trotter. If I am to help you – if we are to help each other – then you must open your affairs to me.'

Widow Trotter hesitated. Had she already revealed too much? It was hard to know how else she could have broached the subject.

'You must understand I have to be circumspect, Mr Henriques. This business concerns matters beyond myself. The full story cannot be laid out to you – not yet ... Mr LeRoy spoke of you as a friend, else I would not have approached you.'

'So, you are a friend of Robert LeRoy, are you?'

It was spoken with a slight asperity, which surprised her.

'No, but I have *tangled* with him.'

She awarded the word a similar sharpness. The response was as she hoped. His face broke into a smile of recognition:

'I see. Things are becoming clearer.'

'Did you not encounter him moments ago? I saw him here at the Exchange.'

'Here – now?'

'Yes. He departed in some hurry. I was observing from the gallery.'

'Well well! You clearly have a *choice* of professions open to you, Mrs Trotter – trader? – or informer? Do I take it you have been keeping watch on us? ...'

There was more admiration than accusation in this. He was thinking hard.

'... Mr LeRoy did not make himself known to me ...'

Both were silent for a moment. The conversation was more like a game of chess. At some point they would have to be open with one another.

'... It is clear we have some important matter to discuss, Mrs Trotter, and I'm eager to know how you might help me ... If we are to make a bargain, then this is the place for it – perhaps with a solemn handshake when the deal is done?'

His words struck home. The Exchange was casting its influence over her. She was becoming a trader, and a spy.

And so, she told him about the Bay-Tree basset table and her entanglement with Robert LeRoy – about the unexpected arrival and 'deep' play of George Sturgis, the severe loss she had sustained that night, and the discovery that her tallière's notes proved to be nothing but paper – that the whole debt had to be borne by herself...

It was a sad tale, and Michael Henriques listened intently, not moving a muscle while the intrigue was played out.

'The men were accomplices, Mr Henriques – and I have since learned more about Robert LeRoy – about Mr *Leary*, I should say ... *Bob Leary – of Dublin* ...'

She watched him closely, and it was evident that the shock had registered. His head jerked up.

'... Does that surprise you?'

'It does indeed! – Another story, no doubt! I have to say I always thought him a performer. He never spoke much of himself. Ours was a relation of mutual advantage – a customary one in 'Change Alley! We shared information – the universal currency of the place.'

'Did you trust him?'

'You trust any man who holds a razor to your throat! Mr LeRoy was my barber ... I am sorry to hear of your misfortune – but I cannot see how I might help. As you will have gathered, he and I have gone our separate ways ...'

She was looking at him inquiringly.

'... I came to have my doubts of the man. He showed a pressing interest in the coal-gas scheme when it was first mooted, but I found cause to believe that what I had confided in him was finding its way to others – and not to my benefit. There was no open breach, but since then my suspicions have hardened. I have had occasion to think him the cause of my recent troubles.'

'Your father spoke of the *villainy* you've encountered. Could I ask – could there be a connection to Vandernan's?'

'There was. I discovered that a "difficulty" I had mentioned to Mr LeRoy was circulated in Vandernan's as a dark rumour. I assumed he had spread the word among his gaming friends. I suddenly found my clients deserting me. It has taken me to the brink, Mrs Trotter, and I am only now recovering. Whether it was accident or malice, I know not, but it seems Mr LeRoy knows to stay clear of me.'

'And yet it was he who urged me to bring you my problem.'

Michael Henriques was thoughtful at this:

'You speak of his collusion with Mr Sturgis. It does not surprise me in the least. Vandernan's is a sink-hole – and one I have succeeded in avoiding! I take my chances with the stocks, Mrs Trotter, but the machinations of the gaming-houses are not for me. Yes, wealth circulates there, but it is all extravagance and vanity. No public good comes of it.'

'Yet there is corruption and deceit in the City also, Mr Henriques. I suspect public benefits play only a minor part.'

She wondered if she had pressed too far – and indeed his response was a sharp one:

'That's easily said, and I won't dispute it. 'Change Alley is a thieves' den. I frequently despair of it all! But money can be well used if directed aright ... I have an interest in the material and the practical, Mrs Trotter. Thanks to my father, the Exchange has been a second home. Just think what *benefits* this place brings to our nation! Wealth flows across the seas, our trade expands, and all countries bring their goods to us!'

This was her opening:

'I'm always struck by the walks, Mr Henriques – such a gathering of nations!'

'Yes, the walks – twenty-three of them! And what characters arrive here, many of them fresh off their boats. A motley crew. All those languages – and those titillating smells – so much snuff billowing about!'

'There was one man who struck me particularly ... in the Dutch walk, I think it was. A striking figure in a long black coat and scarlet breeches – a woollen hat pulled over his head.'

There was a telling pause.

'You truly have an informer's eye, Mrs Trotter. I marvel at you! That is Willem Oosterhout. I'm impressed that you single him out – a formidable gentleman! He is a tobacco merchant – but that's not the sum of him. The Dutch are great traders, and he's the shrewdest of the lot. Any business you have with the Amsterdam market, then Oosterhout is your man ...'

At that moment his own shrewdness peeped out:

'... Your curiosity about him does you credit ... I do hope my answer has told you what you needed to know?'

Widow Trotter was momentarily lost for a reply. She had met her match. The look he shot her was intense, but sympathetic.

'There's no denying you, Mr Henriques! I came to the Exchange to find you but have been distracted by seeing Bob Leary – the very last man I expected to be here. He was in close conversation with your Mr Oosterhout. It was the briefest meeting. Mr Leary received a small parcel from him and left suddenly.'

'A Good, concise report, Mrs Trotter. I take it you witnessed this in dumb-show?'

'Exactly, yes ...'

This was awkward, but the young man was compelling her honesty. For all his astuteness there was an innocence of heart there. She saw only one way forward – she must be open with him and trust they would both be gainers. She settled onto the bench, oddly relieved that she could share something with him:

'... I owe you the full story, Mr Henriques – one in which Mr Leary and Mr Sturgis both figure. You will see that Vandernan's is the nub of it. We are convinced that some plot is being hatched that will affect the stocks – and be of particular danger to yourself ...'

And so, she told him all that Will Lundy had learned in the gaming-house. Michael Henriques shook his head sadly:

'So, Vandernan's people are up to their tricks again! You say they are pushing the gas project hard, for a double play – a bubble no less! I confess I had my suspicions. A great wave of interest is building behind the stock, and its price mounts ever higher. But they are about to engineer a fall?'

'Yes, a *put* – is that not the term?'

'It is indeed. And are you certain this is a fixed plan of theirs?'

'Two gentlemen were heard in Vandernan's discussing it as something resolved upon. It smacks of conspiracy, does it not?'

Widow Trotter noticed a bead of sweat forming on his forehead. Clearly the young man felt the danger that was fast approaching.

'Do you know who these people are, Mrs Trotter? Not Leary, surely? – he does not have the means to do this.'

'No, Mr Henriques, it was two others – people who have more than enough power to do you harm – Lord Parham and Philip Roscoe.'

He looked at her in astonishment:

'Roscoe – and Parham? – Yes, they are indeed both subscribers to the scheme – substantial ones! Do you understand what you are telling me?'

'I think I do.'

'Conspiracy is the word, Mrs Trotter ... and is the Bank involved in it? Mr Roscoe is a Director!'

'I know it ... You say Vandernan's are up to their tricks *again*. You have previous experience of their plotting?'

'Yes – and the pieces are fitting together. I see that my own brush with Vandernan's and Mr Sturgis needs to be told ...'

Now it was her turn to hear a tale. What followed was a story of bribery and threats together. Henriques recalled how he had been approached by George Sturgis some months earlier and a scheme proposed that would be to his advantage – an offer richly profitable for all, except for those innocent people who would be tricked out of their money.

'I refused him, Mrs Trotter – and in such terms as seemed to cause offence. Certain threats were made – not physical ones, but to the family's business. They evidently knew my father's trade was precarious and easily a prey to malicious stories. Nothing was simpler than to attack our credit – and as you know, in the City your credit is everything. I revealed all to my father, and he stood by me. Since then we have worked hard to counter the gossip, and our friends have rallied to us. Fortunately, things are improving – but it is a difficult path, and a continual distraction ... This new plot is distressing.'

'I'm glad I have been able to warn you – though there may be little or nothing you can do.'

'Forewarned – forearmed, Mrs Trotter!'

'I wish to think so.'

'From what you have told me, Sturgis and Mr Leary (as I must now call him) have been accomplices. Another fact slips into place! I never thought there could be a connection between them. And you tell me Leary was here just now to meet Willem Oosterhout ... What business could they be doing together?'

'I have a hint, Mr Henriques ... Bob Leary is about to take ship for Amsterdam.'

'You mean he is fleeing the country?'

'I confronted him yesterday in Islington. He has quarrelled with Lord Parham and the cabal at Vandernan's, and after George Sturgis's murder he fears for his life.'

'Murder? But it was a gamester's quarrel, was it not? That's what I heard.'

'That was the appearance, certainly – but it seems Mr Sturgis had become an embarrassment to his erstwhile friends.'

'Someone in Vandernan's had him killed?'

'This is only conjecture – but a strong one. It fits what facts we know.'

A sudden deep frown told her Michael Henriques had recalled something else to trouble him.

'But what if there is a Dutch connection, Mrs Trotter ... if Mynheer Oosterhout is part of this ... where does the thing end? ...'

He gave her a look of encouragement:

'... A moment ago, you said there were things you could not reveal. I hope you don't feel you cannot be open with me.'

'On the contrary, Mr Henriques – I have said more than I intended. But I trust you to make right use of it. I like to think we now have you as an ally.'

'You say *we* ... Do I take it you have friends concerned in this affair?'

'Yes, close and dear friends. I hope you will be able to meet them – but at this moment it would be dangerous to tell you all. We are facing threats of our own. It is not from distrust, you understand ...'

'Say no more, Mrs Trotter – I shall not enquire. But I hope to have the full picture when you feel it is right. You have been a great help – I wish you would allow me to do more.'

'One valuable thing you can do, Mr Henriques, is to investigate Mr Oosterhout for us – his reputation and his history. You say he is an important figure in the Dutch trade. Who are his friends and connections? Do any rumours or suspicions adhere to him? ... But you must do so guardedly, without any open inquiry. It would seem he is a powerful man.'

'In that, I am happy to be your agent, Mrs Trotter ...'

The look on the young man's face was a mixture of emotions: wonder, gratitude, and also a touch of amusement.

'... I am lost for words. You have given me much to think about. A woman of business, and a master spy – and you excel in both. A formidable combination!'

Chapter Twenty-Nine

⸻

'THE LOTTERY!'

Tom caught the word from across the Popham dinner-table and was all attention. The cry had come from his Cousin Lavinia, who bounced in her chair with a mixture of amusement and delight. Beside her, Lady Melksham bridled, showing a hint of a double chin:

'Yes, your brother seems to think a windfall of two thousand pounds would *set him up in life!* ...'

Her look showed she found the idea – and the phrase – more than a little distasteful.

'... You are sounding like a shopkeeper, Frank. What put that idea into your head?'

But Lavinia wasn't finished:

'I think he shows great consideration, Mamma. Frank is thinking of his independence – and a Member of Parliament has great expenses if he is to do the job properly ... there are so many people he needs to *recompense*.'

She looked at Frank with a knowing grin. His face began to glow. It reddened even more when from the other end of the table, Lord Melksham gave a judicious response:

'I recall, my dear, that last year Lord Kilcoole won mightily – a thousand a year for life! ... and it is, after all, an *Honourable Adventure*.'

'Honourable? I do not think so, John! The lottery is an act of desperation. The Kilcooles were facing ruin – why, their furniture was practically stacked on the pavement!'

'Even more fortunate for him!' said Frank, showing some defiance.

There was a moment of silence before another voice was heard. Opposite Tom, Lady Norreys spoke:

'There is nothing to despise about *Chance*, Sophia! She can be a most discriminating deity. I have been on visiting terms with her for some years, and the lady can be very grateful!'

Tom had always enjoyed the banter round the Popham dinner-table, but on this occasion he was finding it hard to be at ease. He looked around at the agreeable company and saw everything to unsettle him: Cousin Frank facing ruin – or something worse – his uncle threatened with the family's disgrace, his Aunt Sophia and Cousin Lavinia unaware of the storm clouds gathering over their heads – and there, facing him across the table, Lady Norreys, perhaps the most disquieting figure of all. How much did she know of her husband's doings? Trapped in a marriage with no love or respect on either side, she was left to take her pleasures where she could, in amusement and distraction. Such a strong woman as he knew her to be, yet what pain might be there … Would he be able to talk with her about Sir Charles and the Vandernan's enterprise? Her presence at dinner had been a surprise, but should he exploit the occasion?

Tom was full of apprehension. What could he say to Lord Melksham, and what more might he discover when the company adjourned? Since his arrival, there had been no chance to learn how things stood with Frank's affairs – and his cousin was now thinking of turning to the *Honourable Adventure* to recover himself! Alas, his aunt's accusation was truer than she could know.

'You are pensive, Mr Bristowe.'

Lady Norreys was looking at him encouragingly. He knew he must dig deep into his resources of good humour and stir himself:

'I was recalling our adventures at the May Fair, Lady Norreys. I try not to think of you as one of the *Fates* – but I wonder, do you perhaps have some lingering influence with the lottery?'

'Fate and Chance are seldom on speaking terms, Mr Bristowe! No, no – I leave lotteries well alone! At least with cards you hold your fate in your hands – unless of course there is other intervention *from above* ...'

There was a pause.

Somehow, he could tell by the look ... She knew.

'... I hesitate to ask after Mrs Trotter. I understand she has found herself under some embarrassment after the basset business. It grieves me to think of it. There was double dealing that evening, was there not? ... You must convey my good wishes and encouragement to her.'

'I promise to do so. I know she admires you very much.'

'And I her. We made a good team at the May Fair, did we not! She is resourceful and will come through this, I'm certain ... I hope you and I shall be able to talk *à deux* a little later?'

She glanced at Lord Melksham, who was seated between them and responded:

'You and Tom? Yes of course. You have things to chew over, I'm sure ... and I suspect Tom is here for more than the leg of mutton – delicious though it is.'

Lady Melksham's voice rang out from the other end of the table:

'The mutton? I was concerned it would not *stretch*. But Tom appears to have left his appetite behind him.'

'He is waiting for the apple pudding, Mamma,' said Lavinia. 'I know that look of anticipation.'

They were suddenly back in the world of genial table talk ...

It was the best part of an hour before Tom, with his Uncle Jack and Cousin Frank, accompanied by a decanter of brandy, found themselves settled before a low fire in Lord Melksham's closet. The setting was deceptively comfortable given the heavy matters they needed to confront, and Tom was worried that the seriousness of the situation may not have been understood. All three of them knew what the topic would be – but where to start? He felt he ought to defer to his uncle, and so held himself back while Frank did the honours with the brandy and Lord Melksham lifted off his tumultuous dress-wig. Unlike Tom's previous visit to this room, it was not to be a formal discussion.

'Well, Tom,' said his uncle, lowering himself into his favourite armchair, 'I am very glad to have you here. What a story we have to piece together! … I hear Frank's gaming-house was invaded last night and the gamesters taken into custody. And George Sturgis dead! So much has been happening. What news do you have for us?'

The question was asked with his usual good humour; but there was an edge to the voice, and without the wig his pinched brow and anxious eyes were at once noticeable. Tom wanted to ask that very question himself, but he had to be patient a little longer and try to disentangle the events of the past two days:

'Will Lundy was there, uncle …'

'What! In Vandernan's – last night?'

'Yes – he was our Bay-Tree spy, and before the mob arrived he learned a lot about what goes on there. You'll not be surprised to hear that the hazard-table isn't to be trusted. It serves a larger purpose. On Sunday nights Vandernan's is an outpost for City men – bankers and gentlemen of note settling their affairs. There's some kind of *system* for dubious dealings – Will caught a whiff of it. They are a cabal of lace-cuffed thieves, all with large purses! George Sturgis and Robert LeRoy were part of the system and served it. But something unforeseen appears to have occurred, and now Sturgis has been killed, and LeRoy is fleeing the country! Will picked up hints of a strong City connection ...'

And so, piece by piece, Tom gave them an account of his friend's adventure in Vandernan's – his play with the false dice, the revelations of Lady Rastell, and the drama of Widow Trotter's promissory note. Along the way Tom managed a digression onto his own expedition with Widow Trotter into the wilds of Islington, and their interview with the man who was in reality Bob Leary of Dublin. Frank and his father were a rapt audience, and as the fuller picture established itself there were several intakes of breath. But for Lord Melksham, the great surprise was the fact that the Commissioner of Vandernan's was none other than Sir Charles Norreys:

'What is this, Tom? – Sir Charles? I can hardly credit it! – not his involvement in shady dealings but the fact that he would appear to run the place. I had not thought the man could run a pie-shop! ...'

His head suddenly turned aside with an anxious look, and Tom knew he was thinking of his other guest.

'... Poor Lady Norreys – do you think she will know of this? How could she not? ...'

He answered his own question with unsteady voice.

'... And Lord Parham, you say? ... Now there I am less surprised. The man is a plotter, if ever I knew one! A slippery creature – and a great *whisperer*. What was his role, do you know?'

Tom allowed himself to smile:

'You hit it exactly, uncle – plotter-in-chief, it would seem! It was Lord Parham's *whispering* that brought the greatest revelation of all ...'

And with that, he proceeded to tell them of the conversation Will had overheard between Parham and Philip Roscoe, and about what they had come to think of as 'the enterprise.' During the telling, Lord Melksham's face was like a child's before the turning pages of a story-book:

'But this is extraordinary, Tom! Philip Roscoe, you say? The man is on the Treasury Committee – a Director of the Bank! He is also the Duchess's *broker!* … And this scheme for extracting combustible air from coal … what if I told you the Duchess has been interesting herself in it? Not only that, but she has committed some of Her Majesty's funds also.'

'But I thought the Duchess was not concerned with Privy Purse investment?'

'Not routine ones, Tom – ever – but this was a special purchase …'

'So – do you think the Duchess knows? She must surely have been guided by Roscoe … Does this not put Her Majesty in risk of embarrassment?'

Tom had no sooner spoken those words than all three of them felt the danger. They were coming to see how the events in Vandernan's were growing into a scandal of national dimensions.

'The Duchess wouldn't entangle the Queen in the plot, would she?'

'Not directly, Frank. But I begin to think the worst. If word were put about that the scheme had the support of Her Majesty it would run through 'Change Alley in an instant. The news would be enough to raise the price to the heights …'

Lord Melksham suddenly stood up and reached for the tobacco jar on the mantelpiece.

'… It would be hard to keep the Queen free of blame – of a suspicion that there had been royal connivance in the scheme.'

He sat down again and began filling his pipe while Tom and Frank looked intently at each other. There was a tense silence while Lord Melksham's pipe-lighting proceeded. Finally, tobacco smoke began to billow round him and shroud his features. The two of them froze as if in the presence of the Delphic oracle.

'… Did I say the *worst*, gentlemen? … I fear there may be a more severe danger in all of this – a more momentous consideration. When I think of what is being plotted – Parham and Roscoe's *enterprise* – and ask myself what the motives for it are, I see an even bigger picture forming …'

He began to shake his head.

'… The matter resolves itself into money, of course – a great deal of it! I suspect this play with the coal-gas subscription serves a larger purpose. When I think back to that Treasury meeting, I'm convinced that supporting the Bank – I almost said *rescuing* it – is the prime motive.'

'Rescuing? But surely the Bank of England is stronger than ever? – you said so yourself.'

'No, Tom. I said it was more *powerful* – not the same thing at all! We are talking of debt here. And after that loan to the government – a million and a half, remember! – the Bank's indebtedness is huge, and it calls upon the wealth of the City to support it – the credit of those who stand behind the loan and guarantee it – the Bank's directors in particular.'

'And you think this credit may be in question?' said Frank.

'Just as with a man's reputation – or a woman's – any doubt can leave a mark, it is even so with the Bank. As I remember telling you, it is at daggers-drawn with the Sword Blade company, and it was their intervention that brought the crisis. The Bank's offer of a million and a quarter at five per cent was trumped by the Sword Blade, who offered the government *a million and a half!* This was wholly unexpected, and to counter their offer the Bank had to find a quarter of a million very quickly. That is no small sum! The Sword Blade loan could be secured by land, but the Bank has no *substantial* value of that kind.

'It may be a temporary embarrassment, but in this modern world the credit of the City of London – the *nation's* credit – can be a fragile thing, especially in time of war. Funding the war is the big political necessity!'

'The *Whig* necessity, father!'

'Yes of course – and the more urgent for that! Whig and City are synonymous, and their reputations are one. We may scoff at the *Cits* with their coaches and their processions and scarlet robes, but the Common-Council men – Heathcote and his friends – are the backbone of the City. Any scandal over the loan – any doubt of its secureness – would endanger London's reputation.'

'And *is* there doubt of it?' asked Tom.

His uncle laid his pipe on the table and knitted his hands together as if trying to grasp a thought:

'On Saturday I had a visit from a member of the committee … He came to me in some anxiety, believing me to be someone he could trust for advice – and what he told me (in the greatest secrecy, you understand!) was troubling. He felt he could not keep silent, and yet to speak of it openly would bring the very consequence he wished to avoid.'

'And what is that, uncle?'

'A scandal, Tom! No mere one day's wonder either, but something to set a mine beneath the bulwark – the credit of the City! There has been great foolishness. Damage has been done, and surreptitious efforts are being made to rectify it. It is doubtless a temporary problem, but they are trying to buy themselves some time … The quarter of a million had to be raised immediately, and my informant told me the lottery funds were pledged as security – a desperate measure!'

'But surely, uncle, the lottery will have to pay out large sums at the end of the month …'

Tom saw his uncle wince.

'… All those prizes!'

'Yes, Tom. Exactly. They need capital quickly … And now I hear your news about the coal-gas business, and that these people are using the lottery funds to speculate on the scheme. I think I see what they intend – to play the market ruthlessly. The major stocks – Bank stock, East India, or Hudson's Bay – will not do, and so they look for a small, volatile stock that will take wing and deliver swift and huge returns – a subscription that can be manipulated by a handful of people working in concert.'

'But this is full of risk,' said Tom.

'Indeed it is! The whole thing is a dangerous structure, and on unsteady foundations. It is a pyramid reversed. Can you picture it? The great weight of the war loan supported by the lottery funds, in turn supported by the coal-gas speculation … It is a ridiculous idea – like a child's spinning-top! … And yet the reputation of London is at stake. I can picture them smiling broadly in Amsterdam! In so many ways, their market would feed on our humiliation.'

While Lord Melksham's account took shape, Tom's thoughts had been turning on the urgent question of his uncle's resignation. No reference had been made to the possibility, and nothing had been said about Frank's sojourn in the sponging-house and the terrible ultimatum. It was becoming clear that Frank had not confronted his father on the matter. For Tom to raise it himself was impossible, and yet he saw with increasing clarity why these money-men would want to silence his uncle – and even more why the Duchess and her advisers could think him dangerous. Tom shivered at the thought. A hired ruffian would quickly remove the problem … But why was nothing being said? He reached for his brandy and held his peace.

Little did he suspect what was about to happen.

Frank glanced briefly at his cousin – then, without warning he sprang forward in his chair, his eyes bright with the urgency of the moment. He placed a hand on his father's knee:

'Father, I beg you! Please be careful! … What Tom has told us about Vandernan's confirms your fears, does it not? – about the Duchess, Heathcote, Sturgis and the Bank. The story hangs together ... But can you see how extremely dangerous this conspiracy is for you – for all of us? Your family ...'

Lord Melksham looked startled and was about to speak, but Frank surged on.

'... These people are to be feared! One bloody murder has already been committed. I have been threatened directly, and you have been sent an urgent message by them. You cannot defy these people! You must think of mamma – of Lavinia ... Think what these men might do! They are not playing a game. *You* did not have a hand at your throat and feel a sword pressed against you! ... Believe me, father, you must think carefully and act wisely. More than ever now, you need to consider drawing back – for all our sakes ...'

Frank was unrelenting and glanced urgently at his cousin.

'... I know Tom will join me in begging you *let things be!* Would not your life be happier if you were to relinquish your duties? You know how laborious you find them and how uncomfortable your position is – the vindictiveness of the Duchess, the bad blood at Court ... Nothing would be more understandable ... I'm sure Tom will support me in this.'

Tom felt his neck tighten. Once more he was appealed to, and the look was an intense one. For the first time since Frank had returned from the Grand Tour, Tom could envisage him as having a political career ... He felt duty-bound to speak out before his uncle could reply. It was time to join forces with Frank ... and yet ... What to do? ...

'Frank speaks with passion, uncle ... but there is reason and sense in what he urges. You must at least consider it ... but it must be done at once, before the week is out. To delay will only draw you further into this unsavoury business. When the scandal breaks, no-one's reputation will be untainted – your own included. You must see this. Your resignation *tomorrow* would be judicious and dignified. I say this, uncle ... because I know it is what in your heart you want to do.'

There was silence.

Lord Melksham reached once more for his pipe, and with the help of a candle he set the inflammatory ritual in motion. It was impossible to say whether Frank's eloquence had moved him – or in what direction. Tom thought it best to let the moment last while his uncle pondered what had been said. With his pipe alive again, he responded in deliberate tones:

'You speak kindly, Frank – and Tom too. Believe me, I feel the force of what you say. With the news Tom has brought, the picture has darkened and the threat become much greater ... But the more persuasive your argument is, the more I see a threat to Her Majesty that must be resisted. Were the Queen not being entangled in this, I assure you I would walk away at once! All your reasons are powerful ones – I cannot disagree – not can I fault your motives for urging them. But ... do you not see? ... The more you speak of danger, the clearer my duty to the Queen becomes.'

Frank's argument had been turned around. The greater the fear he tried to convey, the more his father's resolution strengthened.

But one card had not been played. There was still no word of the Devil's bargain extorted in the sponging-house. On that Frank remained silent, afraid of what the story would reveal about himself. His father's firmness made his own acquiescence seem an act of cowardice.

Tom felt his cousin's desperation and struggled to know his own mind. He admired his uncle's stand – heroic principles were to be applauded – but he couldn't help thinking they needed to be placed in a just perspective and tested to the furthest consequence. He was becoming convinced that Lord Melksham must be told of the direct threat to Frank ... If only he could have a few moments alone with his cousin! The two of them would stand together and confront him.

But before anything could be said, matters were decided for them. While Tom's thoughts veered like eddying leaves, Arthur the footman was opening the street door of the Popham residence and taking in a note from a breathless Jeremy who had run as fast as he could from the Bay-Tree. The scene, with all its perspectives and consequences, was about to change. Finely judged scruples were to be swept aside and events resolve themselves.

Chapter Thirty

⚉

THE CLOSET DOOR opened with a sharp knock, and Arthur was inside the room with the note before Lord Melksham could respond:

'For your urgent attention my Lord – from Covent Garden. The messenger can hardly speak he's run so fast!'

If the Pophams' footman wanted to command notice, he succeeded. Overlooking the breach of decorum, Lord Melksham got to his feet and took the note in his hand, flipped it open, and saw the name of Elias Cobb.

Tom and Frank looked at each other in alarm. Lord Melksham read it quickly, and before the blood could drain from his face he swung round to his son:

'Frank – you must leave at once! It is from Constable Cobb. You are to be arrested – the sheriff's men are on their way …'

Frank looked baffled:

'The debt, father? That cannot be! This makes no sense …'

'No, no! Not your debt. They are coming for you on an accusation of *murder*.'

'But …'

Frank looked at Tom in horror.

'… Tom! Surely, this cannot be?'

'You have minutes only …'

His father was thinking rapidly.

'... Leave now – take Silvertail.'

'But what shall I pack?'

'Nothing – there's no time for packing. Make for Brentford – the White Horse – we shall have some things sent you ... Go now! The note says they are only minutes behind ... I shall explain to your mother ...'

'Is there nothing more?'

'No, it's a hurried scribble. We shall deal with this, Frank! ... Arthur will help you – Go!'

'But ...'

'Go!'

His father simultaneously embraced him and pushed him through the door, then hesitated and turned:

'Remain here, Tom. I'll send Lady Norreys to you ... I need to speak with Sophia alone.'

For an instant Tom and his uncle faced each other in silence – there was too much to say.

'You must let me know what I can do, Uncle,' said Tom weakly.

'Yes – and we must talk ... Stay here. I shall need your advice – something I was intending to mention, but ...'

He broke off, his mind leaping to his wife, whose voice Tom could hear in the distance.

'... We shall talk!'

And with that he was gone.

Tom remained alone in the room, thunderstruck. A few scribbled words on a scrap of paper and all had veered into chaos. So much for Frank's sponging-house bargain! Any thought of drawing back was now out of the question – these people were making their own rules.

But they themselves were not without resources. They knew the chief players and what an intricate game it was, and if Frank were able to elude his pursuers it would buy them a day or two. Perhaps Widow Trotter had learned something useful at the Royal Exchange? And Will might be having a profitable meeting with his father. Judge Lundy's City connections could be useful if the nation's credit was under threat.

And now another scene was about to begin – Lady Norreys's interview *à deux*. Tom wondered what was prompting her and what he might discover. For his part It would be an opportunity to raise the subject of her husband – but how to do it delicately? She was a strong and determined woman, but he must not assume this wouldn't be a hurtful topic for her.

The door opened – and there she was, her eyes beaming darkly from under a turban of ruby-coloured silk. Without hesitation or formality, she strode in and met his gaze directly:

'Well, Tom, what are we to make of this? – Frank leaving us so suddenly! Your aunt is having to be pacified – I was ushered from the room!'

And, as if to illustrate the remark, a distant cry of alarm rang out. She looked at him for explanation – and Tom knew he had to supply it.

They sat down. Lady Norreys didn't decline the offer of brandy. An intelligent listener, she grasped at once how matters stood with Frank and his misadventures in Vandernan's. When the name of George Sturgis was spoken the gravity of the moment registered. Her response was brisk:

'So, Frank is suspected of murder because George had bought up his debt? A flimsy circumstance! The pair were amicable enough during basset – though George was in his cups. Surely the killing was a robbery? He would have had a fortune in his pocket – a temptation for any street thief! ...'

She paused. Her voice lowered as a thought struck her.

'... Ah, but this is no simple arrest, is it, Tom? There is malicious intent behind it. Am I right? ...'

Tom's silence confirmed it.

'... You are uneasy about revealing too much, but I suspect the three of you have been conferring about some danger. I wondered at Frank's diffidence during dinner, and you seemed a little distracted yourself ... The Pophams are in trouble, are they not?'

Tom longed to confide everything in her, but for the moment he held himself back:

'We are facing ruthless men, Lady Norreys. You know something of Vandernan's and its people ... well, last night the place was invaded, and my friend Will was caught up in it all. What he encountered was sinister – the distinct smell of corruption. City men were herding like swine at the trough, taking payment and plotting their schemes. The place breeds conspiracies. There was a confidence about them.'

'Ah, this was a Sunday night of course! ... Yes, Tom, I have some knowledge of Vandernan's and have been known to venture there – an indulgence I am happy to be rid of ...'

She averted her gaze and drew breath slowly.

'... My husband discourages it ... He has his reasons – which may not be unconnected with your suspicions about the place.'

'They are more than suspicions, Lady Norreys.'

They had reached a stage in the conversation where openness beckoned as a relief. Talk of 'suspicions' made them both feel that the truth might be risked between them.

'Surely my husband was there last night? He is Commissioner of the place and was no doubt superintending the proceedings?'

'Indeed he was ... and in that he was seconded by Lord Parham ...'

Tom paused to let the name achieve its full effect.

'... Are you acquainted with that gentleman?'

'*Gentleman?* What can I say? My husband's friends – if that is the appropriate word – are not mine. We have our separate circles and do not entertain together ... But I have certainly encountered Parham. He and Charles are part of the fast set at White's, though Vandernan's is their own concern – a convenient adjunct to the mother-house, as it were. What goes on there is more *enterprising*. I have ceased to be either suspicious or astonished at my husband's capacity for deception. Don't be anxious about offending me ...'

She stopped. A smile of contempt showed itself.

'... Enough of dinner-table politeness! ... What *crime* has my husband committed?'

Tom swallowed. He knew Lady Norreys's ability to disconcert. But on this occasion she was anticipating him. He seized the opportunity:

'He and Lord Parham are forwarding a plot – one that amounts to a fraud on the public funds – and there would seem to be some collusion with the Bank. Last night Lord Parham was discussing arrangements with one of the Directors, and Sir Charles was paying the man through the hazard-table, which is effectually Vandernan's accounting system.'

'The Bank? The Cits were at the trough, were they?'

'It would appear so.'

'Hmm – it does have the smell of a Whig plot – and ripening fast! Charles likes to cultivate his City acquaintances in Vandernan's. Your story does not surprise me ...'

She saw a look of apprehension on his face.

'... Don't be uneasy, Tom. I'll not pester you for the particulars, which are no doubt sordid in character ... But what has it to do with Frank Popham? He surely cannot be caught up in this?'

'Alas, Lady Norreys – he is thoroughly entangled, not for his own part but on account of his father.'

'What are you saying? Lord Melksham? That is even more extraordinary!'

Tom saw that he would have to explain. He was beginning to fear Lady Norreys was drawing too much out of him. But it couldn't be contained:

'My uncle – in all his innocence – has stumbled on the conspiracy and finds himself threatened – not directly, but through Frank. My poor cousin has become a kind of hostage – a means to attack Uncle Jack ... It is despicable! ... And now they are pressing the murder on him ... They are hunting him down! It is too much to bear! It will destroy the family ...'

Tom was catching his breath.

'... Forgive me, I should not be telling you this – I fear for everyone concerned ... Frank has to get away! – It will give us the time we need ... We have to stop these callous people!'

Lady Norreys set down her brandy. She looked intently at Tom and saw a colt frisking and chafing at the bit. A few calming words were needed:

'Remember you have friends, Tom. Constable Cobb is an ally – he has taken a great risk in writing that note. And what I know of you and your friends makes me believe you'll come through it all ... Urgency and boldness will have their time, but right now you must be cool and deliberate. Remember, a confident villain is often a blundering one, and if you deploy your resources carefully ...'

Wise words, and Tom noted them:

'Yes, I must think of a hand at cards, mustn't I!'

'Exactly. A perfect parallel in the circumstances ... And perhaps I can help in a small way too ...'

Tom was curious and his spirits lifted.

'... I have an interest in this myself. You see, it touches on the very suspicion I was intending to put to you. You have gone a way to explaining what puzzled me – some words of my husband's which I happened to overhear ...'

'By Chance, was it?'

'Yes, Tom – I told you the lady was a good neighbour of mine! And on this occasion perhaps she can help warn *you* ...'

Lady Norreys caught her breath and raised a finger to her ear as if unconsciously reliving the scene.

'... Charles did not know I was anywhere near – until the floorboard creaked. It was Lord Melksham's name which made me start, and I lingered outside the half-open door – it was quite like a stage comedy! Your uncle's name was coupled with the Duchess's, and it was spoken in snarling tones. It appears that *Her Grace* is angry with your uncle, and from what I could pick up there is some financial irregularity involved ...'

'There certainly is – as I told you. A fraud is being perpetrated.'

'No, Tom, it was not that. Piecing together the snatches I heard, it seems the intent is to accuse Lord Melksham of making a personal gain at Her Majesty's expense.'

'What!'

'I was concerned your uncle might have made some inadvertent mistake, but this is surely a fabrication. As you say, they are ruthless people. Your Vandernan's plot would account for it.'

'But this is outrageous! Did you hear anything particular?'

'No, it was alluded to in general terms. The other gentleman appeared the instigator – though it was hugger-mugger between them.'

'This other man, Lady Norreys – did you see who it was?'

'I heard him, certainly, and it was a voice I recognised. It was the Duchess's secretary himself.'

'Arthur Maynwaring!'

'The very same. I would know those tones anywhere. He's a sly rogue, is he not? – and one you have encountered before.'

'To our cost, yes – though in the end his scheming came to naught. He has resented my uncle ever since.'

'These two attacks are certainly connected.'

'Without a doubt. And your husband is the link.'

'It's a disquieting idea, Tom, but it must be right. I had been wondering why Charles was concerned with the Duchess's affairs – but now a picture is forming.'

'Yes, a murky one. And if we had any doubt of her connivance you have removed it! Maynwaring surely sees his opportunity. Politicians love cabals. These men are moving their plots forward, and we are left trying to work the pieces into a pattern. There must be one. If only we could confront them!'

Lady Norreys raised her hand – it was meant to be calming, but it was almost a fist:

'*Know thine enemy* is a good motto, Tom. Don't be precipitate! You can exploit their weakness and lay your plans accordingly. Remember, every strength is paired with a small weakness. It is often out of sight – but it is there somewhere. You have to discover what it is.'

'There speaks a practised card-player. But must we not play by the rules?'

'By no means – not if your opponent uses trickery. A sharper must be met on his own terms. You have to counter their plot with one of your own.'

Tom recalled Will's adventure in Vandernan's and smiled to himself. Yes, they were already building their own coalition, and must make use of it.

'But the threat these people are making is a powerful one.'

'Of course it is – and so you must threaten in your turn. Find where they are vulnerable. Once you know what game they are playing, you can outwit them. Your big advantage is knowledge – knowing more than they think you do. And while that is the case you must exploit it to the full. Be patient and careful. Only move when you are sure of your ground.'

Tom was beginning to feel a little less desperate. He looked at Lady Norreys who was taking a deserved shot of brandy, her fingers curled around the glass as if she were grasping a thought. At that moment he came to a decision: he would keep nothing back from this determined lady! Thanks to her devious husband she had a stake on the table herself – a considerable one. And from what she had said, it seemed she would welcome being recruited to their cause.

⸻

Frank's escape was a narrow one. Silvertail's impressively greyish tail waved at the sheriff and his men as they mounted the steps of the Popham residence; but they didn't turn around, and a well-muffled Frank was able to begin his flight westwards along Pall Mall without incident.

Inside the house a degree of guile was necessary. Lady Melksham was being comforted by Lavinia in an upstairs bedroom, well away from the hall where Arthur was left to admit the family's unexpected visitors. The footman was dignity personified and showed the party into the reception-room as if they were a Duke and his Duchess. Lord Melksham received them full-wigged and with his business-face on. The forms were preserved. A statuesque Arthur continued to stand watch in the doorway while the scene unfolded.

The eyes of the two under-officers were exploring the ornate plasterwork of the ceiling, but the Sheriff put his no-nonsense question directly, without any polite niceties. There was a moment of silence while His Lordship's eyes widened to express an appropriate astonishment. The 'lie direct' was avoided when he replied that his son was *on the road* and not expected for at least twenty-four hours …

He was fighting to remain composed and inquired as calmly as he could at whose accusation the arrest was being attempted. But he was given no answer, only a vague reply that *evidence had come to light* and the investigation was being *pursued at the highest level* – that a charge of murder would be pressed. It was hard to say which of them felt more awkward: Lord Melksham was still reeling at the shock of events, and Sheriff Kirk was uneasy about demanding a search of the house. But Lord Melksham's indignation could no longer be contained, and he left the law officers in no doubt of his son's innocence and of the offensiveness of the charge:

'There is evil intent behind this, gentlemen! – a malicious accuser determined to destroy my son's career. Do you understand that to accuse a member of Her Majesty's parliament of murder is a star-chamber matter? I'm certain Mr Popham will have no difficulty in refuting a charge that has so little ground to uphold it.'

The speech was well made; but the Sheriff knew the forms well enough and merely narrowed his eyes and asked the uncomfortable question:

'From what you say, my Lord, it appears you already know the ground of it. You have tested it, have you? And find the evidence unsound? ...'

Lord Melksham swallowed hard. Under the pressure of the moment he had forgotten that simple injunction voicing an ancient wisdom: *the less said the better*. This was turning into an interrogation.

The Sheriff pressed on.

'... Perhaps, my Lord, you can account for your son's whereabouts when the murder was committed. There would surely be no reason for Mr Popham to be walking the streets of Covent Garden while decent folk were abed. Are you able to vouch for him?'

Lord Melksham hesitated. He knew he could offer Frank no alibi and was forced to admit as much. Other questions followed, and some further uncertainties didn't work in his favour. He was unable to be specific about what road his son was on and found himself promising that the suspect would present himself for questioning immediately on his return. He was informed that a dispatch was already on its way to the local Wiltshire magistrate at Winterbourne Monkton to ascertain whether Mr Popham had taken refuge at Monkton Court ...

It was a sobered and shaking Lord Melksham who returned to his closet, where Tom and Lady Norreys were waiting for news. By now she had received the full account of the Vandernan's enterprise, and Tom prevailed on her to stay and re-tell her eavesdropping scene for his uncle's benefit. Her report was a bitter blow and confirmed that he was under attack personally. The fact that Arthur Maynwaring, M.P. was the mischief-maker added a sinister political shadow to it all. It also placed Maynwaring's patroness the Duchess firmly in the picture.

Lady Norreys asked to be excused and slipped away to offer comfort and a glass of brandy to her friend upstairs, leaving Tom and his uncle to discuss family matters between themselves. The two men sank back into their chairs, and Lord Melksham distractedly took up his pipe again. But he made no attempt to light it. He was staring into the distance, well beyond the walls of the room.

'So! ... The Duchess and her lapdog Maynwaring! They are bent on ruining us! I must have it out with her! I cannot stand by and let disaster overtake us ...'

'Please, uncle – no!'

'... This can't be allowed to go on, Tom ...'

He swung round.

'... I intend to confront the Duchess directly. You must not try to stop me!'

'I beg you, Sir – not in the heat of the moment! We must be circumspect and move carefully – this is not the time for a cavalry charge.'

'I think it is *exactly* the time! I need to blow my bugle! If these people are afraid of what I know, then I am going to confirm their fears. If I am to be accused, I shall make my accusations first. I shall warn the Queen of the conspiracy – I shall demand to see Heathcote – I shall tell the Duchess everything I know until the blood rises in her face. All this secrecy is poisonous, Tom. The tricksters in Vandernan's have to be exposed – the bankers and stock-jobbers mustn't win. This is no time for *circumspection!*'

Tom was now genuinely alarmed. His uncle was set on a desperate course:

'Uncle, listen to me! I feel the frustrations myself – poor Lady Norreys has just had to endure them. But she gave wise counsel ... Forgive me, Sir, but I must speak plain. The actions you are proposing will serve only to unite everyone against you! For one man to accuse the many – however justly – is dangerous. You become the single enemy, and all will weigh against you.'

'I see! – first Frank tells me I should resign my post – and now you counsel me to do nothing – when my family is being destroyed and my Queen placed in danger ... What am I supposed to do?'

It was a pertinent question, and it gave Tom pause:

'The moment for action is very near, uncle. You know how much our friends are doing. Constable Cobb's note has given us some time, and we must use it carefully. If I ask you to be circumspect, it is because we need to build the larger picture. We do not have it yet but are very close – we are forming our own alliances even as we speak. Both Widow Trotter and my friend Will are at work on this. Mrs Trotter is over in Exchange Alley, and Will is meeting with his father.'

'So ... everyone is allowed to be busy except me! Our family faces ruin – Frank is like to be hanged – my wife is in hysterics –

and I must be quiet! You and your friends are all a-bustle while I am forced to sit on my hands. How can you ask this of me?'

'In truth, I cannot, Sir. All I can say is … what we have stumbled on is not a simple conspiracy but a more involved corruption. There is a mechanism to it – something like the workings of a silk mill with the threads spinning and twisting. There are connections still to be made and questions answered. The plot is an intricate one, and we have to wait until it reveals itself. Then will be your time, uncle – once we have all in place! You must be patient. We must not alert these people to what we know.'

Lord Melksham looked at his nephew and saw a young man of fearsome tenacity. The eyes were ablaze – not with anger but with sheer belief. Tom really did have faith they would find a way through. And his words were persuasive – no need of a bugle.

'I can be patient, Tom – it is somewhere in my nature. But it is *not* in my nature to turn my back. How can I? My son would have me slink away from my duties. I cannot do that!'

Tom knew there was more he needed to tell his uncle:

'There is something you should know, Sir – something that Frank would have told you himself had he not been hurried away. It will explain the fervour with which he urged resignation on you …'

And so, Tom told Lord Melksham of Frank's escapade in the sponging-house and his encounter with the strange messenger – the terrible threat that had been made and the bargain that had been wrung from him.

'Ah, I see, Tom – no wonder the poor boy was desperate for me to surrender my post! But he should have been open with me.'

'I think he wanted to keep the dilemma from you, uncle – he did not wish to force you to decide between the family and your position at Court.'

'I see. But the attempt to arrest him says these people are not to be bargained with – that they have no good faith, or rules.'

'It could be they are themselves divided. There may be little loyalty between them. Like many who lie and cheat, these men are forced to be watchful at all times. The Truth is waiting to ambush them. When we find Sturgis's killer …'

'When?'

'Yes, uncle! – *when* we find the killer, this whole deception will be exposed.'

Lord Melksham found himself offering a slight smile. Tom was sounding like his friend Will – a rousing advocate! Perhaps he should take the advice and not be precipitate – let things unfold … He gave a sigh:

'Frank has fine talents, Tom. I know he is impulsive, but he has such prospects ahead of him. I cannot believe it will all come to an end – that he will be destroyed by this evil charge. The thought is too much to bear.'

'We must be circumspect, uncle. The threats are coming from all sides.'

'A Hydra!'

'Yes – and remember, that creature was not to be destroyed unless you struck off all its heads at once. I doubt that can be achieved! The thing will forever be there, where money is – but we can hope on this occasion to rescue ourselves and our friends from its clutches. We cannot look for more.'

'I see your hopes are not fanciful ones, Tom … You have won the day. I promise to exercise self-control. But in the mean-time is there not something in a minor way that I can do? I would not be idle.'

Tom thought for a moment:

'It would be useful to know if anything is stirring among the Tories and their friends – if Mr Harley has had wind of anything about the Bank. But please …'

'Ah, political gossip! Yes, this is something more in my line, you think? … I'll see what I can do – and don't be concerned! I swear to be discretion itself. There shall be no confrontations – not yet anyway!'

Tom took this as a promise rather than a threat. It was good to see his uncle momentarily cheered. He only wished there was something that could bring comfort to Aunt Sophia and Lavinia, who must be devastated by the sudden turn of events. Although he longed to be back at the Bay-Tree, he wanted to see if there was anything he could do to reassure the two of them. News from Widow Trotter and Will would have to wait a while.

Chapter Thirty-One

———∞∞∞———

AN ENCOUNTER WITH his father was always something Will approached with apprehension, but on this occasion the term seemed inadequate. He could only hope that His Honour Judge Lundy had not been alerted to his son's escapade in Vandernan's. Well, he would soon know! As he crossed Brick Court and mounted the stairs to the first-floor chambers, he felt a tightness in the stomach that told him he was about to enter the world of the Law in its full magisterial character.

Fortunately his father was surprised to see him, and Will stepped into the room without a blast of outrage striking him. There was even hospitality of a sort – his father pointed to a chair and went to retrieve a bottle of elderflower cordial from one of the cupboards.

Will looked about him. Dark volumes occupied the bookshelves on every side – layers of historical precedent bound up into legal writ – and a nose-tingling dust hung in the air. In this place, he thought, you could imagine you were inhaling the judgments of the centuries, a feeling reinforced by the presence near the door of a kind of double lectern. This ecclesiastical furniture was not for a Bible but to support weighty tomes that could be set side-by-side for comparative purposes. As it happened, Oliver Lundy had a preference for working on his feet. In his view, labour was not to be performed in what he termed an 'after-dinner posture.' Will had never been able to decide whether his father's perpendicular character had found a natural home in the Law or been shaped by it.

Given that his own little eyrie at the top of Pump Court was so very near, the two men met rarely. His father refused to climb up to Will's garret. When Will had entered the Middle Temple the year before, they had agreed that the son should maintain a certain distance from the father. Being the offspring of a senior bencher prompted comments enough, and Will was happy to pursue his studies more independently. An active barrister, Richard Sumner – Lady Norreys's brother – became Will's guide and had benefited from the young man's diligence and quickness of mind. Will's meetings with his father tended to be accidental encounters in Middle Temple Lane.

This main chamber of the set was functional. The only concession to anything decorative was a fearsome stuffed owl that watched over the room from a high shelf – less a symbol of the Law's wisdom, Will thought, than a predator alert for the slightest rustle in the grass. Judge Lundy shared something of that bird's unrelenting gaze.

For their conversation, father and son were seated in leather armchairs that faced each other – but not near the hearth, which wasn't the heart of the room. This was no place for convivial fireside chats. And there was no fire in the grate.

'So ... ,' his father began. 'To what do I owe this visit? Nothing untoward, I hope?'

'A mixture of news and confession, Sir – and a request for help, if you are able.'

The word *confession* was nicely hidden, but the judicial brow twitched:

'Confess? You will need a magistrate for that. I hope it is not a hanging matter?'

If this was humour, then it was artfully disguised. His father's sobriquet of 'Hemp' Lundy had not been acquired without reason.

'The threat of the rope is not against me, Sir, though I am concerned in the case – a potential one. This is what prompts me to seek help.'

Will felt he had executed the manoeuvre well, and Judge Lundy's interest was engaged:

'This is not a case likely to involve me, is it?'

'No, father, but it does involve my friends – people you know and admire – who are under the gravest threat.'

'*Gravest?* You do not play with words? A capital offence?'

Will assured him it was, and that corruption and conspiracy were at the heart of it – always things to stir his father's interest.

And with that, he began to relate the story of Frank Popham's Vandernan's disaster, and how thanks to her basset table Widow Trotter had become caught up in the trickery. His father was shaking his head in distaste at the very idea.

Mention of George Sturgis caught his attention:

'Sturgis – Baron Cray's brother? Is this what you allude to? A street robbery, was it not? Have they apprehended the assassin?'

'No, father – but Frank Popham has been threatened with the accusation. He is to be arrested on a charge of murder – unless Lord Melksham resigns his Treasurership.'

There was a burst of sound as Judge Lundy stifled an unholy exclamation:

'What devilish coercion is that? Do they have evidence?'

'They say it can be procured – a Knight of the Post.'

'Bought-in? An affidavit man?'

'Exactly, yes – this is their plan – I assure you they have nothing more – but Frank is unable to account for his whereabouts during the night. It makes him open to any imposition.'

'His whereabouts? ... But Lord Melksham ... Has he been confronted with this? Does he know of his son's shame? The hazard-table!'

'He does not yet know – but Frank must tell him. It is a desperate situation. Frank was attacked and threatened.'

'But who has made this threat? You mentioned a conspiracy.'

By now his father's curiosity was aroused, and Will did his best to convey what he had discovered without running into too many particulars. As he spoke, the ground grew unsteady beneath his feet, and his father's look darkened:

'And where were you when you overheard this plotting?'

Will hesitated slightly too long:

'... In Vandernan's, Sir.'

The pause was enough. It sounded like an admission of guilt. Judge Lundy was alert to such things:

'The *gaming-house*? What in God's name ... ? You have been *gaming*! When was this?'

'Last night, Sir.'

'The sabbath! What are you telling me? I will not believe it! Have you come here to brazen it out with me, Sir? Rather than slink away in shame, you hurry to tell me the news! Are you proud of your adventure? What if the benchers hear about this? I shall be made a laughing-stock!'

'You must understand, father – this was an investigation ...'

'I *must* understand, must I? Well, you will have to help me!'

'I was there to discover what was going on, and what was known about George Sturgis. Vandernan's is a place that breathes corruption.'

The phrase was well chosen – out of his father's lexicon.

'Indeed it does! – but did you need to expose yourself to it? Who introduced you? You cannot have gone to the place alone?'

'I was taken there by a friend, Sam Rivers.'

The look on his father's face told him this was not the reassurance he had intended.

'I might have known! His father despairs of him – the boy is altogether dissolute! He appears to have made gaming his profession.'

'You are acquainted with his father, then? I wondered …'

'Of course. I have connections with the Mercers – especially Alderman Rivers. Indeed, I dined with him a fortnight ago. He is a City Coroner. You must know this – did you not encounter him at that inquest on the murdered press-man?'

'Yes.'

'Well then, tell me! – what part did young Rivers play in this gaming adventure of yours? And what was your role? You said you had a confession to make. I take it you didn't just sit in an armchair nursing a dish of coffee?'

Will knew he would have to negotiate the next step with care. He explained his presence at the hazard-table, but in his father's imagination the scene was wreathed in the choking flames of Sodom. However lofty the motive, the activity didn't look good. (Wisely perhaps, he neglected to mention the false dice.) … His father's silence became unsettling, and the more Will said, the less confident he grew. It didn't help that he was having to censor himself as he spoke – it was not a world his father understood. His casting of dice for Widow Trotter's promissory note began to sound like a cheap trick.

Will eventually collapsed into silence, feeling like a witness whose testimony has served only to incriminate himself.

There was no immediate response, and Will waited for the mortal blow. But as the seconds ticked by, the parental silence became easier. A kind of thoughtfulness appeared to be taking over:

'I see … This tale has a happy ending, then – at least for Mrs Trotter? Well, I am glad of it …'

Will was a degree reassured – the axe was still raised, but his head remained in place.

'... As for the basset – you say she has learnt her lesson?'

'Well and truly, Sir ... although ...'

Here was a sudden awkwardness. Judge Lundy stirred. He always found syntax revealing, especially when left unresolved:

'Although ... *what?*'

'The night ended badly, and I lost the note.'

'Lost it? What do you mean?'

'It was taken from me ...'

Will had hoped he could avoid telling the story of the raid, but in the end it was wrung from him – the whole dramatic scene – exactly what he should have avoided! His confidence had ebbed away. From the very start he had thought himself in the dock, and feelings of guilt had coloured all he had said. He had let himself be browbeaten and hadn't asked any of his own questions. Admonishing himself, Will looked away, only for his eyes to catch those of the owl. It was remarkable, but – somehow – the creature appeared to be smiling at him. Was it a gloat – or could she be bidding him learn from the experience?

All was not lost – perhaps it was now his turn? Will's mouth was dry, and he reached for the untouched glass of elderflower cordial. It was too sugared for his taste, but it fuelled him for what was to come.

His father was still talking:

'... This has been a wild tale altogether! But what possible help could I give you?'

Will knew it was time he told him:

'Let me enlighten you, father! You have treated this whole episode as an adventure of my own. It is not. I entered Vandernan's with a sinking heart, unwillingly, but I told myself that if we were to confront these evil people, then we must know how they organised themselves. It happened that last night was their Sunday accounting night – an occasion when bad men are paid off and illicit funds paid in … Vandernan's is a place to call forth your indignation, and I had hoped my report would find encouragement from you …'

'Hemp' Lundy's eyes scrutinised him, silently.

'… You understand the intricacies of the criminal world, father, especially its relations with power – the State and our warring parties. You are also acquainted with the zealous Benjamin Hector. It was he who led the invasion last night – to the fury of its Commissioner, Sir Charles Norreys, and his henchman Lord Parham. They appear to run the place together. You have said nothing of them, and it makes me ask what you know of their circle of influence. It was clear they considered Vandernan's to be under protection from the authorities.'

'Ah, the authorities! Yes, William, you put your finger on the nub of the matter. It is not clear where authority lies. These are City men, and their world is largely free of responsibilities. Their sort fled the regulation of the Exchange and they have not yet been brought under full control: laws are passed only to be ignored, and the Justices connive at it – many of them are active in the stocks themselves! No, William – there is effectually no law that regulates monetary practices. And these men's allegiances are as fluid as their funds. Their business is *play* – whether in the gaming-house or Jonathan's. You will have noticed how their language bestrides both worlds – the vocabulary of play – of *dealing, banking* and *staking*, of *risk* and *fortune*.

'As for Hector – it is easy to call the man a zealot, but as a Magistrate he is that rare thing – incorruptible. Those who look for a quiet life find him an obstacle. He refuses to bask in the world of inducements and favours. Our politicians of course avert their eyes from this – after all, what are their elections but exercises in monetary persuasion? It is the system, William.'

'The *system!* – that is what Sam Rivers talks of. He has set himself to oppose it – his gaming is his way of challenging it.'

A look of incredulity crossed his father's face:

'Ha! – a strange notion, and a forlorn one! Too many men are *invested* in it … I suspect Samuel Rivers is too – if he would but admit it …'

Will turned his head away.

'… This is not cynicism, William, but sound sense.'

'But we need practical advice, father … We have detected a fraud – not a small thing, but one of national concern. Appropriation of funds. I cannot say more, except that Lord Parham and his cabal would seem to be instrumental in it. It would help us to know about him and how he might be vulnerable – how we can come at him.'

'You don't ask much, William. But be truthful now … Beyond this fraud business, I suspect you have a further concern – a bigger one. Am I right? …'

Will was not expecting this.

'… You are troubled about your friends, the Pophams. It seems to me you are not mentioning your suspicion that George Sturgis's killing is at the heart of all this. Am I right? You would not otherwise be concerned with irregularities in the funds. No-one will ever defeat those!'

His father had made the next move for him, and Will acknowledged that saving Frank was indeed the priority – though the lottery fraud could be the key to it.

'You ask about Lord Parham's circle, William – I don't know the man personally. But I wonder … perhaps there is something …'

Judge Lundy glanced up at the owl, almost as if he were acknowledging her presence. Will was intrigued. Perhaps the bird served as some kind of inspiration to him? Or was she an encouragement at moments of conjecture? It was a fanciful idea – a conjecture of his own.

'... Yes, perhaps there is something ... My one encounter – if that is the word – with His Lordship was early last year when he was a witness in a case I was trying – or rather, he was meant to be. He was to supply the decisive evidence. But at the last minute he found himself indisposed. Needless to say, the case collapsed.'

Will was curious:

'What might the connection be, father, do you think?'

'The case was a serious one – against some Dutch merchants. I shan't enter into the *minutiae* – but it occurs to me that you might explore this – a Dutch connection, I mean. There were suspicions at the time that some pressure had been exerted upon Parham – that he had been persuaded to withdraw his co-operation ... I am of course thinking about Vandernan's – I had not seen the link before! ...'

Will was looking blank.

'... The *name*, William! That should be enough to alert you. There is a Mynheer Vandernan, you know – he is a considerable personage at Amsterdam.'

'Can we be clear about this, father? You are suggesting that the position Lord Parham holds at the gaming-house ...'

Will paused. He wasn't sure how to phrase it. The Judge helped him:

'... was a lucrative reward, William – a return for services rendered – or *not* rendered in his case! Perhaps he still owes allegiance to the Dutch? You asked about Parham's *circle*. This is something you could look into, is it not?'

His father's conjecture was thought-provoking:

'Yes, we shall, Sir ... But I wonder what steps we should take? It is hard to know where to begin.'

'Begin, William – as I have always told you – with the facts that you know and let them guide you to the facts you do *not* know – the gaps they leave. Think yourself at Westminster Hall and piece together the evidence! Remember, the Dutch are powerful in the City – perhaps a little less so than in our Dutch king's time, but their interests remain considerable. This war continues to strain our relations with Holland, and they need allies more than ever. So ... there may be larger interests involved here – political ones, perhaps? There may also be a link to your *funds?* You will know about this. Surely it is a line of thought you could follow? ...'

At moments like these Will glimpsed something in his father that lay deeper than the rigours of the Law. He would make a formidable investigator himself.

'... But there is something you could do immediately, William ... You tell me that Samuel Rivers has been hauled off to Bridewell? That is a humiliation! I would like to know why that young man was the unlucky one while you went scot-free?'

Will's answer came immediately, in the hope that the alternative explanation would not arise:

'Constable Cobb, father – he was there. I understand he used what influence he has.'

The judicial look was hesitant:

'I trust that was the only *influence*, William? If I thought for a moment you invoked my name in this affair, I would be very angry ...'

'I never mentioned it, Sir, believe me! ... But you say there is something I should do?'

'Yes – should you not pay a call on Alderman Rivers? He may be anxious about his son, and an explanation from you about what occurred last night would surely be welcome? ... And, who knows, you might use the occasion to ask him about Parham and his friends? ... It is a thought. I leave it with you.'

Will could see intriguing possibilities, and he began to feel lighter of heart. An idea had emerged which could be useful, and he looked forward to sharing it with Tom and Widow Trotter. But his prime feeling was of huge relief. It had been a gruelling interview, but he had survived. Indeed, the Judge had given him something to ponder.

From this point on, the two men's talk modulated onto less urgent matters, and by the end Will and his father were unconstrainedly sharing thoughts – and a second glass of elderflower cordial.

Tuesday

26 October 1708

Chapter Thirty-Two

❦

O N   T H E   P R I N C I P L E that serious matters deserve serious
food, Mary Trotter had decided that their committee on
this chilly morning should convene over a long and substantial
breakfast. There was plenty of coffee and toast, a plate of eggs
and slices of roasted bacon, supplemented by Mrs Dawes's
spiced ragoût from the previous day warmed through to its full
perfection. If her plan were agreed, then her two young friends
would need fortifying – and dinner might be a problem for them
…

All three had returned from their Monday expeditions
with news to share – Widow Trotter from the Exchange, Tom
from St James's, and Will from the Temple, and in the convivial
setting of the Bay-Tree's parlour they were ready to pool their
discoveries. Each reported in turn. Tom's tale of the dramatic
events at the Pophams' took priority; then followed Widow
Trotter's summary of her interview with Michael Henriques;
and finally, Will contributed a lively account of the meeting with
his father.

Given Frank Popham's flight and the impending charge of
murder against him, the urgency was clear. There was a lot of
new information to pull together, and as each of their stories was
told they saw that what they were confronting was less a single

DAVID FAIRER

organised conspiracy than an interlocking of particular interests. This gave them hope: any system of self-interest risked splitting into factions, and they were beginning to suspect it was already happening with the cabal.

Tom scooped out a generous helping from the stew-pot – a mixture of small pieces of beef with slices of carrot, onion and turnip – and a pot-ball dumpling – and as he did so, he drew a less than dignified analogy with the nature of their investigation.

But Widow Trotter demurred:

'No, Tom, not a ragoût! We should think of it rather as a hand of cards – that is surely the more fitting image? ... We need to arrange them carefully and think how we might best deploy them.'

At this, Tom and Will looked at her in invitation, and she knew that with those words she had set a challenge for herself.

'You have our full attention, Mrs T,' said Will, mischievously.

Tom was more direct:

'We have each told our tale – it would be a help if you could sum it all up for us and tell us where things stand ...'

She had to admit it was a trap of her own making.

'I fully deserve this, gentlemen, do I not? Well, let us see what emerges. You are both welcome to set me right or make suggestions ... I shall try to limit myself to what we *know*. We can leave conjecture for later ... Where to begin ... ?

Widow Trotter reached for the coffee pot and resupplied herself. She felt a little like a military general about to survey the battlefield with the action at its height.

'... Until now, gentlemen, Vandernan's and the Bank of England have been foremost in our minds. We have discovered that the gaming-house provides some kind of service – a highly suspect one – for money-men to settle or receive funds, to pursue irregular deals and more 'informal' ends – things which the Bank couldn't countenance officially. I picture the place as the dirty backyard of the institution where things can be hidden and through which escape is possible.

How far the Bank itself sanctions this is hard to say – but we know that one of its Directors, Philip Roscoe, is involved – he was being paid off on Sunday night and is a participant in the coal-gas 'bubble.' The fact that he is also the Duchess's broker and (we now know) a member of the Committee of the Treasury makes him a leading player in all of this. We know that the two controllers of Vandernan's, Lord Parham and Sir Charles Norreys, are in league together, and that Bob Leary and George Sturgis had been a part of the arrangements there. The pair of them were damaging Mr Henriques' business, it seems because of his refusal to co-operate on one of their tricks. But something occurred to sever the bond between Leary and his patron Parham, and Sturgis too had given offence. Something happened to drive Sturgis and Leary away.

'Let us return to the Bank and its manoeuvrings … The hurried negotiation of the government loan, and the need to find a quarter of a million quickly, has led to a foolish plan to pledge the lottery funds and, in turn, to the desperate expedient of exploiting the coal-gas scheme – a precarious arrangement altogether! The Duchess has subscribed, and they are intending to lend the Queen's name to the enterprise … How official this is, we cannot be certain, but it risks embarrassing Her Majesty, compromising the City, and damaging the Nation's credit.

'This takes us into a larger field – a national one – involving the funding of the War. The new revelations about the Dutch connection are significant. We have learned that for years Bob Leary has been spying for the Dutch, and that he maintains a bond with Willem Oosterhout. Our tobacco merchant is rather more than that – an important figure in relations with Amsterdam who is perhaps prepared to serve its interests above those of the City of London?

'The idea is strengthened by the suspicion that Lord Parham also has interests in that direction. Judge Lundy hints that Parham was paid off by the Dutch merchants, and this would make sense of his bond with Leary. It appears that Vandernan's was a Dutch creation in the days when England and Holland were close friends.

'This means that the 'plot' – if we can call it that – is likely to have national repercussions, and in this Dutch connection we perhaps have something that is subverting the alliance between the Bank and Vandernan's ... but there I am on the brink of conjecture! ... These are heavy matters, gentlemen ...'

Mrs Trotter paused and took some more coffee.

'... This is the national scene. But we are forced to look closer to home, to what concerns us more nearly – I mean the dire threat to Mr Popham and through him to Lord Melksham. Your uncle, Tom, is under attack from the Duchess's secretary, Arthur Maynwaring, who along with his patroness has an old grudge against him. We might consider this a separate issue, but Sturgis's closeness to the Duchess suggests it is more than a personal matter. Lord Melksham's discovery of secret communications between the Duchess and Sir Gilbert Heathcote reveals that Sturgis was acting as her go-between with the Bank. Someone clearly thinks your uncle has dangerous knowledge about this and must be silenced. And Vandernan's was to play its part: Parham fully intended that "Captain Hazard" would break Mr Popham, and he was angry when Sturgis obstructed this. For these reasons, I think we can be confident that the attempt to bring ruin to Lord Melksham and the Pophams is part of the picture ...'

Widow Trotter sat back in her chair with an air of satisfaction.

'... In this way, gentlemen, it is possible to trace threads from the Bank to Vandernan's, and on to the interests of Holland and the Amsterdam merchants. The whole thing is a kind of spider's web, is it not? Leary's flight and the murder of Sturgis may make us suspect that these threads are now being strained and broken – with violent consequences! Mr Popham is under attack – Leary is fleeing the country – and Sturgis is dead.

'The answer to the question, *who killed George Sturgis?* (such a simple one!), is bound up with these circumstances – and understanding them should lead us to the killer ...'

She paused, suddenly aware that her last remark made it sound easy, as if everything could be worked out by reason and common sense. She knew in her heart that they also needed luck – a nice, big juicy slice of it – and more than a little help from their friends.

For a moment there was stillness at the table. Mary Trotter narrowed her eyes to the ceiling as if straining to see what might lie ahead, while the young men on either side gazed at her in silent wonderment. Together they composed a striking picture. The triptych became even more sacramental when she picked up the ladle and delved into the pot of stew:

'There you have it, gentlemen. Is that a convincing account, do you think? Drawn together like that, it almost seems doable.'

'And we *shall* do it, Mrs T! We have friends working in our cause, do we not? Your Mr Henriques promises something more on Oosterhout; and with Lady Norreys alerted to Sir Charles's part in the plot, we might learn more from her.'

Will brightened:

'And we mustn't forget our poor friend languishing in Bridewell! Sam longs to know the truth about Sturgis's killing, and at this moment he is surrounded by resentful gamesters – Bridewell is virtually a Vandernan's-in-exile!'

Widow Trotter was quick to respond:

'I had not forgotten him, Mr Lundy! Indeed, you anticipate the very plan I was going to put to you both ...

Mr Rivers is sure to have heard some Bridewell gossip about Vandernan's and its system. And for that reason ... could I suggest that an immediate visit from you and Mr Bristowe might *pay dividends* – if that's not too tainted a phrase? ... I sniff an opportunity!'

'I suspect it's not the only thing to be sniffed in Bridewell,' said Will.

Tom was happy to assent:

'Your team is ready harnessed, Mrs T ... Shall we venture there this morning, Will?'

'As I understand it, visitors are permitted from noon,' said Widow Trotter, who had clearly prepared the ground.

The mood had become almost cheerful; but while she was speaking it struck Tom that she was herself in danger of being arrested at any hour, and her beloved Bay-Tree remained under the gravest threat. Little had been said on the subject of the promissory note – he knew she must be holding off the thought ... Nevertheless, his curiosity got the better of him:

'Mrs T – you told us someone had called at the Sword Blade office with your note, but that he left no name ...'

Tom noticed a slight lowering of her head.

'... It would surely help if we could discover more about him.'

'He was not a figure of any distinction, Mr Grigsby said, and certainly not a man of business, or a gamester – someone more at home on the street. I'm trying to remember the phrase – it was a striking one ...'

She thought for a second.

'... Ah yes, a *fashionable costermonger*. That was it. Probably an emissary from Vandernan's. The note had come from there, after all.'

Tom was alerted:

'But, I wonder ... You recall Cousin Frank's messenger at the sponging-house – didn't Frank tell us the man was a polite ruffian? it's a similar idea. Do you think the two could be one and the same?'

'Oh goodness – you may be right. Perhaps we could take this further?'

At the same time Will's mind was cast back to Sunday night's raid, and to the man who had seized the note from his grasp. The fellow was grim looking enough, though on that occasion he had no cause to polish himself up. Will broached the idea tentatively.

'Ah yes, if the man *is* from Vandernan's,' said Widow Trotter, 'then our Mr Rivers may be able to put a name to him?'

'Perhaps he's a gaming-house bully?' said Tom, 'employed to eject its more troublesome victims – and carry threatening messages too?'

By this point they were beginning to feel the limitations of fact. Deduction was proving hard, and Conjecture, its amusive cousin, was beckoning. It was clear they had work to do. It was action that was needed – something to propel them forwards.

The interruption, when it came, was therefore welcome.

There was a light knock on the parlour door, which opened to reveal Jenny's bright-eyed face. She delivered her message briskly:

'Apologies for the interruption, Mrs Trotter, but Toby – Mr Mudge – is here asking for you. He says he has some news you'll want to hear … He's come from Constable Cobb.'

Suddenly, along with a smell of pies baking, there was expectation in the air.

'Send him in!' said Widow Trotter, 'and bring us another bowl, Jenny!'

The young watchman, who was dressed for the street, was invited to shed his greatcoat and take a chair. Such hospitality was a little alarming, and he hesitated awkwardly. But the three of them did seem happy to welcome him to their table – it was as if they knew the importance of what he had to tell them … As he sat down, he tried not to look around in any obvious way: this was the famed inner sanctum of the Bay-Tree – a room where it was said you trod softly and spoke quietly.

'Greetings, Mr Mudge!' said the polite hostess. 'Have you breakfasted? We have dispatched the bacon, but I trust a little of the ragoût will be acceptable?'

Toby was nonplussed, but then he caught the playfulness in her tone and was put at his ease:

'I didn't intend to disturb your meal, Mrs Trotter – but I do have an empty stomach …'

'Excellent! We are not convened in form, Toby – in fact our deliberations are at a stand. Perhaps what Elias has to say will be useful. From the look on your face it is not ill news?'

'On the contrary, Mrs Trotter … but it's not Mr Cobb's news …'

He hesitated, helping himself from the pot.

'… He told me you'll want to know what I've discovered.'

'You've been doing some investigating yourself, Toby?' said Tom. 'On the death of George Sturgis, is it? We're eager to hear anything you've been able to find.'

Without waiting for an invitation, Toby seized a piece of bread and thrust it into his stew.

'Yes, Mr Bristowe. I've been doing my rounds – but with a thought to the murder. I've been making enquiries of my own.'

He looked pleased with himself as he spooned the soaked bread into his mouth.

A contented watchman was always a reassuring sight, and the three of them were happy to sit for a moment while the pangs of hunger were assuaged. Expectation was high, and the cheerfulness suggested that his news would lift their spirits.

Several mouthfuls later, Toby was ready to talk, and they were more than ready to listen. He wiped his lips on a handkerchief and looked at them:

'I think we have our killer!'

This was news indeed … Tom and Will glanced at each other with raised eyebrows. Widow Trotter smiled at the word *our*, happy in the thought that he had made their cause his own.

'This is something we want to hear, Toby!' said Tom.

'You've found some vital evidence, have you?' asked Will.

'Take your time,' said Widow Trotter. 'Unfold it to us! …'

The young watchman was not accustomed to having people hang on his every word. But he took this as encouragement. He thought of them as friends and was eager to help:

'Do you know The Flagon? It's a pothouse … There are steps down to it off Hawker's Yard. The thing used to be a coal-cellar.'

'A low place, then?' said Will.

'I've not had word of it, Toby,' said Widow Trotter. 'But such things come and go by the week.'

'It's a cramped cellar, Mrs Trotter – just a few tables …'

He paused, ready to enjoy the moment.

'… and it's not twenty strides from Vandernan's …'

'Ah! This is leading somewhere, Toby!' said Tom.

'… As I said, since Mr Sturgis's killing, I've taken it upon myself to ask about a bit. And last night on my midnight round I showed my face down there … It's not a place you'd take your sister …'

The eventuality was an unlikely one, but they got the point.

'… I tried a thimble-full of ale – which was very good – and put the question to the serving-man about what he could remember of Thursday night. He said he'd been there through most of that night – the place never seems to close! … Being so near, they often have one or two Vandernan's people drowning their sorrows at ungodly hours …'

'This is even better, Toby!' said Will.

'… Well, during the night on Thursday – the man remembers it well – your Mr Leary paid them a visit.'

'Leary? But what time was this?'

'About two o'clock, Mrs Trotter. It seems he is something of a regular there … and that night he was with another gentleman …'

The silence was broken by a distant crash from the kitchen – but none of them moved a muscle.

'… I asked him for a description – and there's no doubting it was Mr Sturgis … he was very drunk!'

'Leary and Sturgis together? – at two in the morning? Near Vandernan's? This doesn't square with Leary's story!' said Tom, looking at Widow Trotter.

Toby pressed on, warming to his task:

'The man recalls it particularly because there was a dispute between the two of them – a furious one, not your usual drunken quarrel. At one point, the other gentleman – Mr Sturgis – took a paper from his pocket, and they were arguing fiercely over it. It got torn in two. There were heated words – and then he hurried off, with Mr Leary pursuing him up the steps – fearfully angry he was!'

'Toby! You prince among men!' declared Will. 'You know what this means?'

'I think I do, Mr Lundy – that's why I've told it you.'

'It is evidence,' said Mrs Trotter a little obviously, 'circumstantial, but directly to the point – damning evidence! I think our Mr Leary was telling us a tale, don't you, Tom? If this is true, then we have to suspect him. It is as close as we'll come to an eyewitness account of the killing.'

Tom was thoughtful, but Will was eager to press the point home:

'This is just the revelation we need, Tom! If we have our killer … how much this will mean for Frank!'

Tom held himself back, not daring to hope:

'If Leary can be found …'

But there was more. As if his revelations had not been startling enough, the watchman had a postscript to offer:

'There's something else you might find useful …'

Toby hesitated, recalling that he was in a holy place. He reddened slightly.

'… The Flagon – you should know … caters for gentlemen of a certain *taste*.'

'Ah! …'

The exclamation came from Widow Trotter. Enough had been said. It was not a taste in art and music.

'… I see. Yes, Toby, that adds some colour to the picture … I wonder if it might tell us something about Bob Leary's relations with his patron, Lord Parham?'

'Do you mean there had been a lovers' quarrel?'

'I wouldn't venture that far, Will, but it's a thought. There's been a strong personal bond between them. Leary spoke of it.'

'It might make the break more bitter, but there were other bonds too – the plotting and deception.'

'Quite right, Tom, we mustn't let it distract us – but we need to store the thought away.'

'Whatever the case,' continued Toby, 'the hunt is on for Mr Leary. Mr Cobb says you saw him up in Islington, Mrs Trotter?'

She sighed and felt annoyed with herself:

'Yes, on Sunday – Mr Bristowe and I had a long talk with him. He spun us quite a story, it seems. How much was the truth is impossible to say.'

'It was *dash'd and brew'd with lies!*' said Tom, quoting his favourite Dryden. 'But one part of it was surely true – he is making his escape to Amsterdam. Mrs Trotter had confirmation yesterday …'

The watchman listened while she told him of her visit to the Exchange, and what she had learned of Leary's Dutch interests – and particularly his meeting with Willem Oosterhout:

'He received a package from the man, Toby. It was a small one – perhaps a bundle of letters … He had told us he was taking the Dutch packet from Harwich on Friday.'

'*Oosterhout*, you say?'

'Yes, a tobacco merchant. He is an important figure in the Amsterdam trade. I learned yesterday that Mr Leary has a history of spying for the Dutch. It seems those activities may have continued.'

Toby was delighted. He felt emboldened:

'Mrs Trotter! – If I am a prince, then you are a *Queen*. Mr Cobb will want to know of this at once.'

'And, Toby … The gentleman I met at the Exchange told me that Oosterhout has his office on the wharf – by Custom House Quay. Elias could well pay him a call? He might know of Leary's whereabouts.'

The watchman beamed with pleasure, and as he savoured the last spicy mouthful of Mrs Dawes's ragoût he settled back in his chair. The fire glowed, and after his nocturnal labours he was in the mood for an after-breakfast nap … But duties had to be performed, and it was with some reluctance that he got to his feet and reached for his greatcoat. It had been a memorable visit. Not only had his own discoveries been welcomed, but he could now return to the constable with even more revelations. Tobias Mudge began to think he was an apprentice no longer – rather something of a *detector*. The notion appealed to him – and so, when he took his leave of the parlour, warm and refreshed, he promised he would call back soon with any further intelligence.

Chapter Thirty-Three

———

'DO YOU THINK we have our man?'

The thought had remained unspoken while Tom and Will made their way up Fleet Street. They had been brooding on the question, but the noonday traffic – human and vehicular – wasn't favourable to discussion. It was hard to be heard above the rattle of carts and carriages and the shouts of pedestrians sidestepping and colliding on the pavement. Will had led the way, with Tom sticking close to his back allowing his tall friend to steer them through.

But now they had paused on Fleet Bridge and were leaning side-by-side over the parapet, contemplating the less than picturesque prospect of the Fleet River, which after a costly renovation was now returning to its true character of a muddy dyke channelling detritus southward to the Thames.

It was Tom who voiced the question. Will, who was accustomed to hearing verdicts confidently pronounced, looked at him with a smile:

'So, you're having doubts, are you Tom? Perhaps you'd be a little more confident if Toby's witness had seen the blade strike home? He could hardly have told us more, surely?'

'I thought you would be circumspect, Will, given your schooling in the nature of evidence?'

Will's smile grew broader – a nice legal argument was beckoning:

'But there's now no reason to doubt Leary's quarrel with Sturgis – the tearing of the promissory note, the pursuit up the steps, Leary's anger! A violent scene was bound to follow, and the place and the time answer perfectly. We can see what happened next – a jury would need little convincing. Show them the picture and they'll give you the rest of the story. A prosecutor couldn't ask for more!'

'But must *we* believe it, Will? Can we trust what our imaginations tell us?'

'A jury will.'

'But I'm asking if *you* believe it. Do you think Leary killed Sturgis?'

'And my answer must be – what I think is of no consequence. On that evidence the jury would convict … but I appreciate that you and Mrs Trotter had the privilege of hearing Bob Leary's story from his own lips. He must have been convincing – whereas I have only encountered *Robert LeRoy.*'

Tom was pensive:

'Yes, the man hasn't exactly earned our trust, has he?'

'But … you are right to give him the benefit of your doubts, Tom. I admire you for it – and I want to share them. Alas, I have seen too much of juries and court-room casuistry. I think it must have done its work on me!'

'We are both committed to Truth, Will. Isn't that what drives us in this whole business?'

Will was silent and nodded his assent. Not for the first time Tom had reminded him of a principle – and had reminded himself too. It was no mere innocence on his part – no simple faith in mankind. Quite the opposite. Will knew how his friend struggled to understand Providence, to trust in the benign order of things.

Will drew himself upright and turned to survey the busy scene that continued noisily behind them. Tom remained leaning on the bridge, his eyes drawn to a dead dog caught in the weeds below:

'And I admire your good sense, Will! Perhaps I just want everything to be ideal? It's a nasty battle out there. Everything is brought into question – while we can afford to indulge our virtues.'

'Never be embarrassed by your virtues, Tom. Please do not! I value them above anything …'

Tom laughed:

'What a parcel of rogues we're faced with! Let us hope we can find our way through all of this. One thing is clear – we have to trace Leary!'

'Toby said the hunt is on. They'll surely send an officer to Harwich – if Leary sticks to his plan to take ship for Holland?'

'If that's his intention. But we cannot be certain anymore, can we? It's a hard lesson to learn.'

Will slapped his friend on the shoulder:

'Enough of that! For the moment we can leave it to Elias and the excellent Mudge – a young man who is determined to solve our mystery single-handed! We must set our thoughts to Bridewell and the unfortunate Sam. I wonder what we're going to find there? I feel for the poor fellow! If the place lives up to its character he's sure to be hurting – inside and out …'

He paused, and his voice became quieter.

'… By rights I should have been with him, Tom – I'm ashamed to think of it. Let us hope he is not too cast down.'

'He will need some cheering.'

Will's eyes lit up:

'And I know one certain way to do it … *gingerbread!*'

He pointed to a figure who was wheeling his moveable shop across the bridge towards them. The man was one-eyed, and his cry of 'Fine Gingerbread!' grated on the ear, but his wares were displayed invitingly and there was a spicy aroma heralding him.

The cakes were moulded into ingenious shapes of animals and fishes, some gilded and decorated with nuts; Punch and Joan were there, and a smart infantryman; but taking pride of place was Queen Anne herself, complete with golden crown and sceptre. After some debate they decided on simplicity – Will chose a wicked-looking gingerbread cat, and Tom a handsome stag complete with its antlers.

Stowing their confectionary tributes, the pair turned and made their way along the side of the Fleet. It aspired to be a broad avenue with a canal as its centre – but Venice or Versailles it was not. It didn't help that the ditch was bordered with cellars on both sides, designed as warehouses but now accommodating little but rats – and an occasional Thames lighterman unloading himself.

To their right, the Tudor walls of Bridewell towered over them. It was no longer a royal palace but still declared itself with a degree of pride. The masonry had resisted the worst of the Great Fire, and as they entered the wide quadrangle it was like a down-at-heel college with narrow archways and mullioned windows recalling what used to be. What it was now, was a 'house of correction,' a title that spoke of a desire to reform as well as punish; but as they strolled across the courtyard a distant drumming sound spoke more of the latter, and angry shouts lent a military air. The thuds grew louder as they approached, and they soon found themselves peering through a barred window into a substantial workroom.

This certainly spoke of prison. The inmates were in rows, bent over the severed trunks of once-mighty oaks that served as anvils for the hemp-beating. Large coils of the stuff were being slowly pounded into their fibres. This was no eager workforce, and wrists were limp and arms aching as the heavy beetles were lifted.

Will swallowed hard:

'Poor Sam – he hasn't the frame for this. I should have gone in his place.'

'I don't see him here – perhaps he has been spared it?'

They surveyed the prisoners. They were a miscellaneous contingent of ruffians and vagrants – but a couple of them sported lace cuffs, now torn and dirty, which almost gave a touch of elegance to their pummelling.

'I do believe I see a pair of gamesters!' said Tom.

'Ah yes – that distinctive look! And indeed, the one on the left is Humfrey, one of the Gray's Inn boys, the keeper of Mrs Trotter's note – until I won it from him. I must say he's handling his mallet very delicately! But there's no sign of our Sam ... Ouf! ... Did you see that?'

He winced. The overseer's rod had given Humfrey a sharp reminder that beating hemp required muscle and force. The man's eyes were ablaze, and the lesson was being reinforced by shouted obscenities and a second full-arm stroke across the buttocks. The men were stripped to their shirts as if haymaking, but this was no summer's field-labour. Heavy timbers lowered above them. The walls were stained, and hooks in the stonework hinted at an older time of state torture. A padlocked chain hung from one of them, offering its silent encouragement; and from another a satiric wag had suspended a length of rope knotted into a noose.

'One thing I'll say,' said Will, 'I'll not speak my father's nickname in jest ever again!'

The spectacle was not one to detain them, and they were glad to move on.

After a few inquiries they were finally able to locate Samuel Rivers. They found him in one of the long wards taking his ease on a straw pallet. It was not the picture they were expecting – and certainly not the glass of red wine he held to his lips. The moment he saw them, he raised his hand in a toast:

'Gentlemen! You have not forgotten your friend. You are just in time for my *levee!*'

The pair of them were momentarily lost for words. An ambiguous figure confronted them. The face was smiling, the voice warm, the gesture welcoming, but more than ever the bloodshot eyes glared from the pale skin like an admonitory ghost, and the thin arm could surely never wield a hammer. Sam swung his legs from the pallet and made to rise. Tom and Will were hesitating.

'So, you're keeping to your accustomed regime, Sam?'

'Yes indeed, Will – though they make it damn'd difficult in here. I was downstairs beating hemp at seven this morning – an awkward interruption to my day! But I am now contemplating breakfast – though I have to say the choice is somewhat restricted. The bread is chalky, and the water I suspect is drawn from our neighbouring channel! I have bespoke a mutton cutlet and a hot ginger pudding, but they are a long time arriving. The service here is extremely lax.'

'Then it seems we have chosen the perfect moment, Sam,' said Tom. 'You have the wine, and we … have the provisions!'

He swung the wallet from his shoulder and carefully reached in for their gingerbread treats.

'Ah, Mr Bristowe! How exquisite! That is certainly a wily-looking cat – and a stag – a noble animal I always think … but this creature seems to have been in a fight.'

Tom saw to his chagrin that one of its antlers was broken off. Will made the best of it:

'But he is a heroic creature, Sam – and sacrificed it in a good cause!'

'Ah yes, the rutting!'

Tom delved a little deeper into his wallet:

'Perhaps this dish will suit your wine better – from the kitchens of the Bay-Tree no less! …'

He extracted a cold venison pasty.

'... Speciality of the house!'

Sam seized it eagerly, and they were soon squatting together in the chill space like watchmen round a brazier. Sam was continuing to talk animatedly. They kept off the subject of Vandernan's for a while lest business matters darkened the mood.

'I see no sign of the Fair Sex, Sam,' said Will. 'I expect for good reason.'

'You're right. Our lady guests have their quarters in the western courtyard, a more commodious building than this mouldering pile. Theirs is a place of elegant entertainment with a gallery for the governors to witness the whipping of the whores, a daily duty which I understand the men perform punctiliously. It is an attraction for visitors – something like a cock fight. Theatre at its simplest!'

'We have seen the workroom, Sam – the hemp-beating.'

'Yes, Tom, the "smithy" we call it. I confess I am a great disappointment to our overseer. He has a reformer's face and a deep grudge against us honourable debauchees. He bares his teeth at cravats and lace cuffs! The man has an unshakeable faith in the redemptive power of the birch.'

'How long will this go on, Sam?' Will asked.

'I look to have my freedom by Saturday – they tell me a week suffices to make us good citizens again! But I have to say, Bridewell is a fine place for plots – for making new alliances over a hand at cards.'

'Cards?'

'Yes, Tom, cards are brought in – though we are actively discouraged from dice. And there is enough gin and brandy from the visitors to make our evenings quite convivial. It helps take your mind off the rats and fleas. At night this is their playground. The bedbugs are affable creatures and snuggle down with us, but altogether I'll be well rid of such companions. You could say I'm itching to leave.'

He managed to crack a smile but shivered as he thought of the night to come.

'You speak of plots, Sam,' said Will, turning the conversation sharply.'We are anxious to know if you've heard any Vandernan's gossip in here. We saw Humfrey in the workroom, and there must be others.'

'Yes, we are a huddle of gamesters, all nursing our back-aches and sore bums. We've talked about how the house came to be attacked and why certain people found themselves released and others not. There's a deal of anger over it – resentment loosens men's tongues! I've busied myself by thinking of this as a spying mission and have gleaned a few snippets for you ... But first I want to hear what progress you've made. What's become of Frank Popham and the esteemed Widow Trotter? ... I must say, it's very cheering to see the two of you!'

And so they talked. Allowing Sam time to enjoy his pasty, Tom and Will entertained him with their parcel of news, and why they were more than ever convinced Vandernan's was at the centre of a web of plots.

'We've begun to ask,' said Will, 'if there's a group working against the interests of the City. Bob Leary has his Dutch connections, and we suspect Parham does too. We are wondering how this squares with the Bank's official business – with Philip Roscoe in particular ... We're baffled by the intricacies of it all, Sam!'

'And well you might be! I've made a study of Vandernan's *system*, as you know, especially our friend Captain Hazard. Its mechanisms excite my curiosity! And it's clear that all is not well amongst our plotters. You're right about the "intricacies," but I would choose another word --- *faction*.

'The whisper amongst my fellow-gamesters is that Sunday night's attack is a sign that Vandernan's arrangements are no longer working as they should. This causes great concern, as you can imagine. The place cannot exist without the *settlements*. I've been told the arrest of poor Jack Beech was part of the new demands.'

'You mean he was sacrificed?' said Will.

'Let us say he was the price, and they came to collect him ... But it turned out a higher tariff was to be exacted ...'

Will whistled as the thought struck home.

'... Certainly, we gamesters are being pressed as never before. The Reformation of Manners people are full of confidence. The zeal of the righteous oozes from them like sweat. You saw how Mr Hector commanded the field, quoting scripture for his purpose... And we had a fine display of indignation from Sir Charles, did we not?'

'He was furious,' said Will.

'Yes, though it was little more than bluster. The Commissioner seemed assured Vandernan's had the State's protection – on what terms we cannot know. But the *system* appears to be breaking down.'

'That's a fine way of telling us their bribes haven't been enough!' said Tom a little churlishly.

'Perhaps bribes no longer do the business. There's a new mood in the air. It seems our "Great Britain" has to be worthy of its God-given future! And so, all the doings of the City are in question. "Stock-jobber" is the vilest term of! I suspect the reformers have not just the gaming-houses in their sights but the whole of 'Change Alley too. We are all to be *reformed*...'

Tom and Will glanced at each other. They had heard such sentiments before, and their hearts sank.

'... Lord Parham's partiality to the Dutch is known about – he has friends among the community and attends the Dutch church. And there's nothing seditious about that – they are our allies, after all ... But I had not thought the allegiance might work against his own nation. What you've told me about Leary's spying is important ...'

Half-smiling, Sam reached for his glass.

'... Leary and Parham are *particular* friends – or have been – and from what you say, their connection has been more than personal. Perhaps they have been leagued in something more villainous?'

'This is what we are beginning to suspect,' said Tom.

'I knew the intrigues in Vandernan's were organised but had not thought them seditious. My sojourn in Bridewell has taught me much! Believe me, gentlemen, this house of correction is a gossip's feast – there's something about this place that unlocks men's tongues.

'The system at Vandernan's is a union of interests that reaches beyond the gaming-house to 'Change Alley. They work in combination and make stock-jobbery an art. At Jonathan's and Garraway's several men operate together by buying or selling stock among themselves – and making a great noise of it. In that way they are able to sink a stock or bubble it according to plan, so the same stock can fall to fifty in a few hours, then soar to a hundred and fifty the next day. Every swing can be calculated because they make the market themselves, and the brokers co-operate. They will take a loss in order to gain more for their friends at the turn. It is precise and effectual ... and there is nothing illegal in it!'

'One thing I do know,' said Will, 'is that brokers cannot purchase stock.'

'They have no need to – though many do! They can be recompensed in other ways. They make the market to suit the association. You speak of a spider's web – well, these men weave a sticky one, and flies are easily caught.'

'Can a man not trust his broker, then?'

Sam gave a laugh:

'Trust? … You have much to learn, Tom. It is said that you must trust your broker as you would trust your wife.'

'To remain faithful?'

'No, Tom – not to lose you money! …'

Sam reached for his injured gingerbread stag and squinted at it suspiciously.

'… And you know how easily false news can set a hare running – I had great success at the Bay-Tree, did I not, Will? The brave town of Lille fell on Saturday morning – for a few minutes at least! And I was just a single voice. You may imagine what could be done if there were a union of interest and people worked together. Remember the wreck of the Albemarle! The goddess Rumour is said to have a thousand tongues – but in truth you need only three or four.'

'So Vandernan's plays this game of false news too?'

Sam was about to attack the stag's remaining antler, but paused. He suddenly frowned, and an earnest look told them they had reached a point of importance:

'Yes, undoubtedly. It has been known – in hindsight of course. This is where Vandernan's system is discreet to the highest degree.'

'So, you can tell us nothing?'

'My resentful informant couldn't say … but he detects a growing disquiet. Something is being planned. No-one knows – but there is apprehension … Perhaps it is like the air on a summer's afternoon – a sudden clamminess that tells you a storm is approaching.'

'This is enigmatic,' said Will.

'What you've both been telling me does nothing to dispel the idea – quite the contrary. Who knows but Roscoe and Parham may be the instigators? But this is merely conjecture.

You overheard the pair of them in Vandernan's, Will. Perhaps they make a habit of putting their heads together on a Sunday evening? Who can say?'

Sam could wait no longer, and the gingerbread antler snapped off. He began chewing happily.

Tom turned to Will:

'Roscoe? A director of the Bank would be well positioned for playing such tricks with the news.'

'No-one better. And Sir Gilbert Heathcote too, possibly?'

'With his line of communication to the Duchess …'

'Through Sturgis, the go-between.'

'The link in the chain … I wonder …'

They slipped into silent speculation. Sam looked at his two friends:

'Of course, you both know my thoughts on 'Change Alley and its doings. Jobbery is a dirty trade!'

'But you said the stocks had done very well for your father,' said Will. 'The Rivers fortune?'

'*Touché!* … Yes, my father esteems the market, and he plays the game boldly enough – though I grant he has a murmuring conscience sometimes. The wilder misdoings trouble him. Being such a big City-man, he knows where the bad smells are and is careful not to lift too many stones! But on Friday he will be wearing his scarlet robe with the rest of the Aldermen.'

'Ah, of course, the Lord Mayor's Show!'

'Yes, Will. The City of London in all its pomp! Word is, the parade will be the most magnificent ever seen, and the pageant undoubtedly the most *glittering*. The Goldsmiths have charge this year and are determined to impress. Let us hope the sun keeps hidden, otherwise we shall all be blinded!'

'*Robes and furred gowns hide all*,' muttered Tom, darkly.

'It will be the triumph of riches!' continued Sam. 'The

Goldsmiths' Company will see to that. The poor Skinners and Fishmongers, Drapers and Cordwainers, will hang their heads!'

Sam was smiling broadly, contemplating the spectacle to come.

'Perhaps Mammon will be driving the leading chariot?'

'No, Will, much too satirical! I understand it is to be a very earthbound *Apollo* playing his lyre while he trundles along the cobbles, enshrined in a marble temple!'

Tom was grinning:

'What need for satire? Such extravagance is a burlesque on itself.'

'We can leave that to the apprentices,' said Will. 'But the populace will gawp and cheer, as ever.'

'What about the Mercers?' asked Tom.

'Oh, nothing will abash *them* – they have precedence over all the livery companies. The Mercers do honour only to God! And Alderman Rivers will be upholding their reputation. This is the season for celebration, and on Saturday he hosts a gathering of the great and the good in Mercers' Hall ... Well, the *great* at least – I'm sure our men from the Bank will be there! ...'

He paused.

'... Now there's a thought! A perfect stage for plotters!'

'Does your father know you are here?' said Tom.

'Word must have reached him, alas. My disgrace is sure to confirm his contempt for all gamesters ... But I wonder ...'

Sam was looking into the distance, a smile beginning to form.

'What are you plotting, Sam? You have a conspiratorial face on you.'

'... I've been thinking how sweet it would be to turn the tables on Rivers Senior, and perhaps the time is ripe. He deserves to know what we have discovered ... What if we three were to smuggle ourselves into Saturday's assembly? There might be some sport to be had? ... You could be my guests ...'

Tom and Will looked at each other in alarm.

'... A couple of lavish wigs, and there'll be no problem. You must let me think ... If I could only get out of this godforsaken *bastille!* It's no place for a fine mind to exercise itself in ... !'

Will knew he had to speak:

'Yesterday my father had the idea I should call on Alderman Rivers and ease his mind about you – explain to him what has happened ... I could prepare the ground for us, perhaps?'

'Aha, yes! You can be my advocate, Will! No-one better to plead my cause!'

It seemed that out of nothing a plan was taking shape which would be hard to resist. Certainly, Alderman Rivers was a man of considerable influence in the City ...

By now, Sam had recaptured his old fire, and the three of them were settling down for some genial talk. But from the far end of the ward a sudden commotion told them that visitors were being shooed away. The dreaded hemp was calling again. Sam physically shivered, and all animation suddenly left him.

As they got to their feet, Will remembered an important question:

'There is something we need to know – if you can tell us, Sam.'

'What is that?'

'An unsavoury individual at Hector's right hand during the attack – do you recall him? – the one who impounded Mrs Trotter's promissory note. Did he arrive with Hector, or is he known in Vandernan's?'

'No, the man is not Hector's – I think he was there to guard him! He's a bully of Parham's. You don't see much of him in the gaming-house, but he tends to appear when things get *uncomfortable* ... He's called Harkins – *Joel* Harkins, I think. Why does he interest you?'

'For a very good reason, Sam. We think he's the man who tried to redeem Mrs Trotter's note at the Sword Blade yesterday morning.'

'Ah! Then Parham must have sent him.'

'That's what it looks like,' said Tom. 'Had Mrs Trotter been half an hour earlier she would have encountered him.'

'Perhaps it was fortunate for her that she did not! It would have been an awkward meeting.'

'Then let us hope she doesn't meet him again.'

Their talking had to end. Sam looked terrified. All gaiety had left him.

'Do your best for me!' he whispered.

They felt the air turn cold as a grim-looking figure strode towards them swirling a cane. The eyes blazed and heavy jowls bulged out of his neckerchief. This man meant business ...

Chapter Thirty-Four

※

L ATE THAT AFTERNOON, over in the Bay-Tree the talk
had turned to the lottery, which was due to be drawn at
the end of the month. Expectation was rising throughout
the metropolis, so that a mere mention of *The Honourable
Adventure* was enough to stir the imagination. In places of
public conversation people were eager to assess their chances
and let the dream take them over for a while – of a coach and six,
a fine house, or improved marriage prospects. The happy topic
floated free with little of fact to tether it. Rumours abounded
of prominent adventurers who were aboard the scheme. The
Duchess of Newcastle, it was reliably reported, had purchased
eleven tickets, and the Earl of Halifax fourteen. It was a
most respectable subscription. Drapers in Lombard Street,
prosperous butchers in Hackney, spinsters in Clerkenwell or
Chelsea – all were in play with a ten-pound ticket, or possibly a
half or a quarter share of one. Even porters and servants could
come aboard for a few shillings by purchasing a part share of a
ticket divided into thirty-two.

In the coffee-room of the Bay Tree it was discovered that
Gabriel Winch the broker had invested a full thirty pounds in
three tickets – a fact that was reassuring to some but aroused a
degree of suspicion too. He had always dismissed the lottery as

a 'sordid enterprise,' but had clearly decided to take his chance like many another.

Numbers became talismans – they were compared, and judgments offered. Seated by the far wall of the coffee-room, two young Scotsmen, David Macrae and Gavin Leslie, were eager to join in the talk. They had been finding their year down in London increasingly expensive and had joined together to purchase a ticket in hopes of a more extravagant style of living or simply a new wardrobe. They announced their number with a degree of pride: One thousand three hundred and forty-eight.

It certainly had an impressive sound – until Laurence Bagnall (author of *The Shoe-Buckle*) intervened:

'Alas, gentlemen! I heartily wish you success with your ticket. However, I cannot but think it an ill-omen'd one.'

'On what grounds, Sir?' said a surprised Gavin.

'It is the year of the Black Death, Mr Leslie! I foresee only doom for it! Nothing good can come of 1348! … Now, were it One Thousand Four hundred and fifteen …'

There was general laughter, but the two Scotsmen exchanged uneasy glances. David reached for his dish of tea:

'Are you taking a chance yourself, Sir?'

A slight frown touched the poet's face:

'I did consider it, Mr Macrae – but concluded that the excitement of the nerves would be too high a price … No, no – securities are the thing for me – the blessings of sure and regular interest!'

'But just think what you could do with a thousand pounds!' offered Gabriel Winch by way of encouragement.

'*Thinking*, Sir, should be directed at matters of substance. I would rather have a cottage on the ground than a castle in the air.'

'Mr Bagnall has no need of riches,' said a cheerful Joe Garvey. 'His verses would not be improved by luxury. They would cease to have that simple strength we so much admire.'

Laurence Bagnall beamed, and his wig gave an approving nod:

'You speak wisely, young man. Poverty is the Muse of Poetry – always has been!'

Gavin Leslie leaned forward:

'In your *Shoe-Buckle*, do you not allude unkindly to the silk stocking?'

'Indeed I do – a courtly extravagance! Good English worsted is an honest cloth. Our native wool would clothe any monarch to advantage.'

Behind the bar, Widow Trotter overheard these exchanges and smiled sadly. By custom she would have ventured for a half-ticket herself, and the possibility troubled her – it would indeed be a last, desperate throw, would it not? In her mind she was back at the basset table with her eyes fixed on those turning cards, sweat tingling her neck.

Fortunately, at that moment Jenny Trip bustled in from the kitchen and recalled her from the melancholy associations. She placed a dish of shelled filberts on the bar:

'I see Mr Bagnall is smiling,' she said. 'Does he hold court?'

'Yes, he is wearing his laurels today. They have been debating the lottery, and our poet will have none of it. He finds it too *exciting* to the nerves!'

'But that's the joy of it! – I dream of a prize myself.'

Mrs Trotter could not help raising an eyebrow:

'Are you adventuring then, Jenny?'

'For a small sum, Mrs T. I've taken a sixteenth share in a ticket: number *seven hundred*. Don't you think that's a very *aristocratical* number?'

Her voice swelled with pride – a year behind the bar of the Bay-Tree had given Jenny the tricks of a satirist herself.

'Yes, Jenny, seven hundred is sure to have precedence. I wish you success – though I would not wish to lose you to St James's …'

There was more laughter coming from Mr Bagnall's table, prompted not by jollity but by amusement. Mary Trotter was aware of the difference, and her heart warmed to it. She wished Tom were there conversing with them, prompting and responding to the wit. With that thought she was instantly carried to Bridewell and its discomforts, and for a moment she regretted sending her two young friends on their mission; but she felt sure they must return with something useful.

Hardly a minute passed before the coffee-room door opened, and there was Tom himself, unfurling his muffler and showing every sign of contentment that he was back in the chocolate house. He strode over to the bar and smiled broadly. He had been dreaming of hot spiced chocolate all the way from Fleet Bridge where he had left Will, and he had his penny ready. It was Jenny who took it:

'Is Mr Lundy not with you, Mr Bristowe?'

'No, Jenny, we parted in Fleet Street – Will has another call to make. I, however, am craving a large chocolate with a generous pinch of cinnamon!'

'It shall be brought you directly. Mrs Trotter has just stepped into the kitchen. She said I was to tell her when the two of you returned …'

Ten minutes later, and Tom had settled matters with Widow Trotter. He promised her a full report on their Bridewell visit once Will had arrived back from Ironmonger Lane, where he was making a chance call on Alderman Rivers. With luck he might pick up news about the grand assembly in Mercers' Hall on Saturday. Widow Trotter's eyes had lit up at the mention of it, imagining a scene of general reckoning not unlike the Last Day.

Now Tom was taking a seat at Lawrence Bagnall's table. The convivial group was debating the competing claims of sociability and self-interest, and Tom's arrival prompted a turn in the argument. Gabriel Winch was in full flow and at once offered the young man as an illustration of his point:

'... And here is Mr Bristowe, gentlemen! He is joining us for a sociable conversation, ready to listen and smile and help move our thoughts forward – once he has satisfied his physical hunger ...'

Tom had just bitten into a slice of Mrs Dawes's chicken pie which had accompanied him to the table and was thus unable to reply.

'... Man's bodily needs,' continued Gabriel, 'will always outweigh the delights of the mind. Food for the mind is a luxury – food for the body a necessity!'

He sat back in his chair, point made.

'As animals, we need food,' opined Mr Bagnall. 'But should we not aspire to more than that? Man's greed is a sad fact, but we are surely more than pigs! Can we not lift our eyes from the trough and look toward the heavens?'

Tom glanced at the faces round him. His enjoyment of the pie was becoming seriously compromised by the intensity with which each movement of his jaw was being scrutinised.

Joe Garvey had been listening closely, pipe in hand:

'You and your City friends, Mr Winch, selfishly pursue their own interests – I concede that. Yet when prices rise, they do so not through individual greed, but by a shared belief in the value of the stock.'

'A subtle argument, young man – almost serpentine ...'

'Yet it holds, does it not? A man who invests with no thought for others will leave himself exposed when the general sentiment is against him. All *value* – even in 'Change Alley – depends not on private, but on common interest?'

There was a moment of silence while the thought was digested. Tom, who had begun to satisfy his bodily needs, was ready for the fray:

'A pleasing notion, Mr Garvey, but does it not flatter 'Change Alley? What you call *shared belief* may be a mercenary collaboration. Individuals may come together for their own ends and create a sentiment of greed or fear – and exploit it. We cannot call such manipulation selfless – quite the contrary. That is surely how conspiracies work? A group's interest may be equally selfish.'

Gabriel Winch thought he recognised an ally:

'You have the wisdom of a stock-jobber, Mr Bristowe! I take it you have experienced Jonathan's? I am sure you must have!'

'Never, Mr Winch … I am *unsullied* and have never entered the place.'

It was an unwise turn of phrase, and Tom at once knew it.

'You imply, then, that Jonathan's is a *brothel?*'

It was said with a wicked twinkle. There was no retreat possible:

'Of a kind, Sir, yes … Bargains are easily concluded; a stock passes from hand to hand and is *thrown over* without compunction. Trust and loyalty are left at the door, and new attractions continually lure the eye.'

It was a bold assertion, and Tom was not sure how much of it was rhetoric. But it seemed to impress the company. Gabriel Winch warmed to the idea:

'Then let me make a dangerous suggestion to you, Mr Bristowe. You must meet me in Jonathan's tomorrow, where I promise to introduce you to the traffic of the place – and to some of the practitioners. We might even find an attractive *bargain* for you.'

There was laughter, but Tom saw an opportunity:

'I shall welcome the chance to experience it, Mr Winch. I am sure you will be an excellent guide.'

And so, Tom unexpectedly found he had an assignation for the following morning at ten o'clock. The more he thought about it, the more it seemed a good idea: they needed to know how Jonathan's functioned and what went on there. His curiosity about the place was mounting, though there was a twinge of disquiet when he recalled its reputation. The place was a cockpit where hot passions and cold calculations fought it out …

⁂

Will Lundy duly arrived at the Bay-Tree in the early evening. He had been fortunate in finding George Rivers in his office in Mercers' Hall, deep in the business of settling arrangements for the Saturday assembly but happy to break off and hear news of his son.

As the three of them settled around the parlour-table, Tom and Widow Trotter could see that Will had been cheered by the encounter. Success was written on his face. But there was much else to tell, and as she poured their coffees Widow Trotter made it clear she wanted to have an account of everything in due order, beginning with their visit to Sam Rivers in Bridewell and what they had learned there.

She knew the place only by reputation, and so the particulars intrigued her, especially its mixture of discipline and laxity. The image of Sam enjoying his wine and gingerbread at one moment and facing the lash and hemp-beating the next struck her as peculiar – she certainly doubted anything in the way of correction would come of it.

Bridewell was also fertile ground for gossip; and from what Tom and Will began to reveal, there could no longer be any doubt that Vandernan's was a dark extension of the Bank, where tricks and cheats were planned, a devious commonwealth that allowed a group of prominent men to pervert the market and impose their will on it. The propagation of false news was the most blatant device and one that was especially hard to counter. The very nature of 'Change Alley encouraged it.

It turned out that during his meeting with George Rivers of the Mercers' Company Will had encountered a rather different aspect of the City. As a Common-Council man, Alderman Rivers was on the governing body of the City of London and took pride in its history and institutions. While they listened to Will's account, Tom and Mrs Trotter saw that in Rivers Will had found someone who knew the workings of the trade from the inside and understood its tricks:

'When he heard I was studying the Law he was happy to admit its impotence in matters of deception. Anyone can solicit subscriptions for a hare-brained scheme – even a fictitious one – and make off with the funds. The Lord Chief Justice himself has declared that the Law is not required to *save a man from his own folly!* And so, there is no protection. Any false pretence of this kind is free of regulation. The City is proud of its rules and standards, but in this it is helpless.'

'So, 'Change Alley really is a wild place?'

'Yes, Tom, it is the home of bulls and bears – and of snakes and foxes too.'

Widow Trotter raised a point of concern:

'How much did you tell him, Mr Lundy? How open were you about what we have discovered?'

Will knew this was an important question, and he approached it with care:

'I was guarded at first, until I felt I had the measure of him. Frankly, I had not expected to find a man so open to talking about the corruptions of the Exchange – it was not the impression Sam had given us! He was anxious to know how his son was faring. The news of the arrests had reached him, but he had concluded that a few days in Bridewell might prove a sobering experience.'

'A harsh way to treat a son,' said Widow Trotter.

'Yes. But he thought the humiliation would be the worst part and was uneasy about the beatings. He felt the disgrace of it, but there was sorrow rather than anger. I put Sam's case as best I could – that he had been my chaperon in Vandernan's. It was then that I spoke of our suspicions about the links between the gaming-house and the Bank – which he knew nothing of. I told him his son was helping us expose its wrongdoings.'

'You could do nothing else,' said Tom.

'I could see he was disturbed by what I had to tell him – his brows began to crumple like paper! It was he who introduced the subject of cheating. It was my mention of Captain Hazard's game that did it. The mechanism interested him, and he was shocked at what we suspect of Lord Parham's connections to Philip Roscoe ...'

Will shifted in his seat and pushed back his hair. For a moment Widow Trotter glimpsed a court advocate readying himself.

'... Alderman Rivers is an ally, Mrs T! He knows how the jobbery in 'Change Alley works. "A complete system of knavery," he called it. He began to sound remarkably like his son. He is no defender of the Bank of England either. It seems there is a growing feeling in the City that it has become too powerful. It is being likened to a standing army – something necessary in a crisis but dangerous as a permanent arrangement. His opinion is that all monopolies are prejudicial, and what was designed for our defence now serves to over-awe us.

'It was revealing to hear him talk. I learned a lot about the Bank and its business. He says it is sucking money out of circulation because of the interest it pays. The Bank is drawing huge funds from private tradesmen and diverting them for their own ends. The Directors, he says, are a mixed bunch; but as a body they are able to set what rates they please and hold sway over the Government. The State is becoming mortgaged to the Bank. Instead of being the last resort it has become the first port of call.'

'This fits with what Uncle Jack told us – that the Treasury Committee had concerns about Sir Gilbert Heathcote and the Bank's powers. Did you say anything about Heathcote and the Duchess?'

'No, Tom, I thought best to hold off from that – but I told him what we knew of the plot to bubble the coal-gas scheme, and how the lottery funds have been compromised. This drew him to the edge of his chair. His eyes widened when he saw the enormity of what these men were risking. But he doubts it is the policy of the Bank. He suspects it may be Roscoe and his friends who have dug a hole for themselves. He was shaking his head in disbelief! It was at this point that I knew he saw us as allies. It's odd to think we could tell him anything and prompt him to action.'

'Action?' said Widow Trotter. 'Does that mean he is going to act himself?'

'I'm not sure – but he is prepared to help us. He is anxious that we work secretly and keep him informed. Evidence needs to be collected. He says that the *conspiracy* (it was his word) is bringing the affair within the remit of the Law.'

'But I thought you said the Law's hands were tied?'

'In the common run of things, yes – but he thinks these men may have reached the point where private practice shades into public treason. The stakes are high because the nation's credit is being put at risk. The City of London is founded on fair dealing. Aberrations are common enough, but once the City is found to be *rooted* in corruption, London's credit will suffer. He is eager for us to continue our investigation. He wants us to be sure of our evidence and help put a case together.'

Tom was impressed:

'I think we can say this is your first lawyer's brief, Mr Lundy!'

Will checked himself:

'Ha! You may be right. It is an important commission! But the best thing is, it clears a path for us, do you see? The

City of London is hard to puzzle out. As a corporation it
values its independence – it governs and polices itself, elects
its own Members of Parliament – even keeps its own militia.
A mercantile republic! Why do you think these men are using
Vandernan's over here in Covent Garden?'

The point was well made.

'I had not thought of that,' said Widow Trotter. 'But that
does not make our task any easier. Can he help, do you think? If
Sam Rivers opened the doors of Vandernan's to us, perhaps his
father could do the same with the City? It sounds like a fortress.'

'I put that very question to him, Mrs T – and that was when
the subject of Saturday's grand assembly arose. It seems Mercers'
Hall will convene some of the most powerful people in the City –
men who have such dexterity in tricking and cheating one another
that to bring them together could prove lively. He said Heathcote
and other Directors of the Bank will be there – including Philip
Roscoe. And Lord Parham too! The new Lord Mayor – if he
survives Friday's parade – will be the guest of honour. Also, several
members of the Treasury Committee will be attending with their
spouses ... And there is a further distinguished courtier with
responsibilities of that kind who is on the guest list – a gentleman
who handles the Queen's finances ...'

Tom's thoughts had run ahead. He knew that look on Will's
face:

'No! ...'

'Why of course! – Her Majesty's Deputy Treasurer is one of
the Great and Good – and unlike many, he will be there on both
counts. Your aunt is also invited!'

Tom shook his head:

'I knew nothing of this.'

'There is more! – and this was where my boldness had some
success ... To this point we had been remarkably open with each
other, and I could see he trusted me – and so I hazarded a direct

request … I asked if it would be possible for him to invite one or two people who have wind of the plot – our *witnesses*, if you like. I told him much could be gained from bringing us together.'

'Us?'

'Yes, Tom. Did I not say? … You and I are to be there! Along with Sam – and four others … I hope you will think I chose well …'

'Four?'

By this time Widow Trotter was beginning to picture the scene. What would she not give to be amongst them!

'Who might these people be?' she asked tentatively.

'I know you will be pleased, Mrs T … He has agreed to ask Michael Henriques – a young man who may have something to say about Vandernan's and its ill doings – and also his friend, Benjamin Levy – the gentleman you said understood the deeper workings of the City's finances.'

'You could not have chosen better!' said Mrs Trotter brightly … But you say there are two more?'

'Yes – a couple I think we cannot afford to be without … Lady Norreys and her husband. I could never forget Sir Charles.'

Tom gave a low whistle:

'I know how persuasive you can be, Will – but this ascends to the statesmanlike.'

'We might almost call you a politician,' added Widow Trotter.

'It is a confident plan, certainly,' said Tom. 'But do you think we shall have gathered our evidence in time?'

'It will be the greatest incentive to do so.'

'Then we have a resolution, gentlemen!' declared Widow Trotter. 'This has given us something to aim for. I think it calls for the madeira, don't you? …'

She jumped from her chair and turned her attention to the sideboard and the decanter and glasses.

'… This will help turn our minds to things closer to home …'

She poured the sweet wine slowly and with a determined hand. There were more immediate matters that needed to be addressed.

Tom spoke out:

'Ah yes, Will – we have some news of our own for you … I have just received another invitation – though the occasion is a far less brilliant one … from Gabriel Winch, no less!'

'Tell me!'

Tom tried to sound eager at the prospect:

'I am to pass tomorrow morning in Jonathan's. Gabriel promises to introduce me to the workings of the place.'

'Ah, Tom! Beware the bulls and bears – I don't know which will be worse! … But what an excellent opportunity – venturing into the enemy's camp to spy out the land! You can discover what forces are gathering, and what the hot stocks are.'

'Tom will only be an observer, Mr Lundy. We cannot afford another of us facing ruin.'

It was spoken calmly enough, but her words recalled the two of them to something that was literally close to home for her. There was a moment of silence.

'Oh, Mrs T …'

Tom spoke quietly.

'… I'm sorry. I don't know how you keep your spirits up. You encourage us to keep good humour – but the Bay-Tree …'

'It must be hard …' said Will, looking down.

'It would be a great deal harder without the two of you, believe me – I cannot contemplate the thought of it! But the last thing I want is any awkwardness. You must not be glum and hold back from the topic. These things have to be faced, and good humour is the pulse of life. I hate anything stiff and flat. No buckram!'

Tom gave Will a glancing look, which prompted him to continue:

'… It happens we do have news – about the man who tried

to redeem your promissory note. We were waiting our moment to tell you ...'

'Ah! I was wondering if anything had occurred.'

'... Sam has identified the bruiser who seized the note from me in Vandernan's, and we think it must be the same man.'

'My "fashionable costermonger"?'

'Yes – it seems he is one of Parham's bullies and must have been sent from Vandernan's.'

'And if Parham used him as an envoy,' said Tom, 'then he surely was the ruffian with the cane and snuff who threatened Frank at the sponging-house.'

'His name is Joel Harkins. That's as much as we can say at present. Perhaps Mudge or Mr Cobb will know of him?'

'Excellent. It's always good to have a name,' said Widow Trotter, thinking hard. Her smile faded, and despite her best endeavours there was the hint of a frown.

'What is it Mrs T?' asked Tom, noticing.

She recalled herself immediately:

'Only a passing fancy! I was picturing myself receiving my own visit from this Mr Harkins. I doubt he will march in through the front door.'

Tom tried to be encouraging:

'But there is no need for him to confront you, Mrs T ...'

'No – I suppose the bailiffs will be called in to arrest me. It will be Frank's humiliating scene repeated. In that case I think I must keep our finest brandy on hand and make it a sociable occasion ...'

Her countenance brightened. It could not be said that Mrs Trotter didn't practise what she preached.

'... But we must certainly ask Elias about this Harkins. He sounds quite a character ...'

The two friends were relieved to see her smile return and raised their glasses of genial madeira:

'No buckram!' they declared in unison.

Wednesday

27 October 1708

Chapter Thirty-Five

———

THE FRONT DOOR of the Chocolate House served more than a routine purpose – it had a dramatic character too. The more businesslike devotees of the Bay-Tree always kept half an eye on it, and like a theatre audience glancing at the side-scene, they registered a newcomer's face and what it might bode for good or ill. When that figure was Elias Cobb, his jaw set and his eyes searching the room, it spoke of news – and not of a reassuring kind.

It was Tom Bristowe who saw him first. He was setting out on his visit to Jonathan's and was nearing the door when it opened sharply, and Elias stood before him.

'Mr Cobb!' he said in greeting, but at once checked himself.

'Where is Molly?' was the immediate reply. 'I have news – and you need to hear it too, Mr Bristowe.'

Several heads turned. He lowered his voice – though not soon enough to avoid causing a stir in the room. But the customers were to be cheated of their expectations as Tom led the constable past the bar and into the kitchen, where they found Widow Trotter in consultation with Mrs Dawes, a jar of honey pressed to her nose. Elias's look was enough to dispel the sweetness, and a moment later she and Tom were in the parlour, braced for what the constable had to tell them. He didn't sit down:

'I cannot stay, but thought you should know at once – it's Toby,' he said. 'He's been over at the wharves. He wanted to report to you himself, but … he says he was on a mission …'

'He was … What has happened, Elias? We were hoping to find Bob Leary. Did he tell you?'

'Yes – I've heard of the goings-on at the Flagon. Poor Toby was so full of himself about it – about the new evidence …'

'*Poor* Toby?' Tom swallowed hard.

'I fear he's been attacked, Mr Bristowe – last night, on Custom House Quay.'

Widow Trotter blanched:

'How badly, Elias? Tell me …'

'He'll survive, thank God. No knife – but it was a severe beating – fists and boots. There were two of them – big fellows. Toby had been asking questions about our runaway and his Dutch friend Mr Oosterhout. It seems they did not welcome his curiosity!'

'So it wasn't a random attack?'

'No, nothing random about it, Molly. He says they gave him some important news before turning on him …'

It was clear Elias had more to tell them.

'… Bob Leary is dead.'

The words struck home, and Widow Trotter was surprised to feel a pang of sorrow, despite all the ill the man had brought her. Tom didn't hesitate:

'How, Mr Cobb? Was it at their hands?'

'According to the bullies, he took a false step on the quay – an unfortunate accident, they said – hit his head on the way down and was swept away. Toby pressed them for more, and that was when they turned on him without warning … He would have met the same fate but was able to reach Tower Stairs and hold on for his life – there was a strong tide flowing. Our Toby is a buoyant piece of God's handiwork!'

'Thank the Lord!' said Tom.

'So, he will survive, you say?'

'Yes, Molly. But he wants me to tell you he's disappointed for you ...'

'*Disappointed?*'

The two of them looked at each other.

'... in how it ended ... He had been thinking Leary could be brought to trial – I do believe he hoped to make the arrest himself! He's concerned that with Leary dead it will make things harder for Mr Popham.'

'That's to be seen ... but you must take Toby our commiserations – and a consoling bottle of our best port. We have a great deal to thank him for – and you too Elias. You're both heroes in the cause!'

Tom was eager to speak:

'Your note to Pall Mall arrived in the nick of time, Mr Cobb. I was there when Jem delivered it. Frank was able to slip the sheriff's men with minutes to spare.'

'It's as well he did, Mr Bristowe – the hunt is on for him. There are those who are pressing hard with this. They think they have the case against your cousin already made – all tied up with ribbon ... but of course there's one piece of evidence they lack.'

The response came from Tom almost as a whisper:

'Frank's torn promissory note ...'

'No-one knows of it, Mr Bristowe. I keep it safe, believe me! Mr Sturgis's pockets were found to be empty.'

Widow Trotter was thinking:

'It was surely meant to tally with the dice in Sturgis's mouth – to announce that Mr Popham was the killer. It must point at Leary. In the Flagon, he and Sturgis had been arguing about the note, and Leary must have taken it with him. It was a bone of contention between them.'

This could only be conjecture. The three of them knew how thin were the threads holding their case together. But the thought cheered them a little.

Constable Cobb's mind, however, was turning to weighty matters. The attack on his watchman was alarming: it confirmed that Robert LeRoy had been leading an exceedingly perilous life – a man with dubious friends and dangerous enemies. And the previous night he had evidently been down at the wharves ...

'Toby told me of your discoveries about Leary and his career of spying ... He says you're looking into the Dutch connection?'

Elias narrowed his eyes – the Bay-Tree militia were not short on ambition.

'Yes Elias, we have some City people with an interest in learning more about Oosterhout. Is he someone you've encountered? He's a considerable merchant at the Exchange.'

'That's not my corner of the world, Molly. I leave that to the City constables. They go about things their own way – when they choose to do anything at all.'

'Mr Bristowe is venturing there this morning – to Jonathan's in 'Change Alley, taking his chance with the stock-jobbers ...'

Elias gave a sound something between a grunt and a growl.

'... He'll be in the capable hands of Gabriel Winch.'

'Hmmm! In that case, Mr Bristowe, I've a piece of advice for you: *Eyes and ears* – and nothing more! Mr Winch is full of his schemes, as they all are. Don't buy anything, and don't *sign* anything!'

'Wise words, Elias,' said Mrs Trotter. 'I've already sounded the alarm. We all know how much can hang on a signature.'

Elias's words were echoing in Tom's mind as he turned from Cornhill into the narrow passage of Exchange Alley. He was conscious of an adventure beginning, and all the apprehensions he'd held at bay suddenly crowded in on him like the buildings themselves. It was not a place he knew, though he had hurried through it on a previous occasion. This time he was here to listen and observe. Jonathan's coffee house was on his left as he approached, and his stomach was telling his legs to keep moving, past the crowded doorway and the huddles of people in conversation along the pavement.

It was the prospect of 'Change Alley talk that concerned him as much as anything. He was at ease with the languages of coffee house, dinner table and church, of politics and the Law – even of the Court – but the jargon of Jonathan's was sure to be something alien, a traders' lingo from a world of mechanism and trickery. He halted and took breath, risking a slight smile: he was a child again, hesitating at the schoolroom door.

'A word, Sir! ...'

The sound was behind him, and he instinctively looked round to find a figure almost jogging his elbow. The man's face was pale, and there was a searching look in the eyes beneath a dark hat pressed down on his forehead.

'... I speak as a friend, Sir. Do you have business here?'

This was an unsettling *friend*, and the voice was rasping. Tom's first thought was to ignore him. But there was no escape save the door to Jonathan's.

'I do – I am meeting with my broker.'

Tom convinced himself with the phrase, but he knew he had already said too much – and too pompously.

'Have a care, Sir. This place is a nest of vipers! There is poison here – nothing but lies and cozening. All is pretence. Do not enter, Sir, I beg you! ...'

The man's eyes were intense, searching for his soul.

'... You have an honest look – you must leave before it is too late. I beg you! They will destroy you ...'

The man suddenly flinched and there was terror in his eyes.

'... Look at them – serpents all! They took everything from me, Sir! I once had a fine estate and kept a coach – but I was cheated of all I possessed. Those men took all I had – I signed it all away! I tell you – *all!* – you must not enter the place!'

The man was now clutching at Tom's sleeve. Heads were turned and people were looking at them. Tom was lost for what to say or do.

One man broke off from his group and strode towards them, annoyance in his face. He pushed the wild-eyed friend away:

'Be gone, Jasper! Do not trouble the gentleman!'

Tom's rescuer reached out and began to guide him in the direction of the door. Part of him was grateful for the intervention, but the familiar anxieties were stirred and he hesitated to speak.

'You must not mind Sir Jasper! He picks out any new face in the Alley. The poor gentleman tells his story to anyone who will listen. It is an unfortunate tale, I grant, and its moral is sound enough – you should indeed be careful here. But fortunes are to be made as well as lost, and the wind can change in an instant. If this is your first visit ...'

There was a momentary pause, but Tom was still tongue-tied.

'... then you must give thought to the advice you are offered. Not all is to be trusted ...'

Tom tried nonchalance:

'I am to meet my broker inside ...'

'Excellent! In that case I wish you good fortune. Are you a Bull today – or a Bear? I have to say the Bulls are having the upper hand – but there's still a good run to be had if you pick wisely.'

'I am a Bull for quality, Sir – but a Bear for anything flimsy. I suspect there's a good deal of insubstantial stuff floating around.'

'It soars and sinks, indeed! You speak shrewdly, Sir! May I ask who your broker is?'

'Gabriel Winch.'

There was a moment's hesitation.

'He's your man for a wager, certainly, if you are in a bold mood. The siege of Lille is the buzz today. We hope for news by the next Holland mail. It is your hottest topic. *When* is now the only question for some – there are wagers on the very hour of surrender! But who knows? The delay goes on and anxieties mount. Bank stock is slipping for want of confirmation. People are becoming fidgety … Lottery tickets are quiet this morning, but I expect things to change before Monday's draw – some players are sure to be squeezed out …'

He lowered his voice.

'… Word is, there are contracts made for twice as many tickets as there are in the whole lottery! Men sell what they haven't got and buy what they don't wish to keep … It's settling day on Saturday, so we can expect some fireworks.'

Tom was trying to keep up with all this news. He was determined not to be thought a novice:

'I am something of an experimenter, Sir, and have an interest in mines and water … I hear of a project to extract combustible air from coal. It is something that greatly interests me.'

'You and many others! The Alley has been echoing to cries of *Coal-gas! Coal-gas!* …'

Tom's garrulous acquaintance had been overheard and at this moment he was halted by a voice from the huddle:

'*Two hundred and eighty*, Ned!'

He whistled:

'Ever higher! If you wish to ride the stock, Sir, then you should jump aboard at once. There was a trial of strength earlier this morning, but the Bulls have conquered. We hear the Queen herself is supporting the project and the Bank is solidly behind it. In that case it can hardly fail. My friend Mr Grimes here is dealing in bundles of fifty shares – I'm sure he can give you a good price … Over here, Jack! …'

The man stepped over briskly.

'… What price fifty?'

'I can do it for one thirty, Ned.'

'That's a good price! …'

He turned to Tom:

'… My friend here will discount you ten pounds, Sir.'

'And for December.'

'*December* too! …' Ned's face was animated. 'And is that not your last bundle, Jack?'

'The last on the books, yes. There is little to be had, I tell you!'

Tom had been hearing this exchange with mounting alarm. The cynic in him said it was an accomplished performance by the pair of them and he was not to be caught – but another voice whispered that these men might soon be dangling from a hook themselves. Who could tell?

By this time Tom was eyeing the door of Jonathan's as an escape route:

'I see I must consult Mr Winch on this. Do give me your card, Sir, if you will.'

The words sounded composed – but this was part of his own performance.

'Here is Mr Grimes's card, Sir. I am Ned Hitch. We must talk more about the coal-gas. I appreciate you must weigh matters, but delay could be costly. It is a remarkable scheme – and the patent is highly spoken of!'

Spoken of – yes, Tom thought, words were hard at work:

'I mustn't tarry, Mr Hitch – but I thank you for your advice. I'm sure we shall talk further …'

Tom doffed his hat and made the man a slight bow. He was beginning to feel part of the scene already. As he stepped towards the door, he ran the two names across his tongue: *Grimes and Hitch* ... There was an oddly comic trick in the conjunction – like a pair of fairground conjurers.

Tom pushed open the coffee-house door, and there they all were – the notorious 'jobbers' in restless congregation. He could sense the electric atmosphere, and his skin shivered. At once a booming cry of 'Coal gas!' to his right drew his attention to that side of the room, where an odd-looking character was doing some brisk business. The man appeared to be a walking office – pencils perched behind his ears, a sheaf of papers stuffed into his hatband, and several pouches dangling from his waist; a large calfskin budget was slung around his neck, into which he was delving as three or four figures crowded him. Across the room, other groups had formed, and noisy chatter was echoing from every direction. Suddenly 'Coal gas! Two ninety!' became the competing cry to Tom's left, supplying the tenor to the other man's bass. There was an antiphonal drama between them.

Tom's eyes searched for the familiar figure of Gabriel Winch, but the place was crowded. No tables occupied the centre of the room, though there were benches and a few desks along the walls for closer consultation. Everything discouraged calmness and collected thought. Every body was busy. There was a palpable expectation in the air as if some great event were awaited, some secret about to be divulged, some disaster imminent, some new opportunity there for the taking. Yes, he thought to himself, the very premise of this place is the future. Every mind here is attuned to expectations, prospects, assurances, promises – endlessly swinging between confidence and doubt. It was a system that had to keep moving or die – an urgency that was emphasised by a giant clock fixed into the cornice. Unlike the Bay-Tree, this was not a room for weighing your thoughts. Indeed, it was the very opposite. He was reminded of one of the outer rooms at

Kensington Palace where anxious petitioners congregated. Yes, he smiled to himself, this is an eternal *ante*chamber – with Fate giving birth in the adjacent room!

Tom had been standing in wonder with these notions playing in his mind when he saw Gabriel Winch beckoning from the bar. He made his way over, feeling some relief that he could station himself with company. Notebook in hand and a pencil between his fingers, Gabriel was in a jaunty mood:

'Welcome, Mr Bristowe! – I thought you might have had second thoughts about visiting this house of illicit pleasure!'

'With you to chaperon me, Mr Winch, I'm sure my virtue will remain intact.'

'Come, come, Sir! You must not fly the field before the engagement begins! You must surrender your tuppence – unless you intend to deal yourself, in which case you'll need a sixpence. In this place any man can be his own broker for the day!'

Tom winced at the thought and was content to hand over a couple of pennies in return for a dish of dark chocolate and the addition of a small almond biscuit.

'You have arrived at a febrile moment, Mr Bristowe. Jonathan's is often a busy place but not always *fermenting* to this degree. The place is putting on a show for you.'

Tom had to raise his voice:

'What is the cause, Mr Winch? Is it the coal-gas project? I hear it being called in every direction.'

'Yes – confirmed news has just come in of a Royal interest in the scheme. We knew the Bank was supporting it, but this is unlooked for. Men are understandably apprehensive of projects, with new subscriptions being offered daily and patents by the dozen. But such support as this is very rare. The stock is flying.'

'India stock! *Who buys?*' came a plaintive cry from behind them. 'You shall have them at *fourteen!*'

There seemed no general hurry in the man's direction.

'I'm a seller of *a hundred!*' was an unhelpful echo elsewhere. 'Take them at *thirteen!*'

Tom leant over to Gabriel's ear:

'That's a big fall in price, is it not?'

'Not as great as it sounds, Mr Bristowe. The difference is ten pound thirteen to ten pound fourteen. The men are saving their lungs!'

Tom saw he had much to learn. Around them, men were moving from group to group as inquiries and offers were being more discreetly made. Gabriel's ears were alert and his eyes darting around to see where the activity was.

'Mr Winch, is it? ...'

A young man was pressing in on them. He was breathing hard and his heavily-powdered bob-wig was slightly askew.

'... Do you have a price on the Prince?'

Gabriel cut him short:

'My book is closed on that, Sir!'

'But for *today* – that he'll not see the morrow? Can you give me odds?'

'That is what I cannot do, Sir. It seems the Prince's odds are soon to be made even – but we must leave that to God ... I have closed my book.'

Gabriel lifted up his notebook to emphasise the point. The young man couldn't hide his disappointment and departed more slowly than he had arrived.

Gabriel shook his head:

'He has the look of a court flunky, does he not, Mr Bristowe? It would seem things are very bad at the Palace.'

'Prince George?'

'Yes, poor gentleman.'

Tom thought it best to move things on:

'I met a jobber outside who told me you were the man for a wager, Mr Winch. Does it keep you busy?'

'As things stand I could make a good living from that alone. It seems everyone is eager to *prophesy*. I'm happy to receive their money, so long as they don't take a hand themselves. I draw the line at any wager on the death of a parent – when a simple pillow could make a man's fortune … I've learned my lesson on that!'

This was a dark view of the world, though Gabriel's mouth curled into a grin as he spoke. But this flicker of amusement was short lived:

'There's something I should perhaps tell you, Mr Bristowe. I've been hesitating – but as the subject has arisen … earlier this week I had an inquiry about an insurance – you know it is becoming quite a rage just now … It was on the life of Mr Popham. He is your cousin, I understand?'

'On *Frank?* …'

Tom reeled.

'… You mean someone has wagered on Frank's death?'

'Not a wager, Mr Bristowe – a formal insurance. Such is not my line of business, so I sent him elsewhere. I have since heard that your cousin is being sought … for a murder. Is that so?'

The chilling word was almost lost in the hum of the room.

'Who was this man?'

'He wasn't known to me. I don't know if he was successful elsewhere …'

Tom was about to exclaim in protest, but Gabriel cut him short:

'… You must not trouble yourself over this, Mr Bristowe. It is common knowledge that insurances, like wagers, are entirely unregulated. Anyone can seek to insure any life – including I've no doubt Her Majesty's – though to my knowledge that treason has not arisen …'

This was little comfort. News of Frank's perilous situation was evidently circulating. It was becoming the talk of the coffee houses.

Gabriel Winch thought it best to change the subject, and for the next ten minutes Tom received a mixture of instruction and advice. His questions were answered, and he began to appreciate the mechanisms of Jonathan's – how, beyond all the swirl of activity, something like equilibrium was being maintained – a balancing of needs and desires sustained by endless adjustments of value. It was an economy, but a monetary not a moral one. Hope and fear alternately pumped through its heart. Tom was familiar with the spiritual idea, and clearly the kingdom of Mammon had its equivalent.

But Tom had other questions too, and when the feverish activity relented a little, he succeeded in drawing Gabriel to the side of the room. His mission to Jonathan's was well begun, but there were more pertinent things he needed to know.

There was one particular matter Tom was curious about, and he decided on a circuitous approach:

'I was expecting to encounter more of our foreign friends, Mr Winch. It seems this is a very English affair. But is that not a Dutchman over there? He's very animated!'

'Across the road is their place – but that *mynheer* is a familiar face in here. He's a broker with many Dutch clients and deals in stocks for them. Mr Jansen is forever dashing to and from the Exchange.'

'In the Bay-Tree on Monday you were talking severely about the Dutch traders – do you truly think them more dangerous than the French?'

'You have an excellent memory, Mr Bristowe ... Yes, I was not speaking for effect. You may call me suspicious, but I have some grounds for it.'

'As I recall, you were about to tell us a tale, but your offer was cut short.'

'A tenacious memory indeed! ...'

Conscious of the implied flattery, Gabriel gave Tom one of his enigmatic smiles:

'... Well, let me satisfy you now, Mr Bristowe – with unaccustomed brevity. I swear!'

Tom hadn't time to congratulate himself on the deft manoeuvre before he was deep into a story of Dutch wrongdoing. The heart of the complaint, it appeared, was the stranglehold they had on news from Europe:

'Intelligence always arrives in Amsterdam before it reaches us, and you can imagine how this works to their advantage ...'

Gabriel told of an occasion when Dutch duplicity came close to breaking him. The story was nothing to the purpose, but it gave Tom the chance to take the subject a little further:

'And do you believe there is a trade in intelligence that takes the opposite direction – from England to Holland?'

Gabriel hesitated slightly:

'*Secrets?* yes! ... I always suspect the Dutch know more than I do! It is not something people like to talk about, Mr Bristowe. It reflects poorly on the City and tastes of sour grapes, as they say.'

'And you must not inquire why I ask you this, Mr Winch ... Is the name of *Willem Oosterhout* familiar to you?'

Gabriel's face registered something close to astonishment, and he gave Tom a searching look:

'But ... you forbid me to ask ... How? ...'

Tom stayed silent, waiting.

'... Mr Oosterhout is well regarded by some ... But that is the man who nearly ruined me. He is not to be crossed ... How? ...'

With great effort he was holding himself back. Seeing his evident confusion, Tom relented a little:

'I in my turn must say very little, Mr Winch – but my friends and I wish to know more of him.'

'Oosterhout is a man with connections, Mr Bristowe – and influential ones. But I'll have nought to do with him. I do know he has friends in the City. But I no longer meddle with such matters.'

It was clearly not a topic that Gabriel Winch wanted to pursue.

Tom was intending to press on, but they were interrupted by an elderly gentleman with a clergyman's manner who politely inquired if he could wager on the next Dean of Windsor – another matter, it turned out, with which Gabriel Winch did not meddle.

The interruption broke their conversation, which had become uneasy. Tom thought the best thing he could do was ask a final question brazenly:

'I have just one more name for you, Mr Winch. You've been generous with your time, but I must ask it: Michael Henriques.'

'Mr Henriques? Why yes, of course. The gentleman is not five yards from you at this moment! But you must expect no more tales of chicanery. He and his father are respected in these parts, though their credit has come under question. Do you wish me to introduce you? I really must see to my business …'

'I would like that very much, Sir,' said Tom, almost disbelieving his good fortune. After Widow Trotter's report, this was a young man he wanted to meet.

Chapter Thirty-Six

⸺

THE MENTION OF Mary Trotter's name brought a glint to Michael Henriques's eyes and warmth to his voice:

'Ah yes, Mr Bristowe, the two of us had a profitable conversation over at the Exchange – she's a woman who would not be out of place in this room. Mrs Trotter has a dealer's wits – I was tempted to invite her into partnership!'

It was said with a smile, and not entirely whimsically. Tom could only agree. It was the best introduction, and the two young men were soon chatting freely together. The stock-jobbers were a-bustle all around them, so they found a bench by the wall on which to perch. The general hubbub was continuing and there were fewer takers for seating.

A cry rang out:

'I sell coal-gas – *Two ninety-five!*'

There was an immediate waving of papers. Tom flinched as the man by their side leapt to his feet.

'I was expecting you to be dealing in the stock yourself, Mr Henriques – a little like our friend the street-hawker over there.'

'Mr Rawls is pushing the stock hard today – but I cannot deal in it with a good conscience, Mr Bristowe – and I think you know why ...'

Tom's look signalled that he knew only too well.

'... It was my darling project, and I was happy to be its first champion. But now some mighty powers have taken hold of it. A Royal interest is spoken of, and the Bank is letting its support be known. Nothing would seem to stand in its way ... Of course, your Mrs Trotter warned me and made me step back. I only half-believed her conspiracy could be real – but since Monday the evidences have confirmed it ...'

There was a sudden burst of noise in the corner of the room, and another cry cut through it:

'Who buys Coal-Gas? *Three hundred!*'

More waving of papers. With each rise in price, the demand seemed to increase. Tom was momentarily distracted. If only he had taken Jack Grimes's price! ... He caught sight of this particular seller and recognised him from the alley. The man had been a buyer not half an hour earlier! Why would he sell so quickly – unless to help nudge the price ever higher? Buy in the alley and sell in the coffee-house – was that the game?

Michael Henriques was smouldering:

'Mrs Trotter is right. The whole business has the stink of Vandernan's about it. Of course, the irony is not lost on me. The subscription I helped establish is mounting in air beyond my reach. I cannot deal for myself and can only wait for the bubble to burst ... I want none of it, Mr Bristowe! I cannot in good conscience urge people to invest. In any case, my voice counts for little. A couple of jobbers grinned at me and called me the *little bear!*'

'*Ursa minor?* I think you should take that as a compliment – let them look up to you! My friend Will Lundy heard the plans being laid in the gaming house – but I think you know this? Lord Parham and Philip Roscoe – they were putting their heads together.'

'Yes, Roscoe! The more I think about it, the surer I am that he's the prime mover in the business – putting the Bank's weight behind the stock … But let us not dwell on that sordid topic. I have news for Mrs Trotter and was about to write to her. You can be my messenger, Mr Bristowe! She asked me to inquire further into Willem Oosterhout …'

There was no escaping that name. Poor Toby Mudge had discovered how dangerous it could be to utter it unguardedly.

'… I cannot say who – but I have talked with someone with a nose for the darker dealings about the Exchange. The stock-jobbers may have been exiled from the place, but the trading there still has its own sharp practices, its protected interests – like any fraternity.'

'The City companies, you mean?'

'No, Mr Bristowe – nothing so regulated, and the more powerful for it. You must think how trading works, and what may be concocted among greedy men to their mutual advantage.'

Tom looked at Michael Henriques. There may have been a cynical edge to his words, but the eyes told a different story. This was a man who knew the enemy.

'Where does Mr Oosterhout figure in the scene?'

Henriques grinned:

'Mynheer Oosterhout looks beyond these shores. His reach extends across Holland, Flanders and Germany, and he uses his forces well.'

'You make him sound like the Marlborough of Trade … Such men have enemies, do they not?'

'Competitors, yes – and, like states, they form and break alliances when it suits them … Mr Oosterhout has agents in many places. They serve his legitimate business, but perhaps other purposes too.'

At that moment Tom's mind turned to Bob Leary – a man who had served Oosterhout's purposes. Had he been cruelly dispensed with? – or been the victim of Oosterhout's enemies?

'And Robert LeRoy was one of those agents?'

'It would appear so – and may still be. Mrs Trotter told me he was taking ship for Amsterdam – but surely to serve his master's interests there?'

Tom saw he had his own news to give:

'Alas, Bob Leary is serving no-one now – except his maker. He has met a violent end at Custom House Quay.'

Henriques was genuinely startled:

'Dead? But that is ... Oosterhout's office is at that very wharf ...'

Tom glanced around, and in a low voice proceeded to tell him of Mudge's violent encounter of the previous night and the news he had brought back.

'I'm shocked, Mr Bristowe! It was no mere misadventure, then? Leary has been murdered?'

'Yes – and like as not by the pair who attempted to consign the watchman to a similar fate. It could have been no accident. Toby had been inquiring about Leary and Oosterhout – a dangerous conjunction!'

Henriques took breath almost with reluctance:

'My news won't contradict that, Mr Bristowe. My informant has wind of something going forward out of the way of Oosterhout's regular trade. Our Dutch merchant has several vessels, large and small, and not every cargo is confined to tobacco. It is said that Mynheer Oosterhout has friends in the Custom House – a valuable resource when you look to diversify your activities ...'

By now, Tom was beginning to despair. He could feel the events of the past few days weighing on his spirits. Everywhere he turned, men were looking to exploit the system, whatever it might be – whether taking a chance, working an advantage, cheating and deceiving ... He longed for the moment when he and his friends could leave behind this world of winners and losers. He found himself craving a simpler reality – a life of substance and honesty – and generosity too ... But there was no escape just yet. There was nasty work to be done.

'You are thoughtful, Mr Bristowe ...'

His downcast look had been noticed.

'... This business disturbs you, I think? – and (forgive me) it makes me wonder if you are more deeply involved? Mrs Trotter was open with me about her plight, but she hinted at troubles beyond her own – that her friends were threatened in some way. She was guarded on the subject and promised to tell me more when the time was right ... Since then it has occurred to me that the killing of George Sturgis lies at the heart of the matter – though I do not know how ... I am a practised listener, Mr Bristowe, and it is always helpful to have the full picture.'

It was a kindly invitation, and at this moment they were the words Tom wanted to hear.

'Perhaps that time is now, Mr Henriques! It is good to share a problem ... But be warned – once I begin there may be no stopping me. Thanks to my friend Will Lundy, plans have already been laid which involve yourself.'

'Curious indeed! Why did I half suspect something like this?'

It was said genially, and Tom was encouraged to continue. With a sense of huge relief he began to unfold the Popham side of the story – the desperate plight of his cousin Frank and the threats to his uncle – how he and his friends had managed to hold disaster at bay – but for how long? Their golden opportunity was the gathering at Mercers' Hall on Saturday, which Tom knew could be decisive one way or another.

Throughout the story, the young broker was intent and held his peace, and Tom spoke as low as the noise would allow. Together they made an incongruous spectacle. Within the room, all was urgency. The restless ebb and flow of business continued, and they were the only figures in the place whose thoughts were concentred elsewhere.

But the *little bear* was gripped, and his looks registered both surprise and recognition. He and his father were well acquainted with what the Vandernan's cabal was capable of.

Tom closed with the anticipated Mercers' Hall assembly, and Henriques nodded slowly:

'That's a powerful story, Mr Bristowe, and it would be more than satisfying to bring it to a just conclusion. You and your friends have some plans in place, but you leave a lot to chance. If all your villains are to be gathered together, then you need to set a trap for them. Perhaps you could take a hint from the old dramatists? ...'

It was an appealing analogy, and Tom was all ear.

'... The surest trap is one that will entangle them in their own devices. In recent months my father and I have had cause to defend our business, and I can tell you that all is not well with the Bank! By the year's end a new Chairman is to be appointed, and there is no small struggle going on. Sides are being taken. Your story confirms what we have concluded – that the Bank is riven by faction.'

'Two candidates, do you mean?'

'Exactly so. The state of affairs is almost parliamentary! You'll not be surprised to know that the mighty Heathcote is the favoured man, with his strong Whig connections – and what you've discovered of his closeness to the Marlboroughs shows it. But he has a rival in Philip Roscoe. Sir Gilbert has stirred up a deal of resentment by using his riches to turn the Bank into his own fiefdom – and has made huge profits from it. Who knows what power he could wield as Chairman? I understand there is some resistance to placing him at its head – a role he has long coveted!'

'So, Roscoe and his allies are the opposition?'

'In practical terms, yes. But there is no good and bad here, just competing powers! What we have in Vandernan's is an outpost for the opposition to organise themselves.'

'But how can we exploit this division?'

'*That is the question*, as Mr Hamlet says!'

Tom's smile died on his lips:

'Sturgis *and* Leary – both killed. Were they dispensable? As the rift grew wider and the game more urgent, did they become inconvenient?'

'It is a dark story, Mr Bristowe, but no less convincing for that. What you and your friends have chanced upon is decisive – it fills out the picture my father and I have formed. The pledging of the lottery funds to underwrite the government loan! – the foolhardy idea of bubbling the market! – all this smacks of a panic. And now with a second killing … Something has gone badly wrong. I cannot believe that Heathcote would permit such helter-skelter stuff …'

'Do you mean, the whole plan was contrived by Roscoe and his allies?'

'It is certainly possible – though "plan" is a flattering word. Perhaps it was a move to outflank Heathcote? Once the hasty loan had been agreed, the desperate expedients followed … A plot is often a way of managing deception …'

'Coal-gas! *Three twenty-five!* Who buys?'

The cry reached them over the dealers' heads. During the past few minutes Jonathan's had filled even more, and the two of them were being hemmed in by the crowd. The frantic ritual was continuing at a faster pace; wigs were askew, and a sword scraped against Tom's knee. The room was becoming increasingly warm and sweaty. The floor was littered with scraps of paper being trodden underfoot, with a dropped snuffbox now adding its choking incense.

Tom sneezed – and he wasn't the only one.

'I think we should move, Mr Bristowe. Let us leave these men to their merry antics! And I know to where we must direct our steps ... There is a gentleman we have to talk with.'

It was a determination rather than a suggestion, and Tom was happy to comply. As the door of the coffee house swung closed behind them, they breathed more freely, though there was still a huddle in the alley outside. Tom recognised Grimes and Hitch continuing to ply their less official trade, and in close consultation with them was another familiar figure – none other than Sir Jasper, the tragic victim. Something in Tom made him smile at the audacity of it. The man was the Betterton of 'Change Alley!

'Our destination is just around the corner,' said Michael Henriques as he led the way.

Lombard Street had a distinctly prosperous character, but there was nothing showy about it. The well-regulated buildings on either side vied with each other by the brightness of their paint and the glow of their brass door knockers. Even the cellars were worthy of respect – not the haunt of servants but a location for additional offices. Lombard Street had no need to display itself, and this reticence served as a guarantee of probity and soundness. Its riches were hoarded out of sight in vaults fortified more securely than any prison. *You can trust us,* these houses declared, there is true value here, not subject to the vagaries of that disreputable alley nearby ...

Michael Henriques was being reticent himself, and it was only when the pair of them halted outside a house with glowing brickwork, handsome sashes and a lion's head door-knocker, that he gave any hint of whom they were visiting. A small brass plate stated discreetly that this was where Benjamin Levy conducted his business affairs.

'Ah!' said Tom. 'I've heard something of this gentleman from Mrs Trotter. She spoke of him warmly.'

'Mr Levy is a good friend of my father's, Mr Bristowe. Without him our business might not have survived these past months. He has been helping us find a way through our troubles. I think you'll find what he has to say of interest, and I know he in turn will want to hear from you.'

This was revealing little, but Tom sensed that something important was about to be added to the picture. As they mounted the steps it struck him that his visit to 'Change Alley was turning into an expedition.

After all the seething activity of Jonathan's, they were relieved to find themselves in a room of ordered quietness, something closer to a library than a busy counting-house. Ledgers occupied the shelves, and a pair of clerks were seated at desks absorbed in their book-keeping. Carpets and heavy curtains lent a muffled solemnity to the place, and a reassuring privacy.

It wasn't long before a door in the far wall opened to reveal Mr Levy himself. He was bidding goodbye to an elderly lady garbed in black, a substantial wallet of crimson morocco cradled in her arms. She made a dignified figure and nodded at Tom as she passed, leaving a waft of jasmine behind her. A tale there, surely! … It struck him how many stories besides their own must be playing out in these streets – futures being decided, hopes raised or crushed.

Mr Levy's study was a place of business, but it was not all books and papers. As Tom settled himself, his eye was drawn to an ebony cabinet intricately veneered in ivory and tortoiseshell – a piece of furniture to grace any Venetian palazzo! And occupying the fourth wall, a large Flemish tapestry told its own story in glowing colours. It was nothing heroic, just a harvested field of wheat and a woman gleaning while a commanding figure gazed at her with outstretched arm. Tom wondered if the Old Testament scene held particular significance for its owner – another story perhaps? He was beginning to see plots everywhere.

Benjamin Levy gave them a warm welcome, and they were soon deep in the subject that concerned them all. Tom was pressed to take the lead, and his evidence of the relations between the Bank and Vandernan's was received with a look of wise despair. For Mr Levy it was a confirmation of the dirty manoeuvres that passed for monetary dealing when politics and power were the motives. Over the years he had encountered much bad faith and ingenious deception. Every line on his face spoke of it. What was slightly surprising was the gleam of delight when he saw how neatly Tom's account fitted with their own:

'And so, the great game goes on! ... Is it not a thing of wonder, Mr Bristowe, this ability to conjure riches out of thin air? These men are *hocus pocus* – fairground jugglers! First there is nothing – the fingers move – and lo! Now there is something! ... How confident these tricksters are that they can escape the trap they set for others! ... Well, we shall see ...'

The last words were said almost in a whisper.

'... You tell a good story, young man. What you and your friends have discovered is a scene of desperate ingenuity. How these men struggle to escape the consequences of their folly and ambition!'

'So, you do believe the Bank's loan rests on shaky ground?'

'The final quarter million of it? Yes, I do. There has been a suspicion here in Lombard Street that it was a piece of *cobbling* – the Tory Sword Blade had to be fended off at all costs. The Whigs were determined it should be their loan! I don't need to tell you that lending money brings influence – and in time of war the need is pressing ... But, but, but! ...

He began shaking his head as if over a naughty schoolboy.

'... Mr Philip Roscoe and his friends had to show that their Bank of England is more than Sir Gilbert Heathcote – the tyrant in waiting! ... and see where it has landed them!'

Michael Henriques leaned forward:

'We have just come from Jonathan's, Sir. The coal-gas has risen to three twenty-five ... The price is being pushed higher by some eager gentlemen. By tomorrow it could be four hundred!'

'A sublime thought, is it not, Michael? Imagine! Someone is bespeaking their coach and six this very moment ...'

The grin on Mr Levy's face was hard to read. He looked at Tom:

'... Michael told me of his meeting with Mrs Trotter – and since then we have been considering what we can do to frustrate this play with the coal-gas. To my mind, the thing is a dubious venture – but my young friend here has great belief in it, and so I would not wish to see it fail ...'

He gave a warm-throated laugh.

'... But is it not amusing, Mr Bristowe? It is the perfect project for these men – an image of their own affairs – a gas! A mere nothing – but a nothing out of which great power may come! There is something adventurous about a scheme of this kind which appeals to me – I am not always counting my gold! Nothing I have earned in my life has been without risk, but I am a believer in making that risk as small as can be. And I don't like to play someone else's game.'

As an underwriter of other men's adventures, Benjamin Levy was exposed to the risks of trade, whether in goods or paper – and over the years with that risk had come great profits and unlooked-for losses. Life was a lively ride. As he continued to talk, Tom was intrigued by the playfulness of his manner, the eyes that flickered with irony from a countenance that bore the imprint of his dealings with the world. It was the record of countless questions, anxieties and doubts, yet could still come to life in childlike wonder at the folly of the human race.

'Timing, Mr Bristowe! That is the key. A strong position may become weak in an instant, and what is valueless at one minute can be priceless the next. Wheat and chaff! Sentiments change with the breeze as it rises and falls. These people are set on exploiting this for their profit – and if all works as it should, those profits will be great indeed – and other men's losses all the greater. Of course, they are co-operative – they work in concert to move the market, and this gives them confidence ... Let me explain what I think they are planning ...'

Tom was all ear.

'... It may seem a nonsense, Mr Bristowe, but these men are staking what they do not have. It is possible to make money without money ... you look confused! – rightly, because you are a practical and rational being – but what these co-operating gentlemen have purchased is a *right*. Let us say they did this when the price of the stock had sunk to *eighty*. What they bought was the right to *buy* an agreed number of shares at, say, *one hundred and twenty* by the settling day at the end of the month, when the option will close ...'

'By Saturday, then?'

'Yes, the thirtieth ... This timing is important. So, whenever they choose before that date, they will be entitled to buy at *one hundred and twenty*, whatever the price may have reached ...'

Tom made the calculation and whistled.

'... And, at the same time, they purchased the opposite right – the right to *sell* – let us say at *seventy* – by the same date. This is called a *put*! Now, if they can ensure that the price swings wildly in the hours before settlement, they can win twice – ideally exercising their right to buy at one hundred and twenty when the price is four hundred – and then, if the stock has collapsed, use their right to sell at *seventy* when the price is fifty – or indeed *ten* ...'

Tom thought he could grasp the idea, which was certainly ingenious. But he was puzzled:

'But you say they can do this without money?'

'Yes – and this is the clever thing! – they borrow their stake for repayment after the settling date – so they can pay it out of their gains. The profit can be huge – much more than simply buying a stock and selling it in the usual way. The option to buy or sell can be traded and become immensely valuable – or, if you are not careful, worth nothing at all.'

'I never thought of a *right* in those terms, Mr Levy. It is a very mercenary one. And I see the illusion in it. They make a fortune from another man's inventiveness and toil, and perhaps cost him his business.'

'Yes, exactly – without ever touching coal, or having a whiff of gas …'

He chuckled, but Michael Henriques was looking gloomy:

'And knowing nothing of the business themselves, Mr Levy. The original subscription was to support Mr Broughton and Mr Darby's scheme and allow them to establish a manufactory … It was not designed to pour a fortune into the pockets of lazy gentlemen with no interest in the business and nothing to contribute to it.'

'And yet …'

Benjamin Levy's brow was contracted. He paused, his mind elsewhere, running over possibilities. The others waited.

'… Truly, I cannot but think we are missing something. This plan of theirs is precarious, is it not? So much is at stake, and yet they cannot control what is to happen, however organised they are … This scheme of the coal-gas is full of possibilities, and the sums involved are great – but I question whether they are enough to cover what is required. This puzzles me. To have such confidence as they do! They must have some assurance they will succeed … And our *Mr Sturgis* …'

The fatal name brought another pause, this time electric.

'… Did he stumble on something? … And where did his loyalties lie? If you can discover this, then perhaps his killing will no longer be a mystery. Perhaps the coal-gas play is part of a larger deception? You must pursue this while I ponder the problem. I shall make further inquiries myself. I shall set about it at once ...'

He turned to Tom:

'... Meanwhile, can I ask, Mr Bristowe ... will you convey a message to Mrs Trotter? Tell her she must not despair. The Bay-Tree is not forgotten! She made no mention of her plight when we met, but her jeopardy is part of this pattern, and once all our pieces are fitted together, she will share in the success.'

'Thank you. I hope you are right, Mr Levy. Perhaps things will become clear on Saturday?'

'Ah yes, the settling day!' said Michael. 'A most apposite conjunction! Perhaps that day's gathering in Mercers' Hall will see other things settled also?'

He gave Tom a knowing glance. Mr Levy was alerted:

'Mercers' Hall? ... Aha! ... An unlooked-for invitation was delivered here not an hour ago ... Do I detect a device, gentlemen? It came from the Mercers – a grand occasion to welcome the new Lord Mayor ...'

Tom's spirits lifted. So, the further invitations had gone out – Alderman Rivers had been as good as his word.

This called for a full explanation, and thankfully the Lombard Street banker was more than happy with the thought of what was to come. As Mr Levy heard the names of those attending, his appetite for the occasion grew:

'All the players! ... I congratulate you, Mr Bristowe. I shall be content to play my part also – whatever it may be ... Can it be that unbeknown to Alderman Rivers, Providence is working itself out? It is an intriguing prospect. What a last act we are like to have!'

Chapter Thirty-Seven

LAVINIA POPHAM RESTED the book on her lap and paused for reflection. She loved Shakespeare, and the comedies above all, especially the darker colours against which their final healing and happiness shone brighter. In the comedies, Tragedy was always ready to make an entrance. Joy was precarious, and the more precious for it. She smiled when she recalled what she had often noted: how much of this depended on the resourcefulness of women. It was they who steered things towards the light … But in this play especially (her eyes returned to the book) what obsession, cruelty and mental pain would have to be lived through first – and how uneasy the final joy would be! …

A sudden knock – quiet and hesitant – made her start.

'Who is it?'

The bedroom door opened slowly to reveal the figure of Arthur the footman, who, without speaking, stepped into the room and closed the door after him. This was unprecedented, even a little alarming.

'What is the matter, Arthur?'

The footman put a finger to his lips, and there was a moment of silence.

'Don't be alarmed, Miss Lavinia. You have a visitor …'

The voice continued hushed.

'... Your brother has returned.'

'Frank – here? What has happened?'

She herself was now whispering.

'He will be able to tell you himself – he is at present in the wash-house. Mr Popham has fled his hiding-place at Brentford and has nothing with him ... He is in some distress – frantic ... Mrs Walker is watching over him and feeding him cake.'

'But – can he not come into the house?'

'He is anxious to avoid his father and Lady Melksham ... He is not yet in a state to explain things to them. He has asked to see you.'

'I shall come down, Arthur ... We must settle him in the kitchen. Cake is good.'

'He thinks he may have been followed.'

It was an uncomfortable thought. She set her heavy volume of plays on the adjacent table and followed him, slipping off her shoes so as to tread softly on the wooden stairs – unlike the Popham footman, she was not lightly shod.

What confronted her down in the servants' area was an instructive picture – something like a moralised scene of 'the Fugitive Gamester.' The subject was seated on a three-legged stool, his head disconsolately propped on his hand as he contemplated a half-eaten slice of cake, his other hand cradling a bottle of ale. Lavinia paused at the wash-house door to take in the portrait, complete with its expressive details: the large washtub and linen-horse by his side, and the pile of sheets against which his shoulder was resting. It really was a sad, instructive sight ...

'Sis!'

He swung round and there was a wildness in his eyes.

'My dear brother – what has been happening? You are home now! – Can you not come into the house?'

Two days earlier Frank had fled with no chance even to bid goodbye, and what Lavinia had learned since then was only patchy – without Arthur's secret intelligence she would have been completely in the dark. The wash-house wasn't the best place for a heart-to-heart talk, and there was too much to be said at once. But now, as if a dam had broken, the words poured out of him. The account of his predicament was headlong, but it made sense of what Lavinia had picked up as rumour. As for his adventure of the past two days, the White Horse at Brentford had become an uneasy refuge when word of the fugitive spread along the road from London and the looks and whispers began.

'I could stay no longer, Sis! I was beginning to be suspected. I had to slip away without notice. And the thought of home was too strong … I have to know what is happening! Am I still suspected? Have matters begun to resolve themselves? I need to see Tom! …'

He was flushed and still sweating from what had been a desperate ride.

'… I've had no news, and nothing to do but fret and fume all day long! Not venturing out – imagining the worst – I can't stand it, Sis! – I must be doing something, or at least know that something is being done.'

Lavinia was trying to think practically:

'Yes – we *both* need to see Tom. But you must calm yourself. We'll send a note round to the Bay-Tree.'

'Sidney!'

'Yes, we'll send Sidney – a verbal message only. I've arranged to pay a call on Julia Norreys, but I promise to be back in half an hour – and from what you say, she may have her own news for us … I'm sure Tom can be found.'

'We'll have a conference, Sis – just the three of us! It will be like the old times, will it not?'

There was a spark of hopefulness here that boded well. But it was clear Frank needed to rest. He was persuaded into a chair in the kitchen, more cake was provided, and the boy was sent off eagerly with his secret message, while Lavinia made her way to Charles Street and Lady Norreys, trying to grasp the import of what she had just heard. Drama on the page was all very well but living it could be alarming. She had now been swept into what appeared to be a national plot of murder, fraud and corruption. And Heaven only knew what further revelations Tom might have …

Lavinia returned to Pall Mall with a more coherent account than her brother had provided. Julia Norreys had been reticent at first, but once she knew her young friend was aware of the seriousness of Frank's plight she was happy to tell her all, which included a lurid picture of Vandernan's and its conspiracies. It was clear Lady Norreys hadn't been idle, and Lavinia was carrying back some information to advance their cause …

Their cause! – within a single hour she had not only been pitched into an intrigue but found herself an active player!

She made her way to the rear of the house, half expecting to find Frank in the custody of the sheriff's men. But there in the kitchen was the newly-arrived Tom with his own bottle of ale, already in deep discussion with his cousin. He had obeyed their summons at once. Out of consideration for Mrs Walker (who was hard at work with the family baking) the two young men had wedged themselves into the chimney-corner, an appropriate nook for telling tales and speculating on the nation's ills.

Somehow Lavinia was able to squeeze herself in, and the three of them became a close huddle. This meant that anything which aspired to conversation was impossible. It had to be confidences spoken in a low voice – the very image of conspiracy. Given what Tom was ready to reveal, this was not inappropriate.

He began with the wider political story they had managed to piece together. He told them of the power struggle within the

Bank of England, the secret Dutch interest that was working through Vandernan's, and how the coal-gas bubble was being exploited; the misuse of the lottery funds, and their hope that the powers-that-be in the City might be prepared to take action. It really did seem they had a convincing picture of the enemy's manoeuvres which were designed to reach their climax by the end of the week.

Frank was impressed, but also anxious to know how all of this related to the threats he and his father were facing. Tom was able to satisfy him that the Bay-Tree militia had been active in that direction too:

'What we can be sure of, Frank, is that the Vandernan's people believe your father has stumbled on their conspiracy and are attacking him through you ...'

Tom paused. This was the moment for him to reveal what they had learned from Toby Mudge's enquiries at the Flagon – the violent quarrel between Leary and Sturgis. Tom knew it would come as cheering news, and indeed Frank was overjoyed:

'You mean it was witnessed? *George and Leary were arguing?* ...'

It was a glimpse of salvation – the two men had quarrelled only moments before Sturgis was stabbed – and there was a witness! His spirits leapt.

'... Surely, Tom, this is conclusive? Bob Leary killed him!'

'You must not build too many hopes on it, Frank. There has been a complication ...'

The mood changed at once as he broke the news of Leary's killing down at the wharves. Frank was open-mouthed, and Lavinia couldn't stifle a gasp of horror. Mrs Walker glanced round – Tom gave her a reassuring smile, and she turned back to her kneading.

Lavinia blanched and lowered her voice to a whisper:

'*Another* murder? This is deadly dangerous, Tom! Does father know of it?'

'Not yet – it is not general news. The attack happened only last night … But we can't think this lifts the threat from you. The evidence of the quarrel is strong – so much stronger than the case against you, which is entirely circumstantial – but we have to assume Parham and his cronies will not relent. We know there's nothing that links you *directly* to Sturgis's killing, and must build our hopes on that.'

Frank was feeling hemmed in. His frustration was mounting. He longed to pace about the room and swing his arms around:

'Ah, Tom! If only they hadn't found that damned promissory note! What was it doing in his pocket? And with my name on it. It was surely put there to point the finger at me!'

He was trying to hold his voice in. Their talk was threatening to become boisterous.

Tom looked puzzled:

'On that point I can reassure you, Frank. They didn't find any note. Thanks to our quick-thinking friend Mr Cobb, that piece of evidence is wanting! No-one knew it had been there – not even Toby.'

Now it was Frank's turn:

But … my visitor in the sponging-house made it his clinching threat – that a fragment of the promissory note had been found in Sturgis's pocket … How could he think that? …'

He broke off as the realisation struck him. At the same instant it had struck Tom also:

'Frank! – do you see what this means? We now have our own evidence. It's indisputable. It must point to the killer …'

Lavinia was caught up in the drama of all this:

'Will somebody explain?'

'… It surely means, dear Coz, that this bully in the sponging-house assumed the note had been discovered *because he had seen it there*. It was Parham's man ... And we know his name – Joel Harkins.'

There was a moment of silence while the significance sank in. Frank was beginning to blush:

'Would you believe it? Five minutes ago, I despaired of having any evidence at all, and suddenly we have two suspects – Leary and this fellow Harkins! Each tells a different story!'

'Both could be true of course,' said Lavinia, whose thoughts had now raced ahead, '... and the link is Lord Parham. You say this Harkins is Lord Parham's man? – Well, from what I've just been hearing from Julia Norreys, that also describes Mr LeRoy?'

'That's true, Coz! You say true. Leary was very close to Parham ...'

'Well, Lady Norreys has been working hard on our behalf, and she wanted me to bring you a message, Tom – she thinks it could be significant ... You have a close ally there! ...'

She gave her cousin a look full of meaning – a provocation he chose to ignore.

'... Julia told me she had overheard her husband talking with Arthur Maynwaring and plotting to accuse papa of fraud ... Well, since then she has been determined to do what digging she can – you know Sir Charles treats her abominably and she's happy to return his contempt ... Well, she has discovered a note! He keeps his study locked and is secretive about everything – but she found it in the pocket of his coat ...'

Lavinia paused, relishing the moment. This was perfect chimney-corner stuff and deserved the most surreptitious of whispers. By now Tom and Frank were leaning in to hear.

'... It is a note to Sir Charles from the hateful Maynwaring – it must have been written yesterday ... it's only short, and she copied it.'

'This is wonderful, Coz!' said Tom as he watched her open her purse and extract a small folded piece of paper. She handed it to him. Frank hung over Tom's shoulder as the two of them read it together. The thing was enigmatic in its brevity, and was undoubtedly secret in nature:

> *Fear not! It seems Her Grace knows nothing. All is still well, and*
> *by Saturday matters will be set right again – and no harm done.*
> *A.M.*

Lavinia remained silent. Tom and Frank looked at each other. It was Tom who spoke first:

'So, Maynwaring is going behind the Duchess's back! Her faithful secretary is playing some game that must be kept from her – *until Saturday* … What can that imply? Whatever they are planning is imminent.'

'Can it be the plot against father?' said Frank.

'But that would not need to be kept from the Duchess, would it?' said Tom. 'No, I think this is something else – something larger? … *Until Saturday* …'

He repeated the words, thinking what they implied.

'… Is this to do with the stocks? With the bubble? But why are the two of them anxious to keep it from her?'

Silence fell as each of them pondered the question. Tom was wondering if the note concerned some Vandernan's deal; Frank was sure it had something to do with Maynwaring's malice against his father; Lavinia was thinking of Julia Norreys and imagining what sweet retribution might be awaiting her faithless husband. And as they pondered, the only sound was the thumping of dough on the kitchen table as the strong-armed Mrs Walker went about her business.

After a few moments Frank was readying himself to speak when a distant cry rang out – a woman's voice. It appeared to come from upstairs – and suddenly, unmistakeably, there were men shouting …

They knew what this meant. Frank was trapped in the chimney-corner, nowhere to run.

'They've come for me!' he said quietly.

Lavinia sprang to her feet, allowing Tom to squeeze out of the ingle so as to give Frank room. By now they could hear the clatter of boots on the stairs, coming closer. It was hopeless. But Mrs Walker wasn't going to surrender. She seized her rolling pin and strode towards the door, ready to confront the invader of her territory. As if given heart by this, Frank instantly unfroze and ran for the back door. Whatever happened, he must not be found hiding from the Law – better to give himself up with dignity. If only he had done so earlier!

It was a noble resolution; but Frank Popham's fortunes had arranged themselves differently. What was waiting for him as he ran across the yard was a giant of a man, armed not with a rolling-pin but a stout oak staff, which he held aloft ready to crash down on the fugitive's head.

There were no formalities, just force – although little resistance was being offered. The officers were making brisk work of it. Handcuffs pinioned Frank's wrists behind his back, and the protesting young man was hauled up the stairs to the entrance hall, to the accompaniment of Lady Melksham's frantic entreaties. It was rough and unceremonious, with no pause to explain. Tom's pleas for the officers to wait until Lord Melksham could be sent for were ignored: the runaway had forfeited such considerations and would not be allowed to escape again.

Tom could only stand and watch as the Honourable Francis Popham, M.P. was led across the pavement towards a waiting coach, protesting loudly at the indignity of it all. Tom was thinking hard. It occurred to him that in his desperation his cousin might reveal something of what they knew. He shouted a warning:

'You had best say nothing, Frank! Don't be tempted to defend yourself to them – *you must answer only to the sheriff, do you hear?* No-one else! Say as little as you can. You must leave things to us!'

His words echoed along the street as Frank was bundled into the coach. Seconds later with the crack of a whip the vehicle rattled away, past groups of amused pedestrians who had been enjoying the entertainment.

———∞———

Lord Melksham was sent for, and in the interim Tom and Lavinia did what they could to pacify Lady Melksham – but to little effect. Brandy served only to enliven her distress, and the polite ritual of the tea-table, rather than calm her, made her feel the social disgrace all the more keenly. Her hand shook, and tea spattered over her dress:

'We are ruined!' she declared. 'The family will never recover!'

To this point she had been shielded from the worst of her stepson's plight, and so the blow was especially severe. The word *murder* had been a terrible revelation.

Tom spoke reassuringly to her about how malicious the accusation was, but what he said seemed to make things worse. The horror and shame of the threat to the whole family could not be concealed.

Lord Melksham's return did nothing to dispel the gloom, and Tom took it upon himself to answer his uncle's immediate questions and give an account of the past hour's drama.

This was too much for Lady Melksham, who protested she could take no more of the 'frightful story.' And at last, at the very moment of rising from her seat, her tears, which until then had somehow been held back, flowed freely and copiously. Lavinia led her stepmother from the room, leaving Tom and his uncle to talk between themselves.

At once Tom sensed a chill in the air. They were back in his uncle's study, but there was no offer of brandy, no genial reaching for the tobacco jar. Lord Melksham's face settled into a frown and he began pacing round the room, grunting to himself. What had just happened was everything he had feared, and Tom's opening explanation seemed to increase his annoyance. He waved a hand and stopped his nephew in his tracks:

'All of this is well enough, Tom. Still you speak of *progress*, of your *investigations* – but where is the evidence? I don't wish to hear of Dutch plots and bubbles in 'Change Alley. There is nothing solid here! You begged me to be patient and wait on events – and look what has happened. An event indeed! An event to remember! Yes, things may be moving on – but only to Frank's certain ruin and the disgrace of the family. There is one way to end this. I *shall* have it out with the Duchess! All must be laid open! Nothing you can say …'

Tom interrupted him in full flight (not something he could recall ever having done before):

'But, Sir! – I was about to tell you – we *do* have evidence. We have not been idle. Since our last meeting we have made important discoveries. I could say nothing earlier, but there is a great deal more to tell you …'

His uncle gave a hum and looked Tom squarely in the eyes for what seemed an eternity. He had stopped pacing the room:

'In that case … You must sit down and tell me everything. I shall listen carefully …'

He reached for the decanter of brandy and began pouring two glasses.

'… I fear for poor Sophia. This has struck her very hard. Perhaps I should have opened it out to her, but I wanted to protect her from the worst … And now the worst is suddenly upon us. I only hope you can bring some light into this.'

Tom received his glass.

His uncle now seated himself and reached over for the tobacco-jar:

'You must have a pipe with me, Tom, and we shall contemplate the worst together. You must not let me smoke alone.'

There was a note of despair in the genial gesture; but the mood was changing, and Tom was glad of the chance to reassure him. As the story began to unfold, his uncle saw that the Bay-Tree militia had been hard at work forming alliances and mapping out the ground. Other *events* had been occurring too, and there was, at last, firm evidence of Sturgis's murder.

By this time Tom's pipe had gone out, but his uncle continued to puff away, eyes bright at the scene that was forming:

'So – you have *two* suspects? And that fellow Leary is dead? ...'

He shook his head.

'... You are right, Tom. These Vandernan's people are desperate men – a faction within the Bank, and one that seeks to make its own rules. They delight in play – but for them, cards and dice are not enough! No, they must play their dangerous game with people's lives, and for the highest stakes.'

Tom saw his uncle understood what they were facing:

'Yes, Sir, and their game is about to reach its *settling day* at the month's end. We are arriving at the moment when accounts are to be concluded, and other things reach their culmination also: the Lord Mayor's Day on Friday, the lottery draw on Monday ... and the reception in Mercers' Hall on Saturday ...'

Tom stopped. His words had the desired effect.

'Mercers' Hall? ...'

Lord Melksham narrowed his eyes.

'... What are you about, Tom? Did you know your aunt and I have been invited? Is this somehow part of your plan?'

With no little climax, Tom told him of their alliance with Samuel Rivers and of Will's interview with his father:

'Alderman Rivers is one of the City's governors, uncle. He has the authority to take action – and on Saturday all the chief players will be there. We are to report and lay our evidences before him. He has extended some other invitations with that in mind ...'

With relish Tom revealed what was being planned, and who would be gathering in Mercers' Hall – what awkward confrontations there could be, and what cards might be on the table. By now Lord Melksham was feeding on his nephew's words:

'This is ingenious, Tom – an impressive strategy altogether. I can see I underestimated what the Bay-Tree militia could do. It is a pity your Field-General cannot be there also ...'

Tom detected a smile forming.

'... I wonder if we might adjust the arrangements?'

'What do you mean, uncle?'

'I mean that poor Sophia will certainly not wish to attend. The last thing my wife wants at this moment is to display herself in public ... And in that case, I think Mrs Trotter would make a highly appropriate substitute, don't you agree?'

This was perfect. Tom could already picture Widow Trotter's face lighting up in anticipation. He would delight in telling her the news! It was clear that his uncle was alongside them in this enterprise and ready to play his part. Lord Melksham felt easier too. Now for a while they could relax themselves into genial conversation and enjoy each other's company.

'Let me pour you another brandy, Tom. You must stay for supper. I shall need you to cheer Sophia!'

Chapter Thirty-Eight

⸺◦◦◦⸺

THE INSTANT THE men entered the Bay-Tree's coffee-room the mood changed. During the past hours Widow Trotter had been anxious for Tom's return, concerned to know what had happened in Pall Mall to call him over there so urgently; but when the door opened and she saw the three pairs of eyes coming towards her, she knew this was the moment she had been dreading. These people had no thought for coffee and genial conversation. They had come for her.

It was a formidable group. A bewigged gentleman holding a document wallet was flanked by figures whose appearance at once spoke *bailiff* to her – not least because of the staves in their hands. Around the room newspapers were being lowered; talk died, and heads turned. Widow Trotter's heart was suddenly like ice, her face a picture of fear. She had temporised and fed on hope, trusting that events would somehow reorganise themselves and she would have time … but here was the assured reality. The scene was now upon her.

She spoke first, before any formal summons could be delivered. Her words were quiet and polite, as if she were greeting guests:

'Let us go into the parlour, gentlemen – we can talk there.'

A sharp nod was the only reply. The men followed her round the bar and into the kitchen, the domain of reassuring warmth and enticing aromas where Mrs Dawes presided. On this occasion she was poised, carving-knife in hand, over a roasted chicken, and was about to speak – but the inquiry died on her lips and she looked on apprehensively as the strangers made their way to the parlour door. Preserving the forms, Widow Trotter invited the three men inside and offered them seats. They declined.

She nonetheless took a seat herself and allowed the men to stand over her, challenging them to register the awkwardness of it. She was almost choking as she thought of the many congenial gatherings she had enjoyed around this table – all the ideas that had flowed, the thoughts exchanged, the challenges that had been faced and overcome. Over the years it had been a place of laughter and encouragement, but also of quiet contemplation when she had been alone with her thoughts.

The bewigged gentleman introduced himself as Edward Barnes, the Sword Blade notary, and after stating his credentials he came to the point without any elegant preliminaries:

'I have brought the necessary documents, Mrs Trotter, so that we can dispatch matters without any fuss ...'

His voice was colourless. Widow Trotter remained perfectly still and made no reply. The look on her face told him to sit down at once.

Somehow the message carried, and a few seconds later Mr Barnes drew a chair towards himself, and his knees performed the operation. He placed the wallet in front of him. They were now eye-to-eye.

'... I understand from Mr Grigsby that you acknowledge the state of affairs and know what is required of you. Financial embarrassment is always troubling. Let me say that I am glad you have chosen this course of action. A loan is easily arranged, and there will be no need to call on the assistance of these capable gentlemen. It can all be completed here and now.'

She tried to remain calm and reasonable:

'But why is this pressing, Mr Barnes? I was given to understand that the person who presented my note for payment on Monday morning did not urge the matter. Since then I have not heard from him or his representatives.

'I cannot go into detail, Mrs Trotter. But the note has been presented once again – this time the party has given firm instructions. These two fellows are here to ensure that the loan is properly arranged.'

'And if it is not?'

'If it is not, then I shall leave you in their capable hands.'

There was no equivocation here.

'You speak of a loan, Mr Barnes. Do I take it you are demanding security?'

'I thought you understood the terms, Mrs Trotter ... If you look at this paper, you will see that the money will be paid into your account on the security of this property and its connected business ...'

Connected business! An empty phrase, yet full of meaning. How jargon drains away the life of things, she thought. Was that all the Bay-Tree was?

'... The title to this property will revert to the Sword Blade bank, and the funds – three hundred pounds – will be released to you ...'

Again – what a neat idea. She was to sign and be free! And the document was *security* – such a warm notion. She longed to *release* some well-chosen words in his direction, but she knew Mr Barnes was trapped in the language of his trade. He was making the client easy.

The man had stopped talking and was looking at her:

'You should read the document, Mrs Trotter ...'

He pushed it towards her.

'... I see you have pen and ink handy ... Take your time.'

She glanced at the two grizzled presences towering above her. They were leaning on their staves and eyeing the madeira on the sideboard.

'Yes, Mr Barnes. I shall do so.'

She forced herself to read through the paper. There was more jargon, and yet the thing was clear enough – chillingly so. Her eye stopped moving, but her thoughts moved on. This was a decisive moment. The paper was not just a document to be signed, but a mortgage on her future independence and comfort. Yet there was no alternative.

She signed.

The moment had passed. Mr Barnes and his henchmen were ushered from the rear of the building, leaving Widow Trotter leaning against the closed door, doing her best to calm herself and breathe slowly. It took some courage to straighten her back and make her way to the coffee-room. She opened the door and was welcomed by a convivial hum and the warmth of the Bay-Tree's evening crowd. Here was her *connected business*, as full of life as ever. Nothing had changed, and yet all had changed. It was no longer hers.

It was well past eight o-clock, and still there was no sign of Tom – a thought that carried a disquiet of its own. Time was dragging heavily. Widow Trotter stood behind the coffee-room bar sipping an almond-flavoured chocolate and thinking how little she had eaten during the day. Customarily at a moment like this she would collect some food from the kitchen and retreat to her parlour – but somehow that room was not the refuge it had been – the thought of solitude was not appealing.

She told herself not to be fanciful and was about to make her way through to the kitchen, when the coffee-room door opened, and a squint-eyed youth peered inside. His dirty linen shirt and canvas breeches attracted glances from the bewigged gentlemen at the adjacent table. But after only a slight hesitation he directed himself confidently to the bar. She saw there was a note in his hand.

'Mrs Trotter?'

She nodded, and the note was held out to her. The youth's fingers were begrimed and had left their imprint on the paper, which had been hurriedly folded and sealed. Her own name was soiled but legible. This was no polite invitation.

She took it from him, and paused, looking into his left eye:

'Where has this come from?'

The youth may have appeared suspicious, but there was no guile in his answer:

'At the wharf – by Custom House Stairs. I know nought of the man. Had an odd way with him – said to be sure and give it you – very pressed he was! – '

'No reply?'

'No – but he said the thing was *important* – and you'd certainly reward me for bringin' it safe …'

Her curiosity was kindled.

'Very well. You're sure the man expects no reply?'

'No, Mistress.'

'Well, you have brought it safe, indeed.'

She handed him a penny. The youth hesitated and seemed to be eyeing the large wooden snuff box by her elbow. With a degree of amusement she took the small spoon and tapped some grains into his open hand. With a smile, he lifted it to his face and snuffled loudly. It was inelegant but effective. With a disconcerting wink, he turned away and left.

She looked again at the note, hesitating as she re-read her name. She was not going to retreat into the parlour – if this was more bad news then she would confront it here. Contrary to custom, she took a pinch of snuff herself, and broke the seal. The thing had been hastily written, and the underlinings added to the urgency. It was unsigned:

Mrs Trotter!

I am no ghost – but you will certainly think this a summons from the dead. I cannot explain here and must be brief. I am aboard ship – and it has been resolved we must leave for Amsterdam on the ten o'clock tide – there is no time to lose. I cannot stay in England, yet am troubled by what may be awaiting me at journey's end.

I may be going to my death – my true *death, that is – not the false demise that has been announced. It was none of my doing but I discover I am now the late Robert LeRoy – an idea that frightens me! It is said to be for my safety, but it may equally be for the convenience of others. Who could be charged with killing a man who is already dead? I am between nations and between allegiances, doubtless an enemy on both sides.*

I must see you before I leave. I beg you to come! – and I swear it will be to your advantage. Believe me, I AM MOST SINCERE.

I know what wrongs have been done you – and not only by me! At this moment I need to confide – and to offer you restitution. You also need to know the truth – such as I can tell it you – the truth about George Sturgis and about Vandernan's. It has been a tissue of lies – – – and I must forewarn you of something that is about to happen. Perhaps the intelligence will allow you to repair the damage done you.

I can say no more here. I BEG YOU, let me see you before I depart. I am aboard the Groene Draeck – a vessel moored at the east end of Custom House Quay. It has a green dragon on the prow. I have so much to explain – not least what – and who – has brought me here.

I must see you!

Widow Trotter was transfixed. Nothing had prepared her for this. The note was genuine – no doubt of it – but she knew she must not go. Every ounce of her good sense spoke against it. It would be the height of folly! Here was an immediate summons to the wharf, and in the darkness. She thought of poor Toby and what he had met with at that very spot the night before when he enquired about Leary ...

But she hesitated. She looked at the coffee-room clock, which showed a quarter before nine. Was there time to summon Elias to arrest Leary – would that be the answer? Would it serve their turn, or bring only embarrassment? ... In a hackney it would take her at least half an hour ... No, no! Again she told herself not to be foolish ... But then she looked down at the note, and the words beckoned to her: *advantage – truth – restitution!* – It seemed he wished to explain and to forewarn her of something ... These were not the words of a man fleeing punishment. Why did he not simply slip away? What was so important that he must see her? The more she thought of it, the odder it became. What could Leary gain? Or was it a guilty conscience speaking? Did he truly want to see Justice done and Evil punished? It could not surely be a trap? He had nothing to gain from that ---

She looked at the clock again. The minute hand was tilting itself towards nine. Her eyes glanced down. Was she truly to be given *restitution?* ... At this moment her state was so abject that the note appeared a gift from above – a hand reaching down to her at her darkest hour, offering the possibility of release ... If she ignored it, she would always wonder what might have been ...

She turned quickly and hurried back into the parlour, throwing off her tiara and seizing her hooded cape. She rapidly sealed the note up again.

In the coffee room she beckoned to Jeremy:

'I have a mission for you, Jem! You must take this to Constable Cobb immediately. Put it into his hands and no-one else's, do you understand? Tell him I'm gone in haste to the wharf. *This is of the utmost urgency.*'

'You can trust me, Mrs Trotter.'

'I know I can, Jem. You must find him. It is important.'

The hackney coach rattled over the cobbles, swaying wildly. Inside, Widow Trotter listened to the crack of the whip and held tightly onto the sash, wondering if she had been right to request 'all haste' to the coachman. Fortunately, there was little in her stomach. The journey was taking her deep into the City, up Ludgate Hill and along Fleet Street, past the Temple, round the churchyard of St Paul's, and then south to Thames Street which led eastward, parallel to the river. She looked out to her right. They were now passing a succession of alleys which ran down to the Thames itself, each one giving a glimpse of masted ships. After London Bridge the river had transformed itself. Upstream it was a local waterway busy with small boats ferrying passengers to and fro; but here it looked east, out toward the oceans of the world and all the riches of distant continents: tobacco, timber, silks and spices – not forgetting the coffee, tea and chocolate which would find their way to the Bay-Tree. Her thoughts darkened for a moment – if she needed an adventure right now, then this was surely it.

The coach jolted to a halt, shuddering from side to side as the horses settled themselves. The journey had been rapid, and Widow Trotter's arm was beginning to ache. She descended warily, paid the coachman, then looked around to take her bearings.

It was still Thames Street, and she was at the head of one of the alleys that descended to the quayside. Throughout the journey she had kept her disquiet under control, but now she couldn't avoid imagining what awaited her. It was a desperate chance, but she knew she had to take it.

She drew her cloak around her, pulled up the hood, and began making her way down the slope towards the river, trying not to slip on the muddy cobbles. The distant wharf was illuminated, but this made the alley all the darker, and the gloom made the shouts more threatening. She told herself this was Thames-side, not St James's, and men were at work here. Indeed, an alarming rumble at her back was a man jogging with a two-wheeled cart behind him loaded with crates.

She reached the riverside, and the prospect opened. There, against a backdrop of the Tower of London, was the torch-lit Custom House, its elegant proportions contrasting with the busy confusion before it. As far as the eye could see the wharves were crowded with ocean-going vessels, a forest of masts bobbing gently in the uncertain river, caught between ebb and flow. The tide was about to turn, and ships were being readied. Her destination lay beyond the Custom House, but there was no clear path. The quayside was in a ferment. Great winches were swinging out to those vessels still being loaded, their crewmen hauling on ropes and setting the sails. The wharf was piled high with stores, and large canvas bundles were offloading from a row of carts.

All this made it difficult to negotiate a course along the quay. Men were manoeuvring barrels across her path, and as she stepped around a heap of tarpaulin she encountered a pair of sailors exchanging obscenities; a push was answered by a blow, and the next moment the men were on the ground pummelling each other. No-one cared to intervene. This was not a place where violence drew much attention.

The end of the wharf was in sight. By now Widow Trotter was close to the water's edge, stepping over ropes tethered to a succession of stone bollards. She peered into the darkness at the prows of the ships, one after another, searching for the elusive green dragon. Finally, at the very last berth of the quay, she found it – though the colour was not to be discerned. And a fearsome creature it was too, the eyes threatening death and the tongue protruding like a serpent. The thing was attached to a single-masted sloop whose name was painted boldly in a gothic script: *De Groene Draeck*.

And there, watching in silence, stood a single figure, a ghost-like form looking down at her from the deck. It was Bob Leary.

Chapter Thirty-Nine

———

'YOU CAME!'

Widow Trotter was looking into a face that had a story to tell – and not a happy one. The bruising gave Bob Leary a lopsided look, and he had limped across the ramp to help her aboard, wincing with every step. The deck hadn't been the ferment of activity she expected, given the vessel was about to set sail: two men were chatting nonchalantly by the bowsprit, and a third figure, half-hidden behind the fore-rigging, had watched them as they descended the steps into the hold. It seemed the Green Dragon was readied for the journey, its cargoes of Maryland tobacco and finest Norwich worsted all well stowed.

Leary had no cabin, just a curtained-off sleeping-berth in a corner amongst the piles of corded bales, and here they were now, seated on a pair of wooden boxes. It was almost a stowaway's quarters. And the man who faced her was not the confident Bob Leary of old, but a more cowed and anxious character – someone with a great deal to say who was uncertain where to begin:

'You have come alone?'

'Yes I have – a frantic journey, and perhaps a foolish one. Your summons came not forty minutes ago. But my curiosity proved too great – especially as I had heard of your death …'

She gave him an accusatory look.

'... This is one of Willem Oosterhout's ships, is it not? ...'

No preamble – and immediately Leary was startled. How much did she know? And what was to follow? It was going to be an uneasy encounter. Certainly, Widow Trotter had determined on yielding nothing in the way of sympathy to this man who had brought disaster on her. She had come, in spite of the obvious danger, not only to listen but to demand answers, and the force of her feelings was such that once begun she found it hard to stop:

'... You must tell me *all*, Mr Leary – because *I have lost all*. Today I have been forced to sign away the Bay-Tree – and with it my hopes for the future. And I am not the only victim. My friends, the Pophams, are facing disgrace – young Mr Popham is being hunted as a murderer ... All of this has your seal upon it. None of it would have happened but for you and your friends. You owe it to me – to all of us – to speak the *truth* at last. The deception has to end! When we talked at Islington, you gave a lively account of your history – but we find you concealed the most adventurous part ...'

She was becoming heated – ready to let fly and enjoy the release of it. She longed for him to feel the lash ... . . But at this moment a voice (was it Tom's?) whispered a warning in her ear: 'Have a care! You are on board a ship which might head out to sea at any moment – alone, at night, with a man who may be a murderer ... Threats and accusations will simply antagonise him. Make him your ally. Remember the contents of his note – the contrition of it ... He has a message for you – give him time to deliver it ...'

Thought is quick, and the moment was enough. She pulled herself up:

'... I'm sorry, Mr Leary. You will understand my anger – I signed that paper not an hour ago and the pain is fresh ... But

I have come here at your summons, to listen, not to rail … I see that your own adventures continue – you have had a few painful blows yourself.'

'Mrs Trotter …'

He faltered again.

'… Like you, I have a deal to say … You have come! – I scarce expected it, given the short notice – but I knew I had to see you …'

She cut through his hesitation:

'Who has attacked you? That would be a good place to start.'

Without his bob wig and silk waistcoat Leary was no longer the fashionable Covent Garden tallière. His hair was uncombed, his coat torn at the sleeve, and the once bright eyes were now reddened – watchful rather than lively.

'At Islington I was honest with you, Mrs Trotter – at least I spoke no serious untruth, though I may have left part of the picture concealed.'

'The truth then, but not the whole truth?'

'Indeed – and Mr Oosterhout was on the dark side of the picture. I see you've been well informed – I am wondering how. Was it perhaps Michael Henriques? I did my best to help you and Mr Bristowe – to set you on the trail. I think I succeeded all too well …'

Widow Trotter allowed herself a nod of assent, but kept her counsel.

'… Ah, well perhaps it is time I gave you an honest account of my loyalties, such as they are. I do have them – though the world I have passed through is not known for its fidelities …

'My foremost allegiance has been to Lord Parham. We were united by our Dutch connections at a time when King William's two nations were the closest of allies. Since my days in Paris I have been concerned in the affairs of Holland, and in France I led a life of subterfuge – professing the necessary

Catholic sympathies while in communication with my Dutch friends ...'

'A spy – and a bold one I should think?'

'Yes – and finally over-bold. I was forced to flee for my life. Willem Oosterhout found me a job in Exchange Alley.'

'Dressing hair ...'

'And keeping myself informed on trade and the stocks – you would scarcely believe how indiscreet men are when you are shaving their chins.'

'Is that how you came so close to Lord Parham?'

'Yes – we discovered we had similar interests as friends of Mr Oosterhout. Parham found him to be a valuable connection, and their debt has been a mutual one. Vandernan's was begun a dozen years ago as a club for the Dutch community, but under Anne it has found a different character ...'

Widow Trotter enjoyed euphemism and acknowledged the phrase with a half-smile.

'... But the two nations have begun to diverge – allies in the field yet increasingly enemies in trade. The land war binds them together, but there is another war beginning. The ports of Holland and Flanders suffer while *Great* Britain looks to press its advantage. She increasingly commands the seas, and the mighty Bank of England is determined to make Marlborough its own. The Dutch are being placated, but the Duke is impatient, and they have become an annoying distraction. In truth, his victories have done little for us ...'

'Us? ...'

Widow Trotter's eyebrows lifted.

'I am no traitor, Mrs Trotter – but the word comes naturally to me.'

'You speak of your allegiance to Parham and the *interests* that bind you both to Mr Oosterhout. What are they? And why have you become his secret cargo, stowed here like one of his bales of cloth? What are you fleeing? And who has done this violence to you? I have so many questions ... I comfort myself with the thought that if you were a killer evading justice you would not have sent for me.'

'Nor would I – you are right. It may be that I have a more generous motive ... But you must wait for my tale to unfold.

'The first thing to understand, Mrs Trotter, is that Willem Oosterhout trades in many things. Tobacco and wool are the staples, but his agents handle other commodities too – ones that demand speed and secrecy, not least matters of intelligence. As you know well, in this world of universal business, news is a currency and can be richly exploited. It has its system of envoys' dispatches and the like, and conveyances by post – the riders and packet boats. But of course there are secret channels too. Mr Oosterhout has his own system of communication, and it has connections everywhere – people like me whom he can call upon when needed. And he has the transport, particularly the small boats that may be pressed into service. You may picture it as a web of intelligence, the shuttle drawing the threads back and forth, importing and exporting. Even I, who have served him for many years, know not the extent of it.'

But Mrs Trotter already had her picture:

'I think you are exporting something tonight, are you not, Mr Leary? Perhaps this journey is not in fact a flight – but a mission. Am I right?'

He didn't falter in his response:

'Ah, Mrs Trotter – *thou has searched me, and known me!* Yes, I do have a commission, and a very simple one. I am a messenger taking the latest news over to Amsterdam ... You must not be aghast – I am no government spy! There are no concealed douments! I am merely a man with a remarkable memory perfected by years of card play. I am useful because I need no cyphered letters that could be intercepted, no paper to be overlooked. I carry all the minute intelligence *here* ...'

He placed a finger on his forehead.

'... In this affair I have been entrusted with informations that will be of value to Oosterhout's banking friends in Amsterdam. You are not to know this, but the Bank of England is about to be severely embarrassed. Certain dealings will be shown to have been badly-managed and loans ill-secured. It is a complicated matter, but I assure you, the particular news of it will be of immense interest on the Amsterdam *Beurs* – I carry particulars of the Bank's false accounting, the names of the people, the sums involved, the extent of the scandal – all this will be put to good use – and believe me, Vandernan's and its activities will be a considerable part of the account.'

'You have remarkable mental powers, Mr Leary. But – in the way of the whole truth – might you also be carrying something *substantial?*'

She knew this was a risk, but the question needed to be put. Leary was visibly taken aback. He knew Mary Trotter to be an astute lady, but once again she was a step ahead, as if he were being led:

'What prompts you to ask this?'

'I happened to be at the Royal Exchange on Monday and caught a glimpse of you there. I was in the gallery and it was all in dumbshow ... but it appeared that a small package was being entrusted to you – by Mr Oosterhout I think?'

The effect of this on Leary was something between consternation and awe:

'But how ... ?'

He needed to gather his thoughts. There was no concealing anything from this woman.

'... You are unerring, Mrs Trotter – and have found your way back to your opening question – what prompted the attack on me.'

'And what is the answer?'

There was a teasing pause … ..

'Diamonds! …'

He spoke it with some satisfaction – now it was her turn to be surprised.

'… You will have heard of the Albemarle?'

Widow Trotter felt a slight shiver down her spine:

'Who has not!'

'Then you will know about the diamonds, supposed lost in the wreck – the very finest stones from India. They are being sought everywhere from Cornwall to Kent, and descriptions of the stones have been circulated. Finding a buyer in London would be impossible …'

'But in Amsterdam …'

'Exactly. Where better to dispose of the stones than at the heart of the diamond trade?'

She looked at Leary's heavily-bruised face and knew there was more to be said:

'You were entrusted with them? But that is a huge fortune!'

'I was given one of the five bulses – the sealed packages – that had been carried by the Albemarle. A prize enough! – but, as you will see from my handsome countenance, it is no longer in my possession.'

Widow Trotter felt his pain:

'You were robbed – by a gang?'

'Of a sort, yes – a pair of customs men, here on the wharf …'

He could see she was startled.

'… Mr Oosterhout has an associate in the Excise, and payment had been made – but word of it must have escaped, and retribution followed. The diamonds were taken from me by force. The two men were of course off duty.'

'So, the stones have disappeared again? What did Mr Oosterhout have to say?'

'Fortunately I had witnesses, so he could not suspect any collusion on my part – and my face told its own story. He is furious, and I didn't escape a tongue-lashing. However, he trusts to my honour and knows I would not betray him.'

Widow Trotter had always thought *honour among thieves* a specious notion, a compromise between cruelty and fear – nothing honourable about it.

She gave his story the tribute of a nod, but her thoughts were moving on:

'These are indeed wild events, Mr Leary – but forgive me if I wonder how they can assist me and my friends. We are trapped in a drama of our own – and one that promises to be a tragedy. It is a play in which you have taken a leading part ...'

Her voice darkened.

'... To this point you have said nothing of Mr Sturgis. I need to know what occurred that night, after you and he left the Bay-Tree. When Mr Bristowe and I found you in Islington you told us that Sturgis spoke of being in trouble – that he was fearful. You mentioned his high political connections but professed ignorance of them ... I now ask you for the *whole truth* – what those connections were and what really happened that night.'

Widow Trotter's challenge was as direct as she could make it – though at this point she was herself holding something back. She longed for a full and frank account.

Leary was momentarily disconcerted, but he shot her an intense look which seemed to bode well:

'First, Mrs Trotter, you must understand one thing. As I told you before, *I was not responsible for his death*. I would not have sought this meeting had I been a murderer, believe me!'

'I do, Mr Leary.'

She was surprised how easily the words came.

'George Sturgis had his own allegiances, and they were no less strong than my bond with Lord Parham and Oosterhout.

But George moved in loftier circles. He mingled freely with the Marlborough set, and his devotion – *fealty* would be the truer word – was to the Duchess. They were card partners, and there was a friendly converse between them that few were allowed. But George's devotion was no chivalrous ideal – there was advantage on both sides. You see, George had strong connections with the Bank – through his cousin, Sir Gilbert Heathcote …'

'His cousin?'

'Oh yes, and the relation was useful for all parties. Both Heathcote and the Duchess gained from it – and it did George's finances no harm at all …'

Widow Trotter smiled to herself. Yes, this made sense. The story tallied with what they knew of Sturgis the go-between.

'… To know Sir Gilbert is to have a finger on the pulse of the market – not only that, but he is someone who can move the stocks by himself if he determines to do so. And Vandernan's was well set to exploit George's connections. He played a full part in its enterprises. Altogether it was a thriving concern: Heathcote and Sturgis – Oosterhout and Parham. Such alliances made the house a powerful forum for intelligence, but it also encouraged more inventive possibilities. How can I put it? Vandernan's was a formidable *coalition* of interests.'

'*Cabal* is perhaps the better term? Michael Henriques was a victim of such an enterprise was he not?'

Once again Leary was jolted by how much she knew:

'Alas, yes. George pressed it very hard with him …'

He caught a look of disgust in Widow Trotter's eyes.

'… I fear the Henriques business has suffered by it.'

'And now there is a play with the coal-gas scheme, or so I understand? Tom Bristowe tells me that Jonathan's was in a ferment today.'

'That project does offer some tempting opportunities … but I have not been directly concerned.'

'I trust you would take the credit if you were ... Do I gather from this that you and George Sturgis were in alliance?'

'Yes, but the co-operation was coming under strain, as it was in Vandernan's itself. Men's ambitions there were mounting, and it was only waiting for one controversial enterprise to blow the coalition apart.'

'You speak dramatically, Mr Leary. That is a violent idea ...'

'But a true one, I fear ... and this is where we come to the present crisis – the moment when all is won or lost. Everything will rest on it, and fates will be determined.'

'You speak as if that moment is approaching.'

'It is here, Mrs Trotter! Everything is in place – but all is precarious to a degree. The slightest puff of wind may blow the structure over – like a house of cards.'

He had reached for the image before recognising its irony. Widow Trotter understood. The news of Tom's meeting with Benjamin Levy was fresh in her mind:

'Yes – I hear the coal-gas enterprise is about to reach its climax.'

Leary gave a hum, and lifted his head:

'True indeed – but I don't allude to the coal-gas play. No, no. This is a far bigger thing, believe me. More daring by far!'

As if to emphasise the point, at that moment the boat swayed and its timbers creaked. She put out a hand to steady herself and recalled where she was. She felt the precariousness of her position. Why was Bob Leary confessing all this to her? Was it the need to disburden himself of Vandernan's and all it represented – or was there some other, possibly darker, motive?

'Rest easy, Mrs Trotter – I am not about to kidnap you and transport you to Virginia! ... It is the swell of the river. I think the tide is turning.'

She was relieved at the lightness of his tone, but began to wonder how his story would continue. Was he about to impart something that would be dangerous to know?

Chapter Forty

'WHAT I AM to tell you is of the utmost secrecy ...'

It was spoken in hushed tones. But rather than think this a privilege, Widow Trotter frowned slightly. Bob Leary sensed her unease:

'... I know you are wondering why I should take you into my confidence – indeed, why you find yourself here at all. But hear me out, and then you can decide what you will do.'

'You speak of it as a responsibility – but why are you telling me this?'

'Because you ask for the whole truth. If you wish to know about George Sturgis and the events of last Thursday, then you must have the full story.'

Widow Trotter's natural curiosity reasserted itself – and at this moment it could hardly have been greater:

'I am all ear, Mr Leary.'

He needed no further invitation and looked around him. Nothing was stirring in the hold, but he kept his voice low:

'I spoke of Mr Oosterhout's network of intelligence and the gains to be made in these speculative times. Being first with the news can be highly profitable – and being the *creator* of news can make your fortune! The wreck of the Albemarle is a case in point, as the lawyers say.

'Yes, notoriously. False news can be a cruel thing, Mr Leary – it is an imposition on trust and honesty.'

'I cannot argue with that – especially against the hostess of the Bay-Tree. I wouldn't dare to … But you will never prevent it. So long as people believe in hearsay and have a desire for gossip, it will continue to be fed. 'Change Alley will always thrive on rumour – no law could ever stamp it out.'

'I will not allow an equivalence between gossip and lies, Mr Leary. Hearsay is one thing – falsehood another.'

'I am duly admonished, Mrs Trotter. I do not pretend this is a virtuous world. Honesty often has a hard time of it …'

Widow Trotter was giving him dark looks, anticipating that his revelation would be of this kind. She was not wrong.

'… As I said, the system at Vandernan's is well placed to sow the seeds of false news – for good or ill – and it has seen remarkable success. Thanks to Mr Oosterhout's agents, secret intelligence from the Bank, and a co-ordinated group of traders and brokers, it has been possible to influence the sentiments of the market. From what you and your friends have discovered, this will come as no surprise.'

'Sadly not. I dread to think what ingenious fraud has been planned.'

'The news is to arrive tomorrow by the Dutch packet – not as a rumour to be discounted, or delivered in some conspicuous way by a rider galloping down Cornhill – no, no, it will come through the official channels.'

'But how can this happen?'

'It will happen by the envoy from Lille being seized on the road. He will be bringing welcome intelligence of the taking of the town – but his packet will be opened, and the dreadful news substituted.'

'What news is that?'

'The death of Marlborough. Nothing less. Shot from the redoubt at the very moment of his triumph.'

Bob Leary wasn't smiling. He was clearly not triumphing in the announcement.

Widow Trotter was groping for words:

'But … the shock of it! … it will make havoc with the market.'

'Exactly so – I don't need to say how violently the news will be received, and what opportunities there will be for anyone who knows the secret. Believe me, plans are in place, and fortunes will be made.'

Widow Trotter thought quickly. She was forming her own picture:

'… But surely, if George Sturgis knew of this …'

Leary began nodding:

'That is why it was kept from him. It has been the most inviolable secret. Only a handful of people know of the plot.'

'This is Oosterhout's doing, I take it – with Parham's connivance? A double satisfaction – a blow at the Duke and at the London market. For people to be hoodwinked in such a way will surely damage confidence?'

'Yes, there will be consequences …'

'Are you telling me that Sturgis discovered the plot? I can imagine his anger – at the effect the news would have upon the Duchess …'

'You are there before me, Mrs Trotter. That unfortunately is what occurred that night when I was with him … I confess to misleading you a little as to what transpired … After a whirl in his chariot George was determined on returning to Vandernan's. It was after one o'clock, and he had a sudden longing to be gaming again. He was quite set on the idea. At the Bay-Tree he had been frustrated – made to quit before he could make the ultimate play …'

Widow Trotter was choking slightly. Leary warmed to his story:

'… I tried to dissuade him. We were in a pothouse hard by Vandernan's. George was well liquored and pugnacious – that is why I didn't want to leave him. His talk was loud, and it drew the attentions of a young man who had wandered over from Vandernan's. The fellow began forcing himself on George and provoking him. The chat became foolish … The man said he had overheard something that evening – some trick to be played with the stocks. Lord Parham's name was mentioned … The man began toying with him.

'I could see George was about to boil over, so when he went to piss, I warned the fellow to high-tail it before he had a fist in his face.

'Well, George reeled back, and in the man's absence he turned his resentment on me and began accusing me. "You and Parham are planning something," he said. I denied it, but nothing I said would shake him off …'

Leary winced and put his hand to his cheek.

'… I'm sorry, my face is hurting again … the thought of what happened next troubles me. Had I only kept silent, Mrs Trotter! – it would never have happened … George would not have died … But I became provoked in my turn. He spoke accusingly of Lord Parham and me – in disgusting terms. The fleecing of Frank Popham was added to the charge-list. He took Mr Popham's promissory note from his pocket and waved it at me … then he ripped it in two. He said he was determined to frustrate the plan to ruin Frank and his father – that he was sick of all the deception. He had already crossed swords with Lord Parham about it.'

'About the settling of Frank Popham's debt?'

'Yes. His Lordship had been angry when George intervened. The plan was to embarrass the Pophams – George said it was some dirty political feud and that Arthur Maynwaring was behind it. He began cursing him too – said that he was an evil influence on the Duchess … Oh Mrs Trotter, he said so much. It poured out of him … And that was when I told him of the plan to announce the Duke's death. Lord Parham had let it slip to me in one of our moments of intimacy and had sworn me to secrecy. But I thought it a dubious proceeding ...

'George was incensed and marched off to Vandernan's determined to have it out. I was fearful what he would do should Parham be there ... "Her Grace will know of this!" he was saying.'

'And that was the last you saw of him?'

'Yes – and the last I saw of Vandernan's too. It seems Lord Parham heard I had blabbed ...'

'There's no wonder he was hunting for you ... But tell me, if the note had been destroyed, how could they pursue Frank Popham for the debt?'

'Deception, Mrs Trotter – the first note wasn't destroyed, but kept – the one Mr Popham made out in favour of Vandernan's.'

'Just as we thought ...'

She gave a small sigh, this time for herself.

'... These promissory notes are evil things, Mr Leary! Money is created out of thin air! Men sign away their wealth and watch it pass into a stranger's hands. Anyone may have a claim on you.'

Bob Leary knew this was said from the heart:

'The business of the note was Sir Charles's doing. He has charge of the gaming side of Vandernan's – the running of the place, the settlements ...'

'The playing of Captain Hazard's game?'

'Yes, and takes delight in it. He was happy to sanction the design against the Pophams. He knows of his wife's allegiance to them.'

'There is no love lost there, I fear. Lady Norreys is certainly an ally of the family – and of our cause. But I had not thought her husband's antagonism quite so open.'

'Sir Charles is not the easiest man to rub along with. His suspicions are quickly roused – indeed there is now bad blood between him and Lord Parham.'

'Is that so? The falling out of thieves! What prompted it?'

'Sunday night's raid on the gaming-house. Word is that Lord Parham had come to an arrangement with a friendly magistrate for a token visit, but our Puritan reformers got wind and seized their chance … As the Commissioner, Sir Charles was furious – felt he had been left to pick up the pieces.'

'Well, that is a breaking of ranks indeed – and useful to know.'

It was an encouraging thought, but Widow Trotter breathed in slowly. By this point she was finding it hard to raise her spirits. Thoughts of the Bay-Tree had returned, and her own troubles were weighing on her. Bob Leary detected it:

'You are downcast, Mrs Trotter. All this is intended to help you and your friends. I understand how hard matters are.'

'But why now, at this last moment, do you wish to help us?'

It was the unavoidable question.

There was silence between them. The sound of the creaking ship's timbers filled the emptiness. Then a distant shout from the quayside found its way in. Leary stirred and drew his hands together, clasping one of his wrists:

'Sometimes we do things not for a particular reason. The prompting can be a deeper one. A simple choice may have intricate motives, and for once they are my own. *This is something I do for myself.* I am not someone's agent or serving others' ends. Believe me, I have thought hard on this and have come to a determination. The beating was decisive. I have always taken my chances and ridden my luck as if right and wrong do not matter. To speak truth, I am sick of plots and deceptions …'

Mary Trotter heard this with astonishment.

'… What you do with the information about the false news, I leave entirely to you. It is a dubious charge. Before this moment I have told but a single person – and that man is now dead …'

She was thinking about her reply, but he continued:

'... That evening at the Bay-Tree's hazard-table I was happy and playful, surrounded by your friends. I felt how different it was from Vandernan's. Chance is delightful when it is genuinely itself, free of fate and calculation – and when it is accepted with grace and good humour. I never want to return to Vandernan's. In Amsterdam I shall perform my trick of memory and see my commission through – but at present I have no plans on returning. I am blessed with talents that will allow me to make my way anywhere.'

An immodest claim, but it was spoken with a beguiling honesty.

'I don't know what to say, Mr LeRoy, except that you have certainly helped us, and I am very glad I came. You carry my hopes that life will treat you well.'

He stretched out his arm:

'There is something more ...'

Deftly, and with a precise turn of the hand, he took the buttoned cuff of his coat between his fingers and squeezed. A thread broke, and in only a few seconds he worked a nail into the hole and withdrew a small crystal.

Widow Trotter watched fascinated, hardly breathing, as he held the thing up to her. Even in the gloom of the hold it caught the play of the candle flame and came to life. She was entranced.

'This is the most remarkable of the stones, Mrs Trotter – the one described in the newspapers, singled out for its beauty and value ...'

'But how ... ?'

'It was my insurance. It was a considerable challenge to extract it from the bulse and then seal the package up again – these things are scrupulously secure, as you would expect. But I employed all my skill in it. No-one will guess.'

Mary Trotter remembered to breathe:

'Light-finger'd Bob!' she murmured in quiet tribute.

'Keep it safe. Do with it what you will – but be assured of its value. It is a table-cut diamond of the first water, and perfect – just above twenty-six carats.'

He reached into his fob and took out a small square of silk, placed the stone in the centre, and magically twisted and knotted it.

'Take it – it is yours.'

'But your insurance ... Can you not trade it in Amsterdam?'

'It cannot be delivered as arranged, and word would get round if I tried to sell it. The thing would hang heavy on me. Besides, ... I really think it should be entrusted to honest hands. You will know what to do. Let it be the pledge of my innocence.'

Widow Trotter took leave of Robert LeRoy – as she once more thought of him – with new heart and a fresh determination to see her mission through. For all his protean reinventions and capacity for trickery, she had glimpsed an essential integrity too – a principled sense of himself that could be thought of as conscience. She knew he would never return to Vandernan's.

As she stepped onto the quayside she paused, and turned to look back at the Green Dragon. Her eye was once more drawn to the ship's carved figurehead. It was indeed a fearsome beast, but now she could see something defiant in the creature, ready as it was to breast the ocean waves and face the storms ahead. Perhaps it should be her token also?

So much had just happened. It had been a momentous interview, and Mary Trotter was slightly dazed at the thought of what she was carrying with her. She had been entrusted with news that might shake the state, and deep in her inner pocket was a diamond to grace a queen – a glittering fortune. Twenty Bay-Trees! She was also bearing a heavy responsibility and facing choices such as she had never confronted before. If only she could sit quietly and take stock of all she had learned!

Her steps slowed as she ran the scene through her mind. The quay was thronged as before, and she was making her way back along it in a desultory way, her thoughts busy. She needed to decide how to get home. A wherry from the nearby stairs was convenient and would take her to the Savoy and the Strand, but she could see the river was gathering pace – negotiating the arches of the bridge against the tide would be near impossible. She hesitated. Better return to Thames Street and the possibility of a hackney …

Only then did she notice the man's eyes, unblinking, fixed on hers. He stood in her way, not moving. She knew that look – she had seen it often enough in the alleys off Drury Lane – a smile of anticipation, a kind of contractual recognition of what she was and what he expected. Almost on him, at that moment she turned to the side – only to feel his arm sharply threaded through hers and her body drawn close. She tried to push him away, but with a laugh he hugged her tighter. There was so much bustle around them that her struggle went unnoticed.

'*You mistake!*' she shouted as he drew her along with him. It was a stupidly polite thing to say, and she knew it – this was no sociable encounter and the words were easily lost in the noise. But she was clever enough to know that a street expletive would only confirm and encourage.

The man was murmuring endearments. She tried to turn and punch him, but this was met with a knowing grin, shared by a group of sailors lounging by the wall.

Then she heard his sudden 'down here!' spoken more gruffly. They were at the corner of an alley, and the darkness stretched ahead. She knew she had to act now or lose all.

But once he had pulled her into the alley and they were out of sight, he stopped, and she had a new sensation. Something extremely sharp was being pressed into her side. The endearments ceased, and through the pain she heard three simple and direct words, spoken low but clearly:

'*Mrs Mary Trotter …*'

This was more chilling still – it was no random encounter.

'… You are a long way from home, Mary Trotter. Strolling the wharves late at night, all alone … What can you be in search of, I wonder?'

Her instinct was to scream an alarm, but caution told her the man would immediately finish the job with a single thrust and melt into the night. No, she needed to stay calm and try to talk with him:

'The same as brings you here, I assume – we are both friends of Robert LeRoy, are we not?'

This was taking a chance, but it might initiate an exchange – anything to hold him off …

'Ha! A sociable visit, was it? An intimate *tête à tête* over supper? … I think not.'

It was spoken with a sneer, and for the first time she got a purchase on the voice. Although the man's figure was rough, and the features craggy and damaged, the voice had an urbane manner that was incongruous …

'What have you come for? *Tell me!*'

She hardly heard the words. Her thoughts were busy – back with Mr Grigsby at the Sword Blade, and recalling Frank Popham's phrase, *polite ruffian* … At once she knew who it had to be … Surely this was Joel Harkins?

'I wished to ask his advice …'

An absurd idea, she knew, but the words were the first that came to her lips. She dared not move, the knife was pressed so close. Even breathing was painful.

'Well, I was told the famous Widow Trotter might be paying Mr LeRoy a visit. Jack said he had taken a letter over to Red Lion Court ...'

So – her cheeky young messenger was one of a team.

'... Jack has been helping me keep watch over our mutual friend. We are concerned lest any visitors delay his passage. I have been told to ensure his ship leaves safely and on time – and with him aboard ... You were a good while talking. Perhaps I should call on him myself ...'

Then, in an instant all pretence to politeness was gone:

'... *What did he tell you?* Answer me! Or this blade will settle it!'

'To speak truth – I came for money. Mr LeRoy is in my debt for several hundred pounds – and he promised to arrange things before he left for Holland ...'

She felt the man pause as he registered her words. It gave her a few precious seconds. Now was the moment to give him more to think about:

'... It was an innocent meeting, I assure you! ... I have his promissory note right here ... Let me show you ...'

He drew back a few inches and freed her arm. It was now or never.

'... I have it – Look! ...'

With that, she made a leap, pushing him away with one hand and attempting to run back to the quay.

'*Rape!*' she shouted as loud as she could – but the man's hand was over her mouth and he was dragging her back. She couldn't see the knife, and was expecting a searing pain to strike at any moment. Her elbows were thrusting and she was biting into his fingers.

Suddenly the man's body shuddered, his neck twisted, and his arm fell down. There was a second figure behind him, and she saw a staff waving ... A blow had been struck from behind, and the man was staggering. Then there was a voice – a familiar one – from a third figure running up to them:

'Molly!'

Her assailant was still on his feet, and the knife in his hand swung wildly. The blade caught her arm, but she clutched his wrist and held on with all her strength, trying to prevent a second thrust. And then another fist, large and powerful, joined hers. The man's wrist was bent back, there was a cry of pain, and the blade fell onto the cobbles.

Widow Trotter couldn't speak, and could only watch as Harkins was pushed firmly to the ground, a large boot pressing into his neck while handcuffs were being attached. She caught her breath:

'Elias!'

'My Lady! … What adventure is this?'

'Jem found you – thank God!'

'Yes, he gave me Leary's note – said you were off on a wild mission and would be sure to need help.'

This showed little trust on Jeremy's part, but how right he was.

Bob Turley, the watchman, was now bending down over the struggling body:

'Well well – Mr Harkins! Assaulting respectable ladies in a dark alley? Or were you about some other business?'

So, she was right – it was Parham's henchman standing guard on Robert LeRoy and his secret.

'He is known to you, Mr Turley?'

'Oh yes. What will your protectors say, Harkins? I doubt they'll trouble themselves with your fate. You're on your own now.'

Widow Trotter longed to hear more. But Elias was supporting her arm and pulling back the sleeve. There was a quantity of blood, but it was a clean slash and hadn't reached an artery.

'You've been exremely lucky Molly,' he said, in a disapproving voice. 'You should have found me first, not rushed off on your own.'

She was only too happy to be admonished. Huge relief outweighed everything.

She watched as Elias and Bob held the prisoner down. Someone ran for the local watch while Elias reached into the man's pockets to discover what he might be carrying. There was just enough illumination from the quay for Widow Trotter to see a folded sheet of paper emerge.

'Here, take this Molly,' said Elias, before delving further.

She took the paper from him and stepped over towards the light. It was some kind of formal document. She lifted it closer and tried to focus her eyes on the text. It was possible to make out the name 'Vandernan's' and a large sum of money … and then her eyes jumped to the foot of the page where a bold signature was defiantly visible. At once the throbbing in her arm was forgotten, and the sheet of paper became as precious as the diamond in her pocket. She read the unmistakeable, familiar words – 'Francis Popham.'

Chapter Forty-One

———∞∞∞———

IT WAS MIDNIGHT when Widow Trotter returned to the Bay-Tree, physically exhausted but with a mind that couldn't rest. She knew she had to see Tom at once, however deep he might be in Morpheus' embrace. The news of the Marlborough plot was simply too urgent. Sleep wouldn't come until her thoughts had settled and she had decided what to do with the dangerous knowledge. Nothing had been said to Elias and Bob, who were taken up with Harkins's arrest, and it was clear that Tom must be the first to know ... As for the diamond, it remained deep in her pocket. The Trotter fingers had not even dared touch the little silk parcel since leaving the ship. She wanted to preserve its mystery a while longer, as if the thing were exerting some power over her. It was Mary Trotter's own secret in what had become a genuine adventure – 'the Curse of the Albemarle Diamond' she thought to herself, and the idea was strangely stirring.

Now, as she mounted the narrow stairs to Tom's chamber, an immediate curiosity surged back. There would surely be news of his summons to Pall Mall – and something told her that between the two of them was a story to be unfolded. A midnight conference seemed appropriate. She looked down at her tray – alongside the candle was a bottle of honest burgundy and two slices of veal pie ... It was good to be home.

There was no need to knock – simply her tread on the squeaking stair was enough. There was the answering sound of hasty steps within the room, and Tom's door swung open to reveal not a yawning figure roused from slumber, but a fully-clothed young man with joy and relief in his eyes. Widow Trotter had been bursting to speak, but it was Tom's words that tumbled out:

'You're here! – Thank the Lord. We've been concerned – Jeremy said you'd hurried off to the wharves on some urgent summons. Poor Jem was shaking his head as he told me, as if it were an assignation in a dark alley! ...'

Tom stopped. The expression on her face told him he had touched on something little short of the truth.

'I hardly know where to begin, Tom – such happenings! And you must have news yourself? Your summons to Pall Mall was as sudden as mine!'

Tom swung his desk chair round and offered his guest the armchair, and as they settled themselves they looked at each other in eager anticipation, two adventurers ready to share a bottle and tell their tales ...

Each of them could speak of a dramatic reappearance – one a figure returning from banishment, the other from the dead. Tom's news of Frank's return and arrest for murder was the first of the revelations, and the darkness didn't lift with her own tale of Bob Leary's activities. Tom was amazed to hear of his defiant survival – the man's resourcefulness was remarkable. His career of spying and deceit was evidently far from done and smuggling was now to be added to the score. It was yet another episode in the *Tale of the Irish Trickster!* Leary's picaresque antics gave them enough to talk about, even without mention of the diamond in her pocket ... Widow Trotter was holding back on that, still unsure what she should do.

Not that there wasn't enough to occupy their thoughts. Tom's suspicions of Leary's motives appeared confirmed:

'What a prodigy, Mrs T! ... So, the man's memory has a full record of the Bank of England's embarrassments! ...'

He gave a low whistle at the idea.

'... The scandal will play well in Amsterdam – but what a betrayal of his friends in Vandernan's! All their deceptions laid bare! It shows where Leary's allegiance lies. I can't help seeing the irony. For once the man is telling the truth – and he'll do more damage with that than with any of his falsehoods.'

'But you've not heard all yet, Tom. Leary was revealing about other things too. The factions in Vandernan's are serious ones, and there's not a little malice in their ranks. Now I understand how George Sturgis may have met his death ... there is something about that fatal night you have to know – a great secret that may have cost him his life ...'

It was a dramatic remark, and the midnight darkness was right for talk of secrets. The room was wrapped in silence, and the two flickering candles added a gothic melancholy to the scene. Tom listened with rapt attention as she related Bob Leary's story of the quarrel at the pothouse and what had prompted it.

Now Tom could see the scale of the divide that had opened up between Lord Parham with his Dutch interests and George Sturgis with his allegiance to the Marlboroughs. Parham's attempt to ruin Frank at the Hazard table had certainly provoked Sturgis, but hearing of the plot to announce the Duke's death must have been decisive. Tom was astonished – it was a hazardous undertaking even for Vandernan's! These men were playing for the highest stakes! Given Sturgis's closeness to the Duchess, the revelation had made his anger at Parham all the greater.

'We must be very cautious,' said Widow Trotter solemnly. 'These are dangerous hours. The packet with news of Marlborough's killing is expected in the morning, and the plot is an intensely-guarded secret.'

Tom now knew he had evidence of his own:

'Yes, Mrs T, and it is a secret from the *Duchess* too! ...'

She raised her eyebrows.

'... I have something to share with you. Lady Norreys has been helping our cause and has made a discovery – a message to her husband from Arthur Maynwaring. We were puzzling over it, but now the meaning is clear. It seems he and Sir Charles are also involved. Read this ...'

Tom had the paper in his hand and gave it to her.

'... This must be the Marlborough plot, don't you think?'

Widow Trotter's eyes scanned the thing in astonishment:

'*Her Grace knows nothing* ... I can hardly believe it, Tom! Maynwaring – her own secretary – colluding with the plotters! *by Saturday matters will be set right again – and no harm done.* What extraordinary assurance! ...'

'What Leary told Sturgis about this in the Flagon was incendiary, was it not, Mrs T?'

'Extremely. But one thing I'm sure of – Bob Leary did not kill Sturgis. He would never have sent for me and told me so much – and everything he said had the ring of truth. It was quite a confessional. Had you been there with me, you wouldn't doubt it. And Leary's story of their quarrel tallies with Toby's account.'

Tom listened and nodded – yes, there could be little argument with that. He also knew that he had more evidence of his own to offer – evidence from Frank that pointed directly away from Leary and toward that other figure who was haunting their speculations. Now it was Widow Trotter's turn to listen intently, and when the name *Joel Harkins* was spoken, her eyes glittered. She lowered her glass of wine and savoured the moment.

'... And so, Mrs T, what Harkins said to Frank in the sponging-house can mean only one thing – that he assumed the torn promissory note had been found in Sturgis's pocket ...'

'So Harkins must have put it there – or been told it was there … No-one but Elias knew … Wonder of wonders, Tom! So at last we have the link in our chain – one that ties Vandernan's to Sturgis's killing. We have known it must be so, but the proof has eluded us … this is surely conclusive? …'

There was a thrill in her voice, not lessened by the thought that a revelation of her own – more dramatic still – was about to follow. Knowing this was the moment, she settled herself more deeply in the armchair:

'… This brings us back to Custom House Quay … My adventure didn't end with the Green Dragon, Tom. Tonight's drama was only beginning … I had an encounter …'

She could see Tom was on tenterhooks and drew breath slowly:

'… Joel Harkins tried to kill me.'

Widow Trotter was no Mrs Barry – but her delivery of the line was worthy of that great actress and certainly deserved a bigger audience. Tom felt the authentic thrill and set down his glass:

'I cannot believe this!'

As if any more were needed, she revealed the evidence. Tom watched agog as her left sleeve was rolled up. The bandage was not large, but in the half-light it showed enough blood to command attention.

'Mrs T! What *have* you been doing?'

'My message to Elias bore fruit, Tom – it was he and Bob Turley who were my rescuers. Jem's concern must have played its part too – they saw me just in time.'

Tom demanded to know more – every detail of the scene – and as the full picture emerged his relief was such that he became almost angry. He admonished her for taking so great a risk – though he conceded the gains had been great.

'But I gained even more, Tom! …' she continued, unabashed. 'And this discovery has a direct bearing on you and your family …'

This was masterly.

'... Remember who it was seized my promissory note from Will and tried to redeem it at the Sword Blade ...'

'Joel Harkins again, yes – sent by Parham, we have assumed.'

Tom wondered where this was leading.

'Well, it seems promissory notes have been our Mr Harkins's stock-in-trade! Elias found another one – in his pocket.'

Tom was becoming almost baffled:

'So many notes – and so many pockets, Mrs T!'

'Yes, but this one is something special ... It is the first note that Frank signed at the gaming-house. Vandernan's didn't destroy their original, but kept it and used it to have Frank arrested ...'

'Do you mean ... So, Frank's debt might now be cleared?'

Delight was bubbling up inside him.

'Well ... Elias impounded the note and is keeping it *safe*.'

It was a cheering thought. Tom was now grinning broadly:

'So, taking all things together, Parham's bully has a lot of questions to answer! ... Surely the evidence points to Harkins as the killer? How can they still hold Frank as a suspect? Perhaps the nightmare will soon be over?'

He beamed brightly at Widow Trotter and received an answering smile – it was indeed a smile by definition, but it somehow lacked radiance. There was a tautness of the brow. She was trying so hard to share his joy, but the eyes told him a thought was tugging at her.

'Oh, Mrs T ... I'm sorry – I was thinking only of the family ... I haven't asked about the Bay-Tree. Do you have any news?'

There was a pause. Widow Trotter was trying to find the right words:

'Let us say, this evening I put my name to a piece of paper – a far from flimsy one I fear. I even attached my seal to it. My debt is cleared, Tom ... but the Sword Blade is now the legal owner of the Bay-Tree ...'

Tom gave a spontaneous groan.

'… Payment has been demanded – and the two bailiffs gave me no choice. Had I not signed I would now be in the Fleet.'

Any good cheer they had accumulated now slipped away, and for a few minutes their talk lost purpose and direction. Both of them knew why despondency was pictured as a quagmire: words of commiseration, frustration, and indignation covered the ground but didn't seem to be getting them anywhere … Finally it was Widow Trotter who found the way back. Whether thought of the diamond in her pocket had anything to do with it is hard to say, but there remained enough to be hopeful for. It was time to think of practical matters:

'Well, Tom,' she said, pouring the last of the wine, 'our midnight chat has been useful I think. Two profitable excursions! Our little band has achieved so much, and we must hold onto it … But now decisions have to be made – and one urgent decision above all … The news of Marlborough's death is to arrive in the morning. We must think hard what we should do – or whether we should do anything at all …'

Her voice had already decided the question.

Tom had no doubts. Head and heart spoke with one voice, and he knew what he must do … It would certainly be the boldest of moves – an all-or-nothing venture! – and it would go against everything he had previously advised – but surely this was the moment for it? He could see how it might work …

'I have an idea, Mrs T …'

Somehow Widow Trotter knew that he meant business.

'… Prince George is dying – there is no hope of his recovery – and the Court is assembling at Kensington. Uncle Jack is going there in the morning … Also in attendance will be the Duchess of Marlborough …'

'Tom! …'

She stopped herself from saying more and let him continue.

'The Duchess must be warned about the news that is about to break. Uncle Jack has been pulling at the leash, Mrs T, determined to have matters out with her, and I have repeatedly stopped him … but perhaps this is the right moment. The Duchess must be told!'

'By Lord Melksham.'

It wasn't a question. She felt the rightness of it.

'Yes, I've repeatedly urged him not to confront her – but now he won't be accusing her, but advising her. He will have the most important news … I also think he should take Maynwaring's note with him …'

Widow Trotter's eyes widened.

'… She needs to see how her secretary has gone behind her back – and on a matter of such grave importance.'

The move was certainly a bold one, and its decisiveness appealed to her. She was sure Lord Melksham would be willing to play his part.

'But how might she react, Tom? She is your uncle's sworn enemy, is she not?'

'Yes – well, she certainly thinks that *he* is *hers* … but how much of this has been Maynwaring's doing is impossible to say. We don't know what poison he has whispered in her ear … But whatever the case, she needs to be prepared. She has to be saved from hearing the news of her husband's death – for compassion's sake if nothing else.'

'You are right, Tom – and it would cause a terrible scene. At the Prince's deathbed too … Unthinkable!'

'I must hurry over to Pall Mall at first light. Uncle Jack must know of this. I shall leave the decision to him, of course …'

By now, the two candles were burning low and it was time to end their *tête à tête*.

'Well Tom, we have put together an intricate picture! But I think we are prepared for what is to come. After everything we have learned these past few days, we now know our enemies – and, just as important, we know who our friends are.'

'Yes – and friend and foe will be assembling on Saturday in Mercers' Hall … A volatile mixture, perhaps?'

'It is sure to be! I cannot but think there will be some drama … Oh, if only I …'

She stopped herself in mid-sigh. She had never been one for impossible dreams …

'But *you* are coming too, Mrs T …'

Thursday

28 October 1708

Chapter Forty-Two

⸺∽∽∽⸺

OUT WEST AT Kensington the morning air was fresh, and as Lord Melksham stepped down from his coach he breathed in deeply. He was struck as always by the peace and order that reigned over the place. There was a lot of sky, and birdsong in the trees – a blessed calm after the bustle of London. More a country estate than a palace, the modest buildings were almost dwarfed by the neatly trimmed parterres which stretched out before him – Dutch domesticity, he thought, gesturing to Versailles.

There was the sharp scent of box on the breeze, and the gravel crunched under his feet as he strode towards the apartments of poor Prince George – though with his mind very much on other matters. It was a difficult occasion in prospect, with many possibilities for awkwardness and embarrassment. The Duchess would surely be there – though Her Grace was now an uncomfortable presence at Court, haunting the world where she had once ruled as the Queen's intimate. She was no longer Anne's strong right hand. The privy chamber and bedroom had been exchanged for the drawing-room and the long gallery – to which he himself was now heading.

His steps slowed, and moments later he found himself idling in contemplation, thinking back over Tom's surprise visit and the extraordinary revelation he had brought with him.

The daring of these people! The Vandernan's money-men were indeed ruthless – what would they not do to exploit the stocks? What might they invent next? They were like children who had discovered a new game – one without rules and therefore free of annoying sanctions on cheating and falsehood. Such notions couldn't touch them. Their fictions would be more powerful than others' truths.

As for Tom, what a reversal it had been! Lord Melksham smiled to himself when he recalled the ardent look on his nephew's face as he urged the meeting. He had heeded Tom's earlier injunctions with good grace – and how wise the advice had been! A headlong accusation would indeed have been disastrous. But now he had come with vital news to warn and advise the Duchess. It struck him how judiciously his nephew had handled their talk. Tom had allowed him to think it was his own initiative – that this moment was of his choosing!

Of course, he must prepare to be confronted in his turn – some of what he had to say would be unwelcome to the Duchess's ears. But if he handled the business carefully he might put his case and even secure favourable terms. He hoped she wouldn't turn her back on him …

After a long climb he emerged from the Queen's Staircase into the long gallery to find a respectable number of courtiers – about forty of them – some gathered in groups and talking in low voices, others standing quietly or looking out of the windows. There were a couple of naval uniforms, a red-coated officer, and a clergyman in pudding sleeves, but the general dress, like his own, was sombre rather than funereal. Muted tones had been chosen over black – this was no wake, and it would have been thoughtless to anticipate.

He looked down the full length of the gallery but there was no Duchess. His heart sank. Many of the faces were familiar, though at this moment he didn't wish to be drawn into conversation. It was not an occasion for witty sociability, and solitude was an acceptable option. The mood was quiet enough to tell him that no dramatic news had broken.

Lord Melksham looked around and gathered his thoughts together. The Queen's Gallery was part of the Prince Consort's apartments, not a room he knew, and he was struck by the splendour of the place. Rich turkey carpets covered the floor in glowing colours and served to muffle the sounds even more. Along the facing wall, embroidered silk hangings were a backdrop to a display of fine Chinese porcelain, some of the vases several feet high. Queen Mary's collection was evidently still housed here! It hardly reflected George's hearty naval enthusiasms, but no doubt the private rooms would be stamped with his masculine character. One thing stood out. Occupying its own table alongside the central fireplace was a fully-rigged model of one of the Prince's flagships, on this occasion making something of a sad statement amidst all the oriental luxury.

Minutes passed. Lord Melksham turned from the window and walked across to the ship, inspecting its fine detail and admiring the workmanship. Miniature figures were busy on the vessel, hauling ropes, carrying provisions, and setting the sails – there was even one tiny moustachioed individual occupying the crow's nest. He began to feel easier in his mind.

Suddenly all talk in the room died. At the far end of the gallery the door to the Prince Consort's apartments had opened, and every eye turned ... There she was, the Duchess of Marlborough – something of a stately galleon herself – in a gown of deep green, edged with gold, her flaxen hair gathered up and bound with dark ribbons. She strode into the room, looking straight ahead, and even from a distance he noticed that her chin was quivering slightly. She acknowledged no-one and continued to walk along the gallery, unhurried, avoiding all eyes. There was a hectic flush on her cheek which he took to be anger. Without pausing, her strides carried her past a group of courtiers who turned and pursued her with their gaze. Others drew back. Only a brave man would intercept this determined progress, and as she came closer Lord Melksham felt the chill of a front-line infantryman facing the advancing enemy.

Appropriately, it fell to the intrepid army officer to make a move. Hand on sword and with a clink of spurs, he swung to face her and offered a polite inquiry. Alone and without any covering fire he had succeeded in securing her, albeit briefly. Lord Melksham distinctly heard her first words, delivered in lofty indignation: *'She would not see me!'* – it was a stifled cry that deserved to be shouted at the winds.

He took a tentative step forward. The Duchess's eyes flashed toward him – only for an instant, but enough to tell him she had registered his presence unfavourably. Words were being exchanged with the officer, but she was eager to get away – her body needed to be on the move. Lord Melksham braced himself. This was a meeting he was determined to make happen, however bruising it might be. The opportunity would not occur again, and he must take his chance. He was experienced enough to know that on this occasion nothing of courtly politeness would serve the turn – nor could it be an ambush. He would have to be bold – begin brusquely, draw her fire, and press in close with his all-important news …

She gave him another look – this time a warning – and a moment later she broke free of the Colonel to continue her progress.

Lord Melksham moved to her side:

'Your Grace!'

The words came confidently from him, but with a kindly warmth.

'I have nothing to say to you!'

Her stride remained resolute, and he found himself pacing alongside. He had her ear – at least her left one – and only seconds to claim her attention …

'I have news you need to hear. You must give me a moment of your time. It cannot wait, I assure you.'

'I have no mind for business today, Lord Melksham – let alone for any political nonsense. There is nothing to know, and I have nothing to answer for.'

'There is much to be answered for on both sides, Your Grace – some bad blood to be purged, I know it well … But now I speak to you as a friend. It is in your interest to hear. If I say it is life and death I do not exaggerate. You must listen …'

He could do no more. They were now at the very end of the gallery, poised in front of the open door. The stairs were waiting.

'… I have come here to find you.'

It was spoken almost as a whisper.

She was about to move on, but stood still and faced him. The long gallery with its many peering eyes was behind them. They were together in a corner, an arm apart, and her gown was over his shoes.

The Duchess lifted her head proudly and scrutinised him. Her jaw was now resolutely set, but he caught a sadness in the eyes. Could it be she would welcome a chance to talk?

Seconds passed like hours. Then she turned away:

'I suggest the parterre, Lord Melksham … There are things best said in the open air. No echoing walls.'

There was a touch of wit in her words which gave him hope. But as they descended the staircase nothing was said. The only echo was the clatter of shoes on dark oak. It was not until they reached the palace garden that talk resumed. Whether it would become a genuine conversation was uncertain.

'What do you have to say to me? … I am ready.'

Her tone was brisk and forthright. She began to walk, more slowly this time, and he paced the gravel alongside her.

'I do not come with news myself, but to forestall others' news ...'

'Enigmatic! You wish to have priority with your informations? If this is some political scheming, I do not wish to hear it ...'

The irony of this from such a consummate schemer was not lost on him:

'Not for my part, Your Grace. I have hurried here to prevent the shock of false news – it will be brought you at any moment – but it will be an imposition.'

He had caught her interest, but her suspicions were not allayed:

'Ha! One man's false news is another's true! – if life has taught me anything, it is that. Are you competing for my ear, Lord Melksham? I want none of it! I have had nothing but trouble from you and your Tory friends. Is this some trick of Harley's?'

There was contempt in her voice. Lord Melksham began to feel he was losing the initiative. Something had to be done.

He halted, challenging the Duchess to continue walking on alone. The awkwardness had the desired effect. She too paused, and turned to face him. She was intrigued by the game he was playing:

'Well then, what is this false news I must be wary of?'

It was said almost casually.

'That the Duke is dead.'

He allowed the blunt words their full effect – he was not prepared to gloss them for her. There was a moment of stunned silence.

'*False*, you say? Are you certain? But who would wish to spread such a rumour?'

'It is no rumour – that is the trick. It will come as certified news from Lille – arrived this morning by the official packet. But it is an entire fiction …'

'You are *certain* this is untrue?'

She was unable to suppress alarm.

'Completely, I assure you. It will be the sensation of an hour – hardly that – but enough for the plotters to mount a raid on the stocks – to make their fortunes. The shock to the nation, and especially to yourself, means nothing to them. Word reached me of the plot at dawn this morning – I knew I must come and forewarn you. It is a desperate business.'

'Cooked up in 'Change Alley, no doubt?'

'Yes, but its origins are in Vandernan's. It has been organised from Holland. The mail has been intercepted and the official packet substituted to bring the appalling news. Jonathan's and Garraway's may be in a ferment at this very moment.'

This was a lot to take in. She couldn't resist narrowing her eyes:

'Why are you so concerned for my feelings, Lord Melksham? This was exceedingly thoughtful of you – something I would not have looked for …'

He did not respond but waited for her to continue.

'… What is your motive? …'

Her Grace was clearly thinking out loud.

'… Hitherto you have shown no such consideration – indeed you have been set on discomforting me. You have pried into my secret affairs and encouraged malicious talk. It was brought to my notice that you have been reading my private correspondence and using it to feed my enemies' resentment – to make unfounded allegations …'

'I found a letter.'

'Yes, indeed you did! – and what did you do? Fold the thing

up again and discreetly ignore its contents? No, you thought it prime matter for gossip amongst your friends ...'

'But I ...'

'... Not only that, but I understand you placed a construction on it that impugned my character and that of my dear friend George Sturgis ... Oh yes! It came to my notice, my Lord ... and now I find you are concerned for my welfare and anxious to guard my feelings. You may wonder why I ask what has brought you here!'

This combative response had been half-expected, but it was more direct and circumstantial than he had bargained for. It called for a determined reply:

'I assure you the death of Mr Sturgis has affected me also, and in the most painful way. You must know that my son Frank is arrested for his murder – an *unfounded allegation* of the foulest kind! In these circumstances you should understand why I interest myself in Mr Sturgis – why I seek to discover who might want to kill him – who his enemies were ... Any evidence may be vital. Need I say more? Is saving the life of my son and preventing the ruin of my family not motive enough?'

He let the question hang.

The Duchess looked away, turning her eyes toward the parterre with its intricate interwoven patterns:

'You believe your son is innocent – I understand that. But you must see how the imputation against him plays with me – how it adds to my suspicions.'

'We both have our suspicions, Your Grace. You ask what has brought me here – well, I shall answer you as directly as I can. This daring plan to announce your husband's death is not a singular adventure. No, it is part of a larger enterprise in which Mr Sturgis himself played a part, and from which he sought to extricate himself. This is what we have discovered – and that is how we had wind of today's plot.'

'Vandernan's has been the source, you say? It is a vile place – the resort of tricksters and highwaymen! Jack Beech was snatched there on Sunday, was he not?'

It was spoken with a shrug – she was making light of it.

'He was indeed. But the true vileness of the place lies elsewhere – as I think you know ...'

He hesitated, but there was no response. This was hazardous terrain.

'... Vandernan's is a nursery of frauds and plots, and George Sturgis was a part of it. A cabal of money-men run their own system from there – a faction within the Bank. If you want *political nonsense* – as you call it – then you need look no further.'

'But how should this touch me? The affairs of the Bank are hardly my concern.'

'Perhaps they ought to be, given what is being practised on you this very day ... Do I take it Sir Gilbert Heathcote has expressed no disquiet about Vandernan's and its antics?'

This touched her. Her eyes caught fire:

'Your suspicions again! I don't know why I tolerate this! You are trespassing on my private affairs, Lord Melksham. I will not be questioned!'

The Duchess turned and resumed her walk along the path. He was in danger of losing her. Perhaps he had been pressing too hard? He remembered what Tom had said – that he was here to warn and advise, not accuse ...

He drew alongside her again:

'Forgive me if I spoke too boldly, Your Grace. I came to alert you, not to harass you.'

'Well, you have delivered your message, and I am grateful for it ... But now I think there is nothing more to be said.'

'Alas! ...'

The word came out before he could stop it. She read the tone at once:

'What? There is more? Cannot I shake you off?'

'There is more you need to know, Your Grace – which it is in your interest to hear.'

'You presume too much, Lord Melksham – and have done so from the beginning. Why do you persist in this? It is not for you to decide where my *interests* lie.'

'Of course. All I can do is inform – you must decide your course of action. I think you will be surprised by what I have to say.'

This was exasperating but also intriguing. They were approaching a stone bench. If the annoyance was to continue, then it were best endured sitting down.

'Well then,' she said, settling on the bench. 'What more is there? Yet more suspicion? A further imputation in the guise of advice?'

'Coal gas ...'

Simple words, but the Duchess looked genuinely puzzled.

'... The new project for extracting combustible air from coal – it has been taking 'Change Alley by storm.'

'Ah yes. Mr Roscoe assured me it was a great scheme – and it seems many others are of that opinion. The gains have been remarkable ... Why are you frowning? Does it meet with your disapproval? How I invest my money is surely my own business.'

'I am thinking of Her Majesty. You took it upon yourself to commit the Queen's funds to it ...'

'Ah! I see where this is leading. My relations with the Queen– that inexhaustible topic of gossip and speculation! I have been sorely tried this morning, Lord Melksham – perhaps you wish to vex me even more? Or do you intend to reassure me and make me easier in myself? Am I to benefit from my deputy's fund of wisdom on the matter? Pray advise me!'

There was no retreat possible in face of these sarcasms, and so Lord Melksham gave her the full benefit of his insight on the matter of the coal-gas bubble and much more besides. He was unrelenting. As each item of evidence accumulated, piece by piece, there formed a vivid picture of the Vandernan's enterprise and the machinations of Roscoe and Parham. All the natural colour drained from the Duchess's face, leaving only the cosmetic behind.

He was prepared for the onslaught to come. He had decided there was nothing more to lose, and he would stake everything on speaking the truth as he knew it. He bestowed it all upon her.

He waited.

'I see ... And you say my own broker knows of this conspiracy? ...'

'Not only does Mr Roscoe know of it, but he has been the prime mover – he and Lord Parham between them.'

'... And this is driven by his ambition to be the next Chairman of the Bank?'

Lord Melksham nodded. The calm was making him uneasy.

'... And today's raid on the stocks – my husband's supposed death – is a part of their plan?'

It was like a spring coiling remorselessly. He needed to break the tension:

'Alas, Your Grace, Mr Sturgis has already been their victim. The moment he discovered the plot to announce the Duke's death he swore to expose their secret and warn you himself ... This was only minutes before he was killed.'

'*Minutes?*'

'Yes – so much we know. It could be no coincidence.'

The Duchess was thinking hard. He detected a sudden resolution in her, a coolness. She crossed her hands and straightened her back:

'It is a good story, Lord Melksham – and you make a lively drama out of it! ...'

The tone was brisk.

'... But these facts of yours are hardly that, are they? Everything you tell me arises from hearsay – from what men have said and what they have overheard ... Do you have material evidence for any of this? There is much supposition, much knotting together of scraps. It is such a daring and involved scheme – I am sure Mr Maynwaring – my eyes and ears! – would have had wind of it. I cannot believe such an ambitious conspiracy could have gone on undetected. My secretary must have sniffed it out.'

'He did not need to, Your Grace.'

'What do you mean? ... What are you implying?'

The heat had suddenly returned – her look was urgent, a frown intensifying her gaze.

Lord Melksham slowly reached down into his pocket:

'False news is a curious thing, is it not? It may appear so trivial, a mere sporting with the truth – a hint can be enough. But its poison runs deep. And a playful lie can be more powerful for being outrageous ... Today's false news about the Duke will hardly disturb the heavens – its bubble will quickly burst and merely make a few men extremely rich ... Perhaps that is how Mr Maynwaring thinks of it?'

'What?'

He unfolded the paper and handed it to her:

'This note was sent to Sir Charles Norreys, the Commissioner of Vandernan's.'

The Duchess read it silently to herself:

Fear not! It seems Her Grace knows nothing. All is still well, and by Saturday matters will be set right again – and no harm done.
A. M.

Her fingers trembled. He thought for a moment that she was about to tear the thing to shreds. But she handed it back to him calmly:

'This is not Mr Maynwaring's handwriting! What game are you playing with me? Here is yet another flimsy thing. I cannot believe you wish to build so much on this piece of paper. It is a forgery ... How do I know this whole exercise has not been an elaborate fabrication?'

'You may wish to think so – I can understand it. But uncomfortable truths have to be faced.'

'Where has that scrap come from?'

'It was copied by his wife, who discovered it in Sir Charles's pocket.'

Suddenly the supposed truth appeared a trivial farce. The Duchess gave a cry of vindication:

'Ha! The inquisitive Lady Norreys! And what can Lady Norreys have to do with the truth? Do you not know she regards me as her inveterate enemy – she and her satiric friend Mrs Manley! The pair of them are prime conspirators themselves, I would suggest ...'

It was a challenging response, and hard to counter – the grain of truth in it troubled him. Lord Melksham's spirits sank. Was everything a fiction? He was beginning to understand what he and his friends were battling with. They had found themselves in a world where Truth was somehow negotiable – much like a bill of exchange, of value to anyone who could use it. Substantial things had lost their status and must fight it out with wild notions that were all the stronger for their currency – active and impossible to suppress. How could they find Truth in such a world and persuade others to accept it?

He was close to surrender:

'I can do no more, Your Grace. I have done what I can to tell you all I have learned – and you are at liberty to reject every word of it. To you it seems an unlikely fiction – but at least you have heard my story. I would wish to have a similar recognition from you... I and my family are under the gravest threat – victims of a lie that you have it in your power to challenge. You in your turn must surely question what Mr Maynwaring has been urging on you. It is hearsay, I agree, but I am given to understand that he has been inventing some charge against me, just as he and the people in Vandernan's are conspiring to convict my son of murder. I appeal to your humanity. These people are masters of fiction, and very soon you will appreciate what damage untruth can do. I'm glad I have been able to warn you of this and lessen the shock and grief they were prepared to inflict on you.'

Lord Melksham stood up, feeling battered by the confrontation but satisfied he had done all he could to press their case. He felt he had served his friends well – Tom, Will, and Mrs Trotter – the three stalwarts who were active in the field, tirelessly trying to hold Justice and Truth together.

The Duchess was also thoughtful. It took a moment for her to rise, but he detected a look on her face that suggested his words had found their mark. He knew he must say no more but await the outcome.

At that moment, as his eyes scanned the palace gardens, he could make out a distant horseman riding full gallop along the London road towards them.

Chapter Forty-Three

‑∞‑

'I THINK THE pulse of things is quickening, gentlemen!' said Widow Trotter as she poured out the coffee. Her two callers, Tom and Elias, had arrived at the Bay-Tree simultaneously – Tom to report that he had set his uncle on the road to Kensington, and Constable Cobb bringing news of how matters had resolved themselves during the night at Custom House Quay. Between the three of them there was much to tell, and one revelation followed another. Nods and raised brows alternated with intakes of breath and startled exclamations – most of these latter were from Elias, who was struck by how rapidly events had moved on. The audacious Marlborough plot brought a special gleam to his eye:

'That trickster Leary has been a fortunate fellow. What secrets he carried with him! – the Bank intelligence, those smuggled diamonds, the false news about the Duke – It's impressive. No wonder he was under protection. Violence seems to follow him. The man is safer out of the country ...'

He looked at Widow Trotter.

'... Well, the adventurer is gone now – off to his friends in Amsterdam. And I say good luck to him. You're well rid of the rogue!'

'The Green Dragon sailed, then?'

'Yes, it slipped anchor without a by-your-leave, and the tide carried it away. Much to everyone's relief I've no doubt.'

'I thought it best to leave Mr Leary out of the picture.'

'Well, I took my cue from you, Molly. I said little to the magistrate altogether. I made it an arrest for theft and not an attempted rape – to keep you free of the sordid affair. There can be half a dozen such attacks on the wharves in a single night, and your presence there would have been questioned. No, my story of the stolen note and pursuing him from Covent Garden did the business. Bob Turley played his part too. The magistrate's eyes popped when he saw the sum – two thousand guineas! And when Harkins claimed it as his own there was unconcealed hilarity. He wasn't in his gentleman's togs last night!'

'I'm glad you didn't destroy the note,' said Tom. 'It will surely be useful in tying Harkins to Vandernan's?'

'Exactly! It gives him a lot of awkward questions to answer – and our Mr Hector will be certain to ask them.'

'Hector?'

'Yes, Molly, you'll be pleased to hear that the local justice was only too happy to consign the case to a Covent Garden magistrate. What a reunion that is likely to be! Harkins was at Hector's side during the raid on Vandernan's. It couldn't have fallen neater, could it?'

'So, Parham and Sir Charles will have a lot to explain – why their man Harkins was in possession of Frank's promissory note. Do they explain the circumstances – or do they expose him to a charge of theft and let him hang?'

The constable looked at his two friends:

'As I said, awkward questions! And from what we know of Mr Hector, he is sure to be tenacious in the matter.'

'Now that Harkins is in our net, Mr Cobb, can he not be charged with murder? We can prove he tampered with Sturgis's body. That is a great thing ... We are nearly there, Mrs T!'

'Nearer, certainly. But there is much to do. Vandernan's will not be easily outwitted – and the Bank … We must remember what powers we are facing, and what influence they can call on.'

Elias had no doubts:

'Well, if our zealous magistrate wants to expose the evils of the gaming-house he could hardly hope for more.'

'And there's a battle to be fought in the Bank too, surely?' said Tom. 'They may come to see Vandernan's as an embarrassment.'

Widow Trotter's eyes brightened at the idea:

'Yes, and that is something we must try to encourage on Saturday. After all, we shall have the players at our disposal – ready to set one faction against another.'

'Saturday?'

The constable was baffled. There was a plot brewing, he was sure of it …

Widow Trotter gave her old friend a knowing smile and proceeded to tell him of the Mercers' Hall assembly and their hopes for it.

'Well, well, My Lady! This is momentous. You will be mixing with the City's finest!'

'More than mixing, Mr Cobb – Mrs Trotter is sure to be stirring the pot herself. *Fire burn, and cauldron bubble!*'

The allusion wasn't a flattering one, but she took it in good spirit. As for Elias, the constable began to appreciate for the first time what large forces their investigations had brought into play:

'You're in very deep, all of you – I'm concerned how you're putting yourselves in danger. This is no sport! You hazarded your life last night, Molly, and very nearly lost it … just an inch further with that blade …'

His voice softened, as if to blunt the painful thought.

'… I don't wish to think of it.'

'I've already been angry with her,' said Tom. 'But don't we need to be a hero at least once in our lives?'

'Yes, but you have to be vigilant! … Toby, Bob Turley and I take risks every day – it's our occupation – and that fellow Leary lives a life of adventure – diamond smuggling indeed! … You must allow me to be concerned.'

It was a shaky argument, he knew, and he admired Mary Trotter's courage – but it was something he felt needed to be said.

A little more vigilance on his part would have told him that the word *diamond* had brought a catch in Widow Trotter's breathing – she could have sworn the stone had twitched slightly in her pocket. The tiny packet had remained there untouched exactly as Bob Leary had tied it, waiting to reveal its treasure again. But the temptation had been resisted. She had amused herself with a dream of wealth, picturing how she would trade with some dubious Clerkenwell jeweller and transform her fortunes. But it was not to be. Now was the time for her to play her magic trick, and she made the most of it:

'Mr Leary left something behind him, gentlemen …'

There was a puzzled silence while she delved into her pocket for the silk parcel and held it out to them.

'… He presented this to me – a generous and thoughtful gesture – but perhaps one of contrition also.'

The silk parted to reveal the diamond, and the effect was as theatrical as she could have wished. The three of them were in awestruck communion as it passed from hand to hand. Almost an inch across, the gem displayed itself to special advantage at the centre of Elias's rough palm – it didn't need a soft white skin to do it justice.

'Stolen goods,' the constable murmured, '… but how beautiful. It deserves a fine silver chain.'

He looked at Mrs Trotter.

'Yes, stolen, alas – and not for me, Elias. India's finest! But I cannot keep it. You must hand it in to the authorities.'

She gave him the silk bag.

They knew she was right, but an unsuppressible *what if* was in their minds ... For a moment they toyed with the thought, unwilling to let the diamond pass from them.

'I shall deliver it to Mr Secretary's office this very day – and I'll not breathe easily until it's safe. The thing has had a remarkable journey. I trust its final mile will be uneventful.'

The mood had become sober, but with the diamond's fate now settled a sense of urgency returned. Their thoughts moved to Bob Leary's other secret – the news of Marlborough's death.

'The lightning will strike at any moment, Tom – if it has not already done so. Cannot we intervene in some way?'

'I'm off to 'Change Alley to watch the drama play out – but I'm not sure anything can be done. A lone voice can hardly contradict an official announcement. The news won't be arriving as rumour, remember.'

'If only we had more time! It will be seen as a national disaster.'

'The fox amongst the chickens! Let us hope there will be no serious consequences.'

Widow Trotter remained uncomfortable:

'To toy with Fate like this is very dangerous. It may be a game with the stocks, but people will be hurt.'

'I'll do what I can, Mrs T. I'll try to find a familiar face – Gabriel Winch perhaps? I hope most to see Michael Henriques or Benjamin Levy ... But I need to send a note round to Will – he's busy in court today. I've so much to tell him!'

'You'd best go at once, Tom – every minute could be important. Leave the note to me – I'll ask Will here for a dish of tea at *six*. We must have a committee ... Go now – the alley awaits! ... But please bring us back some cheering news!'

What Tom would find when he arrived was nothing short of chaos. In the City it was suddenly a day like no other. The shocking intelligence of the great general's death had swept through Whitehall like a conflagration – the dispatch could not be clearer! Ministers were white-faced and frozen in disbelief – wands of office shook in their hands. A messenger was dispatched to Kensington with the news. While men of power were paralysed in indecision, the word flew across to 'Change Alley with lightning speed. In Jonathan's and Garraway's, anxieties that were already tinder-dry burst into flame. The unlooked-for disaster appeared at once to change everything – the future of the war – the hopes of the nation and its allies – the safety of Europe. All was thrown into doubt.

Down 'Change Alley the scenes were frantic. Bank stock lost a third in an instant – and other stocks collapsed also. Confidence was no more. The floor had given way, and no-one knew where a solid ground of value was to be found. Suddenly value itself was melting in the heat of the panic.

But in the alley, there were certain individuals who had planned for this moment with ingenious skill. While the price of stocks plummeted, the grand design of the Vandernan's cabal was being achieved – and remarkably beyond their hopes. Knowing that the rebound would shortly come made the ride all the more exhilarating. The plotters were finding it hard to suppress their elation. While everyone around them sank into despair, they fought to conceal smiles of satisfaction …

That was the scene as it had been planned … but it is not what happened.

The truth is, Tom arrived in 'Change Alley to find that news of the Duke's death had not yet broken, but another report had arrived to dampen the mood of the place. There was despondency in the air, and faces were downcast. The cause was an announcement that the much anticipated Lord Mayor's Show would not be taking place on the morrow. The City of London's grand celebration was to be cancelled! There had been no offical notice of Prince George's death, but it was evident that their day of civic triumph was not to be. The festive crowds would not be filling the streets; holidaying apprentices would not be chasing after the procession and mimicking its solemnities; the Goldsmiths would lose their chance to dazzle and display their wealth, and the carts would not be creaking under the weight of their allegorical decoration; the scarlet robes and furred gowns of the liverymen would remain in their cupboards; the decorated company barges would not proceed along the Thames to volleys of gunfire from the City grenadiers; the City's Champion in full armour would not lead the company of armourers; the golden-crowned Apollo, robbed of his throne, would miss out on his great day ... and poor Elkanah Settle – London's ten-pound laureate – would never see his magnificent design realised. The good citizens would have only his illustrated pamphlet to gaze at the engravings and wonder at what might have been. What a world of civic pomp and pride would be lost!

This disappointment was quite enough to occupy the minds of the stock-jobbers, and as Tom made his way down 'Change Alley he felt the contrast with his previous visit. He had expected uproar, but instead there was casualness – no sense of eager purpose. His knowledge of what was to come made him scrutinise the faces around him, and he searched for a hint that something momentous was awaited. But there was nothing – until he noticed a group of three outside Garraway's, their bewigged heads huddled together, eyes wary and scanning the alley. He wondered who they were. One of the men consulted his watch, and brows were furrowed. Will Lundy would have recognised two of them immediately, though Tom did not ...

But it was enough to confirm expectations. He was convinced they were waiting for the scene to burst into frenzied life.

Tom began thinking there might be something he could do. Perhaps there was time to put his knowledge to work? Should he grasp Opportunity by the forelock and purchase some stocks at their lowest – then sell when universal joy and relief had lifted the market to a height? He would never have such a chance again …

It was a tempting thought, and it became stronger when he saw someone he did recognise walking down the alley towards him. At once his spirits lifted. He gave an urgent wave of the hand, and Michael Henriques raised his in response. It was a welcome meeting on both sides, and within seconds Tom had pulled him aside out of earshot of others and told his secret.

'But this is madness, Mr Bristowe! – the wildest scheme I ever heard! Are you certain of it?'

'They are daring men, Mr Henriques, and ready to ride the thing hard and make their fortunes. Could we take advantage of this ourselves, do you think? You know how trading works …'

It was spoken impetuously, and Tom looked for a similar response – but Michael shook his head:

'No, you must not think of it, Mr Bristowe! Never leap aboard another's horse – it is far too dangerous!'

Tom was deflated by the response:

'So, you think we should simply wait and observe the drama? Would we not be risking very little? The cabal will be making that play, will they not? … If only Mr Levy were here …'

Michael saw this was serious. He spoke quietly into Tom's ear:

'Compose yourself. You do not know what particular ploy these men will adopt – though from what Mr Levy told us, they will have their puts already in place, waiting to pounce when the disastrous news arrives – and at the same time they will purchase options that will soar when sentiments change. The price of these will multiply their gains many times.'

This merely fanned the flame.

'But surely we might consider doing something?'

'Forgive me, Tom. You must let me speak frankly, and not take it wrongly … You say this wild scheme is the brain-child of Willem Oosterhout and his Vandernan's cronies – and that it was revealed to Mrs Trotter by Bob Leary … ?'

Michael's voice made this sound the most dubious of pedigrees.

'… And you speak of it as a certainty – as a thing undoubtedly in place?'

Tom's confidence ebbed a little. Phrased in that way the idea sounded highly suspect. He began to see that an impulsive move might be ill-advised.

'I accept it is a risk – but, do you see that huddle outside Garraway's? I have been watching them. They are on the lookout for something – the picture of expectation!'

Michael turned to look:

'Well well! – a little cabal of their own, I see! Those are two familiar faces, Tom, and you know them well by reputation … The gentleman in the flaxen wig is Lord Parham – and the fellow in plain worsted is Philip Roscoe … You may be right about this plot of yours.'

Tom was transfixed. So, there they were, the chief plotters gathered for their great adventure! He felt vindicated – and even more apprehensive of what was about to happen.

But at that moment another voice sounded behind him:

'Mr Bristowe! You are back with us again! …'

Tom swung round to find Gabriel Winch's satirical smile beaming at him.

'… The lure of 'Change Alley was too great for you, was it? We'll make a jobber of you yet!'

Gabriel and Michael nodded acquaintance. Tom was suddenly anxious about what had now become their secret. He felt he had to say something to steer the talk:

'I came to see what news was stirring, Mr Winch. I enjoyed the hum of the place on my first visit – though I find it much duller today.'

Gabriel's look sharpened a little more. His eyes narrowed:

'Yes indeed, the alley is at its best – and most profitable – when chaos reigns. But in my experience, calmer waters have possibilities of their own. You have time to think and observe. The master-jobber can smell things in the quiet air.'

'You're being philosophical, Mr Winch! Perhaps you'll tell me that during a lull men's thoughts turn to wagers?'

'Ah! A shrewd point, Mr Bristowe! You are beginning to master the ways of the alley ... As it happens, this morning has given me food for contemplation ...'

Both Tom and Michael stirred at this.

'Something *in the air?*' said Michael.

'Possibly – though I am a cautious man: I like to grasp things before I put weight on them ...'

He hesitated – then, in a quieter voice, made the move.

'... I have taken a wager this morning – for a considerable amount – that the price of Bank stock will sink below one hundred today ... Now what does that tell me? ...'

Gabriel paused, but neither of them hazarded an answer.

'... Perhaps little in itself – such things are common enough ... however, in my various idle conversations during this *quiet* time, I discover that several other brokers have taken wagers of a similar nature – once again for very large sums ... This provokes thought.'

Tom felt a sudden tremor and glanced at Michael. It was Michael who spoke:

'Perhaps keeping quiet is the best plan, Gabriel – not to draw notice.'

'Hmmm ... I agree. To tread softly is best ... I see that the gentleman who placed the wager with me is over there talking with Mr Roscoe ... Now, what brings a director of the Bank to the alley this morning, do you think? And why is he exchanging words with someone who has wagered a large sum that the stock will plunge today? ... Am I wrong to be suspicious, Mr Henriques?'

'This is how rumours begin, Mr Winch! You have a difficult choice: do you stay silent and wait on events – if there are to be any – or do you reveal your suspicions and feed the rumour, which would itself bring about the collapse of the stock.'

'You understand my dilemma. Do you think these wagers are intended to unsettle the market? Or might these men know something we do not?'

Gabriel and Michael went silent, both chewing on the same bone. Tom's mind was working quickly. It seemed the plotters were not able to resist placing side-bets of their own. This was reckless, and more than ever he appreciated how Vandernan's and 'Change Alley were learning each other's ways.

But what occurred next ensured there was little time for contemplation. Instantly the mood of the alley was transformed by the arrival of a horseman. The animal was in a sweat, and when its rider leapt from the saddle and tethered the reins to a post outside Jonathan's, the shouted inquiries began. The rider, who was himself perspiring, remained dumb; and when he hurried into the coffee house all the faces around him knew something dramatic would follow. This was *news* – urgent news. But of what kind?

Tom glanced toward Garraways and saw that Lord Parham and his two companions were already hurrying over. All eyes in the alley – and many of the feet – were directed at Jonathan's. The coffee house doorway was jammed with people eager to hear the message delivered, and Gabriel Winch was one of them.

With the nimbleness of a dancer he had bounded over there, leaving Tom and Michael to exchange looks of apprehension.

The atmosphere was fevered. By now, Jonathan's was full to bursting, and those who were left outside were beside themselves with curiosity – longing to ask questions while needing to hold their peace and catch what was happening inside. A tense silence descended.

Tom was curious himself, and his mind was working hard. While every eye was glued to the coffee house, his were directed at the horse, and in particular at the saddle cloth. It was of a purple colour, trimmed with gold, and in one corner he could make out a heraldic beast, part eagle, part lion, its claws in the air. He had seen it before – a griffin … This was no government post-man or hired messenger. No, that was the crest of the Duke of Marlborough.

Chapter Forty-Four

⟨⟨⟨

T HE TENSE SILENCE in the alley was suddenly broken by a shout from within the coffee house. People outside the door began to murmur and exchange glances, uncertain what the sound portended. Tom had been unsure what to expect, but as he listened there was no doubting it – the noise, growing by the second, was one of jubilation. There were even a few cheers. Jonathan's was celebrating!

Alongside him one figure was breathing through gritted teeth and pushing his way forwards. Lord Parham was beginning to think events were not going according to plan.

The coffee house door opened, and a jobber shouted the news:

'Lille has fallen! The town has surrendered!'

Tom and Michael looked at each other, wondering whether to share in the relief.

'Parham looks fearful,' said Michael. 'He was clearly not expecting this.'

'But it will make the ill news worse, surely?' said Tom, '– when it comes ... *if* it comes?'

Others around them were less uncertain. Trading within the coffee house resumed with fresh urgency, and they could hear stocks being shouted – potential buyers were crying out for sellers.

There was now a skirmish going on at the entrance, with those inside wanting to leave and spread the word, and those outside anxious to join the action. Any thought of forming a plan to exploit the situation was out of the question. This was Gabriel Winch's profitable chaos, and Tom could picture him busy in the thick of it.

He was surprised therefore to see Gabriel squeezing out of the door, a look of puzzlement on his face. He was coming towards them, clearly with the intention of sharing something. After their earlier conversation perhaps he was baffled too?

'Gentlemen! I take it you have heard the news from Lille. Our jobbers are in a fine frenzy!'

'But you are not joining them, Mr Winch?' said Tom.

'I am holding off, Mr Bristowe. I have been a bull these past days and see no cause to adjust my strategy. All is in place, and I shall *tarry the grinding* ... But I have just heard something extraordinary – I know not what to make of it ... An announcement!'

Tom glanced again at the steaming horse:

'This was no government dispatch, was it?'

At this, Michael gave him an inquiring look, but Gabriel merely grinned:

'No indeed – once again you speak shrewdly, Mr Bristowe – and what the messenger delivered may surprise you – or it may not ... I recall yesterday's conversation when you showed an interest in the Dutch system of intelligence. You told me your friends wished to learn about the activities of Willem Oosterhout ... This was when you were looking for Mr Henriques here ...'

Tom was uneasy at the direction of Gabriel's thoughts. This was a man who was himself extremely shrewd – and well practised in reading the omens.

'... Our courier has brought news from Lille – but by way of Kensington, would you believe – and directed here by the Duchess herself! ...'

Gabriel paused to gauge their response. Tom was silent, hanging on every word.

'... The Duke has sent a message from the field of battle with a note to his beloved wife – he knows not to rely on the post! And Her Grace has redirected him here to announce her husband's success ...'

This made sense – but there was more to come.

'... The Duke was concerned the post would be intercepted – and with good reason it seems, for the Duchess has added a message of her own. It has come to her notice, she says, that a false report of the Duke's death is to be circulated – and that *Dutch* interests might be behind it. Her Grace wishes us all to know that any such report is false, and that the general is in exceptional health! ... What do you make of that, Mr Bristowe? I have never heard the like. A Dutch plot, eh?'

There was an unspoken surmise behind Gabriel's words – Tom knew he had been fitting the pieces together:

'I think our suspicions agree, Mr Winch! Your wagerers surely have a stake in this plot? Well, we now have our answer – it appears you are not going to be out of pocket after all. I congratulate you!'

While he spoke, his thoughts were over in Kensington. This must surely be the fruit of his uncle's meeting with the Duchess? – but had he also prevailed on other matters?

'And I congratulate *you*, Mr Bristowe! I detect some relief – and in you also, Mr Henriques. It is always good to see conspirators routed, is it not? ...'

There was a teasing glint in his eye.

'... I wonder, are we to expect a second sweating horseman at any moment? I do hope so! – they add to the theatre of the place. What a busy mart this is, and what ingenuities are abroad! I must off and see if there's more to be sniffed out ... If the two of you have wind of any sequel I would be grateful to know of it.'

And with that, he left them for other conversations. They

watched him melt into the swirling crowd.

'Now there's a man who delights in business, Tom! He loves the twists and turns of his profession ... And what a turn we have just witnessed! I know one gentleman who will be furious at what has occurred.'

'A certain Dutch merchant?'

'Yes indeed. Mynheer Oosterhout will not be happy. After all their planning, everything was in place – but *somehow* the secret escaped!'

Michael gave a laugh. Tom was beginning to register the scale of their success:

'Can you believe it? Their false news has been exposed before it arrives – and from a source not to be contradicted!'

'I must apologise for doubting your story, Tom – it seems your own lines of communication have been impeccable. But what a huge blow to Roscoe and his faction – his ambitions have taken a knock! I suspect the plot was also meant to strike at the Bank and reveal how vulnerable it is – and at the same time set up the market for the biggest play possible.'

'I assume tens of thousands are at stake?'

'We cannot know, but you could add a zero to the figure and be nearer the mark. These men have been badly hit – ruined even ... Yet the affair is surely not over? Like a wounded animal they can still do damage. They have been frustrated in their false news, but other plans may have been laid – and of course there remains the coal-gas scheme ...'

'I hope we shall find out more in Mercers' Hall.'

'Indeed, Tom – and I assure you Mr Levy and I are preparing the ground. I must hurry over to Lombard Street and report on what we've just witnessed. He's sure to be astonished. Will you accompany me?'

'I think I had better wait here a while longer – to see if there are repercussions ...'

Out of the corner of his eye Tom had seen Lord Parham and Philip Roscoe emerge from Jonathan's. They looked deathly pale and were with two other gentlemen. There was some close whispering going on.

'... I might be able to exploit my anonymity in this place. Who knows but I may overhear something to our advantage?'

'I wish you luck, Tom. But have a care!'

The alley had quickly become crowded as the hot news from Lille spread to Cornhill and the Royal Exchange. People were gathering in animated groups, and so it was possible for Tom to steer himself within range of Lord Parham and his associates. With their solemn faces drawn into a circle they looked like physicians consulting over a sick patient – and after the Duchess's message their enterprise was certainly at death's door.

With lively talking in all directions it wasn't easy to make out more than a few words, but the ones Tom was able to catch told him these men could still make trouble. He distinctly heard *coal gas*, and there was something about a *plan* for *Saturday*. There was some nodding – and then *We shall follow your lead ...* A few moments later a frowning Philip Roscoe spoke of *Sir Gilbert* and *the Duchess* in the same breath – and Tom distinctly caught the words *his doing!* delivered emphatically. It seemed they suspected the message from Kensington had been prompted by Heathcote! If they needed evidence of a faction within the Bank, then this was it.

Tom was standing as near as he could risk without raising suspicion, and he strained to catch more, half-expecting to hear the name *Melksham*, but the general hubbub was now so confused that any further words were inaudible. Sad scraps indeed! But he had managed to pick up something. It was clear that the men's plans were still proceeding. There was deep shock and suppressed anger in their looks.

As the news reverberated round the alley, Tom felt the

excitement pressing in on him and found it suffocating. He felt it in the warmth of the crowding bodies, the whiff of expectant human breath, the electric feeling that anything was possible here. It was a magnetic force not unlike the pull of the gaming-tables. And around him were the alley's people – the tribe of jobbers, agents, scriveners and middle-men, the hangers-on who congregated to breathe the air of the place, all rubbing along with each other, ready for any opening to exploit … It was all so very stimulating. But for Tom at this moment it brought to mind a string of scavenging kites hovering over a carcase – and he himself was one of them … Suddenly he knew he wanted to be gone.

Widow Trotter's invitation for a 'dish of tea' didn't do justice to the spread that confronted Will when he arrived at the Bay-Tree. A welcoming feast was laid out on the parlour table. Mrs Dawes's newly-baked orange cake was supplemented with apple tarts, buttered buns, almond macaroons, and quince preserve, with a few small dishes of things to nibble. It was partly an acknowledgment that much had happened since Tuesday evening and there were two whole days of activity to report on; but there was also an element of defiance in the hospitality – Mary Trotter was determined to be the generous hostess for as long as she was able and make the two young men feel at home.

Tom and Will were happy to enjoy a convivial banquet after their exertions – the one returned from the confusion of 'Change Alley and the other from the tedium of Westminster Hall. Will in particular had a great deal of catching-up to do, and the first half hour was an epic tale of adventures and discoveries – of *moving accidents* and *hair-breadth 'scapes*. He was rapt with astonishment as Widow Trotter told of her expedition to

Custom House Quay – the death and resurrection of Bob Leary, Harkins's attack, and the gift of the Albemarle diamond. The story gathered pace with Leary's revelation of the Marlborough plot, a drama which reached its catastrophe with the Duchess's message to Jonathan's and the confounding of the Vandernan's plotters ...

Will was spellbound. He had spent the day enduring a series of tedious recitals and labyrinthine arguments that finally led nowhere – but this was different. Tom and Mrs Trotter told a wonderful tale. Not only that, but their account was beginning to make sense of all the circumstances of the past week and build them into a credible plot.

He gave a sigh:

'What can I say? I've missed a whole lifetime of adventures! I feel I've been idling away my time to no purpose.'

'Don't despair, Will,' said Tom. 'There's surely more to come – and from that look on your face I'm beginning to suspect you have something of your own to tell us. I know that look! You're pulling at the leash – am I right?'

Will grinned as he helped himself to an apple tart.

'How can you tell? I've been trying for *sang-froid* – but it's not easy to hold news in, is it? ... Yes, something has come my way in this last hour and I'm bursting to tell you both ... We still have the small question of a murder to resolve – and I think this is going to bring us closer ...'

Widow Trotter took this as her cue and suggested that with the tea now drunk they might perhaps graduate to the madeira – it was the best accompaniment to cake.

Will took this as a tribute to his dramatic abilities. The audience was readying itself and the curtain was being raised ...

'It happened just now, Mrs T – I had arrived back in Pump Court and was reading your message when I had a visitor – Sam Rivers.'

'So, he's been released! I'm glad of that.'

'Yes, it appears Alderman Rivers may have had something to do with it – fathers can be very helpful sometimes – and it seems the other Vandernan's debauchees will shortly be following him. A few days of hemp-beating will have made them virtuous members of society.'

Widow Trotter couldn't suppress a loud 'ha!'

'A judicious summing-up, Mrs T! Sam says the indignation of the Bridewell gamesters has been intense – not just the pain and humiliation, but real anger at how Vandernan's has treated them. They know they were sacrificed for some behind-the-scenes deal while gamesters of more influence were allowed to go free. The talk has been mutinous!

'Well, you'll recall Humfrey Corbet – the young fellow I won your promissory note from. It seems he's taken his Bridewell entertainment badly and is now happy to point the finger at the Vandernan's system. He confirmed to Sam that their funds are the fruits of theft and fraud – all kinds of dirty work – and he's been forthcoming on how your promissory note reached him. He made question of it at the time and was told it had been brought into the place by Joel Harkins! There's only one way that could have happened ...'

'Just as we thought – Harkins must have taken my note from Sturgis's body but left Mr Popham's note behind to incriminate him. We now have the double evidence.'

'Yes, what we legal men call *corroboration* ...'

Will said it with mock-formality. Tom smiled:

'This is gold dust, Will! The net is closing in on Harkins – and we have him in custody too. Mr Cobb will be glad to know of it. Surely they cannot hold Frank for much longer?'

Widow Trotter could see her strategy achieving success:

'It's the best news, Mr Lundy. I knew Bridewell gossip would yield something.'

'But there's more, Mrs T ... There is another person suffering in Bridewell who is even less happy than Humfrey, and who is ready to speak out ...'

'Someone else?'

Widow Trotter nearly choked on her cake.

'Yes, the doorkeeper of Vandernan's – Mr Travis. I encountered him at the gaming-house on Sunday night. Sam tells me he's been employed there for years – a man who sees all its comings and goings! He's a trusted gentleman who has been close to Parham and whose discretion ought to command a high price ... But now he has been dismissed, would you believe!'

'Not a politic move,' said Tom.

'Extremely foolish! It seems Sir Charles Norreys blamed him for letting the rioters enter the building ... But it turns out that Parham had ordered him to allow Jack Beech's arrest, not telling him it meant going behind the Commissioner's back! So Travis feels he has been tricked. He is furious with both of them.'

'Oh dear – no wonder there's bad blood between Parham and Sir Charles.'

'Yes. Joe Travis has been made to bear the blame, and Parham refused to defend him. As you can imagine, he's pawing the ground and swearing revenge!'

Widow Trotter's pulse leapt at this. She could see possibilities ...

'Just think, gentlemen – what if we could make use of this anger and give Mr Travis the chance to take his revenge on Lord Parham ... Am I being fanciful? The doorkeeper of Vandernan's ...'

'Yes – what doesn't he know!' said Tom, relishing the thought.

Will had already been thinking along these lines:

'No, it's not fanciful, Mrs T – not at all! Indeed, Sam put the idea to me himself ...'

Will paused, conscious of the importance of what he was about to tell them.

'Sam has talked with Mr Travis and says the gentleman is ready to tell the truth about what happened the night Sturgis was killed ...'

Tom broke in:

'About the murder itself?'

'Sam isn't sure. It's not yet clear how much the doorkeeper knows, but it must be damaging.'

'Do you mean he's prepared to give evidence?'

'It's not that easy, Tom. Travis's word could easily be challenged. Any accusation would be seen as resentment at his dismissal – The motive of revenge would invalidate his testimony.'

'We're back with your *corroboration*, are we not?' said Widow Trotter with an uneasy smile.

'We are! But how to achieve it? ... Sam is such an ally, Mrs T! These past days he has been working on our behalf. He has arranged for Travis to call on him when he is released tomorrow ... The plan is that Sam will bring him over here to the Bay-Tree! ... Now, what do you think of that?'

The hostess of the Bay-Tree thought highly of it. Widow Trotter was now beaming from ear to ear:

'I like it very much, Mr Lundy! We must organise a cosy reception for him. Mr Travis will be among friends – and if we play our cards well, we may find him an invaluable ally. Surely, between the five of us we can come up with a plan?'

Friday

29 October 1708

Chapter Forty-Five

※

FRIDAY MORNING, AND Widow Trotter sat in her parlour snatching a quiet moment. The coal fire was already beginning to glow in the grate, and her eyes were drawn towards it. She was amused to find herself searching in its flickerings for some hint of what the day would bring. She was not an especially contemplative person and usually relished this early time of day for its vitality. A moody pensiveness didn't suit the hour at all.

That morning the breakfast trade had been happily busy. It was good to see her customers greeting the day like a new acquaintance, and the air alive with possibility. She had something of those feelings herself but hardly dared acknowledge them – stirrings of hope were always precarious, and hers were mingled with unquiet thoughts that needed working out. It helped to shut the parlour door for a few minutes and be alone with them.

It had been a blustery night with a whistling wind and rattling windows, and the rain was still driving down – the Lord Mayor's Show would have turned out a bedraggled affair! The Bay-Tree's customers were stumbling in with damp clothes and dripping umbrellas, relieved to be somewhere dry and warm, and as always she had been there to welcome them. More than ever the chocolate house had become part of her identity, not just stirring memories but feeding her aspirations too. That was the cruel thing – she still had plans! With the loss of the freehold her grip on the place was precarious, but all the more tenacious for it.

Little more than nine months earlier, on a stormy day much like this, her life had changed. Suddenly, and under circumstances tinged with terrible comedy, she had become 'Widow Trotter.' And what a time it had been since then, for her and the old Good Fellowship! The place had been rejuvenated – much like herself – into the Bay-Tree, and had taken on a more varied and lively character. New friends had been made, new prospects opened, and during these months there had been challenges she could never have anticipated.

And now here they were, she and her friends, approaching the climax of another adventure – one that touched her directly and threatened everything she valued. They had been drawn into the world of *Mammon* – a power she had often dismissed but which she now recognised as the god of this world in all its self-serving deception and trickery – its refusal to be held to account by what was real and true.

These recent days had told Mary Trotter something important about herself. She realised how much she valued substantial things – things to which, and for which, she was responsible. She recalled Elias's prophetic words about paper money – that he preferred something *to have and to hold*. Yes, how very slippery paper was, and the world of endlessly shifting allegiances it served. How it loosened connections and brought confusion! All those notes – exchanged, hidden, stolen, burnt even – those precarious token promises – what power they had! A handful of words scratched on a sheet of paper, or a tiny image printed on a piece of pasteboard, could change lives for ever – whether it was a bill magicked into a coach and six, or a single playing-card, its corners turned over, converted to a country estate.

There was something ludicrous in it all – substance rising from abstraction, solid things melting away to nothing. It was not a world she felt comfortable in. Credit was edging out Truth, just as paper credit was replacing coin. She shuddered at the prospect of Mammon's eventual apocalypse – what a universal loss of belief there would be when the whole magnificent cloudy structure evaporated and people saw there was simply nothing there. Perhaps it would be a kind of universal darkness?

Lofty thoughts – and easily indulged! She had begun with glimmerings of hope and had managed to work her way to the horrors of the Last Day – so much for Trotter's contemplation! This would never do. With conscious effort she pulled herself back to the here and now and tried to think practically about the immediate challenge that faced them.

She was beginning to have hopes of this Joe Travis – the doorkeeper of Vandernan's no less! Perhaps he would open the door for *them*? But they must be careful not to push him too far. It was all very precarious. She was eager to meet the gentleman in the flesh and gauge his character – how far they might trust him. Well, she would soon know. He and Sam Rivers might be appearing at any moment.

Elias must be involved too – his genial presence would reassure Mr Travis and signal how seriously they were taking what he had to say. And Will would be ready with legal guidance in what was sure to be a tricky interview. What their meeting must not become was an interrogation. They would be there to support the doorman's anger at Lord Parham with evidence of their own and, If things went to plan, to direct his revenge toward legal retribution. Was that too much to hope?

She stood up with fresh determination and looked around the parlour at the six empty chairs. Everything was set. The table had been pushed to one side and the chairs arranged in a convivial circle between the fire and the well-stocked sideboard

– a setting in which Mr Travis would feel comfortable. Tom and Will were in readiness upstairs, and Constable Cobb had promised to call with the latest news. All she could do was wait.

But things had moved swiftly elsewhere, and there wasn't time for her to grow impatient. Only seconds later a distinctive rat-a-tat at the parlour door announced the arrival of Constable Cobb. The action was beginning ... or was it?

The door opened and Widow Trotter's smile froze. Elias was standing there with a look of such grimness that he hardly needed to announce unwelcome news. In awkward silence he looked around at the rearranged furniture and felt even more the weight of what he had to tell her.

'What's the matter, Elias?' was all she could say.

The constable didn't take breath:

'Mr Popham has been charged with murder.'

'No! ... But surely – not now? Not with what we know? ...'

'Alas, Molly, they have made their move. Someone has been found who will supply the evidence they need – a man who will swear he saw Mr Popham fleeing the scene with a bloody sword in his hand ...'

'But that is absurd – stage antics! – like something from the Theatre Royal ... it makes no sense at all.'

'Sense or nonsense, Molly, they have found their *affadavit man*, their *knight of the post* ...'

The constable spat out the euphemisms with contempt and sank into a chair with a sigh.

'I can hardly believe this, Elias – just when things are moving in our favour. I was about to tell you of our new hope – our own witness ...'

'Ah! – so this is your meeting, is it? I see you've made ready. Am I about to encounter the gentleman?'

'That is the plan. Tom and Will are waiting upstairs, and we are expecting Sam Rivers to deliver him here shortly.'

She was standing stiffly, gazing at nothing. Elias beckoned her to sit down beside him:

'You mustn't despair, Molly. The charge against Mr Popham is vexatious, we know it is – and it will be proved so. This new witness of yours may make all the difference. You must tell me about him, and how you discovered him.'

'It is all thanks to Sam, who encountered him in Bridewell. He is the doorman of Vandernan's – or was until the raid. His name is Joe Travis ...'

Mrs Trotter looked at Elias, expecting his eyes to light up at the news. What she saw was something like bewilderment.

'Tell me you are jesting! ...'

Her look told him she wasn't.

'... But this is their knight of the post – Joe Travis! ... And you say the man is coming *here*? ...'

Widow Trotter was aghast, gripped by the chilling thought that Frank Popham's false accuser would soon be seated in one of these chairs – welcomed here among her friends ...

'... What game is the man playing, Molly?'

Her mind was reeling – it was hard to grasp what it all meant:

'I cannot believe this. Do you think Sam Rivers has been misled? He told Mr Lundy that Vandernan's has dismissed Travis and the man is now thirsting for revenge on the gaming-house, and Parham in particular ... That was the story. We are hoping to recruit him for our cause ...'

'I don't know, Molly. Perhaps he is playing two hands at once? ... Or has he decided to throw in his lot with the cabal? The dismissal could be a pretence.'

'Well, he must know of our connection with the Pophams – perhaps the offer to help us is a trap? ...'

After her experience of recent days she knew such double-dealing was all too plausible. Her heart sank, and with it a portion of her faith in humanity. In her mind's eye she saw a second Bob Leary – another chancer who was not what he seemed.

'Whatever the case, Molly, it doesn't bode well. There is some deception going on … It's clear I have to stay for your meeting … We must be careful what we say to him.'

'Yes, we need you here, Elias. Such a man could be dangerous.'

The arrival of Joe Travis didn't allay Widow Trotter's fears – quite the contrary. As Sam Rivers guided him into the parlour and made his introductions the uneasiness in the room was palpable. Tom and Will were trying to look welcoming, but after the constable's revelation they were searching the man's eyes for a hint of his intentions. Elias himself was unable to conceal a scowl, and silent questions were being asked by all of them. Travis glanced around him, sensing this was a commission of inquiry masquerading as a genial gathering. His features didn't lessen their apprehension – square-jawed and thick-boned, he was less scarred than Joel Harkins but appeared to be from the same stable – deep set, untrusting eyes, and a hunching of the shoulders added to an impression of guardedness. This was not a man naturally at ease.

But judgments are often better postponed, and it occurred to Widow Trotter that someone with the smell of Bridewell still in their nostrils deserved a suspended sentence. Coffee was poured and politely handed round while Will Lundy – always looking to strike the right note – recalled his arrival at Vandernan's the previous Sunday. He remembered the doorkeeper's wit and risked introducing the topic with wry humour:

'I don't know what I expected that evening, Mr Travis – but you were a most good-humoured *Cerberus* and made me feel welcome at once. The best-natured of watchdogs!'

It seemed to work, and there was the hint of a smile on the tight lips:

'You saw but one of my heads, Mr Lundy – I kept the other two for more troublesome customers …'

Widow Trotter glanced at Tom. The word *kept* had slipped out – an encouraging sign?

'And you had great trouble that night, Mr Travis. Mr Bristowe and I had the full story from Mr Lundy – you don't need to recall it for us. It must have been distressing, and not something you wish to dwell on.'

There was a hesitation. Sam Rivers jumped in:

'That's thoughtful of you, Mrs Trotter – but I assure you, Mr Travis and I have been talking of little else. Neither of us intends to let the matter rest … Indeed, we are here to join forces with you. I've told Joe what I know of the Bay-Tree militia and how Parham and his cronies are threatening your family, Mr Bristowe …'

Tom could hardly contain himself at this and kept his eyes fixed on the doorkeeper, looking for the slightest flinch. Sam continued:

'… Parham, Roscoe, Norreys – the whole gang – Parham especially! The man is an evil schemer and deserves to be called to account.'

Sam was certainly an eloquent mouthpiece, though they would have preferred to hear those sentiments from Travis himself. He was drinking his coffee in silence and gave a reflective nod. There was tension in the air.

Tom had every reason to resent the man's calmness and was doing his best to hold back from a confrontation. They needed his help. Accusation would surely come; but first the doorkeeper had to be encouraged to speak for himself:

'How long have you served Vandernan's, Mr Travis?' Tom asked.

The reply was terse:

'Ten years. Back in King Billy's time. It was a different place then.'

'Its Dutch character was strong, was it not?'

'It was a club for merchants and traders. But it became a gaming-house pretty soon ... And then the bankers and stockjobbers moved in. Parham and Norreys saw to that. They began using it for their friends.'

'You've been close to Lord Parham, Mr Travis? And a trusted servant of the place ...'

'If you mean I did a good job – yes. But trust works both ways ...'

He looked Tom full in the face.

'... You have to trust me, and – even more – I have to trust you ...'

He looked at the others. It was clear that Mr Travis had not come simply to help, but to bargain.

'... The killing of Mr Sturgis!'

Will responded immediately:

'Yes, Mr Travis, that is what concerns us. We are determined to see justice done.'

'And Joel Harkins is in custody, I understand. Do you build your hopes on that?'

Unease was growing in the room – it was becoming an interrogation, but not in the way they expected. Elias shifted in his chair:

'Mr Harkins is now charged with a serious theft, Mr Travis. It is clear that Milord Parham and Sir Charles Norreys have disowned him and are happy to see him hang. Now that *is* a serious breach of trust! A promissory note in his pocket – no doubt entrusted to him – has signed his death warrant.'

The doorman shook his head:

'So, it has come to this? Vandernan's throws its scraps to the hounds – anything to distract their pursuers. It is a clever trick in many ways ... But I think you believe theft may be the least of Joel Harkins's crimes. You suspect him for the murder, do you not? ...'

This was a turn they had not looked for. The doorkeeper was supremely well informed – or simply very astute.

'... But I have to tell you this ... Joel Harkins did not kill Mr Sturgis.'

Tom went cold. The words were spoken with such certainty. Was Travis sure of the man's innocence – did he know of another's guilt? It struck Tom that he might indeed believe Frank did the deed. This made him hesitate.

Will, however, spoke out:

'*Then who did?*'

The others were alarmed. Will was suddenly in court examining a witness – a dangerous all-or-nothing tactic in the parlour.

The question was met with silence. Travis reached for his coffee, and savoured it:

'Do you want an immediate answer? Or do you wish to hear the story?'

'Whichever will bring us to the truth.'

'Ah, the lawyer's assurance!'

Tom could take no more of this:

'There's only one story we want, Mr Travis! Why are you intending to swear in court that my cousin killed Sturgis? ... Can you deny it? Parham's affadavit man! It is you who speak with assurance. I don't know what tale you wish to tell – but if it is to accuse Frank ...'

'Mr Bristowe! This is why you need to hear me ...'

He noticed Tom's clenched fists.

'... Your anger is understandable – but the truth is in my *tale*, as you call it. I did a lot of thinking in Bridewell. Talking with Sam here I learned enough about recent events to confirm my contempt for Parham and his friends. Yes, His Lordship and I had been close – very close – which made it the worse betrayal.'

'That's a strong word to use, Mr Travis,' said Widow Trotter. 'But are you not serving his ends in this?'

'The contrary! ... You need to know that mine was a twofold dismissal: Sir Charles was furious and demanded it – a doorkeeper who didn't keep the door! – but Parham was determined to be rid of me for another reason – a more politic one. The day after the killing he had pressed me to swear I had seen Mr Popham that night outside Vandernan's with his sword drawn. The vast sum of a hundred pounds was promised ... He spoke persuasively, and said that Joel Harkins would confirm it – that Harkins had seen the whole thing, but as a witness in court he would be immediately suspect, given his *unofficial* activities in Vandernan's ...'

'As Parham's bully, you mean?'

'Yes, Mr Lundy. You catch my drift ... Harkins swore the truth of it to me. But I kept my own counsel ... I have long known him, and he's a wheedling, dangerous piece of work – not to be trusted. And so I said *no* – I refused to lie on oath.'

Elias's scowl was deepening:

'But Mr Popham has been charged on the expectation of your evidence. How can that be?'

'I told you I had been thinking hard in Bridewell – especially during the hemp-beating. Every blow of my hammer was a determination – driving home the thought how I could turn the tables with Parham – play his game. I decided I could do it best by agreeing to be his witness. It would bring him close to me again – lower his guard ...'

Joe Travis now had an attentive audience.

'... It would be satisfying indeed to reverse the play. You should know that Harkins and I began as Parham's cubs – the two of us were his team in the early days – prize-fighting ...'

There was a hint of an old mischief in his look.

'... His Lordship followed the sport and had an eye for a boxer with a strong fist. The two of us fought for him and put many a guinea in his pocket at Moorfields and Hockley Hole, but especially when we fought each other at country fairs where we were not known. It was a profitable arrangement – the odds were always in Parham's favour ...'

'So it was later you became his bruisers at Vandernan's?' said Tom.

'Harkins, yes – but unlike him, I lost the taste for violence ... I had suffered bruises enough – though I could still buffet it, when needed.'

Widow Trotter couldn't stay silent:

'I have felt Harkins's own *buffeting* directly, Mr Travis, and carry the scar. Two nights ago I was near to being his victim myself ... And yet you insist he is not our killer. What makes you certain? What is it you know?'

The doorman was jolted by her revelation, which made the question a vital one:

'I don't absolve Harkins, Mrs Trotter. But you must hear me out ... I learned that he had been paid to persuade me to perjury – in full knowledge of the falsehood. Truth was, he had not seen Mr Popham that night. Harkins said little on the matter, but I knew him for a liar. He had been busy about the place when the murder took place. I was at the door and saw the comings and goings ... Well, I confronted him, and he became angry. I later learned he had Mr Popham's promissory note – part of his bargain with Parham no doubt. There is a secret between them. Both have a stake in Mr Popham being found guilty.'

Tom's spirits lifted:

'You mean, they share the guilt?'

'What I do know is there was a lot of confusion that night – but it's clear to me what happened – I know how George Sturgis died ...'

The simplest words – but they were enough to hold his audience in thrall. Was the curtain finally to be lifted?

'... It was the small hours, and the place had been quiet –

all the noise and company was down in the hazard-room. But things changed when Mr Sturgis made his appearance – he came out of the darkness ranting, and demanding to have it out with Parham. The man was spoiling for a fight – liquor'd as a mash-tub, scarce able to stand! I refused him entry, and soon there was all hell going on. He was crying plots and accusing His Lordship of treason – and worse. "Where's the sodomite?" he was crying. "I know everything, Parham! – all your schemes!" Parham had left the place ten minutes earlier or there would have been an almighty fight … Harkins was restraining him, and checking himself too – I think he was ready to administer a thrashing there and then …

'Sturgis was like a mad preacher threatening hell-fire, and Parham was in his sights. From what I heard of the charges there was quite a list, but little of it made sense. He saw plots everywhere – against the Duchess – against the Bank – and against Mr Popham. Conspiracy, treason, sodomy – all jumbled together. The fuse was hissing, the barrel was raised – but no Parham … After some ticklish minutes he was persuaded to take himself off before the Watch settled matters with their staves. Harkins saw him from the premises …'

Travis paused. The scene had been swiftly sketched, but they could see in caricature what dangers Sturgis had been provoking. Will winced at the picture of a man with a grudge all bundled up in resentments and frustrations. He had known such moments of wild accusation in court – always with a bad result. Sturgis had been a danger to himself – and not many minutes later, murder would silence him.

'But, the killing!' said Tom urgently. 'Did you see the killing?'

'I was not an eye-witness, Mr Bristowe. But what I *did* see …'

He broke off to finish his coffee, the others scarcely breathing. '… I thought the commotion was over – and indeed all was quiet again. But after a quarter hour or so His Lordship appeared and slipped back into the house – not a word to me – with Harkins close behind him. The two of them went to his office – some business to be transacted, I thought …'

Another pause, as if he was struggling to make sense of events. He was breathing faster, and hesitated.

Widow Trotter gave voice to their frustration, but did so quietly, prompting him:

'These are suspicions, Mr Travis – nothing more, unless …'

'There is more, Mrs Trotter. I saw more … The face I saw – Parham's face – he was flushed, with a haunted look. A doorkeeper has eagle eyes – he scans a body instantly, looking for anything irregular – it is a routine, done almost without thought – and I had scanned him … I saw blood on his sword.'

'Blood?'

'Yes – we notice such things.'

'But can you be certain of this?' asked Will, '– that it wasn't simply dirt?'

'It wasn't much – but I'm certain … What I do know is, when I saw him leave, his sword was clean – shining as new!'

There was silence while his audience took in the implications of this.

'You say he returned with Harkins? I take it he wore a sword too?'

'Yes, Mr Lundy. We wear them as uniform – but Harkins is no swordsman, I assure you. Harkins would have killed Sturgis with a single blow – not a thrust of the sword. That would not be his way. No, I know what I saw – and it can mean but one thing.'

Elias spoke:

'You said you'd had it out with Harkins – confronted him. Did you challenge him with that?'

'With the blood? No, not that, not directly. I thought it best to keep it to myself – dangerous knowledge! A lesson Mr Sturgis should have learned ... I simply asked Harkins what he'd been doing. He resented the curiosity but tried to brush it away – said he'd sent Sturgis packing, then popped into the Flagon to wet his whistle and had found Parham there ...'

Tom and Will glanced at each other – it was a scene they were trying to imagine – an unlikely one, but the idea lodged in their minds.

'... Of course, I didn't believe him for a moment – and he knew it. As I've said, I later discovered he had in his possession the note Mr Popham had made out to Vandernan's. I'm sure it was negotiated between them – Harkins's payment for keeping quiet! A fortune!'

'Mr Travis, you are making a serious allegation here – before an officer of the law. Such a statement cannot be ignored.'

'I do not wish it to be, Constable. I have not spoken of this to anyone, and I do so now, to you and the others, because I have come to a determination. Hearing about the charge against Mr Popham has made up my mind. I wish no innocent man to die ... And yet, the matter is not simple.

'I spoke of *negotiation*. Until this moment I have had two truths to offer you – contradictory ones. The first is the truth of what I saw – the evidence of a doorman's eyes. And the second *my* truth – the convenient testimony it would suit me to speak ... As you can see, this morning I have made my choice. But if my evidence is to have any weight, then it must find support. I am a solitary witness – a single pair of eyes. And to a jury they would be the eyes of a man who has been dismissed – someone with a lodged resentment against a peer of the realm. In court, my evidence would meet with scorn. That is why I have told you my *tale*, Mr Bristowe.'

Tom blushed slightly:

'You are seeking corroboration? ... but how can we give you that?'

He glanced at Will, who raised an eyebrow. Travis pressed on:

'There is a way, Mr Bristowe – and one that would confirm Parham's responsibility – prove that it was his sword, and his hand, that did the deed.'

'And this would involve us, Mr Travis? Is that what you intend?'

'Yes, Mr Cobb – notably yourself. The word of a constable – an officer of the law – is absolutely necessary.'

'But how can I supply it? I may believe your story – but that is not enough.'

'No – and that is why I have thought of a meeting – a surreptitious one – between Parham and myself. I have already sought one, to settle what my evidence shall be and how things may be set in train. If I am to step forward as a witness I shall need Lord Parham's instructions …'

Will was intrigued by this grim parody of the legal process – like an attorney and his client in Westminster Hall:

'And you need to have this meeting on record, of course – with Mr Cobb here as your witness.'

'Yes, Mr Lundy.'

Over recent months the Bay-Tree militia had made themselves expert in eavesdropping, and Will was already forming a picture:

'Do you have some arrangement in mind?'

There was a pause while the doorman looked around him – all eyes were asking the same question.

'The Flagon … I have proposed it as our rendezvous tonight. It is a suitably private place for delicate negotiations.'

Widow Trotter saw that Elias was looking distinctly uneasy as the plan began to be sketched out:

'But surely it is public – at least to a degree, is it not, Mr Travis?'

'Yes, but ...'

Travis, who had glimpsed the constable's mounting alarm, thought it best to tiptoe towards his idea.

'... The Flagon does have a private space – a room for hire by the hour – for more *discreet* meetings.'

Mary Trotter was unabashed but still doubtful:

'That's all very well, Mr Travis – but you need your assignation to be witnessed ...'

'That is done easily enough, Mrs Trotter. Mr Morson, the proprietor, aims to profit doubly from his clients – to let the room – and also let the little closet adjacent to it ... The closet is conveniently furnished, and the small spyhole nicely placed and well disguised by the wallpaper. Mr Morson expects to make more money from the closet than the chamber.'

Now all eyes had turned toward the constable, who at this moment was shifting uneasily in his chair and longing for a few minutes alone with his pipe. Elias knew the floor was his, but saw the difficulties at once. The proprieties of the thing troubled him:

'Such evidence would be valid and sufficient, Mr Travis, I concede. But for a constable testifying in a court of law – the method of gathering the evidence ...'

He stopped. He was finding it hard to complete the thought.

Will gave assistance:

'You need not say more, Mr Cobb. We understand your scruples and what a delicate matter this is ... But the witnessing of a crime or confession is not compromised by the means. A trap is a legitimate procedure if it exposes the truth. The ingenuity does not detract from the legality.'

Elias, for whom *delicacies* were a tricky matter, remained hesitant. This ploy was fine in theory – but in practice?

'But ... the character of the Flagon ...'

'You are mindful of your dignity, Mr Cobb – and properly

so,' said Tom. 'Yet would this not speak of your daring spirit – your enterprise in the detection of a crime?'

Elias looked at Widow Trotter, who smiled approvingly at the thought.

The constable came to a resolution. She could almost detect a twinkle in his eye:

'Do you understand what you are asking of me? ... But if this device is necessary to bring a murderer to justice, then ... so be it. I shall spy on your *tryst*, Mr Travis.'

Chapter Forty-Six

⚭

CONSTABLE COBB LOWERED himself onto the deep blue velvet and took stock of his position. It was certainly a comfortable one: the single-sided couch had a downy softness, and his thick legs stretched out languidly before him, the picture of patrician repose. Apart from an exquisite little side-table alongside, it was the only furniture in the cramped closet but enough for the customary purpose, and in normal circumstances he would have been relapsing into slumber within minutes; but a combination of fear and embarrassment gripped him. His mind was busy, and his first thought had been to flee.

He was conscious of the comic potential of the scene. All was set for an elegant farce of closets, spy-holes, concealed doorways, and the various ingenuities of a stage gulling. The 'arrangements' were ludicrous, and part of him was amused at the sheer luxury of aristocratic lewdness – the spurious ease of it, with everything served up and ready for the taking. It was a seductive style in every sense.

Down in the cellar the pot-house offered conveniences of a lower order – it was a rough affair, sawdust on the floor, a Smithfield smell and not the least gesture toward comfort. But that had its decorum too: the very sordidness of the setting was a licence for indulgence. So, in the Flagon all tastes were catered for: it had a dual character of high and low – ermine and vermin, as the saying went.

In his own little *cubiculum* Elias found he was perfectly positioned for the job in hand. He adjusted his eye to the spy-hole and through it took in what was a distinctly opulent scene. Against the far wall of the chamber, framed by fluted pilasters, was an oriental sofa upholstered in crimson plush, with splayed, nicely-turned legs, and over it, a large mirror was embraced by *putti* waving gilded fronds. Alongside, invitingly, a laquered tea-table held a pair of wine glasses and an opened bottle. The room was illuminated by an elaborate stand of candles – the clients must be expected soon? He shifted his eye slightly and was disconcerted to find the bed was immediately before him, unencumbered with curtains – no need for privacy here. But with an eye to practicality the right-hand wall was sheathed in folded drapes which added to the feel of luxury while helping muffle any excessive sound.

Elias was starting to sweat. He dreaded to think what the next hour would reveal and prayed the drama would be confined to verbal exchanges. His mind turned to the report he would be expected to give of this encounter, and at once he wished he had never taken the business on. Humiliation lay in wait. But he wanted to think there was an odd kind of heroism in it too – he should see himself as an adventurer, and remember the cause he served.

These contemplations were cut short by the sound of a door opening and a shuffling movement from the chamber. Immediately, as instructed, he extinguished the candle and held his breath. A sharp cough told him there would be no difficulty in hearing what was said, and when the figure came into sight he knew the view was more than adequate. He was in his own private theatre.

It was Joe Travis. Elias half expected him to walk over and wink at the spy-hole, but a second creak of the door told him that Lord Parham must have entered too. Indeed they were in mid-conversation:

'So, how much do they *know?* …'

It was Parham's voice, brisk, holding back anger.

Elias was surprised. He had anticipated a more tentative encounter, but this was a man ready for business … and as for the question – it was an extremely alarming one.

Parham took the bottle in his hand and began pouring the wine.

'… You said you would have something to report – well, let me hear it.'

Travis had his back to the spy-hole, but Elias heard the reply well enough:

'Harkins is suspected – they are pinning their hopes on that.'

'Good, yes – as I thought. His arrest changes the game somewhat … I think a new plan may be called for … Take off your coat …'

There was silence while Travis disrobed. Lord Parham presented the second glass to him and smiled. For a moment the tone changed:

'… I'm glad you have come to see sense, Travis. These past days have been awkward ones – for us both. Bridewell was an unfortunate interlude …'

He swung round, and his eyes took in the whole room, sweeping slowly past the spy-hole. Elias felt his mouth dry – he was near to coughing.

'… But what about that fellow Cobb – the one who arrested Harkins? Is he done interfering?'

'The man is a busybody right enough. His friends at the Bay-Tree have set him on.'

'Ah the Bay-Tree, yes – the *Honourable* Mr Popham's friends! The young man has allies – and they have been active … And that damn'd troublemaker his father – word is, it was he who turn'd Her Grace against us. Mr Maynwaring is convinced of it.'

It dawned on Elias that these two were confederates – or had been. Joe Travis must be playing a skilful game here? – he trusted that was so. Surely they hadn't been misled? The men's contempt was certainly convincing. He was hearing the genuine voice of the Vandernan's cabal.

Lord Parham drained off his glass:

'Why do you stand there? I didn't intend you to stop with your coat.'

He began unstrapping his sword.

'We have things to discuss, my Lord. You said so yourself. The plan needs to change.'

'That can wait, Travis …'

'No – I need to know now – if I'm to change my story. This has to be settled. We must discuss it.'

Parham eyed the doorman suspiciously:

'*Discuss?* Have you come here to *confer* with me? To *canvas my thoughts?* Perhaps you wish us to *reconsider* matters?'

The tone had become sarcastic. Travis responded:

'You know I'm prepared to testify … I have dismissed my scruples, and place myself in your hands …'

'Exactly so.'

Parham put down his glass and began loosening his cuffs.

'… But, as you say, this business with Harkins changes things. I have an idea, my Lord …'

Parham paused and narrowed his eyes. The doorman was presuming a great deal.

'An *idea?* Well, well! – you must permit me to share it. You seem remarkably anxious to resolve matters. Perhaps you should tell me your thoughts on the Sturgis affair at length – and then we can take some tea …'

Elias was scarcely breathing. He tried not to blink (another part of Mr Morson's strict instructions). This made the scene even more intense. He had already decided Parham was an obnoxious character.

Joe Travis persisted:

'Do you confirm my payment – one hundred pounds? The account has to be settled before the trial comes on ...'

'So, Travis – you wish to negotiate with me? I would advise caution ...'

He gave a dismissive flick of the hand.

'... Yes, the hundred is assured – and I shall not be ungenerous beyond that. I can make your life easier in other ways.'

'In that case, if you are buying my evidence – would it not be put to better use ... if I turned it against Harkins instead of Mr Popham? ...'

Travis was waiting for the outburst, but it didn't come. Lord Parham lifted his head and looked toward the ceiling, as if weighing the suggestion. Travis was emboldened:

'... You would still be protected – but conviction would surely be more certain, would it not, given what has happened? Harkins is in custody, charged with stealing the promissory note – Mr Popham's original note that Mr Sturgis thought had been destroyed ... What if I had seen Harkins challenge Mr Sturgis with it? ...'

Parham's interest was roused.

'... Offer to sell it back to him – for a considerable price? ...'

He paused. Parham's eyes were bright:

'Say more ... with what result? What did you *observe* next?'

'Anger of course – that the note had not been destroyed – that his friend Mr Popham was still under threat. Mr Sturgis was wildly drunk and tried to seize the note – there was a violent struggle ...'

Travis paused and left the vivid picture unfinished. Something almost of a smile was the response:

'There is something ingenious in this – over ingenious perhaps ... My concern is the dice – how do you explain the dice? Harkins's idea was to implicate Mr Popham with them.'

'Exactly – that remains the idea. If I said I *saw* Harkins place them in Mr Sturgis's mouth – that he did it to divert the blame from himself – rather than from you ...'

At this, Parham looked uneasy:

'Are you sure you would be believed? Could you carry it off?'

'Certainly – if I swore I heard it – *saw* it ... after all, I am no hired affadavit man, am I? I am the doorman of Vandernan's, who had followed Harkins and Sturgis out of the gaming-house ...'

The picture was filling out. His Lordship gave Travis a look that was part admiration – and part suspicion.'

'You have been thinking this over, haven't you? Imagining the scene for some time?'

'As soon as I heard of Harkins's arrest, yes – I thought it a surer way of saving your skin – of lifting you out of danger.'

The phrases chimed awkwardly. The implied accusation struck home.

'You are remarkably certain of my guilt, Travis. You take it for granted ... But I am prepared to indulge your fancy.'

'Of course, I will say nothing, my Lord – I have no intention of announcing what I truly saw ... and I do have an abiding loyalty to you – though in recent days you have sought to destroy it ...'

There was a tone of regret which suddenly turned the mood of the scene. Elias peered at Travis, who was now in profile, and saw a wide-eyed openness that spoke of sincerity. His admiration for the doorkeeper increased further.

'... You rejected your servant, my Lord – but he still has your interest at heart. I can remove the threat from you – decisively.'

Lord Parham looked doubtful:

'You speak of some certain knowledge – as if you know the very truth of the matter – a witness in deed ...'

This was a dangerous moment.

' ... Perhaps you do speak from genuine devotion – but is there not an accusation concealed in what you say? ... Would you dare to make some kind of allegation yourself?'

'No, no – I would not dream of such a thing ... But I have known the truth all along – that you killed him ... But I would never, *ever* say so. You can be sure of that ... I would be a fool even to hint at it. I would not be believed! ... That is why the story I am to tell must be made convincing – do you not see?'

Lord Parham's face was darkening. This whole conversation had veered onto treacherous ground. He was suddenly fearful, astonished. He moved closer:

'What did you see, Travis? What is this *truth* of yours?'

The two men were now only inches apart, but the doorkeeper stood his ground:

'I saw Sturgis's blood on your sword. No doubting it.'

Parham was shaking slightly – whether from anger or fear Elias couldn't determine. There was a moment of silence as Parham's thoughts began to re-order themselves:

'Was that *all* you saw – or was there more? You have a remarkable interest in the scene.'

'Only because I want to protect you, my Lord. I do not wish to see my patron go to the gallows!'

The dread word had been spoken. Travis was risking all ...

Lord Parham said nothing, but turned away and lifted off his wig, laying it over the arm of the couch. Elias was startled by what was revealed – a completely bald head glistening with sweat.

'So, Travis ... you offer to save me, while threatening to betray me ...'

'There is no such threat, my Lord.'

'Is there not? All I am hearing is an accusation.'

Parham was now removing his coat.

'The truth must be faced – or Harkins will seize that ground. Do you not see? Together we can protect you from his allegations – he is sure to accuse you – that is why we must deliver *him* to the Law, not Mr Popham ...'

Travis reached out and touched Lord Parham's arm.

'... Harkins will protest that it was you who ran Sturgis through – that he merely helped arrange the evidence – that you gave him the Vandernan's dice and ensured the torn note was left behind. *Is this not what happened?*'

There was a breathless pause.

'How can you know this, Travis? You were no witness. I cannot allow such a thought to be spoken! ... And yet, the true threat lies in what you do not say – that together you and Harkins can see me hang. Are you truly ready to offer your evidence against Harkins? ... Do you think to name your price? How can I trust you?'

Elias stifled a grunt of disgust. What a game was being played here! All this talk of *trust* – when the truth was twisting like a curtain in the wind. He shifted slightly on the couch.

Lord Parham looked around the room once more, only this time suspiciously:

'You are play-acting, Travis! This is no court-room. It is indeed a fine chamber – beautifully appointed for its purposes, for intimacies and revelations. But I did not come here to confess – and yet you appear to expect that of me.'

'You still cannot trust me, my Lord – after so many years! Why would I seek this meeting unless to help you when you needed it most? If I intended to bear witness to what I saw that night, I would have done so – to a magistrate. Can you not understand that? What is done is done. You must build from here.'

Parham, almost in relief, was caught up in the feeling of the moment:

'Yes – what I did – on a second's impulse – is done, and cannot be recalled ... but I was provoked to the limit ...'

Constable Cobb, whose neck was starting to ache, stopped breathing. Was this what he'd been waiting for? He pressed closer to the spy-hole.

'... I was returning to Vandernan's when I found Sturgis blocking my path. He had been thrown out of the place and was wild-eyed and furious – the man could hardly stand! Yet he held his sword firm against my chest and let out a stream of foul accusation against me and against Vandernan's. He would tell all! He would go to his cousin Heathcote the next morning and reveal everything – the *stinking conspiracy*, he called it. He had just learned of our plan to play the market with news of Marlbrough's death – our challenge to the almighty Heathcote! He would *reveal every trick*, he said ... But there was more ...'

Lord Parham hesitated and instinctively lowered his voice.

'... He would expose me as a sodomite. He said he had chased Mr LeRoy off in a panic – that he knew well enough what had existed between the two of us. "You and your catamites!" he shouted, and the words rang out. I expected windows to open at any moment. Of course it was the eloquence of the bottle, but ...

'I should have drawn on him there and then and fought him face to face – but I held my peace. He spat at me in contempt, sheathed his sword, and turned his back on me ...

'There was no-one observed it – except Harkins. He had followed Sturgis and hung back inside the arch of the alley watching the confrontation ... and it seems you have guessed the rest ... Our friend Harkins was very resourceful and thought more clearly than me. But of course, it placed me in his power ... And now you – you with your sharp doorman's eyes! Do you make the same play?'

Joe Travis said nothing. The scene had worked itself out, and he was uncertain what to do.

But Parham, as if a weight had lifted from him, did know. Travis, now with his back to the bed, found his shoulders gripped hard, and he was pushed down onto it, legs apart. Parham leaned over him and began unbuttoning the doorman's shirt.

Elias's eyes widened – and he blinked …

He shouldn't have done so. At that instant Lord Parham glanced up and saw the flicker. An eye, cunningly concealed in the pattern of the paper, was staring at him.

Behind the wall Elias choked. He swung off the couch, sending the side-table crashing to the ground.

In an instant Parham leapt back and reached for his sword.

'You bastard, Travis! This is all a trick! What have you done?'

There was a note of bafflement in his voice, but desperation too. Travis jumped from the bed as Parham made a rush at him. The sword's point scraped his arm and slashed a pillow.

Elias's shouts echoed beyond the wall and somewhere a door banged.

Parham was frantic:

'You lying dog!'

He gave another thrust, swift and direct. Travis made a boxer's feint and grabbed the arm, but the sword jerked, and in an instant the blade was hanging over his throat as the two of them fell onto the bed.

'I'll take you with me, Travis!'

With every ounce of his strength Travis clutched the blade and held it from his face. Parham pulled it to the side and sliced through the hand.

Travis gave a cry of agony:

'You're mad! *All's not done!* – don't you see? …'

The point of Parham's sword was now touching Travis's neck.

'... I can save you still! ...'

It was a last, desperate cry.

The blade trembled against his skin. Behind it he saw the terrified eyes glaring down on him.

There was a moment of hesitation – Parham had heard the words.

'... The truth can save you!'

But no response came. At that instant a floorboard creaked, and an oaken staff struck Parham's skull from behind. The body sank silently down in a heap.

Travis lay on the bed. Blood was pouring from his hand, and he was shaking. Unlike honest fists, swords had always frightened him – there was something cruel and dishonest about them.

Bob Turley dropped his staff and tore at the bedsheet:

'You're a lucky man!'

Seconds later Elias burst into the room, having negotiated the twisted passageways of the Flagon. What he saw told him the action was over. He paused for a moment to take in the picture: Joe Travis was propped on the edge of the bed, grimacing with pain while the watchman bound his hand tightly with the sheet – and at their feet was the body of Lord Parham, crumpled awkwardly on the floor, the eyes closed, the distorted face pressed into the Turkey carpet.

It resembled the final tableau of a tragedy, and certainly the scene that had just played out between the two men had been a riveting one; but Elias sensed he had witnessed only the culmination of a longer story of passions and jealousies. Who could say?

It looked like an ending, but the constable knew there was a larger drama still to resolve. Frank Popham was safe, thank God – at least from the charge of murder. As for Parham, the constable knelt down by the body and noticed the trickle of blood that was beginning to augment the carpet's glowing colours. Was all done with him? It would appear so – one way or another. From his secret vantage-point he had heard a convincing account of the fateful night, and they now had their killer. The evidence was clear ... But a *murder?* ... who could say how Justice would work itself through? Experience had taught him never to take the machinery of the Law for granted. And beyond that, tomorrow's grand gathering in Mercers' Hall would no doubt add its own complications, and then, on Monday, there was the draw for the lottery. Much remained to be settled ... Perhaps the Fates might yet have a say?

Saturday

30 October 1708

Chapter Forty-Seven

THE END OF the month – 'settling day', the day when terms expired and contracts were wound up – was always a busy one in 'Change Alley. Stocks could move feverishly, and the jobbers were wary of convulsions. On a day like this there was something physical about the market – its nervous system was at a stretch, its animal spirits excited by hopes of gain or a last-minute reprieve.

There had been no reprieve for Lord Parham. He had been unlucky – just an inch to one side and His Lordship would have been able to take his chance with a jury against a vengeful doorman and a peeping Tom. But the blow to the head had been decisive. Poor Bob Turley was deeply distressed by it, however much Constable Cobb insisted the watchman's intervention may have cost a life but had also saved one ... the loss and gain had been finely balanced.

In Jonathan's coffee house there were grim faces among the cabalists when the shocking report reached them, but as the minutes passed the concerns of the market took over. The grand plan of the Vandernan's cabal had been shattered by the Duchess's intervention, and when the intelligence of the Duke's death arrived – a little tardily – it was seen for the imposition it was. The malicious intent of the Dutch added to the swell of patriotic feeling. It seemed the great general had triumphed over both his enemies and his purported allies.

On this morning the cabalists were well represented in Exchange Alley. Besides Philip Roscoe and Sir Charles Norreys, both Sir John Simons and Dr Wakefield were in Jonathan's to keep an eye on their interests and see the working-out of at least part of their plan. It turned out to be a dramatic day for coal-gas stock, not least because the cabal poured ever greater funds into their play, looking to compensate with tumultuous gains. Their 'troops' among the jobbers had been busy. Options were being shuffled, and by late morning the strategy was maturing beyond their hopes.

In recent days the dazzling success of the coal-gas scheme had been cleverly managed and its rise exceptional. Now the cabal's 'puts' were in place, so that on this day a collapse of the stock would reap untold rewards. All their gains were transferred and ready for the slide. It was no coincidence that developments during the morning had played into their hands. The Duchess's broker, Roscoe, had been busy, and all her shares were sold. Moments later it was revealed that Her Majesty's holding had likewise been liquidated. In an instant, confidence evaporated and the scheme suddenly appeared to be less a feasible business than a will o'the wisp. The death blow came from a nicely-timed satirical broadsheet being cried outside the Exchange, which declared that knowledgeable opinion considered the project's claims fanciful and impractical – all gas and no substance. It was a disaster for the stock. There would be no way back.

And so, when the cabal made their way to Mercers' Hall for the grand assembly their faces were suppressing smiles and the mood was quietly confident. As for the occasion itself, the Prince Consort's death meant that the original plan for a formal banquet had been adjusted. A gathering that would have indulged itself in everything that was golden and glittering had been refashioned as a more sober affair. Official Court mourning would not begin until Monday, but with the Lord Mayor's Day celebrations cancelled, the City of London was concerned not to flaunt its pomp. Some restraint was in order. Instead of a grand banquet, it was decided that an extremely grand buffet would suffice.

The Bay-Tree contingent had readied themselves early. Tom was accoutred in his Popham suit, solemnised by his best ebony wig and a black waistcoat that Widow Trotter had retrieved from her late husband's wardrobe. The garment had been cleaned and taken in, but its sombre associations lingered. The pair's mood was unsettled after Elias had called in early with a mixed report – the joyful news of Frank's deliverance from the murder charge set against the grim business of Lord Parham's killing.

'A heavy price, Tom,' said Widow Trotter, '– but I suppose it saved His Lordship from the gallows.'

Their sense of relief, however, could not be disguised, and they were looking forward to sharing it with Lord Melksham, whose carriage would be arriving at two.

In her own preparations the patroness of the Bay-Tree had shunned finery, conscious of the melancholy undertone of the occasion and knowing that any display from her would appear presumptuous. The keynote was simplicity – her dark blue muslin gown shorn of its additional lace trimmings, a modest headpiece of woven silk, and her jet necklace.

Over in the Temple, Will Lundy's best Westminster Hall suit was serving the turn. With a slight shudder he took down his second-hand dress wig from the top of the cupboard, sniffed at it suspiciously, and put it to one side. It might be a grand occasion, but his own newly washed and brushed hair would have to suffice – that was the only display he needed. In him, cheeerfulness had begun to have the upper hand and he found himself whistling as he retrieved his sword – another item usually left undisturbed.

Earlier, a note had been sent over to the Temple, and Will was able to break the latest news to Sam Rivers as they walked together to Mercers' Hall:

'What are we to make of it, Sam? Is it a kind of justice, would you say? Parham killed as he was about to kill a second time?'

'More Fate than Justice, I'm inclined to think. Parham thought he could control everyone and everything – determine events. Such men always end badly. They are bent on mastering their Fate, and it consumes them. Don't meddle with it, I say! Far better to steer through the accidents of this world and try to make the best of things – in the end it's a safer path.'

'Yes, his malice against Frank Popham was unrelenting.'

'Politics, Will!'

'True enough – Parham and Sir Charles were in league with Maynwaring there. They were determined to bring down Frank's father.'

'Malice is the true word for it. Let's not mourn him. Think about Frank – he's a fortunate young fellow, and I trust has learned a valuable lesson.'

'Well, it's an awkward start to a political career. A cloud can hang over a man.'

'But what excellent training for the cockpit! You cannot carry your innocence into parliament – and there's a peg for your principles at the door.'

'Ever the cynic, Sam!'

'No, Will, a student of human nature.'

'Speaking of which, we'll be seeing the full pageant this afternoon. The Cits in all their glory. Your father presiding!'

'But not quite the glory there should have been. The Goldsmiths lost their chance to shine yesterday, and today the gold will be shrouded in black. But I don't expect the Mercers will weep at that.'

'The new Lord Mayor will be there, I hear.'

'Yes, it's in Duncombe's honour ... Now there's a man with a cloud – and a dark one too ...'

Will looked blank.

'... An infamous case. Sir Charles was impeached by parliament for appropriating public money. His friends in the Lords saved him – by a single vote! These things are not forgotten.'

'But no hindrance to eminence, Sam. I wonder if our Vandernan's bankers will be equally fortunate? My interview with your father was a shock to him – hearing about the cabal and what we suspect of their fraud on the funds. He's set on learning more, and today we look to lift the curtain on their plotting.'

'A fine plan it is, Will – and from what you tell me, you have the actors assembled – Mrs Trotter among their number! I'm sure she'll steer through it all with her customary grace.'

'But as matters stand she is like to be the cabal's chief victim. She has surrendered the freehold of the Bay-Tree.'

'No! I hadn't heard – lost her business?'

'Signed away to the Sword Blade. Things are suddenly precarious. But somehow she keeps her spirits up. I can see no way out for her.'

'Well, who knows what accounts will be paid today? – it's settling-day, remember. Our City friends will have one ear to the goings-on in 'Change Alley. There may be some anxious faces.'

'Yes, with their grand plan in ruins they'll be looking to salvage what they can ... I only hope your father will be convinced by our evidence – we have witnesses enough.'

Sam suddenly pointed ahead to a couple of figures about to enter the grand doorway of Mercers' Hall:

'And look who's there, Will – two of our cabalists! You encountered them in Vandernan's taking their pay from Captain Hazard.'

'So I did. The Hockley Hole gamester – and Dr Convex. Unmistakeable!'

Sam Rivers laughed:

'Have a care, Will. In the hall they will be Sir John Simons and Dr Wakefield. The money-men deserve your respect! Remember, the City is a place where wealth is held in great credit – and your credit is your wealth. Here it is not sunk in land but grows with the funds. It is *cent per cent* that counts. A *zero* adds hugely to a man's reputation!'

Now in a sportive humour, the two of them turned under the entrance arch and began making their way up a handsome broad staircase of dark oak. Will was usually confident enough in public places (and none was more public than Westminster Hall), but when he walked into the grand space his pulse quickened.

Mercers' Hall didn't match Westminster for scale, but on this occasion it compensated by the atmosphere of wealth and dignity it breathed. He scanned the gathering and to his embarrassment saw it was a veritable sea of lofty wigs, all bobbing together in groups, interspersed here and there with the gowns of ladies. Unlike Tom and the Pophams, he was not acquainted with Kensington or St James's, but he knew at once that this was the Court of Mammon. There were certainly courtiers enough, and over to the right was an impressive gentleman in robes of office attended by some of the guests. His scarlet and furs set him apart as did the resplendent gold chain that hung heavy from his neck.

'That's our new Lord Mayor,' whispered Sam. 'Sir Charles Duncombe.'

Will suddenly felt like a shabby intruder, and a half-naked one too! Smell or no smell, he should have donned his old wig. A generous spattering of ambergris oil, and he could have held his own against anyone in the room.

In the midst of it all was Alderman Rivers, the host of the occasion, who was occupied in greeting his guests, briefly interrupting their progress towards the table of drinks. These were in lavish supply. But other long tables at the side of the room were sparsely provisioned – practically empty. No rich banquet this, but distinctly frugal commons! – little more than a scattering of nuts and biscuits, so far as Will could see. His face fell:

'I've brought an appetite with me, Sam. Don't tell me we are to be sent empty away?'

Uneasy glances from some of the other guests carried the same thought – that condolence for the dead prince was in danger of being stretched too far. But Sam was reassuring:

'Sympathy in grief, Will ... but I suspect our mourning will be of short duration once the Cits have done with the solemnity – dad will have seen to it. The hungry will be filled with good things!'

'Indeed they shall, you rogue! ...'

It was Sam's father. He grinned at his reprobate son and gave Will a nod.

'... Be assured the tables will be groaning when the time is right. We are determined to have a banquet in all but name ...'

In an instant the aldermanic brows darkened. He turned to Will's ear, lowering his voice:

'... I am glad to see you again, Mr Lundy. I have things to tell you – and you in turn have more news, I hope? Your friends will be here soon?'

'We shall gather our witnesses together, Sir.'

'Good! This is a difficult moment – a day of great danger. I have taken soundings, and your suspicions have only been confirmed ... The crisis has arrived, Mr Lundy – but more of that later ...'

Alderman Rivers turned and surveyed the lofty hall.

'… What a convocation we are – all the might of the City in one body! Everything appears worthy and substantial, does it not? – yet how fragile it is – how precarious the credit by which we thrive … There are cheats and scoundrels among us!'

He went silent. Will detected a shudder of contempt – or was it fear?

Sam's attention was caught by an especially substantial figure conferring with two of the larger wigs:

'I see Sir Gilbert Heathcote is looking grave, father.'

'And with good reason – I have consulted with him! He will have a part to play in our scene … But you must be patient a while longer. Once the tables are plenteously supplied and our guests have received their rations we shall slip away to my study and thresh out the truth.'

Will and Sam moved further into the room, reassured that some kind of confrontation was promised but also apprehensive of how it would all work out. Was the reputation of the City so vulnerable, its finances so insecure? Much of the institution's power came from confidence – a fragile underpinning at best – and if that were lost what kind of collapse might follow? … These were dispiriting thoughts.

At that moment three newly-arrived guests were in a more sanguine mood as they hesitated at the threshold and took their first view of the hall. Widow Trotter was smiling as she surveyed the tall dress-wigs along the skyline. The scene at Custom House Quay somehow came to mind:

'A lot of stately vessels, Tom – and some fine rigging! Do you recognise anyone?'

Tom did, and instantly felt a chilling touch as he recalled the task they were facing:

'Yes – that's Sir Charles Norreys over there to the right, in a huddle with Philip Roscoe, the squat gentleman in the purple coat.'

'Sir Charles? Oh goodness – yes, I recall his brief visit to the Bay-Tree! … and that's Roscoe, is it? I must say he looks distinctly *imperial* – a touch of silver too! I thought Will said he was a plain, no nonsense worsted character?'

'Not in this place, clearly. Perhaps he's letting his ambitions show.'

'Does he not bid to be the next Chairman of the Bank?'

Lord Melksham stepped forward and smiled in his turn:

'Indeed, Mrs Trotter – and if you want to see a true prize fight you would do worse that bring him head to head with that jowly gentleman who is scowling across the room at him. Sir Gilbert Heathcote!'

'There you have it,' said Tom. 'Heathcote and Roscoe. Two contenders for the crown. Shakespeare might have made something of this!'

'You say right,' said Lord Melksham. 'You see before you the grand cause of our drama – the warring parties of the Bank in the flesh. Faction and murder, vaulting ambition and unscrupulous plotting – our play has it all, does it not? And what violence and tragedy have sprung from it? A contention indeed!'

'The Vandernan's pair are looking exceedingly pleased with themselves.'

'Information from 'Change Alley perhaps?' said Widow Trotter. 'Look, there's two more of them!'

Sir John Simons and Joshua Wakefield joined the group, and whatever news they brought appeared to add to the complacency that played across their faces.

'So much for Lord Parham,' said Tom. 'No dropping eyes here! I think their minds are set on other matters.'

'This is a theatre, Tom – audience and actors caught up together. Are we ready to play our own part, gentlemen?'

There was no time to reply. Their host was bearing down on them, hands extended in greeting. After the introductions

Alderman Rivers confirmed his plan for a conference in his study once the formalities had been attended to:

'I have heard of your exploits, Mrs Trotter – you and your friends. Sam tells me the Bay-Tree is a veritable *bureau* of inquiry and investigation. I look forward to gathering you together ...'

His smile sank a little.

'... I have to say, playing the genial host is difficult today. I am training my face into good cheer but the muscles are beginning to ache. We are holding off an almighty scandal ...'

He allowed himself a little sigh before the cheeks lifted again.

'... Mr Lundy and my son have already arrived. No doubt you will want to congregate? Meanwhile, I must offer a formal welcome to our guest of honour and then summon the magic banquet ...'

He caught Mrs Trotter's glance.

'... We *Mercers* know how to do these things! It will be like the old court masques ... There will be no need to provision yourselves – I shall have a platter sent to my study.'

And with that he turned in the direction of Sir Charles Duncombe, now positively garlanded with well-wishers.

'Well,' said Tom, 'we may have missed the parade, but it seems we are to be given a show ourselves.'

Lord Melksham was impressed:

'This will be an informed committee, Mrs Trotter.'

'I'm taken with our host – a most businesslike gentleman! We must gather our party together, my Lord. We have to find Michael Henriques and Mr Levy. Perhaps they are with the others ... And Lady Norreys also. I very much want her to be there ...'

Alderman Rivers's speech of welcome was a nicely calculated performance. A solemn opening allowed precedence to the late

Prince George, to whom he paid twin tribute – as the faithful consort to Her Majesty, and as Lord High Admiral *thanks to whom our navy continues to be Great Britain's pride! ...* Given the disaster of the French blockade, this rhetorical licence brought suppressed smiles throughout the hall and an audible rustling of wigs. But when he called for a minute of silence they dutifully nodded in unison. Will, who was always amused by ritual, looked around the room and imagined a congregation sleeping through a tedious sermon.

A polite pattering of applause drew the solemnity to a close.

Then at once, as if to banish the forces of doubt and despair, their host declared that they also had something to celebrate. If the City of London had been robbed of its day of triumph, they might on this occasion be allowed a small degree of festivity to assert the City's eminence in the nation's affairs and remind themselves of *the duties and responsibilities this trust carries with it.*

The sentiment was congenial and elicited warm growls of approval. Then, judging his moment perfectly, this civic Prospero raised his hands and called upon *London herself* to give sanction to the occasion.

Instantly a trumpet rang out from the gallery, and all heads turned to see an apparition enter the hall. It was a female form garbed in silver and bearing a lofty turreted headpiece complete with battlements and miniature union flag. Given this weight of symbolism, the figure negotiated her entrance with some trepidation, a hefty spear clutched in one hand and a shield bearing the red cross of St George in the other.

In language that laboured to match the vision, *London* offered welcome to the many distinguished guests *who have done so much to increase my wealth and guard my honour,* before she turned to pay relentless tribute to the new Lord Mayor. Duncombe beamed back at her and raised a glass as the scroll of his virtues unwound – his wisdom and munificence, his patriotism and public spirit, his nobility and probity, his almost divine charity; the Lord Mayor was a sun-like figure ready to *cast his radiant beams* on the City and *advance my glory* ...

It was exalted stuff, although the audience was a little distracted by the tendency of the city walls to lean with increasing precariousness. There was universal relief when the address came to an end with the fabric intact, though the sidelong tilt of London's head told them it had been a close call.

There was more masque-like ingenuity to follow. A tall gentleman in a golden robe entered, sporting an elaborate crown that wreathed his brow with a circle of radiant beams. The lyre clutched to his chest told them this was *Apollo*, bereft of his chariot and six horses but here performing heroically on two long legs.

'It's Elkanah Settle!' whispered Tom. 'He's going to have his moment of glory after all!'

And sure enough, the laureate of the pageant delivered his lines with a proud smile, giving Duncombe his approval and greeting him as a fellow deity:

> ... *Fill you your Seat, my Lord, as I fill mine.*
> *With wisdom govern, and with glory shine!*

Sympathetic cheers greeted Mr Settle, who bowed and moved aside to allow the final figure to enter and deliver her blessing. This was *Astraea*, the embodiment of Justice. She was a sparkling sight, garbed in a blue shift richly beset with imitation diamonds. On either side, two young boys carried a canopy over her head fringed with gold and surmounted by white and scarlet feathers. Astraea declared that Duncombe would be her guardian and they would rule together as one:

... My golden scales I offer as your own.
Justice and her great lord shall fill one throne!

And with that she presented her gift to a bemused Duncombe, who couldn't avoid offering an ambivalent picture – the Scales of Justice in one hand and a glass of claret in the other.

And now, not before time, the banquet was borne in, dish after glorious dish, all applauded spontaneously by the company. Everything from turkeys and shoulders of mutton to capons, ox-tongues, pheasants and larks. A waft of exotic spices tickled the nostrils, and eyes darted everywhere. Interspersed along the tables were silver chargers piled high with salmagundi, salads and savoury creams, garnished with lettuces and coloured eggs. And in the very centre of the hall, a table was set up for sweet things: various fruit creams, blancmanges and syllabubs, all arranged around the central feature – a handsome model of the Tower of London executed in sugar-work and marzipan.

As the feast materialised Tom and Will were open-mouthed, while Widow Trotter couldn't conceal an ironic smile:

'Well, gentlemen, the City of London pays tribute to its new monarch! In this place Royalty is overmatched, is it not?'

'Especially at a time of national grief,' said Tom. 'It's good to know the Cits continue to be well provided for.'

'Plump and well stuffed!' said Will.

'The turkeys also,' added Tom. 'Fine birds all! ...'

He was watching Roscoe and his circle, who were whispering between themselves as they surveyed the wealth of provisions.

'... I see our cabalists are in celebratory mood – all smiles and good cheer.'

'That's ominous,' said Widow Trotter. 'They most certainly know something we don't ... But we must resist temptation and gather ourselves together. We have our own little party to attend. We have things to tell – and to learn...'

It took but a few minutes for Mercers' Hall to become thoroughly bustling. With no place-settings the guests were free to dart hither and thither along the buffets in search of delicacies, manoeuvring round one another, arms and elbows reaching out, wigs dangling over the food. It was not the most orderly of gatherings. Individual plates had been provided, along with ingenious tools combining a fork at one end and a spoon at the other, so that diners could stab and ladle to their heart's content. Every palate was catered for, and choice morsels offered themselves from every direction. The bounty was all for their enjoyment! Conversation rose and fell; murmurings of pleasure and exclamations of delight alternated with the slurping of cream and the crunching of larks. The City fathers and their train were in the mood to celebrate.

Yet there was an element of unease creeping in: the pleasures of one dish were immediately forgotten at the prospect of another, and the very plenitude was frustrating – being able to have anything, yet not have all. Human appetite excited, but it limited too. Perhaps there could never be enough ...

Chapter Forty-Eight

⟨≈≈⟩

WHILE THE HALL seethed with indulgence, the mood in Alderman Rivers's study was one of apprehension and unease. The sound of the feeding throng could be heard beyond the wainscotting, which made the stillness more striking. As people took their seats no-one spoke, but from every face it was clear that unsettling news was ready to break and stories were waiting to be told. Michael Henriques had a haunted look, and Lady Norreys glanced anxiously toward Widow Trotter, who in turn was frowning into thin air as she tried to order her thoughts. The other young men felt the formality and ceased their talk. Only Lord Melksham appeared enlivened by curiosity, looking around at the silverware and items of company regalia on display. The platter of food on the table before them spoke of business rather than pleasure.

Alderman Rivers had his coroner's face on, as if preparing for an inquest – which given the circumstances was fitting enough. He had just been told of the death of Lord Parham in the molly house, and he began with that chilling news. Its sordid character troubled him, but he was more concerned that it might somehow be connected to the Vandernan's conspiracy and Parham's recent activities.

As she listened, Widow Trotter realised there was a great deal more he needed to know. She could either reveal the truth gently or let it explode in his face. She chose the latter:

'The dubious character of the Flagon is the least of it, Mr Rivers. His Lordship died at the moment *when he was about to kill for the second time* ...'

She chose her words for maximum effect and allowed the alderman to register the full horror of the idea:

'Kill? ... the *second* time? What can you mean?'

'It is a terrible story, Mr Rivers, and you need to know the whole of it ... Lord Parham killed George Sturgis – and he himself died intending to make another man hang for it. The assignation in the Flagon was to settle the arrangements. Frank Popham was to take the blame ...'

This was a lot to take in, and not only for Alderman Rivers. Lady Norreys and Michael Henriques looked at each other in astonishment.

'Terrible indeed! – you must tell it all, Mrs Trotter. Do not spare us. This is a revelation, but it answers to what I have begun to discover of the Vandernan's machine. It perverts trust and equity, and without those, we in the City are in a parlous state. Every valuation is doubtful. No contract is free of suspicion. Without trust we cannot conduct our business.'

And so, the full circumstances of Sturgis's killing were told: Parham's confession to Joe Travis, and Constable Cobb's witnessing of the drama. The climax came with the Marlborough plot and how it had been designed to cause a convulsion in the market.

'So, that too was spawned around the hazard tables at Vandernan's! – I should have known. This is vital intelligence, Mrs Trotter. And the Dutch connection is most alarming ... We came close to a collapse of the market, did we not?'

Lord Melksham stirred:

'Yes, Mr Rivers – and Sturgis was about to expose the conspiracy. His devotion to the Duchess made the plan abhorrent to him. But Parham could not afford to let it fail – they were so near to achieving their goal. Had Mrs Trotter not discovered the secret at the Wharf, and my nephew here not conveyed it to me, then the false news would have suceeded. Our chain of intelligence held – but it was a close-run thing! At the eleventh hour the Duchess played her part.'

'I rejoice to hear that George Sturgis set himself against it. In spite of all, he had a conscience about such things ...'

Michael Henriques, who had to this point maintained a glum silence, was forced to interrupt:

'Ha! Easily said! – If he had a conscience, then he wore it lightly. Believe me, my father and I learned that to our cost! Sturgis was part of the Vandernan's machine and happy enough to do their work – twist our arms and threaten us with ruin if we did not co-operate ... and he was near to succeeding ...'

Michael spoke of his entanglement with Sturgis and how the cabal preyed on businesses and manipulated them for their own ends – a picture of trickery and exploitation that Alderman Rivers was coming to understand all too well. He shook his head:

'Alas, this tallies to what I have been hearing. I do not exempt Mr Sturgis from blame, I assure you! Such men move from the gaming-tables to the stocks with ease. It is all play to them – a sport without rules, and the Law washes its hands! ... But the Vandernan's cabal has even bigger ambitions. They have entangled themselves in matters of national importance. Four days ago I had an instructive talk with Mr Lundy ...'

He acknowledged Will with a respectful nod.

'... And what he told me of your investigations, Mrs Trotter, set me on a trail that has led to some disturbing discoveries ... Vandernan's is no small operation – indeed they extend their reach into the very heart of the City. They are a faction, yes – but one that aspires to much more. Their ambition is to seize control of the Bank of England itself …'

These were dramatic words. But as Rivers drew the evidence together, an all-too convincing picture began to form.

'… These men are a tightly-knit association. They understand how the system can be made to favour them if they work together. We know how money breeds money, and how its mechanisms can be manipulated. But these people make this a science. They are a corporation in themselves – an exchange within the exchange …'

'You mean that Vandernan's aspires to be another Jonathan's?'

Widow Trotter's question drew a shake of the head:

'No, this is more secretive – a kind of Freemasonry. We think of Jonathan's and Garraway's as lawless places, and indeed they are. The principle of the Vandernan's cabal is that this anarchy can be turned to advantage by a group which operates by *rule* and discovers the laws that work unobserved within the system. Master those, and you master the system itself. You use others to forward your ends.'

This was an intricate idea, and a striking one. The brightness in his eyes told them he felt its force.

Will knew where this was leading:

'And these people look to become a power in the Bank. Through Philip Roscoe, no doubt?'

'Yes, Mr Lundy. Your suspicions of him have been borne out. Sir Gilbert Heathcote is aware of a faction within the Bank – Simons, Wakefield, and others, and how they are working in Roscoe's interest …'

'But, forgive me, Mr Rivers …'

It was Widow Trotter. She leaned forward, chair creaking, her hand pressed to the table.

'… Might it not be said that there are *two* factions in the Bank – and that Sir Gilbert himself has overmastering ambitions?'

There was an uncomfortable silence. The Alderman breathed deeply:

'Ah! ... You are not wrong, Mrs Trotter. There is doubtless ambition on both sides. But Sir Gilbert has the Bank's reputation at heart. That is why the machinations of the cabal have horrified him. The *lottery funds* ...'

Rivers stopped in his tracks, hesitant about introducing a topic that was fraught with danger. Lord Melksham siezed on the hiatus:

'Yes, I heard it whispered that the lottery funds have been used to underwrite part of the war loan – a quarter million of it – and that the Vandernan's people were responsible for pushing this through.'

Rivers saw he could not draw back:

'Alas, my Lord, this would apppear to be so. The Bank was alarmed at the Sword Blade's intervention ... Well, the Vandernan's people sniffed an opportunity to make money for themselves and their friends – to trump out the Sword Blade and assert their own power within the Bank. It was arranged quickly with little thought to the risk involved ... Only when the transaction was completed did they see the danger – that the credit of the City had been thrown into hazard. From what you tell me, the news of the Duke's death was part of the plan, and the coal-gas business was another game for them. These wretched people! How it has all come crashing down! I hear the gas stock has plummeted this morning!'

This was a topic close to Michael Henriques's heart, and he had been sunk into despondency at the latest news from 'Change Alley. Many good people would lose badly, and he felt partly responsible:

'Yes, Mr Rivers. All confidence in the project has gone ... but I assure you, this is the cabal's own game – and the most daring part of it. Their bull is now a bear! They have reversed the play and are about to garner rich rewards. This settling day will see them make their fortunes.'

It was a painful thought. Where was the justice in it? If only *Astraea* would bestir herself!

The mood was now decidedly gloomy, and Widow Trotter knew her next words would darken it further:

There is more you need to know, Mr Rivers ... My adventure down at the Wharf on Wednesday yielded something else. It will not bring you any comfort I fear ...'

She saw the alarm on his face but couldn't draw back. Calmly, almost unwillingly, she told him of her meeting with Bob Leary aboard the Groene Draeck – not the full story (Heaven forbid) but what she had learned about the chief purpose of his voyage – to carry a wealth of embarrassing revelations to Amsterdam – the deceptions and frauds, the names and the numbers – the sum of all he had discovered to the detriment of the City's credit and the reputation of the Bank. The implications were grave, and her final words struck home:

'... I fear Mr Leary is an accomplished spy, Mr Rivers. He has worked for the Dutch over many years ...'

A deep, pitiable groan came from their host:

'So, the Beurs will know every item of our folly ... Matters could hardly be worse! This is *treason!* ...'

The word brought a hush. Eyes shifted anxiously – no-one dared break the silence.

Then Rivers stirred himself and spoke again, quietly and with deliberation:

'... I have to tell you – some spying business has been suspected. Sir Gilbert Heathcote has become aware of it. I find he has had his own suspicions of Vandernan's activities ...'

There was another pause while he chose the right words.

'... Perhaps you know that Mr Sturgis was his relation ... well, it appears Sir Gilbert was able to draw on his cousin's knowledge of the gaming-house and what went on there – anything that touched on the interests of the Bank. In recent days he had been sent some disquieting reports ...'

This was one revelation too many! Tom could hold his peace no longer:

'Are you telling us Sturgis was Heathcote's agent in Vandernan's?'

Widow Trotter was confounded too:

'Was he not serving the cabal's ends? Surely, all the evidence ...'

Michael Henriques jumped in:

'Yes, it's impossible! The threats Sturgis made to us were real enough, believe me!'

Alderman Rivers felt his feet sinking in the mud:

'It is hard to say this, Mr Henriques, but the fact must be faced – it seems that George Sturgis was a servant with two masters. Vandernan's valued him for his links to Sir Gilbert – and *vice versa*.'

Lord Melksham couldn't be left out of the chorus. He joined his voice to theirs:

'Two masters – and one *mistress* also! He was very close to the Duchess, as events have shown.'

By this time Alderman Rivers was rather lost for words:

'It is a murky picture, I confess ... but Mr Sturgis's prime allegiance was to Sir Gilbert and Her Grace. Of that I've no doubt.'

'This does make some sense,' ventured Will. 'The Marlborough plot had been kept from him, and Leary's revelation that night must have been a terrible shock because it was something Sturgis ought to have known – absolutely diamond intelligence! At that instant he could no longer conceal where his loyalties lay ... Of course, being blind drunk didn't help matters.'

'Yes,' said Tom. 'The pretence fell away. A lot of pent-up anger must have burst from him – like a volcano!'

It was a dramatic image, and at that moment, as if in response, some shouts were heard coming from the hall – things were getting lively there.

'Can I speak, *gentlemen?*'

The words were delivered from over by the door, where Lady Norreys was seated. She had been listening intently to their conversation, intrigued by the revelations and the sense of foreboding that had settled over the room. It was a dark picture and an instructive one. She could only conclude that the City's system of money and power was running out of control. Yet it appeared to her a remarkably playful world: the jobbers and money-men were like children squabbling over a new toy and peevishly flinging it around the room.

'Of course, Lady Norreys!' said Alderman Rivers. 'Forgive us. I fear we have been wrestling with a difficult state of affairs – such entanglements!'

Lady Norreys knew all about entanglements, and she was not untouched by the antics of the Vandernan's cabal. But she knew his words were well meant and responded graciously:

'Whether it is out of delicacy or embarrassment I do not know – but none of you has spoken of my husband and the role he has played in this affair. As the Commissioner of Vandernan's he has of course been close to the centre of this web of corruption …'

She didn't mince her words, and they struck home.

'… I have lived with this plotting for too long. Of course I have not been privy to all the play-acting – but I have picked up enough to turn my stomach. To be dismissed and ignored can prove an advantage, gentlemen – a woman can listen and observe the comings and goings. Sir Charles's friends have always been polite but are inclined to be careless – and our footman

Alexander has sharp eyes and remarkably keen hearing … He is also an ally of mine …'

Suddenly the mood in the room was different.

'… Servants, as you know, are invisible, and I have made sure they regard me as someone who can be trusted with information – I am both discreet and generous …'

Alderman Rivers was looking at Lady Norreys with a degree of wonder, his mouth slightly ajar. Tom and Widow Trotter smiled at each other.

'… There have been meetings, surreptitious ones – at least in their eyes – and I can confirm all your suspicions. The plotting would seem to be very much as you have pictured it – an unedifying mixture of selfish greed and political manoeuvring. The political motive should not be forgotten. Arthur Maynwaring M.P. needs to be added to your roll call of conspirators – a man who breathes the air of party-plotting and who has been eager to use the Vandernan's cabal for his own advantage, particularly against Lord Melksham. My husband, I regret to say, is very taken with Maynwaring and has willingly co-operated …'

She turned to Lord Melksham, who at this point was hanging on her every word.

'… Mr Maynwaring's Whig masters have been fighting a war, have they not? But now their troops appear to be attacking each other! The enemy of course is Mr Harley and his darling project. Yes, we know the Sword Blade threatens the Bank's monopoly – but the challenge is surely one of principle – of doctrine even? – a Tory land bank countering the Whigs' floating paper! … Would you not agree?'

Lady Norreys paused, aware that a woman talking politics was an exotic species. Lord Melksham cheerfully nodded. Alderman Rivers was impressed:

'You put the matter very clearly, my Lady.'

'The Bank and Vandernan's – Heathcote and Roscoe – ought to be allies, and yet these men are hammer and tongs against each other. The Tories have lost the battle and their troops have departed – but the fighting is as intense as ever. The City has to take a stand, Mr Rivers. The Vandernan's cabal must be exposed and punished ... Its poison cannot be allowed to spread any further! It is sapping the strength of the nation ...'

She stopped in her tracks, aware that her confidence may have taken her a step too far.

'... Forgive me, Mr Rivers – I do you the credit of speaking my mind! ... But do you not agree this madness has to end?'

The apologetic turn was rhetorical, of course – a compliment dressed as a rebuke – and at this moment its effect was decisive.

'My lady, you express what I think all of us in this room believe. *England and St George*, eh? ... Well, I shall try to do my part.'

Another shout was heard. Their host looked apprehensive, but remained polite as he rose and gestured toward the door.

'I think we should hurry. Thank you all for your deliberations. It has been a most instructive meeting. I have learned a great deal and have come to a resolution ... We must now return to the *fray* – and judging by the mounting noise in the hall I think that word is the right one.'

Chapter Forty-Nine

⸻

Something had happened in the hall. As the group emerged from the Alderman's study they could tell the mood had changed. The sound was different – the polite hum had become a confused rumble; male voices were booming, and the air was troubled, with huddles forming and re-forming like an anxious crowd waiting for news. It felt as if a threatened storm had begun to break, and all the talk was now of finding shelter.

Widow Trotter allowed the men to stride off and join the hubbub while she hung back to appraise the scene. Lady Norreys was standing beside her, and the two women shared a moment of rueful contemplation:

'This is not a happy place, is it, Mrs Trotter? All is so very restless. Fear is never far away.'

'Yes, I sometimes think these City men take delight in turbulence. Is uncertainty not the very thing they seek? ... I confess a part of me finds it stimulating too. There is much greed and lazy privilege here, but also what possibilities for enterprise and endeavour! ... They have the resources to make things happen – to make things *better*. I tell myself these are fortunate people.'

A note of sadness had crept in, which turned thoughts of what might be into regrets for what might have been ... Lady

Norreys sensed it and knew she had to seize the nettle and tell Mary Trotter her sombre news. Delicacy and a degree of cowardice had held her back. But the thing could be postponed no longer ...

'Mrs Trotter ... I have not had the chance to express ...'

She hesitated, and the words petered out. The look on her face betrayed an anxiety of her own.

'... Damn it – what can I possibly say? I have heard about the Bay-Tree – that you have signed it over to the Sword Blade ...'

There seemed no gentle way to introduce the topic – but the words came out clumsily.

'... I had the news from my husband this morning, and I regret to say he was gloating over it ... You know how things stand between Sir Charles and me! The man has nothing to recommend him – especially when he takes pleasure in another's troubles – but there was some reason behind his malicious satisfaction ... Oh, Mrs Trotter, what can I say? ... He has purchased the Bay-Tree!'

The noise in the hall was considerable, so that Widow Trotter's involuntary cry was hardly audible. She was lost for words and a chill ran through her. An uncertain future had been facing her, but this was the very worst, beyond imagination. She was trying hard not to picture it ... She was frozen in a kind of reverie.

Lady Norreys was watching in dismay, feeling helpless and not knowing what she ought to say. But words came from somewhere:

'We must do something, Mrs Trotter! This cannot be allowed to proceed ...'

It was an involuntary determination, and none the weaker for that – but an instant later it had become a firm resolve.

'... He must be made to revoke the deal. There must be a way ...'

At this glimmer of possibility Widow Trotter found her voice:

'Has it been done out of malice, Lady Norreys? I cannot think of another motive.'

In truth, she was finding it hard to think of anything at all.

'Vandernan's, Mrs Trotter! He has plans, it seems. He sees the Bay-Tree as a joint establishment – the gaming house's reputable twin.'

'*What?* No!'

The audacity of this almost took her breath away. It was a monstrous idea, a travesty. A part of her found a grain of comfort in the very absurdity:

'... But, that would destroy *everything!*'

It was a shout of despair. Widow Trotter looked across the hall and her throat tightened – she could make out Sir Charles some way off, still huddled with Roscoe and their co-conspirators. A sudden anger took her, but she fought it back ... Lady Norreys was right. There must be a way if only they could find it. She had to collect her thoughts ...

In her own mental ferment she hadn't registered the increasing ferment in the hall. She now realised there was a general commotion. Lady Norreys was frowning at the scene:

'There is something amiss, Mrs Trotter – there truly is ...'

Before they could say more, at that moment a familiar voice rang out above the din:

'Mrs T! ...'

It was Tom, who had emerged from the press looking concerned, eager to tell them something. His wig was slightly askew, and behind him were the beginnings of what could almost be called a scuffle, with bodies shuffling awkwardly, hands gesticulating and voices raised.

'...The word is out! ... There's panic about the lottery – a rumour that the funds are unsafe. I could be back in 'Change Alley!'

Widow Trotter in turn was reminded of the Royal Exchange – but that place was ordered and quiet in comparison:

'Has Alderman Rivers made his move?'

'He's in close conference with Heathcote, who is scowling like thunder. People are taking note. The coal-gas news has unsettled them – and now the lottery ... This thing can't be contained any longer.'

Lady Norreys didn't need to ask what he meant:

'Yes – it truly is a *thing*, Tom, isn't it. Perhaps these people need to bruise their shins before they can understand – feel the pain of it?'

There was a note of disgust in her voice. Widow Trotter's attention was on the far side of the hall:

'I see the cabal are becoming involved ...'

She began to move forwards.

'... I think this is something we should observe, don't you?'

Suddenly there was a shout. A swirl of coats and wigs parted to reveal the almighty Sir Gilbert Heathcote striding over towards Philip Roscoe, who was shrugging off someone's arm and looking apprehensive at the approaching figure.

What happened next was a true confrontation – head to head, the two men outfacing each other. Physically it was an uneven match; but Roscoe stood his ground and was meeting Heathcote's accusations with a pacifying smile. This annoyed the great man even more – he was not ready to be reassured, let alone indulged like a child.

What had been a polite assembly was now a crowd offering commentary on the dispute. Other skirmishes were happening as arguments stirred into life. Around the hall it was a scene of confusion and indecorum. Women's voices too were ringing out as people fought to be heard. With such a thickening atmosphere of accusation and counter-charge it was hard to gain any details of the conflict, but the two protagonists were continuing to duel away – thankfully without swords, though their hands were poised over the hilts. Tom was picturing a pair of turkey-cocks puffing out their chest feathers at each other. They were on the brink of violence, words clashing blade on blade.

Voices in the hall began to subside as eyes turned toward the main dispute. People were straining to hear what was being said. With the general hubbub lessening, some words became audible:

'Yes – it *was* audacious! We acted boldly! And at that moment boldness was needed! ...'

Roscoe was pitching his own indignation directly against Heathcote's:

'... The Bank was sleeping! Over-confident! We had let the enemy regroup. Do you not see? We had to move surreptitiously, and apace ... *We would have lost the loan!*'

'You had no right to take matters into your hands, Roscoe! – It was against all form and process. The Board was not consulted!'

'Hah! The Board! ...'

Roscoe's shout rang out confidently.

'... You mean *yourself!* ... And indeed you were content enough with the result. Only now do you complain – eating sour grapes! You are anxious only for yourself, Heathcote – not for the City. It is *we* who had a care for that ...'

'Nonsense!'

'... All is now working out ... and this is what troubles you, I think? Someone has encroached on your estate – you cannot bear a rival near your throne!'

There was contempt in Roscoe's look. Heathcote was almost steaming as he fought his corner:

'*Appropriation*, Sir! Does that term mean nothing to you? You and your gang have made lottery funds your own ...'

'No – we have *invested* them – and to excellent effect, as you will soon see!'

'It is a *fraud*, Sir – nothing less! And it is you who have directed this adventure – your own *dis*honourable adventure – heedless of the risk. You are flirting with danger!'

'This is hypocrisy, Heathcote! You have pursued your own devious ventures many a time! Some of them not to be peered into. Tricks worse than this!'

Widow Trotter looked at her friends – it was as if this performance was for them alone. It confirmed their discoveries. Everything was pouring out – all the accumulated grudges and resentments – and in public too! It was foolhardy.

And now Sir Charles Norreys was intervening, his arm outstretched between the two men:

'The funds can cover it, Sir Gilbert ... the Coal-Gas will deliver. We shall have the resources ... it can all be *managed!*'

That placating word! – a word which always had a reassuring currency in the City. His tone was complacent, attempting to bring calm. Sir Gilbert was not appeased:

'But the lottery ...'

'The funds are secure. As I say – it is being managed.'

Heathcote, however, was far from finished and at once opened up another front:

'And the false news about the Duke? Another contrivance of yours, Roscoe – a contemptible one!'

'How dare you! What are you saying?'

'It was you and your gang. You cannot deny it. The truth has become known ...'

'What nonsense!'

'... You imperilled the nation, you and your Dutch friends. Deny it if you can! Parham was your plotter-in-chief – and what a noble sacrifice he has made for your cause! Dead in a molly-house brawl, by all accounts ...'

This was reckless. Heathcote was becoming unwary. His indignation had spilled over into contempt, and his words brought gasps around the hall. Roscoe, who had remained the cooler of the two, saw his chance. The bout had swung their way and he sensed the outrage in the room. He spoke solemnly:

'I do deny it, Sir. It is a foul accusation – beneath even you. I demand you withdraw it!'

His fingers closed round the hilt of his sword. Heathcote countered in similar fashion. Their sword-knots shook.

'Gentlemen! ...'

Alderman Rivers had had quite enough of this. The unseemly dispute was threatening to bring dishonour to the City, and the Mercers' company in particular.

'... There will be no fighting here! ...'

His words gained in authority from two broad-shouldered footmen who had moved close, ready to intervene.

'... You must cool yourselves. On every count the City of London is the aggrieved party here, and the Court of Common Council is the body best able to judge these matters. You can be sure I and my fellow Aldermen will inquire thoroughly. All wrongs shall be punished ...'

He had found himself in the role of judge, and surveyed the assembly with as much dignity as he could muster.

'... And Sir Gilbert assures me the Bank itself will investigate the business. The reputation of the City – the very credit of the nation – demands it. However successful your manoeuvres, Mr Roscoe, your methods need to be questioned ... There are more pieces to be put together, and Sir Gilbert and I shall make it our chief concern. It is important we sound the matter thoroughly ...'

He looked questioningly at Heathcote.

'... We must find some way to regulate these things – otherwise it is anarchy, and our institution will lose all respect!'

A warm murmur of assent came from the body of the hall. Somehow Rivers's declaration had caught the mood. Heathcote looked slightly uneasy at how things had developed but felt duty bound to nod his agreement. There was mounting relief all around. It seemed the dangerous rapids had been negotiated well enough for the time being – Vandernan's would face a reckoning in due course. Rivers was beginning to think the assembly would now calm itself and a degree of harmony be established.

It was a laudable hope – but it was not to be.

At that moment Widow Trotter and Tom were startled to see a familiar figure emerge from the crush and step forward onto the scene ... It was none other than Benjamin Levy! They had regretted his absence from their earlier meeting, and were now to discover what had detained him.

Levy stood still and looked around him. A hush descended. It appeared the drama was not yet concluded. Rivers turned in surprise, and his heart sank when he saw a face that carried its own silent message. It did not bode well.

'I hate to be the bearer of ill tidings, gentlemen ...'

Levy's countenance was wise, careworn. He knew the solemnity of what he had to say and felt it as a burden on his own shoulders.

'... There is something further you all need to know. It changes the picture greatly – and not for the better. My news is grim – but you cannot be shielded from it ...'

Levy was speaking quietly, and his words commanded absolute silence.

'... In recent days I have been conducting my own inquiries into Mr Broughton's coal-gas scheme. It has been a remarkable phenomenon, has it not? – a whizzing rocket illuminating the sky! The centre of so many expectations, with so much of hope – and of money – invested in it. And what a portent it has proved! ... I fear the adventure is over ...'

Spontaneous murmurs sounded from every direction. Roscoe was at once alarmed:

'What do you mean, Sir?'

Levy turned to face the room:

'Mr Broughton has disappeared – and he has left nothing behind him. The coal-gas project is no more. It is not that the stock has become worthless – *there is no stock – there is no project*. Everything connected with it – all contracts, all negotiated funds, options – all is mere paper. You may as well light your fires with them!'

'But …'

'There is nothing material – no goods or machinery, no assets to be realised – not even a wooden privy! And there is no patent! Naught of value can be salvaged from the wreck. All that remains is the idea – an excellent one, no doubt, and one whose time may come – but the thing has disappeared along with Mr Broughton. A projector to end all projectors, is he not!'

'But is he not being sought?'

'Oh yes – after a fashion. But the gentleman has slipped away. Shropshire cannot hold him! Perhaps England cannot either? He may be in Ireland – or at the Pole … Abraham Darby knows nothing of his whereabouts. It seems Broughton's scheme was an imposition on him from the beginning. Yes, the man aspired to be his collaborator – but there was no contracted agreement between them. Mr Darby's suspicions grew – and our projector vanished, along with the funds, before he could be sent packing. There is … *nothing!*'

There was silence in the hall as the implications sank in.

Roscoe, Norreys and the others froze like ghosts. This surely couldn't be happening? *Nothing?* The word continued to echo around the room.

'But we have contracted options …'

'I'm sure you have, Mr Roscoe, but there can be no further dealing in the stock – sale or purchase. The paper is utterly null and void …'

'No, no! This cannot be! …'

Suddenly there was movement.

'… We must to the alley at once! No! *This cannot be!*'

Above the noise in the hall came a cry of terror as Roscoe, flanked by Sir John Simons and Dr Wakefield, hurried half-running towards the door – only to find their way blocked. A signal had been given by Alderman Rivers:

'I would ask everyone to remain calm …'

His voice commanded the room.

'… We need to take advice on these developments. At this moment, any panic will simply start a fire that will be impossible to extinguish. For all our sakes, I urge you to remain in the hall until a course of action is decided. There shall be no running off to Jonathan's!'

The assembled dignitaries saw the sense in it, and a murmur of assent was heard. Those who knew about such things understood the significance of this catastrophe. Rumour had been vindicated: the lottery funds were not safe – far from it. And the draw was to be made on Monday! The whole nation was expectant. If the funds could not cover the prizes, there would be outrage and chaos … Minds were working this out and the implications became clearer.

Alderman Rivers was back consulting with Heathcote, both men in sombre deliberation like a pair of hanging judges. There was nodding and shaking of heads between them as they confronted the situation. Their fears had been entirely justified – but what to do? …

Widow Trotter, Tom, and Lady Norreys had been watching it all in silence, awestruck at how Nemesis seemed to be directing the scene. They longed to exchange thoughts – but as they continued to observe, something told them the drama was not yet over ...

Sir Charles Norreys had still not moved. He was a forlorn figure, standing alone, slightly stooped, staring at the floor, figuring to himself the enormity of his own plight – how much he personally was invested in the gas scheme and what the working-out of these events would mean for him. Disaster – nothing less! Violent curses were stifled under his breath ... Of course, the project had been sheer folly – a mad undertaking from the very start! But Sir Charles, who was not a man to indulge in self-reproach, directed his accusations elsewhere: his anger was levelled at the caprice of Fortune, his contempt at the gullibility of others, and his resentment at Mr Broughton's overwhelming success.

Lady Norreys was watching her husband closely. His face and figure were eloquent. He had always been a secretive man, but there was no disguising the play of passion now. The performance needed no words.

Widow Trotter had noticed him too:

'Sir Charles is suffering, I see. He has been hit hard by this.'

Lady Norreys touched her on the arm:

'There is something I must do.'

It was spoken with quiet determination, and she made her move across the hall. Widow Trotter and Tom looked on as she approached Sir Charles who was still held in a kind of trance.

He became aware of his wife standing there and flinched as if startled that someone wished to address him. His frown became more intense ... Not for the first time the hostess of the Bay-Tree longed to be an invisible spirit – if only she could fly over there and hear their conversation ...

She was spared this frustration by the return of Lord Melksham with Will and Sam, all eager to rehearse Mr Levy's Shakespearean entrance and the great confrontation between

Heathcote and Roscoe. Sam Rivers had enjoyed his father's performance:

'I must say my old man played a good hand, did he not? Judicial discipline! But he robbed us of some serious action. I was hoping for a duel, or at least a bout of fisticuffs. Heathcote and Roscoe – champions both! Now, wouldn't that have been something?'

'A new thing for Mercers' Hall, certainly,' said Will. 'But the lawyer in me is glad dignity prevailed. This whole business is not to be settled by a blow – there's a great deal to be remedied and a lot of healing to be done. What we have uncovered is a serious matter – one for the City fathers to settle.'

'That scene makes it more likely, don't you think?' said Tom. 'It was such a public display! There can be no *cabal* any more. Their secret is out, and the gang will be watched closely in future.'

Widow Trotter was rather less confident:

'Yes, Tom – but we must trust the City to take a stand. Your father will have to be bold, Mr Rivers. This will require some determination.'

'I think something is being determined as we speak,' said Will. 'Heathcote and the Alderman make a formidable alliance …'

The two great City men had withdrawn to Rivers's study and were evidently still deep in consultation …

Meanwhile, out of earshot, another scene was playing out at the far side of the hall, where Lady Norreys and her husband were exchanging words:

'*Ruined?*'

'Yes – we are ruined!'

'*We?*'

Just a single syllable, but it was unexpected. Sir Charles looked askance. Her expression unsettled him and he hesitated … there was no alarm in his wife's voice, and if he looked for sympathy he was going to be disappointed.

'What are you implying? …'

No elaboration came.

'… This damn'd project has sunk us – I am head over ears in it. When I say *ruin*, that is exactly what we face …'

'You have overspent, Charles. Always such confidence! … So, you have made your own play with the coal-gas? I'm disappointed in you. It was a stupid scheme from the beginning. Anyone with a solid understanding could have seen that – and I'm sure you did see it. You and your gang selected it for that very reason, did you not? – a stock that would bubble away like sparkling champagne, with nothing to weigh it down … And see where this has got you all! You thought you were masters of the game. You have played on others' folly without seeing your own!'

'Off you go again – the old tune! … as if you were averse to risk yourself!'

'True – but I am careful, Charles. I wait my moment – and I don't rely on the stupidity of others. The coal-gas has done well for me – very well indeed …'

'*What?* …'

The effect on her husband was electric.

'… *What have you been doing?*'

'I understood your plan from the beginning, Charles, and thought to benefit from it. I knew the Vandernan's cabal would push the stock as high as could be – but that was enough for me. I did not wish to pursue the game beyond good sense.'

Sir Charles, who was beginning to perspire, adjusted his wig, trying to comprehend what had happened:

'You bought … and sold?'

'Yes, Charles. That is the way with the stocks, is it not? …'

She couldn't disguise the sarcasm.

'… it is really very simple.'

'But … to make a great gain you must have had a great outlay. The money … ?'

'My pearls, Charles.'

'Your pearls? ... But ...'

'Yes – I pawned them, would you believe? A very superior pawn-broker – someone with Royal connections who was happy to receive them into their care ... And it gave me all the capital I needed ...'

By this time Sir Charles was dumbfounded. But somewhere a hint of relief was making itself felt.

'... Don't be alarmed. The pearls are back in my possession – along with a great deal of money – although strictly not *my* money, you understand ...'

'What do you mean?'

'I thought it best to make my brother my broker. It has all been done in Mr Sumner's name, and it is his bank account that has benefited – though I have the sole use of the funds of course ... I can do with them what I will.'

The meaning was clear: this was not money her husband could lay hold on. Sir Charles saw that his wife held a winning hand – but the look on her face and the slightly teasing tone in her voice suggested she might be willing to negotiate ...

There was still no word from Alderman Rivers, who remained ensconced with Heathcote in his study. Throughout the hall apprehensions were mounting, not least among Widow Trotter and her friends when she told them about the sale of the Bay-Tree. To become an outpost of Vandernan's! The idea was too dreadful to contemplate. She tried to reassure them that Lady Norreys thought something might be done, but the news was alarming ... All they could do was turn and observe Sir Charles and his wife in conversation and try to draw meaning from the minutest look and gesture. Certainly, something was being warmly debated ...

And then, suddenly, the bargaining was over. Lady Norreys was striding in their direction, leaving Sir Charles behind, stiff and frowning into space. As she came nearer they could detect a glow of satisfaction on her face, and when she spoke her voice had a confident ring to it:

'Well, Mrs Trotter. What can I tell you? ... After some brisk negotiation, a treaty has been agreed between Sir Charles and me. I have to say his position was exceedingly weak and he had little choice but to subscribe to my demands ... For my own part, I don't want a bankrupt husband – and so I agreed to come to his rescue ...'

With a degree of relish she told them of her adventure with the coal-gas stock and how greatly she had benefited from the investigations of the Bay-Tree militia.

'... Being privy to the Vandernan's plot gave me an advantage – a debt that I'm happy to repay, Mrs Trotter ... You will be pleased to hear that my husband has agreed that being proprietor of a chocolate house is not for him – especially now when he has not three farthings to his name. His debts will be called in, and *retrenchment* is the word of the hour. He is cancelling the purchase!'

Widow Trotter gave a cry of delight and was beginning to pour out her thanks when Lady Norreys stopped her:

'You must wait, Mrs Trotter – there's more ... I said *retrenchment* – a useful term that can involve a *pruning* – a cutting back of entanglements ...'

She had her audience gripped.

'... I was able to make my husband see that in recent months he had extended himself too recklessly – had taken on unnecessary responsibilities – I think *dirty dealings* was the phrase I employed ...'

Widow Trotter could believe it.

'... I helped him see that to divest himself of a few of them would help re-establish his credit, which at this moment is quite exploded ... With this end in view, he has agreed that one or two of Vandernan's more slippery bits of paper should be disposed of … Frank Popham's duplicate promissory notes in particular have become an embarrassment …'

By this point Mary Trotter was hardly breathing – and she was not alone.

'… I am pleased to report that Vandernan's intends to declare them no longer valid. Sir Charles will be happy to see what is left of them committed to the flames …'

A spontaeous *hurrah!* rang out from Lord Melksham and was greeted with relief all round. But Lady Norreys still had her serious face on:

'… But there is another promissory note that has been troubling me – one that has had some wild adventures, passing from hand to hand and becoming ever more soiled in the process …'

Will smiled at this.

'… My husband acknowledges that from the very beginning the note's circumstances were unfortunate. The thing was part of a sordid episode and has brought hurt and injustice to an innocent party …'

Lady Norreys couldn't prevent a broad grin from breaking out (throughout her report she had been finding it hard to sustain the judicial style).

'… I speak of your promissory note, Mrs Trotter – the crucial article of our treaty! … I am happy to say we had success there also. Be assured, an explanation to the Sword Blade will be given – they are your bank, I know. You can rest easy. The matter will be settled. Your mortgage arrangement will be cancelled. The freehold will again be yours.'

The simple phrases chimed like holiday bells. For Widow Trotter they were the sweetest music she had ever heard.

Her *thank you! – thank you!* brought smiles to everyone. Her whole body was animated by joy and it was hard to keep still.

Had the circumstances been less formal she would have resorted to dancing.

Thankfully perhaps, at that moment there was a general stir. The study door had opened and Alderman Rivers, followed by Sir Gilbert Heathcote, processed into the body of the hall. There was a marked solemnity to their gait, and when the two men positioned themselves side by side it was clear some form of announcement was to be made.

There they were, the Council and the Bank, shoulder to shoulder, closing ranks. There was no need for allegory – the meaning was perfectly clear: here were two sterling characters who would say what needed to be said. The City of London was ready to assert its authority.

A cautious Alderman Rivers thought it best to avoid any more direct accusations, especially with the Vandernan's contingent glaring at him so fiercely. Other faces in the hall were eloquent too – a mixture of hope and fear. In many minds there was just one question: was the lottery safe? Everyone knew that the fate of the *Honourable Adventure* would affect great numbers – not only the rich and the not-so-rich, eager to play for a fortune, but thousands more who saw their fraction of a ticket as the passport to a new life.

But others understood that more was at stake. Modern *honour* was a currency of uncertain denomination, easily claimed and readily traded. In the City of London, however, the principle ran deep. Honouring debts was the Golden Rule. But more fundamental still was *credit*, the arterial blood of the organism which allowed wealth to grow as if by magic. Value accumulated as it flowed, and to lose faith in it would expose the trick by which the financial system worked.

Alderman Rivers of the Mercers' Company knew the lottery was the public face of the City's operations and was quick to announce that the mounting fears were groundless. The

Honourable Adventure would be drawn on Monday as planned! The funds were available, and all prizes would be honoured.

Spontaneous cheers showed that many in the hall were relieved and satisfied ... but Rivers was not yet done. Alongside him, the imposing figure of Sir Gilbert Heathcote seemed to represent assurance, and the trace of a smile that played across his countenance wasn't quite enough to reveal the secret – that he had guaranteed the funds personally. Thanks to him, the Bank of England would avoid scandal, and Philip Roscoe and his cohort would be exposed for what they were – a subversive faction whose dark manoeuvrings had imperilled the institution. No announcement was needed – Heathcote knew that word of his self-effacing generosity would quickly spread. In his mind he was already rehearsing his role as saviour of the Bank. This was an exaggeration of course, but Heathcote's mind was a capacious one and always found room to accommodate his pretensions. At this moment the future Chairman of the Bank was radiating confidence and success.

Alderman Rivers raised an arm and swung round to encompass the whole audience. A hush fell. A speech was coming:

'Gentlemen – and ladies! We are gathered together on this auspicious day to celebrate the City of London – an ancient institution that thrives as never before! As this mighty metropolis grows in strength and influence, our new nation of *Great Britain* looks to extend its interests across the globe. Trade expands, and the Thames is increasingly a river for all mankind. With each tide the materials of every continent come to our shores and British ships carry our wares to all points of the compass. Here at home, our Royal Exchange is a universal mart, a temple to the glories of commerce; our livery companies guard the traditions and skills of every trade; and the Bank of England is the bulwark of the nation's credit ...'

Rivers acknowledged a beaming Heathcote at his elbow.

'… Never in the nation's history has there been such promise of future prosperity … … . But this new greatness brings with it new responsibilities …'

The words signalled a shift in tone. His look grew darker as he turned the coin to reveal its obverse image:

'… Here in this hall we have been given a warning, my friends – a reminder that our world of commerce has its darker side … I speak of the labyrinth of Exchange Alley and the activities pursued there …'

A slight shudder ran through the hall.

'… It ought to be the glory of our city – a place where enterprise and endeavour are supported, and where companies can spread their gains and bring prosperity to the land. What it must *not* become is a mere *gaming-house!* …'

Rivers almost spat out the words.

'… the mores of 'Change Alley are under attack from many quarters. We all know that *Jobbery* has become the insult of the hour – and I may say, not without cause! – and unless something is done, the very mechanism of trading in stocks may break down. This would be a disaster. It is clear that some *reform* is needed! …'

His voice had risen. Glances were being exchanged amongst his audience, who were undecided whether such an investigation should be encouraged.

'… I shall say nothing further on this occasion … but I can assure you that along with my friend Sir Gilbert Heathcote here, I intend to press for some inquiry to be made. The Bank of England and the Court of Common Council will find common cause in this, and any misdemeanours that are discovered will be punished …'

A sudden silence suggested that many of his hearers were recalling the fate of naughty schoolchildren.

' ... But, my friends, such considerations are not for this moment. Let us take pleasure in our society. Let us celebrate our past achievements and the glories that await us. I invite you all to continue to enjoy the Mercers' hospitality – there are further provisions to be sampled! Be light of heart and assured of the future! The City of London has ridden out many a storm in the past – has resisted fire and pestilence – and it shall do so again!'

The applause that followed was a token of relief as much as thanks. Standing together in the circle, the Bay-Tree platoon – Widow Trotter, Lord Melksham, Lady Norreys, Sam Rivers, Tom and Will – were momentaritly lost for words. They had heard a rousing speech which answered to the drama of recent days – and indeed had been prompted by their own discoveries. There was much to be proud of. As a group, they had achieved far more than they might have expected. The matter was no longer theirs, but it appeared to be in safe hands. Alderman Rivers had pronounced encouraging words, certainly ... they must hope his speech had been a prologue, not an epilogue ...

The audience began roaming the hall again in search of more wine and the new delicacies that were arriving. As Widow Trotter looked across to the far tables she caught sight of a figure who had been forgotten in the disturbance of the hour. Leaning against the buffet, a glass cradled in his hand, was the other Sir Charles. For all his finery he made a disconsolate figure, perhaps brooding on the thought that once again a day of mayoral triumph had become an anti-climax. Had the determinedly practical Duncombe been a man for symbols, he might have found a degree of reassurance – and perhaps an exhortation – lying there on the floor beside him. Between his left shoe and the table leg were Astraea's handsome scales, now laid awkwardly on their side, but perhaps waiting to be taken up again?

Monday

1 November 1708

Chapter Fifty

—∞∞∞—

Tom made his way over to Guildhall early and found that the dignified building had been transformed into something between a courthouse and a theatre – a place of reckoning but of entertainment too. This was no incongruity. After the extraordinary events of the past fortnight the mixture seemed appropriate – the constitutional heart of the City of London given over to the drawing of a lottery!

A grand drama of the passions was about to play out, with the audience as the actors, and Tom was mingling with the throng in the equivalent of the pit. Along the sides of the hall were balconies from which the Quality were surveying the scene, fans a-flutter, with cards and wine in readiness to while away the time. Above his head the colourful banners of the City companies hung from the roof – standards not won in battle but boasting achievements of a different kind. Tom smiled to think that among them must be the ensign of the Worshipful Company of Playing-Card Makers.

It was all part of the human comedy, and somehow it made sense. Everything he and his friends had encountered during their recent adventures could be summed up in this spectacle of a crowd gripped by the dream of riches and waiting for Dame Fortune to favour them. Yes, he thought, there was no escaping money and its pursuers! – those who desperately needed it, those who had plenty but craved more of it, and those who enjoyed the sport.

Then he laughed. How tempting to moralise on the spectacle! What poetic satisfaction in the neatness of the thought! But it wouldn't do – that kind of thing was surely more Bagnall than Bristowe? He knew he was part of this scene himself: young Thomas Bristowe was eager to take his chance with Fame; he had an uneasy allegiance to Fortune, and he surely pursued his own refined version of greed? It was time to stop sermonising and give way to the thrill of it all.

There was a busy hum in the hall reminiscent of theatre-goers waiting for the curtain to rise. The metropolis itself was on display all around him – substantial City figures and country squires, gamesters and tradespeople, housewives, lawyers and clergy, several valets and tall footmen perhaps keeping watch for their masters, and chambermaids handsomely dressed in their mistresses' cast-off gowns, each of them a single chapter in a vastly bigger story – one that would take lifetimes to do it justice.

Tom opened the sheet of paper on which his list was written, every number carrying the hopes of a chocolate-house player. He had come as the emissary of the Bay-Tree, where Widow Trotter was preparing to host a lottery celebration – though he couldn't help thinking a commiseration was more likely. He was to be the messenger and return with as much news as he could collect – in a sense he was playing Fortune himself.

His eyes scanned the paper. At the head of the column was Gavin Leslie and David Macrae's ill-fated 1,348 (was it to be the Black Death for them?), followed by Jenny Trip's noble 700, of which she had a sixteenth share; the three merchant friends, Jack Tapsell, Barnabas Smith, and Samuel Cust, had each laid out ten pounds for a full ticket – 819, 1,233, and 2,260; Captain Roebuck had paid a premium for a quarter share of 1,704 in the hope his hero Marlborough would triumph for him; Adèle Ménage had one eighth of 429; and Mr Denniston and Mr Pomery had each a half-share of 927, their fates entwined. There were several other numbers that he was being asked to look out for – but at the bottom was the most important one of all, which he would have no difficulty in remembering – 1,551. When the scale of Mrs Trotter's disaster was confirmed he had organised a secret subscription and had succeeded in raising the sum of five pounds for a half-ticket. She knew nothing of this and would continue to know nothing unless the Fates decreed otherwise. Although the freehold of the Bay-Tree was hers again, all her three hundred pounds of savings had gone – a bitter blow in itself.

Tom gave his attention to what was happening on the stage. There was a ripple of applause as the five judicial figures began to take their seats at a long table spread with papers and ledgers. Their ample wigs and serious looks gave every assurance that things would be conducted with the utmost probity ...

The draw was about to begin, and he was fascinated to watch the machinery of it. Towering over either side of the stage were two huge wooden cylinders in the form of a wheel balanced on a metal axle, turned by handles around the circumference. Fortune's wheels indeed! But rather than a fickle goddess, in front of each stood a bluecoat charity boy in his long tunic waiting to extract the tickets from a small flap in the side. It was clearly important to believe in the innocence of Chance – perhaps as something closer to Providence? Like altar boys assisting at the sacrament, they were there to bring purity and grace to the ceremony. Behind them the Gothic windows added a further ecclesiastical touch, and before them was the numerous congregation saying their silent prayers.

A cheer went up as the wheels began to move. The ritual was under way. From the left wheel was drawn the ticket number, and from the right wheel its outcome. To almost complete silence, the first announcements rang out over the hall: 'eight hundred and five ... *blank!*' ... 'two thousand one hundred and seventeen ... *blank!*' ...

The antiphonal voices continued, and during these moments the expectation was palpable. From the left came a surge of hope – and then from the right a crushing disappointment – a blank. Until suddenly there was something different: 'one thousand one hundred and forty-two ... *five hundred pounds!*' At this, a wild cry rang out and a couple flung their arms round each other. The drama had begun! There would be moments of elation and despair, though Tom was soon resigned to the fact that the day would be a challenge to his stamina. He straightened his back and checked himself: what were a few hours under the eye of eternity? The thought brought a momentary chill ... Yes, in its secular way this was the sorting of the damned and the redeemed. The scene before him was like some animated fresco of the Last Judgment.

Three hours later Tom was leaning disconsolately against the wall, still listening to the droning of the numbers and the repeated anti-climax – *blank – blank – blank* ... He had been hoping for the opportunity to hurry back to the Bay-Tree with good news for someone, but one by one the numbers on his list had been echoed by an intoned *blank*. It was as if a knell were tolling to recall everyone to the futility of hope. The moments of rejoicing served only to interrupt the cries of despair and sighs of resignation.

Then suddenly the voice appeared to be speaking directly to him ... *Seven hundred!* it declared ... this was Jenny Trip's number ... The seconds of silence that followed seemed to last for ever ... He was waiting for the call of *blank!* Instead, he heard the words *Eight hundred pounds* ...

Well, well! Tom could scarcely believe it – something to cheer at last! He worked out the arithmetic: a sixteenth share would be fifty pounds – a handsome sum for her, a full two years' wage! Her number had indeed served her nobly. He was tempted to carry the news to the Bay-Tree at once but was conscious that 1,551 had still to be called, and he knew he mustn't break off now. Something – his fancy rather than his faith – told him the stroke of good fortune was going to be repeated. He could almost hear it.

He listened with fresh attention, but the announcements continued their predictable path – until another sound, a man's voice, broke over him:

'There he is! *Cousin Tom!*'

He turned to see the beaming face of Frank Popham, who was accompanied by Lavinia. Without words, the two men embraced joyfully, then Tom stepped back, shaking his cousin by the shoulders:

'Frank! – this is a happy chance! You are a free man!'

'Entirely due to you and your friends, Tom. Widow Trotter's flying brigade came to my rescue. I have yet to hear the full story but am promised it a little later – We've been invited to the Bay-Tree for something called a *celebration* ... if Mrs Dawes is given her head it will certainly be that.'

'Believe me, we shall tell you all ... but what brings the two of you here?'

Tom looked at Cousin Lavinia with narrowing eyes. She in turn was shaking her head in mock disapproval at him:

'That is what I must ask you, Tom! Have you joined the gamesters? I thought you rejected Chance – but it seems the lady has some attractions after all? ...'

Tom reddened slightly, but turned it to advantage:

'I am merely the Bay-Tree's messenger, Lavinia, though I blush for you ... I promise not to tell – perhaps you are spying on behalf of Aunt Sophia, the Pophams' lottery broker?'

Lavinia assumed a mock firmness:

'No, Tom. Certainly not. I'm here to observe the pageant. I've been told all of human life is observable at the lottery – and looking around I could almost agree, though there is a scarcity of beggars.'

'Not for long, perhaps. Some of these around us may soon be holding out their bowls.'

It was not a comfortable thought, but it prompted Frank to speak. He glanced uneasily at his sister:

'No, Tom, I have to confess – the ticket is mine! Have the winners been posted yet? I have five pounds on this particular horse – I'm told it is in high form. I have expectations ...'

He caught a flicker of disapproval on his cousin's face:

'... I assure you, Tom – I reached out for the ticket in my darkest hour – it was meant to be my salvation ... but now it will be a welcome bonus!'

'*Will be?* You seem remarkably confident, Frank.'

'I have Gabriel Winch's warrant – he says it will leave the rest of the field standing!'

'You bought from Gabriel?'

'Yes, a half-ticket – my share of *one thousand five hundred and fifty-one*.'

It was spoken with pride.

'Extraordinary! – a good omen, Frank. Gabriel has done the business. You and Widow Trotter share a ticket!'

The news did seem fortuitous – and Tom had more to cheer them:

'And after three hours of waiting, I have just had a prize-holder – none other than Jenny Trip.'

Lavinia was delighted:

'Hurrah! That's wonderful! Ten thousand, I hope?'

'Her share is fifty pounds – but it will set her up. I'm so pleased for her.'

'Excellent!' said Frank. 'All we need now is for 1,551 to deliver for us ... Shall we pray?'

It was said in amusement, but after a few minutes the three of them were making their silent orisons. They all felt that success would somehow complete the story of the past fortnight, and in such an appropriate way too – give it a satisfying and well-deserved ending.

The moment came a full hour later. *One thousand five hundred and fifty-one* was duly called, and, far from an instant seeming an eternity, the response came all too quickly: *blank*. That was it. A blank. There was to be no final benison.

Tom's conclusion was philosophical:

'Perhaps we have had happy endings enough, Frank. It would be ungrateful to look for more.'

And in that stoical spirit, the three of them set off for the Bay-Tree.

The chocolate house was indeed in celebratory mood in defiance of any disappointments the lottery might bring. There had been no visit from a joyful Tom, which did not bode well, but in the coffee-room there were smiles and congratulations a-plenty. A welcoming banner hung from the ceiling, and along the bar were displayed samples of Mrs Dawes's savoury inventiveness – pewter dishes offering coy glimpses of artichoke, beetroot and mushroom. The enticing aromas of venison pasty and chicken pie wafted from the kitchen to reassure the regulars that there had been no dangerous revolution.

The occasion felt like a second re-opening. In the past few days the Bay-Tree had been a place of dark conjecture, of furtive looks and whispers, and uncertainty had hung heavy; but now the convivial ease was restored. It was as if the place felt a sense of homecoming that was wanting to express itself. The talk was open, the relief palpable, and the conversation seemed to have found its spark again. Behind the bar, Jenny's lappets were swinging gaily as she took orders for speciality drinks, and moving around from group to group, Mary Trotter was in her glory. The place was hers again, and her friends were happy to share in the delight.

There was much to celebrate. Gathered in the room were many of the players who had rallied to the cause and helped bring some order and meaning out of the disturbances of recent days. Explanations were being given and stories told. There was a general feeling that they had emerged from a labyrinth and were at last able to compare notes and make sense of what had happened.

Will Lundy was recounting his adventures in Vandernan's to Lady Norreys, who was fascinated to hear about his dice-play of six and one, and how Lady Rastell had fought Jack Beech over the green baize with the turn of a single card. The two of them concluded that Chance was never an entirely random thing – that skill and astuteness had a role to play, and a person's character, if it could not always defeat the odds, might nudge them in the right direction. In her turn, Lady Norreys impressed Will mightily with an account of her play with the coal-gas shares. Between them they came to the incontrovertible conclusion that a wily and determined female gamester could outwit any male. As a mark of special favour, Will was entrusted with the secret knowledge of how this process worked, and he swore on pain of death never to reveal it to another.

Over by the fire, Lord Melksham and Mrs Ménage were recalling their basset game in the Good Fellowship room where George Sturgis and Robert LeRoy had set the dangerous events in motion. It was another meeting of minds, this time in defence of rumour. They agreed that it demanded a particular skill to prevent it from being mere gossip, and that in practised hands rumour could expose deception and be an avenue to the truth.

They were both ready with instances when an overheard remark or a shrewd suspicion was remarkably prescient:

'It was the man's cuffs!' said Lord Melksham. 'I knew from that moment he was up to no good!'

Wisdom after the event was in generous supply. For many of them, hard experience had been gained and lessons learned – by no-one more so than Michael Henriques, who in a mood of sober melancholy was made to recall his own naivety – how he had allowed himself to be drawn into Mr Broughton's coal-gas project with its disastrous consequences. He found himself explaining to Mr Denniston and Mr Pomery how easily enthusiasm could blind a man to reality, and that allowing oneself to be drawn into another's dream was fraught with danger. The two friends sympathised and became curious as to his line of business. It didn't take long before he was extolling to them the possibilities of rape-oil soap – how gently it massaged the skin and would guard the finest complexion.

'Well, there they all are, Mrs Trotter! …'

Sam Rivers was looking round the room, a cheese savoury waving in his hand.

'… You are fortunate in your friends – what a sociable place this is!'

His voice was almost wistful, though his tightly-drawn features registered amusement too:

'… I have become fond of the Bay-Tree. What characters, eh?'

'You are a *character* too, Mr Rivers – and a friend – a good one. Nothing we have achieved could have been done without you. This is your place now.'

'Part of me would like to think so – yet Vandernan's draws me too. Risk and opportunity are my profession, remember – I am between systems, Mrs Trotter!'

'But here we have no *system*, Mr Rivers – that is our charm. We are a mixed company. Is there not something agreeable in variety? There is no uniformity in this room – whether of manners or ideas. You can always be sure of a good argument here. I relish it – and I know you do too.'

'Ah yes, variety does have its attractions – I detest the predictable! Indeed, I have just been listening to Mr Bagnall giving a disquisition on the subject. He maintains that order and variety are no contradiction – he was waxing lyrical about it – how each needs the other. A philosophical gentleman is your poet!'

'A genuine Bay-Tree character! … But I would like to think you could find yourself at home here, Mr Rivers. During recent days have we not together challenged the system, as you call it – exposed its workings? That has been your project from the beginning has it not? I like to think you are pleased with what we have achieved. Mercers' Hall must have given you satisfaction?'

'I wish I could be so sanguine, Mrs Trotter … Your friends have certainly done some good. They have exposed corruption and prevented injustice – and that is no small thing. But the system will survive. I suspect our new nation will turn out to be much like the old … Politics will continue to be a cockpit – the preachers will still rant – and filthy lucre will always cast its spell. It is the way of the world, Mrs Trotter! … But the Bay-Tree will survive too – at least its spirit will, I trust …'

He gave her a radiant smile.

'… And speaking of variety, I have promised myself a venison pasty … I must tell you, this is the tastiest breakfast I have had for a long time!'

With a parting wink Sam was making his way back to the bar when the coffee-room door opened to reveal Tom and his Popham cousins. The long-expected messenger stepped inside, suddenly aware that many eyes were trying to read his face and gauge what news he had brought from Guildhall. The paper he held in his hand was a portent. A hush descended.

He handed the list to Widow Trotter and whispered in her ear:

'Just a single success – but one to be celebrated! I hope our other friends will not be excessively disappointed ...'

She saw the numbers and fought to suppress a smile, then she turned to face an expectant room:

'My friends! Thanks to our agent here, I have the bulletin from the lottery ... I fear it is what in our heart of hearts we expected – with one notable exception ... The Bay-Tree does have a winner ...'

She was enjoying being the reporter of good fortune.

'... The successful number is *seven hundred* ... Jenny! ...'

There was a whoop of delight from behind the bar, and the lappets whirled crazily as congratulations came from every quarter.

'... Your share of the prize is the sum of *fifty pounds!*'

Jenny was grinning from ear to ear:

'The prize is more than that, Mrs Trotter – my mother has a share also – and my brother too! ... We are suddenly a rich family!'

No-one held back. Jenny was brought into the body of the room and made to sit down. Widow Trotter formally handed her a glass of punch, while Jeremy held out a tray of delicacies. She looked around her:

'I am my own bank, Mrs Trotter! I think I should call at 'Change Alley tomorrow. That is the thing, is it not, Mr Bristowe? ...'

For a moment people were startled – until she began laughing.

'... But from what I hear, that place is a den of thieves. No, I shall keep the money safe. You must advise me, Mrs Trotter!'

The remark was thrown out innocently enough and received a warm smile in return – though it drew an uncomfortable thought from the hostess of the Bay-Tree: what would she not give for fifty pounds herself! Things were going to be hard ...

'Miss Popham, welcome! ...'

With a lift of the spirits she had turned toward Lavinia, who was looking around in some bemusement, intrigued to find herself in a place of which she had heard so much but never thought to enter.

'... What do you think of our Bay-Tree?'

'I think it in a good way to flourishing, Mrs Trotter. With some new leaves, I see!'

'Yes – ladies! They add a civilised touch, don't you think? I have to take care lest I upset some of the gentlemen – but for this special occasion ...'

'It is your domain once again, Mrs Trotter ... Tom has told me of your difficulties. He has been very troubled by them. Everyone is so happy you have come through.'

'It has been a terrible time for your family too.'

'Yes – but somehow we have survived – the Bay-Tree and the Pophams together! We owe you so much, Mrs Trotter. Poor father has been in torment and mother quite distracted. I feared for them ... But from what I hear, things are set fair – though brother Frank is beginning to talk politics again, so our dangers are far from over. I think the experience will be a bond between our families.'

'Yes, I do think of this place like that.'

'Yes, I know. Tom has said the same.'

'But how we should have fared without Lord Melksham ... I don't need to say ...'

Widow Trotter paused. There was so much to be said – too much for that moment.

'... But you must tell me news of Arachne's Web. Are you

and your friends writing again? What plans has Mrs Manley? I was going to ask Lady Norreys when I had the chance...'

'We are never short of materials, Mrs Trotter, especially now. We must not allow these gamesters and jobbers to escape! Satire is readying itself. Arachne's voice will soon be heard again.'

'Excellent! ...'

She looked into Lavinia's eager young face, and an idea stirred:

'... I have been thinking about the Bay-Tree ... Our upstairs chamber is always at your disposal should you need a place to meet. It has been fitted out very comfortably – and I'm selling the basset table ...'

'Take care what you offer, Mrs Trotter! We shouldn't wish to overthrow the reigning laureates of the house – Bagnall and Bristowe!'

They both laughed.

Tom overheard and took the words as a summons:

'What do I hear, Mrs T? Are you scorning poetry? You must not listen to Lavinia.'

But his cousin was too quick for him:

'We were talking of poetry, Tom, not your georgics – not kale and turnips – though I think you describe them very prettily. Will you be returning to *Covent Garden*?'

'It cannot be soon enough, Coz. After the madness of recent days – all that cheating and deception! – I shall take up my pen with relief. I'm sick of airy speculation. I long for things of earth – *grounded things*.'

Widow Trotter heard his words and warmed to them.

'Yes, Tom, I think we have had more than enough of Vandernan's and 'Change Alley – of trickery, spying, smuggling and double-dealing – I am happy to shut the door on it all. I want to hear no more of them!'

The door, however, had other ideas.

It opened to admit Elias Cobb.

The constable looked happy enough to be among friends, though the news he delivered was nothing to cheer them: Joel Harkins had been released.

When she heard this Widow Trotter went momentarily pale, and Will, who had come over to join them, gave a groan and shook his head:

'So, that villain comes off scot-free?'

'There was no cause to hold him, Mr Lundy. The charge was theft, and Vandernan's will not press it – the promissory note is cancelled. It has been such a tangled affair – but we can be pleased that Mr Popham has gained from it. I'm sorry, Molly. It seems your attacker down at the wharf will walk away.'

Widow Trotter sighed. It was, she supposed, inevitable:

'I don't question the Law, Mr Cobb, but it does seem hard. The two men who have done real harm to me – Joel Harkins and Bob Leary – both have eluded its judgment. I shall bear Mr Harkins's scar, and thanks to the other, the loss of my savings. It seems I cannot even have your *poetic justice*, Tom. The good are supposed to end well while the bad are punished ... but only in fiction it seems!'

'You ask too much, Molly. This is the real world, not the stage of the Theatre Royal.'

They were sobering words – but she noticed that his smile grew broader as he spoke them.

'What are you up to, Elias? I know that mischievous look! I've had enough of plotting.'

'Ah – but some plots are more satisfying than others, my Lady! ...'

He gently took hold of her hand, and with a twinkle in his eye resorted to their old language of romance.

'... I have been venturing on your behalf.'

The others were intrigued at this game-playing between them.

'Surely not at the tables, Elias – that is something I cannot believe!'

'No, no, I did not sink to that – I risked nothing in the business, I assure you! I have simply been pursuing the Justice you thought so elusive. It is in a way poetical ... It concerns a certain diamond ...'

The word sent an electric charge through the group. Widow Trotter was startled:

'No, Elias! You were given the jewel to return – you have surely done so? That is not the way! I want nothing to do with it.'

'But I did return it, Molly – and Mr Secretary received it gratefully. And Leary's information about the customs men – well, it has led to a couple of arrests. There was a conspiracy, and they are now confident of tracing the other diamonds also.'

'Where is this leading, Elias?'

His smile became broader still.

'Do you not remember? – a reward was offered for the diamonds' return. Well, your magnificent gem is the star of the collection, and along with the clue that came with it ... I have secured you a quarter share of the reward money. What say you to two hundred and fifty pounds? ...'

'What do I say? ... '

There was a moment of rapt silence while she allowed her mind to take in the news.

'Very neat indeed,' said a smiling Tom. 'And no trickery in it!'

'That's true Justice, Mrs T,' said Will. 'A deserved reward!'

'And honestly earned too, Molly,' added Elias.

Widow Trotter was on the verge of choking:

'Yes, I really think it has been. How remarkable – almost ridiculous! You've succeeded in rendering me speechless ...'

The others glanced at each other and wisely held their tongues.

But each had the same thought, and with the thought came laughter – from all of them. It was a spontaneous celebration. Bright, refreshing, contagious laughter. Something had given way, and for a moment all strains and anxieties seemed to have vanished. The game had come to an end. There was so much to be lived through again in recollection, so much left to explain and express ... but at that moment nothing more needed to be said.

THE END

Historical Note

—◦◦◦—

Captain Hazard's Game

This Chocolate House Mystery takes place in the days following 21 October 1708, and once again the novel's fictional plot is interwoven with events and issues that were the hot topics of coffee-house conversation at the time. During these twelve days the eyes of the new nation were turned to the war in Europe, a continuing struggle to check the ambitions of Louis XIV which had been dragging on for seven years. The Duke of Marlborough was besieging Lille and the Dutch were proving to be demanding allies. After the Battle of Oudenarde (11 July) the decisive initiative had been lost and prospects of a French defeat had receded. Peace was no nearer, thanks partly to a huge loan from the *Bank of England* which would continue to finance the allied forces.

The Whiggish Bank had been established in 1694, and by 1708 it had achieved a monopoly of government finance, making itself indispensable to the men in power (who after that summer's General Election were now the Whigs). The previous year it had financed the union with Scotland, and in 1708 the renewal of its charter was being contested by its one serious rival, the Sword Blade Company, a Tory 'land bank' which challenged the Bank of England's monopoly. This was much more than a clash of rival businesses – it was a political and constitutional struggle between the older 'landed interest' and the new 'moneyed interest', and it shaded into a pro- and anti-war dispute.

The Whigs' power base was the 'City', the world of finance, business and trade over which the Aldermen and the ancient livery companies ruled. This walled 'mercantile republic' whose liberties and customs had been guaranteed by Magna Carta was largely self-governing, with its corporation, its members of parliament, its ward constables, and its own militia. The 'Cits' (as the wealthy city-men were called) might be sneered at by the satirists of the fashionable 'Town' further west, but they were determined that Great Britain would grow rich through an expanding world trade and the new financial economy that was developing.

The long-established Royal Exchange in Cornhill was the nation's merchanting centre, but over the road was a more lawless world. In 1698, in reaction against stringent new rules, the 'stock-jobbers' ('a low wretch who gets money by buying and selling shares in the funds' – Johnson's *Dictionary*, 1755) had decamped to two coffee houses in Exchange Alley, Jonathan's and Garraway's, where share-dealing was done and any man could be his own broker. Jonathan's would eventually outgrow its premises and transform itself into the 'London Stock Exchange'.

In these years before the famous crisis of the South Sea Bubble (1720), the fledgling stock market was wild and largely unregulated. Attempts were being made to bring its activities under control through broker-licensing, etc., but the legislation was largely ignored. Enforcement was a huge problem, given that many Justices were themselves profiting from 'the market'. The only effective check was a kind of self-regulation, an informal system based on reputation and good credit; but this was haphazard and easily evaded. In pamphlets like Daniel

Defoe's *The Villainy of Stock-Jobbers Detected* (1701) some of the tricks of this new trade were exposed. Greed, selfishness and deception were rife, and the authorities were concerned that the nation's Public Credit was at risk.

There was good cause. Not until mid-century was 'false pretences' recognised as a crime, and anyone could advertise the riskiest of projects and take subscriptions freely. Wagers were enormously popular and were made on anything at all (Queen Anne later banned them). What we call 'insider trading' was rife, and cartels and syndicates might operate secretly. A special problem in 1708 was so-called 'false news' (the phrase was being used at this time) when the market was turned by baseless rumours and misleading reports in the papers – lost ships, threats of invasion, the death of the Queen being the most infamous examples. The fledgling stock market was a dangerous world from which fortunes could be made or ruination come.

Paper currency (which since 1705 could include promissory notes) was just beginning to establish itself, helped by the fact that coins were in short supply, and the increasing flow of credit led to worries about price-fluctuation. The concept of money was changing, and the new world of paper credit was bringing the nature of 'value' itself into question. A gap was opening up between what was termed 'imaginary' and 'intrinsick' value.

It was recognised that in this regard the stock market was very like a gaming-house – both encouraged risk and both managed to evade attempts to regulate them. The anonymous pamphlet, *An Account of the Endeavours that have been used to suppress Gaming-Houses* (1722), paints a vivid picture. The gamester and the speculator were often compared. In 1708 gaming houses were illegal, but despite frequent calls for their suppression they continued to thrive thanks to influential patrons and co-operative magistrates. The occasional raid did little to discourage them.

The best documented raid of the period was that on Vandernan's in Covent Garden on 21 December 1721, and I have drawn from the vivid account preserved in the Old Bailey reports. There isn't a record of the place as early as 1708, but Vandernan's offered itself as the appropriately local gaming house, and so I have licensed it earlier and given it a character and a history.

In writing about this hazardous world, I have made use of the pamphlets and newspapers of Autumn 1708 and have followed the chronology of these twelve days. The papers offer many suggestive details such as reports of the siege of Lille (Chapter 9) and the particulars of the lost bank-notes for which a reward was offered (Chapter 3) – in this book I imagine these notes finding their way to Vandernan's, and via Robert LeRoy to Widow Trotter. In a couple of cases I have allowed fiction some leeway. The wreck of the Albemarle in fact occurred in early December, although the various particulars – including the false news report and the lost (and later recovered) diamonds – are authentic. News of the capture of Lille arrived in London on 24 October, and the false report of Marlborough's death is on this occasion a fiction.

The contest between the Bank of England and the Sword Blade over the huge government loan is well detailed by John Carswell in *The South Sea Bubble* (1961), and I learned a lot about the Bank, the City, and the conduct of the stock market in these years from his book, and from Bruce Carruthers's *City of Capital: Politics and Markets in the English Financial Revolution* (1996), Sir John Clapham's *The Bank of England. A History* (1970), and Anne Murphy's *The Origins of English Financial Markets* (2009). A fascinating picture emerges of a system struggling to establish itself through law and regulation while confronting repeated ingenious abuses. Defoe's brilliant *Anatomy of Exchange Alley* (1719) lifted the lid on the tricks of the market and set out to prove the 'scandalous trade' of stock-jobbing to be 'knavish in its private practice and treason in its publick.' The infamous Bubble of the following year would make his point for him.

In the world of gaming there was more ambivalence about sharp practice, and tricksters, like highwaymen, could be seen as resourceful rogues. The gamester was a kind of hero, as in *The Memoirs of the Lives, Intrigues, and Comical Adventures of the Most Famous Gamesters and Celebrated Sharpers* (1714), a volume that has helped bring alive the world of Vandernan's and its clientele. The instruction manual, *The Compleat Gamester* (1709), contains the first full account in English of the French game of basset. The tricks of card and dice play were the subject of study, and handbooks advised and warned those taking part. A pamphlet I found useful is *The Nicker Nicked; or, the Cheats of Gaming Discovered* (3rd edn, 1669), and like my fictional Sam Rivers I learned especially from the Dutch mathematician Christiaan Huygens, whose study of probability (translated into English as *Of the Laws of Chance, or, A Method of Calculation of the Hazards of Game*) was influential. As for lotteries, an undated pamphlet, *Calculations of the Numbers most likely to attain the capital prizes in the ensuing lottery deduced from mathematical demonstration* tells us that the lottery-loving public believed there was a way to outwit Fortune and improve their chances.

In chapter 22 I took a chance myself with Will's head-to-head casting for six and one with Humfrey Corbet. The successive throws of the dice as described are exactly my own as I played out the scene while writing. It was fascinating, and a little eery, to find that the probability described by Huygens was perfectly reproduced.

Stage drama of the period can help enliven the picture. James Shirley's old play, *The Gamester* (1637) remained popular, and along with Susannah Centlivre's two comedies, *The Gamester* (1705) and *The Basset-Table* (1706), they give a flavour of the world of gaming and the language of the tables. Centlivre's later play, *A Bold Stroke for a Wife* (1718), has a lively share-dealing scene set in Jonathan's, as does the anonymous farce, *Exchange-Alley: Or, The stock-Jobber turn'd Gentleman* (1720).

The novel's grand assembly in Mercers' Hall is fictional. Besides gathering the various protagonists together, the occasion has allowed me to convey some idea of the Lord Mayor's Show that never was. My original intention was to conclude the novel with that brilliant climax to the City's year when it celebrated itself and gave the people a holiday. But in 1708 the event was cancelled at the last moment because of the death the previous day of the Queen's husband, Prince George. Staged by the Goldsmiths Company, the parade would have been a glittering sight, and indeed we have a full and detailed description of it – with illustrations – in Elkanah Settle's *The Triumphs of London For the Inauguration of the Right Honourable Sir Charles Duncombe, Knight, Lord Mayor of the City of London . . . Performed on Friday the 29th of October, Anno 1708* (London, 1708) which was printed for the occasion. This has misled some scholars into assuming the pageant took place – but alas it did not. Instead, in the novel's fictional reality the great and good of the City come together in Mercers' Hall, and some of the pageant is enacted there, with Settle himself taking part. The verses are his, though the allegorical figure of London is my own addition. Whether we call it Chance, Fortune, or Fate, the cancelling of the pageant shows that novel-writing may also be subject to life's uncertainties.

The Chocolate House Mysteries no. 1:

Widow Trotter has big plans for her recently inherited coffee house, not suspecting that within days her little kingdom will be caught up in a national drama involving scandal, conspiracy, and murder.

The new 'Great Britain' is in crisis. The Queen is mired in a sexual scandal, spies are everywhere, and political disputes are bringing violence and division. The treasonous satirist "Bufo" is public enemy number one, and the Ministry is determined to silence him. Drawn into a web of intrigue that reaches from the brothels of Drury Lane to the Court of St James's, Mary Trotter and her young friends Tom and Will race against time to unravel the political plots, solve two murders, and prevent another.

Praise for Chocolate House Treason:

<hr/>

"A stunning debut novel."
— *Sandra Callard*

"Deftly plotted, historically accurate, richly descriptive, and wittily written – this is a charming and compelling mystery. I loved it ... A fabulous debut!"
— *Cynthia Wall*

"Fairer certainly brings the period to vivid life, so much so that as a reader you feel as if you're living the action as much as the characters ... The action is fast-paced and incredibly believable."
— *Jonathan White*, Highlights Magazine

"This is an extremely entertaining and civilised read, richly characterised, stylishly written, and cleverly plotted. A well-paced and suspenseful murder mystery is set with originality and wit in a confidently evoked early eighteenth-century London and excitingly investigated by a most unusual and engaging trio of amateur sleuths."
— *Alistair Stead*

"This deeply informed, engaging, and wonderfully literary novel captures its social and personal dramas with Swiftian insight and the amusing urbanity of Addison. It is a compelling story narrated expertly."
— *John Sitter*

"As a lover of literary detective fiction and a long-bereft fan of Bruce Alexander's Sir John Fielding mysteries, I am delighted to have found David Fairer's Chocolate House Treason. This novel offers an immersive 18th century experience thanks to Fairer's clubbable characters, pitch-perfect dialogue, and vivid period detail. Murder and political intrigue. Betrayal and loyalty. Suspense and surprise: Chocolate House Treason has it all!"
— *Kate Ravin*

"If you enjoy stories of political and courtly intrigue, excellent characterisation, and a good murder mystery, then you will love this book."
— *Debra Davidson-Smith*

"David Fairer has created a group of original and attractive characters, and given them a genuinely exciting mystery to solve, in the beautifully evoked, larger-than-life surroundings of Queen Anne's London. A hugely entertaining read!"
— *Linda Bree*

"This is a wonderful book. Chocolate House Treason is rich in descriptions of the time. David Fairer has a gift for them. Every sense of the reader is in play ... The chocolate house becomes a character all its own, full of political intrigue ... This is a terrific first novel. I look forward to many more!
— *Jody Price*

The Chocolate House Mysteries, no. 2:

Theatre Royal, Drury Lane, 24 April 1708. A performance of Macbeth is under way when disaster strikes and the stage becomes a scene of elemental chaos – and for Widow Trotter and her friends at the Bay-Tree Chocolate House a new adventure begins involving murder, poison, fire, and a rogue elephant . . . the book moves among the eccentric characters of the Theatre Royal company in Drury Lane and at the exuberant May Fair, where the actors moonlight in the fairground booths.

The puritanical reformers are seeking to close the theatre and abolish the Fair, and 'accidents' begin to happen – but Mary Trotter, Tom and Will are determined to expose the conspiracy, and the action reaches its climax at the Fair when the players are faced with the ultimate act of terror.

Praise for The Devil's Cathedral:

⁓

"A hugely enjoyable mystery with an engaging cast of characters and a vivid evocation of the sights (and smells!) of eighteenth-century life. Actors, thugs, puritans, poets, pig-roasts, dastardly deeds in the costume store, and sinister plots to wreck the theatre. Strongly recommended!"
— *Amazon reviewer*

"Having read and thoroughly enjoyed David Fairer's first book, *Chocolate House Treason*, I was keen to read this follow-up. I was not disappointed! The author's passion and knowledge for the period shines through, and I found this a totally immersive read. There is a depth and vividness that brings this world alive, with some lovely touches of humour and humanity woven into the narrative. I just loved it, as did the rest of my book group."
— *Andrew Kelly*

"Fairer's account of the theatre in its cultural, social and practical contexts is compellingly vivid. Again, I had that sense of complete immersion in a world that sits somewhere between the immediately familiar and the strangely different . . ."
— *Richard Boon*

"A rollicking and fascinating tale, cleverly plotted and teeming with a large cast of colorful characters. A story chock-full of life, novel ideas and lots of delicious verbal pyrotechnics."
— *NetGalley reviewer*

"*The Devil's Cathedral* fuses an exciting mystery with an exploration of a vital aspect of 18th century London. Debates about the theatre come alive with an amazing power, violence, and contemporary relevance, and the sounds and smells of the London theatres and fairs are vividly evoked. David Fairer's impressive scholarship is imaginatively translated into a tale that is intellectually and emotionally engaging."
— *Jim McLaverty*

"A wonderful book, recreating all the atmosphere of 18th century theatre life, with a mysterious plot for readers to solve, and a suspenseful climax. I learned how Mayfair got its name: from the carnivalesque street fair and entertainments. David Fairer's thorough research makes the reader feel they are actually there. I particularly enjoyed the author's own renderings of typical plays of the time!"
— *Katie Wales*

"A marvellous fictional voyage that deserves to be enjoyed without any moderation whatsoever!"
— *NetGalley reviewer*